SOON & VERY SOON

SOON &
VERY SOON

THE TRANSFORMATIVE MUSIC AND
MINISTRY OF ANDRAÉ CROUCH

ROBERT F. DARDEN
AND
STEPHEN M. NEWBY

Oxford University Press is a department of the University of Oxford.
It furthers the University's objective of excellence in research, scholarship,
and education by publishing worldwide. Oxford is a registered trade mark of
Oxford University Press in the UK and certain other countries.

Published in the United States of America by Oxford University Press
198 Madison Avenue, New York, NY 10016, United States of America.

© Robert F. Darden and Stephen M. Newby 2025

All rights reserved. No part of this publication may be reproduced, stored in a retrieval system, transmitted, used for text and data mining, or used for training artificial intelligence, in any form or by any means, without the prior permission in writing of Oxford University Press, or as expressly permitted by law, by license or under terms agreed with the appropriate reprographics rights organization. Inquiries concerning reproduction outside the scope of the above should be sent to the Rights Department, Oxford University Press, at the address above.

You must not circulate this work in any other form
and you must impose this same condition on any acquirer

Library of Congress Cataloging-in-Publication Data
Names: Darden, Robert, 1954– author. | Newby, Stephen, 1961– author.
Title: Soon & very soon : the transformative music and ministry of
Andraé Crouch / Robert F. Darden, Stephen M. Newby.
Other titles: Soon and very soon
Description: [1.] | New York : Oxford University Press, 2025. |
Includes bibliographical references and index.
Identifiers: LCCN 2024038790 (print) | LCCN 2024038791 (ebook) |
ISBN 9780197748121 (hardback) | ISBN 9780197748152 |
ISBN 9780197748145 (epub)
Subjects: LCSH: Crouch, Andraé. | Gospel singers—United States—Biography. |
Church of God in Christ.
Classification: LCC ML420.C945 D37 2025 (print) | LCC ML420.C945 (ebook) |
DDC 782.25/4092 [B]—dc23/eng/20240820
LC record available at https://lccn.loc.gov/2024038790
LC ebook record available at https://lccn.loc.gov/2024038791

DOI: 10.1093/oso/9780197748121.001.0001

Printed by Sheridan Books, Inc., United States of America

To the late Pastor Sandra Crouch for giving us her blessing to write this story.
To Bill Maxwell for his generosity and for his
photographic and sonic memory.

Special Thanks
To Mary Landon Darden
and Stephanie Ashe Newby for their support, love, and
gracefully walking with us every step of the way.

Thank You
To the hundreds of musicians, singers, friends, family members,
music executives, producers, scholars, librarians, researchers, and
writers who came before us for sharing their memories, insights,
tears, prayers, and laughter as we sought to tell the story of the
transformative life, music, and ministry of Andraé Crouch.

Contents

Foreword by Dr. Henry Louis Gates Jr.	*ix*
Introduction	1
1. The World That Shaped Andraé Crouch: Southern California, 1940s–1960s	7
2. The COGICs: *It's a Blessing*	25
3. The Addicts Choir	51
4. *Take the Message Everywhere*	75
5. *Keep On Singin'*	101
6. *Soulfully*	125
7. *Just Andraé*	153
8. *"Live" at Carnegie Hall*	177
9. *Take Me Back*	197
10. *The Best of Andraé*	227
11. *This Is Another Day*	245
12. *Live in London*	265
13. *I'll Be Thinking of You*	283
14. *Don't Give Up*	311
15. *Finally*	337
16. *No Time to Lose*	359

17. The Final Years	379
18. Conclusion	395
Index	*407*

Foreword

Andraé Crouch crafted a signature sound that transcended and crossed the borders of nationality, denomination, and genre and produced gospel music for the world. He drew inspiration from Thomas Dorsey and the deep musical traditions of his own Church of God in Christ denomination, filtered what he heard through the ecumenical populism of the Jesus Music era, and delivered traditional gospel music kicking and screaming into the latter half of the twentieth century.

Coming out of Southern California's thriving gospel culture, Andraé Crouch and the Disciples were one of the first multiracial groups in gospel. To achieve the new sounds Andraé heard in his head, he was the first to incorporate horn sections and synthesizers; he made the background vocalists co-lead singers; he experimented with jazz, reggae, funk, pop; and all but created the praise & worship music movement. He didn't just cross over into the mostly white world of American contemporary Christian music, his relentless touring and talent took gospel music to the entire world.

He composed some of most enduring, most performed songs in gospel music history.

And yet, there has been no serious, long-form study of the man's ministry or music.

It was with that in mind that Robert F. Darden and Stephen M. Newby began what would become *Soon & Very Soon: The Transformative Music and Ministry of Andraé Crouch, the Light Years*—a partnership that featured comprehensive interviews with Crouch's family and friends, collaborators and colleagues, and a host of gospel music executives and artists.

The book is the culmination of nearly a decade's worth of research by authors Darden, who is also founder of the Black Gospel Music Preservation Program (BGMPP) and has written extensively on gospel music, and Newby, a university professor and composer with degrees in music and theology who continues to serve broadly in church and para-church ministries and now leads research at the BGMPP and Gospel Music Archives.

Soon & Very Soon is neither a hagiography nor a critical, theory-based analysis. It is instead a highly readable deep dive into Andraé's world, a joyous life-and-works exploration of his influences, collaborations, compositions, lyrics, life, and sometimes tumultuous times.

Dr. Henry Louis Gates Jr.

Introduction

The legendary gospel music star Andraé Crouch was one of the most influential, most transformative, and most innovative musical artists in American music history in any genre. In gospel music he is spoken of in the same "genius" pantheon as Mahalia Jackson, Thomas Dorsey, and the Reverend James Cleveland.

It is hard to overstate the impact of the man *The Guardian* (UK) called "the foremost gospel singer of his generation." At Crouch's death, President Barack Obama and First Lady Michelle Obama released a statement that cited his "extraordinary musical talent" over a fifty-year career and told of how "grateful" they were of his music and celebrated him as the "leading pioneer of contemporary gospel music" whose "soulful classics . . . have uplifted the hearts and minds of several generations and his timeless influence (that) continues to be felt in not only gospel but a variety of music genres."[1]

While Crouch is the bridge between traditional and contemporary gospel, he also all but invented—or, at least, was the first to perform and record—two of today's major modern music formats: contemporary gospel and praise & worship and was a dominant figure in a third (Jesus Music). His compositions ("The Blood Will Never Lose Its Power," "Through It All," "My Tribute (to God Be the Glory)," "I've Got Confidence," "Soon and Very Soon," and others remain featured staples in modern hymnals in thousands of churches around the world, Black and white.

Crouch's musical innovations influenced every major gospel artist who followed him. At his passing in January 2015, the Winans, Kirk Franklin, Tye Tribbett, Jonathan McReynolds, Donald Lawrence, Hezekiah Walker, Yolanda Adams, Donnie McClurkin, and a host of others stated that he was their primary influence and inspiration. With his group the Disciples, Crouch introduced/imported jazz, Western European classical, calypso, Latin, and other musical elements into his gospel stylings. His recordings are unparalleled in gospel music, comprising a musical statement so broad and innovative that scholars are only now unpacking its musical depths, compositional savvy, theological praxis, and lyrical layers.

From a lyrical standpoint, Crouch was the first major gospel music composer and artist to address the most pressing issues of the day in a song—homelessness, AIDS, abuse, prejudice and racial intolerance, drug abuse, marital discord—and tie the lyrics to the redeeming power of the gospel of Jesus Christ. Crouch, who along with his twin sister Sandra Crouch, served as minister of the church his father founded in Pacoima (near Los Angeles), ministered daily to individuals experiencing these issues, and bravely continued to address them in his compositions, despite increasing criticism from vocal elements in the African American church.

Crouch's "Disciples" were the first multiethnic group in gospel music and included female and male members. They were the first gospel group to appeal to racially mixed, ecumenically and multiethnically diverse audiences and appear in primarily white churches and venues, ranging from international mega-churches to Madison Square Garden and Carnegie Hall, as well as network television programs ranging from *Saturday Night Live* and *Soul Train* to the *Tonight Show with Johnny Carson.*

Crouch's influence was so pervasive that he recorded, performed with, and/or composed for some of the most powerful names in popular music as well, including Michael Jackson, Elvis Presley, Elton John, Bob Dylan, Paul Simon, Quincy Jones, Little Richard, Stevie Wonder, and Madonna. Crouch earned seven Grammy awards and was nominated for Academy Awards for his composition, arrangement, and production work on *The Color Purple* and *The Lion King.*

When Crouch died in 2015, his obituary was featured prominently in the *New York Times* and all major American and British newspapers, on the BBC, PBS, NPR, and most major television networks. His funeral was attended by some of the most notable politicians, musicians (gospel and popular), and Black and white religious leaders in the country.

In sum, Andraé Crouch is *the* towering figure in gospel music in the latter forty years of the twentieth century and the early years of the twenty-first century.

And yet, the literature—both scholarly and popular—on Crouch is surprisingly, even shockingly thin. There is no serious biography of Andraé Crouch. There is no academically annotated discography, no analysis of his innovative

INTRODUCTION

compositions or performance techniques, no study of the scope and impact of his lyrics.

Our task is complicated by the seemingly miraculous nature of Andraé's gift. As later chapters will testify, his uncommon talents simply . . . *appeared*. At a time of great need in his church, Andraé's father "called" the necessary gifts from his son. With no musical training or lessons, two weeks later a fourteen-year-old Andraé became the church pianist. Shortly thereafter, with no previous music compositional experience, Andraé wrote one of the great enduring gospel songs of the African American Church, "The Blood (Will Never Lose Its Power)"—and promptly threw it away.[2] It is one of the central stories, perhaps the *original* story, of Andraé and Sandra Crouch. These two events were told repeatedly by the two siblings until their deaths. So great are those gifts that coauthor Stephen Newby, in his many presentations and writings on Andraé, calls them "Mozart-ian." Inexplicable, unknowable.

Fortunately, it is not the duty of the biographers to verify miracles, or even explain them. We perceive our task as to make some kind of order out of chaos, to assemble thousands of interviews, sermons, and articles/essays/reviews—all in hopes of making sense of the uncanny life of Andraé Crouch. Whether or not you believe in the origin story of Andraé's talents, the results of his bountiful creative imagination—hundreds of timeless songs, thousands of life-changing (or at least life-altering) concerts—remain and continue to touch and influence millions today.

Which means biographers must start somewhere. Nature or nurture? A spark of the divine? A musical prodigy? How much of Andraé's innovation, imagination, and identity was due to his relationships with the incredibly diverse group of people that surrounded him?

But if the transformative life of Andraé Crouch truly is due to nature—whether he was born with this gift or received it via what his lifelong denomination, the Church of God in Christ (COGIC), calls the "anointing"—you still must start somewhere. We believe that we all stand on the shoulders of giants and that our lives are at least in part influenced by our surroundings and those who surround us, as well as those who have gone before. Even when telling the story of his gift, Crouch was always quick to cite his relationships, sources, and influences.

With *Soon & Very Soon: The Transformative Music and Ministry of Andraé Crouch*, we sought—as much as possible—to identify those relationships, sources, and influences.

To do so, we proposed to explore Crouch's life and works through historical observation, the basic music theory behind his compositions, the hermeneutics (biblical interpretation) behind his lyrics, as well as a thorough examination of popular and scholarly archives and databases, and—most important—detailed interviews with his family, friends, fellow musicians, singers, composers, pastors, and gospel music scholars, as well as music industry executives.

From this array of incredibly multifaceted sources, stories, and artifacts, we attempted to create a chronology of Andraé's life and works, as revealed through his recordings with Light Records.

As noted above, the paucity of interviews and scholarly and popular work on Crouch and his ministry meant that the next challenge was to identify, locate, and interview as many members of that widespread, disparate group within Andraé's musical, theological, and personal community as possible. For that, we are deeply indebted to the many friends and musicians who made those vital connections and introductions for us, particularly his sister the late Pastor Sandra Crouch and Andraé's longtime and closest collaborator, Bill Maxwell.

In the end, in attempting this biography, we sought to understand, or at least come to terms with, an artist who was one of the most significant musical influences on our lives and careers, from a very early age. We wanted to bring Andraé Crouch to life to the vast array of people who experienced not just his music and ministry, but his larger-than-life personality, whether it was through a deeply felt personal relationship to an individual song or even as a lifelong influence and impact on a musician's life and musical career.

In the process, we hoped to determine/explore/establish the place of the multitalented Andraé Crouch in the highest canon of gospel music's artistry; in short, his place on the mythical "Mount Rushmore" of artists—Jackson, Dorsey, and Cleveland. And, if successful, our hope is to introduce a new generation of musicians and scholars to Andraé's life of ministry and at least a portion of his unparalleled musical repertoire. In recent years, we have repeatedly heard young people sing Crouch's songs but were too often shocked to learn that the singers either did not know the composer's name or had never even heard of Andraé Crouch.

For these reasons and others, we worked for nine years to create an enduring resource for further investigations into Crouch's life and work.

Of course, whether we succeeded with all or any of those goals, is up to the reader and future generations to decide.

INTRODUCTION 5

But along the way, as we worked in a close partnership, we discovered that we brought different strengths to the project. As the manuscript began to come together, we experienced in real time a new modality of study and exploration where a Black man and a white man, a concert music composer and theologian and a rock 'n' roll drummer and journalist, two scholars from radically different backgrounds could, by our close, often daily collaboration, bring to light aspects of Crouch's life and ministry that neither of us could possibly have encountered or even understood alone.

NOTES

1. Steve Turner, "Andraé Crouch Obituary: One of the Greatest Gospel Singers of His Generation, Crouch Was Known for His Choral Work with Michael Jackson and Madonna," *The Guardian*, January 12, 2015, https://www.theguardian.com/music/2015/jan/12/andrae-crouch; President Barack Obama and Michelle Obama, Statement by the President on the Passing of Andraé Crouch, whitehouse.gov (archives.gov).

2. Mike Rimmer, "Andraé Crouch: 64-Year-Old Gospel Legend Cuts 'Smokin'' Church Music," *Cross Rhythms*, January 13, 2007, www.crossrhythms.co.uk/articles/music/Andrae_Crouch-64_Year_Old_Gospel_Legend_Cuts_Smokin_Church_Music/25534/; Bob Gerstyzn, "Andraé's Music Will Never Lose Its Power," *The Wittenburg Door*, no. 192 (March/April 2004), online edition.

I

The World That Shaped
Andraé Crouch

Southern California, 1940s–1960s

If you wanted to transform gospel music and could pick where you wanted to be born in 1942, you'd pick Southern California. Andraé and Sandra Crouch were born into a state in the early throes of inventing—or reinventing—itself. The massive, unrelenting changes already underway in 1942 would provide Andraé an uncommonly rich and diverse background, not just in music, but in virtually every other significant facet of life in the twentieth century—economics, race, politics, the arts, and, of course, religion. In that year, the country was at war, both abroad and with itself. Racial tensions had heightened, fueled by ever more restrictive Jim Crow laws in the South. The declines of the Harlem Renaissance in New York and Bronzeville in Chicago had all but passed. Conversely, the uncommon lives and careers of the Crouches reflected the progressive nature of a state quickly becoming the nation's economic and cultural powerhouse. California was the dream destination of millions throughout multiple Great Migrations by multiple races, all drawn by the booming war-fueled economy, the splendid weather, the mythos of Hollywood, and the opportunity to perhaps—*just perhaps*—begin anew in a place without the old prejudices, barriers, and preconceptions that still plagued the rest of the country. Two young people growing up here saw and experienced an extraordinary melting pot of communities, ideas, and cultures all working out the new parameters in what was, for all intents and purposes, a new world.[1]

Not coincidentally, the late 1950s and 1960s were the years that the planet's musical axis swung from the East Coast to the West Coast. California was America's answer to the tsunami of Beatlemania that had threatened to swamp all homegrown popular music. In a remarkably short time, record labels and artists of every conceivable musical style, taste, and inclination, every race, and every level of ability found themselves there, from San Francisco to South Central Los Angeles, learning from and influencing each other and enriching, in the end, *all* American music. Again, for the young and impressionable Andraé and Sandra, they found themselves in the midst of the beating heart of what popular and sacred music were and were becoming. Country, western swing, music for film, rhythm & blues (R&B), pop, beach music, conjunto, salsa, Mexican American, West Coast jazz, classical concert, and gospel music all found a new and fertile home in Southern California.[2]

Gospel Music

Jacqueline DjeDje's research has revealed something of the complexity and richness of gospel music in California since the 1930s. Far from being dwarfed by the scale (and tradition) of gospel music in its ancestral home of Chicago, Los Angeles developed into a gospel music hotbed, one fully capable of empowering and encouraging a generational artist like Andraé. DjeDje credits the Great Migrations for making California unique. "The environment," she said, "affected the culture and eventually also affected the music." Part of that environment is due to the landscape of Southern California, which did not have, she said, rural areas earmarked for African Americans, forcing most new arrivals to instead live in or adjacent to urban zones. The Blacks who journeyed to California were often better educated and found the middle-class employment there too often denied them elsewhere. "These are the ones," she notes, "who establish the religious traditions." This "anomaly," as DjeDje describes it, a place with a somewhat less inherently racist society with wider economic opportunities, was one of the components that enabled a Black man, William Seymour, in 1906 to found an interracial revival movement at 312 Azusa Street in the Azusa Street Mission. "I don't think a Black man could be able to do that any other place," DjeDje said, in part because the majority of the early adherents to the new movement were white.[3]

As California's population swelled, so did the congregations of its many churches, and virtually all were filled with recent immigrants who, DjeDje writes, were eager to hear the gospel music of their churches back home. As early as the 1930s, these burgeoning new congregations invited various

Chicago gospel luminaries, including Thomas Dorsey, Robert Anderson, the Roberta Martin Singers, Sallie Martin, and others, to lead choir workshops, direct choirs, and perform in concert. Pianist Gwendolyn Cooper Lightner, who opened the Los Angeles Gospel Music Mart in the early 1940s, coached and trained those musicians and singers thirsty for this new sound. From the earliest beginnings, however, as Lightner told DjeDje, those first "homegrown" gospel artists "did gospel in a different way." Lightner attributed at least some of the divergence to a marked distinction between Dorsey's gospel beat and what she called the "Holiness beat" then throbbing throughout the city.[4]

Lightner was soon hired by John L. Branham, pastor of St. Paul Baptist, in 1946. Branham, who was originally from Chicago, also hired gospel singer James Earle Hines as the choir director. The combination and focus on gospel music led to the creation of the Voices of Eden, a gospel choir with more than 100 voices. The Voices were soon so popular that they were given their own radio show, which eventually could be heard in seventeen states. St. Paul's itself became widely popular, drawing African American celebrities and gospel artists alike to its packed services. Lightner's rhythmic piano playing was also enormously influential. DjeDje quotes famed gospel singer Eugene Smallwood as saying that Lightner was the pianist "who put the 'ump' in gospel playing . . . she's about the 'Queen of Gospel' when it comes to playing." St. Paul's success led other Los Angeles pastors and churches to become involved in radio and television, including Thurston G. Frazier, who directed the Voices of Victory Choir, which had a weekly television show that led to a national recording contract.[5]

According to DjeDje, by the late 1950s and early 1960s, Southern California had become a premier destination for gospel. Nationally known composer Doris Akers's Simmons-Akers Singers (with Dorothy Simmons) were in time joined by James Cleveland, Margaret Aikens Jenkins, Clara Ward and the Ward Singers, Cassietta George, Raymond Raspberry, the Gospel Pearls, the Chosen Gospel Singers, and some of the new "hard" gospel quartets, even as the number and size of local gospel choirs grew exponentially.[6] Drawn by increased economic opportunities in the sprawling metropolitan area, gospel artists continued relocating to California well into the 1960s. Gospel artist Bessie Griffin once told DjeDje that when it came to Los Angeles, there was "no other place" where she could live and have a "nice home and nice white picket fence."[7] It was a heady, exciting time, not just for gospel but for all forms of popular music. Legendary singer Linda McCrary was among those who transplanted to Los Angeles. The McCrarys—Linda, Howard, and the other siblings—quickly became "A-list" backing vocalists in the city's competitive recording industry. "In other places we went to," McCrary told Nadra Nittle of PBS, "the opportunities didn't present themselves to us as much as they did in Los Angeles. We knew L.A. was the best place to flourish."[8]

Church of God in Christ

Yet another factor made Southern California the ideal home for a transformative gospel artist—religion. More specifically, the Church of God in Christ (COGIC), the faith of Andraé and Sandra's parents and grandparents, found a mighty home in Los Angeles and would, as the authors hope to show, become an essential element in the genius of Andraé Crouch.

Among those who came to witness the Azusa Street phenomenon firsthand in 1907 was the founder of what would become called the Church of God in Christ, Charles Harrison Mason, who received what the Azusa Street believers called the "baptism in the Holy Spirit." Mason returned home to Memphis and experienced multiple visions, spontaneously composed songs, participated in healing services, and preached a new, more intimate relationship with Jesus Christ. From a few followers, the Church of God in Christ grew to become one of the largest Protestant denominations of any kind in the United States.[9]

To outsiders, the theological differences among the denominations directly influenced by the Azusa Street movement or outwardly similar in precepts and core beliefs—Pentecostal, Apostolic, Assemblies of God, Church of God in Christ, Holiness, Sanctified, Full-Gospel, and others—can range from subtle to bewildering. The gamut ranges from denominations that mildly accommodate popular culture outside the church to denominations that strictly separate themselves from the "corrupting" influences of the outside world. In the beginning, most shared at least to some degree a desire to separate themselves not just from nonbelievers ("the World") but also from other Protestant denominations, including Baptist, Methodist, and African Methodist Episcopal, the largest of the primarily African American denominations at the time. This "separate-ness," or as Horace Clarence Boyer described it, the adoption of "Heaven or Hell" as a "principal preachment," overwhelmingly manifested itself in COGIC worship services, clothing, behavior, daily conversation and language, and the performance of music in the church. As for the music, Boyer writes that gospel music was quickly chosen as the "illuminating force behind this theology." Mason, though not a musician, led his growing denomination in "song fests" and composed a host of songs, most passed informally from congregation to congregation. He also is credited with the composition of two of the denomination's most influential "shout songs," which quickly became staples in COGIC congregations, "Yes, Lord" and "I'm a Soldier in the Army of the Lord," both of which are still performed and recorded today. Boyer describes "Yes, Lord" as a "COGIC chant" to signify the "limited number of tones, unpulsed-*rubato* tempo and simple harmonies." "I'm a Soldier," with its driving rhythmic beat and elaborate movement and clapping rituals, was adopted into both the folk music revival of the early 1950s and by numerous gospel artists in the 1960s, including those not affiliated with COGIC. It continues to be performed and recorded today.[10] Generations of COGIC young people, including Andraé and Sandra, found these and other musical chants to be thrilling, engaging elements of their worship services.

Historian and musician James B. Boyer (brother to gospel scholar Horace Boyer) has posited that the distinctiveness of the COGIC brand of gospel owes an additional debt to the location of the first Church of God in Christ congregations near Memphis's famed Beale Street and the fact that many of the early adherents came primarily from impoverished backgrounds. These early converts were familiar with the blues and later R&B artists performing at the clubs and bars along Beale. Gospel music may well be described as the beat of Saturday night coupled with the words of Sunday morning and—in the voices and hearts of the COGIC faithful—it became a "significant entity" in the church, "sung out of a divine power that lifts men up." It is and has been from the beginning, Boyer writes, "a music of hope."[11]

Early COGIC Musical Missionaries and Influencers

From the first days of the nascent denomination, the evangelical nature of the COGIC faith, coupled with this joyful, rhythmic expression of gospel music, produced a wealth of musicians who traveled widely to share their gifts with enthusiastic other denominations. These early traveling musical evangelists, called "planters," worked with different COGIC elders and bishops, including Samuel Crouch and Riley F. Williams, and helped establish new churches throughout the country. Not much is known about the first and most influential of these planters, "Blind" Arizona Dranes. Researcher Michael Corcoran traced her faint paper trail from the Institute for Blind Colored Youths in Austin, Texas, in 1910, where she was trained as a classical European pianist, to early recording studios where she recorded a bright and lively brand of ragtime, barrelhouse, and stride piano in the 1920s. Corcoran writes that Dranes may have joined the Church of God in Christ in Wichita Falls, Texas, where she began a professional relationship with charismatic preacher Elve Doran. By 1926, she was touring with the then Fort Worth–based Samuel Crouch. It was there that a record executive for OKeh Records' parent company, Consolidated Talking Machine Co. of Chicago, heard Dranes performing on a radio broadcast on New Year's Eve. According to Corcoran, when Dranes went into the studio on June 17, 1926 (shortly before a new group called Louis Armstrong and His Hot Five were scheduled to record), she became the first COGIC female to record what would be called *gospel music*, and her sessions produced many of the piano rhythms and riffs that would influence nearly every major gospel and rock 'n' roll pianist to come. Listening to Dranes's earliest recordings, "Bye and Bye We're Going to See the King," "My Soul Is a Witness for the Lord," "It's All Right Now," and "I Shall Wear a Crown," Corcoran admires the pianist's propulsive "1-6-5-1 octave bass line" and Dranes's "left-hand *ostinato*—constantly repeating a melodic fragment" while the right hand plays a "symphony of harmony"—hints and hallmarks of rock 'n' roll *and* gospel keyboards for decades to come.[12]

But Dranes only recorded a few more sides, usually as an accompanist, in the years that followed, including a handful with popular COGIC preacher F. W. McGee. She lived for a time near the Black music hotbed of Deep Ellum in Dallas and, thanks to Corcoran's meticulous research of fragmentary African American and denominational records, her name is found on major COGIC programs across the United States, including in Cleveland in 1947, where she was billed as the "Famous Blind Piano Player from Chicago," and behind Madame Ernestine Washington at a 1953 women's convention in Chicago. At some point, she joined her longtime friend, now *Bishop* Samuel Crouch, in Los Angeles at the Crouch Temple on South Central Avenue in 1961. Dranes died from a stroke at an assisted living facility in Signal Hill, California, on July 27, 1963. Although she is relatively unknown today, Dranes's expressive, memorable piano playing and keening voice were heard by thousands and influenced generations of COGIC musicians. Terrence Curry, who holds several national music leadership positions with the Church of God in Christ, said that Dranes's chordal style of piano playing—that is, the ability to play distinctively different chordal voices simultaneously—is the common thread that binds Dranes with later COGIC pianists, including Andraé Crouch and Mattie Moss Clark. Those few who did remember her in performance, though, called it a memorable experience. Helen Davis, at age ninety, was interviewed about Dranes in 2003 and recalled seeing the blind pianist at E. M. Page's church in Oklahoma in the 1920s: "She'd get the whole place shouting. She was a blind lady, see, and she'd let the spirit overtake her. She'd jump from that piano bench when it hit her." "She was the Holy Ghost's favorite singer," Corcoran writes, "an otherworldly vessel fueled by faith."[13]

Dranes was not the only COGIC singer, not even the best known one on the road, singing for the denomination. A very young Rosetta Tharp (the "e" in Tharpe was added later) and her mother, Katie Nubin, evangelized for the Church of God in Christ as early as the 1920s. At one point in St. Louis, Tharpe said that they encountered Dranes performing "The Storm Is Passing Over." Joop Visser and others cite Dranes as a significant influence on the young guitarist.[14] Tharpe would become the first artist to record what is recognizably gospel music (before even Thomas Dorsey) to achieve national success, performing and recording well into the 1960s, influencing a host of gospel and rock 'n' roll stars, often while at odds with the COGIC churches as much for her success and flamboyant lifestyle as for her well-publicized marriages (including one to Russell Morrison before 20,000 in Washington, DC, at Griffin Stadium and the resulting commercial release of the music from the event).[15] James Boyer writes that the music-friendly nature of the denomination helped spawn a number of other influential, sometimes best-selling artists in the 1940s through late 1950s: Ernestine B. Washington (1943), Utah Smith (1940s), Marion Williams (with the Ward Singers, 1940s), Marie Knight (recording with Tharpe, 1940s and 1950s), Jessie Mae Renfro (1949), the Boyer Brothers (Horace and James, 1951), the Gay Sisters (1951), Kitty Parham (with the Ward Singers, 1953), the Charles Taylor Singers (1954), and, somewhat later, the O'Neal Twins (1962) and Mattie Moss Clark and the Southwest Michigan State Choir COGIC (1966). Recordings by these artists and more would be welcome in the gospel-friendly confines of the home in Pacoima of the young Crouch twins. Boyer notes that the music of later COGIC gospel artists including Myrna Summers; Timothy Wright; Walter, Edwin, and Tramaine Hawkins; the Clark Sisters; and others would also reflect the same influences.[16]

In retrospect, it was these four facets of the Church of God in Christ that had the most significant influence on Andraé and Sandra: the denomination's continued emphasis, from the church's earliest days, on its adherents being active disciples of the message of Jesus Christ, living in a "holy" manner, the anticipation of the Second Coming of Jesus, and an all-consuming passion for the evangelizing of nonbelievers. Where the Church of God in Christ differed from other Pentecostal belief systems is that those four aspects were coupled with the widespread, enthusiastic support and participation of women in music evangelism as well as in education.

As early as 1917, Mason had authorized the denomination to create the Department of Evangelism, charged with enrolling converts and living by the motto "The Flames of Evangelism Must Never Go Out." One of the earliest stars of the denomination was Lillian Brooks Correy, the "Singing Evangelist," who would later assume the title of General Overseer of Women's Work for the Church of God in Christ.[17]

All these core elements appear repeatedly in Andraé's songs and sermons all of the way through his final recordings decades later. The COGIC tradition on the West Coast verified the vigorous musical evangelism of the denomination through focus on "saving the lost" by any holiness means necessary. While Crouch's family may have owned a dry-cleaning business, it mostly served as an outreach to the community at large . . . essentially, Crouch Sr.'s "day job" that enabled him to passionately preach the gospel. Whereas most COGIC traditions elsewhere demanded and were often dominated by strict adherence to denominational doctrine related to smoking, drinking, and dancing; wearing makeup, jewelry, and "worldly" clothing; and abstinence from all other aspects of popular culture, it appears that Crouch's family was—first and foremost—solely focused on the salvation of the soul, determining that the change on the inside would ultimately influence all outer appearances, whatever that might be or become.[18]

And it was into this rich, turbulent world, at this time and in this place, that Andraé Edward and Sandra Elaine Crouch arrived.

Childhood

Andraé and Sandra were born to Benjamin Jerome and Catherine Hodnett Crouch on July 1, 1942, in the home of his grandmother at 33rd and Compton in Los Angeles, joining their two-year-old brother, Benjamin Jerome Crouch Jr. The Crouches lived behind Crouch Cleaners, at 47th and Compton, for two years before purchasing the nearby Embassy Cleaners, which featured more living space for the growing family. Andraé's slim autobiography (written with Nina Ball, 1974), *Through It All: Andraé Crouch*, says that his father's primary concern was not laundry, but evangelism at nights and on weekends, primarily along Long Beach Boulevard and Vernon Avenue. Significantly, this "bootleggin' street preacher" (as his wife and friends dubbed him) was not a "hellfire and brimstone" street corner evangelist. Instead, Andraé writes, his father consistently preached "the love of Jesus" because he "wanted to spread the gospel, see people saved, and minister to their needs," though he was not yet "appointed" to the ministry. By age three, both Sandra and Andraé regularly accompanied their father on his rounds, shaking hands with addicts and alcoholics, often bringing them home, where they were "cleaned up" and given "surplus" shirts from their dry cleaners. At night, Benjamin Sr. would take his new acquaintances to church (Image 1.1).[19]

At the time, the Crouch family faithfully attended Emmanuel Church of God in Christ at 1399 E. 33rd Street in South Central Los Angeles, founded and pastored by Benjamin's relative, Bishop Samuel Martin Crouch Jr. Sandra said that because Bishop Samuel had been a Methodist before he converted to the Church of God in Christ, he spoke softly, his diction was "classy," and that he was both a "great teacher" and a world traveler. From the prism of eighty years later, it is difficult to know just how significant a role Bishop Crouch played in the ministry of Andraé Crouch. But he certainly plays an outsized role in the annals of the Church of God in Christ, behind only Charles H. Mason, Gilbert Earl Patterson, and a few others. Samuel Crouch was originally from Dallas and eventually pastored churches in Denison, Fort Worth, and Dallas. In 1949, *Ebony* magazine called Samuel the "first known Negro radio preacher" when he began broadcasting on a Fort Worth station in 1924. Samuel traveled to Fresno, California, in 1927, at the invitation of both COGIC evangelist Mother Emma Cotton and his mother, Mother Rose Tucker, who had come to California earlier. Samuel Crouch's name can be found repeatedly through the convention programs at the University of Southern California Digital Library's Pentecostal and Charismatic Research Archive until his death on August 14, 1976. The 1976 program features a two-page spread, "In Memoriam," that lists Samuel Crouch's many accomplishments in the church following his election as "Bishop" in 1940 while still pastor at

Image 1.1 Twins Sandra and Andraé Crouch as they appeared on the back jacket of the *Just Andraé* album. (Light Records LS-5598-LP, administered by MNRK Music Group)

Emmanuel Church of God in Christ. During his life, Samuel achieved some of the highest leadership positions in the denomination. He also initiated and coordinated mission efforts overseas, established more than 250 low-cost housing units in the area, and pioneered the church's California-based radio outreach. However, when the "host pastor" of Emmanuel, Supt. Wilbert Jones Jr., honored Bishop Samuel Crouch's legacy with a special memorial service to mark the fortieth anniversary of his passing, Jones chose to highlight Samuel's efforts to transform his congregation into "personal workers," and how he "dispatched them to hospitals, convalescent homes, prisons, skid row and street corners throughout Los Angeles to minister."[20]

Throughout his career, Andraé felt a special calling to society's outcasts and spent several years working with alcoholics and unhoused people in Los Angeles, making him unique among gospel artists of the day. He later broke long tradition in gospel music by writing songs directly addressing these and similar issues.

Meanwhile, as the family's dry-cleaning business flourished, Benjamin Crouch, who had received a degree from Wilberforce College in Ohio, began taking classes, first at the International Church of the Foursquare Gospel-affiliated L.I.F.E. Bible College in Los Angeles, then Biola College. According to Andraé, his father vowed to "do whatever the Lord wanted him to do," if his legs would be healed following a hit-and-run accident that broke both of his legs and crushed his kneecaps. During his nine-month convalescence, the elder Crouch began preaching as a fill-in pastor at small churches in the area. At age nine, both Sandra and Andraé made public professions of their faith and were baptized by their father. The Crouch family then joined Macedonia Church of God in Christ in Val Verde, more than seventy miles away, with Benjamin preaching on Sundays and again evangelizing at area prisons, addiction clinics, and hospitals. Sandra recalled that their father had his children accompany him to sing, whether it was during a revival service or on a street corner. "We'd sing a cappella," she said, "because my dad said, 'If you can really sing, you got learn how to sing without a keyboard, because you might go someplace and they don't have a keyboard, what are you going to do?" Crouch Sr. also insisted the three children know the "parts"—tenor, alto, soprano—to every song they sang. When Macedonia "called" Benjamin Crouch to become its permanent pastor, he agreed—on the condition that the Lord would "give Andraé the gift of music" since the small church did not have a full-time pianist, an important consideration in the music-dominated COGIC tradition. Benjamin called his son to the front of the congregation and asked, "Andraé, if the Lord gives you the gift of music, will you use it?" Andraé writes in his biography that his response was both immediate and emphatic: "Yes, Daddy. I'll play for the Lord," even though to that point he had neither played a musical instrument nor received any musical training. His mother quickly bought him a cardboard piano to practice on and the family purchased a used piano a week later. It was then that Andraé set about learning the instrument primarily by ear. Two weeks later, Andraé accompanied his father's congregation as they sang the gospel hymn "What a Friend We Have in Jesus," though he had to "run up the scale to find out what key they were singing in." "In our churches," he said later, "they sing in any key, you know, and just take off without a songbook. It was just really a touch of God and I knew that He had a plan for my life." Sandra said that both she and her brother Ben Jr. were "shocked" by what happened that morning. "I had never seen anybody lay hands on someone and God speaks," she said. As promised, his father then accepted the pastorate. Music itself was a salvation for Andraé, who had a childhood stutter, which meant, he said later, that he "couldn't tell anybody about how I felt about Christ." His father, Andraé said, had told him, "You never stutter when you sing." Andraé soon sang his responses to questions, including when asked the time of day. Armed with his newfound talent, Andraé organized a church choir and quickly began performing at COGIC district meetings and youth rallies. Shortly thereafter, he joined brother Ben and sister Sandra in a group they called "The Crouch Trio," even performing at the annual Church of God in Christ convention in Memphis.[21]

Benjamin and Catherine emphasized the importance of family—and this family was focused entirely on church. Both Andraé and Sandra said that their lives revolved around their churches, Emmanuel, Macedonia, and then Christ Memorial. "We had a great life," Sandra recalled. "They made everybody feel that church was the best thing besides heaven. Everything was fun." So much so, that Andraé and Sandra would sneak into the family car and hide when their father traveled to revivals or the prison ministries—and only reveal themselves when it was too late to turn around. Later, at Christ Memorial, family members automatically served as needed, whether it was forming and singing in a choir, cleaning the bathrooms, attending a program, or ushering at services. "You had to do all that," Sandra said. "That's what we did in the family."[22]

Music was at the heart of most family get-togethers. In COGIC circles, particularly in the smaller churches, spontaneous, improvised singing was common: "Writing songs on the spot," Sandra called it, though at the larger, more-established Emmanuel COGIC, the congregation sang from hymnals. But unlike many COGIC families, the Crouches also listened to secular music at home. "My father loved all kinds of music," she said. "He could play a little jazz with his right hand. He loved opera. He kept us filled with all kinds of music. From that, hearing all types of music, that's how Andraé's ear was very sensitive to different styles of music. It wasn't all gospel." Among the artists they heard was Aretha Franklin. When a Franklin song came on the radio or on the turntable, Sandra said her father would turn to Andraé and ask: "'How do you like that? Can you play that? Try to play that.' Andraé had a really good ear and he could play anything he heard. He could pick it up." Of his gospel influences, Andraé often cited the artist he called the "guru of gospel," James Cleveland. Andraé said his father's favorite group was the Davis Sisters: "When I was growing up, they were probably one of my biggest influences because their background vocal sounds like horns to me."[23]

Christ Memorial Church of God in Christ

In 1951, while still commuting to Macedonia in Val Verde, Benjamin Crouch Sr. was approached by members of his congregation who lived in the San Fernando Valley about the possibility of establishing a new COGIC church there. The family relocated to Pacoima while Andraé and Sandra were still in junior high school. Under Crouch's leadership, the new church quickly grew from a small gathering in a congregant's garage to a storefront on Van Nuys Boulevard to what would become the present location at 13333 Vaughn Street, where it became Christ Memorial Church. Sandra attributed the rapid growth to her father's style of preaching. While he could be loud on the street corners, his sermons and personal conversations were "very, very, very gentle." Ola Andrews, a childhood friend of the Crouches, said that Benjamin was a "very good preacher" and a "very loving person." "My father wasn't the type that beat the gospel into you," Sandra recalled. "People love the Lord because how much my father and mother loved God. I think that if you tell people enough about heaven, you don't have to preach about hell. I think we teach that same kind of style. I know Andraé did, even with the music." Singer and longtime family friend Linda McCrary remembered Sandra and Andraé traveling with their father in the back of an open truck, singing and preaching on the streets of Pacoima. When father Benjamin could no longer continue the practice, McCrary said that Sandra continued in his place.[24]

In a later interview, Andraé said that the family's dry cleaners always closed at 5 P.M. on church night, even if there was a long line of people waiting. Andraé and Sandra would walk from school to the cleaners, do their homework, and help around the business until it was time to go home, clean up, and get ready for services. Customers could also expect to be "witnessed to" by either of his parents. "Every person that came into the cleaners," Andraé recalled, "if they could lead into a conversation about the Lord, they not only had that person's clothes but they would be praying for them to meet the Lord. That's the way I grew up."[25]

The "Call" to Evangelism

Andraé writes that it was while playing "His Eye Is on the Sparrow" on the piano that he first heard God's call to ministry, though in what form he did not yet know. Among his early projects at Christ Memorial was to organize a "kickin'" youth choir of ten singers. As described in *Through It All*, when the choir performed at district youth meetings, the ten voices "sounded like fifty." Emboldened by his newfound success, Andraé began singing with his new friends from the junior high school and, later, San Fernando and Fremont high schools. From the beginning, Sandra said, Andraé was the pianist and she was the percussionist, usually with a tambourine. Andraé also manipulated the foot pedal on the piano to make it sound like a bass drum. "He would hit it like that and flap it," she said.[26]

It was not until more than twenty years later, in one of his first interviews with a major African American magazine, that Andraé admitted to *Sepia* that he had actually changed his name while in high school: "My twin sister at birth was named *Sandra* and I was called *Andra*—it rhymed. I hated that, so when I was in high school I took my birth certificate and added the 'e' at the end. Now it's legally Andraé."[27]

"The Blood (Will Never Lose Its Power)"

At some point during late 1950s or early 1960s—neither Andraé nor Sandra precisely remembered the date—the Crouches and young friend Billy Preston were invited to the home of a friend hosting famed gospel artist the Reverend James Cleveland. Based on evidence from other interviews, the twins were about fourteen or fifteen at the time, though they could have been as old as seventeen or eighteen. In 2007, Andraé recalled how Billy, Andraé, and Sandra attended a party for a children's choir Cleveland had formed. From a kitchen window, Andraé said he saw Cleveland in the backyard, hosting a barbecue. Too nervous to introduce himself, he silently admired the legendary songwriter. At one point, Andraé said that he mumbled, "Boy, I sure wish I could write a song." It was the first time he said he had directly asked for the "gift" of songwriting. As the three friends continued to watch, Cleveland poured a red barbecue sauce over a rack of ribs. Andraé was mesmerized:

> All of a sudden, five minutes after I prayed this prayer, my hearing went out and everything turned to slow motion. All I could hear was the blood splashing. It sounded like the blood of Jesus. As they were pouring the sauce over these ribs, I remember speaking the words: "Ooh! It's blood."

Andraé grabbed Sandra and Billy and took them back to the living room, which featured a large piano. Andraé sat down and said, "Billy! Come and play this!" Crouch played a melody as he sang, "The blood that Jesus shed for me," then ceded the piano bench to Preston:

> Billy took that and played it and I said, "Ooh, that's not good." My sister had been writing down the words. I took the paper and balled it up and just threw it in the sink. We threw it in the trash because I didn't think it was anything. I didn't understand what God was doing.

But Sandra fished the crumpled paper out of the trash bin. "Andraé, that's a good song. Play it again." Reluctantly, Andraé said, he complied:

> We started playing it some more and then all of a sudden I got into it and then when I opened my eyes, everybody that was in the back came up and started singing it. They were crying. And the Lord just took that song and took it all around the world.[28]

It was about this time that Andraé began assembling a small group of friends to create a gospel group, one he would name the COGICs.

NOTES

1. Hundreds of books have been written on California in the second half of the twentieth century, particularly Southern California. Some of the more lively histories include Andrew Rolle and Arthur P. Verge, *California: A History* (Chichester, UK: Wiley Blackwell, 2015); Carey McWilliams, *Southern California: An Island on the Land* (Layton, UT: Peregrine Smith, 1949, 2009); and the excellent companion volume by Carey McWilliams and Lewis H. Lapham, *California: The Great Exception* (Oakland: University of California Press, 1999). A host of excellent books examine the economies (and related racial impacts) of the area, including Sarah D. Wald, *The Nature of California: Race, Citizenship and Farming Since the Dust Bowl* (Seattle: University of Washington Press, 2016); and Thomas Patterson, *From Acorns to Warehouses: Historical Political Economy of Southern California's Inland Empire* (Milton Park, UK: Routledge, 2014).

2. Likewise, the books and articles on the music of California, from San Francisco south, would fill a small library. Some of the ones the authors particularly enjoyed: William McKeen, *Everybody Had an Ocean: Music and Mayhem in 1960s Los Angeles* (Chicago: Chicago Review Press, 2017); Barney Hoskins, *Waiting for the Sun: A Rock 'n' Roll History of Los Angeles* (New York: Backbeat Books, 1996, 2003, 2009); Ted Gioia, *West Coast Jazz: Modern Jazz in California, 1945–1960* (New York: Oxford University Press); Steven Loza, *Barrio Rhythm: Mexican American Music in Los Angeles* (Chicago: University of Chicago Press, 1993); Lynell George, *No Crystal Stair: African-Americans in the City of Angels* (London: Verso Books, 1992); and Jacqueline Cogdell DjeDje and Eddie S. Meadows, eds., *California Soul: Music of African Americans in the West* (Berkeley: University of California Press, 1998).

3. Jacqueline Cogdell DjeDje, interview the authors, February 19, 2021.

4. Jacqueline Cogdell DjeDje, "The California Black Gospel Music Tradition: A Confluence of Musical Styles and Cultures," in DjeDje and Meadows, *California Soul*, 130–132.

5. DjeDje, "The California Black Gospel Music Tradition," 133–134.

6. DjeDje, "The California Black Gospel Music Tradition," 140–141.

7. DjeDje, "The California Black Gospel Music Tradition," 140–141; DjeDje interview.

8. Nadra Nittle, "Los Angeles's Role in the Rise and Mainstreaming of Gospel Music," *PBS SoCal Los Angeles*, June 21, 2019.

9. Several informative sources chronicle the history of the Church of God in Christ and its theology, including Ithiel C. Clemmons, *Bishop C. H. Mason and the Roots of the Church of God in Christ: Centennial Edition* (Largo, MD: Christian Living Books, 2020); Anthea D. Butler, *Women in the Church of God in Christ: Making a Sanctified World* (Chapel Hill: University of North Carolina Press, 2007); and Ovell Hamilton, *Sanctified Revolution: The Church of God in Christ: A History of African American Holiness* (Itapira, Brazil: UP Books, 2021).

10. Horace Boyer, *How Sweet the Sound: The Golden Age of Gospel* (Washington, DC: Elliott & Clark, 1995), 18–23.

11. James B. Boyer, "Gospel Music in the COGIC Tradition: A Historical Perspective," *Rejoice!*, Fall 1989, 15.

12. Michael Corcoran, *Ghost Notes: Pioneering Spirits of Texas Music* (Fort Worth: Texas Christian University Press, 2020), 22–30.

13. Corcoran, *Ghost Notes*, 31–33; Terrence Curry, interview with the authors, September 10, 2020.

14. Joop Visser, *Sister Rosetta Tharpe: The Original Soul Sister*, Properbox 51 (four-CD collection) booklet, 8–9.

15. Gayle Wald, *Shout, Sister, Shout!: The Untold Story of Rock-n-Roll Trailblazer Sister Rosetta Tharpe* (Boston: Beacon Books, 2008), 38–39, 125–130.

16. James Boyer, "Gospel Music in the COGIC Tradition," 16–17.

THE WORLD THAT SHAPED ANDRAÉ CROUCH   23

17. Hamilton, *Sanctified Revolution*; Samuel S. Hill, ed., *Encyclopedia of Religion in the South* (Macon, GA: Mercer University Press, 1984), 93.

18. On COGIC theology, see Hamilton, *Sanctified Revolution*; Hill, *Encyclopedia of Religion in the South*; and Stanley M. Burgess, ed., *The New International Dictionary of Pentecostal and Charismatic Movements* (Grand Rapids, MI: Zondervan, 2002).

19. Andraé Crouch with Nina Ball, *Through It All: Andraé Crouch* (Waco, TX: Word Books, 1974), 18–19.

20. Andraé Crouch, *Through It All*, 20; "Emmanuel COGIC Salutes Legacy of Bishop Crouch," *Los Angeles Sentinel*, August 4, 2016 (https:lassentinel.net /emmanual-cogic-salutes-legacy-of-bishop-crouch.html); Butler, *Women in the Church of God in Christ*, 127, 129, 141, 147; "69th Annual Holy Convocation Official Program," Church of God in Christ, November 9–19, 1976, 76–77; "Top Radio Ministers: Negro Preachers, on Air Since 1924, Now Broadcast in Every Major U.S. City to 7,000,000 Listeners," *Ebony* 4, no. 9 (July 1949): 56–61; Louis F. Morgan, "The Flame Still Burns," *Charisma Magazine*, https://myc harisma.com/charisma-archive/the-flame-still-burns/; Sandra Crouch, interview with the authors, November 4, 2020; Stephen Gardner, personal correspondence with the authors, December 22, 2023; Timothy J. DeWerff, personal correspondence with the authors, August 27, 2024.

Note: Both Andraé and Sandra Crouch informally referred to Bishop Samuel Crouch as "uncle" or "great-uncle." But the genealogical research of Dr. Stephen Gardner and Timothy J. DeWerff indicates that Bishop Crouch was, in fact, their first cousin, once removed. Authors Darden and Newby believe that the "uncle" or "great-uncle" designation was an informal one used within the Crouch family, as has happened in both of their extended families, a familiar and affectionate "title" that eventually became codified in the family story. Regardless of Samuel Crouch's official biological relationship with first Benjamin Crouch and later Andraé and Sandra, it is clear from their writings and interviews that he played an important role in their lives.

21. https://newchristmemorial.org/legacy; "Benjamin Crouch; Church Founder," *Los Angeles Times*, December 23, 1993; Andraé Crouch, *Through It All*, 27, 36–40; Sandra Crouch, interview with the authors, November 4, 2020; Ruthie Edgerly Oberg, "The COGIC Minister Who Bridged the Racial Gap in Gospel Music," *AG News*, May 24, 2018; Tavis Smiley, "Interview: Singer-Songwriter Andraé Crouch Discusses His Career," *Tavis Smiley*, June 8, 2004.

22. Sandra Crouch, interview with the authors, November 4, 2020.

23. Sandra Crouch, interview with the authors, November 4, 2020; Bob Gersztyn, "Andraé's Music Will Never Lose Its Power," *The Wittenburg Door*, no. 192 (March/April 2005).

24. Andraé Crouch, *Through It All*, 43–44; Sandra Crouch, interview with the authors, November 4, 2020; Ola Jean Andrews, interview with the authors,

August 6, 2021; Linda McCrary-Fisher, interview with the authors, February 23, 2022.

25. James Abbington, *Direction for Music and Worship in the African-American Church: Interviews with Pastors, Theologians and Musicians* (DMA diss., Church Liturgical Music, University of Michigan, 1998), 16.

26. Andraé Crouch, *Through It All*, 43–45; Sandra Crouch, interview with the authors, November 4, 2020.

27. Patrick Salvo, "New King of 'Pop Gospel,'" *Sepia*, December 1976, 54.

28. Mike Rimmer, "Andraé Crouch: 64-Year-Old Gospel Legend Cuts 'Smokin'' Church Music," *Cross Rhythms*, January 13, 2007, https://www.crossrhyt hms.co.uk/articles/music/Andrae_Crouch_64_Year_Old_Gospel_Legend_C uts_Smokin_Church_Music/25534/; Gerstyzn, "Andraé's Music Will Never Lose Its Power."

2

The COGICs

It's a Blessing

While they were still in their teens, it's barely hyperbole to claim that the COGICs may have been one of the most talented aggregations of gospel artists of any age ever assembled. Over a period of weeks in 1959, Andraé and Sandra were joined by Frankie C. Springs, Billy Preston, Edna Wright, Gloria Jones, and Sondra "Blinky" Williams, all of whom would achieve musical success on their own in the years to come.[1]

Sandra remembered meeting Frankie, who went by Frankie Karl, through his mother, an usher at the Emmanuel COGIC. "We put Frankie in the group because he had a piano and that's what we rehearsed [on]," Sandra recalled. Gloria Jones and Frankie were already friends and Jones credited Karl with introducing her to gospel music. Jones recalled driving in her father's Pontiac with Andraé, Sandra, Wright, Williams, Karl, and Preston, and hearing the Reverend James Cleveland sing "Peace Be Still" on the radio:

> "Gloria, the Caravans are coming into town. Go down to the Olympia Stadium." I knew nothing of this. I would go with them. We were just children. Then we would see Inez [Andrews] come and sing, "Mary, Don't You Weep," Mavis Staples and Shirley Caesar shout across the stage. So Frankie and I grew up around this. This is how we became friends. Mavis, that's who influenced me—and that's who Andraé actually tried to make me sound like.[2]

In junior high school, Jones and another friend, Jeanie Greenlee, sang with Karl as the Wonder Teens. Jones said that Karl was already composing gospel songs and that the trio occasionally performed in area churches. "Frankie was a beautiful child, inside and out," Jones recalled. "His special talent was as an artist and he could recognize talent in a bumble bee." At one point at a

Church of God in Christ convention, Karl encountered Cleveland and asked if the Wonder Teens could sing for him. When the time arrived, the Teens performed the familiar COGIC song "My Soul Loves Jesus." Cleveland kindly encouraged the singers. According to Jones, it was that same summer in the late 1950s that Andraé first talked about forming a group of his own with sister Sandra. Eventually, the Wonder Teens and Andraé's new aggregation merged, though Greenlee's family moved away shortly thereafter. The newly named COGICs quickly began singing in area churches, conventions, and even colleges. When Karl joined the Air Force, he introduced Andraé to Billy Preston, who in turn brought schoolmate Edna Wright to the promising new group.[3]

The unquestioned musical star of the COGICs was William Everett Preston. Born in Houston in 1946, Billy Preston moved with his mother, Robbie Lee Williams, to Los Angeles, where she became the long-tenured organist for choir director Thurston Frazier at the influential Victory Baptist Church. Billy's sister Rodena was married to future COGICs singer "Blinky" Williams's brother Austin. According to Williams, Rodena was a brilliant keyboard player herself. When Preston was still a child, Rodena allowed him to sit on her lap and put his hands on hers while she played. A keyboard prodigy who never took a music lesson, by age ten Preston had already accompanied the "gospel royalty" who regularly visited Victory Baptist, including Mahalia Jackson. In the audience that evening was Robert Smith, the producer of a film in pre-production featuring Nat King Cole. Smith quickly chose Preston to portray a young W. C. Handy in *St. Louis Blues*, released by Paramount in 1958. While he was still in junior high, Preston's electrifying gospel performances at Victory Baptist and elsewhere soon also caught the attention of both Little Richard and Ray Charles. Sam Cooke tabbed Preston to play the organ on his *Nightbeat* album in February 1963 and a month later took him to the studio to record a solo project, *16 Yr. Old Soul*, for his own SAR label. Jones said that by the time Preston joined the COGICs, he was already a star:

> He had already played on "Drown in My Own Tears" with Ray Charles; he had already played solos for Martin Luther King Jr., Clara Ward and Mahalia Jackson. He was able to encourage Andraé not to be discouraged of his not having all of the proper training, but to have confidence in his writing, in his stories, in his life, in his story about telling about God and really believing in those words. Billy had

already been to Europe, seen the world, been around the United States. We had only been from Pacoima to Los Angeles, but he was humble, so gracious that he never made us feel less than him.

Jones said that one memorable incident from the early days with the COGIC Singers came after Catherine Crouch had just bought Andraé and Sandra their first car, a used Ford Falcon. But the Crouches were nervous about driving the vehicle in city traffic, especially if it meant parallel parking or driving in reverse. Preston, then just thirteen, volunteered to drive and did it effortlessly. Jones said she then asked him, "Billy, where did you learn how to back up a car and drive like this?" Billy responded, "John Lennon. I was with Little Richard in Germany and this group opened for us and they're going to be biggest stars in the world. They're going to be called the Beatles."[4]

The four female vocalists for the COGICs were all the daughters of pastors. Like Sandra's father, Benjamin Crouch, Gloria Jones's father, Elder Richard Jones, was with COGIC and had been a childhood friend of Bishop Samuel Crouch Sr. The area COGIC congregations, including the much larger Emmanuel, met regularly, and Jones said she had known the thirteen-year-old Crouch twins since the age of ten. Wright's father was a bishop in the Apostolic tradition and Williams's father was Baptist. "We were all community children," Jones recalled, "growing up in in Los Angeles, enjoying the wonderful world of gospel. That was our football games, that was our lives. We would take a collection if we performed. Sandra was always the treasurer. Then we would go and have our hamburgers and hot dogs and pop."[5]

Gloria Richetta Jones was born in Cincinnati in 1945, and at age four her father asked her to sing at his church. "They thought it was just going to be like a little child getting up there," she said. The results surprised and delighted the congregation. Jones's family moved to Los Angeles in 1953, where she studied classical piano and continued to sing in her church. Jones was soon invited to sing in the choir on Sunday afternoons at Grace Community Church of God in Christ on Compton Avenue. The Sunday afternoon "sings" attracted a host of well-known singers, including Lou Rawls, Thelma Houston, and Merry Clayton. Also a member of the church and in the choir was Sherman Andrus, a future member of the Disciples. It was shortly thereafter that Jones met first Karl, then the Crouches.[6]

Edna Wright, who walked with Preston to and from school during junior high, was the daughter of the Bishop J. W. Wright, pastor of King's Holiness Chapel in Los Angeles. Like the others, she began singing early in her father's church. Wright was the younger sister of Darlene Wright, who later became better known as Darlene Love. Both girls sang in the choir and, unlike in some Pentecostal families, their father allowed them to listen to popular music. "I watched Diana Ross, I watched Martha Reeves, and I said, 'Oh, that's phenomenal,'" she said in a later interview. Her father, Wright said, considered that all music was spiritual. Close friends Wright and Sondra Williams attended Fremont High School and sang in the a cappella choir.

It was during the tenth grade, Williams recalled, that they first met Gloria Jones. "Gloria said, 'Wow, I like the way you sing. Do you guys sing in a group?'" When Williams said they did not, Jones pressed on: "Well, do you know Andraé Crouch? We're looking for a lead singer and an alto, so would you come to our rehearsal?" The first rehearsal was at Jones's house and the Crouches were in attendance. "They liked my voice and they liked me immediately," Williams said. After an hour or so, Williams said she had to beg off and leave before the session wrapped up. "Look, I got to get to church because my choir rehearses tonight and I'm the choir director," she said.

But Sandra and Andraé, who were from the stricter Church of God in Christ tradition, still had a few more questions for Williams:

> They said, "Oh my God, what's the name of your church?" And I told them Rev. Austin Williams'. And Sandra said, "Oh God, we're all preacher's kids, all pastor's kids. Are you saved and sanctified" And I said, "Yes, I'm saved and sanctified." "Are you filled with the Holy Ghost?" "Yes, I'm filled with the Holy Ghost." "Do you play piano? Have you been baptized with fire?" So that's how I met Gloria, that's how I met Sandra and Andraé. We all fell in love with each other and became extremely close. I found out that Gloria lived down the street from me and so we all became best friends.[7]

Originally from Stockton, California, Sondra "Blinky" Williams began singing in the church of her father, the Reverend Austin E. Williams, Friendly Fellowship Baptist Church in Watts. The family moved to Watts in 1959 and Williams said that the first meeting of the young singers who would ultimately compose the COGICs came later that year. "That was just a movement of the Lord, because the moment we became friends and started singing, we didn't really care to be around anybody [else]," Williams said. "We were like sisters and brothers. The Lord just brought us together and made us brothers and sisters."[8]

Early Days with the COGICs

With the final lineup in place, the COGICs began rehearsing regularly, and word quickly spread through church circles about a talented group of teenagers who could galvanize a congregation. "All of us, as far as we were concerned, we were COGICs for a lifetime," Williams said. "We were together every Saturday and every Sunday for years. My ambition was never to become a singer. Our ambitions were to be COGICs forever." The Crouch's church, Christ Memorial, was a frequent venue, in part because Andraé and Sandra had a car, Williams said, and because the group also performed regularly on Pastor Benjamin Crouch's weekly radio show at Christ Memorial, broadcasts which continued well into the 1970s.[9]

Longtime Crouch family friend and musician Carrie Gonzalo remembered an early COGICs performance at influential gospel composer Doris Akers's Sky Pilot Revival Center in 1960, as well as at the monthly "Sounds of Soul" programs at Wilmington Assemblies of God in Wilmington, California, and Glengrove Assemblies of God in La Puente. In Wilmington, the COGICs served as the "host" group and Gonzalo's "Carrie's Company" opened. At La Puente, the Glengrove choir would open. Well-known composer Audrey Mieir had recommended the COGICs to the congregations and sometimes introduced them at the concerts. Equally intriguing is that Carrie's Company, Gonzalo's group, featured "full-blood Filipinos." "Since Audrey introduced him, that opened the door for Andraé to go into the white churches," Gonzalo said. "We had a nice multicultural event going on, which I think for those times was very good." The two concerts continued even after Andraé Crouch and the Disciples was formed.[10]

According to Williams, Andraé was the undisputed director of the COGICs, despite Preston's prodigious talents. "Billy was super big-hearted," Williams said. "Very nice, funny, witty. He looked up to Andraé, he never tried to take over." When well-known pop and R&B singers continued to try and lure Preston away, Williams said that Preston would reply, "No, I want to sing with COGICs." When they would ask him, "Well, can you play on this number?" Preston would say, "No, I must sing with the COGICs."[11]

Jones said that while Andraé was in charge of the music, sister Sandra was the "boss" of the group and something of a taskmaster at the frequent rehearsals:

> Sandra was very much like her father. If she said we had to wear certain robes, we wore those robes. Or if our hair had to be a certain style. She believed in discipline. She believed in us being ladies at all times and that we were representing the Church of God in Christ, even though Edna was Apostolic, Billy and Sondra Williams were Baptist—it didn't matter. We were still singers for God.[12]

The "singers for God" were soon in demand throughout the Valley, performing for congregations from several denominations as well as at various youth-related activities. During this period, Sandra and Andraé became friends with the Youth for Christ director at San Fernando High School, Sonny Salsbury, who also wrote and performed religious music and who would soon play a role in the developing "Jesus Movement" in Southern California. (Sonny's younger brother Ron also became involved in the movement, founding J. C. Power Outlet, an early country-rock group.) The Salsburys invited the COGICs to sing at Nazarene College in Pasadena and remained close to the Crouches through their careers. As for Andraé, he daily juggled singing and performing with the high school choir, the Christ Memorial choir, the COGICs, as well as his schoolwork.[13]

According to Sandra, whatever spare time Andraé carved out of his busy schedule always went to songwriting:

> I don't know how many songs that he started, because whenever he sat down, he would write a song. It's just like talking to a friend. He would sit down at the piano and there was music that always came because. . . . God is always talking. He would write songs and words that we didn't even understand. I'd say, "Where did you get that word from?" He'd say, "I don't know. I just heard it."

Occasionally, Andraé would start a song and ask Sandra for an opinion. If she liked it, he would return to the piano—but not always on the same song. "Go back to that song," Sandra said she often told Andraé. "That's a good song. Don't leave that. Stay right there."[14]

Williams remembered that during the earliest years with the COGICs, however, that Andraé was not yet confident enough to introduce his original songs to the group. Instead, she said, they performed songs by the Staple Singers, the Caravans, Dorothy Norwood, and other gospel artists.[15]

In 1962, Williams said she began working part-time as a receptionist for Fred Smith, one of the owners of the small Tri-Disc label, whose best-known act at the time was the Olympics. After Smith heard that Williams sang in her church, he took her to the studio to record two songs, "A Bird in the Hand" and "Surprise Party" (Tri-Disc 108), under the name of "Lindy Lou Adams." When the Crouches finally discovered that Williams had sung "secular" music while still with the COGICs, Williams said a religious intervention followed, led by Catherine Crouch. During the intervention, members of the congregation prayed for her soul at the church altar. But soon thereafter other members of the COGICs began to be approached by pop and R&B producers as well.[16]

Like Sandra, Williams said that by 1964, the group was singing regularly as far north as Palo Alto and Oakland. In time, savvy churches and local promoters began hiring the COGICs to open for the national gospel artists that appeared regularly throughout Southern California. But Jones said that some of the established gospel artists quickly became wary of the exciting group of teenagers. "We were so good," Jones said, "the stars didn't want us to open." Eventually, she said, Andraé's winsome personality won over some of the biggest gospel artists, including Inez Andrews and Shirley Caesar. "They loved him so much, they still gave us a chance to sing and to open for them," Jones said, "but it was very difficult." Even as the COGICs' presence in the gospel community was increasing, a concert in early 1964 changed their trajectory. The group opened a well-publicized program, featuring the Staple Singers, the Blind Boys of Alabama, and the Caravans, produced by Richard Simpson, a producer/promoter with ties to Vee-Jay Records.[17]

The First Producer: Richard Simpson

The New York–based Simpson's name began appearing on albums and 45s as early as 1960, producing the likes of James Cleveland, Sallie Martin, and the Caravans, first for small gospel labels like HOB and Seg-Way, and then for the much larger Vee-Jay Records in Chicago. Simpson clearly had some clout in the industry and signed artists to his own Simpson label, which was distributed through Vee-Jay. For a time, Vee-Jay was one of the most influential record labels in the United States, with a wide-ranging roster that included the first Beatles record released in the United States, as well as John Lee Hooker, the Four Seasons, Dick Gregory, Jerry Butler, and many others. The gospel line was equally potent and included the Swan Silvertones, Dorothy Love Coates and the Gospel Harmonettes, and others. While Simpson produced a variety of acts, Williams said that his apparent preference for gospel music earned him the sobriquet "Bishop," though he had no apparent religious affiliation, much less a true ecclesiastical title.[18]

The COGICs' appearance at the well-attended gospel program was a huge success. "When [the other artists] came out on stage, they just couldn't believe this young group of kids," Williams recalled. After the concert, Simpson told the COGICs that he was going to produce the Caravans and the other gospel groups performing at the program and wanted to record them as well. "We had to get permission from our families," Williams said. "Two nights later, they had us in a studio." Fortunately for the COGICs, Andraé had been stockpiling original compositions. According to Sandra, the songs on what would comprise the first COGICs LP were written over a period of two weeks. "He would just say, 'Sing this,' and we'd go, 'Oh, OK,'" Sandra recalled:

> He would write those songs really fast because one thing about Andraé, if he got stuck on a lyric or something, he'd say, "Wait, a minute, wait a minute, wait, wait, wait." Then he would have us singing—whoever was nearby—because he loved good voices. Once they began to sing his music, he would get fresh ideas because he always heard fresh music.[19]

The *It's a Blessing* Session

The COGICs met Simpson, Jones recalled, at Harmony Recorders, 1467 North Vine Street, in Los Angeles, in what she described as a "ship-shaped" building, with the recording studio in the basement. From the beginning, she said that Simpson really did not understand the group or its ethos:

> He was the top promoter for Vee-Jay Records and here he had all of these young people and he loved us. But you have to remember, we were different because we were gospel singers who came into rock and roll. He was used to working with your Philadelphia stars and all of a sudden you've got these little young teenagers. We were cute and innocent, but still Christian girls. You've got Andraé, you've got Frankie, who's absolutely gorgeous, and you've got Billy who is the fifth Beatle. So did they really understand us? I doubt it.[20]

Even for the well-rehearsed COGICs, the recording session was a blur. Jones called it "essentially" a live album. "I will never forget, Andraé said, 'OK, let's start with "It's a Blessing,"' and we just went until it was finished. And then he went to the second one. Not even a playback. One take. Amazing."[21]

What would become the *It's a Blessing* album features eleven songs credited to Andraé: "Don't Let It Be Said Too Late," "It Will Never Lose Its Power," also known as "The Blood (Will Never Lose Its Power)," "My Soul Loves Jesus," "Since I Found Him," "Nothing Is Greater," "Won't It Be Sad," "Say Yes," "He Included Me," "Don't Stop Using Me," "He Lives," and "It's a Blessing," as well as Andraé's arrangement of the gospel hymn "There Is a Fountain." Revé Gipson, who would later work with Frankie Beverly and Maze's publishing division, wrote the liner notes. In them, Gipson notes that she asked the group, "What advice would you give to a teenager or perhaps even a friend who is interested in become a gospel singer?" Andraé responded, quoting from a song by Thomas Dorsey and, perhaps, reflecting the pressures the various members of the COGICs were already facing from popular music: "I would encourage them to go on and stick with gospel singing and live the life they are singing about." Gipson called Andraé a "gifted and talented musician," writing that he credited his mother Catherine "for most of his good fortune, for he feels that without her encouragement and advice, success would never have come his way."[22] Jones said that Gipson "inspired and encouraged us as well."[23]

If the lone recording session was rushed, the photo shoot for the cover was even more haphazard. Williams said that shortly after the recording session, the COGICs were scheduled to be photographed. It was, however, the morning after the senior proms for both Williams and Preston—who, as Baptists, were allowed to attend such events. "So, we were out late and hung out," she recalled, and both were late for the photograph. According to Williams, she had left her pink prom dress at Edna Wright's house. When Williams and Preston failed to arrive at the appointed time, Sandra retrieved Williams's dress and gave it to a friend—whose name has since been lost in time. The photograph chosen for the cover has five of the seven COGICs standing at a railing, the young women all in long pink dresses or robes (from left): Wright, Jones, Andraé, the unnamed young stand-in, and Sandra. Neither Preston nor Williams was pictured. Of the much-shorter fill-in, Williams said, "She never sang a note with them, she only took the picture. She's not on the album at all, end of story."[24]

Listening to *It's a Blessing* nearly sixty years after its release is something of a revelation. The album received no promotion and when it was belatedly released some years later, quickly went out of print. But those fortunate few who did find a copy heard a creative, original gospel recording—and not just for a group of singers and musicians barely out of their teens. The maturity and complexity of the arrangements and vocal prowess of the singers are more than a little startling.

Andraé's Greatest Influence

Whether he knew it consciously or not, by going into the recording studio, Andraé's short career had been pointing to this moment. For someone immersed in the gospel music of the 1950s and early 1960s, recording and releasing an album was hugely significant, a pivotal life event. It meant, in many ways, that you had arrived, that congregations would now have to take you seriously. It was all of these things for Andraé, but—perhaps even more so—it was the opportunity he had been wanting to put a soundtrack to his emerging ecumenical worldview. As the authors have argued, Andraé and Sandra emerged from a different world, a completely different ethos than the typical artist from gospel's so-called golden age. Following the family tradition, Andraé desperately wanted to evangelize. But while other gospel artists sang and almost exclusively evangelized *in* the Black church, Andraé wanted, as the title of an upcoming album boldly stated, to "*Take the Message* 'of salvation' *Everywhere*," to the streets, to *all* races and nationalities. He wanted to minister to the world. Andraé's greatest influence was not as much the COGIC church but instead his father Benjamin's passion for street evangelism, speaking directly to those society had dismissed and cast aside.

Dr. Jamal-Dominique Hopkins, now an associate professor of Christian Scriptures at Truett Theological Seminary, joined Christ Memorial Church of Christ as a young man, drawn by Crouch Sr., who was by then a bishop in the denomination. Even late in his ministry, Hopkins said, Crouch remained a "street preacher and a street evangelist" and that calling "colored and informed how he approached ministry." Well into the 1990s, as he had done with Andraé and Sandra as children, Crouch Sr. continued to drive a truck with a public address system evangelizing throughout the San Fernando Valley. "Anytime I think about Bishop Crouch," Hopkins said, "I think of the characters right out of the pages of Scripture." The Valley, including the area around Pacoima, was heavily Latinx, and Bishop Crouch's evangelism was, of a necessity and a calling, broadly ecumenical. "For Andraé and Sandra and anybody growing up in the Valley, it's going to be hard for you to go to a school that's not multi-ethnic, multicultural," Hopkins said, "and that will impact you." It was in this context that Crouch Sr. flourished. "There was a culture or an ethos that was ripe for ecumenicalism," Hopkins recalled. "Evangelism, street evangelism, was given privilege, in a sense." The church services at Christ Memorial COGIC even had two offerings each Sunday—the first being on offering for missions and the second the weekly tithe offering. Hopkins said for Andraé growing up in this environment, and clearly admiring and modeling after his father, his musical ministry would have been almost destined to have this ecumenical mission-oriented thrust. "You have home missions and foreign missions," Hopkins said. "Bishop Crouch was home missions. Andraé becomes foreign missions." It was the driving force of Andraé's career. "It's almost like in some songs, Andraé sings what he saw his father do," Hopkins said. "His father lived it out and Andraé sang out it. His music was a testimony, a testifying, a witness to what his father was living."[25]

The Great "Lost" COGICs Album

Andraé refers repeatedly to this more inclusive calling throughout his biography and in later interviews. But to reach these new audiences, he felt he needed a new "sound doctrine" as well. As the dawn of his recording career approached, Andraé must have intuitively known that in this regard he would have to internalize the language of the world's popular music to succeed. In the pre-Disciples releases, there is already a clear transition of methodology emerging from what has gone before in the genre.

The COGIC tradition, while a lifestyle for "unworldly separatists," which leads to holiness, was still free enough musically to allow Andraé to arrange his musical language in such a way that the world—not just Black churchgoers—would resonate with what he was communicating. These earliest releases were Andraé's first experiments with what the authors call an expansive "Crouch sound doctrine," a musical approach that would fully flower in the years to come. He was clearly gifted, even at this early age, but he was a major talent who was still figuring out the craft of songwriting.

The songs on The COGICs' *It's a Blessing* are arrangements of old hymns, COGIC call-and-response shouts, and Pentecostal spiritual songs. Significantly, it also included a few new works that referenced traditional Black gospel performance practices. All of this was juxtaposed and orchestrated with an instrumental accompaniment composed of a decidedly West Coast gospel quartet sound (piano, Hammond organ, bass, and drums). Other gospel artists, most notably the Mighty Clouds of Joy, were in the very earliest stages of recording with some form of this configuration, but the majority of artists were still only accompanied either with a keyboard (or keyboards), such as Mahalia Jackson, or a single guitar, such as the Dixie Hummingbirds.

Despite the indifferent production values and often murky sound from producer Simpson's rushed recording session, the heavily COGIC-influenced instrumental quartet rhythm section shaped and set the tone for a new type of rhythm section that would eventually transform gospel music's instrumental accompaniment techniques for the rest of the twentieth century.

The album features Billy Preston on the Hammond B3 organ and Andraé on the piano. The names of the drummer and bassist have long since been lost to history, though their contributions are minimal and sometimes amateurish.

On virtually every song, Andraé rarely strays from the black keys of the keyboard. In the instrumental gospel music oral tradition, this physical approach to the keyboard is instinctive. Many Black gospel musicians first learned to play the piano with an attraction to the black keys. From the beginnings of the genre, these five black keys (D♭, E♭, G♭, A♭, and B♭) have been pivotal to the gospel "sound," as well, establishing the key signatures for songs. Crouch's way of engaging the methodology of composition is centered on these black keys on the piano. The authors call this process of attraction "black key pitch centricity." The prominence and importance of this attraction—and engagement—with these five tones are critical for understanding Andraé's creative process, melodic design, and chord selection. Crouch preferred playing the piano in key signatures focused on black keys. In the oral gospel music tradition, this approach to piano performance, with its black key pitch centricity, the authors believe, liberated, rather than hindered, Andraé's creative process. Composing on the five black keys, with the addition of C♭ as a white key tonal center, provided a deep gospel music sonic centering for his songs. This approach is at the heart of how Crouch will establish his sonic vocabulary and enter the world of gospel songwriting. In fact, throughout his career, he composed most of his songs in the keys of D♭, E♭, G♭, A♭, and B♭.

It is possible that Andraé conceived the opening cut, "Don't Let It Be Said Too Late," as an overture, a call to action for the listener. *It's a Blessing* invites listeners to pay close attention to the main theme—salvation. The album is essentially twelve original songs, re-imaginings, and arrangements of the primary COGIC theological tropes, often brilliantly interpolated with simple church language catch phrases.

Side I

The bluesy opening track, "Don't Let It Be Said Too Late," features the familiar gospel $\frac{12}{8}$ time signature and begins in the key of D♭ major. Around Edna Wright's slow and increasingly emphatic vocals, the other singers sing in prime unisons before the verse expands into three-part harmonies. The first part of the song sits around borrowed and colored chords in D♭, while the second half of the piece modulates to the fourth scale degree in G♭, repeating a similar chordal nomenclature. Behind Wright's multi-octave voice, the background vocals have a heavily pop-influenced style, even as Wright adds urgency to their plea, repeating "don't waste your precious time." Written and recorded in 1964, some of that urgency perhaps also comes from the prevailing sentiment of the "Jesus Movement," a youth revival just then sweeping out of Southern California. Led by hordes of young and earnest Jesus People, one of the basic tenets of this evangelical movement was the eschatology that Jesus' return was imminent.[26] "Don't Let It Be Said Too Late" slowly builds, but before Wright can fully launch into a full-tilt gospel vamp, Simpson unexpectedly (and awkwardly) fades at the 3:44 minute mark.

Crouch's ability to arrange and reimagine existing hymns, gospel songs, and COGIC chants is never more evident on "It Will Never Lose Its Power," also sometimes known by its later titles, "The Blood," "The Blood (Will Never Lose Its Power)," or "The Blood Will Never Lose Its Power." One of the enduring songs of the Pentecostal/Holiness tradition is Civilla D. and Walter Stillman Martin's "The Blood Will Never Lose Its Power," which first appears in a hymnal, *Canaan Melodies*, published by the Church of the Nazarene's Nazarene Publishing House in 1914, copyrighted in 1912.[27] According to hymnary.com, at least twenty-five other hymnals include it, most tellingly *Holy Ghost Songs: Church of God in Christ Standard Hymnal*, compiled and edited by Anna B. Crockett, Elder Richard L. Fidler, and Deborah Mason Patterson in 1957.[28] It is difficult to imagine that Andraé was not aware, on some level, of this gospel hymn.

One of the key distinctions of Andraé's song is the contour of the initial melodic line. Here it bears some similarities to the 1914 hymn, at least in the beginning of the verses. Meanwhile, both opening melodies begin with a perfect fourth interval, and the historically perfect intervals, fourth, fifth, and eighth, all represent royalty. For the purposes of a theology of music discourse, musical theory when combined with symbols of *Christology* (the theology of Jesus Christ) may represent theological meaning in the music itself. In this Crouch "blood" song, there are *eschatological* (the theology of hope, bridging the past, present, and future) frames that present the Christian concepts of salvation, especially as expressed in the bedrock COGIC *soteriology* (the theology of salvation through the blood of Jesus Christ). Since musical time is managed by meter, the 1914 hymn and Crouch's piece both share compound time signatures, representing a divisibility of three, symbolizing the Christian concept of the Father, Son, and Holy Spirit at work for the salvation of all creation.

While the Stillman hymn is in $\frac{6}{8}$ time signature, with an up-tempo feel of two beats, Crouch's song is measured with a $\frac{9}{8}$ time signature, with a mid-tempo feel of three beats. The Stillman hymn, in the key of A major, holds all the elements of mid-century holiness hymnody, with a fermata (a musical hold) at the high point, and with text-setting clarity. One of its strengths is that the hymn can easily be performed by a congregation singing SATB (soprano, alto, tenor, and bass) harmonization.

The Crouch version presents Black gospel-styled singing, with an impassioned lead vocal by Gloria Jones. His song, in Ab major, utilizes a harmonic language that imports both diminished and sophisticated 11th chords. This allows Andraé to create new melodic lines, use rhythmically complex syncopation, as well as incorporate standard ii–V–I jazz progressions. Later in the song, new lyrical material emerges: "It reaches to the highest mountain, it flows to the lowest valley, the blood that gives me strength from day to day." There are some resemblances to the Stillman hymn:

STILLMAN/STILLMAN: *The blood that Jesus once shed for me/As my Redeemer, up on the tree.*
CROUCH: *The blood that Jesus shed for me/Way back on Calvary.*
STILLMAN/STILLMAN: (Chorus) *It will never lose its pow'r, it will never lose its pow'r; the blood that cleanses all sin will never lose its power.*
CROUCH: *It will never lose its power.*[29]

As theologian James Cone, the father of Black liberation theology, declared, there are significant commonalities between "the cross and the lynching tree," and Andraé's lyricism directly connects Black liberation theology's articulation of freedom and bibliocentric crucifixion language.[30] For Crouch the key line is "the blood that Jesus shed for me, way back on Calvary." Jesus' death on Calvary was clearly on a cross and not just any tree.[31]

Written several years earlier, "It Will Never Lose Its Power" is the first known example of Crouch's arranging techniques merging with his compositional sensibilities. Here he clearly knows what musical elements to borrow from the hymns of other denominations.

Andraé shifts meters in this version of the popular COGIC chant/hymn "My Soul Loves Jesus," which also bears a connection to the C. H. Mason hymn "Jesus Is a Wonder to My Soul." In Andraé's hands, this COGIC rhythmic chant-chorus is transformed into a gospel song from gospel's golden age. The conversion from the original $\frac{4}{4}$ to a $\frac{12}{8}$ shuffle rides on a bouncy triplet feel with an ecumenical focus that would not be out of place in Black churches outside the Pentecostal tradition. His arrangement highlights several highly styled vocal embellishments, from high pitched growls to lower-level vocal placement, sounds that will not show up on a James Cleveland or Harold Smith and the Majestics LP for several more years. For a comparison, listen to the Cleveland-arranged background vocals with the Southern California Community Choir on the Aretha Franklin concert documentary, *Amazing Grace*, recorded in 1972, though not released until 2018. Cleveland's arrangements are more restrained, more choral, and much more traditional than what the COGICS are doing in 1964. As the soloist, Aretha, a Baptist, however, has the liberty to present complex vocal coloring in the context of worship—thanks in part to the COGIC denomination, where artistic liberation in the Holy Spirit is a paramount consideration.[32]

"Since I Found Him" has some of Andraé's most accomplished arrangements of background vocal parts, something that would eventually become one of his greatest musical strengths. Under Williams's lead vocals, the singers achieve a tight purity and sweetness of tone, with no one voice or part dominating, but with a definite bounce and pendulum-like swing. The graceful triadic harmonies soon mesh into wonderfully articulated prime unison singing. This is one of the earliest examples of Andraé's version of the old gospel call-and-response format, with its layered antiphonal background vocals. "Since I

Found Him" is a foreshadowing of the deep, sophisticated contrapuntal arranging techniques (and interests) still to come.

"Nothing Is Greater" is similar to the song "My Soul Loves Jesus" in that this golden age gospel song in A♭ major features doo-wops with a mid-tempo swing in step with the vocal stylings of Inez Andrews, Albertina Walker, Dorothy Norwood, and the Caravans. The focus is the biblical idea of eternal value: "There is nothing in my life that I possess/that's any greater than His love for me." The song ends with a readily identifiable cadence listeners will hear again and again in Andraé's later work, especially "Bless the Lord." The use of this I–IV–I cadence infers that this song is for "church folks."

Side I ends with Sandra and Andraé trading lead vocals on "Won't It Be Sad," another track that sounds like a driving swing arrangement of an older spiritual or COGIC chant. Interestingly, this is one of Andraé's few lead vocals on the entire album. In the introduction, Preston pulls the organ's black drawbars out, creating a "brittle" sound that grabs the listener's attention, calling "those with ears to hear" to listen "before it is too late." Despite the up-tempo, jump swing rhythms, the song both is a lament and a call to discipleship. The COGIC Singers proclaim the gospel message, but the call is set to very *un*-gospel-like bebop swing vocal stylings.

Throughout the song's short 2:29 minute span, Preston pushes the black drawbars in, pulls the white drawbars out, and supports the singers with a hollow, haloed sound. This inventive technique on the B3 organ again underscores Preston's sensitivity and unique ability to paint a variety of colors on the organ, as well as his fast-moving foot pedal bass lines and the edgy jazzy riffs that would be scandalous in the African Methodist Episcopal (AME) or Baptist churches of that era. The irony is that amid this quite danceable pop-gospel arrangement, the background vocals continue to chant "It's so sad, sad, sad."

Side II

For the beloved hymn "There Is a Fountain," sung in gospel *rubato* (slowly) style, it is clear that lead vocalist Jones grew up listening to songs performed in the dramatic lining-out style called "surge singing" that allowed soloists free latitude to follow the leading of the Holy Spirit in a glorious array of musical swoops, whoops, trills, and dramatic interpretations. It's a Black sacred music tradition that is both passionate and florid and one that counted Mahalia Jackson as among its foremost practitioners.[33]

"There Is a Fountain" was written by William Cowper in 1772, and the music is based on "Cleansing Fountain," a traditional American camp meeting melody first arranged by Lowell Mason in 1830. "There Is a Fountain" has been favored in African American churches for more than a century and, like "The Blood (Will Never Lose Its Power)," "There Is Power in the Blood," and "Nothing but the Blood," is one of the "blood" songs so beloved in the COGIC tradition.[34]

Preston, also well versed in the "surge" tradition, introduces a descending chromatic line on the organ to musically "paint" the text "and sinners *plunge* beneath that flood." Throughout the song, the vocals support a robust three-part style. These vocals are superimposed over other types of chords as an extension of the 7th, 9th, 11th, and 13th scale degrees within a scale. The unique placement of vocal parts, within the keyboard accompaniment, is worth noting because it reveals a deep understanding of one of the important theoretical music foundations in gospel, one that—as self-taught musicians and composers—Crouch and Preston were immersed in through the shared traditions and oral history that is one of the identifying facets of gospel music. Throughout the entire recording there are root movements: A♭, D♭, E♭, and B♭, a tonal centering effect or (again) gospel black key pitch centricity. "There Is a Fountain" is in the key of A♭ major, where the singers sing in one key while the piano parts appear to be in another key. They sing chords built upon thirds as some accompaniment chords are superimposed with diminished seventh chords in the second and third inversions. In "There Is a Fountain," as mentioned earlier, Preston employs the characteristic black key pitch centricity by playing chromatic scales. In just this two-bar introduction, his left hand plays a ii–V–I progression, while his right hand plays a descending chromatic passage. What makes this song unique in gospel music is the idea of extending the harmonic language *above* the tonic, subdominant, dominant, supertonic, and leading-tone chords. In doing so, Preston dramatically pushes the envelope by bringing new harmonic language to the gospel tradition, beyond anything present in any hymnal. As future recordings reveal, Crouch is influenced by both Preston's performance virtuosity and almost otherworldly command of harmonic language.

"Say Yes" is in the key of D♭ minor and is an invitational call to discipleship and the beginning of what the authors believe is—whether intentionally or subconsciously—a liturgical service, a progression not unlike a standard Sunday morning at a COGIC church. From the opening lyrics, Crouch's evangelistic sensibility is declared: "If you wanna know Jesus, all you have to do is say *yeah*." In this musical offering, listeners experience Andraé's commitment to COGIC congregational gatherings, reflecting the energy of the worship services and a robust transparency in the singing. Just as William Banfield posits that Black music is tethered to Black cultural codes found within work songs and spirituals, "Say Yes" works as a derivative form of the shout, the original heart song of an enslaved people that is at the root of the spiritual, first sung in the brush arbors of the American South.[35]

This song's energetic summoning is Andraé's spiritual prelude and preparation for evangelism. He is working the work of prayer, pleading to all those outside of God's kingdom to "say yes to God!" Almost immediately, there are shouts and testimonials: "If you wanna new walk, new talk, just say *yeah*."

Obviously, for the non-COGIC or Pentecostal believer, this is something of a behind-the-scenes view of a COGIC service, an energetic fusion both Holy Spirit–driven and an earnest plea for the sinner. In this, COGIC worship practices are extensions of the shout tradition. The authors suggest that, as the song abruptly, even prematurely fades out, the Holy Spirit showed up in the recording session and the singers "got happy" (as it is called in some Holiness traditions) and Simpson was forced to truncate the performance to keep the track from being too long within the time constraints of the standard vinyl LP—a frustratingly short 2:15 minute *shout serenade*.

Williams is the lead vocalist on "He Included Me," a celebratory traditional gospel praise song in G♭ major with a $\frac{9}{8}$ time signature. Crouch's piano-playing employs extended harmonic language. This language evolves to include diminished chords functioning to support passing other tonalities, minor sixth cadences, inversions of chords, and a variety of harmonic root movements. Andraé's piano playing, with both the pentatonic octave upward and downward gestures in the accompaniment, is a foreshadowing of the trademark punchy, exhilarating piano style to come.

What is clear in the chorus of "He Included Me" are the variety of vocal performance practices executed by the background vocals. From prime unison singing to brassy harmonies, supported with *glissandos* and a clear dynamic range, the singers emotionally convey their gratitude and declare repeatedly that God has "included me" in salvation's plan.

The overall song form of "Don't Stop Using Me" is AABB. The A section performed slowly as an introduction to the B section, which evolves into a $\frac{12}{8}$ golden age gospel call-and-response. What is rare about this second consecutive "me" song is the deep sense of calling to evangelize found in the lyrics: "There's so much that can be done, many souls can be won/So please don't stop using me." Composed in the key of A♭, "Don't Stop Using Me" is a highly personal cry to God, a prayer-song sung with an "in the moment" awareness of Kingdom of God possibilities.

Andraé digs deep into his COGIC roots with the next track on the LP, "He Lives," and the arrangement is once again illumined with Black musical textures. High intensity and rhythmic variations performed at a high level propel the listener to the throne of the Risen Savior. It is as if Jesus Christ is present with the COGICs in the recording session (again, a foretaste of Crouch's way of beckoning the Spirit of God in the moment—working to create a spirit-filled rehearsal recording session). Consequently, the recording transcends the singers performing for and with each other, and what is captured is a sense of renewal and revivalism as one of the singers shouts, "I can feel Him!" A repetitive instrumental section, called the "vamp," fades to the end. The recording process in "He Lives" captures a transcendent moment in time. With a syncopated upbeat hand-clapping fusion, the work presents elements of both pure Pentecostal vamp and shout tropes.

To achieve this, Andraé has called on the familiar old hymn "I Serve a Risen Savior" ("... he walks with me and he talks with me...") by Alfred Ackely. The original is in $\frac{6}{8}$ and A♭ major, but for his purposes, Andraé interpolates this hymn with a G♭ black key pitch centricity, call-and-response vocals, and plenty of COGIC Holy Spirit fire.

The album closes with the title track, "It's a Blessing," a smooth dialogue with lead vocalist Williams and the background singers as they again seek to convince listeners of the reality of a true and living God. As with several of the earlier songs, it is in a $\frac{12}{8}$ time signature; it is an A♭ major gospel power ballad that promises a therapeutic embrace between the audience and the Holy Spirit. Despite her youth, Williams's rich vocals have a depth and creative range that rival some of the best-known gospel singers of the day and Preston and Crouch arrange the instrumentation to create a colorful, imaginative setting. Her vocals veer from a deep, raspy "chest voice" to a more hushed conversational tone that invokes a personal relationship with God as she seeks to convince listeners, once and for all, that God is real and *that* is the true blessing of the title.

It is possible, the authors believe, that the much more personal second side of *It's a Blessing* has been carefully designed and orchestrated into something akin to a symphonic work that surges toward a clearly defined end. The opening hymn "There Is a Fountain" is followed by the celebratory "Say Yes." "He Included Me," "Don't Stop Using Me," and "He Lives" are Andraé's homily, his sermon, if you will—and the central message. "He Lives," with its resonance to older hymns, is the subsequent invitation found in so many Protestant services. The musical "service" ends with the "sending song," "It's a Blessing," which serves as a musical interpretation of the benediction "May the Lord bless you and keep you." It is possible that despite the frantic nature of the recording session that Andraé deliberately conceived and executed Side II in a subtle liturgical format, a musical worship service designed to communicate a very personal message of evangelism and hope.

Andraé's arrangements of "It Will Never Lose Its Power" and "My Soul Loves Jesus" are signposts of his deep knowledge of COGIC hymnody and tradition. The Reverend Charles Mason's hymn "Jesus Is a Wonder to My Soul" and the Martins' hymn "The Blood Will Never Lose Its Power" were simply source materials for Andraé as he created these testimonial arrangements. They mark his deep appreciation for COGIC theological rigor and its tradition of hymnody. Andraé created masterpieces by *arranging* masterpieces, and he would continue to expand his artistic cultural nuances by continually contemporizing his musical prowess and curiosity. There are strong hints and passages on *It's a Blessing* of the acclaimed songwriter he would become and was already in the process of becoming.

It is said in some composition and music theory classes that before someone can be a great songwriter, they must first be a great arranger. With *It's a Blessing*, the great arranger has arrived.

Vee-Jay and Exodus Records

In the end, the confusing cover art and rushed production were the least of the COGICs' worries. Vee-Jay Records, despite the influx of cash from the Beatles releases and other popular acts, was in financial straits from rapid overexpansion, expensive litigation with Capitol Records (related to subsequent Beatles releases), and an unfavorable contract with the Four Seasons, all of which caused the label to careen toward bankruptcy in late 1965. Vee-Jay president Ewart Abner created the quasi-independent Exodus label in hopes of releasing all scheduled Vee-Jay product when the company entered into bankruptcy proceedings the following year. Many of Vee-Jay's existing projects were never released, while others, including the COGICs' *It's a Blessing*, were delayed, some by years. The original release date had been early 1966. When Vee-Jay was liquidated in August 1966, the presiding judge ruled that Exodus was part of Vee-Jay and ordered it to be liquidated as well. (Vee-Jay was later reorganized as Vee-Jay International and released *It's a Blessing* in 1975 as Vee-Jay International VJS-18011, but by then the group had long since disbanded.)[36]

Upon completion of the original recording session, Simpson promptly released a 45 from *It's a Blessing*, "It Will Never Lose Its Power" (with a lead by Jones), backed with "I Don't Need Nobody Else" (sung by Williams) as Simpson Records RS-231 in 1964. Since "I Don't Need Anybody Else" does not appear on the LP, it may have been an outtake from the original session. The group was billed as the "Cogic Singers, The Teenage Wonders." Simpson Records released several more singles in 1964 before releasing a second 45 from *It's a Blessing*, the title track and "Since I Found Him" (both featuring leads by Williams), as Simpson Records RS-273, also in 1964. This time, however, the artists are billed as the "COGIC's" (*sic*) and both 45s were distributed by Vee-Jay. Given Vee-Jay's problems at the time, it's not surprising that neither record made a splash in the industry despite the quality of the performances and songwriting.[37]

The End of the COGICs

Regardless, Simpson and other music industry execs were aware of the COGIC talent pool. "It was such a drag," Williams said, "because recruiting companies were pulling at the COGICs to sing pop because we were so big, so talented, always singing everywhere." Simpson quietly approached Edna Wright during the recording session with a song titled "One Touch of Venus." Fearing that her Apostolic parents might not approve, Wright was dubbed "Sandy Wynns" for the 45. Released on the Champion Record label (14001) and distributed by Tollie Records later in 1964, "One Touch of Venus" was written and produced by Ed Cobb, who had originally offered it to Marvin Gaye. (The single was picked by the larger Fontana label in the UK the following year as Fontana TF550.) The track did well enough that Wright and Cobb returned to the studio to record "Love Belongs to Everyone" for Champion (14002), only this 45 was distributed by Vee-Jay. "But you have to remember," Jones said, "she was Darlene Love's sister. She had seen that world with Phil Spector; 'A Touch of Venus' was a great hit. She was really an icon for me."[38]

Cobb obviously liked working with the COGIC vocalists and asked Jones to the studio to record a song he had written, "Heartbeat" (and the flipside, "Heartbeat 2"), featuring Preston on organ and Wright and Williams on backup vocals. "Heartbeat" was released first on Uptown Records (Uptown 712), then quickly picked up by Capitol (CL 15429). By December, the twenty-year-old Jones was singing the song on the popular TV series *Shindig*. It's a powerhouse of a performance, with an incessant, almost tribal beat fueled by Preston's organ and Jones's confident, sassy vocals and presence. It may have been from this broadcast that Preston was asked to join *Shindig*'s popular house band, the Shindogs. Cobb and Jones then returned to the studio to tape two more of his compositions, "My Bad Boy's Coming to Town" and the B-side, "Tainted Love," for Champion (14003) and distributed by Vee-Jay in 1965. Cobb obviously had a good ear for music—he would later work as an engineer for the likes of Steely Dan and Fleetwood Mac.[39]

Simpson also soon returned to the studio with Sondra Williams to record two songs, "He's Got the Whole World in His Hands" backed with "Heartache," which was released as Vee-Jay Records VJ 941, also in 1964.[40]

Preston's star, of course, continued rising. The public simply couldn't get enough of his full-tilt gospel stylings on the Hammond B3. In very short order, he released *The Most Exciting Organ Ever* for Vee-Jay in 1964 (VJS-1123), *Early Hits of 1965* for Vee-Jay in 1965 (VJS-1142), and *Hymns Speak for the Organ* for Exodus in 1966 (Ex 53 and produced by Simpson), before he finally moved to industry leader Capitol Records in 1966 with *Wildest Organ in Town* (ST 2532, with Sly Stone credited as an arranger).[41]

Gloria Jones and Sondra "Blinky" Williams remembered their time with the COGICs with fondness and not a little regret and mused that perhaps a group with that much talent wasn't really meant to be. Jones said the group slowly dissolved after the recording of *It's a Blessing*, though they still continued performing a few concerts together for another year. Jones said her final concert with the COGICs was at the Los Angeles Gospel Music Awards in 1965:

> That was the year that I would say we all went our way, but it wasn't a breakup. It was more of survival in some cases. Andraé's survival was to continue with the

gospel music. Our survival was to try to make a living because we were older. We were going to college. We didn't have the money to buy the books or to be able to pay for our fees. All of a sudden, we weren't teenagers anymore.[42]

Williams blamed Simpson in particular. "All of a sudden because of so many [producers were] pulling at the COGICs and we started doing sessions for different artists, the next thing you know, there's no more COGICs. And it happened just like that."[43]

It's a Blessing slipped quietly into obscurity, despite the presence of "The Blood (Will Never Lose Its Power)," which remains a beloved standard in Black churches and gospel concerts. Wright, Williams, and Jones all remained in touch with the Crouches, appearing on later projects and concerts. Andraé only devotes a few sentences to the breakup in his autobiography, blaming it on Preston's leaving to join Ray Charles, and then notes that the remaining singers soon found other projects in the world of pop music. There is a certain wistfulness in his words, and it may be that at the time of the writing of *Through It All*, just a few years later, that he's still pained by their departures:

> I often think of the meetings and services where we sang and what an impact we had on people. God really used us. They all had so much talent; each one was a child prodigy and dedicated to the Lord's service. I'd give anything to see them give all their talent to God's glory again.[44]

NOTES

1. Sandra Crouch, interview with the authors, November 4, 2020.
2. Sandra Crouch, interview with the authors, November 4, 2020; Gloria Jones, interview with the authors, December 22, 2020.
3. Gloria Jones, interview with the authors, December 22, 2020; Gloria Jones, personal correspondence, December 15, 2020.
4. Sam Jones, "Billy Preston, Keyboard Player with the Beatles, Dies at 59," *The Guardian*, June 7, 2006; Sondra "Blinky" Williams interview with the authors, December 3, 2020; Richard Harrington, "'Fifth Beatle' Billy Preston Made the Greats Even Greater, *Washington Post*, June 8, 2006; "Preston Lets Soul Music Speak for God," *Fort Lauderdale News*, January 7, 1974, 21; Jon Pareles, "Billy Preston, 59, Soul Musician, Is Dead; Renowned Keyboardist and Collaborator," *New York Times*, June 7, 2006, 10; Gloria Jones, interview with the authors, December 22, 2020. By age six, according to one account, Billy was directing a 100-voice choir at Victory Baptist. Stephen Prothero's *American Jesus: How the Song of God Became a National Icon* (New York: Farrar, Straus & Giroux, 2003), 229–290, as cited in David W. Stowe, *No Sympathy for the Devil: Christian Pop Music and the Transformation of American Evangelicalism* (Chapel Hill: University of North Carolina Press, 2011), 54.

5. Gloria Jones, interview with the authors, December 22, 2020; Gloria Jones, personal correspondence with the authors, December 15, 2020.
6. Patrick Prince, "Gloria Jones Dedicates Herself to Sharing Life and Music," *Goldmine*, August 4, 2010; Stu Hackel, "What Do You Mean You've Never Heard of Gloria Jones?" March 25, 2019, www.udiscovermusic.com/stories/gloria-jones-soul-singer/; Graham Betts, "Gloria Jones," in *Motown Encyclopedia* (AC Publishing, 2014), 228–229; Sherman Andrus, interview with the authors September 3, 2020.
7. Cordell S. Thompson, "Honey Cone Trio Finds It Pays to Advertise," *Jet*, September 2, 1971, 56–60; David Henckley, "Edna Wright Got to Spend Her Life Singing, Put That in the 'Want Ads,'" *The Culture Corner*, September 13, 2020; Ashley Iasimone, "Edna Wright Dead: Honey Cone Singer and Sister of Darlene Love Dies," *Billboard*, September 12, 2020; Sondra Williams, interview with the authors, December 3, 2020.
8. Sondra Williams, interview with the authors, December 3, 2020.
9. Sondra Williams, interview with the authors, December 3, 2020.
10. Carrie Gonzalo, interview with the authors, October 30, 2020. Val Gonzalo, Carrie's ex-husband, also attended several COGICs concerts during this period, and during performances of the song "Searching," Sondra "Blinky" Williams would march down the aisles while she sang: "She'd look in people's purses and say, 'Search and search until you find Jesus.' It was crazy, but it was a good experience. They were such showmen" (Val Gonzalo, interview with the authors, October 10, 2020).
11. Sondra Williams, interview with the authors, December 3, 2020.
12. Gloria Jones, interview with the authors, December 22, 2020.
13. Andraé Crouch with Nina Ball, *Through It All: Andraé Crouch* (Waco, TX: Word Books, 1974), 46.
14. Sandra Crouch, interview with the authors, November 4, 2020.
15. Sondra Williams, interview with the authors, December 3, 2020.
16. Sondra Williams, interview with the authors, December 3, 2020; www.discogs.com/master/605216-Lindy-Adams-A-Bird-in-the-Hand-Surprise-Party.
17. Sondra Williams, interview with the authors, December 3, 2020; Gloria Jones, interview with the authors, December 22, 2020.
18. www.discogs.com/artist/268056/-Richard-Simpson; www.45cat.com/label/Veejay; bsnpubs.com/veejay/veejaygospel.html; Sondra Williams, interview with the authors, December 3, 2020.
19. Sondra Williams, interview with the authors, December 3, 2020; Sandra Crouch, interview with the authors, November 4, 2020.
20. Gloria Jones, interview with the authors, December 22, 2020.
21. Gloria Jones, interview with the authors, December 22, 2020.
22. *It's a Blessing*, The COGICs, Exodus Records, EX-54, produced by Richard Simpson, liner notes by Revé Gipson, 1964; Gloria Jones, interview with the authors, December 22, 2020.
23. Jones, interview with the authors, December 22, 2020.
24. Sondra Williams, interview with the authors, December 3, 2020.

25. Jamal-Dominque Hopkins, interview with the authors, October 13, 2022.

26. Bob Gersztyn, *Jesus Rocks the World: The Definitive History of Contemporary Christian Music*, Vol. 1 (Santa Barbara, CA: Praeger, 2012), 33–61.

27. Haldor Lillenas, ed., *Canaan Melodies* (Kansas City, MO: Nazarene Publishing House, 1914), 209.

28. Anna B. Crockett, Elder Richard L. Fidler, and Deborah Mason Patterson, eds., *Holy Ghost Songs: Church of God in Christ Standard Hymnal* (Chicago: Anna B. Crockett Music Publishers, 1957).

29. Dr. James Abbington, personal correspondence with the authors, February 15, 2022. The authors are indebted to Dr. Abbington for originally identifying the Skillman hymn connection. "The Blood (Will Never Lose Its Power)" by Andraé Crouch, Manna Music, Inc.

30. James Cone, *The Cross and the Lynching Tree* (Maryknoll, NY: Orbis Books, 2011), 3.

31. Braxton D. Shelley, *Healing for the Soul: Richard Smallwood, the Vamp and the Gospel Imagination* (Oxford: Oxford University Press, 2021), 125–126.

32. *Amazing Grace*, directors Alan Elliott and Sydney Pollock, NEON, 2018.

33. William Tallmadge, "Dr. Watts and Mahalia Jackson: The Development, Decline and Survival of a Folk Music Style in America," *Ethnomusicology* 5, no. 2 (May 1961): 95.

34. Melvin Butler, *Island Music: Pentecostal Music and Identity in Jamaica and the United States* (Urbana: University of Illinois Press, 2019), 74–88.

35. William Banfield, *Cultural Codes: Makings of a Black Music Philosophy* (Lanham, MD: Scarecrow Press, 2009), 7.

36. http://www.bsnpubs.com/veejay/exodus.html; "The Vee-Jay Story," Both Sides Now Publications, http://www.bsnpubs.com/veejay/veejay.html; *Record Row: Cradle of Rhythm & Blues*, PBS documentary, Windows to the World Communications, 1997.

37. http://www.discogs.com/label/21829-Simpson-Records.

38. Sondra Williams, interview with the authors, December 3, 2020; www.discogs.com/artist/965778/-Sandy-Wynns; Gloria Jones, interview with the authors, December 22, 2020.

39. Gloria Jones, interview with the authors, December 22, 2020; www.undiscoveredmusic/com/stores/Gloria-Jones-Soul-Singer-/amp; www.discogs.com/artist/262947; www.discogs.com/master/378956-Gloria-Jones-Heartbeat.

40. www.discogs.com/release/6857216-Cogic-Singers-It-Will-Never-Lose-Its-Power; www.discogs/com/release/6857290-It's-a-Blessing; www.discogs.com/master/794499-Sondra-Williams-He's-Got-the-Whole-World-in-His-Hands-Heartache.

41. www.discogs.com/artist/46767-Billy-Preston.

42. Gloria Jones, interview with the authors, December 22, 2020.

43. Sondra Williams, interview with the authors, December 3, 2020.

44. Andraé Crouch, *Through It All*, 45.

3

The Addicts Choir

The First Disciples

Amid the COGICs breakup, Andraé and Sandra were attending Valley Junior College, driving to and from Pacoima in a new car paid for by their parents. Andraé initially wanted to be an elementary school teacher but writes in *Through It All* that the pressures of simply being a Sunday School teacher at Christ Memorial Church quickly put an end to that notion. He briefly worked for RCA Computers but continued to play organ and piano in the church choir, where he also performed from 10 to 11 P.M. each Sunday during his father's broadcast on radio station KHOF. The choir's performances during the Sunday evening broadcasts soon attracted a large crowd to the church.

In 1964, Billy (later Bili) Thedford, a friend from the San Fernando High School choir, began visiting the church regularly. Andraé described him as "a real handsome brother," "tall and slender with hazel eyes and black hair." One Sunday, Andraé invited Thedford to become more involved in the church: "Maybe we could sing together. Maybe God could really use us together." The following Sunday, Thedford joined the church and started singing in the choir. Unlike Crouch, Thedford had already gotten a heady taste of the music industry. For the first few years of his life, Thedford and his sister Carol bounced around California's child foster care system. When Thedford was eight years old, the children were finally reunited with their maternal grandmother, Ann Higgins, who lived with her son Billy Higgins, a jazz drummer. In 1957, the entire family moved to Pacoima, where Thedford formed a small vocal group, the Twi-Lighters. R&B legend Johnny Otis heard the group, took them in to the studio to record four tracks, including "Eternal Flame" (which Thedford composed) coupled with "Happy Days Are Here Again" (Real Fine RI-6236), and sent the quartet on tour. "The company bought us suits and took us on the road with all the grown-up singers," Thedford told one writer. "We were just kids and we got to go out with professionals every night. They taught us how to deal with people and how to handle a crowd. It was great training that is hardly found today."[1]

A few months later at a youth revival service, Andraé introduced himself to another young man, Perry Morgan. Morgan and Crouch met repeatedly over a period of weeks, during which time Morgan also joined both the church and the choir. Perry Morgan was raised Baptist with his family in Texas. They moved to the Los Angeles area in 1959, where Perry soon heard about Andraé and the new choir at Christ Memorial Church of God in Christ. One day shortly thereafter, Morgan recalled that he stood to one side in the packed auditorium as Andraé's choir performed. When the music was over, Andraé found Morgan in the foyer, asked about his faith, then drove him home that evening. In the weeks that followed, Morgan said Andraé checked on him regularly and provided tickets for him to accompany the COGICs to a concert in Oakland. Eventually, Morgan joined the Christ Memorial choir. When Andraé discussed wanting to create an all-male quartet, he asked Morgan to join. "We were like four disciples then," Morgan recalled. "We were pretty lousy. But because the music was so up-tempo and sounded so much like rhythm and blues, the kids really loved it."[2]

Crouch, Morgan, and Thedford became close friends, frequently staying after choir practices to rehearse their parts. According to Crouch, there was an immediate musical connection. "I thought we sounded pretty good," he writes. Howard Neal, another member of the Christ Memorial choir, soon joined the rehearsals, completing the gospel quartet.[3]

The new group began rehearsing to perform on the church's radio broadcasts, with Andraé as the leader, choosing and arranging the hymns and gospel songs and assigning the vocal parts. "Folks started asking about this group," Thedford said, "because we had different *musical* arrangements, and the style was different." Within a few weeks, songwriter and producer Sonny Salsbury invited Andraé to perform at the First Church of the Nazarene in Pasadena. The other three singers agreed to join him. "This was a white church," Thedford recalled, "and then from there it just went on and on and on and on." "We sang four songs that night at the Nazarene church," Andraé adds. "The congregation kept applauding but we didn't know any more numbers to sing. We told them we'd do more next time." After the first performance at First Church of the Nazarene, Morgan recalled that Andraé turned to the group and said, "Yeah, that's good, so we're gonna keep doing this and call ourselves the Four Disciples." The new group enjoyed a similar reception assembling and performing at a special Christmas service on Christ Memorial's Sunday evening broadcast.[4]

Just as the group was beginning to take off, Neal, who was somewhat older, became engaged to LaVern Moore (then LaVern Logan), who herself would later become a pastor at New Christ Memorial. Neal, who was already working full time, soon resigned. He stayed friends with the remaining Disciples and would sometimes substitute for a missing member as needed. Neal was replaced by a young man who had only recently moved with his family to Southern California, Sherman Andrus. Born on June 23, 1942, in Mermentau, Louisiana, Andrus grew up singing in the choir of the Pentecostal Christ Sanctified Holiness Church. In 1963, Andrus moved to California and joined Grace Community Church of God in Christ's choir, where he met Gloria Jones. Andrus said that Andraé and Sandra attended one of the church's famed Sunday afternoon "sings" to hear Jones, who introduced the twins to Andrus. When the choir finished its numbers, Andraé was waiting. Andraé stuck out his hand to Andrus and said, "If I ever get a male group, I want you to sing with me." But Andrus joined the National Guard in 1964 and spent eight months on active duty. When he returned, Andraé got back in touch through one of Sherman's sisters, who also lived in Pacoima. With the addition of Andrus, the new quartet was set, at least for the moment.[5]

Growing up in a more conservative church tradition, Andrus listened to traditional gospel artists and quartets, including Brother Joe May, the Five Blind Boys of Mississippi, the Soul Stirrers, and even some Southern (white) gospel. "As long as the lyrics to a song weren't a bad influence, my parents did allow the seven of us kids to listen to different kinds of music," Andrus told one journalist. "I started listening to the music of B.B. King, Ray Charles, and Sam Cooke, but also enjoyed the singing styles of Frank Sinatra and Patti Page. But Johnny Mathis, Cooke, and Nat King Cole were my favorites." In his autobiography, *My Story! His Song! Blessed!*, Andrus writes that his dream had always been to be a gospel singer and, once he moved to Southern California, Andraé quickly became his musical mentor.[6]

In addition to Andraé's musical genius, Thedford said that the different individual backgrounds and journeys made the early Disciples unique. One other factor was what he described as the "certain style" of gospel music found only in Southern California:

Southern California has a different take on jazz. They have a different take on beat. With all of those styles, that's what we brought to the table when Andraé calls the Disciples together. We started performing an odd form of gospel music. It had to be different than just the basic church. We wanted to stimulate the gospel music industry with a flow.

Thedford said the early Disciples aspired to be more like the Temptations or the Spinners by featuring a "different high energy approach to R&B music." "We wanted to take that from music and make it as eccentric as those others that had been doing *their* music," he said. "So, I think that was really the key to our success."[7]

Andrus cited the Reverend James Cleveland and the Caravans, especially Shirley Caesar and Inez Andrews, as primary influences on the new quartet:

> The thing about that time is that the artist had to do so much, you had to entertain, and you had to sing well. But you also had to perform—and then give an invitation. It was the whole deal. It wasn't just going in with the loud song and a fast song and say, "That's it, folks." I think the biggest [influence] was probably his dad. His dad Benjamin was an anointed preacher and really just a great guy.[8]

Early Performances and New Friends

Regular performances at some of the increasingly larger, primarily white, Southern California churches helped open doors for the young group. Family friend LaVern Moore attributed that appeal, in part, to the Disciples' early relationships with the influential Church of the Foursquare Gospel, as well as songwriter Audrey Mieir, who Moore said was "very much attached to Andraé and the Disciples." Moore also praised the influence and "powerful ministry" of Mieir, who had welcomed them earlier at the churches in Wilmington and La Puente. Mieir, who composed "His Name Is Wonderful," had established the popular "Monday Musicals" in Pasadena as early as 1945. By the 1960s, the musicals introduced a host of gospel artists to the Los Angeles area, including Andraé.[9]

According to Morgan, the Disciples first played the "Monday Musicals" in 1966. "All I remember is that it was a joy to be there," Morgan said. "[Mieir] was so wonderful, so beautiful. I remember the radio station she was affiliated with in Glendale that played some of our songs." Morgan, coming from the heavily segregated Texas city of Kilgore, said he was "not accustomed to white people really treating us with love—it confused me." It was at the musicals,

Thedford said, that he first met pianist Carrie Gonzalo and, later, producer Ralph Carmichael. The popularity of Mieir's musicals enabled the Disciples to appear in still bigger churches. "We were just some kids, man," Thedford said, and compared the musicals to what it would be like to appear on *The Tonight Show with Johnny Carson* a few years later. As a result of the exposure, the Disciples now filled thousand-seat sanctuaries. "They were all white churches, but, well, they *got* us," Thedford said. "They started getting us other gigs."[10]

Andraé writes it was at the 1965 COGIC convention at Crouch Temple that he accepted the "call" to a full-time ministry. After the emotional episode, he was approached by several young men who had heard him perform at Christ Memorial. They invited him to sing at the Teen Challenge Center, a rehabilitation center for addicts housed in a "huge two-story mansion" on Hobart Street. When Andraé, who had only reluctantly accompanied the men to the Center, walked into the building, "I felt like the breath of God was breathing on me." That evening, he met the Center's director, Don Hall, who gave him a copy of evangelist David Wilkerson's best-selling book, *The Cross and the Switchblade*, an account of Wilkerson's work with street gangs in Brooklyn and the conversion of gang leader Nicky Cruz. Wilkerson founded Teen Challenge in Los Angeles in 1963. When Hall invited Andraé to return, he initially declined, saying that he already had responsibilities at his father's church. "But all the way home I heard an addict's choir singing in my head," he writes. Andraé "fought" the call to work at Teen Challenge for six months until he received a "vision" following a choir rehearsal at his father's church where no one showed up. In the vision, he was told to quit his job, sell his new automobile, and form an addicts choir—and that no one would understand. His mother certainly did *not* understand. He had also recently borrowed $300 from his parents to record four songs. When he sold the car, he told his mother Catherine that he would live "by faith." Catherine looked at Andraé in disbelief and replied, "Yeah, you're gonna call my name 'Faith' now, huh? My name is gonna change from Catherine to Faith?!"[11]

A Rare Recording

Few copies are known to exist of the four-song 45 Andraé recorded with the $300 in late 1965 or early 1966. He only mentions three of the songs in his biography—"Nobody like the Lord," "Joy Bells," "I Find No Fault in Him"—which he says were the first three songs he wrote, even before the compositions on the COGICs' *It's a Blessing*, though none of the songs appears on that LP. (The fourth song is titled "I Looked for God.") The extended 45 featured a sleeve with the words "Presenting . . . Andraé Crouch." The EP was released on the "DS—Divine Sounds" label and credits B. & C. Crouch as producers—a nod to his parents, Benjamin and Catherine. Since no address or registration papers have yet been located, *DS-Divine Sounds* was probably Andraé's name for his custom label. Nearly fifty years later, only Sandra, of their friends, family members, or singers, even remembered Andraé recording these songs—much less the actual 45 itself. Sandra said she believed that they recorded the songs in a studio in Hollywood, though she no longer remembers its name or the circumstances:

> Andraé always wanted to record. People would say, "Hey, you ought to make a record." And, so we just said, "OK, we'll do another one. He copied all of those songs. We didn't really care whose name was on it. I certainly wouldn't remember any of the musicians.[12]

There are passages in the four songs that suggest that at least some of the background vocals include some of the former COGICs as well as Sandra Crouch. We believe that the organ heard throughout is played by Billy Preston. The somewhat tinny quality of the recording suggests it might also have been recorded in Harmony Recorders, the same studio where *It's a Blessing* had been recorded. It is not known whether the 45 was sold at Andraé's performances or merely given away to friends and family members. None of the four songs appears on his later releases, but Sondra "Blinky" Williams recorded both "I Find No Fault in Him" and "Nobody like the Lord" on her *Hark the Voice* LP for Atlantic Records in 1967. The Crouch EP may have even served as a demo for the ubiquitous Richard Simpson, who produced Williams's LP. *Hark the Voice* also included three *other* Crouch compositions first heard on the COGICs *It's a Blessing* album, "Won't It Be Sad," "It's a Blessing," and "He Included Me," as well as still another song, "Lord, Don't Lift Your Spirit from Me." In his biography, Andraé writes that he composed "Lord, Don't Lift Your Spirit from Me" in the Chapel at the Teen Challenge Center following a particularly taxing series of performances with the Addicts Choir.[13]

Side I

Andraé had clearly been listening to soul music of the 1950s and 1960s when he recorded the opening track, "Nobody like the Lord." The influences of

Sam Cooke and early Motown can be heard in the lead and background vocals, with rich gospel chord progressions throughout. "Nobody like the Lord" is an evangelistic conversation with Crouch's listeners, where Andraé *sings* his testimony—a precursor to his classic pieces "Through It All" and "Quiet Times." The song is written in A♭ major—a key Andraé often defaulted to throughout his career.

The key of A♭ enables Crouch to "lift up the Lord" to others, allowing him to speak directly and intimately to the listener, calling the listener a "friend" at one point. Whether that listener is Black, white, rich, poor, feeling good about themselves, or caught in a downward spiral of depression, Crouch declares that there is "nobody like the Lord"—and that the Lord can help. The result is a direct invitation in the lyrics: "But I've got a message for you directly from heaven's best." After the bridge, Andraé sings, "He *told* me to tell you."

The song ends with a typical 1950s Black gospel ballad styling, reminiscent of Lucie Campbell's beloved gospel hymn "Something Within." The piano accompaniment rhythmically moves in and out toward a *ritard* and full-stop ending. With rippling piano *arpeggios* soaring and the ever-present Hammond B3 organ's swelling chords, typical in the Black church songs from the 1950s and 1960s, the song pans out as if the doors of the church are now open to receive new members. Andraé has shared his testimony, and the invitation is now extended.

"I Find No Fault in Him" is contemporary Black *metered music* as both Andraé's voice and the music ebb and flow in and out of time. Wyatt Tee Walker calls the Black *metered music* from the post–Civil War era "adaptations" of the "poetry and musicality of the prayer and praise hymns" and spirituals of early Black America.[14] What is both mystically and musically distinct in this piece is that Crouch tethers and channels the spirituals as he compares Jesus' crucifixion to the biblical text of Pontius Pilate saying, "I find no fault in Him" (Luke 23:4 KJV) to the crowd howling for Jesus' death. Crouch again blends various musical genres here—traditional Black spirituals, vocal music performance practices, the background vocals singing the soulful "oohs" with heavy studio reverb, and traditional COGIC piano and organ accompaniment. In doing so, he fuses musical styles and aesthetics that, again, would *not* normally come together in most Protestant white American church settings. This new "genre fusing" is one of the musical hallmarks of the emerging Jesus Movement that Andraé will soon be associated with, as well as the American praise & worship era that will follow in the 1980s.

Side II

In "I Looked for God," Crouch returns to a key that he will use for decades to come, G♭ major, in another intensely personal song with an almost contradictory theme: while he's seeing God in many places, he is also still searching for Him. This level of introspection will find its fullest flower on the *Just Andraé* recording a few years later. To achieve the aching sense of longing, Andraé has the unnamed background singers (but likely some combination of COGICs Sandra Crouch, Sondra "Blinky" Williams, Edna Wright, and/or Gloria Jones) sing the text "He was there, *and* He'll be there" in a striking prime unison D♭ pitch—a minimalistic approach that creates a new sound, at least in gospel music. Preston plays inspired crescendos and decrescendos on the Hammond B3, adjusting the organ's drawbars to create a swelling of God's presence *being there* in the created space and responding to Andraé's declaration of God being present *everywhere.* The lyrics (and overall tone) suggest that God doesn't have to commute to get to places, because God is already there.

"Joy Bells" ("keep ringing in my soul") displays Andraé's continued development as an arranger. "Joy Bells" is not only a typical COGIC shout chorus groove, but this prototype COGIC "hip pocket" song is rebooted with jazz influences. Growing up in the COGIC tradition, Crouch was familiar with the Wesleyan hymn "O for a Thousand Tongues to Sing," and the Methodists and Baptists in that day would typically have sung the piece at quick *tempi*, with jubilation and joy. But in this arrangement, Crouch gives it a theological twist as he reaches toward a more ecumenical approach. As his fellow COGICs would say, it now has Holy Ghost *fire* on it.

In the key of D♭ major, the background vocals "pedal-point" in A♭, singing "*ring, ring, ring, ring, ring, ring*"—"Yes, the Lord keeps ringing in my soul!" Moments later, Andraé declares his twist on his Pentecostal Holiness Wesleyan roots, flipping the meaning of the hymn "O for a Thousand Tongues to Sing": "I have found a joy no tongue can tell/Since He freed my soul from the gates of hell." Within this arrangement, Crouch's text setting paints a clear, distinct direction for the West Coast COGIC trio gospel rhythm section, with hints of a shout chorus and *bossa nova* floor tom patterns on the drums.

More so than the COGICs LP, this obscure four-song EP shows the truest picture of the compositional and arranging prowess that will soon become the hallmarks of Andraé Crouch the artist. Andraé the performer, by all accounts, is already electrifying audiences, Black and white, but he is still feeling his way as a writer and arranger. It's a shame that, as of this writing, these self-produced songs have never been released to a wider audience.

Teen Challenge Center

Andraé writes that he eventually joined the staff of the Teen Challenge Center, beginning a strict regimen of early morning prayer, regular Bible study, and daily chapel services: "When I started to work at the Teen Challenge Center, I was the happiest person in the world." He also began attending L.I.F.E. Bible College with evangelist Jack Hayford in the afternoons, where scripture memorization was heavily stressed. It was during this time that Andraé began to realize his dream of creating a choir composed primarily of addicts, beginning with rehearsals after his college classes. On a staff salary of $27 (Crouch does not specify if that is a weekly or monthly salary), he rented a room from his beloved Aunt Rachael to be closer to the Center.[15]

Andraé remained remarkably busy, continuing to attend the Bible College, working with his father's church, immersing himself in the routine of the Teen Challenge Center where he also did individual counseling, constantly composing new songs, *and* continuing to perform, as time allowed, with the Disciples. Somehow, Andraé found time to involve himself more in the day-to-day operations of the Disciples, including scheduling concerts. He told the *Los Angeles Sentinel* that he very early developed a mailing list that would someday send advance notices of his itinerary to 50,000 names.[16]

Among the people Andraé met at the Teen Challenge Center was David Hall, younger brother of one of the founders of the Los Angeles location, Don Hall. David began volunteering with his brother at the Center after graduating from high school in Hawaii. Andraé and David became acquainted, and David brought friends from college to join them in the ministry. During his college years (1966–1970), David would also bring several carloads of fellow students to the 10 P.M. live radio service at Christ Memorial, more than an hour away in Pacoima. "Most of them had never been to a Black church," David recalled, "but of course the music was great, so my classmates enjoyed it. Andraé would be at the piano, Sandra on the tambourine, their older brother Ben would be in the back operating the sound system. Andraé's dad led the service and usually preached. And *man*, could he preach." On more than one occasion, David would enter the Teen Challenge Chapel for moments of silent contemplation or prayer. "And Andraé would come in and start playing or worshiping the Lord," David said, "or to work on a new song the Lord had put in his mind. Other times, he'd already be in there and I'd come in on him. I felt it was a privilege, even then." After graduation, David and Don moved to Hawaii to found the Teen Center program there and actively scheduled Disciples concerts.[17]

Also at the Teen Challenge Center at the time were Sonny and Julie Arguinzoni. Sonny, who had been an addict in New York City when he encountered David Wilkerson and Nicky Cruz, was one of the first addicts to enter the original Teen Challenge in the City and one of the first to kick the habit. Sonny originally moved to Southern California to attend the Bible Institute of Los Angeles (now Biola University), met his wife Julie, and graduated in 1965. Upon graduation, he asked to join Don Hall as a supervisor in the new Teen Challenge Center on Hobart Street. Sonny said it was Julie's brother Carrie Rivera who first met Andraé and initially encouraged Andraé to attend one of the Thursday night open house meetings. The Arguinzonis, who had by then moved into the Center, said that Andraé quickly became an integral part of their lives:

> I remember Andraé writing a song in the chapel and our little daughter Debbie sitting on his lap. God would really give him songs and he would be fiddling on the piano. I'd ask, "What are you doing?" He'd say, "Yeah, well, I think God is giving me something." He was a tremendous instrument and blessing in the early days. Somehow, there was chemistry there.

When the Arguinzonis established a church building in East Los Angeles, called Challenge Temple (later Victory Temple), Andraé joined them as well. One of Sonny's most vivid memories of Andraé was his constant street evangelism to the addicts and street people, called "pioneering" by the staff:

> And we would have a broken down piano and Andraé would play. He had a calling, there was a supernatural call in his life. He was very sensitive to the people out there, the inner-city people. That's why every time we invited him, he would come. He didn't care about money.

For Julie, she said she most fondly recalled the hours Andraé spent in the living room of the Teen Challenge Center talking to whoever was present:

> [Andrae would] have all of the drug addicts around him and be laughing. He was just a great, great personality. He lived with us for a year. He loved to stay up late—that's when the Lord would give him a lot of the songs. I remember he wouldn't go to bed until about two or three in the morning. He'd be in the

chapel, just playing. Our apartment was right on top of the chapel, so we'd be hearing him every night, playing his music.[18]

Another frequent visitor was former COGIC Sondra "Blinky" Williams, who after leaving the group had completed requirements to become a licensed counselor in California. She too volunteered to work with the recovering addicts, many of whom were also homeless. "It was just something so natural to do," Williams said. "I even had them come to my church to do the broadcasts and my father would have them giving their testimonies on the radio."

Williams said that Andraé spent most nights at the Teen Challenge Center, often sitting up night after night with an addict trying to kick the habit. "He'd be in their rooms with them, helping them sweat, pleading the blood of Jesus and praying over them," she said. "He didn't care if it was the guys or the girls, whatever was necessary for him to do. It was all cold turkey—it was nothing but the Lord."[19]

The different Disciples also found themselves at the rambling old house on Hobart, including Perry Morgan, who had been married in 1966 by Benjamin Crouch Sr. at Christ Memorial. Morgan said that he, Bili Thedford, Ruben Fernandez, and Sherman Andrus would all volunteer periodically, sometimes just informally hanging out, sometimes accompanying Andraé's "pioneering" or singing on downtown's mean streets. Thedford, who lived for a time with Andraé and Sandra's parents in Pacoima, said he remembered making the hour-long trip regularly, though—like Morgan—he was never officially a Teen Challenge staff member. "I was there a lot," Thedford said. "I hung out; I was one of the guys. I consoled them, took them out and talked to them, helped them deal with some of their issues and tried to help somebody to scratch their way back into a stable lifestyle."[20]

Soon Andraé's involvement in Teen Challenge even flowed into the home of his parents. Benjamin and Catherine Crouch had witnessed to and cared for both unhoused people and addicts from the beginning of Benjamin's own ministry. Groups from the Center—counselors and residents alike—found themselves at the dinner table after the Sunday night radio broadcast. "Andraé would fry them fish and cook for them almost every Sunday night after church and just encourage them," Sandra said. "Sonny and Julie Arguinzoni and Nicky Cruz came. They would tell them about how to lead people. They would see [Andraé's] passion and the love of loving people."[21]

Andrus said that most of the Disciples had full-time jobs during the period 1966–1967 and that he had recently married Winnie, who had just moved to

Los Angeles from Texas. Benjamin Crouch had performed their wedding as well, and Andraé and Perry Morgan were involved in the ceremony. Sherman too had become involved with Teen Challenge through David Wilkerson. At one point, Wilkerson even invited Andrus to become the featured soloist on his crusades and rallies. Andrus worked at the US Post Office on the 4:15 A.M. to 12:45 P.M. shift, which gave him more freedom to accompany Andraé, who—despite his grueling schedule—continued to accept more and more invitations to perform, especially on nights and weekends. Andrus recalled one early trip to Seattle that he believed was the first time Crouch used the name "Disciples" in the promotion for the date.

Another Rare Recording

In the early days, when Crouch felt himself again called to the recording studio, only Andrus was available to accompany him. One such session resulted in the 45 "Come and Go with Me to My Father's House" and "Prayer Is the Key to Heaven." The 45 was, apparently, another self-financed recording project, pressed in extremely limited numbers. The authors have been unable to locate a copy.[22]

A song titled "Come and Go with Me to My Father's House" first appears in the 1919 hymnal *Songs of His Coming* and is credited there as an African American spiritual. It has been printed in numerous hymnals, most recently *One Lord, One Faith, One Baptism*, published in 2018. The song has had a long history in COGIC circles as well. Edwin Hawkins, a friend of the Crouches and a lifelong COGIC, recorded it in 1968 as "To My Father's House" on the album that contained his massive hit, "Oh Happy Day."

What Andrus calls "Faith Unlocks the Door" is also known as "(Prayer Is the Key to Heaven) Faith Unlocks the Door" and is found as early as in different 1956 recordings by various artists, including Lawrence Welk, Liberace, the Statesmen, and others. The song is credited to Samuel T. Scott and Robert L. Sande.[23]

Creating the Addicts Choir Album

Despite the time constraints, Andraé soon established a backbreaking schedule for himself and the newly established group. They performed at the Teen

Challenge Center daily and regularly performed at other venues, especially on the weekends. According to LaVern Moore, Andraé was able to turn his musical responsibilities at Christ Memorial over to LaVern Moore's brother James Logan and his wife, Roberta (and former Disciple Howard Neil's sister), herself a talented pianist. "God had his hand on the entire situation," Moore said. "James and Roberta reestablished the music ministry at Christ Memorial, which allowed Pastor Andraé to go and minister at Teen Challenge—and wherever else the Lord directed him to go." Occasionally accompanied by Sandra, a loose grouping of singers began rehearsing in the evenings. "We didn't put that label—that they were 'ex-addicts'—on them," Sandra said. "We didn't say, 'Oh, you're just going to go to hell, you've relapsed again.' We sang songs and we loved people."[24]

As they had with the counseling of the residents, different members of the Disciples and other friends assisted in rehearsing what would eventually be called the Addicts Choir. Andraé frequently invited the newly married Andrus to sing with the residents. Thedford also sang with the choir but on the condition that he not receive credit. "Because this was about Teen Challenge," he said, "it wasn't about us. We were just there in support. Music is a healer. Sometimes you had to hold them up to sing." Morgan also participated in the rehearsals and performances whenever possible. "We didn't do any leading or anything," he said. "We were just backgrounding with them. We were just there basically to support Andraé and also to give our support to the guys who were in the choir." David Hall, who claimed not to be much of a singer, was recruited as well. "But Andraé still found a truthful way to commend," he recalled. "He said, 'With all the people and addicts coming and going in Teen Challenge, I'm glad to have you part of the choir, not so much because of your voice, but because you stay long-term so I don't have to keep teaching you the songs and parts.'"[25]

Even though there was constant churn in the membership with the residents of the Center, incarnations of the Addicts Choir under Andraé's direction sang in various evangelical and secular settings in 1967 and early 1968, usually to a great response. Andrus said that audiences "loved" the Addicts Choir. "Andraé would take the choir out to all these different churches all during the week and on Sunday," Andrus said, "and that's how they raised money for Teen Challenge. He did a great job with it. We did a song Andraé wrote called 'Hallelujah, I Am Free' and boy! that was the end. When the ex-Addicts would start singing, people would go crazy."[26]

One of the people impressed by Andraé's songwriting ability was Tim Spencer of the religious publishing house, Manna Music, Inc. Mieir was one of Manna's best-known composers on a roster that included fellow Southern California composer Doris Akers ("Sweet, Sweet Spirit") and Stuart K. Hines ("How Great Thou Art") and had the capability of widely publishing and distributing Crouch's songs. According to Carrie Gonzalo, Mieir introduced the two men and Spencer immediately began the process of promoting "The Blood (Will Never Lose Its Power)." In the late 1960s, when Christian bookstores were just beginning to be widely established and radio rarely played contemporary religious music, sheet music and sheet music collections were still an important industry staple. Spencer contracted with Gonzalo, a budding Christian artist herself, to transcribe Andraé's songs. Gonzalo was a frequent guest at Benjamin and Catherine's home, often volunteered at the Teen Challenge Center, and remained lifelong friends with the Crouches. "Carl Seal of Manna Music's instructions were to put on paper, just with the piano notes, what represented Andraé's sound," Gonzalo said. "They knew I could do it because I had the understanding and I also had the ear experience with Andraé to learn all those chords. I started playing those G♭s and D♭s—those are the keys that Andraé played in with five and six flats. I once asked him, 'How come?' He said, 'Oh, they're easier, Carrie. Your fingers don't have to stretch so far, and then they fall right in place.'"[27]

Teen Challenge Addicts Choir Album

Eventually, the ragtag assemblage at the Teen Challenge Center morphed into something like a choir. The project was recorded and released on Word Records, then the scrappy newcomer in Christian music. Founded by recent college graduate Jarrell McCracken, Word grew out of a single twenty-minute track where McCracken told the Christian salvation story in a mock radio broadcast of a football game titled *The Game of Life*. In 1968, Word Records featured mostly traditional inspirational recording artists and preachers: Ethel Waters, Billy Graham, Kurt Kaiser, and Burl Ives, as well as various choirs and hymn collections. McCracken, music director Kaiser, and promotions director Billy Ray Hearn were themselves still young men and looking for artists to tap into the emerging youth market. According to the liner notes, Word's decision to release the LP was primarily due to the efforts of Mieir, whose influence extended beyond her popular songwriting: "The album is largely the result of Audrey Mieir's encouragement and support." When the *Teen Challenge Addicts Choir* LP was finally released, Mieir wrote a glowing endorsement. She called it her "favorite choir" and cited Andraé's leadership of this "miracle choir," calling him the "most exciting, dedicated young musician I have ever met. When he touches the piano or sings or speaks, the audience is captivated and becomes involved by his tremendous vitality, dedication, and talent."[28]

The LP jacket features a blurry color photo of some of the choir superimposed over a graphic photograph of a man injecting himself in the arm with a syringe, along with a stylized Bible with hand-lettered calligraphy in the foreground that reads, "Therefore if any man be in Christ, he is a new creature: old things are passed away; behold, all things are become new" from II Corinthians 5:17. In addition to the blurb by Mieir, the crowded back album jacket has thumbnail-sized photographs and biographies of Andraé, Don Hall, a portion of the book jacket from *The Cross and the Switchblade*, a paragraph about the Teen Challenge Ministry, a small picture of the Center at 2263 South Hobart, *and* liner notes by Nat Olson.

Olson's notes, along with the list of songs on the LP, claim that the choir's "progressive sound" has been heard "in churches, conventions, on tour, or at the famed Monday night 'Audrey Mieir Sing' in Faith Center, Glendale, California," as well as including brief information about some of the individual singers.[29]

Side I

"The Addict's Plea" is the first Andraé composition in which neither Jesus nor God is the subject. The tonality is in G♭ minor and the work is theatrical, filled with pensive, sometimes lyrical reflections as Andraé explores the dramatic effects music can have. With these songs, he continues the process of coming out of his musical comfort zone to evangelize a different audience. Several melancholy call-and-responses on the trumpet and acoustic upright bass movements are reminiscent of a late-night club jazz trio, inviting the listener to hear the singer's cry for help. Andraé writes that he wrote "The Addict's Plea" following a conversation with one of the residents, Rosie. Rosie asked him, "Hey man, is there anyone who can help me? Somebody who really knows my needs?" Crouch sang the song so often, he said, that some people in the audience sometimes thought that he was a former junkie. "The Lord gave me rapport with addicts," he writes. "I'd never been there, but I loved 'em so much." It's an intensely personal piece, with Andraé's deep empathy for Rosie and the other struggling addicts clearly evident in the lines "Help me, I'm in despair, it seems like no one even cares."[30]

If "Someday I'll See His Face" had been presented in Andraé's home COGIC church, it would have been as an up-tempo, $\frac{4}{4}$ time signature, musically syncopated celebration. But since Andraé's primary audience for this album is white, he changes his approach. Metrically, the piano and organ accompaniment hint at a $\frac{9}{8}$ compound time signature, but Crouch instead leans into a more reserved $\frac{3}{4}$ time signature and a Doris Akers–Sky Pilot choir-styled arrangement. The loose singing feels congregational, and a close listen to the chorus reveals both professional mezzo-sopranos and amateur first sopranos. To avoid distracting from the melody and the message, Andraé sings the solo with a clear, focused non-syncopated reverence, avoiding bluesy singing or long melismatic improvisatory gestures. His role here, it appears, is to lead the congregation as worship leader, and the song itself is a foreshadowing of the multiethnic praise & worship movement still to come in religious music. The work ends with the hymn-like "amen" found in many hymns.

The key lyric for "The Power of Jesus" is "The power of Jesus can break . . . . every chain." The phrase "break every chain" is briefly interrupted after the word "break" not only to "paint" the text, but also to allow for greater breath support for the tenors, baritones, and basses in the male section of the choir. Crouch arranged for the full spectrum of high-quality voices, as well as singers with a more limited vocal range. The sopranos and altos sing "ahhhs" in counterpoint. The full choir then joins in singing the "amazing grace" passage with call-and-response movements. Throughout, Andraé employs a variety of musical and text setting techniques. "The Power of Jesus" is inspirational, encouraging in both the music and the lyrics, especially the lines "and give to you a victory over shame." The unison vocals are all shouted over Andraé's busy "oom-pah" piano licks, much like a revival chorus led by Homer Rodeheaver, the best-known proponent of full-throated crusade-style congregational singing.

One of the staples of the Billy Graham Crusades, "I'd Rather Have Jesus" has long been associated with George Beverly Shea. In the key of D♭ major, the song emphasizes singer Ruben Fernandez's smooth baritone and lush and pitched-voiced vibrato. The arrangement owes much to Shea's mellow version from a thousand Graham crusades. Somewhat reminiscent of his work with the COGICs, Crouch uses his impressive pedal point techniques on the track. This version feels curiously unfinished, something that no doubt also happened with the rushed COGICs session, and perhaps he was running out of studio time to create more sophisticated background vocals. Still, Crouch, knowing the choir's limitations, in the second half of the song arranges for them to sing an octave unison pedal point backdrop on A♭. This allows Ruben's voice to soar and swell, with the sweetness of his vocal range lifting the text.

For the first time, Crouch's church home roots emerge in the robust piano accompaniment to "I've Got Jesus." In Andraé's sweet tonal centering key of E♭ major, the syncopation, melismatic blues singing, improvisation, and the titanic call-and-responses in the background voices that are more common in traditional gospel music appear. That said, "I've Got Jesus" is an odd addition to the Crouch canon. Though fueled by a rollicking piano and crashing tambourines, it plays like a tribute to the Broadway musical standard, "I've Got Rhythm" ("I've got Jesus, who could ask for anything more?"). This is the song that's closest to traditional Black gospel music on *Teen Challenge Addicts Choir*, complete with a clear-cut $\frac{12}{8}$ compound meter vamp and a full-throttled *ritard* motion toward a church hymn-like ending.

In the key of G♭ major, "Hallelujah, I Am Free" illustrates how Crouch will later develop his popular gospel power ballads. The groove and tenor of Crouch's power ballads will continue to evolve with subsequent recordings. But with a close listen to the meaning within the texts, the gestures of the lead vocal lines, and how the songs are orchestrated, two more elements of Crouch's musical genius emerge—complex, evocative vocal phrasings that do not distract from the purity of text and the use of the vast vocal color palette of musical keys he employs.

Andrus said that "Hallelujah, I'm Free," while clearly aimed at the residents of the Teen Challenge Center, always drew an enthusiastic response when performed in churches. Sherman's clear tenor is featured and the choir sings in the style of a mid-century church oratorio, repeating the title over and over while Andraé's supports the music with jazzy piano fills. The idea of importing an ecumenical "alleluia" creates a common language for a host of different denominations. Again, it is clear that Andraé seeks to appeal to a wider ecumenical audience.[31]

Side II

Side II begins with "Faith Unlocks the Door's" gospel $\frac{3}{8}$ waltz in A♭ major, a sonnet declaring that prayer is the key to heaven drawn from the words of I Kings 8:45— "then hear from heaven their prayer and their plea and uphold their cause" (NIV). This is the second song on the "vanity" 45 recorded earlier by Andraé and Sherman. Andrus said that Andraé's arrangement of this old Southern quartet song was designed to emphasize his strengths as a "crooner." Crouch, he said, had him sing it in the manner of smooth-voiced Johnny Mathis. "That was just Andraé's style of playing," Sherman said; "he could capture so much with just his ability to do all the different styles—and that's how I did that song." This is the first time Crouch creates an instrumental interlude on one of his recordings, which allows for Andraé on piano and who the authors believe must be Billy Preston on the organ to show off their musical chops. They joyfully trade chords and create a reflective, collaborative creative space for prayer (despite the presence of the clearly overmatched drummer mangling what is supposed to be compound meter). Crouch's and Andrus's voices blend beautifully throughout.[32]

In the $\frac{6}{8}$ time signature and in the key of D♭ major, "I Shall Never Let Go His Hand" reflects congregational singing at its most robust. At the beginning of the piece, the choir sings in unison in octaves—this sacred sound is precious to Andraé and it will become a standard rubric or template for most of his compositions in the years to come. The strongest component of this Southern gospel-styled church revival track is the heartfelt duet between Ruben and Andraé. During live performances throughout his career, Andraé would regularly trade voices and mix up solos and duets. Had Ruben and Sherman remained in the Disciples longer, the authors believe that later albums would have featured more of these memorable duets.

With "He Included Me," Andraé begins to masterfully employ new sounds with his use of orchestration. While some all-male gospel quartets utilized the guitar, many conservative Black churches in the North still did not allow the instrument in their worship services. On the piano, the user-friendly key of A♭ major means that the combination of the guitar with Hammond B3 organ produces new "colors," another element that Crouch will frequently import into his musical canon. This is an early example of Andraé's willingness to orchestrate creatively, a unique aspect of his overall musical stylings. As for this particular song, according to Olson's liner notes, Addicts Choir soloist Laura

Lee Myers was a "young housewife who became addicted to prescription pills" and that the lyrics of the song tell her "testimony." "Andraé would look at different people and had heard their testimonies," Andrus said, "and he would write songs for them where they could really embellish their testimonies of what they came through." While passionately performed, Myers's pronounced vibrato gives the song something of the feel of a small-town church recital.[33]

Is the G♭ minor chant-like opening trope to "I Cannot Tell It All" a sly reference to Andraé's Jewish roots? (In a later interview with Mark Joseph, Crouch has said that at least two of his grandparents came from a Jewish background.) The sprightly Pentecostal COGIC dance tempo today sounds like an outtake from the then-popular television musical comedy series *Hee-Haw* and makes good use of the humorous voices affected by the two lead singers. The song also bears a close resemblance to the much older gospel song, "He's Done So Much for Me," by Theodore R. Frye and Lillian Bowles.[34]

One of Audrey Mieir's best-known compositions, "To Be Used of God," has been recorded by singers ranging from Doris Akers to Jimmy Swaggart. In the opening, Andraé's slow and reverent accompaniment owes much to James Cleveland's version in 1965 with the Walter Arties Chorale. Andraé focuses on liberating the emotion of the text with what sounds like a jazz quartet performing with a Hammond B3 organ. With the combination of gospel 11th chords, brushes on the snare drum, and with free-flowing modern melodic gestures sung in the lead line, Crouch blends jazz and gospel styles. He freely recasts tempos and time signatures and builds a lexicon of musical sensibilities. Unusual for his day, especially in gospel music, Andraé listened intently to the mechanics of a variety of musical stylings. These chord substitutions and changes were most definitely *not* in church hymnals. Crouch takes Mieir's well-known chorus and frees and baptizes it with an ecumenical musicality. Crouch's musical liberation would someday enable him to evangelize in such a way that no previous Black gospel artist had done before.

For the finale "Psalms 40," performed in E♭ minor, Andraé has the choir sing a recitative chant reminiscent of both Christian and Jewish texts. "Psalms 40" is both a declaration of victory and the sending-out song to the entire LP. Appropriately, it concludes with the Hammond B3's coloring chords as a postlude to the album's unique closing litany—the words of the beloved 40th Psalm—which are reflective of the old lining-out hymns in the Black church, or even the prayer chants of the Jewish tradition. Taken together, the piece functions as a traditional Christian benediction.

Aftermath

Once released, the lone mention of the LP is in the June 1, 1969, issue of *Billboard* magazine at the end of the "New Album Releases" column, along with four other Word Records. The authors have not been able to locate a review or article on the project, and it does not appear on any year-end lists of best-selling religious albums.[35]

Eventually, once the Addicts Choir was established, Andraé claims that, despite individual success stories, he was forced to move on from the Teen Challenge Center. "I sang for numerous funerals of the kids that didn't make it," he writes. "It really pierces you when you are involved trying to help them. I'm an emotional person and the years at Teen Challenge took their toll. I've never cried so hard in all of my life."[36]

None of the songs from the LP appears elsewhere, and the authors believe that Andraé would not perform any of them in concert in the years to come. But the album enabled him to answer the call of his "vision" to create such a choir at Teen Challenge, and he clearly touched many individuals with his work there. On the surface, *Teen Challenge Addicts Choir* is a one-off project with little connection to the music he will soon record and perform with the Disciples. However, it did provide him with the freedom to musically experiment in various styles, ranging from Southern gospel revival hymnody to jazzy blues and to masterfully create accessible melodies for congregational singers.

Another Modern Liturgy

The LP can also be seen as a kind of musical liturgy for people searching on the road to recovery, from the anguished "Addict's Plea" to the benediction of "Psalms 40." The album established Andraé's deep, visceral connection with two of society's most vulnerable groups, those with housing insecurity and with dependency issues. In that, he connected directly to the life's work of his "great-uncle," Bishop Samuel Crouch, and his father, Benjamin. Both men responded to the scriptural call to minister to the marginalized. When Andraé would write about these topics and other similar issues in later releases, some members of the wider religious community often recoiled in an immediate, judgmental backlash, accusing him of—among other things—the sin of "selling out" to popular culture. But an examination of the earliest beginnings of

Andraé's musical ministry, including the Addicts Choir, proves that this has always been a driving, motivating force in his life.

And it did something else. Every composer needs a playground, a laboratory, a sphere for exploration and musical discoveries. Composers have long explored the notion of new musical possibilities via residencies. The great composers want to experiment, to experience, and to pose the questions *What are the issues? How are we to deal with them?* and *Why?* within the supportive community for whom they are composing. Ultimately, Andraé Crouch was essentially the composer in residence with the Addicts Choir. This virtually unknown recording did not generate attention when it was released and quickly went out of print. Looking back through the lens of more than fifty years, we can see Crouch's growth as a composer, crafting and creating within a relatively narrow framework and with limited resources. The entire recording functions like an oratorio, filled with drama and narrative. In this context, Andraé is more than a songwriter. His grit, grind, and prowess with compositional technique and form, the clarity of his lyrical lines, melodic approaches, cadences, and musical counterpoint are more impressive given the constraints of a small budget and of an exceedingly amateurish and often unpredictable choir. And yet, Crouch still somehow manages to achieve moments of brilliance. His familiarity with a variety of musical genres, colors of keys, and orchestration for the instruments within the community are, by turns, musically winsome, strikingly theological, prophetically innovative, and most certainly biblically evangelical. In the Teen Challenge Center Addicts Choir, Crouch begins to develop as a composer, musical entrepreneur, and producer. His compositional skills are about to catapult his career and ministry to places where both concert music composers and most traditional gospel music recording artists had never gone—and probably would have feared to tread. Crouch will become that rare composer who enters a multiplicity of artistic arenas, multiethnically, intergenerationally, and internationally.[37]

Ultimately, Pastor Sonny Arguinzoni argued that Andraé's greatest gift from his time at the Teen Challenge Center was actually an uncannily empathic ability to relate to people in their pain:

> And then the way that he had a rapport with them that everybody could actually relate to in some of these street people. They were heavy drug addicts that were coming in, looking at Andraé and saying, "Well, he's a square." But, yet you'd see that somehow with Andraé's personality he was able to relate to them—and then God gave him favor with all people.[38]

Once it was completed and released, Andraé at last began to turn his attention to the Disciples.

NOTES

1. Andraé Crouch with Nina Ball, *Through It All* (Waco, TX: Word Books, 1974), 47–48; Bili Thedford, interview with the authors, November 6, 2020; Bili Thedford, interview with the authors, November 6, 2020; https://www.disc ogs.com/release/812892-The-Superiors-Eternal-Dream-Happy-Days-Are-Here -Again; https://easyreadernews.com/songs-sunny-side-jazz-singer-bili-redd-thedf ord-plays-terranea/.

2. Andraé Crouch, *Through It All*, 48–49; Perry Morgan, interview with the authors, March 19, 2022.

3. Andraé Crouch, *Through It All*, 48–49; Bili Thedford, interview with the authors, November 6, 2020; LaVern Moore interview with the authors, March 21, 2022.

4. Andraé Crouch, *Through It All*, 49; Bili Thedford, interview with the authors, November 6, 2020; Perry Morgan, interview with the authors, March 19, 2022.

5. LaVern Moore, interview with the authors, March 21, 2022; Bill Lewis, "KFI in the Middle of a Firestorm—A Look Back on KFI's Coverage during the 1992 LA Riots," April 27, 2017, https://kfiam640.iheart.com/content/2017-04-27-kfi -in-the-middle-of-a-firestorm-a-look-back-on-kfis-coverage-during-the-1992-la -riots/; Sherman Andrus Sr., *My Story!, His Song! Blessed!* (Nashville: WestBow Press, 2021), 17–19.

6. Peter North, "Truly Blessed with a Terrific Voice; Gospel Singer Sherman Andrus Has Sung with Some of the Music World's Greatest," *Edmonton Journal*, January 23, 1998, C3; Andrus, *My Story!, His Song! Blessed!*, 17–19.

7. Bili Thedford, interview with the authors, November 6, 2020.

8. Sherman Andrus, interview with the authors, September 3, 2020.

9. LaVern Moore, interview with the authors, March 21, 2022; mannamusic.com /writers-songs/Audrey-Mieir.html.

10. Perry Morgan, interview with the authors, March 19, 2022; Bili Thedford, interview with the authors, March 22, 2022.

11. Andraé Crouch, *Through It All*, 51–55; David Wilkerson with John and Elizabeth Sherill, *The Cross and the Switchblade* (New York: Bernard Geis Associates, 1962); https://www.teenchallenge.org/about-us/our-history/.

12. Andraé Crouch, *Through It All*, 56–57; Sandra Crouch, interview with the authors, February 25, 2021.

13. Sandra Crouch, interview with the authors, February 25, 2021; Sondra "Blinky" Williams, *Hark the Voice*, Atlantic Records SD R-003, 1967; Andraé Crouch, *Through It All*, 58. Note: The authors would like to thank gospel historian Robert Marovich for providing the copy of this rare 45.

14. Wyatt Tee Walker, *Spirits That Dwell in Deep Woods*, Vol. 3 (New York: Martin Luther King Fellows Press, 1991), Introduction, xiii.
15. Andraé Crouch, *Through It All*, 56–57; Patrick Salvo, "New King of Pop Gospel," *Sepia*, December 1976, 52.
16. Von Jones, "Gospel Greats Have Message," *Los Angeles Sentinel*, March 14, 1985, A1.
17. David Hall, personal correspondence with the authors, September 29 and October 1, 2021.
18. Sonny and Julie Arguinzoni, interview with the authors, December 11, 2020.
19. Sondra "Blinky" Williams, interview with the authors, December 8, 2020.
20. Perry Morgan, interview with the authors, March 19, 2022; Bili Thedford, interview with the authors, November 12, 2020.
21. Sandra Crouch, interview with the authors, November 6, 2020.
22. Andrus, *My Story! His Song! Blessed!*, 19–21.
23. https://hymnary.org/text/come_and_go_with_me_to_my_fathers_house; *Northern California State Youth Choir of the Church of God in Christ*, Pavilion Records BPS 10001, Buddah Records, 1968; Sherman Andrus, interview with the authors, November 7, 2020.
24. Andraé Crouch, *Through It All*, 56–57; Sandra Crouch, interview with the authors, November 6, 2020; LaVern Moore, interview with the authors, March 21, 2022.
25. Sherman Andrus, interview with the authors, November 7, 2020; Bili Thedford, interview with the authors, November 12, 2020; David Hall, personal correspondence with the authors, September 29 and October 1, 2021; Perry Morgan, interview with the authors, March 19, 2022.
26. Sherman Andrus, interview with the authors, September 5, 2020.
27. Carrie Gonzalo, interview with the authors, December 17, 2020; Mannamusicinc .com/history-manna.html.
28. "Word Records Spreads Sacred Music's Message: Now It Plans to Build a Jesus Rock Label with a Mod Sound," *Billboard*, April 19, 1972, T-4; Deborah Evans Price, "Jarrell McCracken, 79: Word Inc. Founder Helped Shape the Christian Music Industry," *Billboard*, November 24, 2007, 10; *Teen Challenge Addicts Choir*, Word Records WST-8403, liner notes, 1968; Bob Gersztyn, *Jesus Rocks the World: The Definitive History of Contemporary Christian Music* (Santa Barbara, CA: Praeger Books, 2012), 105–106.
29. *Teen Challenge Addicts Choir.*
30. Andraé Crouch, *Through It All*, 59.
31. Sherman Andrus, interview with the authors, November 5, 2020.
32. Sherman Andrus, interview with the authors, November 5, 2020.
33. *Teen Challenge Addicts Choir.*
34. Mark Joseph, interview with the authors, December 30, 2020.
35. "New Album Releases," *Billboard*, June 1, 1968, 67.
36. Andraé Crouch, *Through It All*, 60.

37. See *A Commemorative Concert in Memory of Dr. Martin Luther King Jr., 1988–1989*, Programs Presented by Guest Artists, Faculty, and Students, University of Michigan, 1989, 25–31, for a discussion on the importance of residencies for composers.

38. Sonny and Julie Arguinzoni, interview with the authors, December 11, 2020.

4

Take the Message Everywhere

While working and composing for the Addicts Choir, Andraé continued to write for the Disciples. After leaving Teen Challenge, and now freed from his choir-leading responsibilities with his father's Christ Memorial Church of God in Christ, Crouch began introducing the new songs to Bili Thedford, Perry Morgan, and Sherman Andrus. At some point, a fifth singer was invited to join, Ruben Fernandez, who had been featured in two songs on the *Teen Challenge Addicts Choir* LP. Fernandez joined the Disciples from the Messengers (Los Mensajeros), a popular Mexican American gospel group based in Southern California. Singer Gene D. Viale said that the Messengers and Disciples first met during a program at Knott's Berry Farm and the two groups sang at many of the same venues.[1]

Fernandez was popular among the Disciples and their friends, all of whom at times attended services at his home church, La Trinidad. Thedford compared Ruben's lyric baritone to that of Billy Eckstine or Isaac Hayes. "His voice was as big as he was," Thedford said. "He was more than 350 pounds and that's difficult on the long trips on land, hopping planes, flying here, running in hotels. In the beginning, he did some traveling with us." Andrus called Fernandez "a fabulous guy to be around." Morgan said the two men "got along really well." "We used to laugh a lot together and go over to his mom's because she'd cook some really wonderful food for us," Morgan recalled. "We just hung out together a little bit; he was a beautiful guy, a lovely guy who loved to sing." Sandra Crouch agreed with the assessment: "He was one of the nicest guys, such a sweet, sweet guy. But Ruben could sing; he sounded like one of those jazz singers you'd hear in a club."[2]

Early Days with the Disciples

Still, it was a difficult time for the Disciples. With the other members employed full-time, only Andraé was able to commit completely to their new musical ministry. While the group was kept busy performing (primarily nights and weekends), the pay was erratic and Crouch often accepted nonpaying engagements where the sponsoring church or organization would ask the congregation for donations—a "love offering"—that sometimes barely covered their transportation costs. Andraé writes that the Disciples "did a lot of praying—on our knees" as they looked for direction. One other issue in the early days, Andrus writes, is that Crouch was "not a detail person." Sherman tells of one trip to Hawaii where Andraé had neglected to secure accommodations for the group ahead of time. For dates in the continental United States, the available Disciples crowded together in Crouch's recently acquired blue Ford Econoline van, often sleeping in the van after concerts amid the instruments and—later—boxes of sheet music and albums for sale.[3]

Despite the distractions and demands, Andraé continued his constant songwriting, often targeting songs for specific members of the Disciples. Crouch would meet with the chosen singer, usually during the increasingly rare rehearsals, and teach him the new song. Andrus, nominally the "lead" singer in the group, was often the beneficiary:

> He heard what he wanted it to sound like in his head. And I fit what he wanted, for some reason. I was a good student; I was a sponge. I said, "You teach me." I always tried to do his songs the way he wanted me to do them. He might get us all together on a recording or a rehearsal and then start playing something. And then say, "OK, you sing this part." And you'd sing.[4]

After the death of his mother Catherine's sister Rachael, Andraé moved back to his parent's home. Meanwhile, Sandra's newfound success as a Motown session musician enabled her to buy her own home. Their brother Benjamin joined the Navy, married, and soon had children of his own, while their father's rise in the denomination meant that he was frequently away on church business. Crouch writes that it was to comfort his mother in her grief that he wrote two songs, "I Must Go Away" and "God Will Never Leave You, No, No, No, No."[5] (A song titled "I Must Go Away" appears on the *Keep On Singin'* album from 1971 and may be the same song.)

Ralph Carmichael and Light Records

It was during this difficult time that Andraé and the Disciples met Christian music producer and composer Ralph Carmichael, who had founded Light Records and Lexicon Publishing in 1966, a joint venture with McCracken and the larger, more established Word Records. Carmichael had had a successful career in pop music, composing and arranging for Nat King Cole, Peggy Lee, and others, and had served for a time as music director of *The Lucy Show*. A relationship with WorldWide Pictures, the motion picture division of Billy Graham Ministries, led Carmichael to eventually score more than twenty films for WorldWide. In the early days of the Jesus Music movement of the 1960s, he co-wrote two highly popular Christian youth choir musicals with Kurt Kaiser, *Tell It Like It Is* and *Natural High*. Light Records' roster at the time included a number of Jesus Music and contemporary Christian artists, including Jessy Dixon, the Children of the Day, Jamie Owens-Collins, and the Archers. Carmichael was first introduced to Andraé and the Disciples in November 1967 by Manna Music's Tim Spencer. In February 1968, engineer Bill Ball also suggested that Carmichael reach out to the group as a possible addition to Light's roster of artists. Intrigued, he did so:

> The next morning, I started looking for Andraé Crouch. I found him and a meeting was arranged. After the usual amenities, we began exchanging ideas about music—its trends, its potential, and how it can be used to get to kids with the gospel of Christ. I soon discovered under his mild manner and warm smile, Andraé was a guy with a very serious purpose that had reached "do or die" proportions.[6]

The two met at the Manna Music offices in Hollywood. In his biography, Carmichael writes that Andraé was late for the first meeting and the shy, unassuming Crouch spoke quietly about his Christian faith and his work at Teen Challenge. Finally, Spencer suggested that Andraé sit at the piano in the office and play. Within minutes, Carmichael was sold: "Then I knew why Tim had asked me to come to his office to hear this. Andraé was something special. He was far more comfortable singing and playing than he was walking and talking, and probably enjoyed it more than eating and sleeping." Initially, however, Carmichael writes that he worried how his sales staff (Light was distributed by Word in the Christian marketplace) would be able to sell white bookstore owners a record by "a young Black man nobody had heard of" whose music was "a potpourri of rock, jazz, blues and traditional Black gospel," especially an artist, Carmichael noted, whose lyrics were often "street-talk" or "street vernacular"—even though they were also "absolutely scriptural."[7]

The *Take the Message Everywhere* Session

Andraé writes that Carmichael scheduled a two-hour recording session for the group. Carmichael then told Andraé that "anything" that the Disciples wanted to record during that session "would be good" and "left it up to us as to what we wanted to do." This was the beginning of a long, sometimes rocky, relationship between Carmichael's Light Records and the Disciples. Sandra said that she and Andraé met later with Carmichael at his house office to sign the paperwork. "Ralph was very personable," Sandra said of their first meeting. "He really knew music, but he couldn't believe all of those great songs that were coming out of such a young man." In the years that followed, Carrie Gonzalo remembered Carmichael coaching the Disciples on the singing and breathing techniques he'd taught some of popular music's biggest stars:

> It was such a learning experience just to watch everything that happened. Ralph was such a pro and I think that really launched Andraé into a new place musically. Like Audrey [Mieir], he just loved Andraé [and] couldn't do enough to help develop and broaden his ministry. Ralph was one of those people who was just open to new talent. He saw the quality and he saw the conviction in Andraé's gifting and his commitment to glorify God.[8]

Andrus said that the recording session took place at noted organist Lorin Whitney's recording studio in Glendale, which had hosted artists ranging from Aretha Franklin to orchestras working with the Walt Disney studio. Frank Kaymar served as engineer and Jimmy Collins produced, although Carmichael was in the cavernous studio briefly for the recording of "Without a Song." At that time, the studio did not have headphones, so the engineer instead played songs through the speakers. "I had lots of trouble with that," Andrus recalled. "It was hard to record back then because you couldn't play the music too loud because it would bleed into the microphone." Andrus sang "Without a Song" in one take: "I was so glad I didn't have to do it through [again]." (Later, with the Imperials, Sherman said he was nicknamed "One-Take Andrus.")[9]

If the songs on what would eventually be called *Take the Message Everywhere* actually were recorded in just two hours, much of the credit goes to the industry veteran Collins, who, with his wife Carol, composed hundreds of Christian songs, wrote and produced several Christian musicals, including the seminal *Come Together: A Musical Experience* in 1972, and the Grammy-nominated *Ants'hilvania* in 1981, as well as producing a number of faith-based artists. Sandra and Andraé and the Collins family, including their daughter Jamie, who herself would become a contemporary Christian artist, became lifelong friends. Once again, it was Mieir who first introduced Andraé to Jimmy.[10]

When released by Light Records, the first Disciples LP was issued with two different cover versions. The first cover featured Andraé, Ruben Fernandez, Bili Thedford, Perry Morgan, and Sherman Andrus dressed in sharp electric blue suits in front of a blank wall lit with multicolored lights. At the top, the words "Andraé Crouch and the Disciples" are hand-drawn in what the nameless cover designer may have thought was a "groovy" modified cursive. The second cover version features just Andraé, Morgan, and Thedford and adds Sandra Crouch, all in informal poses under an outdoor shed. The back jacket material is identical in both versions. The second cover may have been issued as a last-minute substitute after the Disciples experienced personnel changes following the completion of the LP. In one of the very earliest printed references of a Disciples album, *Billboard* listed the LP in its "4 Star" column detailing new releases in the June 19, 1971, issue.[11]

Once again, Mieir wrote a glowing blurb on the back jacket, including a vivid description of Crouch in performance:

> When Andraé sits at the piano, a light turns on from inside. Sometimes the music is haunting—tugging at the heart. His handsome face glows with inner warmth. The music flows from skillful hands and the message penetrates to the hearts of the listeners. Sometimes the strange pulsating rhythms electrify the audience. One foot beats a hole in the carpet, fingers fly over the keyboard—head back— face aglow, the mood reaches the listeners. Hands clap, feet must pat and "amens" must be said!

While Mieir, whose own compositions were resolutely in the traditional church format, clearly appreciates Andraé's gifts, she continues to struggle to find words to describe exactly *what* it is he's doing: "Some songs are exquisite with pathos, others rich in strange harmonies, yet, again the whole place 'turns on' as the rhythm becomes ecstatic and wild!" *Take the Message Everywhere*, as was the norm in the recorded music industry during this period, was in great measure a producer's medium. While Crouch wrote most of the tracks, Collins and Carmichael created the charts from his original songs,

80 SOON & VERY SOON

hired the studio musicians, and recorded the instrumental tracks separately. When the instrumental accompaniment was completed, only then would the singers come to the studio to record their vocals. This meant, for instance, that Andraé only rarely played keyboards on his early Light recordings. "We never heard the tracks until it was our turn to record," Thedford said. This two-step process on *Take the Message Everywhere* meant that the distinctives of Crouch's piano-playing were either smoothed over or omitted altogether to match what the producers believed were the popular musical norms of the era. Likewise, Andraé's favored black key centricity and gospel styling are often transposed to something much easier for string instrument musicians to play and thereby more familiar, more palatable—at least in the minds of the producers—to Light Records' overwhelmingly white audience at the time.[12]

Side I

"He Never Sleeps"

"He Never Sleeps" is a traditional gospel ballad that receives an up-tempo treatment in Andraé's new arrangement. As the "lead" singer in the quartet, Andrus sings the melody for many of the songs on the LP and, because of his ability to sing in falsetto, his is the highest voice here. "I always was on top," Andrus said. "Andraé had a way of arranging things where you're not in pain. He knew our range without writing it down. He knew what was comfortable for each one of us."[13] At a brisk 2 minutes and 40 seconds, "He Never Sleeps" opens with an E♭ bass groove that undergirds a rhythmically driving vibraphone pattern, marking $\frac{6}{8}$ time with an E♭, to A♭, to D♭ progression as the opening prime unison vocal lines float above the instruments. The lyrics are based on Psalm 121: "Behold, he that keepeth Israel shall never slumber nor sleep" (KJV). The bridge section moves to the key of F minor. Drawing near to a *codetta*, the arrangers embellish on the descending chromatic bass lines, adding a new harmonic twist in gospel music. Finally, the song closes with a descending vocal cascading C minor 7th chord superimposed over an A♭ in the bass. Crouch throughout incorporates more West Coast jazz into this light and breezy number, one that's particularly evocative of 1950s-era close harmony doo-wop.

"Everywhere"

The bright and perky opening notes of "Everywhere" suggest the 1967 opening to The Doors' classic "Light My Fire" with a light arpeggiated harpsichord motif. In the key of E♭ major, the guitarist accentuates a light *go-go* beat style of the popular music of the late 1960s, channeling the Beach Boys, the Hollies, and others. For Andraé, any "secularization" of the gospel sound was always recorded and performed with the idea of expanding the reach of the gospel. Crouch and the arrangers surmised that the more rhythmic grooves, electric guitar riffs (though still an anathema in traditional Black gospel), and pronounced recording studio effects they could utilize, the broader the potential audience the music could reach. Of particular interest in "Everywhere" is the bridge and its text, "Before the Savior left for glory," referencing the work of Jesus as humanity's bridge to God the Father—and as the focus and center of all scripture. Particularly in what sounds like a light pop-gospel song, this is a powerful metaphor—the idea of Christ being at the center of the piece *and* at the center of the bridge in the song.

"The Broken Vessel"

Both the lyrics and the music in "The Broken Vessel" present a significantly different approach in gospel music. In the key of D♭ major, with a slow, pensive $\frac{6}{8}$ time signature, Andraé tells his own Christian testimony, speaking directly to the listener. These lyrics feel particularly personal. After the jazzy, impressionistic opening, the vocalists sing harmonious triads indicative of a compositional technique called *planning*—a method of playing triads up and down a keyboard in succession. In traditional Black gospel performance, *planning* is relatively common and it is found here in both the gospel piano and organ accompaniment. "The Broken Vessel" is the most dramatic song on the LP, something that could have appeared as part of the recovery-based storyline of the songs on the *Addicts Choir* album. Carrie Gonzalo believes that the lyrics, a retelling of Jeremiah 18:3–6, where a master potter restores a broken pot, may have originated during Andraé's time at Lifeway Bible College, where Crouch used music to memorize Bible verses. Sandra said that the song may also have been inspired by his time working with the former addicts at the Teen Challenge Center.[14]

"I've Got It"

"I've Got It" is a fast-tempo, danceable tune with the bouncy Hammond B3 organ riff tied to lyrics with a serious message. It is a musical commentary from the Book of Acts on the event known as Pentecost and the descension of the Holy Spirit. In the introduction, the entire band plays an A♭ blues riff.

The Disciples (and their unnamed guitarist, bassist, and drummer) deliver as they shout: "Something 'bout the power of the Holy Ghost!" Throughout the song, Crouch's holiness roots surge to the forefront as he preaches over a simple (I–IV–I–V–IV–I) harmonic blues progression. The background vocals deliver a bluesy prime-unison five-pitched lick, singing "Hallelujah" over a driving, gritty bass line. "The Holy Ghost has come to us," they shout, and the high-energy closing vamp offers more new chord progressions, all ignited by Sherman's falsetto. The song fades out but the highly charged, spirited passion of the song lingers.

"Without a Song"

Each Crouch release has some form of a power ballad, and "Without a Song" opens with a D♭ major pentatonic *glissando* on the harp, an instrument rarely (if ever) included in classic gospel recordings. This is a point of entry for soloist Sherman Andrus as the song moves into a wonderfully subtle Johnny Mathis– styled ballad. Andraé seems to be saying that his secular audience needs to hear the call to discipleship, too. "Without a Song" features a big ending with the harp, massed vocals, and a soaring falsetto solo in the style of Little Anthony and the Imperials.

"Without a Song" has been popular since its introduction in 1929, with hit versions by Bing Crosby, Billy Eckstine, Perry Como, and Frank Sinatra. The Reverend James Cleveland and the Cleveland Singers (with Viale) released the first "gospelized" version in 1965, and it was Cleveland's rendition that legendary DJ Martha Jean "The Queen" Steinberg used daily at noon on her popular radio show on 1400 AM in Detroit.[15]

"No, Not One"

"No, Not One" takes the LP back to the Black church with a song for the men's church choir. In G♭ major, the ambitious arrangement is only for those congregations with large orchestras. The piece morphs and fades out with a compound meter feel, blending sounds from different church communities. There is no greater friend than the Lord Jesus Christ, Crouch declares, who unites us with his healing love and power. "No, Not One" is fueled by the Disciples' close harmonies. Its inclusion may be Andraé's tribute to a gospel song first published as "There's Not a Friend like the Lowly Jesus" by Johnson Oatman Jr. in 1895. Since then, it has been published in hundreds of hymnals and is now in the public domain.[16]

Side II

"I'll Never Forget"

Religious music listeners in 1970 were doubtless startled by the opening sound of "I'll Never Forget," with its dramatic harmonies and percussive use of vibraphone and piano. Meanwhile, the drummer swings with syncopated rim shots and cymbal splashes, fusing jazz with old school gospel. There is nothing like this in Black gospel music at the time, with the exception of some of the Broadway-influenced compositions of Professor Alex Bradford. (Alas, the liner notes do not list the accompanying musicians, and none of the surviving Disciples could recall their names.) Crouch delivers, with a jazz-like sensibility, this new sound doctrine of praise and worship, moving beyond the long-held traditions of Black gospel and cool jazz. In less than two and half minutes, he delivers a song of redemption, one that references the restoration of the human soul, and the soul of jazz, through his use of a multifaceted harmonic vocabulary. The final chord in the song is one of Andraé's favorite—D♭ major 9th—and once again, it is a musical signpost to how his innovative harmonic language evolves.

"The Blood (Will Never Lose Its Power)"

With "The Blood (Will Never Lose Its Power)," Andraé brings back a song from an earlier project—the COGICs' *It's a Blessing*—and recasts and reimagines it. "The Blood" had been a popular seller as sheet music, but *It's a Blessing*, as we have seen, received virtually no distribution. For his first true national release, Crouch chose to dial back Gloria Jones's gospelized approach and treat the song more like a mainstream Protestant church anthem, with lead singer Andrus hitting the highest notes. But the message remains intact—a theology of salvation that implores the listener to explore the Christian doctrine of salvation. For Crouch, it is literally the shed blood of Jesus Christ that gives him strength. To express this basic tenet of his faith, Crouch chooses a mature harmonic language and the song is filled with complex chords as it inexorably builds to an emotional spiritual tension and release. "The Blood" is still sung in churches today because the elements in the music create tension and excitement that emphasize the power of salvation. There are dozens of recorded versions of "The Blood," and virtually all tap into those musical moments, effortlessly enabling the song to build an ecstatic spiritual euphoric energy. In the hands of a talented, committed singer, as much as any song in Andraé's catalogue, there is a thrilling, majestic tension that crescendos as it closes with a traditional ii–V–I chord progression. "Blood songs" in the African American sacred music canon always carry a *magnum mysterium* spirituality that writers like Melvin Butler and others have long sought to explain and understand. "The Blood (Will Never Lose Its Power)" remains one of the greatest ecumenical hymns of the church.[17]

"Wade in the Water"

Black key dominance and the full band treatment combine to bring the beloved spiritual "Wade in the Water" to life as the vibraphone dances and the guitar glides on the waves of the rhythm. The creative arrangement in E♭ minor feels like a Beach Boys–styled arrangement imported into gospel music. Near the end, the background voices sound as if they are "wading in the water" with a rhythmic text setting that both sounds and feels fluid. For gospel music of this era, the arrangement ends on a E♭ major chord, a Picardy third (the so-called happy third) Baroque cadence. Crouch was immersed in a tradition that treats the spirituals as community music. And as mentioned earlier, despite his innovative, mostly white church–styled arrangements on this album, he does not want his African American gospel music community to feel abandoned.

"What Makes a Man Turn His Back on God?"

"What Makes a Man Turn His Back on God?" again features Ruben Fernandez's warm baritone, and Andraé surrounds him with lush harmonies to accompany the sensitive (though now somewhat dated) instrumental arrangements. When a song begins with a question, it is designed to draw the listener to the singer's voice. To accomplish that, Crouch employs the key of D♭ major and becomes a musical evangelist having a conversation with an unseen listener. From a harmonic standpoint, the song is rich with diminished and 11th chords. Those harmonic progressions distinctively mark this piece for Black churchgoers. He knows his church audience, and the song is crafted to thrill the hearts of his listeners—including, no doubt, his parents.

"Precious Lord, Take My Hand"

For the final song on *Take the Message Everywhere*, Andraé returns to his roots with the traditional gospel of "Precious Lord, Take My Hand." Even so, it's recorded in a radically different form from that of most other versions of Thomas Dorsey's enduring classic. Written following the tragic death of Dorsey's young wife and child, "Precious Lord" has historically been performed slowly and solemnly—Mahalia Jackson's definitive version treats it like a prayer or benediction. But Crouch instead speeds up the tempo with a finger-snapping appeal over a swirling Hammond B3 organ, giving lead vocalist Thedford, who came from a pop/soul music background, room to sound more like Levi Stubbs than Mahalia. The A♭ major arrangement gives hints of Sly and the Family Stone, the sharp guitar strikes on beats 2 and 4 are strikingly modern, and the Fender bass riffs evoke the sound of Motown. The vocal lines by the Disciples float over the arrangement with their clean "oohs" echoed in the call-and-responses. Unlike virtually every version of "Precious Lord," this arrangement encourages listeners to move, tap their feet, and even *shout*. It is a surprising introduction to what would someday soon be called "contemporary" gospel music.

Looking at the album in its entirety, the most enduring song in Andraé's vast catalogue, of course, is the new version of "The Blood (Will Never Lose Its Power)." According to Andrus, when the COGICs performed the song with Gloria Jones singing the lead, "they'd bring down the house every time they'd do it." Andrus said he felt that the Disciples' version did not compare well to Jones's original. "It was just a knockout," he said. "And I don't think ours ever captured the excitement that the COGICs did. I'm just honored that I had a chance to sing it, but it didn't compare to his earlier one with the COGICs."[18]

Among Sandra's favorite memories of this first incarnation of the Disciples were the live performances of "He Never Sleeps," particularly when Thedford and Morgan would join Sherman on the song's high notes. "It was like a dream," she said looking back. "They were all nice-looking young men and when they hit those top notes, all of the women would go '*Huh!*' Bili and Perry were both so tall, 6′3″ or 6′4″, and Bili was just so handsome. The people loved that." It wasn't, however, she said, the type of music typically performed in a Black church. "My father brought home all kinds of music, Black and white, and we would listen," she said. "I think that's why different races could identify with [Andraé's] music—because we didn't sing real hard gospel. After you get everybody on your side, *then* you hit them with the other side." "What Makes a Man Turn His Back on God?," she said, had its origins in their parents' cleaning business, Crouch Cleaners. Customers would sometimes leave nice articles of clothing and never return for them. Then, during his stint at the Teen Challenge Center, Andraé would see struggling addicts relapse again and again. "He built 'What Makes a Man Turn His Back on God?'

from those two experiences," Sandra said. Andraé, she said, could find inspiration "anywhere"—"I'll Never Forget" was even inspired by the syncopation in an upbeat arrangement of "Rudolph the Red-Nosed Reindeer." Gonzalo, who once filled in for an ailing Andraé on piano during this period, said what she remembered best about the songs on *Take the Message Everywhere* are Crouch's extensive use of unconventional diminished chords in transitions between chords. "There is a diminished fifth on 'I'll Never Forget' that's a combination of both hands," she recalled, "that gives the song its unique intro. Andraé's playing was unique, so the changes he used were myriad."[19]

Also worth noting, Sandra added, was that Andraé did not write five of the songs on *Take the Message Everywhere* despite his prodigious songwriting output, which sometimes resulted in the composition of multiple songs in a single day—and night. "You see, when you've grown up during that era, you're afraid that people don't like your music," she said. "So, you do something that they would like—or they would accept." According to Sandra, Andraé even then was thinking beyond Owens and Carmichael in the studio, beyond traditional Black gospel music circles, and out into a wider world of color-blind evangelism. Even though she did not sing with this incarnation of the Disciples at the time, Sandra said she still served as his primary sounding board and critic for the songs that *did* end up on this—and later—albums:

> He used to call me in the middle of the night and say, "Sandra, I've written a song. What do you think?" I would say, "It's 3 A.M., Andraé." And he'd say, "But, do you like it?" I'd say, "It's a fabulous song. Record it." I have the sheet music from songs my father used to sing in my uncle's church and on the back of some of those pieces of sheet music are songs and ideas that Andraé had written.[20]

As the title suggests, Andraé (along with the Disciples and producer Jimmy Owens) *borrowed* music from everywhere, to *take* the message everywhere. For Crouch the composer, this initial release for Light Records allowed him to reinvent himself once again. As he will throughout his career, Andraé intuitively draws deeply from his African American musical heritage even as he restlessly explores all musical genres. Thus, the authors believe, despite the wide variety of musical styles incorporated into *Take the Message Everywhere*, it is still clear that Crouch does *not* want churchgoing African Americans to dismiss his ministry of music. Throughout the LP, though still not as polished or always as instantly memorable as the albums to come, Andraé's compositional approaches and methodologies are never less than highly creative. Working with Carmichael, Owens and the unnamed studio musicians expose and give Crouch access to new musical avenues. Andraé's writing continues to evolve as he explores new melodic tendencies, song forms, arrangement possibilities, and lyrical approaches within traditional gospel music formulas.

Andraé Crouch and the Disciples in Concert

Family friend Val Gonzalo faithfully attended Disciples concerts from the *Take the Message Everywhere* era whenever the group performed in Southern California, as well as the Sunday night radio broadcasts at Christ Memorial COGIC. Gonzalo said that those concerts usually followed a specific pattern. After Andraé and the Disciples came onstage, Andraé would make it abundantly clear what the evening was going to be about:

> His whole purpose was, "My songs—and what I'm singing about—is a tool for evangelism." When he opened, sometimes he sat down at the piano and just started a song that had nothing to do with the whole repertoire of what they were going to do that night. It was like, "I just feel inspired by the Holy Spirit to sing, 'Yes, Jesus Loves Me,' so I'm going to start there and go from that." There was order, yet there was freedom, the great freedom of having the opportunity to say, "What I really want you to know is that Jesus is Lord and He's the Lord of your life and you need to come to know Jesus and to give your life to God."

Val also recalled the emotional response that followed whenever the Disciples sang "The Blood" and the audience-pleasing doo-wop stylings on "He Never Slumbers," which featured each Disciple in turn singing a solo on a different verse. Not surprisingly, he said, the live performances were much looser in person than on the recordings. "Before Sherman joined the group, Andraé would tell them, 'I'll sing the first verse and then someone sings the second verse . . . whoever,'" Gonzalo recalled, "'if it's in your range, you're singing it. When Sherman finally joined, Andraé would star him on a lot of songs, a lot of leads."

Val, who later became a minister himself, said that it was abundantly clear, even at this stage of their careers, that what Andraé and the Disciples were doing was truly unique. "Everything you heard before Andraé was just the same sort of choir music and it just wasn't fitting the times that we were living in," he said. "Andraé brought something outside of the box that had rhythm to it, it had soul to it, it described the tempo of the times." Additionally, the

Disciples were the lone Black group singing to primarily white churches. "Besides the normal white crowd, he was also singing to guys that were coming off the streets," Gonzalo said. "The concerts hosted by Audrey Mieir, because this was Southern California, had Blacks, whites, Mexicans, Chinese, Filipinos, Asians—you had all kinds of people. But Andraé and the Disciples had the only Black Church of God in Christ sound in the concerts."

If the concerts were free-form, virtually improvised experiences, Gonzalo said, the impromptu gatherings after the performances were even more casual. "You'd just walk backstage because you knew the people performing and they're your friends," he said:

> Andraé was very, very hospitable to anyone who would come up to him and would want to talk. I think he had a really powerful spirit of discernment, where someone would come up to him and begin to talk about their life, and they begin to tell him a story about their brother and Andraé would speak into their life right there and say, "You need to give your life to Jesus." They all wanted to tell him their stories and he was so kind to just sit and listen to all of them, every one of them.[21]

Looking back more than fifty years after the release of *Take the Message Everywhere*, Thedford said that he is still amazed at the speed in which everything began to happen following their performances at some of the larger Southern California churches and the release of the LP. "The reason that album even came into play was because we accepted the fact that we were on a musical missionary journey," he said. "All of a sudden, it was like phone call, phone call, phone call. Travel. Pack a bag. Go here. The other guys in the group had never really done a lot of traveling as far as performance travel." It was too much for Fernandez, whose weight and health issues made air travel particularly difficult. He reluctantly left the group. Fernandez died from complications of diabetes and an infection following gastric surgery May 27, 1986. He was just forty-nine. When news of Ruben's death reached Andraé, Sherman Andrus said Crouch was "terribly, terribly hurt and wounded over the death of his friend."[22]

Overseas with John Haggai

One telephone call Andraé and the Disciples had not expected arrived in 1969, shortly after the release of *Take the Message Everywhere*. Evangelist John

Haggai, founder of the Haggai Institute for Advanced Leadership, had a particular focus on missionary work in Asia and his organization trained hundreds of evangelists overseas. When Haggai planned a speaking tour throughout the Pacific Rim and Europe, he asked the Disciples to accompany him. "Someone had told him about our album," Crouch writes. "The Lord had answered our prayers." Andrus writes that while the Haggai organization paid their expenses, the Disciples were expected to provide their own salaries. To that end, the group hosted a benefit concert at the Embassy Auditorium in Los Angeles prior to their departure. Guest performers included members of the Archers and the Children of the Day.[23]

In *Through It All*, Andraé notes that over the next three months, into late 1969, Haggai's tour took the Disciples around the world: Japan, Hong Kong, the Philippines, American military bases in South Vietnam, Germany, India, Egypt, England, and back again. Fortunately for the Disciples, Haggai's team was extremely well organized, and Thedford said that the programs, transportation, and accommodations were scheduled and confirmed well in advance. Crouch's anecdotes in *Through It All* about the whirlwind journey are mostly ministry-related, save for an unsettling mealtime encounter with duck's head soup at the Baptist seminary in Hong Kong.[24]

Thedford has several vivid memories of the tour, which included Danny Diangelo on drums and Steve Conway on guitar and bass. In Indonesia, after playing multiple back-to-back concerts, Thedford lost his voice. In desperation, he picked up Conway's Hofner "Beatle" bass and began teaching himself to play. Thedford, who had played guitar previously, worked tirelessly to master the basics while he waited for his throat to heal. Their next date was at a massive soccer stadium in Jakarta. "There are not too many bass players that will ever get to tell you that their first gig was for 50,000 people," Thedford said. "I think I was too afraid, too scared to be nervous. I just kept playing, listening to Andraé, listening to those changes—because I knew the changes. All of a sudden, I'm a bass player." Thedford, whose voice eventually returned, continued to play bass for all of the live Disciples' performances until 1976. (In Jakarta, Thedford said that the group was singing up to five times a day, traveling from one primary school to the next. Bili believes that the Disciples played for a very young Barack Obama, who was living in Jakarta at the time.)[25]

When the Disciples returned to the United States following the tour, they were exhausted, homesick, and musically a very, very tight quartet. Like the Beatles' Hamburg residency, the months of non-stop performances welded the group into a first-rate close-harmony unit sensitive to Andraé's penchant for improvised songs and choruses—and enabled them to seamlessly play along. The Disciples, all of whom save Andraé were married, scheduled a retreat at a hotel in Hawaii to recuperate together. But a week later, Crouch scheduled another series of performances in the Marshall Islands at the behest of missionary Sam Sasser, who once brought a fifty-voice choir from the islands to Christ Memorial COGIC. On the return flight from the Marshalls to the United States, Andraé wrote the lyrics for a song he had first conceived in Indonesia, "I'm Gonna Keep On Singin'." After still another series of concerts in Northern California, the nonstop travel finally caught up with him and he became gravely ill, at one point spiking a temperature of 106 degrees. He tried to force his way through a concert at a halftime show at a basketball game in the small town of Turlock but finally collapsed. His parents rushed up from Pacoima and checked him into the UCLA medical center, where they prayed over him until he eventually recovered. Meanwhile, the group's booking agency had already scheduled a series of dates in Texas, including one at Baylor University, but Andraé clearly was still physically unable to go. Fortunately, in pre-internet days, there were few readily available pictures of the Disciples, so Sherman Andrus took over the leads, bringing along Christian artist Danny Lee as pianist. Apparently, no one in Waco noticed. "Leading the group gave me great confidence in being able to lead the group and be a soloist on stage," Andrus writes. "I loved being the emcee and interacting with the crowd. This became my strong suit."[26]

Sherman Andrus Departs

But Andraé was not the only Disciple who had been impacted by the nonstop touring. When Crouch began assembling musicians to accompany them on the tour with Haggai, it was Jesus Music legend Larry Norman who had introduced him to drummer Danny Diangelo. Diangelo auditioned for the Disciples at Thedford's house, playing along to an LP of *Take the Message Everywhere*. But once back in Southern California following the grueling tour, Diangelo resigned. Andrus was next. En route to a gig in Seattle, Andrus was involved in a serious automobile accident. As he recovered, his wife gave birth to their first child. The down time, he writes, gave him time to reflect on both the Disciples' backbreaking schedule and his own goal to become a solo artist, or at least featured lead singer. He had already turned down an offer by Columbia Records when he shortly thereafter decided to leave the group. Andrus was quickly signed by Van Woodward Associates, which suggested that bookings would be easier if Sherman formed his own band. After a short stint with a group called the Brethren (with former Disciple Diangelo), Andrus was invited to become the first African American member in one of the most popular Southern Gospel groups in the country, the Imperials. "When I left Andraé and the Disciples, there was no conflict," Andrus writes, "but the Lord was dealing with me and confirmed that my calling was to be a solo artist and merely work on weekends." Andrus and the Disciples remained friends after he left the group, and Andraé produced and wrote eight songs on Sherman's first solo recording, including the hit title track, "I've Got Confidence," for Benson's Impact Record label, released in 1969.[27]

Tramaine Davis Arrives

It was at this point that Andraé began to think about again adding a female voice to the Disciples. For some time, he had been aware of a teenage singer performing with Edwin and Walter Hawkins, Tramaine Davis. While still in high school, Davis and five friends had performed as the Heavenly Tones and even recorded an album for industry giant Savoy's Gospel label, *I Love the Lord.* The Crouch and Hawkins families, both with deep California COGIC roots, interacted regularly, hosting each other at Christ Memorial in Pacoima and at Ephesians Church of God in Christ in Oakland—but it quickly became obvious to everyone that Tramaine Davis was something special. Crouch invited her to join the Disciples and when Bili and Perry were busy for mid-week engagements, it would sometimes be just the two of them in concert. Thedford said that Davis was "a whole new level of vocal" when she sang with the Disciples:

> We had been traveling across the South when Tramaine met up with us and she immediately began wrecking churches. She had people screaming and running up and down the aisles and passing out and falling down. We went to Houston one time and she got the crowd so worked up until the pastor had to come up to the microphone and just stop the whole thing. Nurses were calling and blankets were all over the place, they just kept freaking out. Tramaine's voice was so powerful and so driving and Andraé kept pushing it and pushing it until folks would just go into oblivion.

Almost immediately, Andraé planned to go into the studio again to capitalize on Davis's voice.[28]

Howard Rachinski, founder of Christian Copyright Licensing International (CCLI), heard this incarnation of the Disciples in April 1970 in Everett, Washington. Rachinski, who was working for an early Christian radio station, reluctantly attended the concert at his parents' urging. It was a fund-raiser for the Teen Challenge Addicts Choir. After an interview with Andraé, Crouch invited the young man to pray with the group before the performance and join them for a late meal afterward. Rachinski said the set opened with "Keep On Singin'" and—as would be Andraé's practice throughout his career—he remained after the performance to talk to those in attendance. From the beginning, Crouch never considered what he did as a performance. It was always a ministry:

> One of the things he was amazing at was when he would "read" the audience. "OK, what is this group?" If it was the First Traditional Reformed Dead in Christ Church, he would read that and start with a hymn—and the Disciples would bring great harmonies to the hymn. He said, "I would go to where they were so I could bring them to where He is." [Andraé] would just make sure that he was connecting, that he was just loving on people. He would very rarely do, "The song we're about to sing is a song I wrote about. . . ." He would simply follow the flow, so that the audience was engaged.

From that first meeting, Rachinski and Crouch remained close friends. Rachinski said he heard the Disciples perform numerous times through the years and that there was rarely a set list for a given performance since, as Crouch "read" the audience, he would tailor the songs to the moment— including any in-progress compositions. "He was really engaged in traveling and ministering," Rachinski said. "Andraé might lay out for the Disciples the first few songs but after that the group had to be ready to be spontaneous. Their memory skills had to have a song bank of hundreds of songs because you would not know what Andraé was feeling."[29]

By now it was clear to Andraé that the Disciples were stronger with a mix of voices, male and female. As a favor to her twin brother, Sandra occasionally appeared at the group's Southern California engagements. Andraé writes that he had "always" wanted her to join the Disciples, but by early 1970 he believed that because of her busy recording studio commitments with Motown, it would "take a real miracle from the Lord" for her to do so. By now, Sandra had performed on hundreds of songs for nearly every Motown artist, as well as Ray Charles, Janis Joplin, and others. She was particularly close to Diana Ross, and when Ross performed at the Coconut Grove in Los Angeles, Andraé was invited to attend. Ross introduced Sandra as her "sanctified tambourine player." Andraé writes that Sandra "was just fantastic" that night and "received a standing ovation." "I had never really seen her at work outside the church," he notes. "I looked at her and saw that God had really given her a great gift. The tears came in my eyes and I thought, 'Lord, that's my twin sister. I want her with me.'" When Sandra was able to perform with the Disciples, audience members streamed forward after the concert to tell her what a "blessing" she had been. "It wasn't long until she made a new commitment to the Lord," Andraé writes. "Then singing became more than just helping out her brother and the group." Sandra continued to record with Motown and other artists, as available, and Andraé writes that her extensive experience in the recording studio—and numerous industry contacts—would soon manifest with upcoming tours and projects with the Disciples as she began to clear more time to be with Andraé (Image 4.1).[30]

Image 4.1 Publicity photograph, Andraé Crouch and the Disciples (from left, Sandra Crouch, Perry Morgan, Andraé Crouch, Billy Thedford). Photograph courtesy of Carrie Gonzalo.

Finding Their Audience

While Andraé and the Disciples still sang at Christ Memorial Church of God in Christ, particularly on the Sunday evening radio broadcasts, other dates at—or sponsored by—African American churches were rare. The eclectic nature of *Take the Message Everywhere* may have alienated traditional gospel music lovers in those congregations. Another reason for their lack of bookings in Black churches may have been their connections with both Audrey Mieir and Sonny Salsbury, particularly Salsbury's close relationship to the area Campus Crusade for Christ and Campus Life organizations, which also meant deep relationships primarily with—and, consequently, more frequent bookings with—white churches. The Disciples emerged during a particularly robust time in the life of the primarily Protestant evangelical church, especially in Southern California, the new "Jesus Music movement." The movement had multiple origins, writes Bob Gersztyn, including the hippie counterculture centered in San Francisco in 1967. From a storefront outreach called the Living Room on Haight Street, the newly christened and enthusiastic "Jesus freaks" spread out to Los Angeles and elsewhere. Among the first "hybrid" churches was the influential Calvary Chapel in Costa Mesa, led by Chuck Smith, which had a large congregation of both Jesus freaks and "straight" parishioners. Music was a particular focus at Calvary Chapel, whose membership included musicians who had originally found success in "secular" rock 'n' roll. Jesus Music, as it was soon called, was dominated by heartfelt rock music with particularly straightforward evangelical lyrics. Some early Jesus music artists who gained widespread attention included Larry Norman, Love Song, the Second Chapter of Acts, Nancy Honeytree, and others. Several record labels quickly emerged that specialized in the music, Maranatha!, Good News, and Light. While virtually none of the major artists was Black (save for Andraé and the Disciples), the movement was unusually welcoming to African Americans and quickly spread across the United States. Not surprisingly, the Disciples, who were not yet well known in either Black *or* white households outside of Southern California, found themselves labeled as part of the Jesus Music movement.[31]

Still another issue confronting Andraé during this time was that Light Records, through its distribution agreement with Word, was sold primarily through the new informal network of Christian bookstores and their records simply did not reach many African Americans. Traditional Black gospel labels, such as Savoy, Peacock, Apollo, Specialty, Nashboro, and others, were widely available in African American record stores and outlets and their LPs were promoted and played on the major radio stations that broadcast gospel music, most of which were in the Midwest or East Coast: WLAC (Nashville), WERD (Atlanta), WDIA (Memphis), and others. (Several stations in Los Angeles played gospel, including KFOX, KALI, KTYM, KGFJ, and KRKD, but these focused primarily on traditional artists.) Again, this meant that the Disciples were not yet on the radar of the people who booked concerts in African American churches or venues associated with Black gospel artists.[32]

Andraé rarely spoke publicly about any musical disconnect with the Black church and the lack of bookings. As a lifelong member and active participant in the Church of God in Christ, it must have weighed on his mind, especially since as early as 1966, Crouch had been invited to participate in COGIC music doyen Mattie Moss Clark's influential "Midnight Musicals" at the denomination's annual Youth Congress in Chicago. Clark was the most powerful musical figure in the Church of God in Christ, as a recording artist and director of the famed Southwest Michigan State Choir, as longtime president of COGIC's National Music Department, *and* as mother of Twinkie, Dorinda, and the Clark Sisters. Horace Boyer writes that Clark "had a major impact on the gospel choir in its new form." Through the decades, the Midnight Musicals introduced dozens of younger gospel artists to the COGIC faithful, including Rance Allen, the Hawkins Family, Donald Vails, Keith Pringle—and Crouch.[33]

Musician Jeffrey LaValley was in the audience for the Midnight Musical in 1966. Now a prominent composer himself, LaValley said that Crouch performed his arrangement of "It's Going to Rain" with the COGICs that evening. "I had never heard anything like it," LaValley said. "We called it a 'California thing,' but the difference in the styling is what attracted Mattie to his music—it was totally different from anything we all had ever heard." LaValley recalled that Sandra was the featured soloist on "It's Going to Rain." "She had a drive and an anointing that was on her that night that was really, really something," he said. "That was probably what drew [Clark], as well as the song itself—and the styling of the song."[34]

For all of Clark's fabled influence and clout, by the time of *Take the Message Everywhere*, Andraé Crouch and the Disciples were still receiving very few invitations to Black churches, COGIC or otherwise. For Mattie Moss Clark's daughter and gospel star Twinkie Clark, Andraé's early lack of acceptance among African American churches was particularly disappointing. At her lone visit to his home, years later, she told him so:

> I got a chance to sit and talk with him and let him know how much he inspired me and opened the door for us young musicians to come in with more of a contemporary style. His music reached to all multicultural people, Black and white. He paved the way for me because I know [the Black church] was not ready for the style that the Lord had given me because my style was much more jazzy than Andraé Crouch. It paved the way for musicians like myself and so many others to be creative.[35]

Perry Morgan said that Black audiences were slower to respond to the Disciples not because they were performing "whiter" material, but instead because they were a quartet that sounded more like the Spinners or the Temptations rather than the more traditional Black gospel of the Sensational Nightingales or the Blind Boys of Mississippi:

> Our sound was, in effect, a little more like the top Black rhythm & blues groups— which was new to Black people in gospel music. So they were wowed by our sound, sort of. White people had never heard it because they'd never heard those groups for the most part. They just loved it and embraced us even more than the Black people did.

Morgan said that early concerts ranged from primarily white audiences to half Black and half white. Eventually, the Disciples knew that they had been accepted by at least a portion of the Black gospel music community only when African American audiences finally began to sing along with the Disciples' songs. "In the beginning, the Black people were really slow to come to our concerts, especially because there were so many whites that would come. But the Lord just blessed us and things grew."[36]

A family friend since 1960, LaVern Moore concurred that it was unfortunate that Crouch's own denomination, the Church of God in Christ, did not initially support his musical ministry. "The FourSquare church and others *did* welcome him at first," she recalled:

> They were very much attached to Pastor Andraé and the Disciples. And like anything else, when someone wants you, when someone is accepting you, that's when the [COGIC] church finally opened their arms and embraced Andraé. They eventually anointed him and gave him his ministerial license and licensed him as an elder in the church.[37]

Through it all, Andraé doggedly continued to tour with the new Disciples. As he said in interviews throughout his career, evangelism was his sole calling. Sandra, who was now performing more often with the group, said that that *calling* meant that members of the group always had to be equally committed—at all times:

> We would travel and sometimes we had days off in our bus. We would go through a little town and we'd see a little small church and we'd say, "Let's stop there." They would see the bus and say, "Is that Andraé Crouch?" We'd say, "Yes, and when do you guys have church?" They'd say, "Well, I don't know. . . ." Andraé would say, "I want to sing. Call somebody." We would go there in those little storefront churches and we would sing. "They'd go, 'Wow!' We'd do a whole concert and would have a ball. They'd say, "I can't believe you did this." We said, "This is what we do. This is who we are."

As the Disciples became better known and the crowds and churches continued to get bigger, Sandra slowly resumed her role of being Andraé's "bodyguard." Her assignment became to ensure that he had someone from the Disciples with him at all times, *especially* after concerts. "Because he would talk," she said. "He might talk for two hours after the concert. As long as somebody was listening, he would talk and talk, but he was going to lead somebody to the Lord. Everybody he met, he wanted them to know who Jesus was."[38]

NOTES

1. Gene D. Viale, *I Remember Gospel: And I Keep On Singing* (Bloomington, IN: AuthorHouse, 2010), 54–57; Opal Louis Nations, "'I Shall Overcome': The Gene Viale Story" (2006), http://opalnations.com/Articles.html.

2. Bili Thedford, interview with the authors, March 22, 2020; Sandra Crouch, interview with the authors, June 16, 2021; Sherman Andrus Sr., *My Story! His Song! Blessed!* (Bloomington, IN: WestBow, 2021), 23; Perry Morgan, interview with the authors, March 19, 2022.

3. Andraé Crouch with Nina Ball, *Through It All* (Waco, TX: Word Books, 1974), 66; Andrus, *My Story! His Song! Blessed!*, 19–23.

4. Sherman Andrus, interview with the authors, September 5, 2020.

5. Andraé Crouch, *Through It All*, 67.

6. Ralph Carmichael, *He's Everything to Me* (Waco, TX: Word Books, 1986), 154–155; Liner notes by Ralph Carmichael, Andraé Crouch and the Disciples, *Take the Message Everywhere* (Light Records LS-5504); Robert Darden, *People Get Ready! A New History of Black Gospel Music* (New York: Continuum/ Bloomsbury, 2004), 278; Bob Gersztyn, "Andraé's Music Will Never Lose Its

Power," *Door Magazine*, March 2004 (published online, original in author's possession).

7. Carmichael, *He's Everything to Me*, 153–154.

8. Carmichael, *He's Everything to Me*, 154–155; Andraé Crouch, *Through It All*, 68; Sandra Crouch, interview with the authors, June 16, 2021; Carrie Gonzalo, interview with the authors, December 17, 2020.

9. Stu Green, "Lorin Whitney Studio Sold," *Theatre Organ*, June/July 1978, American Theatre Organ Society, 12–13; Sherman Andrus, interview with the authors, September 5, 2020.

10. Jamie Owens-Collins, "Jesus Music Movement Singer Mourns, Reveals Personal Side of Andraé Crouch," *Charisma*, January 14, 2015, https://charismanews .com/opinion/jesus-music-movement-singer-mourns-reveals-personal-side -of-andrae-crouch; Carol Owens, *Chasing Fireflies in the Twilight: A Memoir* (Newbury Park, CA: SMMI, 2021), 88–89.

11. Andraé Crouch and the Disciples, *Take the Message Everywhere*, Light Records LS-5504-LP; "4 Star," *Billboard*, June 19, 1971, 44.

12. Liner notes by Audrey Mieir and Ralph Carmichael, Andraé Crouch and the Disciples, *Take the Message Everywhere*, Light Records LS-5504-LP; Bili Thedford, personal correspondence with the authors, August 18, 2022.

13. Sherman Andrus, interview with the authors, September 5, 2020.

14. Carrie Gonzalo, interview with the authors, December 17, 2020; Sandra Crouch, interview with the authors, June 16, 2021.

15. Susan Watson, "Broadcasting to the Blacks in Detroit's Melting Pot: Why WCHB Isn't Quite like WJLB," *Detroit Free Press*, January 14, 1973, 128; The Reverend James Cleveland and the Cleveland Singers, "Without a Song," 45 (Savoy 4269, 1965).

16. https://my.hymnary.org/song/dynamic/208/theres_not_a_friend_l ike_the_lowly_jesus?toolkit=veroviostatic&hymnary=1

17. Melvin L. Butler touches on the fascinating topic of the "blood songs" in *Island Gospel: Pentecostal Music and Identity in Jamaica and the United States* (Champaign: University of Illinois Press, 2019).

18. Sherman Andrus, interview with the authors, November 5, 2020. Chris Fenner has written a superb analysis of the often-convoluted history of claim and counterclaim on "The Blood"—aka "The Blood (Will Never Lose Its Power)" and "It Will Never Lose Its Power," including a version by James Cleveland from 1962. https://www.hymnologyarchive.com/andrae-crouch, Chris Fenner, August 25, 2022. Note: Bill Maxwell, Andraé's longtime producer, said that Crouch told him that Cleveland had originally heard Andraé playing the song and claimed it for his own: "And Billy Preston stood up to [Cleveland] and said, 'That's Andraé Crouch's song. Andraé wrote that, not James Cleveland.' And James backed off." Bill Maxwell, interview with the authors, May 18, 2019.

19. Sandra Crouch, interview with the authors, June 16, 2021; Carrie Gonzalo, interview with the authors, December 17, 2020.

20. Sandra Crouch, interview with the authors, June 16, 2021.

21. Val Gonzalo, interview with the authors, October 10, 2020.

22. Bili Thedford, interview with the authors, November 12, 2020; Viale, *I Remember Gospel*, 54–57; Sandra Crouch, interview with the authors, June 16, 2021; Sherman Andrus, personal correspondence with the authors, July 14, 2022. (The authors wish to thank Dr. Stephen Gardner for his genealogical research into the life of Ruben Fernandez.)

23. "Died: John Edmund Haggai, Evangelist Who Trained Evangelists," *Christianity Today*, November 19, 2020, https://www.christianitytoday.com/news/2020/november; https//www.haggai-international.org; Andraé Crouch, *Through It All*, 68; Sherman Andrus, personal correspondence with the authors, July 14, 2022.

24. Andraé Crouch, *Through It All*, 69–72; Bili Thedford, interview with the authors, November 12, 2020.

25. Bili Thedford, interview with the authors, March 22, 2020; Bili Thedford, interview with the authors, November 12, 2020.

26. Andraé Crouch, *Through It All*, 72–73; 84–90; Andrus, *My Story! His Song! Blessed!*, 26–27.

27. Andrus, *My Story! His Song! Blessed!*, 23, 27–28; Danny Diangelo, *A Chasing of the Wind: An Encounter with the Winds of the Holy Spirit* (Vienna, VA: Xulon Books, 2001), 38–43.

    Note: When Andrus officially joined the Imperials in February 1972, it was a significant enough event that *Billboard* magazine documented the event with a photograph, noting that Sherman had originally been a member of Andraé Crouch and the Disciples. This is another very early mention of Andraé in a national magazine (*Billboard*, March 4, 1972, 41).

28. Andraé Crouch, *Through It All*, 93, 95–96; Bili Thedford, interview with the authors, November 12, 2020; Heavenly Tones, *I Love the Lord* (Gospel MB 3050).

29. Howard Rachinski, interview with the authors, October 20, 2022.

30. Andraé Crouch, *Through It All*, 95–96.

31. Bob Gersztyn, *Jesus Rocks the World: The Definitive History of Contemporary Christian Music*, Vol. 1 (Santa Barbara, CA: Praeger, 2012), 1–3. Note: There are several other excellent books on the rise of Jesus Music and its successor Contemporary Christian Music (CCM), including Don Cusic, *The Sound of Light* (Milwaukee: Hal Leonard, 2002); and Paul Baker, *Why Should the Devil Have All of the Good Music?* (Waco, TX: Word Books, 1979).

32. Darden, *People Get Ready!*, 222–223; Cora Jackson-Fossett, "Black History Spotlight: Trailblazing Gospel Radio Announcers," *Los Angeles Sentinel*, February 12, 2020, https://lasentinel.net/black-history-spotlight-trailblazing-gospel-radio-announcers.html.

33. Eugene B. McCoy, *Climbing Up the Mountain: The Musical Life and Times of Dr. Mattie Moss Clark* (Nashville: Sparrow Press, 1994), 50–54; Horace Clarence Boyer, *How Sweet the Sound: The Golden Age of Gospel* (Washington, DC: Elliott & Clark, 1995), 125–127.

34. Jeffrey LaValley, interview with the authors, August 29, 2020.
35. Twinkie Clark, interview with the authors, October 10, 2020.
36. Perry Morgan, interview with the authors, March 19, 2022.
37. LaVern Moore, interview with the authors, March 21, 2022.
38. Sandra Crouch, interview with the authors, November 6, 2020.

5
Keep On Singin'

Liberty Records and "Christian People"

It was during this period that Andraé first met Irv Kessler, then a vice president for the Liberty Records label. Kessler was a well-respected music industry veteran who had had a long career, primarily at Liberty. With several savvy producers on staff, including Snuff Garrett, Si Waronker, and Lou Adler, Liberty had been a powerhouse in the 1950s and 1960s with artists like Jan and Dean, the Ventures, the Chipmunks, Julie London, Johnny Rivers, and others. But by 1970, after being purchased by the TransAmerica Corporation—making its first foray into the music business—the wheels were already coming off. Kessler had first met Andraé at the Teen Challenge Center, where his son had kicked a serious addiction. Over the next few years, Kessler heard the Disciples perform at the Melodyland Christian Center but had been unable to locate a copy of their album, *Take the Message Everywhere*—which he had wanted to give to his son. When Kessler finally found a copy in a Christian bookstore, Andraé writes that he exclaimed, "This group should be heard." Kessler had a profound religious experience in December 1969 and urged Liberty to invest in recordings by faith-based artists.[1]

One of the first photographs of the Disciples in a national magazine features Andraé, Sandra, Bili Thedford, Perry Morgan, and new vocalist Tramaine Davis signing a contract with a smiling Kessler. Printed in the September 19, 1970, edition of *Cash Box*, the caption notes that Liberty/UA is "rush releasing" "Christian People." The Disciples recorded two tracks, "Christian People," backed with "Too Close" for Liberty, with Andraé and Sandra producing. The Disciples and Light had only signed a contract for a single album—*Take the Message Everywhere*—so the group was between labels. According to Thedford, the Disciples discussed the proposal to record more commercial-sounding songs, and—after years of singing primarily in churches and at church-related events—all favored the decision. Thedford said that the group admired the success of Mavis and the Staple Singers, who sang inspirational and gospel music and still opened concerts for the likes of Sly and the Family Stone and Wilson Pickett:

> We wanted to be a part of that. We had come to the conclusion that we had been spending the majority of our careers as Andraé Crouch and the Disciples singing to the choir. We said, "We've got to find a way to make some music that does what we want to do. And what we want to do is reach people." Not for the sake of being a part of the secular move but . . . being involved in a secular market—and reaching people.[2]

The recording session resulted in two songs that sound more like what was currently on American Top 40 radio than anything on *Take the Message Everywhere*—Andraé describes the music as "pop, Motownish," with a more "commercial sound." When the 45 was completed, the Disciples shopped the record to various labels, and had meetings with Herb Alpert at A&M Records, as well as representatives from the Columbia, Mercury, and Liberty labels. With Kessler's support, Liberty made the "best offer." "The music wasn't our traditional form of gospel music," Thedford said. "We were pushing it a little hard. We were trying to reach into the secular market musically. It did well, too. That was the tune that pulled us into the whole festival thing." Morgan liked "Christian People" as well. "It was good," he said, "and the reception was good because it was an 'up tempo' song. We used to sing it everywhere we went, even before recording it."[3]

The 45 was released in September 1970 on the Liberty label, and instead of the publishing being assigned to Manna Music, both songs were credited to "Soul Power Music." Also, unlike Andraé's previous religious projects, the "Christian People" 45 was referenced both in *Record World* and *Billboard*. *Billboard*'s Ed Ochs mentioned the recording in his "Soul Sauce" column on October 17, along with several other R&B singles. A week later, Ochs noted that Liberty/UA was "clicking" with the new release by Andraé Crouch and the Disciples. When the Academy of Recording Arts and Sciences released its Grammy nominations in February 1971, "Christian People" was nominated for the "Best Soul Gospel Performance" award. Liberty quickly reissued the 45 with a sepia-toned sleeve depicting Andraé, Sandra, Bili, and Perry kneeling in a field of tall grass, with the words "Grammy Nomination Best Soul-Gospel Performance!" emblazoned across the top. The record was also credited to the Soul Power label, not Liberty.[4]

"Christian People"

From the opening soulful horns, "ahhh" and "doot-doot" backing vocals, funky bass lines, and prime unison vocals, "Christian People" was created with the Top 40 radio audience in mind. Tramaine Davis, with her highly commercial multi-octave voice, duets with Crouch. Andraé, who listened intently to the radio, knew how to craft a Motown-styled song. It is possible that this may be Andraé's response to Sly and the Family Stone's "Everyday People"—as the Crouches sought to answer the question raised in the lyrics, "Who are we?"— "Christian People!" The song is a stunning leap from his previous releases, one that's much more reflective of what the Disciples sounded like live. It was also an unapologetic attempt to reach a multiethnic audience with an evangelical message. The song's lyrics insist that, for believers, running the race is an essential part of the Christian's identity (Hebrews 12:1). And, because the Crouches are producing the 45 themselves, the song is in Andraé's preferred key of D♭ major (Image 5.1).

Image 5.1 Tramaine Davis singing with Andraé Crouch at the piano. Photograph courtesy of Carrie Gonzalo.

"Too Close"

The flip side, "Too Close," features more of the sharp, punchy horns and a poppin' bass riff—most likely the contribution of the same musicians from the "Christian People" session. The song features beautifully arranged vocals from the uncredited background vocalists, particularly on the bridge, reminiscent of passages in Professor Alex Bradford's signature song, "Too Close to Heaven." The song again employs Andraé's favorite key of D♭, and Andraé and Tramaine sing together warmly on the verses in close, embellished harmonies, alternating major and minor third intervals.

"Christian People" never made the national charts, in part because of the turmoil and personnel turnover at Liberty, which TransAmerica had recently merged with the United Artists label, though the 45 did garner the Disciples their first airplay in Southern California. It also increased their profile nationally, resulting in the song being played on *Dick Clark's American Bandstand* and invitations to open for the larger secular acts, including Santana. But Andraé writes that when label execs at Liberty said that they wanted another "Christian People" as a follow-up single, he balked:

> I knew I could do hip, commercial-type music. But although God had given me the "Christian People" song, I felt like that was another part of me. I believed if I continued with Liberty, I'd have to compromise my testimony, to sacrifice my songs that really ministered to people. I really had to battle the turmoil in my heart. I prayed and fasted, and the Lord told me to minister, so I just rebuked the whole thought of any type of "top-40" song and asked to be released from my contract.

When the Liberty/UA executives denied Crouch's request, Kessler intervened on the group's behalf and he too was told *no*. The Disciples then gathered and prayed for their release. "A few days later," Andraé writes, "I walked into the Liberty office and there was my contract—we were free." The group re-signed with Light shortly thereafter.[5]

But newcomer Davis, like Sandra, still had other recording and performance responsibilities and was not always available to be a part of Andraé's virtually nonstop touring schedule. At a performance at Bethel Gospel Tabernacle in Jamaica, New York, in late 1969 or early 1970, the Disciples met singers Kathy Hazzard and Bea Carr, then in the group Sweet Spirit. Andraé heard the group sing and invited them to tour with him whenever they were available. According to Hazzard, Carr accompanied the Disciples on one trip to Mexico and two weeks after their return, Andraé asked Hazzard to sing on the next leg. "The response at those dates was very, very interesting," she said. "We sang to a lot of white audiences. [Andraé] would say to them, 'I know you guys are looking at me strange—you think that the circus came to town!' "[6]

Tramaine Davis's Departure and Aftermath

Andraé and the Disciples, once again with Davis, eventually returned to the studio to begin work on their second Light album, *Keep On Singin'*. After a couple of tracks had been recorded, including the duet "I'm Coming Home, Dear Lord," with Thedford and Davis, the group left for a short series of dates in Northern California. In Andraé's biography, he writes that over the previous few months he had fallen in love with Tramaine and even bought her a ring—but had not yet proposed because he was afraid of giving up his independence, which included long hours spent composing in the middle of the night. According to Thedford, during the intermission of a Saturday concert in an Oakland church, Davis asked to speak to the Disciples. "Andraé," Thedford recalls her saying, "I don't want to be with you anymore. I'm going back to Walter and we're going to get married." She then turned and left. "Tramaine quit the group and me!" Andraé writes. "She really never knew my real inner feelings about her. I was stunned when she left so abruptly." (Tramaine later married Walter Hawkins and would have a hugely successful gospel career.) Totally bereft, Andraé told manager Bill Murray to cancel an upcoming tour, and work on *Keep On Singin'* was suspended until Crouch could work through his grief. "Andraé totally fell apart," Thedford said. "When we got back home, Andraé went in the hospital. He was just totally broken. If you listen to *Keep On Singin'*, the album has two totally different music styles. Everything changed for him at that point. A lot of music that was produced on that album happened after Tramaine had gone."[7]

Following two miserable days, Andraé received a long, comforting telephone call from friend and former baseball player Albie Pearson. As was Crouch's practice, he then walked to his piano and turned on his cassette recorder. "I'm playing and it's almost like talking in a heavenly language," he writes; "syllables come out as I'm talking to the Lord. It's like a release of something in me—something I've learned I'm not wanting to release, but the Holy Spirit is." When Andraé was finished, he replayed the tape and amid the mix of seemingly random words and syllables was something that sounded like "*truite*" and at that moment, he writes, a musical idea "popped out—the song that became 'Through It All.'" Andraé scribbled down the first two verses, then spent three weeks praying for a third verse. "It came at five o'clock in the morning," he writes. "I was just about through putting it down when my room started shaking and the Los Angeles earthquake of 1971 hit!" "Through It All," which would become one of Andraé's most enduring hits, was still too personal and the emotions too raw for him to include on *Keep On Singin'*— and would not be released until *Soulfully* in 1972.[8]

Sister Sandra Joins the Disciples

Andraé's loss may have been the final catalyst prompting his ever-protective sister Sandra to join the Disciples full time. "One of the reasons that Sandra came in the group was because we knew that she was going to be there," Thedford said. "We already knew that his sister wouldn't come and go, which is the way it worked out. She was in the group from then on."[9] Andraé writes that Sandra's long experience in hundreds of Motown recording sessions was immediately apparent. "She always knows a good song," he notes, "when it has that 'right something.' She's very talented and can play almost any instrument she picks up, even some of the little stringed instruments from around the world." As was their practice since childhood, Andraé writes that he continued to audition his songs for Sandra first:

> "Sing this harmony part," I'd say. She always would, but if she didn't like it, she wouldn't put everything into it. I could always tell right away what she thought. If she liked it, she'd get right into it, as if it kicked off a little "excitement button." Her eyes would light up and she'd say, "You've got another one, Andraé."[10]

Eventually, the Disciples—Andraé, Sandra, Perry, Bili, and a rotating crew of drummers and guitarists (depending on the size of the venue)—resumed touring, even though Andraé still delayed returning to the recording studio. As before, the music performed at the concerts varied widely, depending on what Andraé felt or sensed when the group took the stage. "We barely rehearsed," Thedford recalled. "We barely practiced. We just never knew. Our 'rehearsals' took place, most of the time, a half hour before a concert." Thedford said that if the Disciples had the luxury of a soundcheck, Andraé often used the opportunity to introduce yet another song. At other times, the group would only hear a new song when Andraé started playing it on stage. "We'd hit those first notes, even with the new music, and the crowd would just start freaking out," Thedford said, "and from then on, it was just staying on your toes. Nothing was really planned. In the audience, you'd have different people come up at different times and there's different energies in the air, and there's folks crying for this or that [so] there was never a full program."[11]

For the musicians, that kind of nightly improvisation was either invigorating or terrifying—sometimes both simultaneously. Thedford said he spontaneously worked out many of his most distinctive bass patterns as each song was introduced during those run-throughs—and slowly perfected them with each subsequent performance. While he never played bass on the Disciples' studio recordings, the studio bassists often incorporated his figures and patterns on the final recordings. "Some of the patterns were pretty catchy," Thedford said, "and the musicians would just copy them. Some of the bass patterns would just help them structure their own lines. And some of the patterns I never heard again. Still, I was impressed that some of these 'all that' bassists in the studio liked my stuff."[12]

The spirit of improvisation that pervaded the music was also manifest in the sermons, testimonies, stage banter, and band interaction. Morgan, whose vocal prowess meant that he assumed many of the lead parts after Sherman Andrus and Ruben Fernandez left the group, was regularly teased for his singing. "Andraé used to refer to me and say, 'This is Perry, a white singer. He has no soul,'" Morgan said. "The other Black singers had a lot of curves and did a lot of ad-libbing, but I was more the Johnny Mathis type. I sang straight-ahead, whatever the notes were, no deviating. So I was known as the 'white' singer in the group."[13]

Morgan said he and Andraé sometimes quarreled on the road while touring together. "Mainly because I was so stubborn and obstinate," Morgan recalled. "I didn't really want to be a singer and I didn't agree with a lot of the things he would do. But I loved him. He was my brother." Among the things that Perry admired most about Crouch, he said, was his unfailing belief in the group's evangelistic ministry and his ferocious work ethic, especially on the road. Morgan vividly remembered one incident during this period while the Disciples were on yet another tour:

> [Andraé] had shingles in his throat and he was in such pain, but yet every night we were on the road, he sang his heart out. And you'd look into his throat, and

there'd be bleeding, there'd be ulcers. As soon as we got off the stage, he'd have to go to the hotel and go to bed until the next night for the concert, he was in such misery. That [work ethic] had an impression on me, because my attitude became, "Do whatever it takes to make the ministry successful."[14]

This may have been the illness that Andraé would later reference in the liner notes of the upcoming *Keep On Singin'* album. In response to a question by Ralph Carmichael, Crouch attributes divine intervention for his healing of an unspecified illness. During the "roughest time" of his convalescence, Andraé writes that his mother Catherine kept singing to him a song he had recently written, "I've Got Confidence." "In fact," he notes, "every song on this album is a result of something that I've had to experience, and I believe that every song should have a message."[15]

The group still traveled in the blue Econoline van, now with the words "Take the Message Everywhere" painted on the side. The van, which was designed to hold ten people, became uncomfortably crowded with the singers and musicians, their instruments, speakers, amplifiers, and the LPs and sheet music the Disciples sold at every stop. Eventually, Crouch bought a panel truck specifically to accompany the van and haul the equipment. From the beginning, Morgan was the designated driver, though Thedford spelled him from time to time. "I hated to drive and they took the load off of me," Andraé writes in his biography. Because of his driving style, Crouch said he affectionately referred to Morgan as "Lead-foot." The "Blue Streak," as it was dubbed, lasted more than 200,000 miles. In addition to being the driver, Morgan soon assumed the role as the equipment manager as well, something he continued throughout his career with the Disciples even after the band hired a tour manager. Perry said that he was a "wallflower" and that supporting roles suited his personality:

> I always felt like I was the "lesser" member of the group, in a way. So it was my pleasure to do that while the other guys were doing the other things. They were meeting with people and signing autographs and doing that stuff, and I would be loading the bus and getting ready to go to the next place. I thought that no sacrifice was too great for the cause, and the cause was Jesus.[16]

Recording with Bill Cole

At last, in mid-1970, Andraé felt both comfortable and confident enough to return to the studio to finish *Keep On Singin'*. This time, however, Bill Cole had been assigned as the producer. A longtime music industry veteran, Cole had served as choir director for artists ranging from Andy Williams to André Previn. He also served as Light's head of A&R and was said to have "logged 1500 hours in the control booth" in 1972 alone. With that level of experience, Thedford was immediately drawn to Cole. "I love Bill, man," Thedford said. "He didn't give you the impression that he knew a whole lot. He just told you, 'This is what we're doing. This is how it goes. Let's try so and so.'" Thedford said Cole would "milk" the singers, trying to get their best performance, even if it meant several takes. Unlike some other producers Thedford would work with over this long career, Cole would strike up conversations with the studio musicians and singers. "I realized after a while and listening to Bill that this is how you get to know what you can get out of a person," Thedford said.[17]

Also listed on the *Keep On Singin'* back jacket for his "Arrangements" was Clark Gassman, who was co-credited with Andraé. Gassman was a composer whose credits included the folk-rock mass *In Christ There Is No East or West* and, as a "busy" studio musician, he was reputed to be the first artist to use the new Moog synthesizer on an LP in the religious marketplace, *Ralph Carmichael Presents Clark Gassman, The Electric Symphony*. (Both LPs were recorded for Light Records, and *The Electric Symphony*, released in 1970, includes a version of Crouch's composition "I've Got Confidence.")[18]

One of the first songs Andraé introduced to the group for the recording session was, not surprisingly, "I've Got Confidence," which he had originally given to Sherman Andrus for Sherman's first solo recording, *I've Got Confidence* for Benson's Impact label in 1969. In his biography, Andrus writes that Crouch wrote the song "especially for me as a motto for me because of my confidence in God and his direction for my life." Shortly thereafter, the fabled Southern Gospel group the Imperials heard and recorded the song as well on their *Love Is the Thing* album in 1969. The Imperials were short a member at the time and Bob McKenzie, Sherman's producer, told the Imperials that they needed to consider Andrus. When Andrus joined the group in January 1971, he became the first African American in the previously all-white Southern gospel world. And it was the Imperials, who frequently performed and sometimes recorded with Elvis, who introduced Presley to "I've Got Confidence." Elvis recorded his version of the song on May 18, 1972, and included it in his final and best-reviewed religious album, *He Touched Me*, released later that year, about the same time as the Disciples released their *own* version on *Keep On Singin'*. The differences—and similarities—among the four versions provide an intriguing look into the minds of four distinct artistic approaches. Each interpretation features sometimes striking differences in form, temporal fluctuations, instrumentation, groove, tonal centers, and key modulations (see Table 5.1). What Andraé truly "heard" for "I've Got Confidence" when he composed it would not be known until it was performed live by the Disciples somewhat later.[19]

As Thedford noted, there are stylistic differences both musically and lyrically on *Keep On Singin'* between the songs recorded with Tramaine and those recorded with Sandra several months later. Even the album jacket reflects those changes. For the cover art, Light chose to reuse the photograph from the cover of the Liberty/Soul Power 45 reissue of "Christian People" following the song's Grammy nomination. The photo features Perry and Bili in the back, Andraé and Sandra in the front—but not Tramaine. The slightly darker sepia-toned photograph is also "posterized," blurring, at least to some degree, the racial makeup of the singers. Under the title "Andraé Crouch & the Disciples *Keep On Singin'*" and printed an odd Old West–styled typeface are the words "including I've Got Confidence." Light may have been hedging its bets on an album that would be sold almost exclusively in Christian bookstores in the suburbs. As was the case on *Take the Message Everywhere*, the Disciples recorded their vocals over instrumental accompaniment pre-recorded by producer Cole using studio musicians. Once again, the resulting music sounds more pop/inspirational than what the Disciples actually sounded like in concert. Unlike other songs in Andraé's oeuvre, guitars are often featured more prominently in the final mix, sometimes at the expense of the keyboards. And, as before, it sounds to the authors as if Andraé played keyboards on no more than two tracks.

On the back cover is an "interview" between Andraé and Ralph Carmichael and a photograph of the two men, arm in arm, laughing together. Significantly, though, just above the interview is a note, presumably from Carmichael, acknowledging that the album is "almost a year in the making," the result of Andraé's hiatus from the studio following Tramaine's departure. The "interview" itself contains the breathless promotional material typical of the era. However, in a response to a question about the personnel changes since the release of *Take the Message Everywhere*, Andraé is quoted as saying, "I like to keep sort of loose and be open to news sounds, new ideas, and new talent." Ralph later asks him to expand on that comment and Crouch mentions the contributions of "teenage soul singer" Tramaine Davis: "Occasionally, when

Table 5.1 Four versions of "I've Got Confidence"

	Andrus	Imperials	Crouch	Presley
Year	1969	1969	1971	1972
Form	Intro/VCVCVC-fadeout	Short intro/VCVCVCCC C-fadeout	Short intro VCVCVCCCC-fadeout	Short intro VCVCVCCCC-fadeout
Tempo fluctuations	79–82 beats per minute	81–88 beats per minute	79–86 beats per minute	94–97 beats per minute
Instrumentation	Rhythm section and female background vocals (oohs, call-and-response)	Rhythm section and male background vocals (tertian harmonies)	Rhythm section and male background vocals (oohs, call-and-response, and tertian harmonies)	Rhythm section and male and female background vocals (oohs, call-and-response. and tertian harmonies)
Groove	Backbeat on 1 and 3 musical theater/1960s pop	Backbeat on 1 and 4 country & western male quartet	Backbeat on 1 and 4 Black soul gospel (Early contemporary gospel)	Elvis in his own way (rock, pop, Black Pentecostal) (handclaps on beats 2 and 4)
Key and chord progressions differentiation	D♭ chord progressions on chorus (vi–V/V–V–I)	D♭, then modulations to D, E and E♭ major chord progressions on chorus (I–V–I–V–I)	C major, then modulations to D♭ chord progressions on chorus (vi–V/V–V–I)	B♭ major, then modulations to B major and C major chord progressions on chorus (I–V–I–V–I)

Tremaine's [*sic*] schedule permits, she appears in concert with us." Andraé also brags on the dependability and contributions of Sandra, Perry, and Bili. The interview ends with Carmichael asking about Crouch's recent illness, the nature (and dates) of which is not specified. "Only that I can tell you if God hadn't touched me, I wouldn't be here today," Andraé responds, and adds that the song on the LP, "Take a Little Time (and Thank the Lord)" "sums up" his response to being healed.[20]

Keep On Singin'

Side I

"I Don't Know Why Jesus Loved Me"

The mid-tempo "I Don't Know Why Jesus Loved Me" in D♭ major opens the album. It is one of the two songs on the LP that the authors believe feature Andraé on piano, especially in his signature piano motif (A♭ B♭ D♭ B♭ D♭ B♭ D♭ E♭ F) performed between certain phrases and choruses. The nine-note hook compositionally linking those phrases and choruses will be found for the next twenty years in many of Crouch's best-known songs. At the end of the chorus, the B♭ major chord on the word "did" is a sonic affirmation, an emphatic response to the lyric, "Oh! But I'm glad, I'm glad he *did*." At the end of the second verse, Crouch creates anticipation with each measure before the unexpected interruption of the beat with a 2/4 measure. The point is driven home in the joyful call-and-response vocals between vocalist Morgan and the singers on "So glad he did!"[21]

"I'm Gonna Keep On Singin'"

Producer Cole and arranger Gassman's impact is most strongly felt on the bouncy pop of "I'm Gonna Keep On Singin'" and the next track, "I'm Coming Home, Dear Lord." Cole and Gassman transform Andraé's original compositions into something reminiscent of the popular stylings of the Fifth Dimension, who dominated the charts from 1967 to 1973 with breezy pop songs and whose music appealed to a multigenerational, multiethnic audience. The closing preachy vamp of "I'm Gonna Keep On Singin'" even has the feel of "Let the Sunshine In." The vocalists sing over a soundscape of flutes, French horns, chimes, orchestral percussion, strings, and a harp.[22]

"I'm Coming Home Dear Lord"

Tramaine's vocals on "I'm Coming Home Dear Lord" are hauntingly "head-voiced," increasing to her more familiar "mid-chest" voice—an ethereal preview of what will become one of gospel music's most beloved voices. As she beckons "spiritual drifters" back to a "safe haven" with God, Tramaine sings the lyrics with a Pentecostal fervor. Duet partner Thedford does an admirable job of staying with her. The result is sparkling musical theater in the best "Sound of Philadelphia" sense, dramatic and compelling.

"Along Came Jesus"

After the drama of "I'm Coming Home," "Along Came Jesus" is a fast-paced (approximately 149–154 beats per minute at the quarter note, the fastest tempo on the LP) '60s pop song—more like The Association than Black gospel with its "You know I'm happy now, happy now, happy now, la la la" lyrics. But Andraé uses an abrupt tempo change on the outro to match a tonal shift in the words: "all because Jesus stopped and rescued me." It is tempting to speculate that embedded in the lyrics of "Along Came Jesus" ("I was living on lonely street") is the thought—at least on some level—that Andraé had written this song to encourage himself as he dealt with the devastating loss of his first love, Tramaine.[23]

"Jesus (Every Hour He'll Give You Power)" and "I Must Go Away"

A number of similarities merit considering the closing tracks from Sides I and II, "Jesus (Every Hour He'll Give You Power)" and "I Must Go Away," together as the country & western musical motifs and instruments, including banjo, harmonica solos, a faintly tinkling honky-tonk piano, and Nashville-like guitar strumming and finger-picking, are heard throughout both songs. The musical arrangement accompanying "Jesus" is distinctively simple, with unusually subdued background vocals (mostly wordless "ooh's") and a lovely, intimately personal invitation: "I have a friend I'd like to recommend to you." "I Must Go Away" features similar instrumentation, along with a marimba on the bridge. Throughout Andraé's long career, this is the only example of a verse modulating from B to D major, which is further evidence that Cole and/or Gassman arranged Crouch's original composition.

Keep On Singin' has a pronounced liturgical feel, and the closing songs on each side refer to Matthew 28.

Side II

"Take a Little Time"

Andraé chose to open Side II with a slight return to his COGIC roots with "Take a Little Time." This slow, dreamy ballad is lushly performed and sung in the manner of the two groups that Bill Maxwell said that Crouch "really loved," the Delfonics and the Stylistics. The song is a clever re-telling of the story in Luke 17:11–19 where Jesus healed ten lepers, but how only one returned to thank him: "I just want to take a little time right now and thank you, Lord." One unique element to the number is that it ends with a spoken word section.[24]

"What Ya Gonna Do?"

"What Ya Gonna Do?" is another example of Cole and Gassman's strong influence on the music, perhaps to the point where it only vaguely resembles one of Andraé's own compositions. It's one of the few guitar-driven songs in his catalogue and has hints of the Beatles from their *Sgt. Pepper's Lonely Hearts Club Band* era. Not surprisingly, Maxwell said that Crouch listened intently to the Beatles during these years. The song is particularly theatrical, with a waltz-like $\frac{3}{4}$ time signature, like a carousel. At the song's conclusion, the producers employ a recording studio technique to create a psychedelic-sounding echo.[25]

Lyrically, however, it is all Andraé, especially at a time when Hal Lindsey's apocalyptic book *The Late, Great Planet Earth* was a must-read for Christian evangelicals. "What Ya Gonna Do?" presents a daunting imperative, one that implores the listener to "stop and think it over." "What Ya Gonna Do?" is one of the most vivid examples of the breadth of Crouch's sometimes whimsical creativity, using the seeming disconnect in tone between lyric and music to attract any non-churchgoers who might be listening by presenting the Christian plan of salvation in a fresh and compelling way. For Andraé, sin is oppressive and aggressive and the oppressed *must* be warned to seek deliverance—or else.

"I've Got Confidence"

According to Andraé's longtime producer Maxwell, Crouch always attributed the inspiration for "I've Got Confidence" to a class in self-confidence taught by the Reverend Jack Hayford. It immediately became a hit with the Disciples fans. "Everywhere we went," Morgan recalled, "people would be singing it. And for years they would walk up to the table where we'd be selling albums and start singing 'I've Got Confidence' to us."[26] In the hands of the producers, "I've Got Confidence" is placed in the popular key of C major. It's a happy, upbeat song that builds on the verses to the "money" chorus and it's easy to see why Elvis (and others) would like it—"I've Got Confidence" is catchy and inspirational, with space for dynamic builds and releases. The lyrics follow the Old Testament story of Job, who loses everything and in desperation calls on God, who ultimately delivers him and returns what has been lost.

Along with "My Tribute," it's "I've Got Confidence" that best displays Andraé's deep COGIC roots. The two songs are strongly driven by classic gospel vocals and both feature lyrics positing that Andraé may have been thinking about his musical trajectory. The authors suggest that the lyrics— "God is going to see me through"—may also reflect what's going on his life: the unexpected departure of Tramaine, the pressures and constraints of studio budgets, the influence of producers envisioning very different arrangements to his compositions, recording industry polity, and even, perhaps, the beginnings of his dissatisfaction with their arrangement with Light Records.[27]

"My Tribute (to God Be the Glory)"

Fervently sung by Thedford, "My Tribute (to God Be the Glory)" owes a spiritual debt to Fanny Crosby's beloved hymn "To God Be the Glory," though Andraé changes Crosby's third person to a more intimate first person. Few gospel songs have had the impact of "My Tribute (to God Be the Glory)," a classic that has been recorded by dozens of artists and is featured in at least seven hymnals. In an interview years later with researcher Lindsay Terry, Andraé said that the anthemic ballad had its origins during his time as a counselor at the Teen Challenge Center. Crouch, then eighteen, said that on his first day at the Center he met a young man named Larry Reed, just released from San Quentin prison. When Reed arrived at the Center, he claimed to be an atheist but continued exposure to Andraé's music in time softened him to Christianity. After a time, Reed called Crouch and said, "I dreamed that you were going to write a song that is going to go around the world. It will be the biggest song you ever wrote, to this day." Andraé asked Reed, "Well, what do I have to read?" Reed said John 17:4—"I have glorified thee on the earth: I have finished the work which thou gavest me to do." Crouch said that he read the passage but, feeling no sense of inspiration from it, went to bed.

The following morning, Andraé told Terry that he woke up singing, "to God be the Glory." "Where did that come from?" he asked himself, then sat down at the Center's piano and wrote the entire song in ten minutes. That evening during dinner at friend Carrie Gonzalo's house, Crouch played the song for the first time—and told those present of Reed's prediction. When the group read John 17, Andraé said he exclaimed to Gonzalo, "It's all about glory!" Thedford recalled the song's origin somewhat differently, saying that "My Tribute" was originally written in response to Frank Sinatra's version of "My Way." "We were hanging out and Andraé heard the song and said that the melody would make a good gospel song," Thedford said.[28]

Of "My Tribute (to God Be the Glory)," one writer claims:

> Remarkably, one of the most ignored songs on the album when it was released was the less hooky closing song, a slowly building ballad called simply "My Tribute." Eventually the song would come to be listed in *The Guinness Book of World Records* as the most recorded gospel song in history (over 3,000 versions). In more ways than one it became Crouch's signature tune.[29]

Keep On Singin', ultimately, is an odd amalgamation—Crouch's gospel-heavy songwriting and vocals set to pop/inspirational musical accompaniment. The result is that the orchestral arrangements are rarely in the Disciples' preferred performance keys: "I Don't Know Why Jesus Loved Me" and "I'm Gonna Keep On Singin'" (both in the key of D♭ major), "I'm Coming Home, Dear Lord" and "Along Came Jesus" (both in the key of C major), "Jesus (Every Hour He'll Give You Power)" (key of F major), "Take a Little Time" (C major), "What Ya Gonna Do?" (D minor and F major), "I've Got Confidence" (C major), "My Tribute" (C major), and "I Must Go Away" (B and D major). As with *Take the Message Everywhere*, the LP is a compromise between Crouch's barebones compositions—sometimes uneasily linked with the producers' chords and charts—and the result is heavily weighted toward Cole and Gassman's vision for the final sound of the songs. In Andraé's entire canon (and that includes known live performances), he never modulates from B major to D major. Instead, his piano-playing and preferred keys are always flatted.

It's the authors' opinion that by *Keep On Singin'*, Crouch is becoming somewhat dissatisfied with the results of the collaborations with his musical "handlers," no matter how well intentioned and how talented the producer/arrangers. When the time arrived for his next Light album, Andraé's mind, heart, and talents may have already been moving ahead to other, more satisfying musical projects.

Impact and Influence

That hasn't kept *Keep On Singin'* from holding a beloved place in the hearts of listeners. Claudrena N. Harold asserts that the LP had a "distinctive voice, a groove and message of its own," something both "traditional and contemporary, reverent yet forward-thinking." Mark Powell claims the album is "the aural equivalent of any greatest hits package by Smokey Robinson, the Four Tops or the Temptations" and writes that all twelve songs were "potential blockbuster hit singles." However, "due to the ignorance or bigotry of general market radio, the Jesus People got to keep them all to themselves." CCM blogger Scott Bachmann cites Powell's commentary on the LP and agrees:

> And this time, [Powell] pretty much nailed it. Without *Keep On Singin'*, the racial integration of "white Christian music" and "Black gospel music" might never have happened. And we might all still be attending racially segregated churches on Sunday morning. OK, maybe that's hyperbole . . . but you understand my point. *Keep On Singin'* was a big deal.

Even the influential mainstream music site AllMusic.com notes that *Keep On Singin'* "captures the Disciples at the height of their power and represents both their fierce spiritual commitment and their contemporary take on traditional gospel—a musical choice that helped broaden their appeal to secular music listeners." The album also marked the first mention of Andraé and the Disciples in *Billboard* magazine in the "New LP/Tape Releases" column on December 4, 1971.[30]

Shortly after *Keep On Singin'* shipped to record and bookstores, Carmichael and Light released a 45 with the decidedly odd pairing of two widely disparate artists. Side A featured Richard Roberts & the World Action Singers with the Ralph Carmichael Orchestra performing "Spend a Little Love," written by Carmichael. (Richard is the son of televangelist Oral Roberts.) The flip side is "I've Got Confidence" by Andraé Crouch and the Disciples, with the cutline "From *Keep On Singin'*."[31]

Danniebelle Hall

But by then, the Disciples were on the road once again, with boxes of *Keep On Singin'* in the back of the blue van. On a previous tour date in San Francisco,

Andraé had heard a group called the Danniebelles, featuring Danniebelle Hall, her sister Paula Clarin, Phyllis Swisher, and Jimmye Jackson. Hall began playing piano at the age of three, accompanying her church's congregation on piano at twelve, and by the time she was a teenager was singing and composing her own gospel songs. In 1967 she founded the Danniebelles, which recorded an album (*Making the Most of Today* for tiny Action Records) and even toured internationally with the USO in Vietnam and with World Crusade Ministries before disbanding. Andraé had the Danniebelles drive to his parents' house in Pacoima for dinner and an impromptu—and successful—audition. Tammy Kernodle writes that Hall was one of the pivotal female vocalists who ultimately gave Andraé his "signature sound." Crouch was immediately overwhelmed by her singular alto voice and, coupled with her overseas experience and deep well of gospel music knowledge, quickly asked if Hall would join the Disciples. To be admitted into the small, close-knit group, Danniebelle, of course, had to be approved first by Sandra. Andraé writes in his biography that his sister "really digs" having another female in the Disciples and that "having somebody that can hit those high notes I write reminds me of the good memories when the COGICs sang together." In his biography, Crouch describes Danniebelle as "a real prayer warrior" and that her previous experiences meant that she truly understood the many responsibilities of being a member in a touring band. Later, both Clarin and Swisher (as Phyllis St. James) would also tour and record with Andraé.[32]

But the addition of another singer meant that the old blue van was now simply too crowded, even with the panel truck hauling the equipment and boxes of albums that were sold at each concert. "We'd have to sit up for thousands of miles, sometimes four hundred to eight hundred miles between concerts," Andraé writes, "and our bodies would be exhausted." The Disciples began praying for a tour bus. Finally, at a convention in Nashville, Crouch met Buck Rambo of the Singing Rambos, a popular Southern gospel group. The Rambos had a one-year-old touring bus available for $59,000 and asked for a $10,000 down payment. An unexpected donation by a friend of the band's helped the Crouches raise the down payment, but the remainder still seemed impossibly large. A chance meeting with Demos Shakarian of the Full Gospel Men's Fellowship led to a car dealer agreeing to finance part of the balance. As the tour progressed, Crouch writes that the remainder of the money miraculously arrived and the group secured their first bus.[33]

New Hurdles

While the new bus made touring easier, race relations in the United States in 1970 and 1971 were still a work in progress. Published in 1974, Andraé devotes nearly a chapter of *Through It All* to the hurdles the all-Black Disciples faced in the early days of their ministry. At one concert, members of the audience had been spontaneously singing some of the group's biggest songs prior to the performance, but when the Disciples walked out on stage, more than half of the people left. At a wedding reception, he writes that "Christians" asked members of the wedding party, "What are you letting all of those 'niggers' in your wedding group for?" Perry Morgan remembered having engagements canceled in the South in the early 1970s when the promoters "discovered" that the Disciples were all African Americans. Stephen "Bugs" Giglio, Andraé's longtime road manager, also recalled incidents during their time together, especially in the Deep South, where things were "still pretty crazy" in the 1970s for an all-Black group. In addition to the occasional picketing outside white churches, he said that several times that the group would perform in venues still with Ku Klux Klan posters from a previous event. Later, when the Disciples included white musicians, Giglio said that the group would sometimes be harassed, especially in restaurants. Andraé, he said, managed to remain calm, regardless:

> I don't think there was much influence on him at all. It didn't affect his ability to do what he did. I didn't see him get angry about it, I didn't see him make fun of it or try to make light of it. Never any anger. He'd just put it all out on the stage and talk about Jesus, man.[34]

Prejudice was only one of the issues facing the increasingly popular Disciples. Of the members of the group, only Thedford had had experience with the realities of touring and seen the darker sides of the human condition. At that time, most gospel artists were paid in cash in a variety of informal ways, including the infamous "love offerings" collected at the end of the services. Because of Andraé's call to ministry, there was a constant flow of unregulated people backstage before, during, and after the performances. For Thedford, the new bus only added to the potential for problems. After one concert in Chicago, Bili encountered a group ransacking the tour bus and was forced to confront them alone. Throughout his time with the Disciples, only Morgan knew that Thedford always carried a gun. "I always had weapons, that was my thing," he said. "But when we'd go on the road, we would sell $15,000, $20,000 worth of records." Concert and merchandise receipts were kept in paper sacks or "conspicuous" grocery bags. "You're on the road for a week and a half and you've got $100,000 in cash, mostly $1 bills, and you've got people coming and going in your motel rooms. I always kept the money locked up in a safe place on the bus where nobody knew where it was but the band." For Thedford, as the Disciples got bigger, it was simply a matter of being prudent:

> You got to know where you can't go, you got to know who you can't be around. That was a lot of cash to be driving around the country with, especially when you go to the big cities, mostly in the Black areas. We'd go to Chicago and do something on the South Side; we'd go to Gary, Indiana, to parts of Cleveland. We can't just be so-called Christian leaders and be out here dealing with the world and be naïve.[35]

As 1972 drew closer, the reinvigorated Disciples found themselves at the forefront of a new musical and sociological phenomenon that would profoundly impact their music and ministry. Or as the headlines in one representative article from the influential *Look* magazine stated, "The Jesus Movement Is Upon Us."[36]

Finding Their Audience

Keep On Singin' clearly had an impact far beyond its total sales, which—in any case—are extremely difficult to ascertain with most small, privately held record labels. *Billboard* magazine's first Black gospel-related chart does not appear until October 6, 1973, more than a year after the album's initial release. The initial chart was accompanied by the following short article:

Begin Black Gospel Chart
  LOS ANGELES—"The Best-Selling Gospel LP's," a 35-position chart covering the top sellers in Black sacred music, premieres in this issue of Billboard on Page 43.
  This chart will appear regularly in the first issue of each month of *Billboard*.

Neither *Take the Message Everywhere* nor *Keep On Singin'* is listed in the first chart, which is dominated by the Reverend James Cleveland, Aretha Franklin, Inez Andrews, and other more traditional gospel artists on the main gospel labels—Savoy, Songbird, Nashboro, Peacock, Specialty, and a few others. No other Light Records LP appears through December 1974. The following month, "I Don't Know Why Jesus Loved Me" (Light LS 5546) appears at #10. LS 5546 is the number Light assigned to *Keep On Singin'*, and since that is also the number assigned to "I Don't Know Why Jesus Loved Me" by Light, this must be how the name of the LP was first keyed into the chart-tabulating process. That Top 10 finish is the highest position the album achieved. According to *Billboard*, in the months that followed, *Keep On Singin'*/"I Don't Know Why" remained in the middle of the chart, selling at a slow but steady rate, mostly in the mid-20s.[37]

Years later, Crouch spoke more openly about the special circumstances facing *Keep On Singin'* that impacted both its acceptance and sales, particularly in the African American market. Unlike other gospel artists, he said, both Light Records and Word Records (which handled the distribution) were composed entirely of white staff members, though Crouch repeatedly urged Carmichael to hire Black employees. "They didn't have Black distribution," he said. Additionally, the production of the albums defaulted to what the all-white Light producers and engineers were familiar with: "I felt that a lot of Black people, when we first started. . . . I don't think they thought it sounded Black. I mean [*Keep On Singin'*] sounded white. They just wouldn't hear it from that approach . . . it wouldn't be a high-energy type thing. It was basically a melodic type thing." Crouch said that many Black artists are basically "insecure." "We think that we have to revert back to what we know works rather than being secure in something new that we feel is fresh," he said. That perception, he said, would not change until the release of the *"Live" at Carnegie Hall* album.[38]

NOTES

1. www.bsnpubs.com/liberty/liberty.html; Michael "Doc Rock" Kelly, *Liberty Records: A History of the Recording Company and Its Stars, 1955–1971* (Jefferson, NC: McFarland & Co., 1993), 336–337; Eliot Tiegel, "Pat Boone Opens Center to Aid 'Jesus Music,'" *Billboard*, June 3, 1972, 59; Andraé Crouch with Nina Ball, *Through It All* (Waco, TX: Word Books, 1974), 103–104.
2. "Gospel Go Ahead," *Cash Box* (September 19, 1970), 24; Bili Thedford, interview with the authors, March 22, 2022.
3. Andraé Crouch, *Through It All*, 104; Perry Morgan, interview with the authors, March 19, 2022.
4. "André, Etc., Signs," *Record World*, September 26, 1970, 39; Ed Ochs, "Soul Sauce," October 17, 1970, *Billboard*, 36; Ed Ochs, "Soul Sauce," October 24, 1970, 50; "1970 Grammy Nominations," *Billboard*, February 8, 1971, 12.

5. Andraé Crouch, *Through It All*, 103–104.
6. Kathy Hazzard, interview with the authors, August 19, 2021.
7. Andraé Crouch, *Through It All*, 93–94 (Andraé is referring to what is commonly called the "San Fernando Earthquake," which occurred—as he recalled—during the early morning hours of February 9, 1971); Bili Thedford, interview with the authors, November 12, 2020.
8. Andraé Crouch, *Through It All*, 94–95.
9. Bili Thedford, interview with the authors, November 12, 2020.
10. Andraé Crouch, *Through It All*, 96.
11. Bili Thedford, interview with the authors, November 12, 2020.
12. Bili Thedford, interview with the authors, November 12, 2020.
13. Perry Morgan, interview with the authors, March 19, 2022.
14. Perry Morgan, interview with the authors, March 19, 2022.
15. Liner notes, Andraé Crouch and the Disciples, *Keep On Singin'*, Light Records LS-5546.
16. Andraé Crouch, *Through It All*, 92; Perry Morgan, interview with the authors, March 19, 2022.
17. Bili Thedford, interview with the authors March 22, 2022; Sonlight, *Sonlight* (Light Records LS-5612, 1973); "Lexicon/Light Composer and Artists," *Billboard*, October 14, 1972, W-7, W-13; "Lexicon/Light Expands in Publishing," *Billboard*, October 14, 1972, W-7; Bill Cole with Ralph Carmichael Strings, *Right Now* (Light Records LS-5545, 1971).
18. "Lexicon/Light Composers and Artists," *Billboard*, October 14, 1972, W-7; Clark Gassman, *In Christ There Is No East or West* (Light Records LS-5574, 1972); Ralph Carmichael Presents Clark Gassman, *The Electric Symphony* (Light Records LS-5541, 1970).
19. Sherman Andrus, *My Story! My Song! Blessed!* (Nashville: WestBow Press, 2021), 23, 32; https://www.elvisthemusic.com/track/ive-got-confidence-3/; The Imperials, *Love Is the Thing* (Impact Records HWS 3029, 1969); Elvis Presley, *He Touched Me* (RCA LSP 4690, 1972), Sherman Andrus, *I've Got Confidence* (IMPACT 3019, 1969).
20. Andraé Crouch & the Disciples, *Keep On Singin'* (Light Records LS-5546, 1971).
21. "I Don't Know Why Jesus Loved Me" by Andraé Crouch, Lexicon Music, Inc., courtesy Capitol CMG.
22. https://discogs.com/artist/191325-the-fifth-dimension.
23. "Along Came Jesus" by Andraé Crouch, Lexicon Music, Inc., courtesy Capitol CMG.
24. Bill Maxwell, personal correspondence with the authors, May 18, 2019.
25. Bill Maxwell, interview with the authors, May 18, 2019.
26. Bill Maxwell, interview with the authors, May 18, 2019; Perry Morgan, interview with the authors, May 18, 2019.
27. "I've Got Confidence" by Andraé Crouch, Lexicon Music, Inc., courtesy of Capitol CMG.

28. https://Hymnary.org/text/to_god_be_the_glory_to_god; Terry Lindsay, *To God Be the Glory: 52 of the Greatest Song Stories Ever Told* (Chattanooga, TN: AMG Publishers, 2016), 69–70; Bili Thedford, interview with the authors, November 12, 2020.

29. Mark Allen Powell, *Encyclopedia of Contemporary Christian Music* (Peabody, MA: Hendrickson, 2002), 211.

30. Claudrena N. Harold, *When Sunday Comes: Gospel Music in the Soul and Hip-Hop Eras* (Urbana: University of Illinois Press, 2020), 48; Powell, *Encyclopedia of Contemporary Christian Music*, 211; "New LP/Tape Releases," *Billboard*, December 4, 1971, 5; Scott Bachmann, #45, *Keep On Singin'*, http://greatest70salbums.blogspot.com/2016/10/45-keep-on-singin-by-andrae-crouch.html; https://www.allmusic.com/album/keep-on-singin-MW0000583606.

31. Andraé Crouch and the Disciples, "I've Got Confidence" (Light Records 45, LS-609, 1971).

32. Tammy L. Kernodle, "Work the Works: The Role of African-American Women in the Development of Contemporary Gospel," *Black Music Research Journal* 26, no. 1 (Spring 2006): 90–93; Bil Carpenter, *Uncloudy Days: The Gospel Music Encyclopedia* (San Francisco: Backbeat Books, 2005), 171; Phyllis St. James, interview with the authors, January 23, 2021; Andraé Crouch, *Through It All*, 97.

33. Andraé Crouch, *Through It All*, 97–101.

34. Andraé Crouch, *Through It All*, 106–107; Perry Morgan, interview with the authors, May 18, 2019; Stephen "Bugs" Giglio, interview with the authors, June 18, 2021.

35. Bili Thedford, interview with the authors, March 22, 2022.

36. Brian Vachon, "The Jesus Movement Is Upon Us," *Look*, February 1971, 15–22.

37. "Begin Black Gospel Chart LP's," *Billboard* magazine, October 7, 1973, 3; November 3, 1974, 30; December 1, 1974, 31; January 5, 1974, 18; February 16, 1974, 34; March 16, 1974, 39; April 20, 1974, 38; June 15, 1974, 42; August 10, 1974, 56; September 7, 1974, 38; October 5, 1974, 50; November 9, 1974, 35; December 7, 1974, 41. Note: The disk's B-side is "It Won't Be Long," which would not be released on an album until the following year's LP, *Soulfully*. Light later released a second 45 from *Keep On Singin'*, "Leave the Devil Alone," also backed with "It Won't Be Long" as LS-616. https://www.discogs.com/release/4568922-Andraé-Crouch-And-The-Disciples-I-Dont-Know-Why-Jesus-Loved-Me. (Light also issued a 45 with "I Don't Know Why Jesus Loved Me" as LS-615.)

38. Keith Bernard Jenkins, *The Rhetoric of Gospel Song: A Content Analysis of the Lyrics of Andraé Crouch* (Diss., Florida State University, 1990), 102.

6

Soulfully

The Jesus Movement

On June 21, 1971, *Time* magazine's cover got the country's attention—an artist's psychedelic portrait of Jesus with the headline "The Jesus Revolution." Inside, readers found in-depth stories on the new movement, including a Southern California "wanted" poster for Jesus. For many, this was the first indication that what had started in Southern California had become a national phenomenon. Citing examples from coast to coast, the writer spends a few pages on how music, "the *lingua franca* of the young, has become the special medium of the Jesus Movement."[1]

Using the energy of the Jesus Movement as a catalyst, Bill Bright's evangelical Campus Crusade for Christ (CCC) created an ambitious plan to have tens of thousands of young people converge on Dallas for the World Student Congress on Evangelism in June 1972. The leaders of InterVarsity Fellowship and the Reverend Billy Graham's Youth with a Mission quickly signed on and CCC inundated its members and their churches with more than six million brochures in the months leading up to Explo '72. The Graham organization paid for more than a thousand 16-millimeter prints of a promotional film for the event and the CCC earmarked $1 million of its $2.4 million promotional budget for a syndicated national television broadcast of the concluding concert. The event merited a mention in *Billboard* that noted that Andraé Crouch and the Disciples would be among those performing. An estimated 85,000 young people began arriving in Dallas on June 12, where they were enthusiastically welcomed with billboards and signage across the city. For the next few days, participants were involved in an array of evangelism-related activities and evening concerts in the Cotton Bowl. On Saturday, June 17, 80,000–100,000

126 SOON & VERY SOON

young people converged on an open field just south of downtown Dallas for the concluding concert.[2]

Explo '72 Saturday Concert

The massive Saturday concert was a pivotal moment in both the Jesus Movement and the youth revival that had sprung out of Southern California in the mid-1960s. Following Woodstock in August 1969, large religious music events popped up across the United States, including one of the first, the Ichthus Music Festival in Wilmore, Kentucky, the following year, which featured Andraé and the Disciples. Others included the Faith Festival in Evansville, Indiana, in March 1970, where 6,000 people heard artists ranging from Pat Boone to Larry Norman, and similar events followed in El Paso, Santa Barbara, and Fort Worth in the months that followed. (The Disciples also performed at Hawaii's Diamond Head Crater Sunshine Music Festival in 1971 with Santana and Buddy Miles before 70,000 people.) But it was Graham—the preeminent evangelical in the country—whose support and presence on the stage separated Explo '72 from all that had gone before.[3]

The musical eclecticism of the artists who performed during the week typified the freewheeling nature of the music of the Jesus Movement. After a week of events and nightly rallies and performances in the Cotton Bowl, activities moved to the huge purpose-built stage just south of downtown Dallas. The headliners were Johnny Cash (with the Statler Singers, Mother Maybelle Carter and the Carter Sisters, and Tennessee Three) and Pat Boone, along with country singer Connie Smith and singer/songwriters Kris Kristofferson and Rita Coolidge. The tens of thousands of Jesus Movement adherents in the audience cheered Larry Norman, Barry McGuire, the Children of the Day, Danny Lee and the Children of Truth, Love Song, and Randy Matthews. Somewhat lesser-known artists on the final day included the Armageddon Experience, Turley Richards, the Great Commission Company, Forerunners, and gospel artist Willa Dorsey. Southern gospel fans would have been attracted by the Speer Family. But the performers who drew the greatest response—and who found themselves as the unlikely face (and sound) of the otherwise almost entirely white Jesus Movement—were Andraé Crouch and the Disciples.[4]

Cash and his ensemble began in late afternoon, followed by Graham, who preached and prayed with the vast crowd. Graham included several religious pop music culture references in his sermon. "Put your hand in the hand of the man from Galilee," he said. "When you do, you'll have a supernatural power to put your hand in the hand of a person of another race." Shortly thereafter, the Disciples took the stage. Three high-quality videos of Andraé and the Disciples from Explo '72 are widely available on YouTube. Two feature the group performing songs from the *Keep On Singin'* album, "I'm Gonna Keep On Singin'" (shot during the day) and "I Don't Know Why Jesus Loves Me" (performed under the lights) before a backdrop of brightly colored strips of a sail-like material. Musician Fletch Wiley, who was at Explo '72, said he believes that these two clips were from a Thursday performance, perhaps in the Cotton Bowl or the plaza of the Texas Bank and Trust Company building. Explo '72 organizer Paul Eshleman noted that Larry Norman and Love Song also played during that set and that the three groups "sounded the glories forth through the mod beat." For the third clip, a previously unreleased song titled "Satisfied," the same Disciples wear entirely different clothes and perform during daylight hours in front of the Peter Max–inspired outdoor Explo '72 stage. The lineup included Andraé on piano, Bili Thedford on bass guitar, and Perry Morgan, Sandra Crouch, and Sondra "Blinky" Williams singing backup. The accompaniment was provided by Love Song's guitarist Tommy Coomes and drummer Roger Ford. Backstage, but not visible, were Danniebelle Hall, Phyllis St. James (née Swisher), and the members of the Danniebelles. St. James said that Andraé had invited the group to join him at Explo '72 to "support" the Disciples and meet other musicians and members of the music industry.[5]

"Satisfied"

The live version of "Satisfied" is a Holiness piano-driven gospel vamp that puts an emphasis on the words "Jesus saves" as it moves from D♭ to E♭ major. Crouch's keyboard playing is deeply rooted in Black church performance practices, Thedford's foundational bass has a funk/soul feel, and the rapid-fire tempo means that the audience could (and did) dance a holy dance.

"Satisfied" had been written and performed several months or more earlier. Brian Vachon, who wrote the early *Look* magazine article in February 1971 on the Jesus Movement, turned his experiences into an illustrated book on the topic, *A Time to Be Born*, published in 1972. Vachon writes of attending a Jesus Music concert at the University of Southern California featuring Crouch and the Disciples where he said the reception for Andraé was "almost deafening." The Disciples, he notes, were "one of the few groups of Blacks I had seen at any time while looking at the Movement in California." As for Andraé himself, "a big, authoritative man whose piano was hot soul," photographers Jack and Betty Cheetham include a full-page photograph of Crouch in performance at the piano. The song that Vachon cites is "Satisfied": "It's just like walking in the sunshine/After a long and dreary day." During the performance of the song, Andraé involved the virtually all-white audience in a classic Black church call-and-response in what Vachon calls the "melodious singsong of a Black revivalist." Andraé then shouted, "Praise God," and turned to face the crowd, saying: "Because I trust you're not here just for the foot-stomping and handclapping. We're here singing and talking about Jesus. That's something real. And it's too much sweat to be up here for something that's not real." According to Vachon, the audience agreed "fortissimo" and when the group began the next song, the crowd sang along.[6]

A few months later in Dallas, Andraé and the Disciples launched into "Satisfied" to a crowd a hundred times as large and to the same energetic response. The reaction was similar to what Sly and the Family Stone had generated while performing "Higher" at Woodstock. Sly, like Andraé, had come from a Pentecostal church background, though in the San Francisco area, and even recorded a few gospel tracks in his younger days. One writer said that the Disciples' performance of "Satisfied" "nearly burned down" the venue. Another called "Satisfied" "one of the great highlights" of the festival. The three Explo '72 YouTube clips are the earliest known filmed record of Andraé Crouch and the Disciples in performance, and they confirm what numerous observers, reviewers, friends, family members, and fellow musicians have repeatedly said—Andraé and the Disciples were *electrifying* in concert. Longtime music manager and agent Wes Yoder was in the "nosebleed" seats that day and recalled that the Disciples took the stage following several mostly acoustic "Jesus music troubadours" and suddenly, "you have this powerful energy coming off the stage and the audience was on its feet. You couldn't believe what you were hearing. It was as if he was playing music that you knew but had never heard before. There was nothing like it." Once again, Thedford's fluid bass playing moves easily within gospel, soul music, and even jazz. It's Thedford's driving eighth and sixteenth notes that energize "Satisfied" and set the stage for what's to come with the Disciples.[7]

Thedford said that his memories of Explo '72 have blurred and merged with those of several other subsequent large religious music festivals, save for the resounding response that followed the performance of "Satisfied" in Dallas:

> We started changing our music with "Satisfied," because the audience changed. All of a sudden, you had 400,000 hippies out there and you weren't going to reach them with "How Great Thou Art." You had to come out there with something because they were so energetic and they just wanted to party—and we're trying to share our message at the same time. The way that we wanted to be able to share our message was through the music. If the music wasn't hip enough for the crowd, you lose the crowd.

Thedford said that following the Dallas concert, all Jesus Music–related artists—not just the Disciples—realized that they had been singing primarily to Christians who were already converted. "After '72, it was all about, 'How can we get to the streets?'" Thedford said. "Everybody was kind of fishing for another ride like Explo '72." For Morgan, the performances reflected what Andraé and the Disciples were listening to at that time—Curtis Mayfield, the Spinners, and *not* necessarily traditional Black gospel. "Those were the sounds that he was geared towards, of our music, of everything," Morgan said.[8]

Sonlight

Among the many Jesus groups performing at the various Explo '72 venues were Sonlight, a talented quartet of musicians from Oklahoma City composed of Bill Maxwell (drums), Hadley Hockensmith (guitar), Harlan Rogers (keyboards), and Fletch Wiley (winds and horns). The group backed up several singers during the course of the week, including former Elvis backup singer Jeannie Greene, Connie Smith, Randy Matthews, and Reba Rambo. When Andraé performed at Explo '72, however, Maxwell said the members of Sonlight were immediately struck by the differences between the Disciples and the other Jesus Music groups in Dallas. Crouch had had long experience in involving even hesitant people in the music. "He would sing a chorus once and then would sing it again and have [the listeners] join in," Maxwell said. "Then he'd get them going and he might add a verse and he would go back to the people singing—and he never left that." Maxwell said that only the Disciples interacted with the massive crowd in that manner at Explo '72—it was, he said, one the first instances of what is now called "praise & worship" music.

"Andraé's the only one there that had people singing along and worshiping like that," Maxwell said. "Everybody else was performing their own songs. Then Andraé entered in and that was so astounding. I remember Billy Graham saying, shortly after that, that Andraé was the John Wesley of our times, the hymn-writer for our times."[9]

Maxwell had joined Sonlight from the talented Nashville rock band Barefoot Jerry, which had recorded an album produced by T-Bone Burnett for UNI Records. Maxwell, then twenty-one, had been playing drums professionally since age fourteen, six nights a week, usually with professional musicians, and experienced the usual temptations inherent in the rock 'n' roll lifestyle before having a profound religious experience. The other members of the group, Hockensmith, Rogers, and Wiley, had all gone through similar life-changing experiences in the previous year and all had begun listening to Andraé and the Disciples. When the Disciples performed at Bethany Nazarene College in the city in December 1971, the members of Sonlight were there. After the concert, Hockensmith invited Andraé to drive across town to hear Sonlight at The Open Door—at 11 P.M. "We got kind of bold," Hockensmith recalled, "but we said, 'You might want to come and hear us.' Andraé said, 'Yeah, can you do me a concert?'" They did. The police eventually broke up the impromptu audition because of the late hour but Crouch had heard enough. Hockensmith said Andraé made the offer on the spot: "You know what? I want you guys to be my new band. I'll be giving you a call shortly and we'll start making music together."

When the group returned to Oklahoma, Wiley said that they received a call from an arranger who was working at Explo '72. The arranger said he'd heard good things about Sonlight and asked them to back up various singers during the final concert—which is why Sonlight was in Dallas. Once at Explo '72, Andraé invited the group to the small "green room" backstage and repeated his invitation. What had initially attracted Crouch to Sonlight? "Well, we were all pretty experienced as opposed to just church musicians," Maxwell said. "It shocked him." Andraé, Maxwell added, was the only musician he knew who was making a living while performing contemporary religious music. Wiley's strongest memory of Explo '72 was Andraé's natural generosity. "He was telling everybody he met, 'Oh, man, you should hear this band Sonlight,'" Wiley recalled. "'They are the most incredible musicians. They are amazing. They write the greatest songs.' And he didn't know us from Adam!" Immediately after the festival, Sonlight was hired to be the backup band for a five-day tour with Randy Matthews and Reba Rambo that included several dates in Indiana. After the tour, Sonlight detoured through Nashville to audition for Bob McKenzie and Benson Records. At a restaurant, Maxwell said he felt a compulsion to call Andraé. Wiley recalled that Crouch answered the phone immediately: "Man, I've been trying to reach you guys!" Andraé said. "We're going to play on the Johnny Carson show in like four nights—and I want Bill and Hadley to fly out and play on *The Tonight Show*!" Which meant that Rogers and Wiley were left to return the van full of the band's equipment back to Oklahoma City.[10]

Explo '72 Aftermath and Influence

Campus Crusade for Christ had professionally recorded the Explo '72 concert and released a promotional LP with songs by twelve different artists. The album was only available to viewers of the television broadcast who then requested information about CCC. In addition to tracks by Johnny Cash, Larry Norman, Love Song, and eight other artists, Andraé Crouch and the Disciples were represented by "Satisfied." In a *Billboard* magazine article a few months later, Bob Cottrell, president of a new consortium of religious labels, said that CCC had shipped 175,000 copies of the *Jesus Sound Explosion* album. The sheer number of albums, an almost unheard amount among *all* of the various forms of gospel music at the time, "indicates the growing potential of religious music, which is youth-oriented and directed," Cottrell said. In August, CCC's television documentary on Explo '72, which was edited into three hour-long episodes and featured excerpts both the nighttime rallies in the Cotton Bowl and the concluding music festival, was broadcast nationally on nearly 200 stations in the United States.[11]

Historians have identified Explo '72 as a signature event in the history of contemporary religious music. The festival changed perceptions and accelerated the acceptance of the music in the white evangelical Christian community. As David W. Stowe writes:

> With the media attention to the Jesus Movement peaking in 1971, Crouch's timing was impeccable. Even more than Norman, the Disciples galvanized audiences of Jesus People, especially those with ears for the integrated soul and rock being popularized by Sly and the Family Stone.[12]

Paul Baker, who chronicled both Jesus Music and CCM from the beginning, agrees:

> By 1972, the songs of Andraé were beginning to be accepted by older Christians as well as the youths. Andraé Crouch and the Disciples' appearance at Explo '72 just reassured that acceptance. The hands clapped. The feet stomped. The people sang and praised the Lord with one of the men most responsible for the growth of the Jesus Movement.

"Gospel music would never be the same again," Baker notes elsewhere. "The music programs at Explo '72 gave every visiting delegate a chance to pick a favorite style of gospel music and take home word of what had been heard." Writer Andrew Mall called the event "the Jesus People movement's moment of crossover." "The Explo extravaganza marked the beginning of a new recording industry," John Haines writes, and heralds what would be now called contemporary Christian music. While Marshall Terrill notes in particular the cultural impact of both Love Song and the Disciples at Explo '72 and calls the event the "high-water mark for the Jesus Movement." "Everything was poised for a breakout from Southern California, except a national audience," Terrill writes. "That finally came in June 1972."[13]

Even the members of the Disciples, who by now had performed before several massive concert crowds, were taken aback by the response to their Explo '72 performance. For Thedford, the event had a "surreal" quality:

> Explo '72 was the biggest thing that I have ever done in my life still to today. Nothing had an impact on me as big as that. And it wasn't just about the numbers of the crowd—the energy of that whole thing, the spirit of the people, and what was going on—it was like this is an anomaly. It was like being someplace else in another time. When that week was over, it was like, "Can you believe what just happened here?" I don't know the numbers, I just felt like, "Hey! I got to be a part of it." I was there. I saw it. And I had a hand in it.

Singer Kathy Hazzard, who toured with the Disciples following Explo '72, said the response in the weeks that followed was "overwhelming," especially when the group performed "Satisfied." "As far as getting the crowd going, we'd always perform it at the festivals and it'd be like, 'Here we go!'," Hazzard recalled. Andraé and the Disciples soon found themselves as the featured artists at numerous festivals, including the Ichthus Music Festival, Disneyland, and different gospel concerts and as near-regulars in the popular Knott's Berry Farm concerts. Hazzard said that one of the early tours following Explo '72

SOULFULLY   133

took them to a large church where the pastor immediately objected to the women in the group, Sandra, Bea Carr, and Hazzard, wearing pants. "Sandra said, 'Well, what do you want us to do? Take them off right here?'" Hazzard said. Fortunately, Thedford knew someone in the town:

> Andraé told Bili to call his friend and say, "They don't want us at church; we're going to sing in a park. Find us a park." After a few hours, we'd gotten a permit and the people from the church came to the park. I think at that time about 1,200 people came to the Lord in the park because Andraé said, "Oh no! We didn't come this way for you to tell us we can't sing in your church. We are the church." The pastor had one of those "Aha!" comments and cried and apologized and apologized.[14]

In the weeks that followed, the national media featured a host of articles chronicling and assessing the events in Dallas. *Life* magazine devoted five pages to Explo '72, with numerous photographs of enraptured listeners. In an insightful article on Explo '72 in the *New York Times*, one writer picked up on one of Graham's comments about race at the closing concert—that Jesus would give Christians the "supernatural power to put your hand in the hand of a person of another race." However, according to the article, only "3 percent" of the tens of thousands of attendees had been African Americans. The small numbers were noted by the organizers, as CCC at the time was working diligently to establish a ministry among Black students. Nearly forty years later, John Haines writes that Explo '72 "took place in a predominantly white, European-based religious culture from which African Americans were largely excluded" and that Crouch and the Disciples were a Black "anomaly." Andraé rarely talked about racism, either in interviews or in concert. "But the neatest hat trick was that Crouch's music broke down race barriers between Blacks and whites," Terrill asserts, not unlike Motown concerts. "His audiences were usually mixed in a time when the two races barely fraternized." The overpowering presence of Crouch and the Disciples performing at such an exhilarating level at such a landmark, high-profile event has been indelibly marked by many, including longtime agent Yoder, who considered it a defining moment in the movement:

> I had never seen anything like it. Neither had the church. And it was so necessary, for the awakening that God wanted to bring to the American church at the time, to have someone like Andraé who could bridge the racial thing. You have this African American, Andraé Crouch, and you just fall in love with this. All of a sudden, it starts messing with the racial characters in your head. Andraé had

a tremendous influence, I think unspoken, because racism at that time was not really part of his conversation. But he was still part of the breakdown of the wall of separation that had come.[15]

National Television

The Tonight Show with Johnny Carson was not only the top late night talk show, Carson was one of the most influential figures in popular culture. He had featured at least two gospel artists on the show over the years, Mahalia Jackson and Clara Ward and the Ward Singers, easily the best-known names in gospel at the time. More recently, after "Oh Happy Day" hit the top of the charts and caused a worldwide media storm, Edwin Hawkins had performed on *The Tonight Show* on February 9, 1971. But Andraé Crouch and the Disciples had not yet achieved that kind of audience recognition. According to Maxwell, Andraé went to New York on his own and auditioned for *The Tonight Show's* producers. "No one ever got in off of auditions," Maxwell said, "but he did. They liked him and put him on. He didn't know how great he was. He didn't have any big credits at that time. This was before he exploded. He just went down and auditioned and the talent booker liked him." The producers invited the group to perform on June 27, 1972, just two weeks after the Dallas festival. Once the makeshift group had arrived in New York, Crouch told gospel historian Bil Carpenter that Carson was "very friendly" and worked hard to make the group comfortable. "He knew that gospel wasn't at the top of the charts," Crouch said, "but he could see that gospel was a fresh form of music that was beginning to get more notice." While Andraé and the Disciples would appear at least three times on *The Tonight Show*, Crouch said that that first appearance did much to raise the group's profile in both popular and gospel music. "It gave us clout, but we still had to work for our reputation," Andraé told Carpenter (Image 6.1). Guitarist Hockensmith's memories of the performance are mostly of the positive response afforded the group by music director Doc Severinsen's band. During their number, "You Don't Know What You're Missing," Hockensmith recalled that members of the Severinsen band stood and applauded. Maxwell, accompanying the Disciples for the first time and playing on *The Tonight Show* drummer's kit, remembered that their performance that evening was especially compelling. "It had that Undisputed Truth, Rose Royce kind of feel to it," he said. The choice of "You Don't Know What

Image 6.1 *Soulfully* back jacket with photograph from *The Tonight Show with Johnny Carson*, June 27, 1972. From left, Perry Morgan, Sandra Crouch, Bill Maxwell, Billy Thedford, Hadley Hockensmith, unknown second guitarist. Foreground, Andraé Crouch. (Light Records LS-5581-LP, administered by MNRK Music Group)

You're Missing" from the as-yet unreleased album *Soulfully* was made after careful consideration.[16]

Light Records

Fortunately for the Disciples, Andraé's rising national profile corresponded with the success his record label Light was enjoying as well. To celebrate, founder Ralph Carmichael and his team bought a multi-page promotional section in

Billboard magazine's October 14, 1972, issue to trumpet the rapid growth of the label and its thriving publishing arm, Lexicon. As Light's best-known artists, Andraé and the Disciples were, of course, featured prominently on the first page of the section and the headline of a separate story names them "America's Number One Soul Group." In addition to listing their hits, the article reports that the Disciples' booking agency had booked the group for more than 300 public appearances over the previous year. The article also heralds the Disciples' upcoming album, recorded in Carnegie Hall and reports that the group is now backed by the four musicians from Sonlight, who themselves had an upcoming LP of their own for Light Records. The company's various catalogues, claims another article, includes 60 book and album packages, 500 copyrights, and 2,800 mechanical licenses. According to the article, "product" from Lexicon is sent to "5,000 dealers" (Christian bookstores) via a distribution agreement with Word and another "1,000 more dealers ('secular bookstores and record stores') are being 'converted' each year." Carmichael said he was heavily involved in the cross-platform marketing of all Light/Lexicon products:

> Every album we release turns into a music book, not only containing the same songs as recorded on the LP, but featuring the same arrangements note for note. The converse is also true. For every book we publish, we go into the studio and produce an album—man, we have made some of the most expensive demos in history!

Carmichael's vision and knack for promotion corresponded with the stunning rise of Andraé Crouch and the Disciples' public profile. At the same time, Light's distribution agreement with Word Records saw Word simultaneously expand its sales force and outreach to Christian bookstores. The "admiration" between Light and Word, another article slyly notes, "is probably due to the $4 million gross sales reported for the last year."[17]

The *Soulfully* Album

To capitalize on the Disciples' unprecedented appearance on *The Tonight Show*, the Light promotional team replaced the standard back jacket liner notes of what would be called the *Soulfully* album with a black and white photograph of the band in action on the show. The LP was released during late October 1972, and *Billboard* magazine notes it in the "New LP/Tape

Releases" column on November 11, 1972. However, Maxwell said that the Disciples had actually begun working on the project in late 1971, though the process dragged on until the summer of 1972. Shortly after *The Tonight Show* appearance, Maxwell moved to Southern California and lived for a time with Andraé in the guest house behind the home belonging to Benjamin Sr. and Catherine Crouch, Andraé's parents. It was during the long mixing process for *Soulfully* that the two began working together.[18]

Soulfully's cover features Andraé, Sandra, Morgan, and Thedford standing on railroad tracks in San Fernando staring up at the camera. Crouch told Maxwell that he had been unhappy with the "low budget"–looking album covers on the previous Light LPs. "Light just had cheap album covers," Maxwell said. "And for *Soulfully*, for whoever thought of putting those guys in jumpsuits standing on the railroad tracks thinking it was 'soulful'—well, I don't know *what* they were thinking." As in the videos from Explo '72, the Disciples are dressed in the colorful clothes of the era. Morgan said that by then the band's clothing choices represented an intentional break from the uniforms of dark, matching suits worn by most gospel quartets since the 1950s. "We got to the point, 'Just wear what you want to wear, as long as it's tasteful,'" Morgan said. "We were rebelling against what the church said you had to be. I wore that jumpsuit to death." As early as his time at his father's unusually inclusive church, Andraé had been taught that God "doesn't care what you wear, as long as you come," Morgan said. Once again, Light assigned Bill Cole to produce the album, but the nearly full-page photograph on the back means that no other details—including studio musicians—are noted anywhere. Maxwell recalled that the recording session took place at TTG Studio at 1441 N. McFadden Place in Hollywood. The relatively new studio would, in time, record everybody from Frank Zappa to the Monkees. In addition to the Disciples, the back cover photograph from *The Tonight Show* includes a smiling Bill Maxwell and a second, unidentified, guitarist. Maxwell said that Andraé told him that he does not play keyboards on a single track on *Soulfully*. Keyboardist Clark Gassman, who had worked on *Keep On Singin'*, did some of the arrangements but the other arrangements were charted by various Motown arrangers, including James Anthony Carmichael (no relation to Ralph), all of whom were friends of Sandra through her session work for the label. "The songs are Andraé but the feeling of the music is not really as much Andraé," Maxwell said. "Those are other people's contributions." Crouch's reticence to finish *Soulfully* mirrored his frustration at still not having control over the finished product. Gassman was certainly a talented musician and pianist. But for all of their collective talent, even Carmichael and the other uncredited Motown producers still were not able to—or perhaps were not yet willing to—replicate the sounds Andraé heard when he composed the songs. His frustration over the process—outside producers arranging and recording the instrumental backing by studio musicians that the vocalists would sing over—would manifest with his next project, one he had been quietly composing concurrently with the *Soulfully* sessions.[19]

Maxwell said that the budget for Crouch's Light Records albums was extremely limited, which meant, for instance, that the producers were unable to afford members of the elite West Coast studio musicians known as the Wrecking Crew. Additionally, once the songs were arranged, the unnamed musicians and, later, the Disciples were forced to record them as quickly as possible to keep studio costs low. Andraé told Maxwell that they recorded three songs in quick three-hour segments during the *Soulfully* sessions. "And in three or four sessions, you have all the tracks for an entire album," Maxwell said. "That's the pressure that was put on them." The arrangements mirror a template used by arrangers and producers to spin out completed compositions quickly and seamlessly in the hotbed environment of the various Los Angeles recording studios. With *Soulfully*, Cole's vision was a combination of a primarily white-led West Coast orchestra blended with Black gospel soul vocals to create music with a wide appeal.[20]

Soulfully's Other Message

In retrospect, each of Crouch's albums appears to have an overarching theme or mission, often represented in the choice of title. Both *Take the Message Everywhere* and *Keep On Singin'*, the authors suggest, embody "Songs of Proclamation." *Soulfully*, then, would be "Songs of Liberation." Even the title, *Soulfully*, is indicative of the age. The late 1960s and early 1970s were a time of unprecedented change in America, including the birth of the modern civil rights movement, protests against the war in Vietnam, and the increasing awareness of gender inequality. As a Black man, Andraé, while utterly mission-focused, would have certainly been aware of the ongoing upheaval in race relations, including the rise in African American pride and identity and the adoption of the concept of "soul power" as a shorthand for the Black Power movement. Likewise, this period marks the release of African American theologian James Cone's influential books *Black Theology & Black Power* (1969) and *A Black Theology of Liberation* (1970), two of the first books to articulate theology in a Black social context. Whether Crouch had read these books (or Cone's later *God of the Oppressed* from 1975), they were part of the zeitgeist of the age, at least in some religious circles, heralding an awakening that was permeating the culture, Black and white, and in both the secular and sacred realms of American life.[21]

Through *Black Theology & Black Power* and *A Black Theology of Liberation*, Cone weaves Black poetry, gospel songs, blues, sermons, prayers, Negro spirituals, and a variety of Black cultural codes, immersing readers in the mind of the Black aesthetic and ethos. Cone challenged the status quo within the Christian church, and his message resonated from the pulpits and performance stages of Black America. From the beginning of his ministry, Andraé intentionally worked to reach out to other cultures and other belief systems through his inclusive musical message. Likewise, as an avid radio listener and music consumer, he was keenly aware of the vibrancy of the music of the 1960s and early 1970s coming out of Motown, Stax/Volt, Atlantic, and other labels, which, in a remarkably short time, emerged as a potent emulsifier, bringing together people from diverse backgrounds. More than any gospel artist before him, Crouch explored offering the marketplace of contemporary culture with a multiethnic vision for the Kingdom of God. As a Black artist, he sometimes came under criticism for not more explicitly addressing the issues facing African Americans. The authors contend that a careful reading of *Soulfully*'s lyrics suggests otherwise.[22]

Side I

"Everything Changed"

The album begins with violins, rhythm guitars, and the first of several trumpet blasts heralding another new album. "Everything Changed" is in the key of E♭ major and is heavily orchestrated with Latin-styled percussion and guitar licks throughout. While production values have improved over the Disciples' previous albums, the background vocals, however, are less ambitious than Crouch's earlier arrangements, with mostly basic call-and-response harmonic punches throughout. The prominent chord progression, I–IV–IIIsus4–III–vi–I–IV–IIIsus4–III, and overall arrangement recall the songs of one of Andraé's favorite artists, Steely Dan.

"He Proved His Love to Me"

The slow, Motown-styled power ballad "He Proved His Love to Me" is in D♭ major, again, though it moves to D major. While the song's prominent chord progressions, I–Imajor7–I7–V11–I–IV–I (first inversion) –ii7, echo the musical language of the top funk/soul artists of the time, the vocal unisons and triadic harmonies recall the pop/soul sound of the early 1970s, complete with the lush "ooh's" and the insertion of a string quartet at the break. Theologically, this is another song that directly reflects Andraé's New Testament–based understanding of an intensely personal relationship with Jesus Christ.

"Oh I Need Him"

Morgan is featured on "Oh I Need Him," a second slow ballad, glossily sweetened with harp and strings. The song's common chord progressions (I–iii–vi–iv6–I–II7–ii–v11–ii–V11–I) are reminiscent of the power ballads of the 1970s. While recorded in G on the record, it is published in the Light/Lexicon songbooks in the much more interesting key of E♭ major, which—the authors believe—was Crouch's original key. "Oh I Need Him" builds slowly, with instrumental flourishes that would have sounded at home on a Simon & Garfunkel album.

"Satisfied"

When comparing the *Soulfully* version of "Satisfied" with the version from the Explo '72 video, it's obvious that the live version better captures how Andraé truly conceived the song. Still, the recorded version is bright and lively West Coast soul funk, punctuated by a tight horn section and boosted by more uptempo Latin percussion. The *Soulfully* album version is in B♭ and is based on a standard blues progression but lacks the full-tilt drive and excitement of the Explo '72 performance. The call-and-response lyrics again recall Sly and the Family Stone and refer to Isaiah 53:11—"He shall see the labor of His soul and be satisfied."

"Through It All"

The side ends with "Through It All," the album's highlight and a masterpiece of faith-based songwriting. Performed live, the song strips away the heavy string accompaniment and the hints of Southern gospel vocal stylings. But on *Soulfully*, the background vocals, once again, are relegated to simple supporting "ooh's," even as the arrangement speeds up slightly toward the end. As mentioned earlier, Andraé chose this song title as the name of his biography and the lyrics, detailing his own personal struggles in the faith, have since been adopted by countless performers and listeners.

Side II

"I Come That You Might Have Life"

One of the most overt Motown-styled tributes on the LP, "I Come That You Might Have Life," is fueled by a deep bass groove and soulful guitars. Recorded in E♭ major, the song, laid back and relaxed, once again reveals Crouch's affinity for the silky side of pop music. Here the prominent chord progressions articulate a robust harmonic language: I–I°–ii7–V11–I–ii°–iii7–vi7–ii9–iii7–IV–V–I. As with most of the songs on *Soulfully*, the authors are unsure whether this harmonic evolution comes from Andraé or the producers/arrangers since these are not common chord progressions in the Black church of the 1970s, nor are they progressions Crouch will employ with any regularity in the future. The background vocals are dominated by unisons and the same triadic harmonies that mark much of the music coming from Detroit at the time. It's also one of the songs that is drawn most closely from a specific Bible passage, John 10:10–11 ("The thief does not come except to steal, and to kill, and to destroy. I have come that they may have life, and that they might have it more abundantly.")

"You Don't Know What You're Missing"

Few of the songs in Andraé's catalogue sound more of their time than "You Don't Know What You're Missing," with its very 1970s pop music–framed introduction and even the odd sitar riff. It quickly resolves into more of a standard pop/soul tune, driven by bluesy, pronounced guitar solos and funky horn charts. "You Don't Know" features common chord progressions: I–V–V/III–V/vi–I–IV–I–ii–IV–II–V, is in D♭ major again, and sounds curiously unfinished—more of a riff than a completed, fully realized song.

"Try Me One More Time"

One of the more offbeat songs on *Soulfully*, "Try Me One More Time," suggests a West Coast–influenced interpretation of the hit "Tell Me Something Good" by Chaka Khan and Rufus from 1974. Performed in F major, with an opening chromaticism introduction, the overall Motown feel and the soulful, close-harmony backing vocals enliven the almost novelty nature of the verses before the whole thing resolves, unexpectedly, into a flute solo.

"Leave the Devil Alone"

Another song that would have been a novelty number in lesser hands, "Leave the Devil Alone," with its straightforward blues progressions, ranges from preachy to whimsical in the lyrics as Andraé sings and preaches a cautionary tale about getting too involved with the demonic: "You better leave him alone!" It's slow and funky and with still more of the unisons and triadic harmonies, it sounds less like the Disciples and more like the "B"-side of a song by the Tower of Power or Rufus.[23]

"It Won't Be Long"

The other most enduring cut on *Soulfully*, "It Won't be Long," was inspired by the prominent place in the Jesus Movement given to Hal Lindsey's apocalyptic book of the "end times," *The Late Great Planet Earth*, first published in 1970. The arrangers return to D♭ major to deliver this smooth and otherworldly reflection on the Second Coming, spiced with Asian pentatonic influences and what may be the angular sound of a sitar. The chord progression in this song understandably reflects a fairly standard 1970s Motown formula (since the unnamed arrangers worked extensively with Motown artists): iii7–vi7–ii–ii7 (3rd inversion) –V (first inversion)–IV–I. And, again, these are not the chord progressions normally heard in the Black Church from this era.

Rather than being alarming or accusatory, the lyrics ("Count the years as months, count the months as weeks, count the weeks as days . . .") are performed in a slow and dreamy vocalese, buoyed by a gentle string accompaniment. The orchestration on "It Won't Be Long" slowly swells until Crouch begins preaching about the prospects of Christ's momentary return: "We'll be going home . . . ."[24]

Soulfully as Liturgy

As Andraé himself asserted on numerous occasions, his heart never departed from the church, leading the authors to suggest that, intentionally or not, *Soulfully*'s songs mirror format of a Black church worship service or a contemporary liturgy within a pop/gospel context:

Introit: "Everything Has Changed"

Songs of Love and Contentment: "He Proved His Love to Me," "Oh I Need Him," and "Satisfied"

Song of Testimony: "Through It All"

Songs of Exhortation: "I Came That You Might Have Life" and "You Don't Know What You're Missing"

Songs of Lament and Warning: "Try Me One More Time" and "Leave the Devil Alone"

Benediction/Sending Song: "It Won't Be Long"

On *Soulfully*, Crouch's songs are sermons, his hymns are homilies, and the LP itself is a subtle symphony of liberation in several movements. Even the album title, a subtle reference to this broader view, merges the Protestant church concept of the "soul" with the Black liberation concept of "soul" as a defining element of the African American experience.

Response to *Soulfully*

More than fifty years later, *Soulfully* contains several memorable compositions, songs that are still sung and performed in concerts and in churches even today. Even so, throughout the songs on *Soulfully*, one notable, somewhat puzzling, aspect remains. As noted above, the background vocals, something that Crouch had labored over on previous albums to create imaginative, innovative arrangements, sound almost generic; they're pleasant but unremarkable. The superior quality of the Disciples' voices is still present, but the arrangements resemble those of any given pop or soul album from the era. According to Maxwell, that is an accurate assessment of the situation. At one point in late summer 1972, toward the end of the mixing process for *Soulfully*—and while Maxwell was still living with Andraé—his mother Catherine came back to the guesthouse and said, "Andraé, Bill Cole is at the studio. They're mixing *Soulfully* without you since you haven't shown up yet." According to Maxwell, Andraé said, "I can't let them mix this without me." But ultimately, Cole and the contract arrangers took the vocals, only some of which were finished to Andraé's exacting standards, and in a few days mixed and combined them with the already recorded instrumental tracks. "That became a tendency of Andraé later in life," Maxwell told Bachmann, "he never wanted to finish any record he had started. You'd have to drag him into the studio. Or you'd be getting ready to master it and he'd beg you to let him redo his vocals—and then he'd spend another month on it."[25]

As with *Keep On Singin'*, it is difficult to know how well *Soulfully* actually sold. As noted earlier, *Billboard* did not begin its Gospel LP charts until a year after *Soulfully* was released in late fall 1972. *Keep On Singin'* (or the 45 "I Don't Know Why Jesus Loved Me" LS 616—the listing changes... sometimes *both* appear on the charts) began appearing on November 3, 1973. *Soulfully*'s first appearance is three *years* later, at #29 on September 6, 1975. It appears at #27 the following week, then drops off the chart. It is tempting to assume that *Soulfully* did not receive the promotional push from Light Records that *Keep On Singin'* received, perhaps because of its delayed release or other reasons. But Hazzard said that at least some of "blame" for that lack of success on the charts may also be due to Andraé and the Disciples' popularity as a touring band. After each concert, the Disciples (and touring crew) would dutifully troop out to the lobby or nave to talk to attendees—and sell copies of the latest LPs. "Under the bus, we had boxes and boxes of boxes of *Soulfully* and *Just Andraé* and they would sell out," she said. "We would bring tons of albums and we would come off tour with nothing. There'd be nothing left, especially after the festivals." Albums purchased by the artists—and not sold through the standard record stores—did not appear on the *Billboard*, *Record World*, or *Cash Box* charts, she said. "He was selling hand-over-fist, I can tell you that," she recalled. "The whole time we were traveling on the tour bus, you have the equipment, you have the luggage, and you have Andraé's records." An article on the same topic in a July 1973 issue of *Billboard* notes that gospel singers in particular "have long been regarded as the most capable of salesmen, on and off the stage." Artists "peddle thousands of albums on every road venture," which meant accurate tallies of sales for record charts *Billboard* was invariably problematic.[26]

Despite Andraé's lack of involvement in the instrumental accompaniment and arrangements, *Soulfully* is still somewhat closer to what was to become the signature Andraé Crouch sound than its predecessors. It is beloved by many, including Mark Allan Powell, who cites the "tremendous musical growth" of the Disciples, claims that "Oh I Need Him" is as "soulful as anything Otis Redding or Sam Cooke did," and calls "It Won't Be Long" "hauntingly beautiful." Claudrena Harold writes that the album "remained on the cutting edge of gospel music" and praised the "psychedelic soul" found in "Satisfied" and "Leave the Devil Alone." *The 100 Greatest Albums in Christian Music* ranked the album at #59 and called "Through It All" and "It Won't Be Long" "among the best loved and most covered in his catalog." While Bachmann, in naming

Soulfully as #52 in his list of the "100 Greatest CCM Albums of the '70s," writes that it "raised the bar" and called it a "potent mix of Black gospel and Jesus Music."[27]

Andraé's Growing Dissatisfaction

But in an interview several years later with Maxwell, Andraé's closest musical confidant and producer, Bachmann writes that the frustrations Crouch had been feeling with the recording process had risen to the surface with *Soulfully*. According to Maxwell:

> I think it's one of the worst records Andraé ever did. I thought it was so off-point to who he was. And so did he. It was Andraé's attempt to break free of the bubblegum production that he'd had with *Take the Message Everywhere* and *Keep On Singin'*. And so they kind of turned it into Motown. They took songs like "Through It All" and "It Won't Be Long" and didn't really do them the way Andraé did them. For me, they kind of missed the meat of what the songs were. I thought *Soulfully* just totally missed it. But he let it happen.

Maxwell said that Light Records had been happy with *Take the Message Everywhere* and *Keep On Singin'*, in part, because both *were* so "white friendly." The songs on *Soulfully* were still in the "lighter" *Keep On Singin'*, Fifth Dimension vein. "Andraé wanted [the music] to be more attractive to pop music, to Black music," Maxwell said, "but it didn't fit as much because it still wasn't Andraé."[28]

Longtime singer and friend Hazzard said that Crouch was, indeed, "upset" with Light Records' heavy-handed approach to production. "He was working on *Soulfully*, but that's when he got mad and worked on *Just Andraé*," she said. "He said, 'I'm going to do my own stuff, I can do my own stuff.'" During this period, Andraé also produced the first recording with Hazzard's group, Sweet Spirit, at CAM Sound Studio in Oklahoma City. Maxwell said that Crouch had unexpectedly become part owner of the studio through an unusual business arrangement with a previous associate. "Andraé just flew all of us and the Disciples to Oklahoma City," Hazzard said. CAM, later owned by former Disciple Sherman Andrus, had quickly become a hub of recording activity for Andrus and Crouch's new Shalom label, releasing albums by Sweet Spirit, Pam Thum, the Don DeGrate Delegation, Andrus himself, and others. "This was in 1972," Hazzard recalled. "We had all of the Sonlight musicians, they played everything on the album. We stayed in Oklahoma City for two weeks. Sweet Spirit also did some dates in Oklahoma with Andraé." Sweet Spirit, which also included Bea Carr, Beverly Coy, and Gloria Dolvin, recorded four of Crouch's songs during that span, "Take Me Back," "I Just Wanna Thank You," "Bless His Holy Name," and "If Ever," well before any of them appeared on later Disciples albums. The liner notes credit Sandra and Andraé Crouch as producers, although Maxwell worked on it as well. For Maxwell, it was the beginning of a long career in production. "Well, in a way, Andraé kind of turned it over to me," Maxwell said, "and that's when I felt like the Lord showed me how this worked." Initially overwhelmed by the array of phasers, levers, and buttons on the board, he soon realized that each button took a portion of the music from one place to another. "All of a sudden," he said, "I learned the whole basic things of the board in about a day." The LP also included songs by Harlan Rogers, Hadley Hockensmith, Edwin Hawkins, and Walter Hawkins. Hazzard was present in the studio when Andraé composed "Take Me Back":

> I remember he said, "OK, you all come by the piano and sing this. I don't have the chorus yet." He would start playing it and that's how we did it. He would say, "OK, you guys remember your parts." We'd go to a concert and he'd say, "This is a new song. We just tried it out last night." He'd turn to us and say, "They might not know all the words, but I want you guys to try it." And he had it in his memory and he would play it like he'd been playing it for ten years and we'd just flow with it. That's what I remember about "Take Me Back."[29]

The Impact

Looking back, the songs of *Soulfully* will sound better, more emphatic and energetic—or at least more like what Crouch had originally intended—in the concerts and live recordings still to come. That did not keep many of the songs from having an enduring, transformative impact on their listeners. Legendary gospel music composer Bill Gaither said that whenever he is asked to name his "favorite" gospel song, "Andraé's song 'Through It All' is almost always the first song that comes to mind." Crouch's music, writes Melinda E. Weekes, "brought Blacks and whites of his generation together—albeit in concert halls—for the first time." And in that, she notes, his "career embodies the musical, social and cultural 'integration' of modern gospel music reflective of the social realities of the 1960s and 1970s." Finally, the Hymnary.org website shows that "Through It All" (copyrighted 1971, a year before the album's actual release) is featured in at least two dozen hymnals in multiple denominations—Black *and* white.[30]

Thedford recalled that for each tour with the Disciples, audiences would spontaneously "adopt" a different song ahead of time—and that would become the group's "signature" song for the duration. Immediately after the release of *Soulfully*, "Through It All" was that song:

> We put together a program for every tour and the program would usually start with whatever "hot" tune was that year, whatever the tour's signature song was. We'd think, "OK, we know as soon as we hit a certain chord, the crowd's just going to go berserk." That would really give us a lot of energy. Soon as you got your audience hooked up on the first note that's played, then it's a cake walk from then on.[31]

> Andraé could not have written the passionate and authentic songs he did without some suffering in his life. His music helped me embrace my suffering. My favorite song of Andraé's is "Through It All," a song of God's faithfulness to take us through the valleys and storms. —Melody Green.[32]

> His pen became the word that erased racial and cultural barriers with the birth of the Jesus Movement in the '70s. No matter your color or denomination, the soundtrack of your church life was Andraé Crouch. —Kirk Franklin[33]

Postscript

But amid the furor over Explo '72 and *The Tonight Show* and in the weeks before their movement-defining performance in Dallas, Andraé Crouch and the Disciples slipped in one additional date. On April 10, 1972, the Disciples participated in a unique "dual" concert in New York's famed Carnegie Hall as part of the "Jesus Joy Festival" sponsored by Maranatha. William David Spencer calls the concert "a watershed moment in East Coast, Jesus Movement history." It also was a significant moment in the careers of Andraé Crouch and the Disciples—though they didn't yet know it. The following sentence appears in the previously mentioned promotional package in *Billboard* magazine on October 14, 1972: "They have recorded five albums for Light Records, one of which is an unbelievable live performance at Carnegie Hall, soon to be released." But at the time of the writing, the Disciples had only released three LPs (*Take the Message Everywhere*, *Keep On Singin'*, and the just-released

Soulfully). *Just Andraé* would be released shortly thereafter, but the album recorded at Carnegie Hall—actually recorded *before* both *Soulfully* and *Just Andraé*—was still more than a year and a half away. And it, more so than *Soulfully* or even *Just Andraé*, would cement the group's stature far beyond their original base in the Jesus Movement.[34]

NOTES

1. Richard Ostling, "The Alternative Jesus: Psychedelic Christ," *Time*, June 21, 1971, 56–60, 63.
2. Paul Baker, *Contemporary Christian Music: Where It Came From, What It Is, Where It's Going* (Westchester, IL: Crossway Books, 1985), 53–55; Larry Eskridge, *God's Forever Family: The Jesus People Movement in America* (New York: Oxford University Press, 2013), 169–174; Paul Eshleman, *The Explo Story: A Plan to Save the World* (Glendale, CA: GL Regal Books, 1972); "Monster CCI Talent Windup," *Billboard*, May 27, 1972, 8.
3. Don Cusic, ed., *Encyclopedia of Christian Music, Pop, Rock and Worship* (Westport, CT: Greenwood Press, 2009), 179; Jack Harnish, "'Soon and Very Soon' . . . He's Gone to Meet the King," *Morning Memo*, January 11, 2015, https://www.jackharnish.wordpress/com/2015/01/11/soon-and-very-soon -hes-gone-to-meet-the-king; John Haines, "The Emergence of Jesus Rock: On Taming the 'African Beat,'" *Black Music Research Journal*, no. 2 (Fall 2011): 242; Dani Magee, "Andraé Crouch and the Disciples Are Coming," *Denton Record-Chronicle*, March 17, 1972, 23.
4. Various artists, *Jesus Sound Explosion: Recorded Live at Explo 72* (Campus Crusade for Christ International, 1972); Eskridge, *God's Forever Family*, 173–178.
5. Eskridge, *God's Forever Family*, 173–174; Fletch Wiley, personal correspondence with the authors, August 9, 2022; Bili Thedford, personal correspondence with the authors, August 13, 2022; Phyllis St. James, personal correspondence with the authors, August 27, 2022. Note: The version of the Disciples who took the stage during Explo '72 was already an extremely polished and tight ensemble. The nonstop touring leading up to Dallas had included a strenuous twelve-date tour of Sweden from April 18 to 30, sponsored by the new Scandinavian International Entertainment & Music AB—and the Disciples' tour was the company's first major undertaking. Andraé and the Disciples were one of the few gospel groups who were distributed in Sweden on the new Pilot label. Kjell E. Genberg, "Sweden," *Billboard*, April 29, 1972, 60.
6. Brian Vachon, *A Time to Be Born* (Englewood Cliffs, NJ: Prentice-Hall, 1972), 70–71, 118–119; "Satisfied" by Andraé Crouch, Lexicon Music, Inc., courtesy of Capitol CMG.
7. David W. Stowe, *No Sympathy for the Devil* (Chapel Hill: University of North Carolina Press, 2011), 87; Mark Allan Powell, *Encyclopedia of Contemporary*

Christian Music (Peabody, MA: Hendrickson Publishers, 2002), 211; Wes Yoder, interview with the authors, September 22, 2022.

8. Bili Thedford, interview with the authors, March 18, 2021; Perry Morgan, interview with the authors, March 18, 2019.

9. Bill Maxwell, interview with the authors, May 18, 2019; Fletch Wiley, interview with the authors, October 20, 2020.

10. Bill Maxwell, interview with the authors, May 18, 2019; Scott K. Fish, "Bill Maxwell: A Gift of Music," *Modern Drummer*, August 1983, original clipping in the authors' possession; Hadley Hockensmith, interview with the authors, October 1, 2020; Fletch Wiley, interview with the authors, October 20, 2020; Fletch Wiley, interview with the authors, November 26, 2020.

11. Various artists, *Jesus Sound Explosion: Recorded Live at Explo '72*, Campus Crusade for Christ International; "10 California Religious Labels United in Marketing Venture," *Billboard*, January 13, 1973, 3; Eskridge, *God's Forever Family*, 177.

12. Stowe, *No Sympathy for the Devil*, 91

13. Baker, *Contemporary Christian Music*, 55; Haines, "The Experience of Jesus Rock," 248–249; Andrew Mall, *God Rock, Inc.: The Business of Niche Music* (Oakland: University of California Press, 2021), 50; Marshall Terrill, *The Jesus Movement* (Rocklin, CA: K-Love Books, 2021), 34–39.

14. Bili Thedford, interview with the authors, March 18, 2021; Kathy Hazzard, interview with the authors, August 19, 2021; Cusic, *Encyclopedia of Christian Music, Pop, Rock and Worship*, 182, 185.

15. "Rallying for Jesus: 80,000 Jam Dallas for a Crusade Called Explo '72," *Life*, June 30, 1972, 40–45; Edward B. Fiske, "A 'Religious Woodstock' Draws 75,000," *New York Times*, June 16, 1972, 1, 29; Richard Quebedeaux, *I Found It! The Story of Bill Bright and Campus Crusade* (San Francisco: Harper & Row, 1979), 160–163; Haines, "The Experience of Jesus Rock," 244; Terrill, *The Jesus Music*, 35; Wes Yoder, interview with the authors, September 22, 2021.

16. Hadley Hockensmith, interview with the authors, October 17, 2020; Bill Maxwell, interview with the authors, May 18, 2019; Bill Maxwell, quoted in Scott Bachmann, "100 Greatest CCM Albums of the '70s," http://greatest70 salbums.blogspot.com/2016/02/52-soulfully-by-andrae-crouch-disciples.html; Bil Carpenter, quoted in Gospel flava.com, www.gospelflava.com/articles/johnn ycarson.html.

17. "Spotlight . . . on the Light Label": "America's Number One Soul Group," "LEXICON/LIGHT Expands in Publishing," "Lexicon/Light Composers," "Lexicon Music: Carmichael's Baby," *Billboard*, October 14, 1972, W-7, W-10, W-12, W-14, W-17.

18. *Soulfully* (Light Records LS-5581), "New LP/Tape Releases," *Billboard* (November 11, 1972),70: Bill Maxwell, quoted in Bachmann, "100 Greatest CCM Albums of the '70s"; Bill Maxwell, interview with the authors, September 14, 2022.

19. Perry Morgan, interview with the authors, May 18, 2019; Bill Maxwell, interview with the authors, May 18, 2019; Bill Maxwell, interview with the authors, October 20, 2022; Paul Verna, "From Auto Sound to Infrasound, Hidley's Career Has Been Built on Breakthroughs," *Billboard*, July 1, 1995, 101.

20. See Allan Slutsky and James Jamerson, *Standing in the Shadows of Motown: The Life and Music of Legendary Bassist James Jamerson* (Milwaukee: Hal Leonard Books, 1989), for a good description on studio practices during this era. See also the 2002 documentary by the same name. Bill Maxwell, interview with the authors, October 20, 2022.

21. "Leave the Devil Alone" by Andraé Crouch, Lexicon Music, Inc., courtesy of Capitol CMG.

22. "It Won't Be Long" by Andraé Crouch, Lexicon Music, Inc., courtesy of Capitol CMG.

23. See James Cone, *Black Theology & Black Power* (Maryknoll, NY: Orbis Books, 1969); Cone, *A Black Theology of Liberation* (Maryknoll, NY: Orbis Books, 1970).

24. James Cone, *God of the Oppressed*, rev. ed. (Maryknoll, NY: Orbis Books, 1997), 5.

25. Bachmann, "100 Greatest CCM Albums of the '70s"; Bill Maxwell, interview with the authors, September 14, 2022.

26. "Best-Selling Gospel LPs," *Soulfully*, Andraé Crouch and the Disciples, *Billboard*, September 6, 1975, 56; "Best-Selling Gospel LPs," *Soulfully*, Andraé Crouch and the Disciples, *Billboard*, October 4, 1975, 55; Kathy Hazzard, interview with the authors, September 6, 2022; "Gospel LP's Flood Mkt.," *Billboard*, July 7, 1973, 38.

27. Powell, *Encyclopedia of Contemporary Christian Music*, 21; Claudrena N. Harold, *When Sunday Comes: Gospel Music in the Soul and Hip Hop Eras* (Urbana: University of Illinois Press, 2020), 49; Bachmann, "100 Greatest CCM Albums of the '70s"; *The Greatest Albums in Christian Music* (Eugene, OR: Harvest House, 2001), 178–179.

28. Bachmann, "100 Greatest CCM Albums of the '70s."

29. Kathy Hazzard, interview with the authors, September 6, 2022; https://www .discogs.com/release/2364394-Sweet-Spirit; https://www.discogs/com/label /202626-Shalom-Records-3; Bill Maxwell, interview with the authors, September 14, 2022.

30. https://www.rambomcguire.com/news/2015/6/11/remembering-and rae-crouch; Melinda E. Weekes, "This House, This Music: Exploring the Interdependent Interpretive Relationship Between the Contemporary Black Church and Contemporary Gospel Music," *Black Music Research Journal* 25, no. 1–2 (Spring–Fall, 2005): 47; hymnary.org/hymn; Harold, *When Sunday Comes*, 49.

31. Bili Thedford, interview with the authors, March 18, 2021.

32. Melody Green, "Keith Green's Wife Remembers Andraé Crouch," *Charisma* magazine, January 14, 2015, https://charismamag.com/music/keith-green-s -wife-remembers-andrae-Crouch.

33. Kirk Franklin, "Andraé Crouch: The Man Who Raised the Goal," https://www
/patheos/com/blogs/kirkfranklin/2015/01/Andraé-crouch-the-man-who-rai
sed-the-goal/.

34. William David Spencer, "Afterword," in *Berkeley Street Theatre: How
Improvisation and Street Theater Emerged as a Christian Outreach to the Culture
of the Time*, ed. Jeanne C. DeFazio (Eugene, OR: WIPF & Stock, 2017), 112;
"America's Number One Soul Group," *Billboard*, October 14, 1972, W-14;
Baker, *Contemporary Christian Music*, 55–56.

7
Just Andraé

At some point, during the *Soulfully* sessions, Light Records suggested that Andraé record a solo album accompanying himself on the piano. Bill Maxwell said that Crouch, who was chafing over the arrangements and production methods on the previous LPs, quickly agreed. "Light could then release an album that didn't cost much and they could sell a lot of copies," Maxwell recalled. "But then Andraé threw their plans upside down when he brought Sonlight in. So Light made us a terrible deal—I think they paid the musicians $150 each." Crouch did retain the original concept of recording an album's worth highly personal songs.[1]

With *Just Andraé*, Crouch had, for the first time, virtual autonomy in the studio. Liberated from "outside" producers, he introduced the beginnings of one of the defining elements of his music—the full integration and reimagining of the contribution of a series of astonishing female vocalists, both as background singers and as featured soloists. Side by side with his ability to compose timeless songs, Andraé's ability to write for, arrange for, and utilize background singers in new and creative ways is one of the great hallmarks of his musical genius.

Sonlight Waits

Immediately following Explo '72, however, the members of Sonlight had not yet fully joined the Disciples. Fletch Wiley said some months elapsed, though Maxwell contacted Andraé regularly throughout late 1972 and early 1973. "Bill Maxwell, he's the ultimate schmoozer," Wiley said. "You want to be his friend and he's everybody's friend." In March 1973, the group drove to Southern California in an old Cadillac limo (said to have once belonged to

Elvis) to perform in a tent revival with old school evangelist R. W. Schambach in Santa Ana. "We then met with Andraé and did a demo in Hollywood for Lamb & Lion Records, Pat Boone's label," Wiley said. "Nothing happened with it."[2]

For Maxwell, fresh off being thrown into the fire of *The Tonight Show with Johnny Carson* after only a handful of frenzied rehearsals, *Just Andraé* (along with the *Sweet Spirit* LP) is the starting point of one of the most significant musical collaborations in gospel music history. For all the many compositional treasures in his previous releases, the Crouch legacy begins here.

Maxwell, who had earlier temporarily moved in with Andraé awaiting the rest of his family, said that Crouch constantly auditioned new songs with his house guest. "He would say, 'Listen,' and he would ask me to help him go over things," Maxwell recalled. "It was the start of us, and we started working together. We were friends and he trusted me. I'm just listed as the 'drummer' on *Just Andraé* but I consider that the start of our relationship."[3]

Wiley's role in the creative songwriting process, beginning with *Just Andraé*, was equally unpredictable. Wiley would be invited to the small guesthouse and Crouch would play him a song he was in the process of composing as well. One of the first was "You Ain't Livin' (Until You've Met the Savior)." "He'd play it and I'd write stuff down," Wiley recalled:

> I'd say, "Play it again." He would. We'd repeat the process three times. Then I'd look at my little chord things and I'd say, "Andraé, you just played that song three completely different ways. Which one do you want?" And he'd say, "Really? I didn't know that."

Each time, Andraé would play Wiley the "essence" of the song—but would substitute more and more complex chords and changes with each subsequent rendition. "And he was doing it off the top of his head," Wiley said. "So I'd finally say, 'Well, I'm just going to put what I think you mean and we'll do that. And then if you want something else, we can do that, too.' And that's what we'd go to the studio with." Once in the studio, Wiley also contributed many of *Just Andraé*'s basic rhythm track arrangements.[4]

But there was one last piece of unfinished business before the partnership could officially begin. Andraé wanted Sonlight to meet him at the July 1972 Full Gospel Businessmen's Fellowship International convention in San Francisco. Among the speakers to the crowd of 6,000 people were evangelists Kathryn Kuhlman and Rex Humbard. "It was a wild, charismatic, Pentecostal time," Wiley recalled. *Christianity Today* reported of the event that Crouch and the Disciples "moved the crowds to loud applause and set a few dancing in the joy of the Spirit."[5]

Accompanying Andraé, Sandra Crouch, Bili Thedford, Perry Morgan, and Danniebelle Hall in San Francisco were members of the band that had been performing with him live, off and on, for the past two years. "We knew we were going to fly to Hawaii the following week," Wiley said, "and they were not." Ultimately, it was Wiley who was deputized to "spill the beans" to the previous band members:

> I ended up letting them know that they were fired. I fired the old band and I felt terrible. Andraé is one of these non-confrontational guys. We knew them, and I thought it was horrible. The other band went to Andraé and said, "What's the deal, man?" The next week, we flew to Hawaii with Harlan, Bill, and Hadley and myself and started to be his band in 1972.

After the dates in Honolulu, Wiley returned to Dallas in August and drove his '65 Thunderbird (with no reverse gear) with his wife Kathryn and baby Gabriel to Los Angeles, where they found a small apartment in North Hollywood. Almost immediately upon arrival, the Wileys were invited to the home of Pastor Benjamin and Catherine Crouch for supper. Andraé, who lived in the small house behind his parents' house, was also present. According to Wiley, an uncomfortable conversation with Catherine, who served as Andraé's paymaster at the time, ensued:

Catherine: "Andraé, I understand why you have to have a drummer and a
   guitar player. But why do you have to have this horn player?"
Andraé: "Mama, write the check."[6]

Preparing and Composing *Just Andraé*

Thus began an odd season for the Disciples. As Maxwell noted earlier, Andraé had lost interest in *Soulfully* and was instead touring, workshopping, and occasionally recording with the former members of Sonlight, and the three female singers (Danniebelle Hall, Paula Clarin, and Phyllis St. James née Swisher) he had worked with before, but—initially—not Thedford or Morgan. That was because, Maxwell said, the project was originally envisioned as a "solo album" and that Crouch's irregular recording sessions were done "as quickly and cheaply as possible." Thedford also said that the project was never designed to be a "Disciples" album: "It was just too far out." Wiley remembered the *Just Andraé* sessions themselves as being piecemeal at best. "It was sort of a cobbled-together recording that we did on our own," he said. "*Just Andraé* was more like, 'Let's go on and cut some tracks and we'll just add stuff as we need it.'" But even in the midst of working on the two albums simultaneously, Wiley said the Disciples continued their rigorous touring schedule, in part to capitalize on their recent national media exposure. "We'd be gone at least a week and a half, two weeks a month, sometimes much longer," he said. "That was all of '72 and right into '73—we'd travel."[7]

Andraé Crouch and the Disciples were the label's best-selling artists, so when Andraé showed up with the tapes for another album, particularly one that had been recorded so cheaply, Ralph Carmichael must have been pleased. *Just Andraé* was released in late 1972, hard on the heels of *Soulfully*. At the time, multiple releases by the same artist were not uncommon in popular music. (Creedence Clearwater Revival released *three* hit albums in 1969: *Bayou Country*, *Green River*, and *Willy and the Poor Boys*.)[8]

With the soft-focus matte-finish color cover photograph of Crouch staring wistfully off-camera—but *without* the other Disciples present—it's clear that *Just Andraé* will be different. The back cover features the song list, musician and vocal credits, a beguiling photograph of a very young Sandra and Andraé, and a lengthy letter signed "Mom and Dad." The letter from Benjamin Sr. and Catherine sweetly recaps Andraé and Sandra's musical lives in a few paragraphs and expresses their joy that Sandra had joined the Disciples. It also notes that the group had performed in thirty-two countries over the past two and half years and gives their approval of their son's decision to go it alone with *Just Andraé*. Toward the end, someone (probably Catherine) admonishes Andraé and Sandra to eat right while on the road. The "letter" ends with their prayerful blessing aimed specifically to Andraé:

> Remember, that we love you but more than that we love the God who gave you to us. He has given you a very special gift, that of being able to communicate His love through music. We pray that you remember that blessings are given so that you may again give to others. Your giving in music will bring a song to many a sad heart, a smile to many a troubled face, and hope to many who have lost their way. Praise God from Whom all blessings flow!

Under the list of instrumentalists, the names begin with "Just Andraé (with a little help from his friends: instrumental backgrounds by Sonlight): Fletch

Wiley (horns, flute), Hadley Hockensmith (guitar, bass), Harlan Rogers (organ), Bill Maxwell (drums, percussion), and Sandra Crouch (tambourine and conga drums)." This list is followed by "Vocal backgrounds: Danniebelle Hall, Paula Clarin, Phyllis Swisher and Sandra Crouch."

The credits also list Bill Cole as the producer and Steve Maslow as engineer, with the recording sessions in Abbey Sound Ltd. at 5505 Melrose Avenue in Hollywood. Maslow was at the beginnings of a career that would see him work on a number of gold records, as well as dozens of major motion pictures as a sound engineer, earning three Oscars for Best Sound. Abbey Sound Ltd. had originally been Decca Studios in the 1940s and 1950s (Peggy Lee and the Stan Kenton Orchestra, among others recorded there) before closing. It only operated a few years as Abbey Sound before being bought by Richard Perry and Howard Steele, who transformed it into the popular Studio 55 (Diana Ross, Bob Seger, Stevie Nicks, among many others). Wiley remembered that, at the time, Abbey was both "very stark" and "very cheap." "Which I don't mind because you get a lot more done when people are not playing videogames or having a catered lunch," he said. "So we did it pretty quick, I think. [Andraé] was a writing machine."[9]

Despite having Cole listed as producer, Maxwell, who was at every session, said that Andraé actually "ran" the recording sessions. "Andraé wanted to do an album that showed his versatility," Maxwell recalled:

> He liked different things, so he would do "God Loves the Country People," which was a totally absurd kind of thing for what you would traditionally hear. Then he would do a hymn, like "Bless the Lord Oh My Soul." It was kind of a mishmash of different things—but it was him. It was him being creative. And it was really his first time trying to do things on his own in the studio.[10]

Like Maxwell, Hockensmith had by this time played numerous concerts with the Disciples and had seen Andraé's genius firsthand. He too recalled that the actual recording sessions were loosely structured, highly creative, and always interactive. Crouch would arrive and play his latest composition for whomever he had called to join him in the studio that day. "And we would just write whatever chart we wanted," Hockensmith said. "It's almost like Nashville, except some of the guys weren't using the number system. I was, because that's how I learned how to do it." On later projects, Harlan Rogers or another arranger would create chord charts for the musicians. "But Andraé, he covers the piano so well that we could pretty much hear how this song was supposed to go just by hearing him play it," Hockensmith said. While the musicians enjoyed a great deal of improvisational freedom, Wiley added that the supporting vocalists typically arrived already well rehearsed. "I don't think we ever rehearsed," Wiley said. "He'd just play something onstage and we'd figure it out, figure out what to play," he said."[11]

Maxwell and Hockensmith both said that Crouch often denigrated his piano-playing skills in the studio, though both musicians strongly disagreed with his assessment. Maxwell said Crouch "tried very hard" to "squirrel out" of playing piano on their recordings. "But really, it was Andraé's gift."[12]

Maxwell often called Andraé a "genius." "I don't use that word lightly in music," Maxwell said. "He is the only composer that I've ever worked with who would get everything at once: melody, harmony, and lyrics. Instantly." Crouch's memory for people wasn't nearly as strong, but according to Maxwell he rarely forgot a song. The Hadley Hockensmith composition "In Remembrance" from *Just Andraé* was never a staple of Disciples concerts, perhaps because the song is filled with a series of challenging, complicated chord changes in the key of E major. A few years before Crouch's untimely passing in 2015, Maxwell said he encountered Crouch on the road. "Andraé sat down and played that song and had every chord right and remembered every word," Maxwell said. "He remembered everything musically."[13]

The inclusion of "In Remembrance" on *Just Andraé* was one of the highlights of Hockensmith's tenure with the Disciples. "I was extremely flattered that Andraé even thought about recording the song," he said. "In Remembrance" had originally appeared as one of the songs on the lone *Sonlight* LP and Andraé asked Rogers to play the piano. Both versions are in the guitar key of E, which may explain why Rogers was on the keyboards instead of Crouch, who (as referenced earlier) preferred to compose and perform in other keys. Wiley was also asked to contribute what Hockensmith called a "beautiful" flugelhorn part:

> And it captured the serene kind of quality that I imagined when I wrote the song. It has just a flowing smoothness about it. You don't want anything bombastic when you're giving your sensitive testimony because in that song I loosely referred to the time when I tried to take my own life. I had reached a real rock-bottom situation—and Andraé sang it beautifully. When I first heard his vocal, I thought, "Man, I wish I could have sung it that good.[14]

Chords and Colors

Hockensmith said that among the revelations of touring and recording with Crouch was that Andraé would sometimes say that a certain song sounded "too dark" in a certain key. "He would see it as like light and dark," Hockensmith said. "He would instead say *colors*—maybe one key would be a softer color or another one would be a brighter color." On some occasions in the studio, Crouch would have the musicians play the same song in two different keys. Andraé would listen and say, "This sounds too dark in this key. I want to go with the other key." This ability to intuit what "worked" in a song, Hockensmith said, was another one of Crouch's musical gifts:

> That was Andraé. He played very naturally. He didn't try to memorize a song a certain way and he liked to take liberties. And so even though we had a basic idea of what the chord was supposed to be, he might change it. Sometimes if we could hear it in time, we would go with him. But even if we did, it still sounded great because he was playing with authority and it just—somehow—worked.[15]

Another aspect of Crouch's "natural" ability was in the creation of the chords he used to achieve those "colors." On later albums, pianist Larry Muhoberac was among the musicians who handled the arranging duties. Maxwell said that Muhoberac, who had served as an accompanist for Elvis Presley, said that there were no names for some of the chords Andraé used. "He'd say, 'Those are nine-note chords,'" Maxwell recalled. "'It's this over that over this with this.' It was astounding." The opening chord progression for "If Heaven Was Never Promised to Me" from *Just Andraé* is a good example, moving in a succession with a very sophisticated pitch collection. The song opens with a series of ii7–V7–I–vi7 progressions, and it almost feels improvised as if Crouch was working with jazz musicians in a late-night jam session. "He was unparalleled," Maxwell said. "But one of the problems we had with Andraé was that he was totally free, so he might play 'If Heaven Was Never Promised' one time—and the next time he's not going to play it the same way."[16]

That spirit of improvisation meant that in concert all musicians and singers had to be continually on the alert. Hockensmith said that Crouch would rarely announce what song he was going to perform. "He might just go into a song and just count on us to be there," Hockensmith said. "And it might be real fast like a gospel vamp or something and we immediately had to decipher the key. He kept it exciting. He was fun."[17]

Another song that Hockensmith said that he has vivid memories of is "That's What It's All About," which he considers a "masterpiece." Based on the "love chapter" in the New Testament, I Corinthians 13, Andraé recites a portion of the chapter in the song. "Beautiful chorus, beautiful melody, a beautiful thought," Hockensmith said. "The background vocals sounded really magical when they came in on those choruses. And that's what it's all about, children—that's what it's all about. Beautiful." "That's What It's All About" arrived in the studio much as Andraé had originally conceived it. According to Hockensmith, Crouch "pretty much had all the chords together" when he entered the recording booth. "It was not normal for Andraé to come in with the song unwritten," Hockensmith said. "He may have questions like, 'I don't like the form this is in. I feel like I can do better with the form.' And we would all try to be helpful and make suggestions, but—of course—he was always the deciding factor."

Hockensmith said he was equally impressed with "It's Not Just a Story" the first time he heard Andraé play it on the piano for the other musicians. "I love this song because it is so simple," Hockensmith said. It is, he noted, an example of how great music does not have to be overly complex:

> It starts with, "I heard the story of Jesus, it sounds like music to my ears." I probably haven't listened to that song in twenty-five years, but I still remember the lyrics because they're so great and the song meant so much to me. My mother once said, "That's my all-time favorite song. I just love that song." It's an example of how you can write a very simple song with very simple lyrics, one that's fairly simple musically—but it's almost like the perfect song to me.

The depth of Crouch's songwriting was such that when Andraé first introduced the group to the songs that would comprise *Just Andraé*, those present knew that they were somehow special. "They certainly made an impression on me," Hockensmith said. "I knew I was totally blown away. We all were when we first heard Andraé sing. And I think I knew even then that this music is going to live on and on."[18]

The other track on *Just Andraé* not composed by Crouch is his co-composition with Bili Thedford, "What Does Jesus Mean to You." Thedford said religious-themed musicals, such as *Jesus Christ Superstar* and *Godspell*, were popular during this period and more than a year before the *Just Andraé* sessions, he had begun writing a musical as well. Thedford had completed several songs and just before a Disciples performance played "What Does Jesus Mean to You" on the piano for Crouch. "I said, 'Hey man, what do you think of this tune I'm writing for my musical?' and Andraé fell in love with the tune," Thedford said. "So we sat down and worked the whole song out together. He says, 'Why don't we do so and so and so? Why don't you do this and do that? I want to record that tune.' Basically, his music and my lyrics." Thedford said that "What Does Jesus Mean to You" was too "far-out" for an Andraé Crouch and the Disciples album and the song was the only one they composed together. Singer Kathy Hazzard said the simple, direct message of "What Does Jesus Mean to You" made it one of the most effective "witnessing tools" that the group recorded during this period.[19]

The quirkiest song on *Just Andraé* was doubtless "God Loves the Country People." Andraé had dabbled in country & western with "I Can't Tell It All" on the *Teen Challenge Addicts Choir* LP and country stylings and instruments are sprinkled throughout the *Keep On Singin'* album. Hockensmith agreed with Maxwell that one of Crouch's intentions with *Just Andraé* was "to show that you couldn't pigeonhole him in just one style of writing." Hockensmith called "Country People" a "personality" song. But beyond the barnyard sounds, the lyrics had a serious message. "You don't have to be a real successful person to have a great relationship with God," Hockensmith said. "You don't have to be super-educated. That has nothing to do with it." Hazzard said whenever the Disciples performed "Country People," Crouch would turn and face the audience and say, "When in Rome, you do what the Romans do" and make a show of putting on a cowboy's straw hat. "It was hilarious," she said. Phyllis St. James said that that song was popular during the upcoming tour that included multiple stops in Australia and the South Pacific. "It showed the many sides of this great psalmist whose desire was to relate to all people," she said. "It was sweet but humorous." ("God Loves the Country People" later enjoyed an unlikely resurrection in 1980 when Andraé performed it on the popular *Barbara Mandrell & the Mandrell Sisters* television series with the three sisters. A clip from the show is still available on YouTube.)[20]

Fifty years after the release of *Just Andraé*, two songs from the album still generate a lively conversation among musicians and fans who love Crouch's music—the final two tracks on Side II, "Lullaby of the Deceived" and "Bless This Holy Name." If "God Loves Country People" revealed Crouch's lighter side, "Lullaby of the Deceived" tackles a theme usually found on death metal albums. Andraé's short biography, *Through It All*, devotes an entire chapter to a period in his life when he and Sandra both suffered harrowing experiences with what they believed were supernatural entities. Even as he sang "I've Got Confidence" at concerts during the day, Crouch writes that he was tormented by spiritual manifestations at night. At last, after an intense period of prayer and Bible study, Andraé writes that he was able to banish the presence (or presences). The experience prompted Crouch to write two songs, "Leave the Devil Alone" from *Soulfully* and "Lullaby of the Deceived." The liner notes to *Just Andraé* also include a reference to II Timothy 3:13 ("But evil men and seducers shall wax worse and worse, deceiving and being deceived." KJV) by the song title, reflecting an admonition in *Through It All* against Ouija boards and the study of the occult. Maxwell said that Crouch worked in the studio to "put the fear he had into that song." At one point, the studio musicians even blew into their microphones, trying to create a mournful, eerie sound. "Andraé was sincere about it," Maxwell said, "because that was something that creeped him out." While it started "slightly tongue in cheek," Hockensmith said Crouch's message—"don't be deceived by the enemy"—was serious: "'Don't get sidetracked into believing [and] looking for the devil here and there when you're supposed to be looking to the Lord [and] finding the Lord,'" he'd say. "'Seek the Lord and the devil will flee from you.'" At Andraé's request to make his bass guitar to sound more like a tuba, Hockensmith said that he played his bass with a quarter instead of a pick. And while the original plan had been not to include the other Disciples on the LP, Maxwell recalled that Danniebelle Hall and Phyllis St. James (listed as Eyvonne Williams) joined Sandra Crouch, Perry Morgan, and Thedford on background vocals.[21]

As for "Bless His Holy Name" (mistitled as "Bless This Holy Name" on the back album jacket), Maxwell said that "as a friend" he had to convince Crouch to record the song: "Andraé said, 'It's nothing. It's just a little chorus.' I said, 'You really have to try it.' He did—and it became a big song and so he trusted me after that; that maybe I had an ear for what he had." Maxwell also had a hand in the placements of the songs. "You kept ten or eleven songs," he said, "and then you ordered them. You say, 'Where are you going to place this?' 'Lullaby of the Deceived' is a hard one to place. You're not going to start a side with it and you definitely didn't want to end with it. We knew that we had to end Side II with 'Bless This Holy Name.'" Song placement was intentional and carefully considered:

> You want to start the album up a little bit—you don't want to start at the bottom. What flows after this song? You try them. You listen to them. Does

this key match? How long should we wait between this song and the next one? Should it feel quick or should we have it longer or slower? Then you might move one. You keep messing with it until finally it becomes clear [that] you've made your best choice.

Just Andraé: Impact and Influence

In retrospect, *Just Andraé*, like his earlier releases, appears to have a liturgical sequencing, from invitation to benediction. "With Andraé, intentional doesn't mean that he knew what he was going to do," Maxwell said. "It was really show up and see what happens. Obviously, he didn't want it to be the same old church thing. He was bored with that."[22]

Of "Bless His Holy Name," St. James said the actual recording of the song in the studio was one of the most memorable of her long career. As the singers sang, she recalled, the studio was filled with "a visitation of the Holy Spirit that ushered in an atmosphere of true worship." At the same time, "our vocals just melted down and we began to weep before God. I felt a flushing out of myself and an in-filling of the presence of God Oh, bless the Lord, oh my soul!" The vocalists then stopped singing and "moved into worship." St. James said the experience lasted several minutes and the singers needed additional time to "get ourselves together to get back to singing." She said that she knew that "Bless His Holy Name" had received God's "anointing" at that moment:

> It was definitely a physical manifestation of God's presence in that place. You could cut it with a knife. It was just thick and rich. All of the ambience of the room just changed. It was something that I will never forget for the rest of my life.[23]

"I've sung that song in a lot churches, not just with Andraé," Hockensmith said. "Churches that sing hymns will sing that song. It's always powerful. I consider it a classic song of any age."

Unlike many of the songs on *Just Andraé*, Hockensmith said that Crouch played "Bless His Holy Name" straight through on piano at a rehearsal prior to recording it in the studio. "I think he played it for us to get an idea how he would like to record it," Hockensmith said. "We ended up picking a special studio that had a full-on theater organ with all of the big pipes, all of the different sounds. He had Harlan play that organ just to give it more of a grandiose, in-the-presence-of-God kind of feel." (Whitney Recording Studio in

Glendale, where *Keep On Singin'* had been recorded, was one of the few Los Angeles studios that advertised a large pipe organ.)

During this period with the Disciples, Hockensmith said that "rehearsals" typically consisted of a thirty-minute session conducted between the sound check and the start of a concert where Andraé would quickly play through his latest composition for the group and the Disciples would follow along as best they could. "If it sounded really good, we might even try it that night," Hockensmith said. "Otherwise, we would try it the next night." This was possible, of course, because Maxwell, Rogers, Wiley, Hockensmith, and bassist Thedford all possessed "good ears"—which was an essential element since several of the musicians couldn't read music. "So Andraé would play the stuff and it was the kind of chords I loved anyway," Hockensmith said. "So I could easily remember it after the first time he played it. We were fairly quick to catch on."[24]

As the above conversations suggest, *Just Andraé*, more than any previous Andraé Crouch–related album, is a rich tapestry of thought-provoking theology and boundary-testing musical ideas. It is a rich gumbo of musical influences, recorded without the usual financial and promotional constraints of religious record labels in the early 1970s. While it is not truly a solo album, at least how Light Records originally envisioned it, *Just Andraé* is perhaps his most personal album. And the lyrics, save for "You Ain't Livin'," primarily deal with his own struggles.

Race

One of the criticisms leveled against Crouch—and virtually all gospel artists at the time—was that their music failed to address the ongoing racial conflict that had been roiling the United States for decades. Years later, Andraé said that while he was certainly aware of the issues facing African Americans at the time, he felt that his heavily relational message was, at the very least, complementing what the more outspoken Black artists were singing and saying:

> My music was very inspirational and dealt with a person's one-to-one relations with God—and people felt that relationship. I wrote—and I still write about— "me" or "we" rather than saying "You should do this, Mr. White Man" or "You need to feel this way." I say, "We are going to do this" or "take me back." I'd either say, "Join with me, people of God" or "Friend, you should know the Lord" or I would address myself.[25]

For Andraé to spend most of his career recording and touring with a multiethnic Christian community was itself groundbreaking for a racially divided North American Christian church. Crouch believed that racial tensions could be dismantled through the liberating power of the Gospel of Jesus Christ. Some, though not all, Black scholars and artists agreed. "There is no liberation independent of Jesus' past, present, and future coming," James Cone writes. "He is the ground of our present freedom to struggle and the source of our hope that the vision disclosed in our historical fight against oppression will be fully realized in God's future." From the beginning of his career, Crouch was concerned with a person's one-on-one relationship with God. Through his music, wherever he performed, his goal was to change the environment into a space of healing, reconciliation, and love. As a Black man, Crouch knew racial tensions were increasing, yet he chose to focus on the possibilities of what God's Kingdom *could* look like rather than the current politics of race and racism. Andraé wanted to sing the gospel story with a larger imagination and creativity. He wanted his innovative form of gospel music to impact culture. The authors suggest that Crouch believed that if his music was theologically sound, liberating, attractive, and creative, people would hear the gospel of Jesus Christ differently. And, in turn, his audience would respond to America's race challenges by living together in the peace of Jesus Christ.[26]

Just Andraé: The Songs

Side I

"You Ain't Livin'"

In 1971, Marvin Gaye released "Inner City Blues," which speaks directly to the social ills facing Black Americans and includes the line "This ain't livin." As aware as Andraé was of the popular music of the day, it is possible that he heard this song and created his own response to the spiritual challenges facing the country. Crouch makes his lyric personal, not communal: "*You* ain't livin'." This gospel groove overture *jumps* with a gritty old-time syncopated gospel COGIC piano punch. Over a standard pentatonic blues melody, "You Ain't Livin'" features echoes of West Coast R&B styles in a medium-tempo rock groove. The song begins with an opening repetitive groove on the piano in E♭ minor. With the Hammond B3 organ entrance, coupled with the trap set and tambourine, the groove then morphs into a gospel vamp. A soaring electric guitar improvises in dialog with Andraé's piano improvisations. The result is more jam session than standard gospel song. Crouch's compositional genius can be heard in the obvious tropes of sacred music culture seeded throughout. After twenty-one bars, the jam session evolves into the classic "amen" cadence found in the African American church. Black churchgoers immediately heard the meaning and message in the song. Crouch instinctively fuses Black church improvisation, vamps, call-and-responses, *and* tape deck echo effects on his vocals into one seamless whole. The 1970s pop music–styled background female voicings, with the explicit gospel message of salvation and personal experience with Jesus Christ, deftly illume Crouch's quest for musical excellence in both execution and message.[27]

"In Remembrance"

One of the only times Andraé produced a song in E major is in Hadley Hockensmith's composition "In Remembrance." The warm instrumental brass interpolations, snare drum side stick hits on beats 2 and 4, and light guitar voicings do not really "sound" like an Andraé original, but Crouch's vocals are so pristine and priestly, and deliver this testimony so powerfully, that it's hard to think otherwise. Its melodic shape and harmonic language foreshadow Crouch's own song "Jesus Is the Answer" some years later. Hockensmith wisely creates a separate section within the song and breaks the harmonic sameness with colorful chord progressions set to the words "Think of the love that bought salvation's plan." The slight descending chromatism that emphasizes the words "just to redeem worthless men" is itself an extraordinary bit of text painting. Moving toward a cadence, the first half of the phrase suggests a harmonic language descending downward from heaven that metaphorically lifts humanity. The second half of the phrase, moving upward, then elegantly frames the lyrics "back to the Father."

Maxwell said that Light had not wanted Andraé to include "In Remembrance" because the initial concept was for Crouch to record his own songs exclusively. "But Andraé said he loved the song," Maxwell said. "And he said, 'I'm doing it.'"[28]

"That's What It's All About" (I Corinthians 13)

With a creative background vocal arrangement pushed to the forefront, "That's What It's All About" is another nod to the popular 5th Dimension sound, replete with a dramatic call-and-response with the background vocals on the choruses. In the key of D♭ major, the song's harmonic language, characteristic of pop music culture of the time, begins on a IV chord, with the mystical rhythmic pulse of the carousel drawing listeners toward the lyrics. Midway through the song, Crouch recites I Corinthians 13, slowly building until a dramatic tempo shift near the conclusion. Hockensmith called the song a "masterpiece," praising its "beautiful chorus, beautiful melody, beautiful thought" and "magical" background vocals and compared the composition to those of Burt Bacharach from that era, particularly the unique "jazz waltz" tempo best illustrated by Dionne Warwick's hit version of "Wives and Lovers."[29]

Bacharach and co-writer Hal David had released "What the World Needs Now" in 1965. In Bacharach's 2014 autobiography, he explains how the primary melodic idea, chorus, and $\frac{3}{4}$ time signature had been developed even earlier, in 1962. Crouch's "That's What It's All About" may be a response to "What the World Needs Now Is Love," which itself references—in the gentlest manner possible—the war in Vietnam, the civil rights movement, and even poverty in urban America. "That's What It's All About" beautifully fuses a gospel/jazz rhythm section and pop-sounding background vocals with highly orchestrated strings and brass. For a Black gospel recording artist in the 1970s, this high level of orchestration and musical arrangement is virtually unprecedented—Crouch sounds like a secular artist but one with gospel lyrical tropes. Like "What the World Needs Now," "That's What It's All About" features a bouncy $\frac{3}{4}$ time signature and unusual harmonic progressions. The song's form is similar to a traditional ABA secular song with an accompanying bridge, but with multiple tempo changes and a variety of musical transitions. This suggests once again that Crouch is, indeed, listening deeply to what the musical culture is saying, even as he seeks innovative artistic collaborations and deeply mines biblical and theological resources to enhance the message.[30]

"It's Not Just a Story"

Crouch opens "It's Not Just a Story," in the key of D♭, with a melodic brief borrowing from William Henry Parker and Frederic Arthur Challinor's beloved hymn "Tell Me the Story of Jesus." The song is sermonic as it directly references the gospel. It's not just gospel music, it's music *about* the gospel. It's one of the few songs, Maxwell notes, that feature Andraé on solo piano. The entire track is intuitively engaging, intensely personal, direct, and poignant. Harmonically, "It's Not Just a Story" is simple in song form yet it is sophisticated in harmonic language. Crouch's use of diminished chords, juxtaposed with ii–V–I progressions, is timeless. As he sings "Oh, that plain and simple story, became real to me," the intimacy of the track reflects his personal relationship with Christ.[31]

"Come On Back My Child"

Published in the key of F major in a Lexicon Music songbook, the pentatonic blues melody of "Come On Back My Child" is actually in B♭ on the record. Accompanied by funky, polyrhythmic congas, it is another example of the emerging contemporary gospel sound of the West Coast. Within this context, Crouch uses simplified rock 'n' roll progressions, perhaps suggesting the tension of reconciliation and redemption. The unison vocals are both gospel- and rock-influenced, and while the song isn't particularly contemplative, it demands reflection, including the tongue-twisting phrase, "please believe me, that it would relieve me." "Come On Back My Child" also has playful elements, particularly at the 2.5-minute mark, where there is another quirky instrumental break/jam session. According to Maxwell, "Come On Back My Child" is an anomaly on the album. "The song was cut with musicians *before* Sonlight joined Andraé," he recalled, "though they're not credited on the album. It was a track they had lying around from a previous session."[32]

"If Heaven Was Never Promised to Me"

"If Heaven Was Never Promised to Me" presents a particularly creative approach to a gospel song, painting an aural image of Crouch at the piano in a crowded, smoky nightclub. He sings, "you may ask me why I serve the Lord" and challenges his listeners to think about salvation as not only for the future, but for the present: "If heaven was never promised to me, it's been worth just having the Lord in my life." This concept plays itself out musically through the use of two different tonal centers. The verse has a tonal center of E♭ major (suggesting the future), but the chorus saturates itself in A♭ major (suggesting the present). The thesis of the song, living with Jesus Christ in the present, is worth the relationship, even if there was no heaven promised. Perhaps the song is a sweet-spirited response to John Lennon's 1971 mega hit "Imagine," which posits a universe without a heaven *or* a hell. "If Heaven" concludes with a joyfully gospelized vocal vamp designed to remind listeners that the world is illuminated with the light of Christ. In keeping with the illusion of the late-night club, Crouch's piano stylings are jazzy, introspective, conversational, and yet deeply pensive. In Andraé's theology, the relationality of Jesus Christ is the only rational solution to issues of the world.[33]

Side II

"Lord, You've Been Good to Me"

Andraé begins the Motown groove of "Lord, You've Been Good to Me" by humming instead of singing. This hum is another example of Andraé's intimate, personal relationship with his God and the overall tone is conversational, as if between two old friends. The churchy environment is provided by the prominent place of Sandra Crouch's tambourine in the mix, which flavors the song with a spirited COGIC-styled presence. It is a song of thanksgiving and gratitude with an A♭ major pentatonic (and very catchy) melody. The middle section of the song features a double-time groove where the bass and tambourine play in absolute synchronicity. An instrumental section follows where the entire band plays unison lines in octaves, echoing the instrumental dance breaks then popular on Top 40 radio. Add to this the wah-wah guitar's call-and-response interpolations with a steady groove line and the song fades into the closing vamp, joined by Andraé and his background singers praising God for the Holy Ghost and healing. More than any other piece on this album, "Lord, You've Been Good to Me" displays Andraé's COGIC gospel musical rootedness. The classic gospel church chord progressions and the energetic praise team vocals singing in tight three-part harmony usher in a new era of ecumenical gospel fusion in song.

"What Does Jesus Mean to Me?"

Some of Crouch's most sophisticated harmonizations appear throughout "What Does Jesus Mean to Me?" The song begins gingerly with Andraé's left hand on the piano playing six motifs that chromatically ascend to a gentle cadence, from an F minor 11th chord to B♭ 13th chord. This is a wholly unique harmonic chord progression in gospel music at a time when this type of performance practice was considered "too worldly" for the church—something that had been relegated exclusively to jazz clubs and theater. Crouch and Thedford create extended harmonies that impressively modulate throughout the song.

Their use of D♭ 6/9 chords, with the added 11th and A♭ major 7th chords, creates a startlingly modern tension-and-release component within the song. This tension forces the listener to ponder the words of the text. This intimate slow gospel-jazz fusion power ballad features Andraé alone on the piano and vocals, revealing a scale and scope to Crouch's musical vision that has only been hinted at on previous releases.

"God Loves the Country People"

With "God Loves the Country People," Crouch is clearly having fun with the simple theological premise: God loves *everyone*. No exceptions. In the key of G♭ major and improvising on the black keys, Crouch's orchestration conjures sounds from what he imagines are the country's backroads with washboards, shakers, rooster crows, and various other barnyard animals—all set to a backdrop of the theological premise that all of creation is precious in God's sight. Throughout the song, there are more *Crouch-isms*, such as unison vocal lines exploding into harmony. There are other clever musical tributes sprinkled throughout: In one passage the guitarist mimics Chet Atkins, while in another the barrelhouse piano sounds like Floyd Cramer. Andraé closes with a gospel call-and-response, gleefully vocalizing on top of a triple-time hoedown.

"Lullaby of the Deceived" (II Timothy 3:13)

In "Lullaby of the Deceived," Crouch incorporates a pipe organ sound from a horror movie soundtrack in a $\frac{3}{4}$ time signature, along with the sinister sounds of carousels, calliopes, and seedy carnival arcades. "Lullaby of the Deceived" is one of the most creative, most challenging songs in his entire catalogue. Not many—if any!—gospel songs in any era have dealt with being face to face with demonic activity. Crouch's response is to create music as theology in action. The music functions theologically to encourage listeners to practice their own interpretation on the II Timothy 3:13 passage that provides the basis for the song, imagining what it would be like to experience deception from demons. Andraé sings about dreams turning into nightmares as the sounds of a carousel organ and darkly murmuring clowns give the illusion that someone is dancing with laughing demons. The composition ends with the organ playing fully diminished 7th chords and painting a picture of what it means to sit in a conundrum of deception. Crouch cries, "Jesus, help me!" and the song concludes with a sinister pipe organ postlude. And all this because Crouch is deeply committed to seeing people secure their salvation in Christ. To Andraé, just as Jesus Christ is real, so are the demons in hell and the angels in the heavenlies. As a result, he responds in the only way he knows—to use his imagination to communicate the dangers of spiritual deception.[34]

"Bless His Holy Name" (Psalm 103)

The album ends with one of the foundational songs in the entire praise & worship genre. "Bless His Holy Name" is deeply fused with gospel piano and is set in the practical congregational singing range of E♭ major. With Wiley's majestic clarion trumpet calls, the worship and praise singers gracefully proclaim, "He has done great things." With the full instrumental ensemble present, the singers sing prime unison lines on the chorus, only to explode with three-part harmonious force. As the track builds, Andraé goes into worship leader mode. Under the leading of the Holy Spirit, he creates an ecumenical worship and praise anthem that audiences will sing for the next fifty years. "Bless His Holy Name" has been included in more than thirty hymnals and remains in the active repertoire of many praise & worship–oriented artists and congregations.[35]

The Album as Liturgy

Whether done consciously or not, the authors believe that *Just Andraé* is ordered and designed liturgically, with expressly evangelistic outreach both in format and in contextual design:

> *Introit/Invitation/Call to Worship*: "You Ain't Livin'"
> *Songs of Testimony*: "In Remembrance"
> *Scripture Lesson 1*: "That's What It's All About"
> *Scripture Lesson 2*: "It's Not Just a Story" (which emphasizes the general revelation of the Word of God)
> *Congregational Prayer and Meditation Altar Call*: "Come On Back, My Child"
> *Sermon Songs*: "If Heaven Never Was Promised to Me," "Lord, You've Really Been Good to Me," "What Does Jesus Mean to You," and "God Loves the Country People"
> *Song of Admonition and Warning*: "Lullaby of the Deceived"
> *Benediction/Sending Song*: "Bless His Holy Name"

Response

When released, *Just Andraé* never appeared on the *Billboard* magazine "Best-Selling Gospel LPs" chart, even as his previous albums continued to sell. Despite the presence of some well-loved songs, there are several possible reasons for this absence. It may have been released too soon after *Soulfully*, diluting the market. Likewise, one of Andraé's biggest albums, *"Live" in Carnegie Hall*, would be released just a few months later. It is certainly the most difficult of all of Crouch's albums to categorize, with multiple musical selections, each encompassing different offbeat genres. It is also intensely personal and the theology, at times, is sometimes more challenging than what is found is most three-minute gospel songs of the day. One other consideration, as singer Kathy Hazzard was quoted in the previous chapter, as with *Soulfully*, the Disciples were selling "tons" of the LPs from their tour bus during their nonstop touring, which may—or may not—have prevented either of the albums from charting more highly in the record industry charts.

Mark Allen Powell only mentions *Just Andraé* in passing, calling "Bless His Holy Name" the album's "highlight" and noting the "profound" lyrics of "If Heaven Never Was Promised to Me." *Uncloudy Day: The Gospel Music Encyclopedia* never mentions it at all. Only Scott Bachmann ranks it highly, slotting it at #57 on his "Greatest Gospel Albums of the '70s" blog. After acknowledging the album's "eclectic" nature, Bachmann praises "those beautiful, deep, rich, textured, thoughtful ballads," writing that it is the ballads that make *Just Andraé* "a truly exceptional audio snapshot of what God was doing in 1972." Crouch's peers certainly liked it—in 1973, the National Academy of Recording Arts & Sciences nominated the album in the short-lived "Best Gospel Performance (Other than Soul Gospel)" category, along with groups like the Imperials and Blackwood Brothers. *Just Andraé* was *not*, however, nominated in the "Best Soul Gospel Performance" category for that year.[36]

Just Andraé Today

Some of the songs on *Just Andraé* may sound particularly dated for modern ears. But for coauthor Stephen Newby, the album was profound enough, richly nuanced enough, that as a lifelong fan of Andraé's music he felt compelled to write his thesis at Seattle Pacific University on three songs from the LP, "You Ain't Livin'," "That's What It's All About," and "Lullaby of the Deceived." It's worth mentioning that, for the first time since his COGIC days when he was accompanied by the brilliant Billy Preston, Crouch was surrounded by a diverse community of talented musicians. While doubtless many of the studio musicians from previous sessions were superb artists, Sonlight had quickly become Andraé's community, joining Sandra, Thedford (himself a much underrated bassist), and Morgan. Maxwell, in particular, became an essential element of Crouch's creative process. The addition of Hockensmith, Wiley, Rogers, and Maxwell as the foundation of a regular band/community with the remaining original Disciples enabled Andraé to continue to pursue his dream of reaching beyond the Black gospel music community. The creative spirit found in his African American COGIC roots is, of course, extraordinary. But the authors believe that the multiethnic, musically diverse members of this incarnation of the Disciples enabled Crouch to be—perhaps—even *more* dynamic, *more* creative than had he remained rooted solely in his original gospel foundation, even one as musically progressive as the Church of God in Christ.

Just Andraé, then, is the first time Crouch has all of the musical tools at his disposal, most notably a tightly knit, highly creative band of sympathetic musicians who could now help Andraé "sell" the message of the challenging lyrics. He could "speak" in any secular-styled musical language—and deconstruct it, if necessary—if that's what it took to take the message *everywhere*. His lyrics were firmly embedded in the Christian scriptures to the point it is usually obvious which Bible verse was the inspiration for a given song.

In Andraé's musical universe, music itself does not have an overtly "religious" sound—instead, it is the lyrics of both sacred and secular music that speak directly to each other in the Holy Spirit. *Just Andraé* does not abandon the deep gospel traditions of Thomas Dorsey, Lucie Campbell, or William Herbert Brewster; his music is an extension of that tradition. In order to tell different stories of faith, the authors believe (and Newby posits in his thesis) that Crouch intentionally moved beyond gospel's traditional musical stylings. For much of his career, Andraé would be accused of "leaving" gospel music, though he always protested vigorously that he had not. He had only *expanded* gospel's horizons, just like Arizona Dranes and Sister Rosetta Tharpe before him and like the host of "contemporary" gospel artists who would someday follow him.

As the authors hope to show, to accomplish this often-stated mission, Crouch would increasingly insist that the musicianship, singing, sound production, mixing, and mastering on his LPs be of the highest quality. That alone was a significant leap in a day when gospel artists were forced to record an entire album's worth of material in a few hours, often in substandard studios. Few gospel artists had the financial resources and a multiethnic community's social equity to create such lyrics, such sophisticated musical arrangements, and such a deep theological understanding in creating their art.

As this community of artists evolved in time, his artistic practices and musical traditions evolved with them. The *Just Andraé* album is the first real foreshadowing of what will come to be called "The Crouch Sound," and what Newby describes is a much-heralded combination of balanced theological authenticity, integrity, and honesty—even as his albums continued to receive sometimes vociferous criticism from within the more traditional elements of the Black gospel community.[37]

NOTES

1. Bill Maxwell, interview with the authors, September 14, 2022.
2. Fletch Wiley, interview with the authors, October 10, 2020.
3. Bill Maxwell, interview with the authors, May 18, 2019.
4. Fletch Wiley, interview with the authors, October 10, 2020.
5. Russell Chandler, "Full Gospel World Conclave: With Signs and Wonders," *Christianity Today*, July 28, 1972, 33–34.
6. Fletch Wiley, interview with the authors, October 10, 2020.
7. Bill Maxwell, interview with the authors, May 18, 2019; Fletch Wiley, interview with the authors, October 10, 2020; Bili Thedford, interview with the authors, March 22, 2022.
8. See Hank Bordowitz, *Bad Moon Rising: The Unauthorized History of Creedence Clearwater Revival* (Chicago: Chicago Review Press, 2007).
9. Andraé Crouch, *Just Andraé* (Light Records LS-5598-LP); "Steve Maslow: Biography," IMDb.com: https://www.imdb.com/name/nm0556541/bio; Abbey Sound: https:www.cabusinessdb.com/company?utm_source=595413; Decca Studios: www.discogs.com/label/535617-Decca-Studios-Hollywood; Studio 55: https://www.discogs.com/label/388181-Studio-55-Los-Angeles; Fletch Wiley, interview with the authors, October 10, 2020.

    Note: There is no record in *Billboard* of *Just Andraé*'s actual release date. Assuming (always a dangerous idea!) that Light's release dates in the "LS" series were at least somewhat chronological, and by checking known Light release dates against *Billboard*'s "New LP/Tape Releases, we can estimate generally when an album may have been released:

LS 5581 Andraé Crouch & the Disciples, *Soulfully* (Listed in *Billboard* on November 11, 1972, but doubtless released somewhat earlier)

LS 5598 Andraé Crouch, *Just Andraé*

LS 5602 Andraé Crouch & the Disciples, *"Live" in Carnegie Hall* (Mentioned in *Billboard* on May 12, 1973, but probably released earlier)

And since most sources give "1972" as the release date for *Just Andraé*, that would mean that album would have come out in *late* 1972, possibly between November and December, a few months before *"Live" in Carnegie Hall* was released.

(Thanks to Mike Callahan, David Edwards, and Patrice Eyries, creators of "Light Album Discography," www.bsnpubs.com/word/light/light.html.)

10. Bill Maxwell, interview with the authors, May 18, 2019.
11. Hockensmith, interview with the authors October 17, 2020; Fletch Wiley, interview with the authors, October 10, 2020.
12. Hockensmith, interview with the authors, October 17, 2020; Bill Maxwell, interview with the authors, May 18, 2019.
13. Bill Maxwell, interview with the authors, May 18, 2019.
14. Hadley Hockensmith, interview with the authors, October 17, 2020.
15. Hadley Hockensmith, interview with the authors, October 17, 2020.
16. Bill Maxwell, interview with the authors, May 18, 2019; Hadley Hockensmith, interview with the authors, October 17, 2020.
17. Hadley Hockensmith, interview with the authors, October 17, 2020.
18. Hadley Hockensmith, interview with the authors, October 17, 2020.
19. Bili Thedford, interview with the authors, November 12, 2020; Bili Thedford, interview with the authors, March 22, 2022; Kathy Hazzard, interview with the authors, August 19, 2021.
20. Hadley Hockensmith, interview with the authors, October 17, 2020; Kathy Hazzard, interview with the authors, August 19, 2021; Phyllis St. James, interview with the authors, January 23, 2021; Mandrell.weebly.com/TV-show.html #105
21. Andraé Crouch with Nina Ball, *Through It All: Andraé Crouch* (Waco, TX: Wod Books, 1974), 115–125; Bill Maxwell, interview with the authors, May 18, 2019; Hadley Hockensmith, interview with the authors, October 17, 2020; Bill Maxwell, interview with the authors, September 14, 2022.
22. Bill Maxwell, interview with the authors, May 18, 2019.
23. Phyllis St. James, interview with the authors, January 23, 2021.
24. Hadley Hockensmith, interview with the authors, October 17, 2020.
25. Bob Gersztyn, "Andraé's Music Will Never Lose Its Power," *The Wittenburg Door* (March/April 2004, online).
26. James Cone, *God of the Oppressed*, rev. ed. (Maryknoll, NY: Orbis Books, 1997), 127.
27. Stephen Michael Newby, "Andraé Edward Crouch's Musical and Theological Pursuits: An Analysis of Three Pieces from the *Just Andraé* Album" (2019), *Seattle Pacific Seminary Theses* 15, 27–28.

28. Bill Maxwell, interview with the authors, September 14, 2022.
29. Hadley Hockensmith, interview with the authors, October 17, 2020; Newby, "Andraé Edward Crouch's Musical and Theological Pursuits," 21–31.
30. Burt Bacharach, *Anyone Who Had a Heart: My Life and Music* (New York: Harper Paperbacks, 2014); Newby, "Andraé Edward Crouch's Musical and Theological Pursuits," 27–28.
31. Bill Maxwell, interview with the authors, May 18, 2019.
32. Bill Maxwell, interview with the authors, September 14, 2022.
33. "If Heaven Was Never Promised to Me" by Andraé Crouch, Lexicon Music, Inc., courtesy of Capitol CMG.
34. Newby, "Andraé Edward Crouch's Musical and Theological Pursuits," 36–37.
35. https://hymnary.org/text/bless_the_Lord_o_my_soul_and_all_Crouch; "Bless His Holy Name" by Andraé Crouch, Light Lexicon Music, courtesy of Capitol CMG.
36. Mark Allan Powell, *Encyclopedia of Contemporary Christian Music* (Peabody, MA: Hendrickson Publishers, 2002), 212; http://greatest70salbums.blogsport .com/2015/12/57/-just-Andraé-by-Andraé-crouch-1973/html; "Nominations for the 16th Annual Grammy Awards," *Cash Box*, January 26, 1974, 12, 14.
37. Newby, "Andraé Edward Crouch's Musical and Theological Pursuits," 15.

8

"Live" at Carnegie Hall

The Concert

Andraé Crouch and the Disciples recorded their first live album in Carnegie Hall on April 10, 1972, as part of a "Jesus Joy" package with Jesus Music staples Danny Taylor, Maranatha, Lillian Parker, and Rock Garden. The concert was sold out, so a unique arrangement had the Disciples perform at nearby Calvary Baptist Church for an estimated 1,500 people, then race across the street to Carnegie Hall to record their set. The evening was a riotous success, so much so that organizers scheduled additional "Jesus Joy" events in New York, though without Andraé and his group. Despite their reception that evening, Jerry Davis, one of the coordinators, told *Christianity Today* that the Disciples' set might have been *too* successful. "They went an hour and half over time," Davis said, "and cost us $2,000 extra at Carnegie Hall." The concert was significant enough to merit a mention in Sam Sutherland's breezy "Studio Track" column in *Billboard*. Sutherland noted that Fedco Audio Labs of Providence, Rhode Island, had traveled to Carnegie Hall to record the event. The session "went smoothly," though Sutherland joked that Fedco's Fred Ehrhardt "was forced to watch his language."[1]

Bili Thedford's strongest memory of the concert itself was the response of the audience. The advance ticket sales were so robust that the second concert at Calvary Baptist was quickly arranged and the overflow "packed that church out" as well. "Carnegie Hall came and went," he said. "It was like, 'Wow!'— it was so fast we didn't even understand the importance of doing Carnegie Hall."[2]

The Recording

After the concert, the Disciples resumed their heavy touring schedule and Andraé's attention went first to *Soulfully*, and then to *Just Andraé*. The live album, however, was not immediately released, even though Light Records' Ralph Carmichael raved about the "unbelievable" LP in a spotlight package of stories published in *Billboard* in October. However, as 1972 turned into 1973, there was still no sign of the Carnegie Hall concert. The hang-up was Crouch, who was unhappy with the sound. "He hated it because the band was not good, so he wasn't going to put it out," Bill Maxwell said. "The crowd was so good and actually Andraé was good, but not the sound or the band." Maxwell said that Crouch asked Light Records for permission to work on the master 16-track tape. Carmichael and Light initially refused, then only reluctantly made him a copy of the master. Fortunately, the Carnegie Hall piano had a "boundary" microphone, Maxwell said, with little "leakage" from the rest of the band. Ultimately, the piano accompaniment, along with Andraé's voice and some crowd noise, were salvaged—but nothing else. "His vocals were great," Maxwell said, "the piano was great. But the drummer dropped the beat and turned it around, the guitar player wasn't good, [and] the background vocals were all over the place." As detailed earlier, this is where Maxwell and the rest of Sonlight entered the picture. And, as Maxwell wryly noted, this is where *Live at Carnegie Hall* became *"Live" at Carnegie Hall*, since not *all* of the performances on the final recording were—technically—live.[3]

Crouch and Maxwell finally started re-recording and producing the *"Live" at Carnegie Hall* album nearly a year after the April 10, 1972, concert, a process often interrupted to fulfill pending tour dates. The laborious overdubbing process took place at odd hours at TTG Studio in Hollywood. During different recording sessions, Hadley Hockensmith replaced all guitar and bass tracks, Harlan Rogers replaced the organ tracks, and Fletch Wiley added solos. The most difficult part, Maxwell said, was to augment, match, and then improve on the drums and erratic tempos of the originals. When it came to replacing the drum tracks, Maxwell said that he and Andraé "just tried to figure out what to do." "We didn't know what we were doing, so I would turn everything off and just play with Andraé. If the song sped up, I sped up. If it slowed down, I slowed down. If it dropped the beat, I'd adjust it."[4]

There was one additional substitution from the actual concert, former COGICs member Sondra "Blinky" Williams. Williams was by now touring with Sammy Davis Jr. and recording with Motown. After a chance meeting at an airport, Andraé invited her to sing at the Carnegie Hall concert. Williams said that she was so excited about the prospect that she told Davis that she would not be available for a few weeks. "I lied to Sammy Davis and I lied to Motown," Williams said. "I told them that my grandmother was sick and I needed to go to Houston to visit her." Later, when Light Records contacted Motown about securing permission to use Williams's voice and likeness on the *"Live" at Carnegie Hall* album, Motown flatly refused. "They said, 'Not only can you not use her name, you can't even use her voice,'" Williams recalled. "I was very disappointed and hurt because the album was so big and it was so wonderful." Williams did tour briefly with the Disciples in the weeks immediately following the concert. However, when Davis—who by then was her manager—discovered the deception, she was very nearly fired from the revue. To fill Williams's spot in the harmonies, Crouch turned to Phyllis St. James, who quickly re-recorded the parts. "Andraé didn't really have a soprano between Sandra, Bili, and Perry," Maxwell recalled, "so it made sense for him to bring in a top note. And that was right about when I first met Phyllis."[5]

The mix-down engineer at TTG Studios was industry veteran Eddie Bracken, who the year before had engineered Little Feat's brilliant *Sailin' Shoes*. "I learned so much from Eddie Bracken because he had a lot of experience in doing hit records," Maxwell said. It was Bracken's idea to "loop" the remaining snippets of crowd noise between songs to replicate the feeling of a live album after much of it had to be erased—along with all the other instruments and vocals—save for Andraé's voice and piano. "I learned all of that stuff from Eddie, which I used on all of the live albums I've done after that," Maxwell said. "He was really good."[6]

The Album

The photographs on the LP intentionally feature Andraé, Sandra, Thedford, and Perry Morgan, with only a blurry photo of Andraé on the back jacket. None of the other musicians or singers is included and the liner notes are limited. The notes instead emphasize the exciting nature of the actual concert, stating that the music is "rough and honest," musical flaws and all. Regardless of how "live" *"Live" at Carnegie Hall* is, it represented a breakthrough for Andraé Crouch and the Disciples, in terms of both sales and influence. This was for many of the thousands present—"young and old, black and white, long hairs and white collars, Jew and Gentile," as the liner notes claim—their first exposure to the energy and emotionalism of the Black church musical experience.

It is also the first Disciples album that was unambiguously presented in the form of a worship service. Whereas previous LPs suggested the welcome/message/invitation/benediction format of the evangelical church, *"Live" at Carnegie Hall* is carefully constructed that way, augmented by Andraé's exhortative style of preaching throughout. Few albums—even in the gospel world—would dare to spend nearly as much of their running time preaching as singing. And despite the later substitution of much of the instrumentation and background vocals, the album is an accurate, if somewhat truncated, version of a concert by Crouch and the Disciples. Scholar/musician Raymond Wise said that the album is representative of Andraé's concerts and, in that regard, it is "set up, from beginning to end" to be a worship service:

> Andraé knew he was going to have an invitation at the end. He knew he was going to invite them to the altar to come meet the Lord. He is setting them up, giving them all these things to break down walls, so that they would get there. And that connection draws them then to ask the next question, "Well, you said we're going to heaven. But now tell me how."[7]

For their first live album, another artist might have chosen to reprise their best-known numbers, songs guaranteed to ignite an already primed crowd: "The Blood (Will Never Lose Its Power")," "I've Got Confidence," or "My Tribute (to God Be the Glory)." Instead, Andraé and the Disciples opted not to perform any of the songs from *Take the Message Everywhere*, just one song from *Keep On Singin'* ("I Don't Know Why"), and only two from *Soulfully* ("You Don't Know What You're Missing" and "It Won't Be Long"). No songs were included from the still-to-be-recorded *Just Andraé*. The remaining five songs make their recording debut on *"Live."* Of those, two continue to be performed by artists in a variety of genres—"Jesus Is the Answer" and "He Looked Beyond My Fault."

"Jesus Is the Answer" was not even on the original set list. Andraé told interviewer Tavis Smiley that just before walking on the Carnegie Hall stage, he was struck by the thought that the audience included people from a variety of faiths, not just Christians. "And so I asked God to give me something," Crouch said. "We had never sung the song live. Sandra told me that she wrote the verse, 'If you have some questions from the corners of your mind,' so I told [the Disciples], 'At the end of it say, "He will do it for you."'" Looking back, St. James said the enduring genius of the song is due, in part, to that simplicity. "Andraé doesn't have to preach—'Jesus is the answer for the world today,'" she said. "You can't get any more basic, more simple than that message. And every time I've sung it, I've realized the simplicity of the message. It's like, 'Why didn't I think of that?'"[8]

Singer-songwriter Paul Simon was among those impacted by "Jesus Is the Answer." Simon, who was touring with gospel artist Jessy Dixon, recorded the song during his "Live Rhymin'" October 1973 tour performance at Carnegie Hall. "Jesus Is the Answer," performed by the Jessy Dixon Singers, then appeared on *Paul Simon in Concert: Live Rhymin'*, which was released in early 1974. Dixon once told longtime Christian music executive Lynn Keesecker how much Simon always said he "loved" that particular song.[9]

"He Looked Beyond My Fault (and Saw My Need)" had been written in 1968 by Dottie Rambo and was already a beloved song, with numerous recorded versions. One of the earliest covers of the song was by Sherman Andrus on his Bill MacKenzie/Andraé Crouch–produced solo album *I've Got Confidence*, released in 1969. The Disciples had toured for nearly two years with Dottie's daughter Reba, also a talented singer/songwriter, and Reba's husband, Donny McGuire. Thedford, who sings the song on the album, said he remembered hearing "He Looked Beyond My Fault" for the first time while on the bus with the Rambos. Based on the beloved Irish instrumental theme "Londonderry Air" (also known as "O'Carolan's Lament" and most famously as "Danny Boy"), "He Looked Beyond My Fault" has appeared in eight hymnals and numerous collections of sacred music.[10]

"Live" at Carnegie Hall

"I Don't Know Why"

The album opens with the "Jesus chant" ("Give me a 'J!'"), so popular in previous Jesus Music events, including Explo '72, as the unnamed announcer intones: "Ladies and Gentlemen, Carnegie Hall will never be the same. And it is with Jesus' joy I present to you Andraé Crouch and the Disciples."

"I Don't Know Why" is in one of Andraé's favorite keys, the black key–centric D♭ major, and for a few seconds—two measures in a $\frac{3}{4}$ time signature—Andraé reads the audience. He performs a gentle COGIC meditation on the piano, gingerly drawing the crowd to an awareness of what worship leaders now call an "Audience of One"—Father, Son, and Holy Spirit—in the third measure, then shifts the tempo and a COGIC gospel groove emerges. It's a different introductory approach from both the version on *Keep On Singin'* (where the studio version begins in strict tempo), and the YouTube version from Explo '72 (which begins more robustly). Most of Andraé's recorded piano work since the Explo '72 videos reveal a churchy style of performance where Andraé continually "reads" the audience, shifting tempos, and initiating grooves as the Spirit moves. Throughout the piece, Andraé exhorts the crowd to move from passive listening to deep engagement. The result is that the song is spontaneously rebooted with a new mid-tempo, multiethnic gospel rock feel. Many of Andraé's songs begin with the chorus, especially live, because he has discovered (as many artists have) that people are drawn to music that is catchy and familiar, and the old favorite "I Don't Know Why" is both.

"You Don't Know What You're Missing"

Crouch exclaims that this concert will *not* be the "First Church of the Frigidaire"—instead, Andraé wants to warm up the room with the Holy Ghost. Lyrically in "You Don't Know What You're Missing," Andraé tells his listeners what they *are* missing if they do not meet his Lord. Andraé's approach is explorative and the music plays with the audience, drawing them closer, adding, "this is not a concert tonight, we're having church." Compared to the version on *Soulfully*, Andraé spices it up with some flashy double-time COGIC-styled barrelhouse piano.

The recording features the distinctive sound of the virtually all-white audience clapping on beats 1, 2, 3, and 4. In the often more rhythmically sophisticated Black Church music traditions, most rhythmic hand-clapping centers on beats 2 and 4, with the occasional showy flourish. In many white congregations, if there is any hand clapping at all, the claps are on beats 1 and 3. Andraé's audience is multiethnic, ecumenical, and intergenerational, so he calls everyone to a new rhythmic paradigm—clapping *only* on the downbeats. It's one of several light-hearted moments during the evening. At the same time, creating orderly patterns, such as rhythmic handclapping, is one of Crouch's higher goals for his concerts—and echoes music theorist Leonard

Meyer's notion of implication and music, that "we are explicitly conscious of the fact of implication." Andraé calls his audience to join *with* him. This is one of the hallmarks of the Black church worship experience—the *need* to worship within an oriented, and reorientated, context. Andraé, as he has done throughout his career, reorients the multiracial gathering from "missing something" to "finding something."[11]

As Hockensmith's sharp guitar riffs resound throughout the song, some members of the spellbound audience may have wondered if a guitar could even *do* this in a Christian context? And is it all right to bring the name of Jesus into something that sounds like this? Andraé and the Disciples are the epicenter of change in both Black and white religious music. The double-time feel of the song reflects Black church rhythmic shout sensibilities, where "holy" dancing is inspired and emotional transparency is required. In the ecstatic COGIC tradition, the chant-like "You Don't Know What You're Missing"—and how it is positioned in the concert—clearly requires a vamp, since the unspoken assumption in many Pentecostal traditions is that where there is no vamp, there is no transcendence. For Andraé to take his audience higher, he closes with some spirit-driven homegrown gospel funk. This is new for those who grew up in traditional Black or white gospel music, Jesus Music, *or* church hymnody—unless they were also listening to Top 40 radio, where they would have immediately recognized in Sly and the Family Stone this fusion of spirit, innovation, gospel, and funk. Finally, unlike on the more sedate version on the *Soulfully* LP, there are no studio key modulations in the live performance. Instead, Crouch has chosen a comfortable melodic range in the key of D♭ major to encourage congregational singing.

"He Looked Beyond My Fault"

By now, the energy in the hall is at a fever pitch and it sounds as if the transition from "You Don't Know What You're Missing" was edited to introduce the slower-paced "He Looked Beyond My Fault." Andraé's laid-back, bluesy piano introduces Thedford, who effortlessly croons and testifies to God's "amazing grace." The traditional Irish melody amplifies the warmth and grace of Dottie Rambo's lyrics. Crouch presents the song as a power ballad and it is a good example of how Andraé's harmonic language is continuing to evolve. "He Looked Beyond My Fault" incorporates a rich musical language, including modality, improvisations on pentatonic minor blues scales, borrowed chords, and diminished chords. As the song advances from simple meter to compound meter in $\frac{12}{8}$ time signature, tempos surge toward a COGIC Black worship experience. Finally, Thedford's warm, dynamic vocals soar, rock out, and reach the song's fabled high notes. As "He Looked Beyond My Fault" draws to a close, Crouch borrows the same two broad-brushstroked piano cadenzas first heard on the *Just Andraé* recording at the end of "What Does Jesus Mean to You?"

"I Didn't Think It Could Be"/"Hallelujah"/"Jesus Is the Answer"/ "Andraé Preaching"

The combination "I Didn't Think It Could Be"/"Hallelujah"/"Jesus Is the Answer"/"Andraé Preaching" can be seen as the "worship passage" on the album and features both a congregational worship medley and Crouch's conversation with the audience. On "I Didn't Think It Could Be," built on the harmonic progression ii–V–I–iii–vi, Andraé invites the congregation to sing along. He first asks the women to sing, then the men, dividing them into singing parts and bringing everyone together with a grand gospel funk finale. Then, blending a simple chorus created through some visionary improvisation, Andraé creates a sing-along "Hallelujah" moment, encouraging the congregation to personalize their worship experience. Crouch's words and music ebb and flow as he reads the room, exhorting, directing the people to lift their hands, proclaiming the gospel of salvation, and praising God. While lifting the name of Jesus in the middle of this one-word hymn/chorus, a homily spontaneously emerges as Andraé declares that a "true faith" is a relationship with Jesus. After mentioning other faith traditions, Crouch proclaims that Jesus reigns in power and in healing. As is the case in virtually all of his lyrics, this is an intensely personal concept. The register and tone in his voice rise with exaltation and Andraé stretches his voice to its limits—now high-pitched and preachy, now crying out to God.

From this emotional moment, a new ecumenical anthem rises: "Jesus Is the Answer." Sung in simple unison, and improvised on the spot with a repeated chorus, this is not really a song, it is more like a COGIC chant. The genius is found in a series of sophisticated chord progressions, replicating pop music. The result is effortlessly catchy. The subtle "oohs" of the background vocals, the improvisation, and the diverse chord voicings, with their inversions, are all orchestrated in such a way as to irresistibly draw the audience nearer to the Throne of God.

From there, Sandra leads the song on the verse she composed, and Andraé then plays a piano solo and encourages the congregation to "praise the Lord right where you are." His piano solo, once again an offering to the "audience of One," both sanctifies jazz sensibilities and baptizes blues riffs. This is Andraé as Preacher, evangelizing through a multiplicity of Black musical genres. Like his father Benjamin before him, Crouch wants to tell the world the message of John 14:6, that Jesus is the way, the truth, and the life. The chorus is sung several more times as Andraé resumes preaching: "Let me hear you say 'Yeah!'" he shouts. Through this call-and-response, Andraé whips up the crowd like the Black preachers he's heard his entire life. As the congregation chants "Jesus," Andraé hums and moans along. This extraordinary section reflects a timeless echo of Black lining hymnody and is vividly encapsulated in his vocal gestures, melismatic passages, and cadences. Through it all, the bass, guitar, organ, and drums wail, wait, and watch for Andraé's next cue.

"Can't Nobody Do Me like Jesus"/"Invitation"
In A♭ major, the Disciples roar back with another original song, "Can't Nobody Do Me like Jesus"/"Invitation," a West Coast soul gospel strut fused with rock 'n' roll charm, one that commands the congregation to clap on beats 1-2-3-4. Driven by Maxwell's remastered drum track, the result is another multiethnic fusion that begins with the chorus, rather than the verse. This approach, energetically performed with standard blues progressions, Curtis Mayfield–styled guitar strokes, and Thedford's jazz funk/fusion bass lines, are all years ahead of their time. Andraé's gospel piano supports the vocals' call-and-response in three-part harmony. A big church *ritardando*, a gradual deacceleration of the tempo, is perfect for a live concert—and life within the church outside of the sanctuary.

"It Won't Be Long"
And, in the end, as in all Protestant denominations, Andraé closes with an invitation, "It Won't Be Long." He exegetes on Joel 2:28 and Acts 2:17: "In the last days, God says, I will pour out my Spirit on all people." Perhaps Andraé feels as if he is living out Acts 2:17 as he prophesies in Carnegie Hall. "It Won't Be Long" addresses the eschatology or "end times," the "last days" or "rapture" theology so prevalent in the evangelical church of the day. Unlike his peers in Black or white sacred music, Crouch manages—in remarkably few words—to preach Christ's return to an ecumenically and ethnically diverse audience. This version of "It Won't Be Long" is much more emphatic than the one on *Soulfully*, more melodic, more heartfelt. It begins with the Hammond

B3 organ–driven chorus and fades with the motif, "Goodnight and God bless you." Composer Jeffrey LaValley said he is among the legions of artists and fans who have been touched by the gentle power of "It Won't Be Long," In addition to his own memories of the song, LaValley fondly recalled a radio deejay who for thirty years always closed his broadcasts with "It Won't Be Long."[12]

The Response

As with previous Light albums, the exact release date is uncertain. The first reference to *"Live" at Carnegie Hall* is in a May 12, 1973, article in *Billboard* magazine—but *not* in either the "Best-Selling Gospel LPs" charts or even the "recommended" new gospel releases section. Instead, it can be found on page 56 in the "Latin: Also Recommended" section, where the uncredited reviewer writes:

> ANDRAÉ CROUCH & THE DISCIPLES—*"Live" at Carnegie Hall*, Light 5602 (Lexicon). Exciting entry from this under-rated group. Excellent material that should be programmed at levels other than gospel. Best cuts: "I Don't Know Why," "Can't Nobody Do Me Like Jesus," "You Don't Know What You're Missing."[13]

The album—or some form of it—does not actually appear in the Best-Selling Gospel LPs charts until nine months later, on February 16, 1974, where it debuts at #11. Once again, the listing is actually for two of the songs from the LP, "Jesus Is the Answer" and "Hallelujah," rather than *"Live" at Carnegie Hall*, though the two songs are listed with the same call/catalogue numbers as the album (Light 5602). The error, if that's what it is, was not corrected for another two months. As early as January 5, 1974, John Sippel's "Gospel Gambol" predicted that two releases in the new gospel chart by Andraé Crouch and the Disciples and Rance Allen would pick up "many new, young devotees." *"Live"* moved relentlessly up the monthly chart to #7 in April, #6 in May, #4 in June, #3 in August (there was no July chart), and #2 in September before hitting #1 in October. *"Live" at Carnegie Hall* remained at #1 through January 1975.[14]

Critically, *"Live" at Carnegie Hall* received a strong positive reception. David W. Stowe called it "one of the best live albums produced by the Jesus Movement" and said it was "the first to achieve crossover success outside the

Christian music market." Stowe described the music as "scorching" and likened it to the "infectious, high-energy funk of Sly & the Family Stone." Mark Allan Powell also notes the groundbreaking aspects of the album and agrees it was among the first records from the movement to sell in the mainstream market. He dubbed it one of the "two or three best" live albums ever released in the Jesus Music marketplace and marveled at the "electrifying" performances that made the Disciples an "international phenomenon." John J. Thompson also agreed with the assessment that it was the first religious album on a faith-based label to "cross over" into the mainstream music marketplace. "It put Crouch on the map," he writes. And Scott Bachmann named it the twenty-eighth best contemporary Christian album of the 1970s.[15]

Distribution and Promotion by Word Records

It soon became apparent that *"Live" at Carnegie Hall* would quickly outsell all previous Disciples LPs by a considerable margin. Some of the credit certainly goes to changes in Word Inc.'s distribution system. Word had distributed Light/Lexicon product from the label's earliest days, primarily to Christian bookstores. In 1974, Word was purchased by media giant ABC, which increased founder Jarrell McCracken's financial resources, including more extensive distribution into mainstream record stores and other outlets selling recorded music. *"Live"*'s surge in sales can also be credited to the work of Billy Ray Hearn. Hearn, who directed Word's contemporary Myrrh label, was also instrumental in expanding Light's presence on Black radio and record stores. "I started promoting Andraé Crouch to the white stations and to the Black gospel stations," Hearn said, "Black stations like WQBH in Detroit with Martha Jean the Queen. She had never played Andraé Crouch because he was mainly being sold to the white crowd." Essentially, Hearn recalled, the issue had been that with Light, Crouch "was basically a white artist and I got him to cross over into the Black stations."[16]

Increased Exposure

As the Disciples' media presence increased, the group's name began to appear even in magazines outside the three primary music trade journals, *Billboard*,

Cash Box, and *Record World*. When WCTN in Potomac, Maryland, switched to a "contemporary Christian" format in July, a *Broadcasting* magazine article listed Andraé Crouch and the Disciples first in the accompanying list of featured artists in the format. When another *Broadcasting* article introduced contemporary Christian music to its readers with a lengthy feature in August, it prominently featured a photo of Andraé with the caption, "Andraé Crouch and the Disciples are ranked by many as the Beatles of the Jesus Movement." Elsewhere, when the Gospel Music Association's annual Dove Award nominees were announced in September, Andraé Crouch and the Disciples were listed as one of the five artists in the "Best Mixed Gospel Group" category and Andraé himself was nominated as one of the five composers (along with Bill Gaither and Kris Kristofferson) in the "Gospel Songwriter of the Year" category. Even the venerable licensing organization ASCAP honored Andraé (along with Gordon Jenkins) in a press release, saying that the two composers had "set the pace in the field of gospel music" in having significant sales in country music as well.[17]

Back on the Road

Once Crouch and Maxwell wrapped up the last of the *"Live"* remixing sessions, the Disciples resumed their demanding touring schedule in mid-1973, accompanied on forty dates by the Rambos (Image 8.1). Scattered amid the mid-sized venues and churches, the Disciples, along with the Oak Ridge Boys, headlined the Fourth Annual International Gospel Song Festival in Nashville in July. In August, the Disciples were top-billed at the three-day "Jesus '73" festival in Pennsylvania, which drew 3,000 people to hear many of the same artists who had appeared at Explo '72. Equally important to Crouch's imperative to "take the message everywhere" were a series of widely varied dates in October: Birmingham, Alabama (October 4); Theatre for the Performing Arts, New Orleans (5); Travis Avenue Baptist Church, Fort Worth, Texas (6); a return visit home to Christ Memorial COGIC, San Fernando, CA (14); First Assembly of God, Dallas (17); San Diego (20); Melodyland, Anaheim, California (22); and Maranatha Church, Portland, Oregon (26).[18]

Image 8.1 Andraé Crouch and the Disciples publicity photo, California Gospel Enterprises, Top, from left: Harlan Rogers, Hadley Hockensmith, Bill Maxwell, Fletch Wiley. Bottom, from left: Billy Thedford, Sandra Crouch, Andraé Crouch, Perry Morgan. Photograph courtesy of Fletch Wiley

Overseas

The tour that encompassed most of November and December 1973 (as detailed in *Billboard*'s weekly "Who/Where/When" column) is incredibly ambitious in scope—and not just for a gospel artist. Over a matter of weeks, the Disciples traveled from Canada to Australia and New Zealand before island-hopping across the South Pacific in a series of physically and emotionally demanding dates, sometimes including multiple performances in a single day, in different far-flung island groups. Looking at the schedule years later, Maxwell said that the logistics of transporting the Disciples across thousands of miles of the South Pacific from one day to the next in 1973 would have been challenging even with a full touring road crew, which the Disciples didn't have at the time:

Nov. 1, Playhouse Theatre, Winnipeg, MB, Canada
Nov. 5, New Westminster, BC, Canada
Nov. 9, Bon voyage concert, Hollywood High School, Hollywood, CA
Nov. 16, Phoenix, AZ
Nov. 17, *The Queen Mary*, Long Beach, CA
Nov. 19, Madison, WI
Nov. 23–24, Disneyland, Anaheim, CA
Nov. 26, Honolulu, HI
Nov. 30, Sydney Opera House, Australia
Dec. 1, Sydney Opera House
Dec. 2 Melbourne Dallas Brooks Hall, Australia
Dec. 3, Melbourne, Australia, Town Hall
Dec. 4–5 Sydney, Australia, Bankston Civic Center
Dec. 7, Christchurch, NZ
Dec. 8, Wellington, NZ
Dec. 9, Napier, NZ
Dec. 10, Auckland, NZ
Dec. 11–12, The New Hebrides
Dec. 13–16, Fiji
Dec. 17–18, Tonga
Dec. 19–21, American and Western Samoa
Dec. 23, Hickam Air Force Base, Honolulu, HI[19]

Young promoter Kevin Craik, who was eager to bring contemporary Christian music to his homeland, coordinated the Australian dates. After much expensive long-distance telephone searching, Craik located the Disciple's booking agency, which built the ambitious 1973 tour around a concert at the prestigious Sydney Opera House. "I remember Andraé having the crowd almost up in the ceiling," Craik recalled, "hitting two notes and bringing them back down to earth. I remember having the excitement of having a Black group—African Americans—in the Sydney Opera House so soon after it opened. And I remember the friendships that developed that very first visit."

Kevin and Jan Craik remained friends with the Crouches until Andraé's death in 2015, visiting them in the United States on numerous occasions. Working with the Craiks' organization, the Disciples returned to Australia in 1976 and 1977 as well. "The Disciples, in many ways, changed the direction of Christian music in Australia," Craik said. "And Andraé once told me, 'We've been more accepted here . . . than we've ever been accepted in America as a Black group.'"[20]

For this tour, Andraé and Sandra were joined by Thedford, Perry Morgan, guitarist Jimmie Davis (replacing Hockensmith), Fletch Wiley, Harlan Rogers, and Maxwell. Phyllis St. James assembled a team of touring vocalists that included two other members of the Danniebelles, Bea Carr and Danniebelle herself. St. James rehearsed the singers on a number of songs from Andraé's career, with an emphasis on the *Soulfully* album, including "Everything Changed," "He Proved His Love to Me," "Through It All," "I Come That You Might Have Life," "You Don't Know What You're Missing," "Leave the Devil Alone," and "It Won't Be Long." The vocalists were assigned different "roles." St. James said she sang first or second soprano, Carr was usually assigned the "top" voice, featured singer Danniebelle sang tenor, while Sandra usually carried the "lower tenor" range. "Andraé told me years later," St. James said, "after I'd signed to Motown and wasn't going to be doing many recordings with him, 'You know, I'm really going to miss you. I know you said to call you anytime that I needed you. That's so nice because you were my glue.'" St. James said that while she never sang lead or took a solo on a single song during her time with the Disciples, Andraé told her that she was an essential element to his sound:

> He said that for all of those powerful voices, the solo voices he had discovered, they would come and go. I was the only constant. My voice, my tone, was the glue that brought all those dynamic voices together. I noticed in some sessions he'd say to new singers, "No, no—listen to how Phyllis is doing it. See, she did this. Blend with that."[21]

Memories of the Australian dates remain particularly vivid to several of the Disciples, in part because Light Records had planned on recording yet another live concert at the recently opened Sydney Opera House. To assist, Light flew producer Bill Cole to Sydney. "We were against it because we didn't see much difference between this and Carnegie Hall," Maxwell said, "but they were insistent." Unlike the previous live album, Light had only contracted for an eight-track recorder for the concert. "And [Cole] did the most crazy joining together of tracks I've ever seen in my life," Maxwell said, "where Andraé's piano and voice were on the same track. So if you wanted more piano, you were going to get more voice." The LP was never released. The concerts in Sydney and Melbourne were sold out. "And then you go from that to New Zealand and then to just in the middle of a jungle," Maxwell said. "No equipment, no people; it's just hard. And then you play three times a day. You play some little church and you play a high school and you did something in the evening."

Maxwell said that some of the scheduled dates, such as the concert on the New Hebrides (now the Republic of Vanuatu), were tentative when they were first announced and never actually occurred. In the Kingdom of Tonga, the Disciples performed on several different islands, including one concert in the capital of Nuku'alofa on Tongatu. The flight to Nuku'alofa was on a private plane, too small to carry any of the group's equipment. "On Nuku'alofa, we played in a banana shed with no electricity," he recalled. "We had small amplifiers and an acoustic piano. Andraé sang to the island people—it was serious missionary stuff." The visit to Western Samoa included a stay in a home with no electricity—but plenty of menacing-looking scorpions.[22]

For Thedford, like most of the Disciples, the massive tour was a blur at the time. He does remember that at the Sydney Opera House concert, the audience called for him to sing "He Looked Beyond My Fault." "And it was only then that I realized how big a following the song had," he said. "As for this tour, you don't really realize what's happening, what's going on. You don't realize the importance of the role you're in or the effects of the bubble you're in or how other people perceive you."[23]

Impact and Influence

At the end of 1974, despite its late release, *"Live" at Carnegie Hall* finished second in the final Best-Selling Gospel LPs chart, behind only *Lord, Help Me to Hold Out, James Cleveland Presents the Harold Smith Majestics. Keep On Singin'* was the twenty-seventh best-selling album, and "I Don't Know Why Jesus Loved Me" (probably the misidentified *Keep On Singin'*) finished at #30. With his name attached to six different groups and LPs, Cleveland had six entries in the final top 35 LPs for 1974.[24]

As with many emotion-fueled religious revivals, the Jesus Movement was eventually co-opted into existing or (at best) reformed religious institutions and its energy channeled elsewhere. Jesus Music likewise was subsumed into the more commercial, more palatable realm of what came to be called "contemporary Christian music" or "CCM." Steve Turner asserts that Jesus Rock (as he calls it) had "no effect on mainstream rock 'n' roll" and he's certainly correct that CCM led to a more insular religious music scene where Christian musicians performed primarily for other Christians. The lone exceptions to emerge from that heady era were Andraé Crouch and the Disciples—and *"Live" at Carnegie Hall* was the change agent. Flawed though the recording of the original concert may have been, *"Live"* was a singular breakthrough for an openly faith-driven, uncompromising artist and it took the Disciples into expansive new markets, white and Black, Christian and secular.[25]

If Larry Norman was the John Lennon of CCM, Andraé Crouch was Marvin Gaye, James Brown and Michael Jackson rolled into one.—Mark Joseph[26]

NOTES

1. Andraé Crouch and the Disciples, *"Live" at Carnegie Hall: Sold Out!* (Light LS-5602); Danny Taylor, *Live at Carnegie Hall* (Tempo/Impact TL 7046, 1972); Cheryl A. Forbes, "Jesus Joy Revisited," *Christianity Today*, September 29, 1972, 48; Sam Sutherland, "Studio Track," *Billboard*, May 20, 1972, 8; Paul Baker, *Contemporary Christian Music: Where It Came From, What It Is, Where It's Going* (Westchester, IL: Crossway Books, 1979), 56.
2. Bili Thedford, interview with the authors, March 18, 2021.
3. "America's Number One Soul Group," *Billboard*, October 14, 1972, W-14; Bill Maxwell, interview with the authors, May 18, 2019.
4. Bill Maxwell, interview with the authors, May 18, 2019.
5. Sondra "Blinky" Williams, interview with the authors, December 8, 2020; Bill Maxwell, interview with the authors, September 14, 2022.
6. Bill Maxwell, interview with the authors, September 14, 2022.
7. Andraé Crouch and the Disciples, *"Live" at Carnegie Hall* (Light Records LS-5602-LP); Raymond Wise, interview with the authors, September 6, 2020.

8. "Interview: Singer-Songwriter Andraé Crouch Discusses His Career," Tavis Smiley, June 8, 2004, NPR; Phyllis St. James, interview with the authors, January 23, 2021.

9. "Paul Simon Discusses Upcoming Live, LP, Present & Future Plans," *Cash Box*, February 2, 1974, 7, 22; Robert Hilburn, *Paul Simon: The Life* (New York: Simon & Schuster, 2018), 173–174; Lynn Keesecker, personal correspondence with the authors, September 14, 2022.

10. https://hymnary.org/text/amazing_grace_shall_always_be_my_song; https://godsmusicismylife.com/the-redemption-of-reba-rambo; Bili Thedford, interview with the authors, November 12, 2020.

11. Leonard B. Meyers, *Explaining Music* (Chicago: University of Chicago Press, 1978), 114.

12. Jeffrey LaValley, interview with the authors, August 29, 2020.

13. "Latin: Also Recommended," *Billboard*, May 12, 1973, 56.

14. John Sippel, "Gospel Gambol," *Billboard*, January 5, 1974, 18; "Best-Selling Gospel LP's," *Billboard*, February 16, 1974, 34; "Best-Selling Gospel LP's," *Billboard*, March 16, 1974, 39; "Best-Selling Gospel LP's," *Billboard*, April 20, 1974, 38; "Best-Selling Gospel LP's," *Billboard*, May 18, 1974, 50; "Best-Selling Gospel LP's," *Billboard*, June 15, 1974, 42; "Best-Selling Gospel LP's," *Billboard*, August 10, 1974, 56; "Best-Selling Gospel LP's," *Billboard*, September 7, 1974, 38; "Best-Selling Gospel LP's," *Billboard*, October 5, 1974, 50; "Best-Selling Gospel LP's," *Billboard*, November 9, 1974, 35; "Best-Selling Gospel LP's," *Billboard*, December 7, 1974, 41; "Best-Selling Gospel LP's," *Billboard*, January 18, 1975, 61.

15. David W. Stowe, *No Sympathy for the Devil: Christian Pop Music and the Transformation of American Evangelicalism* (Chapel Hill: University of North Carolina Press, 2015), 93; Mark Allan Powell, *The Encyclopedia of Contemporary Christian Music* (Peabody, M: Hendrickson Publishers, 2002), 211; John J. Thompson, *Raised by Wolves: The Story of Christian Rock & Roll* (Toronto: ECW Press, 2000), 45; https://greatest70salbums.blogsport.com.

16. Earl Paige, "Word Expansion Worldwide in Religious and Pop as Well," *Billboard*, September 7, 1974, 38; Bob Gersztyn, *Jesus Rocks the World: The Definitive History of Contemporary Christian Music*, Vol. 1 (Santa Barbara, CA: Praeger, 2012), 108; Bil Carpenter, *Uncloudy Days: The Gospel Music Encyclopedia* (San Francisco: Backbeat Books, 2005), 107.

17. "Changing Formats," *Broadcasting*, July 30, 1973, 47; "Sounding a New Beat in Radio: The Jesus Rockers," *Broadcasting*, August 20, 1973, 76–77; "Gospel Music Association 1973 Dove Award Final Nominees," *Record World*, September 15, 1973, 58; Ed Shea, "Ed Shea on '73: ASCAP County's Best Year," *Cash Box*, October 20, 1973, 68.

18. "Oak Ridgers Host 4-Day Gospel Fete," *Cash Box*, July 21, 1973, 33; "Shaped Notes," *Billboard*, November 3, 1973, 31; "Intl. Gospel Fest Draws 2,000," *Billboard*, July 28, 1973, 24; Baker, *Contemporary Christian Music*, 84–85;

"Who/Where/When," *Billboard*, September 29, 1973, 16; "Who/Where/When," *Billboard*, October 6, 1973, 12; "Who/Where/When," *Billboard*, October 13, 1973, 15.

19. Bill Maxwell, interview with the authors, September 14, 2022; "Who/Where/When," *Billboard*, October 20, 1973, 18; "Who/Where/When," *Billboard*, November 3, 1973, 14; "Who/Where/When," *Billboard*, December 1, 1973, 14; https://concerts.fandom.com/wiki/Australian_Tours.

20. https://concertarchives.org/concerts/billy-preston-andrae-crouch-and-the-disciples; Kevin Craik, interview with the authors, November 3, 2022.

21. Phyllis St. James, interview with the authors, January 23, 2021.

22. Bill Maxwell, interview with the authors, September 14, 2022.

23. Bili Thedford, interview with the authors, November 12, 2020.

24. "Top Gospel Albums," *Billboard*, December 28, 1974, 34.

25. Steve Turner, *Hungry for Heaven: Rock 'n' Roll & the Search for Redemption* (Downers Grove, IL: InterVarsity Press, 1995), 163.

26. Mark Joseph, *The Rock & Roll Rebellion* (Nashville: Broadman & Holman, 1999), 25.

9

Take Me Back

When does the tide turn? For Andraé Crouch and the Disciples, the release of *"Live" at Carnegie Hall* elevated the group into the highest tier of gospel music, and the Disciples drew ever larger crowds with each tour. More important, at least to Andraé, people outside the narrow confines of religious music were discovering the Disciples as well. He retained his strong ties to the virtually all-white Jesus Movement, began to increasingly add listeners from the realm of Black gospel music, and, as word of the extraordinary live shows grew, even casual music fans now took notice.

Major Tours and Appearances

The Disciples' nonstop touring schedule became even more challenging as additional dates were continually added to tours. One early example in February 1974 is that during a three-day (and night) mini tour in and around Chicago, the group, accompanied by Sweet Spirit, performed six times:

Feb. 5 Northeastern University, Chicago (noon)
Feb. 5 North Central College, Napierville, Illinois (5 P.M.)
Feb. 6 Chicago State University
Feb. 7 Malcolm X College
Feb. 8 Loyola University, Chicago (noon)
Feb. 8 Northwestern University, Evanston, Illinois (8 P.M.)[1]

Not all dates were with the Disciples. In March, Andraé was invited to sing at the Reverend Billy Graham's Crusade in Albuquerque, New Mexico. Massive crowds filled the university's arena for Graham's nightly sermons. On the Graham organization's website is a high-quality video of Andraé alone at the piano singing "Through It All" after telling the story of how he received the gift of music. Crouch's presence that evening even merited a mention in *Christianity Today*'s coverage of the event. Like many of the Graham crusades, the Albuquerque services were filmed and later shown on national television.[2]

Light Records celebrated the Disciples' heightened visibility (and increased sales) with a full-page advertisement in the March 30, 1974, issue of *Billboard* spotlighting "America's Number One Soul Gospel Group." The accompanying photograph is another example of the increasingly fluid nature of the Disciples' line-up, featuring Sandra and Andraé Crouch, Danniebelle Hall, Fletch Wiley, guitarist Jimmie Davis, Bill Maxwell, Bili Thedford, and Perry Morgan.[3]

In the midst of touring, and composing for his next album, Andraé took time off to produce—with Bill Maxwell—Danniebelle's eponymous first LP for Light Records. Recorded at CAM Recording Studios in Oklahoma City in early 1974, the album includes contributions from the members of Sonlight, Clark Gassman, and a few other well-regarded studio musicians. Most of the songs, save for Hockensmith's "In Remembrance," were written by Hall. Another article in *Billboard* notes that Crouch kept an office in the city and was "owner" of Shalom Records.[4]

Preparing *Take Me Back* with Bill Maxwell

Maxwell, now listed as "co-producer," said that the Disciples also returned to the studio in early 1974 to begin recording what would be the group's next album, *Take Me Back*. Because of the Disciples' invariably manic touring schedule, however, the recording process took nearly the entire year, with Andraé and Bill scheduling one- or two-day sessions whenever the Disciples were back in Southern California. The studio of choice was Mama Jo's, at 8321 Lankersheim Boulevard, North Hollywood. Mama Jo's warm vibe, with a recording board designed by noted engineer Vincent Van Haaff, also attracted mainstream artists, including Billy Joel, George Michael, the Alan Parsons Project, Ambrosia, and others.[5]

Maxwell said that among the songs selected for the recording sessions were three that the Disciples had been performing on tour throughout 1973 and 1974, "Tell Them," "Take Me Back," and "You Can Depend on Me." "It Ain't No New Thing" and "You Can Depend on Me" both have 1973 Lexicon Music copyrights, while the remaining songs are copyrighted 1975. Singer

Kathy Hazzard said that "Take Me Back" had originally been written and recorded for Sweet Spirit, with Bea Carr singing the lead vocals:

> We worked on "Take Me Back" during the *Just Andraé* [recording] sessions as well. Once Andraé really liked something, you couldn't stop him. Once he knew that he had the audience captured by a new song, we would play it every night before the album came so that when the record did come out, people knew the song already.

This practice had been part of the Disciples' recording process for as long as Maxwell had been associated with Andraé. "We were constantly trying out new songs during that year," Maxwell said. "In a concert, he wouldn't have a song finished but he'd tell the audience, 'I've been working on a song like this. You guys want to hear a little thing of what I'm trying to work on?'" Crouch would then sing the chorus and say, "I don't have a verse yet." Maxwell recalled that Andraé now had "the whole audience singing." Ultimately, Crouch "got the whole country being a part of the songwriting process." "They felt like that was their song and they were invested," Maxwell said.[6]

An All-Star Lineup in the Studio

For Maxwell, the *Take Me Back* sessions continued a process that had begun with *Just Andraé* and *"Live" at Carnegie Hall*. Early in the sessions, Maxwell contacted specific musicians whose "sound" he or Crouch heard for certain compositions. One of the first to be hired was Joe Sample, keyboardist with the Jazz Crusaders. Fletch Wiley, who attended North Texas State University (now the University of North Texas), also assisted Maxwell in contacting musicians with a shared North Texas background. "I'd known Dean Parks in Texas," Maxwell said; "we were in a band called the Third Avenue Blues Band that was pretty popular playing in clubs around Dallas and Fort Worth." The group hosted a Sunday jam session and the top musicians in the area— David Hungate, Lou Marini, Tex Allen, Tom Malone, and others who eventually ended up in Los Angeles—often came and jammed. Maxwell said Los Angeles–area producers paid the top musicians the same studio hourly rate, "whether they were playing for Barry White or whether you were playing for Bugs Bunny. You get paid the same no matter who you were playing for." That is how Sample, soon a frequent Crouch collaborator, initially arrived at Mama

Jo's. "He just came the first time because he was booked," Maxwell said, "but then he loved it. That's how I got him." Beginning with *Take Me Back*, Parks also became a regular contributor. "He was one of the only guitar players who could play rock 'n' roll [and] who could really read well," Maxwell said. "And Dean helped me get the others." It was Parks, Maxwell said, who often suggested musicians when Crouch needed a particular "sound," including Michael Omartian and Wilton Felder. Once word spread among the close-knit community of studio musicians of the high-quality music being recorded at Mama Jo's, "everybody wanted to play on Andraé's albums."[7]

Maxwell and Hockensmith both said that Crouch, who was keenly aware of his lack of formal lessons, often denigrated his piano-playing skills. "Andraé just was really good at what he did," Hockensmith said. Maxwell said that Crouch "tried very hard" to "squirrel out" of playing piano on his recordings. "He'd say, 'Get another piano player,' " Maxwell recalled of the Mama Jo's sessions:

> But he'd sit down and play it and Joe Sample would just be amazed. He'd say, "Why are you having me? You should do this. I don't play this like you." And Andraé would say, "No, but you bring something to it I don't." Joe Sample once told me, "I've got to be on my A-game here because most of the stuff I play on is just simply pop music. But you never know what you're getting into over here. You could be playing all kinds of things and you better be ready for it.[8]

Despite Maxwell's entreaties, Andraé was so pleased with the results that Sample ultimately played piano on many of the songs on *Take Me Back*: "I Still Love You," "It Ain't No New Thing," "They Shall Me Mine," "Just Like He Said He Would," "All I Can Say," and "Oh Savior." Larry Muhoberac played piano on "Praises," "Sweet Love of Jesus," "Tell Them," and "Oh Savior" (on the Fender Rhodes) and Tom Hensley played on "You Can Depend on Me," while Andraé only played piano on "Take Me Back." The difference with his previous Light albums, of course, was that this time Crouch *chose* to only play on one track.[9]

At Mama Jo's

Even in light of the stellar results coming from Mama Jo's, when the bills from the *Take Me Back* sessions came to the execs at Light Records, Maxwell said he "got into a lot of trouble." "Light didn't pay double scale," Maxwell said. "But to get the best guys, the best rhythm section, players were charging double, something like $110 per hour back then. But that's what it took at first."[10]

In 1974, Mama Jo's was in the process of transitioning from sixteen recording tracks to twenty-four tracks. The studio itself was a small, intimate space, which Maxwell said he liked because the drummer could reach out and touch the piano, resulting in a "better sound." Later, Maxwell said, the owner built a separate room where the drum set could be "isolated." "It was so small, there was no room to include the vocalists during the recording of the music tracks," he said. "We would have the guitar amplifiers out in the hall. The bass and Fender Rhodes would go direct to the board." Instrumental tracks for the songs were recorded first and the vocals were overdubbed later. "But we would have the form pretty right by the time we recorded," Maxwell said. "We'd all know that this is the chorus, this is the verse, this is where they go into the bridge, and this is the instrumental section. We adapted the vocals to that. These were not live recordings."[11]

Hockensmith was at the early stages of a long career accompanying Neil Diamond on tour but continued to record with Crouch whenever possible. Hockensmith joined Parks, David T. Walker, Larry Carlton, and Fred Tackett, sometimes singly and sometimes in pairs, adding "sweetening" to the basic rhythm section tracks. "You add little embellishments and hopefully little hook lines," he said, "lines that people can remember and sing. And then Bill would bring in the other keyboard players [and] synth players that could add pads that would give depth totally different to what Andraé was doing on the piano." Unlike the more casual nature of the *Just Andraé* sessions, Hockensmith said the recording of the tracks for *Take Me Back* felt "a little more sectioned off." "A lot of what I played was just me and Bill in the studio," he said. "I think it turned out well, but in some ways it's harder to play that way." Having the opportunity to record with some of the top guitarists in the country was an added bonus. "I'll confess that Dean Parks was an influence on me," Hockensmith said, "and some of the things I do were from Larry Carlton."[12]

A key addition to *Take Me Back* was arranger/keyboardist Larry Muhoberac. Muhoberac had served as Elvis Presley's keyboard player, including the famed "comeback" special *Elvis* from 1968, and eventually became Presley's music director. Besides being a fine composer himself, Maxwell said that Muhoberac was especially talented at creating string and horn arrangements. "Larry was a Louisiana keyboard player who was really very musical," Maxwell said. "[He] could write anything. If Andraé would sit and play a song, Larry would sit there with his pencil and by the time Andraé played it, the chart was done. No piano. He'd have it exactly. He was very sensitive to Andraé, too."[13]

After the informality of the *Just Andraé* and *"Live" at Carnegie Hall* sessions, Wiley said he too was somewhat taken aback by the *Take Me Back*'s much more structured atmosphere, especially with the rhythm sections, solos, and vocalists all recorded separately. "Bill Maxwell got together with Andraé and they went through a ton of tunes," Wiley said. "Andraé always has a ton of tunes and Bill was good for Andraé. Bill helped him focus." When Crouch discovered that Wiley had a degree in music from North Texas, he asked if he could do arrangements on the album. "I said, 'Yeah, I can arrange music,'" Wiley recalled, "but I really didn't know what I was doing then. I even wrote out all of the bass lines—which was stupid when you have guys like Dean Parks, David Hungate, and Wilton Felder playing bass! But it was really fun to do that with great players." Also different from previous Light releases, Wiley and Muhoberac created their instrumental arrangements with Andraé's input and blessing. Wiley particularly enjoyed working with Muhoberac. "I stole all my string licks from him," Wiley said. "Larry arranged a bunch of *Take Me Back*, including all of the strings, and did the horn arrangements on probably half of the record."[14]

The songs selected for *Take Me Back* were particularly strong, with several later entering the repertoire of Black and white churches and becoming staples of the Disciples' live performances. With Maxwell at the producer's board, an adequate budget, and top musicians available for every recording session, *Take Me Back* also marks the full introduction of vocalist Danniebelle Hall to the contemporary religious music world, with five memorable vocal performances. Sandra Crouch, Perry Morgan, Hall, Thedford, Naomi Beard, and Phyllis St. James were charged with singing Andraé's increasingly innovative background vocal arrangements. The resulting album is, as Hazzard dubbed it, "iconic."[15]

Light Records finally gave the album packaging the attention befitting its biggest star. The sepia-toned cover photograph was taken on a very cold day outside Bill Maxwell's grandfather's church, Union Chapel Methodist Church in Athens, Tennessee, while the Disciples were performing a concert in Nashville and featured Andraé, Maxwell, Wiley, Morgan, Sandra, Hall, and Thedford. "We knew a good photographer in Nashville, Bill Grine, and we needed to shoot a cover," Maxwell recalled. "We had been playing 'Take Me Back' live and decided that would be a good title." For the first time, the

LP has a double fold-out, revealing photobook-styled photographs of the group and detailed liner notes—also in the same gold/tan sepia tone. Even the album sleeve is sharply designed and continues the overall theme and includes—also for the first time—the lyrics to the eleven songs on the album (and their accompanying Bible verses). The significantly longer lengths of the songs on *Take Me Back* (with four of the songs longer than four minutes and three others just under four minutes) allowed Andraé and his collaborators to stretch with more complex arrangements, including several "mini-suites" with multiple interrelated sections or passages.[16]

Take Me Back

Side I

"I'll Still Love You"

"I'll Still Love You" features three distinct sections, beginning with a nod to the opening track on Elton John's *Goodbye Yellow Brick Road*, "Funeral for a Friend," complete with a white noise synthesizer mimicking wind sounds, soon joined by an English horn, harpsichord, analog ARP 2600 synthesizer, and bass trombone—and all coming together in exquisite counterpoint throughout the song. "I'll Still Love You," while it begins on a G♭ major chord, is one of the most harmonically diverse compositions on the album. The song also highlights Thedford's staccato vocal stylings, allowing Maxwell's drum work to shine. The polished performances, arrangements by Wiley and Andraé, and the sheer level of painstaking precision are rare in an era when gospel artists completed entire albums in a day. Andraé's "Team Crouch"—an uncommonly talented group of collaborators—enabled him to orchestrate, explore, arrange, and execute the music he was hearing in his head.

"Praises"

The anthem "Praises" introduces Andraé's theology of worship and praise music. In the key of E♭ major, he returns to the ii–V–iii–vi harmonic progressions he favored in earlier songs, including "If Heaven Never Was Promised to Me." Opening with minimal instrumentation, it's another multifaceted song with distinct sections in a $\frac{3}{4}$ time signature that does not fully "open up" until the chorus. "Praises" showcases Sandra's urgent vocals before the "Hallelujah" section roars in. Buoyed by Muhoberac's challenging arrangements, these first two songs announce a more musical, more confident Andraé.

The recording of "Praises," incidentally, was not without its challenges. Maxwell said that in recording one of the vocal sections, the bass line was inadvertently erased from the first eight bars of the song. Maxwell originally tried to find a bass player on short notice to replace the section but in the end just left the song as it was—sans bass—for those measures.

Raymond Wise called "Praises" "a forward-looking kind of praise song." In the past, Wise said, most African American compositions were *about* God, but rarely addressed God directly:

> They talked about the God who empowered them to make it through their struggles but Andraé's praise songs instead said, "God, now I'm talking to You." That reflects the sense of relationship and intimacy that Crouch often brought to his music. Without that relationship, he could not have written a lot of his music.[17]

"Just Like He Said He Would"

From a theological standpoint, the guitar-driven "Just Like He Said He Would" (which credits John 14:2–3 in the liner notes) speaks directly to the topic of the Second Coming of Jesus, still a popular theme in the evangelical world during this period. For the song, Andraé returns to D♭ major and the vocals—in prime unison—embrace the classic three-part gospel sound. During the opening verse, the song also features Maxwell's signature half-time groove percolating amid a hardcore COGIC funk opening, not unlike the best of Levi Stubbs and the Four Tops. A synthesizer oscillating a pedal point during the audience-pleasing closing vamp allows vocalists Andraé, Danniebelle, and Sandra to really cut loose.

According to singer Hazzard, in the mid-1970s, "Just Like He Said He Would" was often the closing song of concerts. "During this song, Andraé would say, 'OK, I know some of you guys want to clap on the two and four.' But I also know some of you are going to clap on the one and three.' We would just crack up."[18]

"All I Can Say (I Really Love You)"

One of the most memorable power ballads in Andraé's entire musical canon, "All I Can Say (I Really Love You)" features a heartfelt duet between Morgan and Hall. The lengthy, piercing introduction begins with an elongated high E♭ performed on the violins that crescendos and cascades to an A major tonality. The sound of the full string orchestra is cinematic, portraying a dialogue between God and creation—a spiritual love song, rather than the secular love songs of most popular music. This is another example of how Andraé adopts lyrics and contemporary pop love songs for the diverse audiences now attending Disciples concerts in venues other than churches. These were audiences, Maxwell said, that would be well aware of similar arrangements by two of Andraé's favorite groups, the Delfonics and the Stylistics.[19]

"You Can Depend on Me"

The COGIC-influenced "You Can Depend on Me" unexpectedly incorporates Big Band swing elements, Manhattan Transfer–styled vocalese, and a catchy walking bass line. Wiley said that he particularly enjoyed collaborating on "You Can Depend on Me." "It's like a Big Band–era shuffle," he said, "so it lent itself really easily to all of the [University of] North Texas stuff. It's a very bluesy thing." Crouch, he said, constructed the intricate vocal arrangement for the song on the spot in the studio. Hazzard said that "You Can Depend on Me" was particularly popular in their subsequent tours. "That was another song that the audience just went insane over when we started it," she said. "Andraé would start it and it would almost be over. Sometimes he'd say, 'OK, the group doesn't have to sing—you guys know the words.' Bill and the band would play and the whole audience, thousands of people, would start singing the words."

From a ministry standpoint, Andraé's lyrics, which credit Isaiah 6:8, express a mutuality of dependence with God—humanity needs God and God works through humanity. While the song speaks to evangelism, the words now reflect a theology with more of an emphasis on a Wesleyan-styled Holiness tradition, one that declares, as Luke 10:2 says, "The harvest is ripe but the laborers are few."[20] In short, like Crouch is saying in the title, "you can depend on me, God."

Side II

"Take Me Back"

No other song in Crouch's repertoire stitches an entire recording together like "Take Me Back." It is the beating heart of the album, lyrically and musically. From a theological standpoint, the lyrics (inspired by the *Living Bible* translation of Revelation 2:4) challenge listeners to return to God and God's provisions—love, dependence, creativity, responsibility, and promises. In a very direct way, every song examines one or more of those provisions. The slow, majestic full-chorus opening, and the use of twelve powerful voices from Christ Memorial COGIC, makes it clear what's going on here—Andraé is taking the listener to church. In the verses, the soulful brilliance of Danniebelle's voice, with the choir serving as a Greek chorus, sings directly to each listener. The text is Andraé's retelling of the core biblical story of redemption, reconciliation, and return.

The album's title track is also a good example of the collaborative nature of the studio sessions. According to Maxwell, "Take Me Back" was one of the songs that had been created and perfected on tour, incorporating the audience's responses as Andraé worked out the song, one verse at a time. Maxwell said that Wiley created the arrangement from Crouch's original composition and that Muhoberac arranged the strings and horns. "Billy Preston played something inspirational on the organ," Maxwell said, "and Andraé, Wilton Felder, Dean Parks, and I played on the track based on what Billy did. [Muhoberac] was really terrific at taking one of Andraé's melodies or ideas for one of his harmonies and creating an intro and developing it."[21]

Composer Jeffrey LaValley said that as a young man "Take Me Back" captured his imagination from the opening seconds. "I thought it was amazing," he said. "That organ entry intrigued me because I was an organist at that time. So when the piano came in and with that hard chord and organ slide up to that D♭ chord, I said, 'I'm here for this!'" Among the aspects of Crouch's compositions that LaValley said he admired most were Andraé's ability to craft arrangements that were "always perfect" for individual songs. "Nothing was too far out where it took away from the lyrical content of the song," he said. "'Take Me Back' is a really good song. With its changes, it took you to places where you didn't expect that song to go. I loved that album."[22]

Composer Mark Kibble, a former member of Take 6 and a vocal arranger himself, said the "simplicity" of the melody line is critical, which is why a song like "Take Me Back" is so "infectious." "No matter what Andraé does harmonically, you get it," Kibble said, "because the melody and the hook are so simple—easy to repeat, easy to sing that even if you don't know anything about harmony at all, you get that." Kibble added that even when Crouch harmonizes, "he usually does the melody in octave." "You hear it on top and you'll hear it in the bottom," he said, "so that the ladies can sing it and the men can sing it. And at the same time, he will fill the middle with harmony, so that if you hear the harmony, you can sing the inner parts very easily."[23]

Plate 1 The COGIC's *It's a Blessing* album cover. From left, Edna Wright, Gloria Jones, Andraé Crouch, unknown stand-in, Sandra Crouch. Not pictured: Sondra "Blinky" Williams and Billy Preston. From the authors' collection. Exodus Records EX-54, 1965. Images/photos courtesy of Vee-Jay Records.

Plate 2 Andraé Crouch, "Nobody like the Lord" and "I Find No Fault in Him" 45, self-pressed custom disk. Courtesy of Bob Marovich.

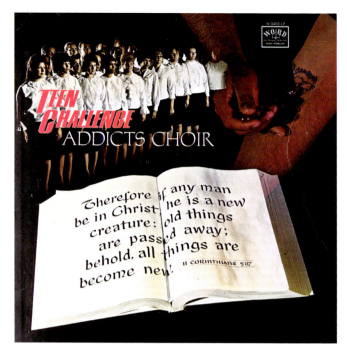

Plate 3 *Teen Challenge Addict's Choir* album cover. From the author's collection. Word Records WST-8403-LP, 1968-69. Images/photos courtesy of Word Records.

Plate 4 Andraé Crouch & the Disciples, *Take the Message Everywhere* album cover. From left, back: Ruben Fernandez and Billy Thedford. From left, front: Sherman Andrus, Andraé Crouch, Perry Morgan. Fernandez and Andrus left the Disciples shortly after this version of the cover was released. From the author's collection. Light Records LS-55-4-LP, 1969-70. Images/photos courtesy of Light Records, a division of MNRK Records LP.

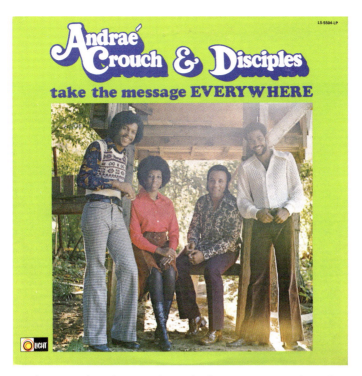

Plate 5 Andraé Crouch & the Disciples, *Take the Message Everywhere* album cover, second version. From left: Billy Thedford, Sandra Crouch, Andraé Crouch, Perry Morgan. From the author's collection. Light Records LS-55-4-LP, 1969-70. Images/photos courtesy of Light Records, a division of MNRK Records LP.

Plate 6 Andraé Crouch & the Disciples, "Christian People" 45. From the author's collection. Liberty/UA 56201, 1970. Images/photos courtesy of Liberty/UA Records.

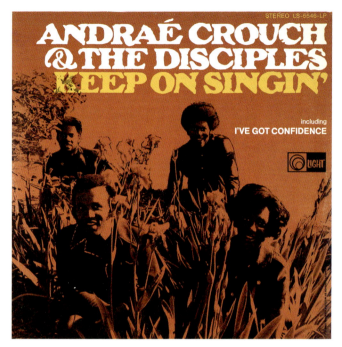

Plate 7 Andraé Crouch & the Disciples, *Keep On Singin'*. From left, back: Perry Morgan and Billy Thedford. From left, front: Andraé Crouch and Sandra Crouch. From the author's collection. Light Records LS-5546-LP, 1970. Images/photos courtesy of Light Records, a division of MNRK Records LP.

Plate 8 Andraé Crouch & the Disciples, *Soulfully*. From left, back: Sandra Crouch, Billy Thedford, Perry Morgan. Front: Andraé Crouch. From the author's collection. Light Records LS-5581-LP, 1972. Images/photos courtesy of Light Records, a division of MNRK Records LP.

Plate 9 Andraé Crouch, *Just Andraé*. From the author's collection. Light Records LS-5589-LP, 1972. Images/photos courtesy of Light Records, a division of MNRK Records LP.

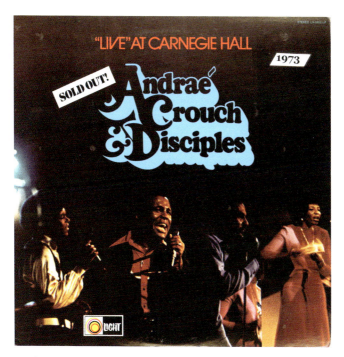

Plate 10 Andraé Crouch & the Disciples, *"Live" at Carnegie Hall*. From left, Billy Thedford, Andraé Crouch, Perry Morgan, Sandra Crouch. From the author's collection. Light Records LS-5602-LP, 1973. Images/photos courtesy of Light Records, a division of MNRK Records LP.

Plate 11 Andraé Crouch & the Disciples, *Take Me Back*. From left, Andraé Crouch, Bill Maxwell, Fletch Wiley, Perry Morgan, Sandra Crouch, Danniebelle Hall, Bili Thedford. From the author's collection. Light Records LS-5637-LP, 1975. Images/photos courtesy of Light Records, a division of MNRK Records LP.

Plate 12 Andraé Crouch & the Disciples, *The Best of Andraé*. From the author's collection. Light Records LS-5678-LP, 1976. Images/photos courtesy of Light Records, a division of MNRK Records LP.

Plate 13 Andraé Crouch & the Disciples, *This Is Another Day*. From the author's collection. Light Records LS-5683-LP, 1976. Images/photos courtesy of Light Records, a division of MNRK Records LP.

Plate 14 *On the Road with Andraé Crouch*, art by Al Hartley. Crouch Music Corporation, 1977. Fleming H. Revell Company. From the author's collection.

Plate 15 DJ Dave Peters interviews Andraé, circa 1978–1980. Photograph courtesy of Stephen "Bugs" Giglio.

Plate 16 Andraé Crouch & the Disciples, *Live in London*. Perhaps the most iconic cover art in gospel music history. From the author's collection. Light Records LSX-5717, 1978. Images/photos courtesy of Light Records, a division of MNRK Records LP.

Plate 17 Danniebelle Hall and Andraé Crouch, heading for the tour bus, circa 1978–1980. Photograph courtesy of Stephen "Bugs" Giglio.

Plate 18 Fans often brought food to the tour bus known as "Ruby" during American tours. One of the most faithful was the "Pie Lady" (center, front). From left, Bili Thedford, Andraé Crouch, Bill Maxwell, and road manager Gary West. Photograph courtesy of Stephen "Bugs" Giglio.

Plate 19 Andraé Crouch, *I'll Be Thinking of You*. From the author's collection. Light Records LS-5763, 1979. Images/photos courtesy of Light Records, a division of MNRK Records LP.

Plate 20 Perry Morgan, captured in a pensive moment while on tour, quit working with Andraé shortly after the Live in London tours ended. Circa 1979–1980. Photograph courtesy of Stephen "Bugs" Giglio.

Plate 21 Sandra Crouch on a tour bus, perhaps during a Scandinavian tour, circa 1980–1981. Photograph courtesy of Stephen "Bugs" Giglio.

Plate 22 Guitarist Jimmie Davis (left) and multi-instrumentalist Fletch Wiley wait for supper somewhere on the road, circa 1980–1982. Photograph courtesy of Stephen "Bugs" Giglio.

Plate 23 Singer Kristle Murden and Andraé Crouch enjoy thumbing through a new magazine, circa 1980–1982. Photograph courtesy of Stephen "Bugs" Giglio.

Plate 24 Andraé Crouch, *More of the Best*. From the author's collection. Light Records LS-5795, 1981. Images/photos courtesy of Light Records, a division of MNRK Records LP.

Plate 25 Andraé Crouch on the tour bus, heading for London, March 1980. Photograph courtesy of Stephen "Bugs" Giglio.

Plate 26 Andraé Crouch goofing around in the Green Room, waiting to go on the *PTL Club* television show, circa early 1980s. Photograph Stephen "Bugs" Giglio.

Plate 27 Andraé Crouch, *Don't Give Up*. From the author's collection. Warner Bros. Records BSK 3513, 1981. Images/photos courtesy of Warner Records.

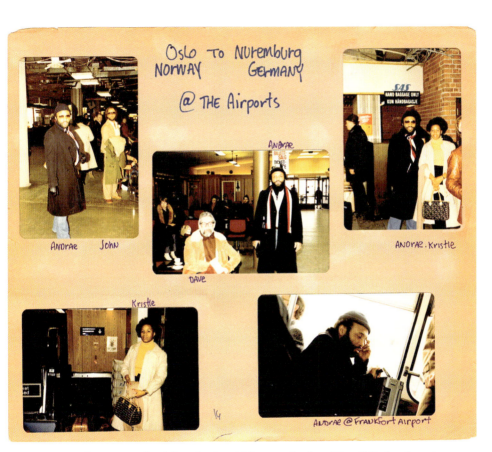

Plate 28 Page from a scrapbook kept by Road Manager Stephen "Bugs" Giglio, featuring airports during Oslo, Norway, to Nuremburg, Germany, transit, spring 1980. Courtesy of Stephen "Bugs" Giglio.

Plate 29 A stoic Bill Maxwell (left) waits for his meal while Andraé Crouch mugs for the camera, somewhere on the road, circa 1980. Photograph courtesy of Stephen "Bugs" Giglio.

Plate 30 Andraé Crouch, *Finally*. From the author's collection. Light Records LS-5784, 1982. Images/photos courtesy of Light Records, a division of MNRK Records LP.

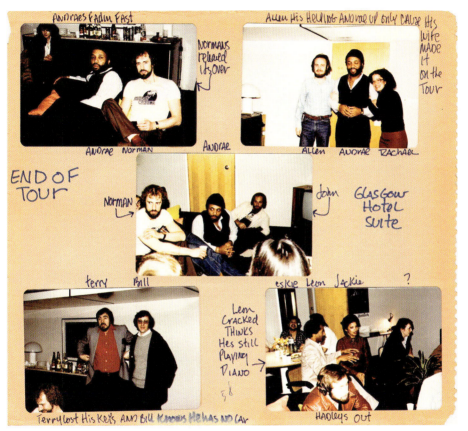

Plate 31 Another page from a scrapbook kept by Road Manager Stephen "Bugs" Giglio, taken in a Glasgow, Scotland, hotel, marking the end of the 1980–1981 European tour, with various band members, family, friends, and crew. Courtesy Stephen "Bugs" Giglio.

Plate 32 Howard McCrary and Sandra Crouch working on a new song, somewhere on the road, early 1980s. Photograph Stephen "Bugs" Giglio.

Plate 33 Andraé Crouch, *No Time to Lose*. From the author's collection. Light Records LS-5863, 1984. Images/photos courtesy of Light Records, a division of MNRK Records LP.

For Wise, the inclusion of "Take Me Back" reflects another important element of Crouch's ministry. Where other songs on an album might show Andraé's command of various musical styles, he always included at least one song that spoke directly to the more traditional elements of the Black church. "He was about ministry," Wise said, "but his ministry took him way beyond the traditional Pentecostal church, way beyond the traditional Black church—but yet he always acknowledged 'that's still my home—and I want to appeal to that audience.'" With that in mind, Wise said, it was important to begin the song with that distinctive Billy Preston "old school" Black gospel riff on the organ. "So there's at least one song that Black church folks can say, 'All right, I don't know about that other stuff, but I like that one right there.' You definitely got the down-home church gospel sound and people are still singing 'Take Me Back' today." It was essential, Wise said he believes, that Andraé make that musical statement on every album. "He's saying, 'Regardless of where my ministry takes me, regardless of where I may go musically, I do acknowledge that it's significant to speak to the community I come from.' He's saying, 'I acknowledge you and I want to honor you in some kind of song.'"[24]

"The Sweet Love of Jesus"

"The Sweet Love of Jesus" is another guitar-driven song, this time in G major, and bolstered by Muhoberac's swelling, string-dominated orchestration as the lyrics revisit I Corinthians 13 (the so-called love chapter). As noted earlier, Andraé avidly followed popular music, listening restlessly for a certain sound, the one best suited to convey a certain message. "Andraé was a storyteller," Wise said. "He was always trying to create images for people. Through the music, he would try to find the right text or lyrics or phrase that would appeal to people's senses." Wise said that one aspect of Crouch's genius was how he made his listeners part of the story he was telling in song. "He's saying, 'My friend, my brother, here's my story. You've got this story, too.'"[25]

"It Ain't No New Thing"

Maxwell said that "It Ain't No New Thing" illustrates how quickly Crouch created and wrote new music. "The songs came almost instantly," he said. "And if he had a song like 'It Ain't No New Thing,' he wanted it to sound old, so that's why we went back and did a Dixieland kind of thing. We tailored [the accompaniment] to what the songs were about." As with many of Andraé's songs, Maxwell said that his unpredictable musical approach was an essential element of Crouch's appeal. "You couldn't pigeonhole him into just saying, '*This* is gospel music.' Underneath that, though, if you took all of the instrumentation off and just played it with Andraé at the piano, the gist of it is that the songs were great." For Andraé, that meant if the lyrics suggested a ragtime feel in D♭ major, then that's exactly what he would do. If he heard brass growls, plungers, Harmon mutes on trumpets and trombones, so be it. If the song further needed banjos, a clarinet, and even a pennywhistle to "sell" it, then he had Maxwell find musicians capable of pulling it off. The presence of several musical styles, including Dixieland, in "It Ain't No New Thing" is one of the reasons that Wise said he uses the song as an example when he teaches gospel music composition at Indiana University. "Students ask, 'This is gospel?' And I say, 'Yes. This is a part of the innovations that Andraé brought to gospel music.'" What Crouch is portraying in the song is that Jesus Christ is not a new thing. To accomplish this, he uses ragtime, an older musical form in the African American musical canon, to reinforce the inspiration he's drawn from Hebrews 13:8, "Jesus Christ is the same yesterday, today and forever."[26]

"They Shall Be Mine"

"They Shall Be Mine" is an up-tempo call-and-response number, but with a very modern feel in the vocals. Performed in the key of A♭ major, the song picks up intensity with a Horner Clavinet D6 funk-driven groove, energized by the Hammond B3 organ on the verses and a sharp Mike O'Neil guitar solo. *Take Me Back* also marks the first time that a synthesizer appeared on one of Crouch's records. For "They Shall Be Mine," Maxwell said that the ARP utilized on the song had been left at Mama Jo's by the pop group Ambrosia (best known for "How Much I Feel" and "You're the Only Woman"). From a lyric standpoint, "They Shall Be Mine" (from Malachi 3:17) returns to the "end times" topic of eschatology as Andraé sings, "He said, 'Behold I come quickly/Got my reward in my hand.'"[27]

"Oh Savior"

"Oh Savior," with hints of Fanny Crosby's "Pass Me Not Oh Gentle Savior," begins with the story of the blind beggar (from Mark 10:46–52), then morphs into an urgent rock 'n' roll attack fueled by congas, screaming guitar lines, and even a cowbell—all bolstering Danniebelle's electrifying vocals in the vamp. To keep things interesting, Andraé plays with the tonal centers of D♭, G♭, and B♭ minor. Wiley's personal favorite on the LP is "Oh Savior," because, he said, it was the most "fun" to record. "It was so sophisticated and so much ahead of its time in 1974 with the synthesizer," Wiley said. "Andraé let me have free rein with the arrangement on it, too, including the horn parts and other breaks that were off meter." Wiley said that he intentionally left "holes" in his arrangement for the synthesizer to fill. "I told Andraé, 'I just hear a crazy synth thing here.'" At the time, synthesizers were still new and difficult to program, which meant that few bands were using them. "Nobody knew anything about them then," Wiley said. "They didn't have these big patches of programs like they do now. So, it's kind of a goofy synth sound." Like many early synthesizer solos, the entire sequence was written and charted ahead of time. "They were building something into [that song] that they've never heard in gospel music," Wiley said. Hazzard said that when Danniebelle left the Disciples to begin her own career, she was delighted to be given "Oh Savior" to sing in concert. It was, Hazzard said, a particular favorite of congregations in primarily African American churches and venues.[28]

"Tell Them"

As seen previously, Crouch loved to end his albums with a liturgical benediction, leaving the departing listeners with instructions for the days to come. "Tell Them" serves that purpose on *Take Me Back*, a lovely closing ballad that features the Fender Rhodes in the key of G♭ major and some of Hall's warmest vocals over an arrangement created by Andraé, Muhoberac, and Clark Gassman.

Wise said that "Tell Them" is one of his favorite songs because he said it contains a "revealing" insight into Crouch's ministry:

> He's saying, "Tell everybody, the homeless, the man who's walking the streets all alone, or somebody who doesn't have a home. Tell them all. Whatever it takes to tell them, we've got to do it." For Andraé, that meant that if it took surrounding that message in the blues or Dixieland or big band or funk or Polynesian music, he's going to use it to tell them, however and whatever it takes. He's saying, "We've got to find a way to let them know that God loves them."

Wise called "Tell Them" one of the "foundational" pieces in Crouch's entire catalogue. "His ministry could be identified or defined by this—Andraé telling people about his God and that He loved them."[29]

While on tour in support of *Take Me Back*, Hazzard said that Andraé usually performed "Tell Them" as the encore number. "He just knew how to get a crowd roused up," she said. "For 'Tell Them,' he'd get up off the piano and come down and pray with the people." When Danniebelle left, "Tell Them" also became Hazzard's song to sing live. "I hardly could ever get through that song," she said. "Andraé used it as an altar call." On one occasion while the Disciples were providing the music for a Billy Graham crusade, Graham stopped the singing of the traditional altar call song. Graham said, "We're not going to do 'Just as I Am,'" Hazzard recalled. "He said, 'I want Andraé to sing 'Tell Them.' People came forward in droves, I've never seen anything like that in my life. So many people have received the Lord as their personal savior because of that song." Hazzard said that sometimes Crouch would bring her forward as he introduced the song. "He'd say, 'The vocalist on this song is Kathy Hazzard—if she doesn't cry.'"[30]

Response

And in that, *Take Me Back* established itself as a plumbline for the future of contemporary Christian music. For the next forty-five years, it was one of the foremost signifiers of sacred musical sensibilities as a kaleidoscope of American pop music culture. The liturgical formatting may be less emphasized than on previous LPs, but the central theme—"Take me back, dear Lord/To the place where I first received you"—has rarely been more plainly stated. Andraé's foundation in Black gospel music, as expressed in the vibrant COGIC musical traditions of his childhood, fuels both *Take Me Back*'s dynamic multiethnic church experience and its diverse international ministerial heritage, not that everybody quite understood it at the time.

When *Take Me Back* was completed, Maxwell said he took the completed tapes to Light Records. "And they told me that they thought I ruined Andraé because it had lost his basic gospel core, his appeal to the audience that he had," Maxwell said. "They thought it was too all over the place." Maxwell agreed that *Take Me Back*, like *Just Andraé* before it, clearly displays and celebrates Crouch's eclectic musical tastes:

> We had a song like "Take Me Back," which was a great gospel song. Everything about it was appealing to the white church and the Black church. Then you had "It Ain't No New Thing," which was Dixieland. Then you'd have something with mandolins, "Tell Them," that sounds like you were in Venice on a gondola. Then you had "You Can Depend on Me," which was kind of a shuffle. There was something that sounded like the Delfonics, with that kind of orchestration—French

horns, strings, and electric sitars. There was no form—but that was one of the nice appeals to [the album].[31]

Maxwell said that Andraé stood his ground when the Light executives challenged both Maxwell's production and Crouch's songwriting. "Bill Cole insinuated that I had 'ruined' Andraé," Maxwell said. "He said, 'You know Andraé had a specific audience and this record is all over the place. I don't know that his audience is going to appreciate this.'" According to Maxwell, Andraé's response to Cole was equally direct and unapologetic:

> Andraé said, "I don't believe there's any kind of saved music. I don't think there's any kind of saved chords. I think the only thing that is unique is the gospel message. So I put this message to any kind of song, any kind of melody, any kind of beat. I'm going to do that. And I like it." And Andraé told me, "I don't care what they say. I think this is the best record I ever did." Andraé was much bolder than I was. If the record company said that they didn't like something, I took it personally. Andraé was more like, "Well, I like it." And we went with it.[32]

Fortunately, the record-buying public loved *Take Me Back* and the album earned Crouch and the Disciples their first Grammy award a year later, justifying both Andraé's vision—and his faith in Maxwell. "There was a lot of pressure on that album," Maxwell said. "That was the first time Andraé was not using the in-house producers. He was in charge of the record himself. The record company was dealing with me and I felt a lot of pressure from them, like it was going to fail." Additionally, Maxwell said he and Crouch disagreed regularly during the entire studio recording process:

> My big fight with Andraé was that he always wanted more; I always wanted less. He wanted more strings, more vocals, "Let's put more something here." You put in so much, it becomes nothing. While I always wanted to skip back to what he was doing. But somewhere in the middle, we found something that worked. It was challenging. And then, once it was a very big success, all of that was gone.[33]

Wiley said that Maxwell had to contend with Crouch's continued "tinkering" to complete any of the songs. "Bill was really good for Andraé just keeping him focused," Wiley said. "He'd say, 'Come on, Andraé, we've got to get this done.' And really, at the end of records, he'd lock Andraé out of the studio just to do the mix because Andraé would say, 'Oh man, we're not done yet.' And Bill would say, 'Andraé, there's nothing more we can do. This thing has the kitchen sink in it.'"[34]

What separates *Take Me Back* from the earlier albums in Andraé's catalogue is Maxwell's production, which focuses on Crouch's strengths—the impassioned performances by Andraé and his team of all-stars, the unique, sometimes idiosyncratic songwriting, and an irresistibly propulsive beat. Crouch was a master of rhythmic articulation in all its many forms, and perhaps it took a drummer as the producer to truly capture that rock-steady pulse found in even the quietest of songs. Maxwell himself, of course, is a superlative drummer, admired by his peers and interviewed in magazines devoted to percussionists. Couple that with Andraé's muscular, gospel-centric chords on the piano, and *Take Me Back* finally captures what the Disciples had been doing live for several years by this point—wrecking churches and auditoriums, night after night after night.

During the months of the on-again, off-again recording process for *Take Me Back*, Wiley and his family moved back to Dallas. He would periodically fly back to Los Angeles and write a horn chart, then fly back home again. If there was a tour, Wiley would accompany Disciples on those dates. Through it all, Maxwell continued to work on the vocal arranging and overdubs. When Wiley was offered a recording contract by Warner Bros. in 1975, *Take Me Back* was his final project with the Disciples. Looking back, Wiley said that the album marked an important milestone in the incorporation of all forms of musical expression in a sacred music context. "*Take Me Back* represented a step forward at that time," he said, "certainly for Andraé. There was a freedom to the album; it was so very different. It was Andraé leading up to that freedom. It was great because he was a very mature songwriter by that point."[35]

For Andraé, *Take Me Back* held a special place in his heart. In an interview thirty years later, he listed receiving his first Grammy for the album as being one of the "high points" of his career in gospel music. "That was the kicker," he said. "When I won my first Grammy, that blew me away." Crouch also received a Gospel Music Association Dove award nomination for "Gospel Songwriter of the Year."[36]

On Tour Again

Prior to the release of *Take Me Back*, the endless touring in support of *"Live" at Carnegie Hall* continued as well. The Disciples' booking agency used the album's success to broaden the group's audience. On June 11, the Disciples performed at Disneyland as part of a particularly eclectic bill that included the Spinners, Flash Cadillac & the Continental Kids, and Olivia Newton-John. Later that summer, they performed to an entirely different audience with Southern gospel stars the Statesmen at the Pine Knob Theater in Clarkston, Michigan, before 5,000 fans. Also in August, the Disciples joined many of the same Jesus Music artists who had performed at Explo '72 for the multiday Praise '74 at the Orange County Fairgrounds in Costa Mesa, California, before an estimated 16,000 attendees. And all this in addition to their usual auditorium and church dates in California, Minnesota, Missouri, Kentucky, Tennessee, Alabama, Texas, Washington, Oregon, New York, Pennsylvania, Ohio, Oklahoma, and Michigan and concerts in Bermuda, Trinidad, and Jamaica in October and November 1974. The Disciples also performed at fifty different colleges, ranging in size from the University of California at Berkeley to Bluefield State College in West Virginia. At the end of the tour, Andraé announced still another nine-day tour, this time of Israel, Cyprus, Syria, and Lebanon, departing December 9. The virtually nonstop touring schedule meant that Disciples Hockensmith and Harlan Rogers eventually returned to Oklahoma, while Wiley "retired" from the road to pursue other opportunities in the music industry in Texas, though Rogers in particular would continue to perform and record with Andraé for the next few years on an irregular basis.[37]

Life on the Bus

Along with the grind and late hours of travel, it was the prolonged absences from his young family that eventually caused Hockensmith to leave. Fifty years later, however, he said he has many fond memories of his last tour:

> We toured on this big bus where we were kind of captives, although it was kind of nice, really. You can have fellowship when you want it. Or you can take your coat to the private room and catch some Zs. Andraé played a lot of music. I remember that he was really in love with Stevie Wonder's *Talking Book* at the time and I think it influenced him in some ways.[38]

Hockensmith said the members of the Disciples also listened to teaching tapes, including some by Jack Hayford from the Church on the Way. Sometimes they'd listen individually and at other times they'd play the tapes over the big speakers on the bus. At other times, different passengers would sing—anything from old hymns to Top 40 hits. The original members of Sonlight often had prayer meetings while on the road or conducted small church services. At other times, he said, the entire band and crew held services together.

"It was a good atmosphere," Hockensmith said. "Throughout the day, we'd wander throughout the bus to different groups at any given time. The conversation would go from music to Christianity to humor. Thank God a lot of the people had a good sense of humor [or] we'd [have] gone crazy on that bus."

While Hockensmith said he remained close to nearly all of the Disciples after leaving, some of his fondest memories were his times spent with Danniebelle Hall. "She was an incredible singer and an incredible person," he said. "Talking about ministry on the road, I don't know how many times I went to her and poured my heart out because she was that kind of person. And she was so wise. She knew the Bible very well and she wrote songs that touched all of Sonlight. We just loved her music."[39]

For the songwriters, including Andraé, Bili Thedford, Hall, and others, the long hours on the bus sometimes gave them the time and space to create. Thedford said that non-musicians assume that songs arrive unbidden, like unexpected gifts. "What happens is you just hear some words and some music in your head and you start writing," he said. Thedford recalled one such instance on the road involving Hall:

> Danniebelle suddenly said, "Hey, I got this new song." We had no keyboards back then on the bus, so she starts singing this tune. Oh man, it just knocked folks out. It was "Ordinary People" and it was probably her biggest hit. Andraé said, "I wish I had been in the spot that you were in when that came."[40]

But the highlight, Hockensmith said, always came at the end of the journey with the concerts themselves. "The spirit was thick at the concerts," he said. "There was no doubt that God was honoring Andraé and honoring our music."[41]

In the Marketplace

Take Me Back had still not been released as 1974 wound to a close, though whether that was due to Andraé's constant tinkering in the studio or a conscious marketing decision on the part of Light Records is uncertain. The year-end sales charts did confirm Crouch's risky decision to completely redo *"Live" at Carnegie Hall.* The album finished second in *Billboard*'s Top-Selling Gospel LP charts, behind only James Cleveland and the Harold Smith Majestics' *Lord, Help Me to Hold Out.* Cleveland continued his marketplace dominance in 1974 with six charting albums in the list of the Top 35 selling LPs (in addition to Aretha Franklin's *Amazing Grace*, which he produced). The Disciples' *Keep On Singin'* ended the year at #27, while "I Don't Know Why Jesus Loved Me" (from *Keep On Singin'*) finished at #30. Light Records was credited with three LPs in the "Top Gospel Labels" category.[42]

1975

Then, as now, of course, a heightened profile often results in heightened scrutiny and critique, particularly from the more conservative elements of the church, Black and white. The criticism of the Disciples' music reached a point in early 1975 where Andraé felt he needed to respond. He told *Billboard* magazine that he had been attacked for using the same instruments as were currently being employed on R&B and pop music albums. "I have been put down by 'severe' gospel lovers for my contemporary gospel style," Crouch said, "but I will not submit to that type of music." His message, he claimed, was unchanged. "I want to destroy the idea that if it's not stereotyped gospel, the music has no soul." Crouch said his character had been attacked for his music and that some of his songs had willfully been misunderstood. Despite the presence of gospel legend Billy Preston on both the album and dates during the 1974 tours, Crouch said that resistance to his music among Black audiences had persisted. He explained this was, in part, because Light Records was distributed by Word, a label that was "not familiar with the soul distribution outlets and we did not get airplay during the early stages of our careers." The success of *"Live" at Carnegie Hall* and the reception afforded new songs from the still-unreleased *Take Me Back* on the tours, he added, were slowly changing that perception. "I can appreciate the standard gospel sound," Crouch said, "because my roots are with that music. But I feel that I can take what I have learned there and move into other dimensions with it." Just a few months earlier, Light's distributor—Word Records—had reported that it was making progress improving the distribution of its product. Word and its biggest competitor, Benson, both claimed to *Billboard* that they had "continued to expand and grow, and to improve distribution." The article concluded with comments from Jim Black of the performing rights organization SESAC: "A huge field exists for major labels to develop acts to exploit them. If the majors get caught up in what is happening [in gospel music], there will be incredible advancement." Whether Black knew it or not at the time, his words had the ring of prophecy, though that success would bring gospel—and Andraé—a new set of problems.[43]

Christian Artists Corporation

The new year also heralded the founding of an organization that would have a significant impact on the Christian music industry, Christian Artists Corporation (CAC). Created by Cam Floria of the Continental Singers, the CAC was created to "unite" Christian artists in "projects and services to further Christian music and communications." Floria said that the new firm would be "owned and controlled" by Christian musicians, authors, speakers, and radio and television personalities. Crouch was among the first to join, along with such influential industry figures as Ralph Carmichael, the Imperials, Kurt Kaiser, Ken Medema, Jimmie and Carol Owens, and others. CAC's first major event, Floria announced, would be an annual music seminar and camp in Estes Park, Colorado, in August, which would include seminars, concerts, demonstrations, and national talent competitions for religious music directors and young musicians. "Estes Park"—as the event would soon be universally called—quickly became an influential force in the Christian music world, and Andraé and the Disciples were regularly and prominently featured.[44]

Andraé as a Friend

In the midst of this incredibly hectic schedule, Andraé received a call in early 1975 from his friends Howard and Donna Rachinski in Vancouver, British Columbia, whom he'd met a few years earlier. The Rachinskis suddenly found themselves with a serious medical problem involving Donna's pregnancy, one that left them shaken physically and spiritually. When Howard mentioned in a letter that the couple would be at Seattle Christian Temple, Andraé dropped everything and flew to Seattle. When the Rachinskis begged Crouch to return and prepare for his upcoming next tour, he forcefully demurred. "He said,

'No, I just want to be with you,'" Howard recalled. "And he just, to put it simply, loved on us." At the worship service, Andraé suddenly turned to the couple and said, "Donna, I think God's going to heal you right now." Howard said that Crouch then began singing "Through It All" to her. Despite the obstacles, their daughter survived to term and today is in ministry herself. "We have story after story like that," Howard said. "A lot of artists, when they walk into a room, they make you feel like they're the most important person there. When Andraé walked into a room, he made you feel like you were the most important person there. He just loved people" (Image 9.1).[45]

Response

Take Me Back was finally released in March 1975. The March 1 issue of *Billboard* featured a full-page advertisement from Light for the album, proclaiming them "America's Number One Gospel Group" (October 1974– January 1975) and noting, for the first time, that the LP was distributed in

Image 9.1 Andraé Crouch and longtime friend Pat Boone, circa 1975. Photograph courtesy Val Gonzalo.

the United States by ABC Records (with Word still handling Canadian distribution). The album debuted at #29 on April 5 on the monthly "Best-Selling Gospel LP" charts. A month later, it was #11 and by June 7, it was the second best selling album on the chart. The LP hit #1 on July 5, fell to #3 the following month, and reclaimed the top spot September 6. *Take Me Back* remained in the top ten throughout the remaining months of 1975.[46]

Stephen "Bugs" Giglio

The success of *Take Me Back* increased the demand for dates yet again, along with the increased headaches that accompany transporting that many people and their equipment from town to town and state to state quickly and efficiently. In May 1975, the Disciples addressed the issue by hiring Stephen "Bugs" Giglio as assistant road manager. Crouch had known Giglio since 1972, when he was employed in a similar capacity by Love Song. "Man, I want you to work for me someday," Giglio recalled that Andraé had told him. For a "sheltered little kid from Orange County," suddenly hitting the road with the Disciples was a revelation. "All of a sudden, Christians of all colors and races and everybody were loving this guy," Giglio said. "They hit the stage with such energy. Even after working for him for years, I was amazed how he could go for three hours and not stop, sweating like a madman. Even though I saw him over and over again, it just never stopped."

Giglio was charged with booking the hotel rooms in each city and had a set budget, which primarily included Sheraton, Hyatt, or occasionally Holiday Inn hotels. If the hotel was beginning to look run-down, Sandra would take charge. "Sandra was a tough cookie, man," Giglio said. "She would sometimes run out of the bus and check the hotel out. If she didn't like it, we'd have to go and find a new one. She'd stand there and say, 'OK, now where are we going?'"

Giglio also coordinated with the volunteers who helped unload the cartons of LPs, caps, posters, and t-shirts.[47]

During this hectic period, Giglio said that to give the band and crew some time off, especially when some of the upcoming concerts were in isolated, distant venues, Crouch began to perform "Just Andraé" concerts, usually only accompanied by two singers:

> Sometimes it was because they couldn't pay enough to support the whole band, but Andraé had a drive for Jesus. He had the motivation to serve the Lord and to

bring it out there. Then we'd meet up with the band again in some other city and we'd start over. I don't care if it was a little hall or a giant arena, he's always the same. He was just on fire.

Giglio said that Crouch's deep passion for evangelism was something that came from his father, Benjamin Crouch Sr. "I'm telling you, Andraé was born with this drive," Giglio said. "He had it in his DNA. His dad was an on-fire preacher in the Valley. His sister's on fire right now in the same church. They don't mess around."[48]

The conditions on the old bus called "Ruby" were cramped but invigorating, Giglio said. "It wasn't fancy, it bumped a lot, and I remember sleeping on the floor with the air conditioner in my face because it was so crowded when you've got twenty people on a bus."

Traveling across the United States in the early 1970s on a bus that included Blacks and whites had its challenges, especially at mealtimes. "Restaurants were a big thing," Giglio said. "Sometimes we'd go into a restaurant between some small podunk towns and we'd come walking in with this crew with every ethnicity and the whole diner is thinking, 'OK, what have we got here?' But we only had a couple of incidents, nothing heavy. Everybody ate together, the whole group." Sometimes, however, Hazzard said that Crouch would remain so long after concerts praying and witnessing that most of the nearby restaurants would be closed. "But that's how we met so many people," Hazzard said. "Until this day, they are family. They knew we'd come through their town. They knew Andraé was going to minister two hours after a concert, so they would just bring food and everything on the bus."[49]

One of Giglio's more unique jobs was to stand in the wings during the Disciples' epic three-hour concerts holding a change of clothing for Andraé. "I don't want to say it was mayhem—it was the Holy Spirit," he said, "but Andraé'd hustle off the stage for a moment and it was like he'd just stepped out of a swimming pool he was so wet with sweat. I'd hand him another shirt, usually a nice '70s-styled shirt with lots of colors. He knew how to sweat because he was working hard out there."[50]

Giglio was also there when Andraé's audiences began to include more and more African Americans, a change that had begun with *"Live" at Carnegie Hall* and accelerated after the release of *Take Me Back*. "I learned that if we did a Black church not to plan on going anywhere," he said. "You're going to a lunch and back again kind of church. They'd have nurses in the aisles because people were going to be slain in the Spirit to the right and to the left."[51]

Giglio maintained a calendar during much of his time with the Disciples, and they provide a unique glimpse into the life of what appears to be one of the hardest-working groups in all of American popular music. This is a sample week, annotated with Giglio's notes in various ink colors from May 1975:

May 25
    Chicago 11:50 A.M.
    Baltimore 2:29 P.M.
    Auditorium
    ACD [Andraé Crouch & the Disciples]
May 26
    Holiday Inn
    Drive to Asbury Park
    Day off for the band
    Andraé fly to Syracuse, NY
    Went with Andraé
    JA [presumably a "just Andraé" performance]
May 27
    Empress Hotel
    Convention Hall 8 P.M.
    Ocean Grove
    Evie
    Asbury Park
    ACD
May 28
    Hilton
    Drive to Buffalo, arrive 7 P.M.
    Everyone to the show, *The Eiger Sanction*
May 29
    Hilton Hotel
    Keinshan's Music Hall 7:45 P.M.
    Buffalo, NY
    ACD
May 30
    Sheraton
    Auditorium Theatre 7:30
    Masonic Temple
    Rochester, NY

ACD
May 31
Hilton
Varsity Arena
Toronto, Canada
ACD

There are other telling details in Giglio's calendars, including numerous notations where he and/or the Disciples drove all night to the next performance. After a particularly grueling series of dates in Texas in July, the group ended up in Oklahoma City on July 31 for a date at the Civic Center Music Hall. At the very bottom of the small space, Giglio has written, "Money stolen."[52]

Back Down Under

In what was becoming an annual event, Andraé and the Disciples left in June for dates in Australia and New Zealand, again coordinated by Kevin and Jan Craik and the Christian Youth Travel Association. Vocalist Phyllis St. James said that she joined a roster that included Maxwell, Sandra Crouch, Perry Morgan, Wiley, Thedford, Bea Carr, and Hall. Performing with the Disciples, and co-headlining, was Billy Preston. The group left Los Angeles on June 9 and returned from New Zealand after more than two weeks of performances. But even in the midst of a demanding overseas travel schedule, Andraé's creative mind never stopped working. Wiley recalled an early morning at a conference center in Australia's beautiful Snowy Mountains. "Andraé could never sleep," Wiley said:

> He's just got a million ideas for a song in his head. He saw me and said, "Hey! I wrote 10 songs last night. Want to hear them?" I said, "Yeah." So he gets his Walkman out, turns it on and begins singing. Andraé would always be writing but he was a little scattered. Bill would get with him and they'd go through the songs.[53]

Year in Review

As 1975 drew to a close, the across-the-boards success of *Take Me Back* validated Maxwell and Crouch's belief in the direction that the Disciples were heading. *Billboard*'s annual Radio Programmers Artists Popularity Poll named him "Best Soul Gospel Artist of the Year" in September, noting that *"Live" at Carnegie Hall* was still in the top 10, nearly six years after its release. In December, the Disciples were chosen to perform in the musical tribute "Hallelujah" at the Forum in Los Angeles. Sponsored by the Ladies of Song, Community Care and Development Services, and Joe Westmoreland's Interdenominational Choir, tickets ranged from $5 to $100 in the 18,000-seat facility. The Disciples were joined by Jane Fonda, Ella Fitzgerald, Marvin Gaye, Sidney Poitier, and nearly another dozen gospel groups. At year's end, *"Live" at Carnegie Hall* also finished as the top-selling LP on the gospel charts, while *Take Me Back*, which had been released in March, charted at #13. Even *Keep On Singin'* charted at #19. And *Take Me Back* was nominated for and won a "Best Gospel Performance" Grammy. There was one other event in 1975, though it was little marked at the time. Crouch had heard a cassette of an album by longtime friends Walter and Tramaine Hawkins. When he discovered that the Hawkins had not yet signed with a recording label, he took the cassette to Ralph Carmichael, with his highest recommendation. Light Records would not release Walter Hawkins and the Love Center Choir *Love Alive* LP until October 1976, and only then with little promotional support.[54]

An Enduring Classic

Take Me Back was an influential touchstone for countless musicians, as well as academics and casual fans. Raymond Wise said that this was the album that "really connected" him to Crouch. "As a younger musician, all these new chords, all of these new things were so exciting beyond the traditional musical and hymn-like sounds that everyone was singing in the '60s," he said. "*Take Me Back*, really, was that first introduction and it took me by storm." Wise said he was immediately struck by the album's "clean, polished" production, especially as compared with all earlier gospel LPs. "*Take Me Back* was the saving grace," he said, "because I remember that around that time that the older folks were complaining, 'Andraé Crouch has left the church; he's doing all this weird crazy music.' But then there was the song, 'Take Me Back,' that redeemed him." For the young musician/singer, Wise said that Crouch's use of an entirely different musical "vocabulary" was incredibly attractive. "It was really that album that brought me to his music in a different way," he said.[55]

Gospel music executive Demetrus Alexander, who has been crucial in introducing a host of gospel artists, including Donnie McClurkin, O'Landa Draper, Kirk Whalum, and others during her career, said that *Take Me Back* was a particularly effective response to what was happening in the world at large in 1974 and 1975:

> He was sensitive to what was going on and what he should say and, in that, he sought God about how to speak into it. Most of Andraé's songs really talk about what we should be feeling from a spiritual perspective in the midst of whatever we were dealing with. Not how we should be with each other because if you get what you're supposed to be doing here, this is going to work out just fine. He wanted to know what God had to say about the matter [asking], "What are we missing?" If things were getting too crazy, that meant that something's going on with us and our connection to Him.

Alexander said that *Take Me Back*'s extended influence was a result of Crouch of being both available and vulnerable to God's will. "His ears were always open," she said. "He never shut his ears to what God was saying, always listening for the little nuggets God was dropping on him."[56]

Take Me Back may be Crouch's most complete theological expression. Every song is linked to a specific Bible passage. Every song points the listener to the overarching themes of reconciliation and redemption, urging—oftentimes pleading—with listeners to ignore life's distractions and return to God.

NOTES

1. "Who/Where/When," *Billboard*, February 2, 1974, 22.
2. https://billygraham.org/story/remembering-andrae-crouch/; David Kucharsky, "Graham's Pow Wow: Springtime in the Rockies," *Christianity Today*, April 11, 1975, 38–39.
3. "Andraé Crouch & the Disciples," *Billboard*, March 30, 1974, *Campus Attractions* section, 99.
4. Danniebelle Hall, *Danniebelle* (Light Records LS 5638); Danniebelle Hall, *This Moment* (Light Records LS 5675); "Oklahoma City Has a Lot of Talented Musical Women Who Give the City a Special Flavor," *Billboard*, November 10, 1973, O-14; Sweet Spirit, *Sweet Spirit* (Shalom Records SH-133).
5. Bill Maxwell, personal correspondence with the authors, October 1, 2022; Discogs.com/label/280685-Mama-Jo's.
6. Bill Maxwell, personal correspondence with the authors, October 1, 2022; Kathy Hazzard, interview with the authors, September 7, 2022; Bill Maxwell, interview with the authors, October 20, 2022.

7. Bill Maxwell, personal correspondence with the authors, October 1, 2022; Scott K. Fish, "Bill Maxwell: A Gift of Music," *Modern Drummer*, August 1983, https://www.moderndrummer.com/article/august-1983-bill-maxwell-gift-music/; Bill Maxwell, interview with the authors, May 18, 2019; Fletch Wiley, interview with the authors, November 26, 2020.
8. Fletch Wiley, interview with the authors, November 26, 2020; Hadley Hockensmith, interview with the authors, October 17, 2020; Bill Maxwell, interview with the authors, May 18, 2019; Bill Maxwell, personal correspondence with the authors, October 1, 2022.
9. Bill Maxwell, personal correspondence with the authors, October 24, 2022.
10. Bill Maxwell, interview with the authors, October 20, 2022.
11. Bill Maxwell, interview with the authors, October 20, 2022.
12. Hadley Hockensmith, interview with the authors, October 17, 2020.
13. Bill Maxwell, interview with the authors, May 18, 2019.
14. Fletch Wiley, interview with the authors, November 26, 2020.
15. Kathy Hazzard, interview with the authors, October 27, 2021.
16. Bill Maxwell, interview with the authors, May 18, 2019; Bill Maxwell, interview with the authors, October 21, 2022.
17. Bill Maxwell, interview with the authors, May 18, 2019; Raymond Wise, interview with the authors, September 6, 2020.
18. Kathy Hazzard, interview with the authors, October 27, 2021.
19. Bill Maxwell, interview with the authors, October 21, 2022.
20. Fletch Wiley, interview with the authors, November 26, 2020; Kathy Hazzard, interview with the authors, October 27, 2021.
21. Bill Maxwell, interview with the authors, May 18, 2019.
22. Jeffrey LaValley, interview with the authors, August 29, 2020.
23. Mark Kibble, interview with the authors, November 20, 2020.
24. Raymond Wise, interview with the authors, September 6, 2020.
25. Raymond Wise, interview with the authors, September 6, 2020.
26. Bill Maxwell, interview with the authors, May 18, 2019; Raymond Wise, interview with the authors, September 6, 2020.
27. Bill Maxwell, interview with the authors, September 15, 2022.
28. Fletch Wiley, interview with the authors, November 26, 2020; Kathy Hazzard, interview with the authors, October 27, 2021.
29. Raymond Wise, interview with the authors, September 6, 2020.
30. Kathy Hazzard, interview with the authors, October 27, 2021.
31. Bill Maxwell, interview with the authors, May 18, 2019.
32. Bill Maxwell, interview with the authors, May 18, 2019; Bill Maxwell, interview with the authors, September 15, 2022.
33. Bill Maxwell, interview with the authors, May 19, 2019.
34. Fletch Wiley, interview with the authors, November 27, 2020.
35. Fletch Wiley, interview with the authors, November 27, 2020.

36. Bob Gersztyn, "Andraé's Music Will Never Lose Its Power," *Wittenburg Door*, March/April 2004, Copy of original online article in the authors' possession; "Gospel's Dove Awards Nominees Reflect Best in the Business," *Billboard*, September 7, 1974, 36.

37. "Crouch, Disciples Perform Gospel at 15 College Sites," *Billboard*, October 5, 1974, 50; "Best-Selling Gospel LPs," *Billboard*, October 5, 1974, 50; "The Setlist Wiki," www.setlist.fm; "Shaped Notes," *Billboard*, August 10, 1974, 56; Paul Baker, *Contemporary Christian Music: Where It Came From, What It Is, Where It's Going* (Westchester, IL: Crossway Books, 1985), 84–85; Fletch Wiley, interview with the authors, October 10, 2020; Fletch Wiley, interview with the authors, November 26, 2020; Hadley Hockensmith, interview with the authors, October 17, 2020.

38. Hadley Hockensmith, interview with the authors, October 17, 2020.

39. Hadley Hockensmith, interview with the authors, October 17, 2020.

40. Bili Thedford, interview with the authors, March 18, 2021.

41. Hadley Hockensmith, interview with the authors, October 17, 2020.

42. "Top Gospel Albums," *Billboard*, December 28, 1974, 34; "Top Gospel Labels," *Billboard*, December 28, 1974, 34.

43. "Gospeler Crouch Ignores Critics with New Sounds," *Billboard*, April 5, 1975, 31; Bill Williams, "Distribution Is Major Problem for Gospel-Specializing Labels," *Billboard*, January 18, 1975, 61.

44. "Christian Artists Corp. Formed," *Cashbox*, January 14, 1975, 14.

45. Howard Rachinski, interview with the authors, October 20, 2022.

46. "Take Me Back: Andraé Crouch and the Disciples," *Billboard*, March 1, 1975, 47; "Best-Selling Gospel LPs," *Billboard*, April 5, 1975, 38; "Best-Selling Gospel LPs," *Billboard*, May 3, 1975, 41; "Best-Selling Gospel LPs," *Billboard*, June 7, 1975, 48; "Best-Selling Gospel LPs," *Billboard*, July 5, 1975, 34; "Best-Selling Gospel LPs," *Billboard*, August 2, 1975, 46; "Best-Selling Gospel LPs," *Billboard*, September 6, 1975, 56; "Best-Selling Gospel LPs," *Billboard*, October 4, 1975, 55; "Best-Selling Gospel LPs," *Billboard*, November 1, 1975, 59; "Best-Selling Gospel LPs," *Billboard*, December 6, 1975, 50.

47. Stephen "Bugs" Giglio, interview with the authors, June 18, 2021.

48. Stephen "Bugs" Giglio, interview with the authors, June 18, 2021.

49. Stephen "Bugs" Giglio, interview with the authors, June 18, 2021; Kathy Hazzard, interview with the authors, October 27, 2021.

50. Stephen "Bugs" Giglio, interview with the authors, June 18, 2021.

51. Stephen "Bugs" Giglio, interview with the authors, June 18, 2021.

52. Stephen "Bugs" Giglio, interview with the authors, June 18, 2021.

53. Phyllis St. James, interview with the authors, January 23, 2021; Fletch Wiley, interview with the authors, November 26, 2020.

54. "Andraé Crouch Honored Again," *Billboard*, September 6, 1975, 56; "'Hallelujah' Gospel Fete on Dec. 18," *Billboard*, December 13, 1975, 41; "Best-Selling Gospel LPs," *Billboard*, December 27, 1975, 42; "Complete List of

Grammy Nominees for 1975 Awards," *Cash Box*, January 24, 1976, 38; Andraé Crouch, liner notes, Walter Hawkins and the Love Center Choir, *Love Alive* (Light Records LS 5686, 1975).

55. Raymond Wise, interview with the authors, September 6, 2020.

56. Demetrus Alexander, interview with the authors, October 10, 2020.

10

The Best of Andraé

With *Take Me Back* (#3) and *"Live" at Carnegie Hall* (#4) still atop *Billboard*'s "Best-Selling Gospel LPs" chart in January 1976, Light Records released the group's first "greatest hits" package, *The Best of Andraé*. The double album debuted the following month at #9 and moved to #2 in March and April before finally hitting the top position in May. For the next few months, *The Best of Andraé* and *Take Me Back* dueled for the #1 position, before *The Best of Andraé* resumed the #1 spot in August through October—a tribute to the Disciples' strength in the gospel music marketplace.[1]

Changes

The Best of Andraé featured Light's most elaborate packaging yet. The cover photo is another closeup of Crouch in full-throated song at the piano, with "The Best of Andraé" written in a large flowing script and "Andraé Crouch and the Disciples" in much smaller letters beneath it. Inside, another gate-fold sleeve boasts two photographs of Andraé on a beach, the Disciples (Sandra Crouch, Danniebelle Hall, Andraé, Perry Morgan, Bill Maxwell, Bili Thedford, and Fletch Wiley), a photograph of an adoring concert crowd, and another photo of Andraé singing. On the back cover is a more formally posed photograph, with Andraé in the middle of a throne-like chair with the other Disciples crowded around him. Whether this was Light Records' intention or not, the focus, beginning with the title, is on Andraé, with the Disciples in a much less prominent position. Despite the many contributions of the other musicians, it was Andraé whom Light Records now marketed, not the group.[2]

Earlier Disciples, including Sherman Andrus and Tramaine Hawkins, had already gone on to successful careers. In addition to Danniebelle's just-released recordings for Light, Wiley had signed a contract with the new Star Song label for a series of mostly instrumental albums, beginning with *Ballade* that featured the members of Sonlight and included "My Tribute." Thedford had been approached by the new Good News label to record a solo LP and when he began recording in Mama Jo's in April 1975, the sessions even merited mentions in *Record World* and *Billboard* (though the *Music of My Birth* album would not be released for another two years). Thedford said that the members of the Disciples could see the changes coming. "When we first started, we formed a corporation," he said, "'Andraé Crouch and the Disciples,' with Andraé, Sandra, Perry, and myself. We had offices in Pacoima with secretaries, promoters, and booking agencies there. We had a nice setup. And after a time, it morphed into 'Andraé Crouch.'" Thedford said that the increasingly longer and more demanding tours were taking a toll on his family. "After each tour, we'd all scatter like a pool hall break," he said. "When you'd come home, the only question that you would get was, 'When are you leaving?'" Thedford finally left the Disciples for good after the second Australian tour, though Maxwell said that Bili stayed in touch with Andraé and the other Disciples, especially Perry Morgan. His departure created an opening for a touring bassist and singer.[3]

Not a Greatest Hits Package

The song selection on the double album was designed to expose the Disciples' newer fans to earlier Light LPs, especially *Keep On Singin'* and *Soulfully*, since those two releases had not received the wider distribution of his later albums. Conversely, only three songs were selected from his most recent release, *Take Me Back*:

The Best of Andraé

Side I

"Take a Little Time" (*Keep On Singin'*)
"Everything Has Changed (*Soulfully*)
"Tell Them" (*Take Me Back*)
"I'm Gonna Keep On Singin'" (*Keep On Singin'*)
"My Tribute (to God Be the Glory)" (*Keep on Singin'*)

Side II

"Bless His Holy Name" (*Just Andraé*)
"I'm Coming Home" (*Keep On Singin'*)
"Just Like He Said He Would" (*Take Me Back*)
"If Heaven Was Never Promised to Me" (*Just Andraé*)
"Take Me Back" (*Take Me Back*)

Side III

"Jesus Is the Answer" (*"Live" at Carnegie Hall*)
"Through It All" (*Soulfully*)
"Satisfied" (*Soulfully*)
"Jesus (Every Hour He'll Give You Power)" (*Keep On Singin'*)
"I Come That You Might Have Life" (*Soulfully*)

Side IV

"I Don't Know Why" (*Keep On Singin'* and *"Live" at Carnegie Hall*)
"I Didn't Think It Could Be" (*"Live" at Carnegie Hall*)
"Oh I Need Him" (*Soulfully*)
"I've Got Confidence" (*Keep On Singin'*)
"It Won't Be Long" (*Soulfully*)

The package included seven songs from *Keep On Singin'*, six songs from *Soulfully*, two songs from *Just Andraé*, three songs from *"Live" at Carnegie Hall*, and three songs from *Take Me Back*. No songs from the Disciples' first Light release, *Take the Message Everywhere*, were included, nor are there any selections from *Teen Challenge Addicts Choir* (distributed by Word Records) or the COGICs' *It's a Blessing* (distributed by Exodus/Vee-Jay). Nor were either of the two songs released by Liberty Records, "Christian People" and "Too Close," included.

In addition to the song listings, *The Best of Andraé* featured a list of the producers and arrangers who had worked with Andraé since *Take the Message Everywhere* and a "thanks" column that included Ralph Carmichael, Light Records, Jimmie Owens, Audrey Mieir, Bill Murray, "and the musicians."[4]

According to Bill Maxwell, Crouch was not given input into the song selection for *The Best of Andraé* collection. "We didn't give much regard to those 'best of' things," Maxwell said, "because there was no new recording going on.

And I was only invested in it if I'm working on it." Maxwell said that Light Records proposed the project to the Disciples in a rather casual manner. "They said, 'This is a way of making money without spending money,'" Maxwell recalled. "'[We'll] take some of your old tracks and put them together and just repackage them.' Later on, we got smarter and started putting a couple of new songs on them to help sell them." Light Records did its part, buying a full-page advertisement in *Billboard* on March 13 with the headline: "Congratulations! America's #1 Grammy Award Winning Gospel Performer" and spotlighting the *Take Me Back* album. The ad, which includes thumbnail photos of all seven of the group's Light albums, including his "latest release" *The Best of Andraé*, also features a photograph of Andraé in action and some breathless encouragement for retailers: "You've never heard gospel until you've heard Andraé! Here are seven reasons why Andraé Crouch & the Disciples are #1 nationwide. Now is the time to order his best-sellers."[5]

The New Horn Section (and More)

Among the trends in popular music at the time were bands that prominently featured horn sections. Blood, Sweat & Tears; Chicago; Dreams; and others were horn-dominated aggregations, while groups like the Tower of Power and Earth, Wind & Fire followed the model of James Brown's Famous Flames in spotlighting an array of gifted horn players as both soloists and as part of call-and-response-styled arrangements. In the mostly hardscrabble financial models of gospel and contemporary Christian music, it was not economically feasible to travel with that many musicians. A rare exception in the mid-1970s was the group Psalm 150.

Psalm 150 quickly attracted top-flight musicians and performed primarily throughout the San Francisco–Los Angeles corridor, where Andraé first heard them. The group even recorded an album for the small Manna Records label in 1974, *Make Up Your Mind*. Trumpeter Allen Gregory said that he first met Crouch when Psalm 150 opened for the Disciples in February 1976 at Melodyland Christian Center in Anaheim, though he said he'd been aware for the Disciples for years. When Gregory finally heard the group in concert, he was captivated—and "completely blown away" by Fletch Wiley's mastery of the trumpet. "He was a Doc Severinsen kind of a player," Gregory said. "He was so good with the high notes—a really, really strong player."[6]

Andraé and Maxwell liked what they heard with Psalm 150 as well. According to bassist/singer James (later Jaymes) Felix, the group introduced themselves to the Disciples after the show. "We were up and coming and young and hungry," Felix said, "and Andraé and Bill took a shine to us. They started our second album, which Andraé funded himself." But the LP was never completed, though Felix said he still has the original two-inch reels in his home. From there, Crouch invited Gregory, Felix, wind player Glen Myerscough, and keyboardist Michael Escalante to join the Disciples. Gregory said his first gigs with Crouch were part of the "Just Andraé" concerts which featured fewer musicians in smaller venues, though Andraé added horns for a few shows as well. Gregory's first concert was in February 1976 in San Luis Obispo at Cuesta College. "I don't remember if Glen and I actually had charts or not," Gregory said, "but I think it was just a thing of trying to remember the [horn] parts. I was glad to be working after Psalm 150 broke up and I'd just gotten married the week before." Felix said he was going through a "rough period" in his life. "Bill Maxwell tracked me down and asked if I would consider joining Andraé's group," Felix said. "Well, obviously, I didn't have to think about it twice because I was a drowning man—I'd leap for the opportunity. The next day, I would show up at Andraé's house and they crammed a bunch of music down my face."[7]

A week later, Gregory, Myerscough, Escalante, and Felix were on the road as Disciples. "I was living in Orange County and my wife dropped me off at a parking lot in Santa Ana where the tour bus was waiting," Gregory said. "We drove straight to St. Louis. This was with the road crew and I didn't know any of these people." The newest Disciples had had little rehearsal time with the group to that point and Gregory said his first concern was finding a place to practice. "And with a trumpet," he said, "you always have to keep your lip in shape. It was a big adjustment."[8]

Gregory and Myerscough had been friends since childhood, and the two helped each other on the "whirlwind" month-long tour. Psalm 150's audiences, he said, had primarily been in the all-white world of Jesus Music in Southern California. The Disciples, on the other hand, performed at a variety of venues to both Black and white audiences. "Andraé just had a way," Gregory said; "he had an appeal to all different kinds of audiences. There was something about him that was disarming to people. He had that ability to make people feel like he was talking to them personally."

Additionally, Gregory said Crouch was "very sensitive to the leading of the Holy Spirit," which meant, as others have said, that—from his very first concert with the Disciples—the performances were never the same from night to night. "Andraé would go from something that was a real 'get-down' kind of thing straight into a praise & worship section," Gregory said. "But his segues were always real smooth. I think that added to his popularity. People left his concerts feeling inspired and lifted up, as opposed just going to a rock show."[9]

Myerscough, who played saxophone, flute, and other wind instruments, said he had no idea what to expect while experiencing extended periods on a tour bus with the Disciples. Fortunately, the group dynamic was both kind and supportive for the young musicians from Psalm 150. "All those people got along so nicely," he said, "and enjoyed each other's music. It was traveling with real believers who understood intuitively that we are family as Christ's followers. They were people who really trusted God and struggled with things in life that they trusted God with." Just as the concerts could be spontaneous, so could life on the bus or in the hotels. Myerscough said that on more than one occasion Andraé delayed scheduled departures for an hour or more so that the group could have a Bible study or pray together.[10]

"Andraé had never had horns like that," Maxwell said. "What I loved about Glen and Allen is that I played in horn bands all my life but arranging [for them] drove me crazy. They took care of that; they figured out their own parts and they were always good." The new members from Psalm 150, including Escalante and Felix, brought a different dynamic to the Disciples on the road. Maxwell said that the mix that had included Black gospel (Andraé, Sandra, Hall, and Perry) and jazz and R&B (Maxwell) now included a jazzy Latin flavor from Escalante and Felix and a "bebop jazz" from Myerscough and Gregory. The result, Maxwell said, was a wholly unique blend of gospel music that ranged from the Tower of Power to Natalie Cole's "This Will Be," from Love Song and the Jesus Movement to the Mighty Clouds of Joy and Edwin Hawkins. "Andraé was different," Maxwell said. "We merged everything together." Singer Kathy Hazzard said that Myerscough, Gregory, and Wiley made up one of the best horn sections of the era, regardless of genre. "Oh, those boys with those horns? You couldn't touch them," she said. "I don't care—Earth, Wind & Fire? Good. But our horns you couldn't touch."[11]

In fact, virtually all of the musicians and singers that Crouch and Maxwell brought in would achieve at least some degree of success in their careers even after leaving the Disciples. Each was a creative, accomplished artist, but Crouch

THE BEST OF ANDRAÉ   233

said he insisted on one additional qualification—each had to have a religious commitment as well. "It has to be," he later told writer Bob Doreschuk. "Otherwise, they could be tearing down what we are building up." Any singer or musician who displayed questionable judgment or actions, Andraé said, "would be a reflection on me."[12]

Andraé's New Home

The year 1976 brought other significant changes to Andraé's life. Crouch had lived in a small guesthouse behind his parents' home until the mid-1970s, when he rented an apartment in Marina del Rey on Admiralty Way, though he spent more time on the road and in the studio than in the apartment. According to Bill Maxwell, it was Andraé's mother Catherine who suggested that he buy his own house. Andraé, who was indifferent to money and left his finances to others, told Catherine, "I don't have the money to buy a house." Maxwell said that she shook her head: "Yes, you do. I've been saving your money. I've been intercepting your checks." From the bank account, Andraé was able in early 1976 to put up a "huge down payment" on a home on Wells Drive in Woodland Hills. In the years ahead, the home on Wells Drive—particularly the kitchen and a grand piano—quickly became the epicenter all of things Andraé.[13]

Family friend Val Gonzalo said the new home was Andraé's sanctuary, decorated like a jungle, with jungle wallpaper, and everything designed around his Kawai grand piano. "He entertained there," Gonzalo said. "It was important to him, to entertain people's lives." As singers who didn't live in the Los Angeles area would arrive for recording sessions, longtime friend and singer Hazzard said that they would often end up at Andraé's house—and sometimes not leave. "We would start at 6 o'clock and go to 6 o'clock the next day," Hazzard said. "When Tata Vega would arrive, she'd say, 'OK, we are not going to bed tonight.' Andraé would start cooking at 5:30 A.M. and then we'd start all over again." Hazzard said that Crouch loved to cook all the staples, but particularly chicken dishes. "He loved the 'gospel bird,'" she said. "He liked hot, hot, hot food." Singer Phyllis St. James said that the creative process often began with fried chicken. "You'd come to his house for rehearsal and he'd go to the kitchen," she said. "He'd get the food on and we'd begin and he'd hear a germ of an idea. Then he'd say, 'Oh, wait a minute' and take his tape recorder to the piano." Andraé's captive audience would then listen to the new snippet of a song several times as they finished their dinner and soon found themselves rehearsing it around the piano. "It's a process," St. James said:

> He's creating it with the energy of the singers around him. I know those antennae are going up, going out and we're connected in as we're flouring the chicken, getting ready to fry it. Or somebody's chopping for the potato salad and he's listening to his cassettes. And that's how he would find different ideas to sit down and play. I spent a lot of time just sitting around and listening to germs until he sparked an idea.[14]

Vocalist Vonciele Faggett said she was a friend of both Crouches long before she began singing with them and the same "process" applied to her. She said that Andraé found his new home to be a particularly creative environment. "I just so admired his gift and prophetic writing in just a split second," Faggett said. "We could be at his house, supposedly having dinner or just socializing, and in the middle of that he would go to the piano and say, 'Oh! Oh! Come here, come here. I need you to sing something right quick.' And he would start writing a song or a chorus and go back and finish it later." "You never knew what you were going to get there," Val Gonzalo said. "He was always saying, 'What do you think about this? Listen to what the Lord has given me here.' With Andraé, hospitality and music intersected with one another; they were connected. You always felt welcome, whether you were a stranger or if you had known him for years." Not that it was all work, of course. Longtime friend Carrie Gonzalo said that after the "ginger chicken and rice" dishes, Andraé would sometimes regale his guests with tales from the road or perform credible imitations of the lead singers with various gospel quartets. Fletch Wiley said the impromptu dinners/sessions at Andraé's new house were incredibly creative times. "All he did was music," Wiley said. "He listened to a ton of records. He'd just kind of cook some chicken and rice and go play the piano and write stuff into his cassette recorder right on the piano."[15]

Perry Morgan, one of Andraé's oldest friends—and the longest serving Disciple by this point—said that Crouch's creativity in his new home was not confined to the dinner table:

> He would stay up all night a lot of nights when he was home. Even on the road, he'd have a piano brought to his room and stay up all night writing and singing. And when we'd get on the bus the next day, he would go to sleep. But at home if he was asleep, he would get up and go to the piano and turn his tape recorder on

and start on all of the songs that the Lord had given him! And when he finished it, he would put it in a drawer.

Maxwell confirmed Morgan's account, saying that new compositions could—and would—arrive after Andraé had gone to sleep. "He'd wake up in the middle of the night and hit 'record' on his tape player," Maxwell said. Crouch would sing or chant some nonsense syllables into the recorder, then go back to bed. "He'd play it back the next day on the tape and I'd go, 'What was that?' And he'd say, 'Oh, it's a song.' Then he'd go to the piano and be triggered. He'd remember exactly what he was hearing."

Even after a decade of touring together, Morgan said he would stand on the side of the stage and marvel as Crouch sang songs composed just hours earlier. "Especially in a church," Morgan said, "his songs would capture me. Most of his songs were special. He'd sing a new song and I would look at him and he'd be really into pouring his heart and soul into this song. He had that gift, that anointing, to bring everybody in."[16]

In Concert

From the beginning of their musical ministry, the Disciples had been popular particularly in the Los Angeles area, regularly headlining a variety of high-profile venues, including Disneyland's "Night of Joy" concerts, Magic Mountain, and Knott's Berry Farm. According to a story in *Billboard*, Disney, "due to numerous requests from patrons over the past five years," turned the park over to gospel music on April 30, 1976. Various gospel artists were showcased outside the park's signature rides and attractions between 8 P.M. and 1 A.M. Bill Long, the park's marketing director, said that ticket sales had been capped at 18,000 and that the event "surpassed" similar events featuring rock, country, and R&B artists. Andraé Crouch and the Disciples headlined, along with Jesus Music stalwarts Love Song, Barry McGuire, Honeytree, and others. As per Long's prediction, the Night of Joy event became an annual event at Disneyland and the Disciples were repeatedly featured.[17]

And then it would be time to hit the road again: another massive festival in April with more Jesus Music pioneers, a June concert in Cleveland at the Music Hall, a sold-out August presentation in the new Raincross Square

Auditorium in Riverside, California, followed by an appearance at the August 1976 Gospel Music Workshop of America in Kansas City with the royalty of the gospel music world—and dozens upon dozens of smaller dates in between (Image 10.1).[18]

Image 10.1 Flyer/advertisement for October 6, 1976, Andraé Crouch & the Disciples performance, Greek Theatre, Los Angeles. Flyer courtesy of Perry Morgan.

Songwriting

Several new songs began emerging during these dates, including "We Expect You," "All That I Have," "Soon and Very Soon," "This Is Another Day," and "You Gave to Me." Typically, Maxwell said, Crouch would tell the group, "I had a little idea for a song. You guys want to hear it?" That snippet would often evolve into the chorus and spark another idea for a song. At that point, Maxwell said that Andraé would introduce the song in skeletal form to the audience, sometimes that very evening. "And people would get excited and be invested in their hearing a new song." The song would grow and change with each subsequent performance and, eventually, Andraé—or someone—would add a bridge. "'Soon and Very Soon' started as just a chorus and then Andraé added the bridge section later," Maxwell said.[19]

As a college student, Donn Thomas was once invited to Crouch's home for dinner, where he found, among others, composer/producer Patrick Henderson. Thomas said that when he arrived, Andraé was still working on "Soon and Very Soon." "Andraé turned to us and said, 'What do you guys think about this song?'" Thomas recalled. "It was an awesome song, but Andraé still needed some lyrics to it." Thomas, who became a pastor himself, said something "very significant" then followed:

> Finally, Andraé lay down on a couch and went deep into his subconscious [for] maybe an hour. And then, as he visited his subconscious, he came out with incredible lyrics. It taught me something. I'm a songwriter and it taught me how to easier go to that place. Not only in the soul but, I believe, he visited his spirit. I believe God would give him lyrics and then he'd begin writing them; lyrics that have lasted for generations to come.[20]

It was during this period that Andraé first met Christian artist Keith Green and his wife Melody when Billy Ray Hearn asked Maxwell to produce Green's first album for the Sparrow label. The Greens and Andraé immediately became fast friends. "Keith and I had no idea God just dropped us into the deep end of the Christian musical genius pool," Melody recalled. "He was soft-spoken and tender and filled with a disarming and quiet humility." Maxwell recruited many of the same musicians and singers to record with Keith, and though Green was still early in his career, Crouch had him open for the Disciples on several important dates. "Andraé was warm and encouraging," she said. "He inspired us to be more like Jesus. We loved Andraé's music, but more importantly, we loved Andraé."[21]

Charts

In the June 5, 1976, issue of *Billboard*, the initial release by Walter Hawkins and the Love Center Choir, *Love Alive*, which Andraé had shared in cassette form with Ralph Carmichael more than a year earlier, unobtrusively entered *Billboard*'s "Best-Selling Gospel LP" chart in the next-to-last position, #34. Throughout fall of 1976, as the Disciples' *Take Me Back* and *The Best of Andraé Crouch* swapped the #1 position, *Love Alive* steadily climbed the charts until in the October 9 edition, when it hit #1. *Love Alive* and its successors would dominate the music charts in the years that followed in a way previously unseen in gospel music history. Walter, Edwin Hawkins's younger brother, was the "driving engine" behind the group's success. Further fueled by the incendiary vocals from his wife Tramaine, the *Love Alive* series would sell hundreds of thousands of copies and add a host of new gospel songs to the repertoire for the multiethnic choral community and the Black church.[22]

Andraé's songwriting for the next album continued, as it had for nearly twenty years, right through year's end, whether on the road or at his new house. Singer Hazzard said that another song that emerged at "one of our famous feasts there" was the meditative "Quiet Times." "It was right after Thanksgiving," she said. "He said, 'I want you guys to sing this.' I said, 'How did you . . .?' Andraé said, 'That just came.' Andraé had the big, big piano in his living room and a regular piano in his bedroom and once he went up to that room, we'd all say, 'Uh oh, he's coming down with a song.'"[23]

Songwriting—and eating—weren't all that went on in the big house on Wells Drive. In 1976, Vinesong founder John Watson, who had met Andraé during one of Crouch's earlier visits to the United Kingdom, became a house guest and de facto personal minister. Watson also began a Bible study that quickly included, among others, Stevie Wonder, Donna Summer, and Bob Dylan. The Bible study grew so large it eventually moved to Andraé's studio. "It was made up of burnt-out actors and musicians," Watson recalled, "and a lot of them pretty wealthy people. One day I counted and found there were sixty-seven people there and with cars parked all of the way down the road, I realized we couldn't have it in the studio anymore." Watson rented a hall on

THE BEST OF ANDRAÉ

239

Hollywood Boulevard and "Andraé's Sunday PM" continued until eventually it eventually transformed into a church under Vinesong's auspices. In time, Watson was called to South Africa, where in 1982 he would eventually encounter Andraé again.[24]

New Media

In December, the popular *Sepia* magazine published one of the first long-form interviews with Crouch, complete with numerous informal photographs taken in Andraé's Woodland Hills home. The interview, "New King of 'Pop Gospel,'" written by well-known journalist Patrick Salvo, caught Crouch in a happy, expansive mode, strumming a guitar, lounging in new wicker furniture from Hawaii, posing in his backyard and, of course, playing the piano. It also gives at least tacit acknowledgment of his long-simmering "feud" with James Cleveland. At one point, Salvo asks Crouch why Cleveland has been more popular with African American gospel music fans, while Andraé has appealed—until recently—primarily to whites. The difference, Crouch says, is that he tries "to do tunes that everybody, Black and white, understand. With some of the Black gospel, white people just don't feel relaxed. The white Christian sometimes feels out of place." Conversely, Andraé adds, "I think it's a much healthier attitude to be concerned with everybody. After all, we're all children of God, and that's what the gospel message is all about." The rumors of the supposed tension between the two popular artists also prompted Andraé to say that he does not believe that there is a competition with Cleveland. "What I want to do is improve the image of gospel," he says, "the whole look. One of my very talented Black brothers, James Cleveland, has done a lot for Black gospel."

The article notes that the Disciples now gross more than $1 million annually from their concerts and album sales and that the royalties from Andraé's 200 compositions have made him one of the "highest-paid ASCAP songwriters" in the United States. Andraé says, however, that, commercial success had never been his goal.

> I never knew I would be so successful financially or fame-wise. I believe in what I'm doing. I'm not singing gospel music because it may be the hip thing to do. I believe in the gospel message, in the Bible, Jesus Christ and God. I believe that's all actually true. I sing it and I believe.

240 SOON & VERY SOON

Not all gospel artists, alas, believe the same way, Crouch tells Salvo. Instead, these artists "just go through the motions. Sometimes when you ask these people if they believe in what they're singing, they say, 'Well, I was baptized, wasn't I?' But they're kidding themselves." In another part of the interview, he scolds—without naming names—Black preachers who he says drive in Rolls Royces and African American celebrities who "stay up all Saturday night snorting cocaine and then go sing in church Sunday morning."

Crouch spends a good part of the interview talking about the influence of his father, Benjamin, and his father's tireless support of society's marginalized and abandoned people.

The interview ends with Andraé's opinion on his longtime label, Light Records. It isn't a ringing endorsement, and the quotes offer insight into their sometimes bumpy relationship:

> Light Records, although a white label, was the best religious label we could find at the time. We found some of the Black religious labels to be total rip-offs. At Light, they're a bunch of nice guys, but they don't seem to know as much as we'd like about promotion. We are going to try to give them a little more time, though, since they are honest. And they're the greatest publishers in the country.[25]

1976 Comes to a Close

Even as *The Best of Andraé* (#2), *Take Me Back* (#6), and *"Live" at Carnegie Hall* (#9) continued to sell extremely well, Light trumpeted the release of the Disciples' upcoming next album, *This Is Another Day*, with a full-page, full-color advertisement on page 2 in the November 6, 1976, issue of *Billboard*. The close-up photograph of Andraé (sans Disciples), dressed in a natty tropical shirt and hat, included several breathless advertising blurbs: "Grammy Award Winners!" You haven't heard gospel . . . 'til you've heard Andraé!" "This Gospel's #1!" The ad also lists the first three singles from the LP: "Soon and Very Soon," "You Gave to Me," and "Perfect Peace." The following month, *This Is Another Day* entered the gospel music charts at #10, behind *The Best of Andraé* (#9), but ahead of *Take Me Back* (#11) and *"Live" at Carnegie Hall* (#12).[26]

The year-end sales report in *Billboard* reflected what the Light Records' brain trust already knew—1976 had been a very good year for Andraé Crouch and the Disciples—but had also introduced a formidable new artist to the label's roster in Walter Hawkins and the Love Center Choir. The Disciples were listed at #1 in the "Soul-Gospel Artists" column, ahead of the Reverend James Cleveland and the Charles Fold Singers (#2) and the Love Alive Choir (#3). In the final tally of the top-selling albums, the Disciples had four LPs in the year-end chart: *This Is Another Day* (#5, despite only having two months on the chart), *Take Me Back* (#10), *"Live" at Carnegie Hall* (#11), and *The Best of Andraé* (#17).[27]

If nothing else, *The Best of Andraé* cemented Crouch's standing as the most musically adventuresome artist in gospel or contemporary Christian music. No one came close to the sheer diversity of songs, either lyrically and musically. Later, Andraé would credit his father, Benjamin Crouch Sr., both for some of his restless compositional creativity and for the freedom to follow his mercurial muse. "Like my pa always told me," Andraé once told James Abbington, "'If you have to hymn it, hymn it. If you have to rock it, rock it. If you have to funk it, funk it. Whatever it takes to get your message over to the people, that's what you've got to do.'"[28]

As for the Disciples, they had one more major tour to close 1976, an epic trip to the United Kingdom where they performed concerts in Wales, as well as in Manchester and at London's famed Hammersmith Odeon to bring in the New Year. The dates were recorded for another live album, though it would not be released for more than a year.

NOTES

1. *The Best of Andraé* by Andraé Crouch and the Disciples (Light LS 5678, 1976); "Best-Selling Gospel LPs," *Billboard*, January 3, 1976, 30; "Best-Selling Gospel LPs," *Billboard*, February 7, 1976, 53; "Best-Selling Gospel LPs," *Billboard*, March 6, 1976, 40; "Best-Selling Gospel LPs," *Billboard*, April 3, 1976, 55; "Best-Selling Gospel LPs," *Billboard*, May 1, 1976, 56; "Best-Selling Gospel LPs," *Billboard*, June 5, 1976, 56; "Best-Selling Gospel LPs," *Billboard*, July 4, 1976, 42; "Best-Selling Gospel LPs," *Billboard*, August 7, 1976, 52; "Best-Selling Gospel LPs," *Billboard*, September 4, 1976, 54; "Best-Selling Gospel LPs," *Billboard*, October 9, 1976, 43.
2. *The Best of Andraé* by Andraé Crouch and the Disciples (Light LS 5678).
3. Irene Johnson Ware, "Gospel Time," *Record World*, May 11, 1974, 27; Bob Kirsch, "Studio Track," *Billboard*, April 14, 1975, 51; Bili Thedford, interview with the authors, March 22, 2022; Bill Maxwell, interview with the authors, November 4, 2022.
4. *The Best of Andraé* by Andraé Crouch and the Disciples (Light LS 5678, 1976).
5. Bill Maxwell, interview with the authors, November 4, 2022.

6. Bill Maxwell, interview with the authors, October 21, 2022; "Congratulations! America's #1 Grammy Award Winning Gospel Performer," *Billboard*, March 13, 1976, 89.

7. https://discogs.com/release/228347-Psalm-150-Make-Up-Your-Mind; Allen Gregory, interview with the authors, August 19, 2021.

8. Jaymes Felix, interview with the authors, August 21, 20201; Allen Gregory, interview with the authors, August 19, 2021.

9. Allen Gregory, interview with the authors, August 19, 2021.

10. Glen Myerscough, interview with the authors, June 18, 2021.

11. Bill Maxwell, interview with the authors, November 4, 2022; Kathy Hazzard, interview with the authors, October 27, 2022.

12. Bob Doreschuk, "Backstage with Andraé Crouch," *Contemporary Keyboard*, August 1979, 14.

13. Bill Maxwell, interview with the authors, October 21, 2022.

14. Val Gonzalo, interview with the authors, October 10, 2020; Kathy Hazzard, interview with the authors, August 19, 2021; Phyllis St. James, interview with the authors, January 23, 2021.

15. Vonciele Faggett, interview with the authors, October 21, 2021; Val Gonzalo, interview with the authors, October 10, 2020; Carrie Gonzalo, interview with the authors, October 31, 2020; Fletch Wiley, interview with the authors, October 10, 2020.

16. Bill Maxwell, interview with the authors, May 18, 2019; Perry Morgan, interview with the authors, May 18, 2019.

17. "Gospel Switch: Disneyland to Experiment with It for Single Night," *Billboard*, May 1, 1976, 54.

18. "The Setlist Wiki," www.setlist.fm; Roland Forte, "Disciples Will Sing Here Monday Night," *Cleveland Call and Post*, June 19, 1976, 12B; "Crouch Gospel Scores Solidly in Riverside," *Billboard*, September 11, 1976, 37; John Sippel, "Booking Agency Formed: Gospelers Will Meet August 22," *Billboard*, August 7, 1976, 52.

19. Bill Maxwell, interview with the authors, November 4, 2022.

20. Donn Thomas, interview with the authors, August 21, 2021.

21. Melody Green, "Keith Green's Wife Remembers Andraé Crouch," *Charisma*, January 14, 2015, https://charismanews.com/opinion/keith-green-s-wife-remembers-andrae-crouch.

22. "Best-Selling Gospel LPs," *Billboard*, June 5, 1976, 56; "Best-Selling Gospel LPs," *Billboard*, July 4, 1976, 42; "Best-Selling Gospel LPs," *Billboard*, August 7, 1976, 52; "Best-Selling Gospel LPs," *Billboard*, September 4, 1976, 54; "Best-Selling Gospel LPs," *Billboard*, October 9, 1976, 43; Claudrena N. Harold, *When Sunday Comes: Gospel Music in the Soul and Hip-Hop Eras* (Urbana: University of Illinois Press, 2020), 88–90.

23. Kathy Hazzard, interview with the authors, October 27, 2022.

THE BEST OF ANDRAÉ

24. John Watson, interview with the authors, October 6, 2021; https:www.crossrhyt hms.co.uk/articles/music/Vinesong_the_globe_trotting_worship_ministry_fr om_South_Africa/39413/.

25. Patrick Salvo, "New King of 'Pop Gospel,'" *Sepia*, December 1976, 50–54.

26. "This Is Another Day," *Billboard*, November 6, 1976, 2; "Best-Selling Gospel LPs," *Billboard*, November 13, 1976, 61; "Selling Gospel Music LPs," *Billboard*, December 18, 1976, 49.

27. "Soul-Gospel Artists," *Billboard*, December 25, 1976, 100; "Soul-Gospel Albums," *Billboard*, December 25, 1976, 100; "Soul-Gospel Labels," *Billboard*, December 25, 1976, 100.

28. Bob Doreschuk, "Backstage with Andraé Crouch," *Contemporary Keyboard*, August 1979, 10.

11

This Is Another Day

Creating the Album

This Is Another Day's packaging was Light's most elaborate yet, as befitting Andraé's status as one of the best-known, best-selling artists in religious music. Artist Rick Sharp created three full-color tropical scenes for the album. The cover—unusual in gospel and CCM because of its lack of overt religious symbolism—depicts a tranquil view across a still ocean, flanked by palm trees under billowing clouds. The inside gatefold is another watercolor island paradise, with an illustrated Andraé staring across the horizon. On the back jacket is still another Hawaiian-styled vista, only set at night, along with a list of the vocalists and various salutations and thanks.

The LP gatefold repeats the palm-tree motif and includes a detailed list of the instrumentalists who recorded with co-producers Crouch and Maxwell, featuring many of the same A-list session artists who had recorded on *Take Me Back*, as well as the Disciples and several unexpected "guest" stars. The album sleeve's front lists the lyrics, while the back sleeve has a photograph of Andraé, surrounded by headshots of the Disciples: Danniebelle Hall, Jimmie Davis, Sandra Crouch, Bill Maxwell, Mike Escalante, Bea Carr, James Felix, Perry Morgan, and, at the top, Bili Thedford. By the time of the release of *This Is Another Day*, however, Thedford had already left the group and did not appear on any of the tracks. Nearly fifty years later, *This Is Another Day* remains a model for album packaging in gospel music.[1]

Clearly, the balance of power between the Disciples and Light Records had shifted considerably. "Whereas the record company didn't have any faith in me or Andraé to do his own work, after we had finished the *Take Me Back* album, everything changed," Maxwell said. "Because that album was so big, for *This Is Another Day* they just left us alone."[2]

Back at Mama Jo's

That also meant a return to the comfortable, familiar confines of Mama Jo's recording studio. "We kind of lived there," Maxwell said. Famed producer Alan Parsons also liked the soundboard and amenities at Mama Jo's and had returned to work on an album by the pop group Ambrosia. Maxwell said that when the Disciples weren't recording, he found excuses to "hang around" and observe a top engineer whose credits included the Beatles. "Alan was kind enough to show me some of his tricks," Maxwell said. "For instance, he showed me how to work the VSO [variable-speed oscillator], where you can speed up a tape or slow it down. We did a lot of that on *This Is Another Day*." One of the songs that benefited from Maxwell's newfound expertise was "We Expect You," where Fred Tackett's acoustic guitar part was slowed down to give the guitar a "strange" sound, Maxwell said, as if Tackett were "popping or plucking the strings." Crouch and Maxwell were so pleased with the VSO effect that they employed it on the background vocals on some songs, giving them a "higher" quality. Parsons also taught Maxwell how to "double" instruments, such as the guitar, on different tracks, creating a "flanging double sound."

Also helpful was engineer Tom Trefethen, who worked closely with Parsons. It was Trefethen who showed Maxwell how to creatively combine different mixes for the same song, an effect that's used on the song "Perfect Peace." "It was our time for experimenting," Maxwell said.[3]

On September 23, 1977, Steely Dan's *Aja* hit the marketplace with such hits as "Peg," "Black Cow," and "Deacon Blues." *Aja*'s influence is heard throughout *This Is Another Day*, and the LP, more than any other Crouch recording, highlights the distinctive sound of the Fender Rhodes piano. The result is one of the most extraordinary gospel, jazz, and funk fusion performance practices of the decade, one that is arguably on equal terms as the justly praised *Aja*.

This Is Another Day

Side I

"Perfect Peace"/"My Peace I Leave With You"
The opening bars of "Perfect Peace" suggest songs by Earth, Wind & Fire or Curtis Mayfield with their combination of soul and funk, stabbing guitar

licks, and the orchestrated hierarchy of soaring strings. The accentuated sixteenth notes on the hi-hat and the uniquely flavorful bass trombone pedal point draw listeners to a new sonic environment, one unmatched thus far in Crouch's artistic economy. And, for the first time, disco, the hot new industry canopy, found its way into Andraé's restless musical curiosity. Maxwell said that Crouch "kind of liked the vibe" of disco. "To me, when I listen to ['Perfect Peace'] now, it sounds like a combination of a Barry White song and the theme to *Love Boat*," Maxwell said. The song was arranged by Fletch Wiley and Andraé, with a swooping string arrangement by Larry Muhoberac. It is Muhoberac who composed and performed the innovative synthesizer passage. "We took a lot of talented people and let them be creative with the music," Maxwell said. Singer Kathy Hazzard said that the instrumentation on the song was especially memorable, even by Maxwell and Crouch's exacting standards. "Take the vocals away, you still have an album," she said. "Those boys *play*. And Bill Maxwell [is] always in the pocket." But Crouch feared that a song with that pronounced of a beat needed more "depth" to keep it from being "trivialized." Maxwell said that Andraé then conceived the chords that would segue into the next song, "My Peace I Leave with You," leaving the actual arrangement to Muhoberac, who wrote and performed the instrumental link between the two songs.[4]

"My Peace I Leave with You" begins with a motion picture soundtrack "soundscape," much like the string orchestral prelude to "All I Can Say" from *Take Me Back*. While navigating the different genres, this interlude prepares listeners for a journey from disco horn lines to a combined ARP and Moog synthesizer–fueled soliloquy based on Isaiah 23:30. No other piece on the album is as outspoken or overtly scriptural and it may be that the listener hears, for the first time, Crouch's taste for film music.

Maxwell said that much of the power of "My Peace I Leave with You" comes from the combination of Andraé's songwriting, Muhoberac's inventive string arrangement and keyboards, and Danniebelle Hall's vocals. "That's as fine, as high as I ever heard Danniebelle sing," Maxwell said. "I never heard her hit those notes like that. Her pitch was just dead on—a really great, great vocal." Hazzard agreed that Hall's vocals on the track are among her best. "Danniebelle always reminded me of Roberta Flack," Hazzard said. "Her tone was like Roberta Flack. All you had to do was darken the studio, let her sit on a stool with her headwrap and go for it. She'd say, 'OK, tell me what to do. Tell me how you want me to shade it.' Just like that." Hazzard, who was known for crying during emotional songs, said that Hall was "another crier." "She'd say, 'I'm crying on my own song!' You could feel her depth."[5]

"This Is Another Day"

The title track, "This Is Another Day," serves as a four-minute master class in piano. When musicologist Guthrie Ramsey writes, "Since the codification of ragtime piano, pianists developed highly idiosyncratic approaches to solo and ensemble-based improvisation that constituted key elements in the generic codes of various black popular music," he could have used Crouch's piano track here as an object lesson. In "This Is Another Day," Andraé presents a COGIC-styled fusion of pianistic right-handed gospel impressionistic harmonic "planning" (chords moving in parallel motion) in covenant with a bebop groove at a slower tempo. The walking bass and versatile horn lines, as well as the interactive call-and-responsive sections, create a praise song for another day, literally. More than any other song on the album, Andraé's rhythmic section leadership is more pronounced, present, and felt on this track.

Andraé's singing and lyrics are especially preachy, and the Disciples' highly embellished background vocals are subtly sophisticated and deeply reverent— somehow melding both rhythmic intensity and a virtuosic vocal dexterity. The gospel music world hears, perhaps for the first time, the introduction to the ethereal sound of a vocal jazz ensemble meeting a gospel praise and worship team. No other Black gospel choir or group of the era was singing this type of challenging style. It was just too worldly.

"This Is Another Day" marked the first horn arrangement by new Disciple Glen Myerscough. The funky bass part was created and performed by Wilton Felder, who, like Joe Sample, was a member of the Jazz Crusaders. Felder, who was equally adept on saxophone, is also known for his distinctive bass lines on such hits as the Jackson Five's "I Want You Back" and "ABC" and Marvin Gaye's "Let's Get It On." Maxwell added that both Mike Escalante and Crouch played keyboards on "This Is Another Day." "That's Andraé playing piano at the end," Maxwell said, "you can tell a mile away." Hazzard said that the piano playing on "This Is Another Day" still moves her, decades later. "Andraé made a piano walk, talk, dance, moonwalk, everything," she said. "I would just look at him and think, 'Is he really playing that?' After this album, he really started getting a lot of calls for studio stuff."[6]

"Quiet Times"

The pronounced modern jazz ballad opening to "Quiet Times" reflects Herbie Hancock's *Maiden Voyage* with its array of minor 11th chords, creating something mellow, soft-spoken, and unassuming, while at the same time cosmopolitan and chic. While there is no mention of "God" or "Jesus" anywhere in the song, it still qualifies, the authors believe, as an instrumental offering of high praise. Andraé's intention is to personalize his relationship with God, and "Quiet Times" reflects both a mystical feeling and theological trope. The song's lyrics are about the work done in the quietness of the soul; conversational, precious, secretive, and settled, while never understating the love relationship. It is a covenant, a promise between God and Andraé, supreme and beautiful.

Maxwell said that "Quiet Times" presented one of the more challenging vocal tracks on *This Is Another Day*. The accompanying piano parts are by Clark Gassman, with Joe Sample on Fender Rhodes, joined by Al Perkins (steel guitar), Dean Parks and Jay Graydon (guitars), David Hungate (bass), and Maxwell on drums. For the vocals, Maxwell said that Andraé's original idea was to create something in the vein of Manhattan Transfer or Lambert, Hendricks & Ross. Sandra Crouch, Hall, Perry Morgan, Bea Carr, Felix, and Hazzard recorded Andraé's intricate vocal parts at Western Studios. "Andraé's group were great singers, but they weren't used to doing those kinds of harmonies," Maxwell said. "It took forever trying to record those background vocals, maybe two or three days." Perkins, whose credits include hundreds of artists including Bob Dylan, Emmylou Harris, James Taylor, and the Eagles, played on a number of tracks on *This Is Another Day*. "What a great guy," Maxwell said. "He can play anything and did everything we asked."[7]

For composer/arranger Mark Kibble, "Quiet Times" is the perfect example of how Andraé took an easy-to-remember musical hook and "painted a picture" with the simple melody:

> You literally felt like, "I'm about to be on a date with Jesus Christ Himself" and the way Andraé painted that picture with the music in the background, it literally feels like you're out on a beach, that you can hear the water going, the seagulls, and feel the cool breeze—and you're not even there. You feel all of that. You feel you can see the table set before you and you're having that quiet conversation with Jesus Christ.[8]

250 SOON & VERY SOON

One of the more beguiling elements to "Quiet Times" is Crouch's sweet-spirited allusion to George Gershwin's "You Can't Take That Away from Me" at the close.

"Soon and Very Soon"

Within Andraé Crouch's extensive repertoire, "Soon and Very Soon" is the song that is closest to musical formulas found in the oldest Black spirituals. The shapes and insignias within the music and lyrics, along with the melismatic passages and cadences, constitute and establish the enduring themes and symbols in the African American spiritual tradition. Theologian Frederick Ware writes that the Black community's use of "symbols and themes" are "vital for the construction of African American theology." The very nature of the piece's existence, the authors believe, is wholly rooted in community. "Though symbols and themes are used and repeated frequently, they are subject to reformulation as new events and challenges emerge in African American experience, which itself is never static," Ware adds. The motif, and even the title "Soon and Very Soon," quickly becomes an African American sacred trope, one that signaled deliverance and determination, hope and empowerment, and finally, faith and love.

The African American church's eschatology, defined as the looking toward the future in hope, as expressed in song, means that the way forward is not through escapism from the trials and tribulations in this world. Instead, "Soon and Very Soon" establishes sabbath, solace, *and* activism through the act of singing. In the authors' opinion, this is something few songs from any genre or era can do as well.

Not surprisingly, "Soon and Very Soon" is one of the very best known, most beloved songs in Andraé's entire catalogue. Over a small rhythm section, the vocalists (Sandra, Morgan, Hall, Felix, and Carr), accompanied toward the end by members of the Christ Memorial Choir, created one of the most atmospheric, timeless songs of Andraé's career. While based on a fragment of an old Church of God in Christ chant/song, one which musician Jeffrey LaValley said he sang as a young man in COGIC services, Felix said that the final version of the song began to appear in bits and pieces while the Disciples were on tour. "We didn't know the songs," he said, "so we learned them on the spot. He did that to all of us all the time. After a while, we got used to how he'd write these chord changes and think, 'OK, you know where he's going to go.' Of course, we really practiced them later on." From those small beginnings, Maxwell and

Crouch laid down a basic rhythm track with Felix on bass and with Andraé overdubbing a simple organ motif to "keep it very, very pure," Maxwell said:

> Andraé said, "It feels like it needs something else." I said, "It'd be great if we had somebody old, like they're going to see the King and they know they're getting ready to see Him—and they're singing. They could moan or something." Andraé said, "We have an older woman in our church, Mother Dora Brackins. She can moan: 'We're marching, I'm going to see the King. I'm going to see the King.'"

As for Andraé himself, he later told NPR's Tavis Smiley that "one of the secrets" of his songs, including "Soon and Very Soon," was that he "never preached" at his listeners:

> It was always a feeling that I had about God. And you will notice in a lot of my music that it's always a "We" and the festivity of seeing Jesus was that we're going to see the king. It was a corporate thing. And so I think that that's the way I got that one going, and the verses speak for the lesson in the song.

Maxwell and Crouch enlisted the Christ Memorial Radio Choir from his father's church and overdubbed a simple snare drum march pattern. Once it was completed, Andraé brought Brackins to Mama Jo's and played the completed track for her. According to Maxwell, Crouch turned to Brackins and said, "Just moan like you do in church." Brackens responded, "Well, I don't really know what to sing. Now, I *do* know 'Soon and Very Soon'—I've been singing that all my life." Crouch later added the bridge and completed the song. Maxwell said that once Andraé turned the completed album over to Light, the label executives—and Light's distributors—immediately pronounced it the "biggest" song on the LP. "And they were right," Maxwell said, "But until Mother Brackins told me, I hadn't known it was an old COGIC chorus."[9]

"We Expect You"

Felix's crooning high tenor voice is featured in "We Expect You." In G♭ major, another song that emerged on a Disciples tour more than a year before the release of *This Is Another Day*. Myerscough remembered first hearing what would become "We Expect You" before a performance in New York City earlier that year. Andraé asked Myerscough to bring his saxophone with him to his hotel room, where he had his electric piano already set up and the vocalists had been rehearsing. "We did a quick rehearsal in his room," Myerscough said, "Just out of the blue he wanted to feature me on this song. And we played

252   SOON & VERY SOON

it that night for the first time—whatever you needed to do to get the music to work."

Months later, when the time came to record the song, Maxwell said he urged Crouch to sing and accompany himself on the piano. But Crouch instead insisted that Felix sing, even as he continued to tinker with the arrangement, recording full-band treatments arranged by Clark Gassman, then Muhoberac. Finally, Andraé agreed to record it with just Felix and piano—but insisted that Joe Sample play the piano. "And Joe goes out and plays great," Maxwell recalled, "but it's not Andraé. And Joe kept saying, 'Andraé, you're the one who is supposed to be playing this song.'" After the multiple recording sessions, Andraé at last relented and recorded the piano—and captured the song in a single take. Maxwell said he overdubbed his drums and additional guitars by Tackett. "We VSO'd it and that's how that came about," Maxwell said. For Felix, however, the session had been anything but straightforward. Felix said that he and the other musicians had arrived at Mama Jo's that morning expecting to record a different song. "But he lays this on us," Felix said. After Crouch had played the instrumental accompaniment to "We Expect You," he turned to Felix and said, "Oh, and you're singing it." "So I didn't really know the song—I learned it on the spot. An hour later, we're recording it." Felix said that he only truly "learned" the song in the weeks ahead while performing it live. Felix was not the only musician surprised during the session. At one point, Myerscough recalled, Andraé turned to him in the studio. "He said, 'I'd like you to play through the melody here, at this point,'" Myerscough said. "After the second verse, he just wanted me to do whatever I felt like I could do. So I just basically played the melody. I just added to it as I could, without getting too crazy or flamboyant." It was, Myerscough said, the first time he was featured in a Crouch composition. "It was a surprise," Myerscough said, "but I was glad to do it. I was grateful and it gave me a chance to do something nice to contribute to the whole. Andraé was very nurturing to everyone to get them to contribute what they could and what they wanted to. He encouraged that." Following the release of *"Live" at Carnegie Hall*, the group had begun to see more African Americans in their concerts and Maxwell said that the Disciples were taken aback at the reception "We Expect You" received in a Black church in Queens. "These people started screaming like they were crazy," Maxwell said. "They did not expect that voice coming out of a Latin dude. It went over so well live." "When James—we called him 'Arky'—got up there to sing, it was totally amazing," Hazzard said. "He was like a rock star. The audiences loved it."[10]

"You Gave to Me"

Crouch and Maxwell brought in another top arranger to handle *This Is Another Day*'s most overtly R&B song, "You Gave to Me," even though the song, in E♭ major, sometimes feels more like a groove than a completed song. The multi-talented David Blumberg, whose previous credits included the Jackson 5, Stevie Wonder, and Gladys Knight, brought a funky energy to the project, fueled by guitarists Dean Parks and David T. Walker, bassist Felder, Joe Sample on keys, and noted saxophone player Michael Brecker. Maxwell said he had been invited to join Michael and Randy Brecker's new band Dreams when the group's original drummer Billy Cobham left. When Dreams later broke up, Maxwell said he stayed in touch with the brothers, whose musical stars were clearly on the rise. When their new group, the Brecker Brothers, came to Los Angeles to perform at the Roxy, Maxwell invited Michael to record two songs at Mama Jo's, "You Gave to Me" and "The Choice."[11]

"All That I Have"

"All That I Have" is an oddity in gospel music in that while the verses are in the key of E♭ major, the chorus and hook are in G♭ major. "All That I Have" became a popular ballad in the 1970s and 1980s, frequently played at weddings, in part because of the sweet duet between Perry Morgan and Danniebelle Hall. Felix said that from the first time he heard Danniebelle sing the song during the session, he knew she was "special." "When she sang, it was with more than just a voice," Felix said. "My goodness, she was so anointed, and it was like second nature to her, whenever she opened her mouth and sang."[12]

Maxwell said that Parks's memorable electric sitar lines on "All That I Have" "were added as a tribute to the Delfonics and Stylistics." The success of *Take Me Back*, he said, had given Andraé the freedom to try still more new musical approaches, including this one. "We were alone to create," Maxwell said. "Not everything worked out, but Andraé was extremely creative. He could always hear another part." That meant, however, that some songs would have ten or more additional passages or solos at any given time. "It gets confusing," Maxwell said. "My job was to try to edit them out and say, 'No, it doesn't need this or that' because Andraé just has things coming at him all the time musically."[13]

"The Choice"

Written by Felix and Greg Eckler (with additional lyrics by Andraé), "The Choice" was first recorded by Psalm 150 and Maxwell said that the arrangement closely mirrors the original, with Felix singing the lead. The piano parts were contributed by another one of Maxwell's friends from Oklahoma, Leon Russell. The two had met through a mutual friend, guitarist Jessie Ed Davis. "Leon was going through a divorce and was in Los Angeles, so I contacted him," Maxwell said. "He said, 'Oh, I'd love to come and play.' At the time, Leon was really one of the biggest acts in the country. He showed up and played great." But for Felix, it was a nerve-wracking experience. He said he was already feeling "under-qualified" to be playing bass when bassists of the caliber of Felder and Hungate were contributing such memorable bass lines. On the day of the session, Felix said his bass guitar had just "died." Fortunately, Ambrosia was finishing work on their own album at Mama Jo's. "So Bill asked the bass player Joe [Puerta] if I could borrow his bass," Felix recalled. "And he said, 'Oh sure.'"

"The Choice" is—obviously—about choices and the community of song writers (the former members of Psalm 150 and others) made several intriguing arrangement decisions. The song musically mirrors what the lyrics suggest. Arranged by Fletch Wiley and Larry Muhoberac, the song dispenses with the traditional eight-measure introduction. Instead, it features the harmonic progressions (I–V7/V–IV7–V7) in A major, a funky bass groove, and Chaka Khan–styled vocalese. These elements work together to suggest that *choices* are up to the listener. Immediately after the tenor saxophone solo, the bridge highlights a piano breakdown, a temporary modulation to the key of C major, and implies a charge to the listener: "those who have ears to hear, let them hear." The song recapitulates the opening, and finally jams with a call-and-response, fading out with the words "the choice is up to you."[14]

"Polynesian Praise Song"

The origins of "Polynesian Praise Song" can be found during the Disciples' first tour of Australia and New Zealand. Following a series of dates in New Zealand, Maxwell said that a group of the Maori people came to the airport to see them off. "It was so touching," Maxwell said. "They started singing these worship songs at the airport as we were leaving, and Andraé wanted to try and recreate that." The song serves as a benediction for the album, a "sending off," island style. With "Polynesian Praise Song," Andraé honors his friends by composing a straightforward praise & worship song. The seashore sounds, ukulele, and pedal steel offerings are deftly couched in a $\frac{6}{8}$ time signature as Crouch reverently declares, "We praise your holy name."[15]

Response—and Impact

Maxwell said he believed that *This Is Another Day* was the "best album" he worked on with Andraé Crouch and the Disciples. "Whatever it is for you," he said, "that one—for me—was the one I liked best. We loved each other very much and we cared about the people. Andraé always cared about the people." Felix said he was a little "star-struck" throughout the recording process. "I knew that everything Andraé did has this anointing and specialness to it," Felix said. "You just knew that people were going to relate because he had a way of making it relate . . . because he had the music in mind [and] because he had a deep ministry mind[set] about what he was writing as well. So the way he correlated those things, obviously—to me—it was just divine orchestration."[16]

Of the most memorable songs in the Andraé Crouch catalogue, "Soon and Very Soon" continues to captivate casual fans and musicologists alike. The song has appeared in more than fifty hymnals and was selected to be sung at the public memorial service for pop superstar Michael Jackson on July 7, 2009, in Los Angeles. The words and music have an indefinable, almost ineffable quality of antiquity about them; it somehow sounds even "older" than most classic gospel songs as the opening lyric reads, "Soon and very soon/We are going to see the king." While Arizona Dranes, who sang and recorded a number of songs and hymns in the earliest COGIC tradition in the 1920s and 1930s, never recorded anything with the title of "Soon and Soon Very Soon," there is a deep connection when compared to the title and first line of one of her best-known numbers from fifty years earlier, "Bye and Bye We Are Going to See the King." "Singability" has been an essential element of African American sacred folk music since the time of the spirituals. Mark Kibble attributed its enduring appeal and "timelessness" to its simplicity and use of repetition. "Not all songs have to be simple to be great, but some of my favorites are," Kibble said. "And 'Soon and Very Soon' has been [translated] in 180 languages." Even legendary gospel scholar and musician Horace C. Boyer, who was no fan of contemporary gospel music, cited "Soon and Soon" as an example of gospel music's importance in providing, among other things, "the sole sing-along in the Black community." "We will sing when we are in a group," he writes. "That's a compliment. That's what they did in our motherland." And in that, like few other songs before or since, "Soon and Very Soon" strikingly encapsulates Frederick Ware's concept of the "symbols and themes" of that motherland.[17]

On the Road Again

The Disciples continued their demanding 1977 touring schedule, including another series of dates in Europe in February. In Holland, the group performed three concerts and recorded a television special, all sponsored by Gospel Music International, the first Dutch gospel label. In all, the Disciples performed twelve dates in Scandinavia and the UK, playing before an estimated "29,000 [people] in halls averaging 3,000 seats, grossing $127,500." Supported by Word Records and DJM Records, the group also taped a BBC appearance. Back in North America, the Disciples resumed their rigorous schedule, ranging from another return visit to Disneyland's "Night of Joy" to a sold-out date in Columbia, South Carolina, among a host of others. It was during those spring tours that Allen Gregory, then just twenty-three, lost his father. "I could tell Andraé was there for me if I needed to talk," Gregory said. "He was never cold or uncaring or any of the other things I've experienced in the music business. I think more than anything else with Andraé, he really loved the Lord and that's what motivated everything."[18]

Amid the Disciple's breakneck pace, Maxwell and Crouch finished up producing Danniebelle Hall's first album for Sparrow Records, which also featured most of the Disciples. *Let Me Have a Dream* followed three successful LPs for Light Records as she launched her solo career with a tour of Australia. Maxwell's stature as a producer was growing as well, and between studio dates with the Disciples and touring, he also found time to produce Keith Green, Jessy Dixon, Fletch Wiley, and the 2nd Chapter of Acts.[19]

The success of *This Is Another Day* also meant that the Disciples were getting noticed, booked, and broadcast in a wide variety of settings outside of traditional religious music. In April, *Cash Box* magazine noted that the group was finally "gaining airplay in regular programming on Black-oriented stations across the country" because of Andraé's "innovative approach to gospel music." The higher profile meant that the Disciples were able to venture into new markets as well. During an appearance in the Bahamas, Prime Minister

Lyndon O. Pinding was in attendance and greeted the Disciples after the show. On May 20, Andraé and the Disciples became the first contemporary gospel music to perform in New York's Madison Square Garden, followed by dates in Washington, DC; Pittsburgh; and Detroit before appearing on the *Dinah!* talk show with host Dinah Shore on May 25.[20]

Before the packed June date at the multiracial Greater Pittsburgh Charismatic Conference in the Civic Arena, Crouch paused long enough for an interview with the *Pittsburgh Courier*'s Mattie Trent. Speaking to an African American writer, Andraé took the opportunity to address two of his ongoing concerns, perceptions and race:

> Not a fad. Jesus Christ is real. People might look at us at this meeting and call us freaked out, but we're not drunk, we know what we are doing. So many are hung up on their hang ups. I'm so glad I don't have to search anymore. Jesus is not only for the red man, the yellow man, but He's for the Black man, too.[21]

The group continued performing across the country during the summer festival season, stopping long enough in July for Crouch to be honored at the Christian Booksellers Association's annual meeting in Kansas City. Light Record's Ralph Carmichael and Word, Inc.'s Jarrell McCracken were on hand to award Andraé a plaque celebrating the sale of more than one million albums over eight Light LPs. Soon thereafter, the Disciples were performing concerts in Anchorage and Fairbanks, Alaska. Or, as a writer for *Record World* put it, "Alaska's cold wilderness recently felt the heat of the U.S.'s hottest soul-gospel singer." From there, the group traveled south once again on another leg of its never-ending tour to include several of its longtime favorite Southern California venues. On one occasion, however, when Felix had already booked a prior engagement on the same night as an important concert at Magic Mountain, Maxwell quickly contracted with another young bassist, Abraham Laboriel. The two had first worked together on the 2nd Chapter of Acts LP *Mansion Builder* earlier in 1977 and had made an immediate connection. After a crash course in Andraé's music, Laboriel said he and the Disciples took the bus to Valencia:

> The place was packed with believers and when we started to perform with Andraé, we were all transported to the presence of the Lord in the most amazing way. Suddenly, everybody stopped using any of the attractions in the park and they all congregated to the outdoor auditorium that possibly held 2,000 people. We did all the classics that night, "This Is Another Day," "Take Me Back," "Soon

and Very Soon," "My Tribute," and a beautiful song that was not recorded until many, many years later, "There Is a Bell."[22]

An Eventful End to a Stellar Year

As 1977 rolled to a close, the Disciples continued to tour to enthusiastic crowds, and Maxwell and Crouch continued to commute to Los Angeles to work on the live album tapes recorded back in December 1976 in the UK. It had also been an exceptional year for Light Records, and the label was represented throughout *Record World*'s lengthy October 1 issue celebrating gospel music. One full-page advertisement featured photos of Light's three top-selling artists, Andraé, Walter Hawkins, and Jessy Dixon, with Andraé's caption written in breathless advertising prose:

> Phenomenal Andraé Crouch has sold well over one million gospel albums. His latest album, *This Is Another Day* knocked the top out of the gospel charts and landed right in the middle of the soul charts. Headlining as a top box office draw, Andraé and the Disciples "wow" the crowds![23]

A few days after the *Record World* articles were published, Andraé and Sandra hosted a special fund-raising banquet honoring their father Benjamin, marking his twenty-sixth year as pastor of Christ Memorial Church of God in Christ in Pacoima. Among the 700 guests at the Century Plaza Hotel in Los Angeles were the Reverend Jesse Jackson and a host of California politicians. One of the highlights was a congratulatory telegram to Benjamin Crouch from President Jimmy Carter and a fiery performance by the Disciples. Money raised from the event was earmarked for the completion of Christ Memorial's new sanctuary.[24]

Andraé and the Disciples closed 1977 with another thirty-five-date tour in November and December. One of the significant stops on the tour was to perform the first Black gospel concert in Nashville's venerable Opry House that was reviewed in *Billboard*'s "Talent in Action" column—also another first for the group. Writer Gerry Wood writes that Crouch could be "one of the biggest soul singers in the business" but instead chose to become "the best" in gospel music. Though Andraé was suffering from a head cold, Wood says that the crowd of 3,500 was quite willing to erupt into "rhythmic applause" throughout. One of the highlights, he writes, was the offbeat combination of the music from the Beatles' "Yesterday" to the lyrics of an unpublished song titled "Calvary." Wood noted that the Disciples' racial mix, five Black and five white musicians and singers, reflected the audience demographics as well. Alternating between preaching and performing, the ninety-minute set closed with "This Is Another Day" and "Soon and Very Soon." It was followed by a three-song encore, "Born Again" (perhaps "You Don't Got to Jump No Pews"), "My Tribute (to God Be the Glory)," and finally, the Disciples were joined onstage by Reba Rambo to sing "Just Like He Said He Would." Following the concert, Andraé stopped by the *Record World* offices in Nashville, where he was photographed with the magazine's John Sturdivant and was presented *Record World*'s "#1 award plaque."[25]

Soledad Prison

The Disciples scheduled two more significant dates to end 1977. Like his father, Andraé had a particular heart for society's outcasts—people with a chemical dependency, people with housing insecurity, and the incarcerated. The Disciples had been performing in various smaller prisons and jails for several years, but in December they received permission to perform at the infamous Soledad State Prison in California. The invitation was due to the work of the independent ex-con outreach organization, The Way Inn. On December 29, Crouch took the full band to perform two concerts in the gymnasium, the only venue big enough to accommodate inmates from all three correctional centers where, since its opening in 1948, eighteen prisoners and four corrections officers had died, mostly in racially motivated incidents. The event was significant enough that *Time* magazine assigned correspondent James Wilde to attend and titled his article "Hosanna in Hell: Andraé Crouch Brings the Gospel to Soledad Prison." Andraé and the Disciples ate with the inmates in the cafeteria and passed "with dignity and ease" among the often-warring Black, Latinx, and white inmates. Using the prison's "beat-up piano," he opened with a prayer: "I come in the name of Jesus. Wash me in your precious blood as I open the door of my heart and receive you as my Lord and Savior." Wilde noted that the prisoners had automatically segregated themselves in the gym, but all responded as Andraé sang "Through It All."

When the concert ended, many of the inmates lingered. "I've been in jail a long time, but I've never seen anyone react to anyone like this," a Latin male told Wilde. "When you can get all these races together acting as a whole," a white prisoner said, "that's good. It was a miracle considering all of the tensions here." Wilde asked Crouch about his motivations for performing at Soledad. "I'll hook them any way I can," Andraé replied.[26]

Andraé's other engagement was a New Year's Eve benefit concert for World Vision, with the proceeds going to the organization's efforts to provide medical supplies in East Africa. According to Bill Maxwell, Crouch had long talked of performing in Africa and, as the calendar turned to 1978, began to explore opportunities to take the Disciples there.[27]

This Is Another Day spent every month high on the *Billboard* "Best-Selling Gospel LPs" chart and finished as 1977's fifth top-selling album, behind Walter Hawkins and the Love Alive Choir's *Love Alive*. Three other Disciples albums charted as well: *The Best of Andraé Crouch* (#8), *Take Me Back* (#10), and *"Live" at Carnegie Hall* (#11). Taken together, the sales from the four LPs earned the Disciples the top position in the cumulative "Soul-Gospel Artists" category, ahead of *Love Alive*. Andraé's peers in the Gospel Music Association also gave *This Is Another Day* their Dove Award in the "Gospel Album of the Year." At the ceremony, Crouch presented CCM artist Evie Tornquist her own Dove as "Female Gospel Vocalist" of the year.[28]

Impact and Influence

This Is Another Day sometimes gets lost in the discussion of Andraé's work, especially since it is bookended by two of the best LPs released by the Disciples, *Take Me Back* and the upcoming *Live in London* double album set. Crouch himself considered the album pivotal in expanding his ministry beyond white evangelical circles and the Black church to a wider audience. Though little remarked at the time, *This Is Another Day* is the first time the message in some of his songs is intentionally multifaceted. A few years later, he told *Contemporary Keyboard* magazine that, in essence, the album "talked about God as being the lover of us all," particularly the song "Quiet Times." "A lot of people don't see God as gentle," Crouch said, "they see him as one who would kill you if you make a mistake. I see him as somebody who really digs me for what I am, so I write songs about him which someone might direct to somebody else they love." In the article, Andraé recounts a conversation with a young woman who called "Quiet Times" "a pop song or love song." "It's like she was afraid of the idea of love between two people and she only thought of

God as being beyond all that," Crouch said. Later albums would be even more overt.[29]

As for religious publications, *CCM (Contemporary Christian Music)* magazine slotted *This Is Another Day* at #24 in their list of "The 100 Greatest Albums in Christian Music," where longtime *CCM* editor John Styll notes that "in the mid-'70s this album stood head and shoulders above most contemporary releases." The album, he writes, "stood the test of time, thanks to great songs, top-notch production and spirited performances."[30]

Those "great songs," most notably "Soon and Very Soon," continue to be frequently sung today, still performed in churches where the young people may not know the composer's name, but they definitely know his music.

> Those songs, those records, you can listen to them right now and just have yourself—as the old church folks say—a Holy Ghost good time.—Kathy Hazzard[31]

NOTES

1. Andraé Crouch and the Disciples, *This Is Another Day* (Light Records LS5683).
2. Bill Maxwell, interview with the authors, November 4, 2022.
3. Bill Maxwell, interview with the authors, November 4, 2022.
4. Bill Maxwell, interview with the authors, November 4, 2022; Kathy Hazzard, interview with the authors, October 27, 2022.
5. Bill Maxwell, interview with the authors, November 4, 2022; Kathy Hazzard, interview with the authors, October 27, 2022.
6. Guthrie Ramsey Jr., *Who Hears Here? On Black Music, Pasts and Present* (Oakland: University of California Press, 2022), 239; Daniel E. Slotnick, "Wilton Felder, Saxophonist for the Crusaders, Dies at 75," *New York Times*, October 3, 2015; Bill Maxwell, interview with the authors, November 4, 2022; Kathy Hazzard, interview with the authors, October 27, 2022.
7. Bill Maxwell, interview with the authors, November 4, 2022; https://www.alperkinsmusic.com/discography.php
8. Mark Kibble, interview with the authors, November 7, 2020.
9. Frederick L. Ware, *African American Theology* (Louisville, KY: Westminster John Knox, 2016), 61; Bill Maxwell, interview with the authors, November 4, 2022; Jaymes Felix, interview with the authors, August 21, 2021; "Soon and Very Soon," by Andraé Crouch, Lexicon Music, Inc., courtesy of Capitol CMG; Tavis Smiley, "Interview: Singer-Songwriter Andraé Crouch Discusses His Career," *The Tavis Smiley Show*, NPR, 2004, http://www.npr.org.
10. Glen Myerscough, interview with the authors, August 19, 2021; Bill Maxwell, interview with the authors, October 21, 2022; Jaymes Felix, interview with the

authors, August 21, 2021; Glen Myerscough, interview with the authors, June 18, 2021; Kathy Hazzard, interview with the authors, October 27, 2021.

11. Bill Maxwell, interview with the authors, November 4, 2022; https://www.discogs.com/artist/12281-David-Blumberg.

12. Jaymes Felix, interview with the authors, August 21, 2021.

13. Bill Maxwell, interview with the authors, November 4, 2022.

14. Bill Maxwell, interview with the authors, November 4, 2022; Jaymes Felix, interview with the authors, August 21, 2021.

15. Bill Maxwell, interview with the authors, November 4, 2022.

16. Bill Maxwell, interview with the authors, November 4, 2022; Jaymes Felix, interview with the authors, August 21, 2021.

17. https://hymnary.org/text/soon_and_very_soon_we_are_going; Randal C. Archibold, "At Jackson Memorial, Music and Mourning," *New York Times*, July 8, 2009; Arizona Dranes, *Completed Recorded Works in Chronological Order, 1926–1929* Document Records (DOCD 5186); Jeffrey LaValley, interview with the authors, August 29, 2020; Mark Kibble, interview with the authors, November 7; 2020; Horace C. Boyer, "Defining, Researching, and Teaching Gospel Music: A Contemporary Assessment," *Black American Culture and Scholarship: Contemporary Issues* (1985a), 36; "Soon and Very Soon" by Andraé Crouch, Lexicon Music, Inc., courtesy of Capitol CMG.

18. Willem Hoos, "Concerts and TV: Holland Welcoming Crouch, Disciples," *Billboard*, February 5, 1977, 54; "Crouch Euro Trek Triggers Wide Exposure," *Billboard*, February 5, 1977, 36; www.setlist.fm/festivals; "*Billboard*'s Top Boxoffice," *Billboard*, March 5, 1977, 35; Allen Gregory, interview with the authors, August 19, 2021.

19. https://www.discogs.com/artist/419312-Bill-Maxwell.

20. "Reflections 'N Black," *Cash Box*, April 9, 1977, 43; Gerry Wood, "Gospel Scene," *Billboard*, June 4, 1977, 66; "Crouch's Gospel Draws Premier of Bahamas," *Billboard*, September 10, 1977, 46; "Crouch Moving Gospel to N.Y.," *Billboard*, May 7, 1977, 62.

21. Mattie Trent, "Sketches," *Pittsburgh Courier*, June 4, 1977, 17.

22. "Gospel Retailers Honor Crouch," *Record World*, August 20, 1977, 58; "Crouch LP Sales Top Million Mark in 10 Yrs.," *Cash Box*, August 27, 1977, 67; Vicki Branson, "Gospel Time," *Record World*, September 3, 1977, 62; Abraham Laboriel, interview with the authors, August 19, 2021.

23. "Light: The Record Company That Has Brought the World Gospel's Greatest," *Record World*, October 1, 1977, 71; "Because Gospel Is Important to Us . . . We've Made It Our Business," *Record World*, October 1, 1977, 59; "J. P. Bradly: PR for the Inspirational Market, *Record World*, October 1, 1977, 86; Paul Baker, "Jesus Music: A New Dimension in Pop and Gospel," *Record World*, October 1, 1977, 88.

24. "Benjamin Crouch Honored in Cal.," *Record World*, November 12, 1977, 78.

25. "Opryhouse Opens Its Doors to Gospel," *Cash Box*, December 24, 1977, 44; Gerry Wood, "Andraé Crouch: Talent in Action," *Billboard*, November 26, 1977, 56; "Crouch Visits RW," *Record World*, December 24, 1977, 60.
26. James Wilde, "Hosanna in a Spot of Hell: Andraé Crouch Brings the Gospel to Soledad Prison," *Time*, January 9, 1978, 14; "Crouch Performs at Soledad State Prison," *Record World*, January 7, 1978, 52; "Crouch & Disciples Sing at Soledad Prison," *Record World*, January 7, 1978, 33; Gerry Wood, "Gospel Scene," *Billboard*, January 7, 1978, 70.
27. Gerry Wood, "Gospel Scene," *Billboard*, January 7, 1978, 70; Bill Maxwell, interview with the authors, November 4, 2022.
28. "Soul-Gospel Artists," *Billboard*, December 24, 1977, 100; "Soul-Gospel Albums," *Billboard*, December 24, 1977, 100; "Gospel Music Assn. Hosts the Ninth Annual 'Dove Awards' Presentation," *Cash Box*, December 10, 1977, 43.
29. Bob Doerschuk, "Backstage with Andraé Crouch," *Contemporary Keyboards*, August 1979, 10.
30. Thom Granger, ed., *CCM Presents: This 100 Greatest Albums in Christian Music* (Eugene, OR: Harvest House, 2001), 104–107.
31. Kathy Hazzard, interview with the authors, September 7, 2022.

12

Live in London

A Busy Season

The Disciples continued their nonstop touring in 1978, even as Bill Maxwell and Andraé Crouch regularly flew back and forth to Los Angeles to work on the *Live in London* tapes. The Disciples' popularity overseas was one of the catalysts for the formation of "Gospel Contact," an organization to promote gospel music in Western Europe. One of the organization's first operations was to arrange and coordinate a multinational tour in January and February featuring the Disciples, Chuck Girard, and the Rambos. The venture debuted in Rotterdam on January 12 with a concert by Andraé and the Disciples, recorded and broadcast in March by the Dutch broadcasting company NCRV.[1]

On the home front, Lexicon's *The New Church Hymnal*, first printed in July 1977, passed the 250,000 sales mark in April—with another 100,000 copies recently reordered—a spectacular number for a new hymnal. Several of Andraé's compositions were featured, along with popular songs by Ralph Carmichael and Bill Gaither. Crouch's success prompted Carmichael to propose a publishing venture with Lexicon Music where Andraé's songs from *This Is Another Day* and the upcoming *Live in London* would be published as part of Lexicon Music, Inc./Crouch Music. Lexicon would administer the copyrights "on all of Crouch's publications."[2]

In late spring, Maxwell and Crouch were at last happy with *Live in London*'s production and sent the completed tapes to Light Records for mastering and duplication. The year-long process was, at last, complete.

A Game-Changing Release

A review of the original concert in the venerable English music magazine *Melody Maker*, published two weeks after the original concert on January 15, 1977, provides one of the few detailed reviews of this classic incarnation of the Disciples. Critic Karl Dallas immediately differentiates Andraé from more traditional gospel artists "who turned our heads around in the Forties and Fifties." "He had barely been onstage at the Hammersmith Odeon for more than couple of bars before the entire theater was literally jumping with joy," Dallas writes. "He even got them clapping on the offbeat, too, which is more than *Black Nativity* ever managed in my experience." Dallas complains briefly about the vocal mix but writes that the "seven accompanying Disciples were so good—especially a real bitch of a tenor player—that there was always something good going on." Dallas adds a comment on the versatile nature of Andraé's preaching and singing voices, then closes with a personal note:

> I entered the hall on New Year's Day feeling as out of place as a Jew at a National Front rally, but I left feeling blessed. Anyone who can do that, in these conditions and at the fag-end of a Hogmanay hangover, has got to be a special kind of witness, and that's what Andraé Crouch is, something really special.[3]

In the United States, Light Records announced the long-promised arrival of *Live in London* with an eye-catching full-color two-page advertisement in the July 22 issue of *Record World*, complete with the iconic keyboard-as-spaceship cover. The ad also featured promotional copy typical of the era, including a blurb that urged DJs to play "these dynamite sounds"—"Revive Us," "If I Was a Tree," "I'll Keep Loving You," and others.[4]

Cash Box magazine also provided one of the first "new release" reviews in any mainstream magazine of a Disciples album, with a paragraph in its August 5, 1978, edition. The writer claims that the Disciples "have performed before millions all over the world" and offers advice for both prospective record stores buyers and radio station programmers:

> It is impossible to single out the secret of the success of the Disciples, but there are common denominators relative to their live and recorded performances. First, the technical excellence of this group is unsurpassed anywhere, Secondly, whether the song is up tempo or ballad, their delivery is full of emotion. People

love Andraé & the Disciples and they love this album. Includes: "I Surrender All," "Take a Little Time," "Hallelujah" and "Revive Us Again."[5]

The Concerts

The original concerts in 1977 had been uncommonly hectic affairs, even by Andraé's standards. After arriving in London from Los Angeles, a bus had taken the group to Port Talbot, Wales, that evening for a concert with Pat Boone and his family, and back to London again the following day for some much-needed time off. The third day was spent on a detailed soundcheck with a mobile recording studio prior to the concert in the Hammersmith Odeon scheduled for that evening. The following morning the Disciples were driven to Manchester for the final concert before flying out—three concerts in four days. Both the London and Manchester shows were recorded, with the bulk of the songs on *Live in London* actually drawn from the Manchester concert, primarily because the singers and musicians, Maxwell said, were less jet-lagged by that point. Maxwell, of course, was both producing and playing the drums. "I didn't know then how stupid it was," he recalled, "but it was very stupid to be trying to play drums with the headset on, talking to the truck, racing back and forth, and making sure all things sounded good." And all of this without another drummer to check the sound of the drums.[6]

Both Glen Myerscough and Allen Gregory, who had never been to Europe before, recalled the high quality of musicianship in the concerts, which meant that Maxwell, as producer, had to do very little overdubbing during the project's mixing stages back in the states. Gregory said that Maxwell arranged for the group to receive triple scale for the two nights:

> but with the condition that if we flubbed anything we'd have to come into the studio and fix it for free. And so Glen and I actually nailed everything. We didn't have to come into the studio and fix anything, which was such an accomplishment! The fact that Glen and I nailed everything on the spot, I think was a sort of miracle in and of itself. But that's how tight the band was.[7]

James Felix, also on his first European tour, said his most vivid memory was of Maxwell's dual role in the concerts. "I always found it amazing that Bill's the producer and he's playing drums," Felix said. "He's got to jump off these drums, run back to the trailer where they're recording, do whatever you got to do, come back, and pick up where you left off. All I had to do was play bass."

That this was even possible, Felix said, was because the Disciples were so well rehearsed. On one or two occasions, when the group was forced to repeat a song, it didn't matter to the audience because, as Felix said, "they loved it."[8]

Live in London boasts the most iconic cover art in gospel music or CCM, an air-brushed marvel depiction of a piano keyboard as a spaceship, hovering over the Union Jack. Inside, the two-LP gatefold features pictures of the band: Andraé, Harlan Rogers, and Mike Escalante (keyboards), James Felix (bass), Bill Maxwell (drums), Sandra Crouch (tambourine), Jimmie Davis and Hadley Hockensmith (guitars), Glen Myerscough (saxophone), and Allen Gregory (trumpet). Vocals are attributed to Andraé, Perry Morgan, Danniebelle Hall, Bea Carr, and Felix. Special thanks were also given to Kathy Hazzard, Phyllis St. James, and Bili Thedford.[9]

The Musicians

Much of the piano on *Live in London* is performed by Rogers, including the impressively fast-paced fingering on "Perfect Peace." Maxwell said that the decision to invite Rogers was because of Andraé's desire to do more preaching. "I needed somebody really strong that could sit in," Maxwell said. "He couldn't play like Andraé but he would play all of the right stuff." Rogers and keyboardist Escalante switched as needed among the acoustic piano, organ, Clavinet D6, and Fender Rhodes when Crouch suddenly bounded up off of the piano to preach or testify.[10]

Escalante had begun playing the Hammond B3 organ while in elementary school and joined his father's Latin-flavored band, along with his two brothers, at age twelve. "Mike had so much experience by the time he was eighteen and joined Psalm 150," Myerscough said. "He was untrained otherwise—he just learned by listening. Everything just came so easily. He added a lot of rich depth to the music." Myerscough called Escalante, who at age twenty was younger than the other musicians, Andraé's "protégé."[11]

The Set List

One of the most striking elements about the double album is the presence of five hymns, gospel songs, or traditional church melodies, "I Surrender All,"

"Revive Us Again," "Power in the Blood," "Praise God, Praise God," and "Hallelujah." Throughout his career, Maxwell said, Crouch would perform the older songs of the church, depending on the audience. "At that period, Andraé was very in tune with the audience," Maxwell said. "And so if he looked out and saw an old white audience, as it was in Port Talbot or Manchester, he would immediately go into those songs that they knew. When we got to London, more Black people came."[12]

To make it more challenging, Maxwell said that even with a prearranged set list, the Disciples never knew which hymns Andraé would start singing. "You'd know what you're starting with and maybe what you're ending with," he said, "and then he'd just change it. He'd start and we would jump in." According to Maxwell, Crouch "felt" each audience within moments of walking on stage. "He would be sweaty and nervous before," Maxwell said, "but once he sat down at the piano, it was like he was locked in with the people. So he would run with that." Interestingly, Maxwell said he believed that Andraé's connection with his audiences was stronger at the piano. "I felt like a lot of that communication left with him when he started *not* playing the piano anymore and was standing up."[13]

An Evangelical Statement

At its ecumenical heart, *Live in London* is Andraé's most ministerial recording—and among the most unmistakably ministerial albums in gospel music history. It tells a story and takes the audience on a spiritual journey. Even as Crouch engages the congregation, his primary concern remains sharing the message of Jesus Christ and discipling the audience—in short, evangelism. It is a remarkably clear-eyed musical and religious statement that addresses and ultimately merges two significant threads in African American faith. In the first thread, the Black theologian and mystic Howard Thurman advocated the use of silence and meditation in worship. But in the second, Black charismatics like Charles Mason charmed adherents into believing that charismatic denominations, such as Apostolic, COGIC, and other Holiness groups, have the corner on Holy Ghost–filled experiences.

Live in London somehow manages to interweave these two radically different threads. The end result is doubtless something new for many of those in the three audiences. The album invites participants to clap, sing, and shout; it expresses new ideas and invites the audience to join in the singing of new songs through improvisation; it mandates communal participation; and it balances all of these elements with moments and songs that evoke introspective reflection. Andraé accomplishes all of this by leading his rapt audience(s) with an uncanny balance of COGIC charismatic sensibilities *and* multiethnic ecumenical charisma. He instinctively reads the audience and meditates in the Holy Spirit, locates doctrinal divisions in the Church, addresses both theological and spiritual challenges, and then effortlessly, almost magically, creates a spirit of unity in communal spaces.

And when this happens, over the course of the four sides of the album, these different ecumenical communities are suddenly preferential to each other through the music and worship. The authors suggest that Crouch certainly believed that when the audience/congregation worships as one body, it is a direct reflection on the desires of Jesus' "unity prayer" in John 17 ("I in them and you in me—so that they may be brought to complete unity," John 17:23). When this happens, the church is now united in common purpose and community.

Five original songs, "You Don't Have to Jump No Pews (I've Been Born Again)," "If I Was a Tree," "I Just Want to Know You," "You Gave to Me," and "Well Done," are not found in hymnals, nor are they likely to ever appear in evangelical hymnody. Yet they reflect, as well as any such grouping of songs can encompass so large a concept, the diverse palette of western Christian doctrine. Together, they comprise what the authors describe as a new and unique genre in gospel music, "Moral Life and Community." As it is so beautifully suggested in Frederick Ware's towering *African American Theology*, being a Christian is not just attending church, and not just for Sunday. At its best, it values and encompasses "life, freedom, justice, community knowledge, truth, family, work, friendship, and democracy." These five songs unapologetically declare that jumping over pews has boundaries, that trees have limitations—and that knowing God deeply is relational and that living a life well done is itself pleasing in God's sight.[14]

Live in London

Side I

"Perfect Peace"

The album opens with a new version of "Perfect Peace," this time in the key of G♭ major and with a distinctively jazz fusion flair. The opening twenty-two-bar instrumental, a D♭ minor piano solo over an 11th chord, captures the audible expectancy of the crowd. It's—again—unusually jazzy for a gospel concert and the music seeks to move listeners to open their hearts to hear what the Spirit is saying. Crouch and Maxwell understand what is at stake here. African American music and jazz have been highly valued in Europe for decades where it has served as a music at once both electrifying and unifying, peaceful and reconciling. Andraé and the Disciples continue and extend in the tradition, just as Duke Ellington and Miles Davis continued and extended jazz. The adoring acceptance by the audience accorded the group is in that tradition. It's possible because, as composer/theologian William Banfield writes, "Music is a movement of views, values, ideas and creativity among individuals"—not nations or people groups. And that total embrace, manifest throughout the album, is one of the reasons that Crouch will return to Europe time and time again throughout his career.[15]

"I Surrender All"

Another surprise addition to the set list was the unexpected inclusion of the old hymn "I Surrender All." With an ethereal vocal by Bea Carr and haunting flute performance by Glen Myerscough, Maxwell said that the beloved hymn would be different each time Andraé played it. "He might do the chorus longer," Maxwell said, "or he might say, 'Sing that verse again.' You had to be on your toes." That included the song's key, which was never indicated until Andraé started playing. Fortunately, Maxwell said, Crouch always began in a handful of favorite keys—B♭, E♭, A♭, G♭. "So, we knew it was going to be in one of those keys."[16]

"You Don't Have to Jump No Pews (I've Been Born Again)"

"You Don't Have to Jump No Pews" continues with some of Andraé's most melodious preaching to date. In the key of G♭ major, this 1970s-fueled funk groove, with its distinctive vamped harmonic progressions (ii–V–I–V/ii), the audience enthusiastically sings (and probably dances) along, especially on the line "I've been born again." Neither Maxwell nor Felix said that the Disciples had either heard or rehearsed what would be called "You Don't Have to Jump No Pews" or "If I Was a Tree" prior to the concerts. "He just pulled them out and we're like 'OK,'" Felix said. "He didn't care whether we're recording or not. He says, 'Oh, I got this new song' and gives us that look. And we're like, 'OK, here we go.' He probably wrote them back in the dressing room and whipped them out." "That song was just a little spontaneous thing he did," Maxwell added. "We never really rehearsed it. He liked it loose. He would just jump on the train and it starts going."[17]

For musician Terrance Curry, despite the laughter from the audience, he believes that "You Don't Have to Jump No Pews" is so memorable because of its strong, unapologetic ecumenical statement. "He was bringing the gospel of Jesus Christ down to a level that people could understand," Curry said. "Salvation is not based on emotional feeling, it's really about your personal experience with the Lord Jesus Christ."[18]

It's also historian Deborah Smith Pollard's "all-time favorite" song by Andraé on her favorite Disciples album. "It has to do with something that just thrilled me as a Baptist child listening to a Church of God in Christ person saying, 'you *don't* have to jump no pews,'" she said. "From the first time I heard that song, I knew he was trying to tell people, 'It's in God's word and believing. *That's* what matters.' And I thought, 'Wow, you are getting this across to people who receive Christ in a variety of different ways. And it seemed to matter because he lays it out so well in that song."[19]

Likewise, music executive Vicki Mack Lataillade said that songs like "You Don't Have to Jump No Pews" are what made Andraé special and set the Disciples apart for younger fans. "He talked about a lot of things young people were thinking about at the time," she said. "And other artists were stuck with stuff that was strictly in the Bible or various old-fashioned themes. Andraé talked just about anything."[20]

"Take a Little Time"
The performance of "Take a Little Time" closely mirrors the recorded version on *Keep On Singin'* from 1971. Maxwell said that he always believed the chorus was a tribute to the Delfonics' "Didn't I (Blow Your Mind This Time)." "He loved their style," Maxwell said, "but he also took a lot of those things that meant something to him as a kid in church, too, and turned it into something else."[21]

Side II

"Tell Them"/"If I Was a Tree (The Highest Praise)"
Following an inspired rendition of "Tell Them," which Myerscough said still gives him "chills" when he thinks about it, Andraé launches into another new

song, "If I Was a Tree (The Highest Praise)," which subtly references composer Margaret Pleasant Douroux's beloved "Trees." Crouch sings it with a whimsical, almost childlike innocence and uses Douroux's original to craft a particularly compelling lyrical hook, "You created me in your image to give you the highest praise."[22]

"Hallelujah"

"Hallelujah," a gentle praise & worship chorus in the congregational friendly key of A♭ major, had been around for more than a decade in various incarnations. On the album, it serves as a meditative transition to "Revive Us Again." When *Live in London* was first released, gospel insider Teresa Hairston said she and her gospel music–loving friends were delighted at the prospect of a gospel artist even performing in the UK, much less receiving such an enthusiastic response. Their favorite song from the album was the new version of "Hallelujah." "We sang that in the church like there was no tomorrow," she said. "You could sing that song anywhere, anything and it was the house record. And we knew that when you came in with 'Hallelujah,'" it's about to be Bedlam. That's it."[23]

"Revive Us Again"/"Power in the Blood"

"Revive Us Again" foreshadows "Oh, It Is Jesus" with its slowly driven $\frac{6}{8}$ compound meter feel. Suddenly, the Disciples explode into "Power in the Blood," a dynamic COGIC stomp driven by Sandra's propulsive tambourine and Felix's driving, walking bass lines. Maxwell said that whenever Andraé launched into the two up-tempo versions of the hymns that close Side II, "Revive Us Again," and especially "Power in the Blood," it was with the idea of introducing the Black church to mostly white audiences, something Crouch had been attempting to do since the composition of "The Blood (Will Never Lose Its Power)" nearly twenty years earlier.[24]

Side III

"I Just Want to Know You"

In the key of G♭ major, "I Just Want to Know You" is the lone song on *Live in London* not originally performed in either London or Manchester. Maxwell said that for album's length reasons, the LP needed another new song. Sometime after returning from the UK, Crouch and Maxwell assembled the Disciples at United Western Studios in Hollywood, where much of the album's mixing was taking place. "It was something that [Crouch had] half-started," Maxwell said. "That's the way it always went. In those days, he'd have something half-written and he'd try it out on the audience—then he'd figure out what worked." Maxwell then tried to match the crowd sounds from London "so it felt like it was done at the same time."[25]

"Just Like He Said Would"/"I'll Keep on Loving You Lord"

Bracketed by two more of Andraé's short homilies to the crowd, "Just Like He Said He Would" from *Take Me Back* is arranged with a driving disco-styled up-tempo beat but transforms into a funkified dialogue between the Clavinet D6 and horn section on the energetic vamp. The song morphs into another short reflection (listed as "Andraé Talking" on the LP) before it leads into another one of *Live in London*'s original compositions, "I'll Keep On Loving You Lord." In the key of G♭ major, this gentle, ethereal ballad "I'll Keep On Loving You Lord" echoes the emotional testimony from his intensely personal "Through It All." In the lyrics, Crouch pledges his love for God even if the "sweetness" in his life has been taken away, even as he pleads his case to God.

Maxwell said that while Andraé had completed "I'll Keep On Loving You Lord" some years earlier, it was only occasionally performed live. The song reflects a deeply personal conversation between Andraé and God. "Andraé was always totally honest in his music," Maxwell said. "He wrote about what he was thinking and what he was feeling." "It's another song expressing his deepest thoughts, his wishes," Myerscough said. "In spite of all our known frailties and ability to disappoint God and disappoint ourselves, he still has this earnest desire. And that's Andraé talking."[26]

"You Gave to Me"

Felix returns as lead vocalist on "You Gave to Me" in B♭ major. The eight-measure introduction is subdivided by an irresistible 8th-note funk groove. The orchestration is driven by the guitars and Clavinet, two instruments that rarely found their way into most Black churches of the era, primarily because they sounded too "worldly" to some ears. Andraé uses them to propel the audience back to its feet and, again, do a little spirit-filled holy dancing in the aisles. But if versions of those dances were taking place in discos, Crouch repurposes and sanctifies them for this worship gathering. "You Gave to Me" shifts to the key of E♭ major as Andraé begins to groove on the minor 6th chord, accompanied by Carr, Hall, and Felix singing along on the catchy "Got to tell the world about You" chorus.

Side IV

"Oh Taste and See"/"Praise God, Praise God" (Reprise)

Then, once again, Crouch changes gear. "Oh Taste and See" feels instead like an old Baptist lining hymn, but it is an improvisatory incantation, one that intersects even older Black traditions with its deep, deep undertone discretely building ecumenical bridges through shared rituals, beliefs, and narratives. The minor melody in A♭ is somehow both melancholy and invitational at the same time. Andraé invites the audience to hum along with him, then sit back, fold their arms, and sing along with him, "Oh taste and see that the Lord is good." In that moment, the African American storefront church is now in Europe. It was a haunting moment, Maxwell recalled. "With 'Oh Taste and See' and then 'Praise God, Praise God' Andraé was doing a call-and-response," Maxwell said. "He's getting the audience to sing like they're in a Black church, a worship chorus, a singalong.[27]

"This Is Another Day"/"Well Done"

As the concert service draws to a close, Andraé returns to still another popular song from an earlier album, "This Is Another Day," stops and again speaks from his heart, then gently leads his congregation into a third reprise of "Praise God." *Live in London* has one last surprise, one more new composition, "Well Done," a joyful closing jam with a host of fiery solos by the instrumentalists. "Well Done" returns to E♭ major, one of Crouch's handful of preferred keys, and opens with Myerscough improvising on his saxophone over a B♭ 11th chord. Andraé urges the audience to offer their applause not to the group, but to the Lord with what he calls their "ten-fingered instruments," their hands. Lyrically, it is another return to his reoccurring themes—his desire for his listeners to strive to live in God's kingdom. More than with any other gospel artist, Crouch's lyric-driven theology manifests James Cone's belief that "Black identity is bound up with God's future judgment" and that the goal of all humankind should be to hear the words "well done" from their Creator. For Andraé Crouch, the hope of someday hearing "well done" is his highest aspiration.[28]

"My Tribute"

As mentioned earlier, *Live in London*—like many of Crouch's concerts before it—ends with "My Tribute (to God Be the Glory)." Nothing Andraé ever released, including *"Live" at Carnegie Hall*, stands as a more explicit statement of his belief that he was called solely to be an evangelistic ambassador, a "Holy Ghost envoy" to the world through his music. Crouch's entire ministry had been couched in diversity and he is compelled, the authors believe, to share that diversity with the world. If that were to happen, then Andraé had no other choice *but* to adopt his unique combination of expansive music with utterly inclusive lyrics—two absolute prerequisites for reaching diverse audiences.

"My Tribute" (to God Be the Glory)" is one of Crouch's signature pieces, a sending song in this context and one he would return to again and again. For years, Perry Morgan, the longest-tenured Disciple, always sang "My Tribute," so it was only appropriate that the last *Disciples* album would end this way. Maxwell said that while nothing was officially stated to mark the occasion, the name "Disciples" was quietly dropped, save for dates that had already been booked under that name in 1979. Through the years, the previous Disciples, Sherman Andrus, Bili Thedford, and Ruben Fernandez had, one by one, left the group. Sandra Crouch's involvement was also lessening by this point, Maxwell said, as her solo career began to take off, leaving only Morgan. "Andraé always used to say that Perry was the sound of the group," Maxwell said. "His sound, his tone *was* the Disciples—his tone always stuck out. It's a great-sounding voice, especially in unison. Without Perry, there was no Disciples."[29]

Live in London captures Andraé at his peak. He is soloist and orchestrator, mystic and practitioner, minister and psalmist, and music director—all at the same time. Andraé becomes an embodiment of reflection, response, and repose to the prayer in John 17. The result is an artist at the pinnacle of his career.

Response

Live in London debuted at #11 on the charts on September 2, 1978, and stayed in that range until year's end. For the Disciples, however, the surging media attention was all but unprecedented. On October 8, the *Los Angeles Times* featured Andraé and the group in a multipage article titled "New Industry Booming: Gospel Music Born Again," and photographs of Andraé and the audience at one of the Disciples' concerts dominate the first page. Writer Russell Chandler referenced the group's earlier concert at the Greek Theatre and filled the piece with facts and figures on the growth in both gospel music and CCM. The flurry of publicity was also accompanied by several high-profile concert reviews, including the Disciples' first review in the venerable show business journal *Variety*. On the same page with concert reviews of Ben Vereen, the Chieftains, and Grover Washington, critic "May" wrote that Crouch was a "highly gifted performer who sings gospel" during the performance at the Greek Theatre in Los Angeles. The reviewer cited in particular "I Surrender All," "Tell Them," and "Hallelujah" and noted that the audience responded with cries of "Praise God!" "May" compared the concert to a service in a Black church, writing that "there was not a moment when the force of the message faded" and that:

> There was not a moment, either, when the force of his presence as an entertainer dulled. None of that is news. All gospel music has pursued the linking of those elements. What is unique about Crouch is that he has done it with contemporary colors, and better than others.[30]

Billboard's review of the same concert was somewhat more muted. Reviewer Jean Williams wrote that the Disciples' concert marked the first time a gospel artist had performed in concert at the Greek Theatre, though it was "difficult to distinguish this show from a secular concert." The audience, which included infants, preteens, senior citizens, church groups, and even the "curious," responded with "dancing, foot-stomping and handclapping." The set opened with an "energetic" "Oh Savior" and included songs featuring Danniebelle ("Tell Them") and Carr ("I Surrender All"); the critic cited in particular the renditions of "It Won't Be Long," "Just Like He Said He Would," "Softly and Tenderly," and the "showstopper," "Soon and Very Soon." But when Andraé declared that the performance was actually "church" rather than a "concert," Williams disagreed, writing "for those who came to have church, that's what they had—others enjoyed a concert."[31]

At the close of the concert, which also closed the Greek's 1978 season, "more than 200 gospel editors, performers and Light Record executives" gathered backstage for a ceremony to honor Andraé's tenth year with Light Records. A photograph in *Record World* marking the event included a broadly smiling Crouch, performers Johnny and Lynn Mann, the Reverend James Cleveland, Gentry McCreary from Light, and Danniebelle.[32]

```
ANDRAE CROUCH AND THE DISCIPLES      NEWSLETTER                    -3-

ITINERARY

May 13          AC        Meadowland Giants Football Stadium
                          Plainfield, New Jersey
                          9 a.m. and 11 a.m.

May 13          AC&D      Symphony Hall
                          Broad Street, Newark, New Jersey
                          8:15 p.m.

May 14          AC&D      Convention Hall
                          Asbury Park, New Jersey
                          7:30 p.m.

May 15          AC&D      Spectrum
                          Broad and Pattison Place
                          Philadelphia, Pennsylvania
                          8 p.m.

May 22          AC&D      Elgin Field House
                          1200 Maroon Drive
                          Elgin, Illinois
                          7:30 p.m.

May 23          AC&D      Performing Arts Center, 929 N. Water Street
                          Milwaukee, Wisconsin, 8 p.m.

May 25          AC&D      Minneapolis Auditorium, Minneapolis, Minnesota
                          7:30 p.m.

June 16         AC        Municipal Auditorium, 705 Grand Avenue,
                          Shreveport, Louisiana, 8 p.m.

June 17         AC        Son Shine Music Festival, Hamilton, Ohio
                          (Outside Festival)

June 30         AC        Albuquerque, New Mexico

July 8          AC        The Rock Church, 640 Hempsville, Norfolk, Virginia
                          7:30 p.m.

July 16         AC        YMCA of the Rockies - Longhorn
                          Estes Park, Colorado, 7:30 p.m. approx.

July 21         AC        Indianapolis, Indiana

July 27         AC        Jesus '78, Little Hocking, Ohio

July 28         AC        Bethel Temple, 327 S. Smithfield Road, Dayton, Ohi

July 29         AC        Little Rock, Arkansas


CHECK YOUR LOCAL BIBLE BOOK STORE FOR VERIFICATION OF CONCERTS AND
FURTHER DETAILS.

ITINERARY INFORMATION IS ALWAYS SUBJECT TO CHANGE, SO BE SURE TO VERIFY
LOCALLY.
```

Image 12.1 Sample page from the Andraé Crouch newsletter with tour dates from 1978. Courtesy of Perry Morgan.

Record World's annual tribute to gospel music section was, unsurprisingly dominated by Andraé Crouch and the Disciples, Walter Hawkins and Love Center Choir, and the Reverend James Cleveland. In the article on Light/ Lexicon, Ralph Carmichael predicted sales of gospel music "doubling and possibly more in the next several years." Another article credited Crouch and the Disciples' "contemporary soul inspirational" sound for gospel's expansion into Europe and "for bringing the sound back and up to the attention of mass audiences." In a full-page interview, Cleveland was asked if Black gospel and white gospel were finally coming together. "Oh definitely," he replied. "Andraé Crouch has bridged the gap between Black and white audiences and done a very good job."[33]

A Year-End Flurry

But Crouch actually spent much of December bridging the gap with still another audience, this time in South Africa. In November and December, the Disciples had toured with the group Living Sound, founded by Terry Law in 1969 as an international music ministry. Law urged Andraé to join him and come to highly segregated South Africa on the condition that all venues would be integrated. "If Andraé is singing in a concert," Law is quoted as saying, "the Blacks are as welcome here as whites. No Black, including Andraé, would be treated as a second-class citizen." Beginning December 6, Crouch appeared ten times as a solo artist, which Andraé called "meetings" since musicians were being urged to boycott South Africa's brutal system of apartheid. The "meetings" were in Johannesburg, Durban, Port Elizabeth, Cape Town, and Soweto. Jason Law, Terry's son, writes that these appearances caused "quite an uproar" and had a "seismic" impact on the country. The experience whetted Andraé's desire to return with a full band to Africa as soon as possible.[34]

When the year-end report sales and airplay charts were published, Andraé and the Disciples found themselves in an unfamiliar position behind both Cleveland and Walter Hawkins. *This Is Another Day* finished 1978 as the #5 ranked album, followed by *The Best of Andraé* (#15), *"Live" at Carnegie Hall* (#17), and *Take Me Back* (#27). Released late in the year, *Live in London* didn't appear in the list of the Top 35 albums.[35]

Crouch rarely discussed—at least publicly—his feelings about the relative "success" of any of his releases, and the authors' interviews with more than 200 of the musicians, singers, family members, and friends who worked with him were remarkably consistent on this point—he was wholly concerned with the ministry and the message. In an interview at the time for an African American newspaper, Crouch admitted that that profound, unrelenting sense of calling weighed heavily on him regardless of the size of the crowd or the sales figure for his latest album:

> I feel very humble before an audience. Sometimes I get nervous when I see all those people standing in line to see us, then I am reminded that it is God they seek, not me. And I relax. I am just an instrument of God.[36]

NOTES

1. Willem Hoos, "Dutch Label Exec Leading Push to Popularize Gospel," *Billboard*, January 7, 1978, 72; "Dutch TV Beams Gospel by Crouch," *Billboard*, May 7, 1977, 60.
2. Sally Hinkle, "Gospel Scene," *Billboard*, April 1, 1978, 52; Vicki Branson, "Gospel Time," *Record World*, August 19, 1978, 68.
3. Karl Dallas, "Caught in the Act: Andraé Crouch," *Melody Maker*, January 15, 1977, 14.
4. "Together in One Explosive Double Album," *Record World*, July 22, 1978, 366–367.
5. "Gospel Reviews: Andraé Crouch & the Disciples," *Cash Box*, August 5, 1978, 29.
6. Bill Maxwell, interview with the authors, November 6, 2022, and January 20, 2023.
7. Glen Mycrscough, interview with the authors, June 18, 2021; Allen Gregory, interview with the authors, August 19, 2021.
8. Jaymes Felix, interview with the authors, August 21, 2021.
9. Andraé Crouch and the Disciples, *Live in London* (Light Records LSX-5717).
10. Bill Maxwell, interview with the authors, September 15, 2022.
11. Glen Myerscough, interview with the authors, August 19, 2021.
12. Bill Maxwell interview with the authors, January 20, 2022.
13. Bill Maxwell interview with the authors, January 20, 2022.
14. Frederick L. Ware, *African American Theology* (Louisville, KY: Westminster John Knox, 2016), 157.
15. William Banfield, *Cultural Codes: The Makings of a Black Music Philosophy* (Washington, DC: Scarecrow Press, 2009), 54.
16. Bill Maxwell, interview with the authors, January 20, 2022.
17. Jaymes Felix, interview with the authors, August 21, 2021; Bill Maxwell, interview with the authors, January 20, 2022.
18. Terrance Curry, interview with the authors, September 12, 2020.
19. Deborah Smith Pollard, interview with the authors, September 26, 2020.
20. Vicki Mack Lataillade, interview with the authors, October 9, 2020.
21. Bill Maxwell, interview with the authors, January 20, 2022.

22. Glen Myerscough, interview with the authors, June 18, 2021; "If I Was a Tree (the Highest Praise)" by Andraé Crouch, Lexicon Music, Inc., courtesy of Capitol CMG.
23. Teresa Hairston, interview with the authors, September 11, 2020.
24. Bill Maxwell, interview with the authors, January 20, 2022.
25. Bill Maxwell, interview with the authors, January 20, 2022.
26. Bill Maxwell, interview with the authors, January 20, 2023; Glen Myerscough, interview with the authors, June 18, 2021.
27. Bill Maxwell, interview with the authors, January 20, 2023.
28. James Cone, *The Spirituals and the Blues* (Maryknoll, NY: Orbis Books, 1992), 5.
29. Bill Maxwell, interview with the authors, January 20, 2023.
30. "Best-Selling Gospel LPs," *Billboard*, September 2, 1978, 51; Russell Chandler, "New Industry Booming: Gospel Music Is Born Again," *Los Angeles Times*, October 8, 1978, 3, 32, 33; May, "Concert Review: Andraé Crouch, Terry Clark, Chuck Girard," *Variety*, October 25, 1978, 74.
31. "Talent in Action: Andraé Crouch and the Disciples," *Billboard*, October 21, 1978, 42, 44.
32. "Andraé Crouch Celebrates," *Cash Box*, December 23, 1978, 28.
33. "Light & Lexicon Lift Their Lamp to the People," *Record World*, November 11, 1978, 36; "Black Gospel: Not Just a Passing Fad," *Record World*, November 11, 1978, 28; "James Cleveland on Expanding Gospel's Audience," *Record World*, November 11, 1978, 32.
34. "Soul Sauce," *Billboard*, December 23, 1978, 43; "Where in the World," *Cash Box*, December 23, 1978, 43; Jason Law, "Andraé Crouch and Living Sound, 1970s, South Africa," https://terrylawspeaks.com/Andraé-crouch-and-living-sound-1970s-south-africa/; https://worldcompassion.tv/about-us.
35. "Gospel: Soul Gospel Albums," *Billboard*, December 23, 1978, TIA-68.
36. Val Benson, "Caught in the Act," *Michigan Chronicle*, November 19, 1977, A6.

13

I'll Be Thinking of You

Good news greeted 1979. *Live in London* finally hit #1 on the *Billboard* charts on January 6 and held the top spot through March, only to be bumped in April by Walter Hawkins's *Love Alive II*, which remained there for much of the year. Andraé and the Disciples received a Grammy nomination for the album (Best Soul Gospel, Contemporary), and Light Records named Bill Maxwell as director of A&R for the label's contemporary and soul gospel artists. The promotion was part of a restructuring at Light, which reported that it had enjoyed a nearly 50 percent sales increase in 1978, due largely to Crouch and the Disciples and Walter Hawkins and the Love Center Choir. In announcing the promotion of Maxwell and others, founder Ralph Carmichael said that label was also signing several new artists, including Tramaine Hawkins. Carmichael claimed that there was a "new excitement" in gospel music. "I believe we'll live to see the day that gospel artists will sell into eight figures."[1]

On the Road Again

However, work on the next album slowed in early 1979 as the Disciples resumed their manic touring schedule. Much of January was again spent performing abroad in Scandinavia, Germany, Holland, and the United Kingdom. The tour included a return to London, this time at Royal Albert Hall. England's *Melody Maker* magazine was present once again, and the reviewer called the concert a "triumphant return." "I wasn't saved," the critic noted at the end of the review, "but I sure had a good time." Northern Ireland at the time, however, was still in the midst of the decades-long "Troubles," with continued violence between Catholics and Protestants. As the bus took the Disciples to the venue, James Felix recalled armed soldiers stationed in streets lined with barbed wire, sandbags, and concrete barriers. Glen Myerscough said that the promoter had booked the group at two different venues, one for Protestants and one for Catholics. Felix said that one of Andraé's standard icebreakers at concerts was to call the names of various denominations present: "How many COGICs do we have here tonight?" "How many Presbyterians?" "How many Episcopalians?" But at the Catholic arena, Felix said, Andraé shouted out, "'How many Protestants do we have in the house tonight?' and I'm like, 'Oh, we're in trouble now.' He hadn't thought that through," Myerscough said, "and there was a moment of silence—but then people started laughing."[2]

Norwegian television network NRK recorded a concert on the tour in Bergen, Norway, that was broadcast in June 1979. Available on YouTube, it's a rare recording of the Disciples from this era, with a particularly potent band: Andraé (piano/vocal), Hadley Hockensmith (bass), Bill Maxwell (drums), Mike Escalante (keyboards), Allen Gregory (trumpet), Glen Myerscough (saxophone), Jimmie Davis (guitar), Sandra Crouch (tambourine/vocals), Perry Morgan (vocals), Bea Carr (vocals), and Kathy Hazzard (vocals). The concert set list—at least as presented on this clip—includes both well-known and relatively unknown numbers: "Oh Savior," "I Surrender All," "It's Gonna Rain," "All of Me," "It Won't Be Long," "Jesus Is the Answer," "Soon and Very Soon," and "Well Done." The singing is superlative throughout and the band is very, very tight. Some of the songs, including a hypnotic version of "It Won't Be Long," are as good as anything Crouch ever recorded. The audience sings along on many of the songs and responds enthusiastically with rhythmic applause.[3]

The group returned to the United States in mid-February long enough to be awarded the Grammy, then embarked on another ambitious twenty-four-date tour from March 15 to April 15 that ranged from Houston and Fort Worth across the South to Atlanta and Miami (Image 13.1).[4]

Crouch vs. Cleveland

To the delight/dismay of gospel music fans, the ongoing James Cleveland/Andraé Crouch discussion flared up again, this time in New York's controversial *Village Voice*. Amid a lengthy article from April 16, 1979, titled "James Cleveland Sings the Horns Off the Devil," Cleveland pondered Crouch's continued success and included an intriguing assessment of Andraé's gifts:

Image 13.1 John Denver and Andraé Crouch, taken somewhere on the road. Photograph courtesy of Val Gonzalo.

There is no musical form that Andraé Crouch doesn't embrace. He can be Dixieland, jazz, soulful; he can be extremely contemporary, then he can be extremely traditional if he wants to be. Wherever his creativity leads him, he goes there. He never allows himself to get boxed in. If he plays on the college circuit, he has a bag of tricks for college students, and if he's in the crusades he has something for crusades. If he's in open air pavilions, he has something for that. Being one of the more fortunate, he can adapt to anything, whatever the call might be.

While that kind of versatility might be an anathema to traditional gospel fans, Cleveland's description perfectly captures Crouch's earliest goal for his ministry, to take the message everywhere . . . including the White House.[5]

Two Pivotal Events

Summer 1979 brought two significant events to Andraé's life. On June 7, he was invited to the White House, along with James Brown, Smokey Robinson, Stevie Wonder, Mavis Staples, and other major artists in a salute to Black music. President Jimmy Carter heard performances by Billy Eckstine, Chuck Berry, Evelyn "Champagne" King, and Crouch. Crowd estimates on the White House lawn ranged from 500 to 1,000 people. Andraé closed the concert, performing several songs, including "Soon and Very Soon" and "Jesus Is the Answer." According to *Cash Box*, "Crouch whipped the audience into a spiritual crescendo. As the Carters sang and clapped, Andraé Crouch called the gathering spot, 'The White House Church.'" A photograph in *Billboard* a few weeks later featured Carter thanking Crouch for the performance.[6]

In the wide coverage of the White House event, no mention was made of the Disciples. And while Crouch had often performed "Just Andraé" solo concerts in smaller settings, the decision to omit the Disciples was, apparently, intentional. For some time, Andraé and his management team had been in contact with Warner Bros. Records, one of the foremost labels in popular music. Days after the White House concert, Warner Bros. announced that Andraé had signed a "lucrative four-LP" deal. *Billboard* noted that, at the same time, Crouch had recently signed another four-album contract with Light Records. The Warner Bros. albums, Jean Williams writes, "will be even more contemporary than the Light product, sporting some minor word changes," primarily the words "God," "Jesus," or "Lord." Nor will the Warner promotion use the term "gospel," though the music "will basically be the same, with possibly some changes in instrumentation" between the two labels. Artists had left gospel for the popular music marketplace for decades, of course. With the new deal, however, Crouch would become the first to try to do both simultaneously, with each label responsible for promoting their album in their respective markets. "Gospel music has been stereotyped for a long time," Crouch said, noting that the term meant "different things to different people." Andraé also said that he would continue to write and produce himself. Williams reported that Warner Bros. had "actively pursued" Crouch for more than a year. Again, no mention was made of the Disciples.[7]

Left unanswered at the time was the question as to whether Crouch's existing—and very protective, often very insular—gospel audience would embrace his new dual approach or see it as a sellout, a charge that had been hurled at artists as early as Sister Rosetta Tharpe and, more recently, Aretha Franklin. The initial news coverage implied that the upcoming releases in the two markets would be solo albums, sans the Disciples. Crouch and Maxwell had already been in the studio—again scheduling short blocks of time between tours—for several months by summer 1979 and the prospect of releasing two versions of the songs added to their workload, particularly for an artist as exacting and prone to remixing and rearranging as Andraé. Light Records tentatively tested the waters with an early release of the single "I'll Be Thinking of You." The 45 debuted at #73 in *Record World*'s "Black Oriented Singles" chart in mid-March, but never rose above #72, and was off the chart by mid-April.[8]

Crouch's new contract was only briefly addressed in *Billboard*'s annual gospel music special section on July 28. Instead, several writers claimed that part of the problem facing Black sacred music was its confusing array of names. One writer asked a hypothetical "multiple choice question" of readers: "Is Andraé Crouch a contemporary Christian artist? Soul? Inspirational? R&B? None of the above?" The answer? "Andraé Crouch is all of the above."

In another article, scholar Pearl Williams-Jones writes that Crouch's "versatility" was the reason why he was chosen to close the "prestigious" Black music concert at the White House in June:

> Andraé Crouch's music can be said to encompass the gamut of Black America's pluralistic styles. He sings and plays a piano style which was hammered out of the Pentecostal roots of the Church of God in Christ but has incorporated the instrumental stylings and vocal arrangements one is apt to hear from any number of sources—whether studio orchestras or an *avant garde* rock idiom.[9]

Live in London, after hitting #1 on the *Billboard* charts January and February, fell to #3 in March and #9 in April, never again broke into the Top 10 album lists in 1979, and was off of the charts completely by December.[10]

The unrelenting cycle of touring with occasional breaks for recording sessions, now at several new studios, continued through the rest of 1979. Andraé made another trip to the UK over the summer to support *Live in London* and received the first major product display of a gospel artist in London's HMV, "the largest secular record store in Europe." He was featured, along with several other mostly CCM artists, at the Fifth Annual Christian Artists' Music Seminar in the Rockies at the end of July. For the August release of *PUSH for Excellence* by Myrrh Records, which benefited the Reverend Jesse Jackson's Operation PUSH, Andraé and the Disciples contributed "Soon and Very Soon," and other tracks featured Walter Hawkins, Edwin Hawkins, Bili Thedford, and Danniebelle Hall, among others. In September, Light/Lexicon released the Spanish-language version of its popular *The New Church Hymnal*, called *Una Nueva Alabanza*, with well-known songs by Crouch and others translated into Spanish. Also in September, Felix, the former bassist and singer with the Disciples, signed a solo deal with Light, with Maxwell producing. And in November, Andraé and Sandra received a gold record as co-writers of "Jesus Is the Answer" from Paul Simon's *Live Rhymin'*.[11]

Onstage with Andraé

Felix said that during 1979's tours, particularly on the more up-tempo songs from *Live in London*, Andraé became increasingly animated on the piano. "When he'd get to going, it's like, 'Man! The piano is going to break!' He'd be playing that nine-foot, 12-foot grand and you'd think it was Jerry Lee Lewis up there. You knew you were in trouble when he kicked that piano seat back and stood up." Felix said that as bassist he stood behind Andraé on stage and, like the rest of the musicians, watched Andraé closely. "I remember those times where he would just have this moment of silence," Felix said. "And he'd play a few chords, then he'd start to speak. That to me was so memorable—it's hard to even express how he did that. He just poured his heart out." What followed could be any song in the Disciples' catalogue, an old hymn, or even something that emerged in the moment. "Those, to me, were the most golden times," Felix said. "The performances were great, but those quiet moments were the key."[12]

As with previous albums, some of the songs for what would be called the *I'll Be Thinking of You* album first emerged during the sometimes interchangeable tours. Myerscough said that he remembered the title track first appearing at the close of a concert. "I don't remember where we were," he said, "but I remember I liked it the first time he sang it to the audience. After that, it was one of the last things he would perform in concert, at least on that tour."[13]

Recording Studio A-Listers

Even more than with previous releases, Maxwell and Crouch assembled a host of well-known musicians and singers for *I'll Be Thinking of You*, most notably Stevie Wonder, but also Patrick Henderson, Billy Preston, Philip Bailey, and others, along with many of the "A-list" session players from previous albums.[14] Other significant additions were Linda and Howard McCrary from the McCrary family of singers and musicians, and singers Kristle Murden,

Tammie Gibson, and Howard Smith—all of whom would tour and record repeatedly with Crouch in the years to come. The McCrarys, who first signed with Light Records in 1972, had recorded several pop albums in subsequent years. Linda and Andraé had met in Nashville and Crouch had told her that the McCrary's album *Sunshine Day* was playing on repeat on the Disciples tour bus. The McCrarys lived near the Crouches in the San Fernando Valley, and when the family group disbanded, Howard and Linda became regular visitors at Andraé's dinner and music sessions. Linda and Andraé remained close friends throughout his life. Crouch once even called McCrary from Europe to play her an early version of "I'll Be Thinking of You." "That album was a mark for me in my heart," Linda said, "because it started changing my life because of what Andraé was saying in those songs. When you relate the songs to your spiritual life, God starts changing you."[15]

Earlier, Murden had written, sung, played piano, and recorded a three-song cassette, which she sent to Light Records. Light's A&R man, Gentry McCreary, later fished the cassette out of a box of unsolicited tapes and played it for Carmichael. When Light declined to sign Murden, saying her voice was "too jazzy," McCreary sent the tape to Andraé, who was looking for a female vocalist for a new song he was recording, "I'll Be Thinking of You." Crouch liked what he heard and flew Murden from Tacoma, Washington, where she was a minister of music, to Los Angeles. "And within an hour of arriving in California, they took me straight down to the studio," Murden said. Maxwell and several other singers were in the studio at the time. Andraé introduced her by saying, "This is Kristle, she's going to sing lead on this song." "Then Andraé stood right in front of me and said, 'This is what you sing, this is how I want it to go,'" Murden recalled. "Then he said, 'You can take your liberty; kind of stretch it out a little bit but stay with the melody.' I'm a melody singer, so I was really happy for that." Murden said she sang the lyrics a few times until Maxwell asked, "Are you ready to sing it?" and pushed "Record." "I sang the verse and they kept the original first take," Murden said. "Once I did the verse, then we took the rest of the song section by section and worked out what Andraé and I would sing."[16]

Murden soon became another participant at the dinner/songwriting gatherings at Andraé's house, along with Howard and Linda McCrary and others. Both Howard and Kristle were excellent pianists and soon the solo "Just Andraé" concerts became a trio or quartet, with their own separate tour dates. "It was amazing," Linda said. "We'd do a cappella stuff that Howard or Andraé would arrange and we had an incredible arrangement of 'Pass Me Not, Oh Gentle Savior.' It was like being with my brothers and sisters again because when you live in the same house, music is always going on, creativity is always going on. Andraé's mind never stopped." Linda, who would in time arrange vocals for other artists, said she learned much about vocal arranging in those impromptu sessions. She had already created some of the arrangements with the McCrarys, but Linda said that her abilities matured around Crouch's grand piano:

> When I met this man, and he's talking about "colors" and how things are supposed to be "delivered," he makes you feel like you are already on stage, and they are looking at you. He took me to a place, even to this very day, that when I get a call to do an arrangement, I always pray about it and say, "God, what do you want to say?" What he taught me in vocal arranging is that you have to listen to the song. The song will dictate what it is trying to say. And if you're not hearing it, if you can't get inside the head of the writer, the heart to the writer, then it's very hard to depict.[17]

As a young man, Howard Smith had had a profound religious experience hearing Andraé Crouch and the Disciples at Henry Ford Auditorium in his native Detroit. "The anointing was so thick, I literally ran out of the room," Smith recalled. Smith soon joined a gospel group composed of members of the Winans family, the Testimonial Singers, then another group, the Followers of Christ—which was when Andraé first heard him and invited him to sing on *I'll Be Thinking of You*. Smith was also instrumental in later bringing the Winans siblings to both Andraé and Light Records. Smith said that Crouch flew him to Los Angeles specifically to record "The Love Medley." "They drove me straight from the airport to the studio and flew me out again," he said. "That was my first time in the studio."[18]

Another new voice on *I'll Be Thinking of You* was singer Tammie Gibson. Gibson joined the sessions while singing with Stevie Wonder's Wonderlove during concurrent recording sessions in Hollywood for *Journey through the Secret Life of Plants* and *I'll Be Thinking of You*. Wonder and Crouch had first met in France, when Wonder invited them to one of his concerts. Afterwards, Crouch told Maxwell, "I'm going to write a song for Stevie to play on." Back in the United States, Wonder agreed to play harmonica on "I'll Be Thinking of You" but asked that the two men come to his home studio. Maxwell said that he and Crouch had been instructed to arrive at 10 P.M., but Wonder wandered in at 1 A.M. "And Stevie wanted to play air hockey first," Maxwell said. "We finally finished about 2 A.M. and did the recording in around thirty minutes."[19]

In the Studio

Of the multiple, sometimes lengthy recording sessions for the album, Howard McCrary said that Maxwell and Crouch had a "very methodical" approach in the studio. "Andraé would tell us, 'I want you to work with people down to a low frazzle.' In other words, 'Just milk it for all it's worth.'" Perhaps no one had a more difficult time than Smith. For someone who had never been in a recording studio before, Andraé's penchant for spontaneously composing intricate background vocal arrangements made the "green" Smith work harder than anyone else. "He comes up with stuff and buddy, if you don't learn it, he gives it to someone else," Smith said. "If you said, 'Wait a minute, what was my part again?' all of the girls would look at you like, 'Oh my God, here we go.' And Andraé would come out and change everybody's parts—and he'd never give you the same part again." Smith and Sandra Crouch often shared the same vocal parts, and Smith said that Sandra had to continually push him closer to the microphone, especially on tour. "And those girls were cutting," he said. "I learned as time went by to cut with the girls. I had to use a more powerful tone with Alfie (Silas Durio), Phyllis (St. James), and Maxi (Anderson) singing. So to sing the tenor part, I had to push and I had to cut. But it was exciting. It was Andraé Crouch, man." Unlike most of the instrumentalists and soloists, Smith said that Andraé had the background vocalists record together. "You get the best singers that you can get in the room and you want their vibe, their energy," he said. "And you want their colors, you want it all on the mic at the same time so they feed off each other. There were no charts for us."[20]

Maxwell also went to England to record the strings parts at Chapel Sound in London with Swedish arranger Lennart Sjöholm. "We loved Lennart and he was a great arranger," Maxwell said. "He was really soulful, especially with strings." Maxwell sent Sjöholm the chord charts in advance, then brought the tapes of the recordings with them to England, where Sjöholm had by then handwritten the string charts for the musicians. This was done, Maxwell said, because studio time was much cheaper in the UK. Even though Light's studio budgets—which were an advance against projected royalties—had increased with each successful album, Maxwell said they were still considerably smaller than comparable popular music projects he'd worked on previously. And, he said, it wasn't until *Take Me Back* that the group had even begun to receive appreciable royalties.[21]

I'll Be Thinking of You

Side I

"I'll Be Thinking of You"

In the key of G♭ major, the musical language in "I'll Be Thinking of You" is more complex and sophisticated than what Andraé's audiences had heard before. Written during an era where events that ranged from the Camp David Accords to the mass suicides at Peoples Temple in Jonestown, it's possible to hear this song as a prayer. Longtime Disciples member Harlan Rogers arranged the track and Hadley Hockensmith augmented Dean Parks's and Larry Carlton's guitar parts, including the intros. Maxwell said that as the recording process progressed, he "felt" that the song, another one of Crouch's famed power ballads, also needed the touch of famed studio bassist Leland Sklar (and, of course, Stevie Wonder's effortless, distinctive harmonica).[22]

"I've Got the Best"

One of the genuinely "fun" songs in Crouch's career, "I've Got the Best," in B♭, features Andraé and Earth, Wind & Fire's Philip Bailey trading vocals over a "Boogie Wonderland" groove, anchored with a funky bass line. Arrangers Crouch and Michael Omartian flip the call-and-response language, with the background vocals leading the lines as Crouch mimics Donald Fagen of Steely Dan's vocalese. Maxwell and Omartian had been friends since Danniebelle's debut album, which Maxwell had produced. Omartian had, at one point, even been invited to join Maxwell's new jazz group Koinonia.[23]

"Touch Me"

Buoyed by Henderson's shimmering keyboards and Sklar's lovely, melodic bass line, "Touch Me" is another one of Crouch's trademark ballads. The song begins in F minor, slowly picks up speed, and only begins to sound like a classic gospel song on the chorus. The song, which channels Lucie Campbell's much-loved (and much-recorded) "Touch Me, Lord Jesus," hearkens back to his Black church roots and serves as both a lament and a prayer for help. The song's closing vamp is highlighted with a deliberately soulful R&B groove under the lyrics "shower down on me."

"Lookin' for You"

Few songs in Crouch's entire catalogue have more of a Steely Dan feel than "Lookin' for You"—including the vocals, which sound to be directly inspired by Donald Fagen's distinct phrasings. To achieve that sound, Andraé again employed keyboardist/arranger Omartian, who had recorded with Steely Dan, and later won Grammy awards for his production with Christopher Cross, Donna Summer, and others. According to Maxwell, Crouch was at the height of his "Steely Dan phase" and finally met Fagen at a recording studio in Santa Monica, much to his delight. When mutual friend Jeff Porcaro introduced the two men, Maxwell said that Andraé excitedly exclaimed, "I can sing just like you! I can sound exactly like you." "And I said later, 'Andraé, why do you care about that? You're better than Donald Fagan.'"

Even so, opening as it does with an E♭ minor 9th chord, the sheer musicality of "Lookin' for You" stunningly depicts the depth and weight of how God travels with believers—even as they look for God. Spurred and inspired by such Steely Dan songs as "Glamour Profession" and "Peg," the song also serves as a "coming out" party for Crouch's new rhythmic devices and meticulous tonal materiality. For the next four albums, Andraé embarks on a musical and lyrical expedition. Throughout *I'll Be Thinking of You*, he takes the listener through a range of musical genres, but it's only when listening to the entire album in order, the authors suggest, that a liturgical format once again appears. "Lookin' for You" invites and evangelizes—a conversation composed in a sermonic format *without* mentioning God.[24]

Side II

"Bringin' Back the Sunshine"

If *I'll Be Thinking of You* is, indeed, framed in a liturgical format, then "Bringin' Back the Sunshine," in D♭ major, is invitational. In an attempt to expound on the ineffable, unknowable theology of the Holy Spirit, it references Matthew 6:34, Lamentations 3:2–23, and Revelation 21:4, and returns to the musical device of *musique concrète*—the process of using nonmusical instruments in a composition to create the accompanying thunder and wind sounds. It's something Andraé has done through the years but never in such a dramatic fashion. To "discover" Crouch's playful way of communicating—the authors believe—he intentionally placed "Bringin' Back the Sunshine" at the beginning of Side II as an invitation to discovery. In the days of vinyl LPs, listeners physically turned the disc over. The physicality of this gesture, and movement of this song, is a subtle declaration to "to turn to the other side" because God is bringing back the sunshine. Patrick Henderson, who had previously written songs for the Doobie Brothers and Aretha Franklin, was a much-in-demand producer in both the religious and mainstream music worlds and had the unique ability to likewise "turn over" genres, where musical secular and sacred aesthetics meet. And like Andraé, Henderson was a keyboardist who grew up in the COGIC tradition. He had studied under Mattie Moss Clark and served as the worship leader and resident composer for the famed West Angeles Church of God in Christ. Finally, like "Polynesian Praise Song" from *This Is Another Day*, 'Bringing Back the Sunshine" has a decidedly "island" feel, including sounds of the seaside in the background.

For Maxwell, in retrospect, the song's highlight is the ethereal vocal by Danniebelle Hall, who he said is "one of the five best singers" he worked with in his long career as a producer. Maxwell said that when legendary arranger/composer Marty Paich heard Danniebelle sing on a religious television program, he asked to meet her. When Maxwell arranged the meeting, Paich also brought his son David, later of Toto fame, to the studio. "Marty said, 'She's better than Sarah Vaughan'—he just went on and on about her,'" Maxwell said. "She never over-sang anything, but the sound of her voice was just so soulful—she was a great soprano."[25]

"Jesus Is Lord"

"Jesus Is Lord," inspired by Philippians 2:10–11, interprets a scripture on the weighty topics of salvation and the lordship of Jesus Christ in a remarkably fresh way. It blends gospelized R&B funk in the verses with a chorus that includes horn arrangements that mirror the Beatles' "All You Need Is Love." The background vocals emerge as a tight, high-voiced power package, while the Earth, Wind & Fire–influenced bass and drum grooves create a joyous Sunday morning feel. The song constantly circles and dances around its neighboring chords, creatively switching between the keys of A♭ and D♭, and with even a small section in B♭ minor.

As the most enduring song on the album, Maxwell said that "Jesus Is Lord" has, in time, become a "foundation in the R&B community." So much so, that QuestLove and the Roots, in their capacity as house band for *The Tonight Show with Jimmy Fallon*, performed the song the week of Andraé's passing in 2015. Howard McCrary, who jointly arranged the vocals on "Jesus Is Lord" with Andraé, as well as most of the other tracks on the album, called the song "explosive." "Bill Maxwell refers to Andraé as the 'George Gershwin' of gospel music," Howard said, "and rightly so because Andraé had the ability to come up with these amazing tunes. These ideas would come and there was nothing like it at the time. The only other composer I know of that magnitude at the time was Stevie Wonder." When Wonder or Crouch would compose a song, McCrary said, "it's like that song had been written a hundred years ago. It's like a comfortable pair of shoes or a nice, comfortable sweater." For Howard, "Jesus Is Lord" is a prime example:

> It was just so bouncy and had a great groove to it. The song writes itself but also the arrangement writes itself. The nuances are very important on Andraé's productions because the way that he composed and wrote the song, the background vocals were committed to follow that lead. That's why I said it was "explosive"—it was like the magic just came together.

Maxwell's memory of the "Jesus Is Lord" session is marred by a serious gallbladder attack he suffered in the studio during the recording of the song. After recovering, he said that he kept the loose, church-styled keyboard interplay between co-composers Andraé and Patrick Henderson and added "live" horns with Steve Tavaglione, Glen Myerscough, and Allen Gregory. "It was more like a live song," Maxwell said, "it was simple, we didn't overdo it and it ended up being a live staple. And Andraé really sang it. That's what I was always trying to get Andraé to really sing and—on that one—he did."[26]

The second chapter of Philippians is considered to be the "Christ Hymn" in theological circles. Few songs in Crouch's catalogue make such a definitive statement. The authors believe that, with the upcoming albums with Warner Bros. that will be assailed in the Black church community for their lack of overtly "Jesus jargon," Andraé is using "Jesus Is Lord" to make clear exactly what he believes—and Who is in charge of his life.

"The Love Medley" ("There's No Hatred")

The first track of the sophisticated medley, "There's No Hatred," opens in E♭ major. Harlan Rogers arranged the song and played the Fender Rhodes on the track, along with Billy Preston (organ), Dorothy Ashby (harp), Abraham

Laboriel (bass), and much of Andraé's touring band for 1979 and 1980, as well as guitarists Hadley Hockensmith and Dean Parks. Maxwell said that one of the unique aspects about "There's No Hatred" is that "The Love Medley" has three different tempos. "We cut it live at United Western Studio #2," Maxwell recalled, "which also has a balcony. I put the horn section up in the balcony and they were live—everyone was live, everyone was in the room. We cut it with all the tempos changes in one or two takes."[27]

Looking back, Smith said he was never sure if his appearance in the studio for the recording of the medley was planned or happenstance. "Andraé just threw me out there to kind of show me off to the background singers," Smith said. "He said, 'Hey, go out there and just improvise. We'll play a track—just go out and sing a little something on this.' So I went out, put on the headphones and started improvising." Smith said that Andraé had originally planned to sing the lead vocal himself. "I never understood it, but Andraé really didn't like his voice," Smith said. "He was always giving away songs and it would frustrate Bill to no end. But he ended up giving it to me and it turned out pretty good."[28]

When Howard McCrary heard Smith record the lead vocal on "The Love Medley," McCrary said that he immediately thought that Smith possessed "one of the most beautiful" voices he had ever heard. "It's kind of like if you could put Johnny Mathis, Al Jarreau, and Mel Torme into one body, you'd get Howard Smith," McCrary said. "We were very, very happy to have him on the project."[29]

The primary theological reference in "The Love Medley" is found in the fourth chapter of Ephesians. But musically, at least within the genre of gospel music, the song pushes the boundaries by echoing the timeless R& B power ballads of the 1970s by Stevie Wonder, the Bee Gees, and Donny Hathaway, among others.

"Dreamin'"

More than any other instrument in Christian scripture, the presence of the harp is used to signify peace and tranquility. With the harp as the focal point, Crouch places "Dreamin'" in a pentatonic, all black key pitch centricity, awash in harp and piano *glissandos*. Andraé sings that while he doesn't know the date of Christ's return, all Christians continue to dream about it. For Crouch, the Rapture, as interpreted in John 14, Matthew 24:30, and I Thessalonians 4:17, has been one of his most persistent and treasured themes, beginning with his earliest albums. Though the eschatology, the theology the future of the Church and heaven, of the fevered early days of the Jesus Movement had largely abated in most Christian circles, Andraé returned to the topic again and again. "Dreamin'" is still suffused with the same sense of longing first heard in "It Won't Be Long."[30]

For "Dreamin'," Maxwell said they hired Ashby, an African American harpist from Detroit who had been featured on Stevie Wonder's recent albums. "We'd all fallen in love with Dorothy," he said. "So 'Dreamin'" was cut where it was just Dorothy and Andraé." Maxwell said that at the end of each recording session, if there was still time, he would ask her, "Can you play me a song?" "When we'd done eight or ten of them," he said. "I gave the tapes to her and said, 'Now you have a new album.' But she died of cancer shortly after that and we lost her. She was a soulful person who played beautifully."[31]

More than forty years later, Howard McCrary said that listening to "Dreamin'" still makes him tear up:

> Because whether you're working with Andraé in the studio or putting together songs in his home, it was like a dream. It was almost surrealistic. There is this chromatic motif running through the song that's very dream-like. He made a relationship with Christ something personal, something so endearing, that you hear that melody, you just knew you were in heaven. There is nobody like Andraé, nobody.[32]

A Broader Audience

In an interview with the *Los Angeles Sentinel* in support of the LP, Crouch said the use of new singers and musicians was an effort to broaden his sound—and audience. "I like to showcase new talent," he said. "You'll never hear a solo album just me on there. I see no point in that. I don't need the ego trip of just singing alone." Andraé also praised the "fantastic" talents of Murden, saying she possessed "one of the clearest voices" he had yet heard. "And what she did on my album is only a grain of sand compared to what she can do in the future."[33]

I'll Be Thinking of You was released on both Light Records and the Warners (WEA)-distributed Elektra label (Elektra E1-60078) in October 1979. Despite the attention generated earlier in the year by the announcement that it would be a joint release, the album generated relatively little response in the popular music arena. *Record World*'s short review in its list of that week's new releases is one of the few that marked the event in either the religious *or* trade markets:

> Crouch has equally strong appeal in both the contemporary/inspirational and soul/spiritual gospel fields. With the help of fellow artists Stevie Wonder, Kristle Murden, Michael Omartian and the Disciples, Crouch has assembled another highly polished, commercial package.

But *I'll Be Thinking of You*, which was released at the same time as Wonder's *Journey Through the Secret Life of Plants* and other top-selling LPs, did not immediately appear on either the Soul-Gospel or Soul charts. At year's end, *Live in London* finished 1979 at #4 in the Soul-Gospel chart, while *Take Me Back* finished at #26. In overall sales, Crouch was ranked behind James Cleveland, Walter Hawkins, the Gospel Keynotes, and Shirley Caesar.[34]

Road Warriors

As 1979 ended, Andraé served as both a performer and presenter at the 13th Annual NAACP Image Awards December 7 at the Hollywood Palladium. Crouch, who was also named "Best Gospel Artist," sang "Through It All" as civil rights hero Rosa Parks received the organization's Humanitarian Award. Andraé (billed with the Disciples) then resumed touring, this time to Great Britain and Scandinavia, where the response was so enthusiastic that the group would soon be booked abroad two or three times in a year. Gibson said that in the weeks after *I'll Be Thinking of You* had been released, she had a profound religious experience and left Wonderlove. She called Andraé and asked if he had any work for her. "He told me, 'I'm going to Europe again in six days,'" Gibson said. "'I want you to come to Encino and see if you can blend with the rest of the singers.'" Gibson, who had attended school with singers Vonciel Faggett, Alfie Silas, and Jean Johnson and had worked with them on other projects, immediately agreed. "And I did blend," she recalled. The touring group, which at the time included Maxwell, Perry Morgan, Howard McCrary, Geary Faggett, Howard Smith, and others, left six days later. Gibson said the dates in Reykjavík, Oslo, Stockholm, and Helsinki were "thrilling." "They *love* gospel in Scandinavia," Gibson said. Looking back decades later, while the various musicians and singers said that they have trouble differentiating among the many different European tours that occurred regularly through the mid-1980s, nearly all vividly remembered the passionate responses of the audiences. Howard McCrary said that even though *I'll Be Thinking of You* had only been released for a couple of months and was not always readily available abroad, the European audiences often sang along with the new songs. "These are Andraé's fans, Andraé's followers," he said. "To see the people come out and fill these auditoriums with 5,000 to 10,000 people was just mind-blowing. I think Europe had a deeper appreciation than Americans did. They loved him in America, but they were crazy over there in Sweden, Germany, and England."[35]

Abraham Laboriel's Impact and Koinonia

One of the stalwarts of the tours was bassist Abraham Laboriel. Maxwell said that legendary sax player Ernie Watts had highly praised Laboriel at the time, saying, "He plays things no one has ever played." In 1979, Maxwell and Laboriel (who had met via producer Omartian) formed Koinonia with Harlan Rogers, Hadley Hockensmith, Dean Parks, Alex Acuna, and John Philips. Though there was frequent turnover among the musicians, Maxwell said that Laboriel was a constant creative presence. Koinonia toured whenever Maxwell was not working with Crouch. "And when we went, we were astonished with the crowds," Maxwell said. "Musically, it was very creative because when I'm producing Andrae, the last thing I'm thinking about is my drumming. It helped me get better."

Laboriel said that during his 1979–1980 tours with Crouch in Scandinavia some songs—to his surprise—were performed differently for those audiences, including "There Is a Bell," a version of which, retitled as "Until Jesus Comes," was not released until more than decade later. "Andraé always did versions of 'There Is a Bell' on those tours by himself on the piano," Laboriel said:

> and I'm almost embarrassed to use the words, but with an anointing. He would play the piano—honestly—better than the greatest pianists of all time. Sounds would come out of the piano that I never knew were possible and while he was singing. People talk about angels appearing when people sing so beautifully and that they were reinforced by the sounds of angels singing. Andraé could do that with his piano. It felt like several anointed people were playing the piano at the same time.[36]

Life on the Road

Alfie Silas Durio, who joined the touring group after the *I'll Be Thinking of You* sessions, had been introduced to Andraé by fellow singer Marti McCall. At another impromptu backyard barbeque at his house, Crouch asked Durio to join the European leg of the tour. "One memory in London was that after we'd performed and got on the bus, people started shaking it," she said. "They're rocking the bus and shouting, 'Andraé! Andraé! Andraé!' And I was thinking, 'Man, are we on the road with Rod Stewart or somebody?'" Durio was soon given the intimidating task of singing the beloved "My Tribute (to God Be the Glory)" with Andraé to close many of the concerts on the tour. "I remembered many times when I would finish singing that song it was as if I could not move afterwards," she said. "The anointing of the Lord was so powerful and the atmosphere was charged with the presence of the Lord in such a way I had never experienced before."[37]

Singer Russ Taff also toured at different times with Andraé, both as a member of the Imperials and as a solo artist, into the 1980s. Quartets like the Imperials typically followed a strict schedule, which made Taff's experiences with the Disciples all the more memorable, particularly since Crouch was chronically late. "Andraé would wander in with his cup of coffee, smiling and happy to see us," Taff said, "and we would forgive him every time." During the Scandinavian segments of the tours, Taff said the group would perform with large gospel choirs at festivals during the weekend, but sometimes play larger nightclubs and similar venues during the week, which, he said, "was a new experience for this Pentecostal boy." On one tour, Taff was the opening act—"the designated rocker"—at a club in Helsinki, Finland, filled with noisy, restless patrons. After a riotous reception, Taff said he left the stage with the crowd still agitated and talking loudly:

> Andraé simply walked onto the stage alone, sat down at the piano and started singing, "Jesus is the answer for the world today/Above him there's no other/ Jesus is the way." The room went completely silent and everyone's attention was focused on the stage. He moved to "Through It All" and "The Blood Will Never Lose Its Power" and the crowd started singing along with him softly at first and then with all their might. The entire atmosphere of the room changed, you could absolutely feel it. Eventually the band joined him onstage and he brought the house down as usual. But what stands out in my mind is that unforgettable image

of Andraé at the piano, lost in the power and beauty of his own songs, and taking all of us with him.[38]

1980

Finally back from still another European tour that included multiple dates in England, Holland, Germany, Sweden, and Norway in late January, Andraé appeared with a nine-piece version of the Disciples at a "Tribute to Martin Luther King" on January 15, 1980, at the Music Center at Chandler Pavilion in Los Angeles. The *Hollywood Reporter* noted that actor Paul Winfield hosted the event and Crouch was joined by Dionne Warwick and Maureen McGovern. *Billboard*'s review of the event, however, said that Crouch's attempt to bring "church" to the venue "failed miserably." Citing a bad vocal and instrumental mix throughout the performance, critic Eliot Tiegel called "Perfect Peace" and "Dreamin'" "more Tin Pan Alley than religious statement." In late February, the National Academy of Recording Arts & Sciences awarded Crouch the Grammy for Best Soul Gospel Performance, Contemporary for *I'll Be Thinking of You*. Former Disciple Bili Thedford had been nominated in the same category for *More than Magic*, as had the *PUSH for Excellence* LP. Andraé and the Disciples were asked to perform on the televised Grammy Awards ceremony, in a show that included performances by Bob Dylan and the Mighty Clouds of Joy. Kristle Murden said that the network had originally approved her duet with Andraé on the title track but decided at the last minute to feature "Jesus Is Lord." "To this day I don't understand why that went the way it did," she writes in her biography *It Took a Miracle and Then Some*. 'I'll Be Thinking of You' was the biggest song off of that album." Toward the end of the performance of "Jesus Is Lord," Murden writes, Crouch approached her and unexpectedly placed the microphone in her face: "I had no idea what to do in that moment because it was so impromptu," she said. "I opened my mouth and let out a squeal. Seriously, I think it was supposed to be a quick ad lib but came out so high that it was more like a squeal." The heightened profile resulted in an appearance on NBC's *Today Show*, with interview segments recorded at his home, Christ Memorial Church of God in Christ, and during the "Tribute to Martin Luther King" concert. Host Boyd Matson would become another one of Crouch's longtime friends.[39]

Success for Light Records

It was also a golden period for Light Records and Lexicon Music. Buoyed by the strong sales of releases from Andraé, Walter Hawkins, Jessy Dixon, and others, the label reported that gross sales for November 1979 had increased 51 percent over the previous year. The ASCAP check for performance royalties for radio and television airplay had increased by 100 percent over 1979. Most important, Andraé's success abroad prompted the label to significantly increase exposure in the UK, Europe, Australia, Asia, and Central and South America. "There is no doubt about the demand going up and little doubt of our ability to supply," Carmichael said. Among the list of upcoming releases, Light touted new signees Tramaine Hawkins and Murden.[40]

Saturday Night Live

Andraé enjoyed another milestone on May 24, 1980, becoming the first gospel artist to appear on the enormously popular *Saturday Night Live.* The episode marked both the end of the fifth season of the show and the last appearance by many of the regular cast members. Frequent host Buck Henry welcomed Crouch and the Voices of Unity—clearly not the Disciples—as they performed "Can't Nobody Do Me Like Jesus" with the *SNL* house band. The appearance on the often controversial show, which included a sketch with Henry's risqué "Uncle Roy" character, would quickly become another point of contention between Andraé and more traditional gospel artists.[41]

Crouch continued his practice of each summer performing at the larger American music festivals, as well as numerous smaller dates. With the increased exposure, he performed for the first time at Red Rocks, Colorado, in July before 8,600, joined co-headliner B. J. Thomas a few days later in Tulsa, Oklahoma, to perform before a sold-out crowd of 12,000, and finally appeared as the featured artist at a heavily promoted concert at Six Flags over Georgia. The increased coverage paid off for Andraé and *I'll Be Thinking of You.* After moderate sales during the first part of the year, the album jumped to #2 in April and May, fell slightly to #4 in July, finally hit #1 in August, and remained in the Top 10 in *Billboard*'s "Best-Selling Gospel LP" charts for the remainder of 1980. The Elektra version, however, languished in the middle 60s in the first part of the year, before dropping off the "Soul LPs" chart completely by July.[42]

Crouch vs. Cleveland II

In September, the editors of *Billboard* magazine's regular gospel music special section chose to print lengthy parallel interviews with Cleveland and Crouch, continuing (and perhaps abetting) the differences between the two artists. In the Cleveland interview, writer Ed Ochs mentions that Andraé had appeared on *Saturday Night Live* in May. Cleveland's response reflects that of many in traditional gospel music and the Black church itself:

> They called me to go on "Saturday Night Live" but I wouldn't go because I felt the show was, number one, too controversial, too risqué. Andraé went on and I think he did a very good job for gospel music. I enjoyed Andraé's performance—it may have done something for Andraé as an artist—but I don't think it did anything for the cause.

Cleveland adds that despite the overtly religious nature of the song—"Can't Nobody Do Me Like Jesus"—Crouch was presented as a "performer, not a religious personality."

In Crouch's interview, Andraé asserts that a "spiritual warfare that fights against the new thing" exists in gospel music and that there are those who claimed that he was "not a gospel artist anymore, but a pop artist singing gospel lyrics" and that he is "too fancy" and is "neglecting of what gospel music is all about." In response, Crouch admits that the term "gospel" has become something of a problem itself because of the "stereotypes" associated with the music. "I think gospel people—we, ourselves," he tells Ochs, "have done more damage in keeping gospel down than what any secular radio station has done by taking it for granted." Andraé says that he'd received hate mail following his appearance on *Saturday Night Live*. "I don't see how a Christian would ever believe that or really could feel that way when Jesus said, 'Go unto the highways and byways,'" Andraé adds. Of his upcoming "secular" releases, Crouch "is preparing" his listeners "for the day gospel songs may not mention Jesus or God," but instead talk about a "Christian kind of song, a love song, how good it is to have a girlfriend [who] like you [ ] loves God." Elsewhere in the interview, he says that he had been asked to sit on the Presidential Commission for Energy Conservation co-written a song with Stevie Wonder, and was in the process of writing songs for his upcoming albums for both the Light and Warner labels. "I can't say one album will be different from the other," Crouch says, "just wherever I am musically, wherever I feel I am musically, whatever I feel each album will communicate with the most people. Warners told me that they just wanted good music. They don't care what I say."[43]

More Never-Ending Tours

By fall, Andraé was on the road again. Perry Morgan's personal files include a faded packet of daily instructions for a brutal tour that extended from October 8 (in Spokane, Washington, with Huey Lewis and the News opening the first half of the tour) to November 10, a total of twenty-four concerts. The tattered pages contain the excruciating details of transporting a large band and crew from town to town, hotel reservations, venue details, and contact information. At most of the concerts, the promoters were required to provide four four-door sedans and drivers, along with an equipment/luggage van and driver. The performance halls ranged from the 18,000-seat Pacific National Exhibition in Vancouver, BC, and the 15,000-seat Forum in Inglewood, California, to the final date in the packet, the 12,300-seat University of South Carolina Coliseum (Image 13.2).[44]

Image 13.2 Andraé Crouch in a pensive moment in his dressing room. Photograph courtesy of Stephen "Bugs" Giglio.

An Eventful End to the Year

The year 1980 wound to a close in much the same way as previous years, with Crouch continually touring and writing songs for upcoming releases. In addition to the unnamed (and never released) song composed with Wonder, Andraé reported that he had already completed three others, "No Room for Rumors," "Handwriting on the Wall," and "Waiting for the Son." In October, he participated in an all-star concert titled "ShowVote" designed to promote voter education and participation. The sold-out crowd in the Los Angeles Forum also featured performances by Wonder, Smokey Robinson, and Buddy Miles. The following month, Crouch was one of the first performers on BET's *Bobby Jones Gospel* program, said to be the first "commercially sponsored gospel music program" to be nationally televised on cable. The *Saturday Night Live* controversy—which only extended to the small world of gospel music—did not keep Andraé from appearing on several national television programs as TV became an increasingly viable aspect of his ministry. Appearances on the PBS series *More of the Good Ol' Gospel Music* and the syndicated talk and variety series *The Toni Tennille Show* culminated with a featured spot on NBC's year-end limited series, *Barbara Mandrell & the Mandrell Sisters*. Andraé performed with the sisters and with the Christ Memorial Choir. Nineteen-eighty ended with Crouch purchasing a 15-acre ranch, 20 miles from Kona, Hawaii. At the time, Andraé said that his plans were to build a "leadership training center" on the site.[45]

From the standpoint of record sales, the Light Records version of *I'll Be Thinking of You*, which had debuted on the "Best-Selling Spiritual" LP charts in January, methodically worked its way up the charts, finally peaking at #1 in August, remained in the top six for the rest of the year. The album ended 1980 as the #5 top-selling "Spiritual Album," and Andraé, sans the Disciples, finished as the seventh best-selling gospel artist. However, the Elektra Records version peaked in the chart's mid-60s and by late summer had fallen off the "Best-Selling Soul LPs" chart completely.[46]

Time and time again, for the artists who had both worked and worshipped with Crouch, sales—or lack of sales—for a project like *I'll Be Thinking of You* were the last thing on their minds. "He is a universal artist, a universal songwriter," Murden said. "And even though he was a gospel artist, he wrote these

Hints of a New Direction

Listening to *I'll Be Thinking of You*, more than fifty years after its release, however, it is possible to hear—once again—Andrae's growing dissatisfaction with the status quo in gospel music. As noted above, some of the songs clearly reach beyond the evangelical church. For an artist who continued to proclaim his overwhelming desire to take the Christian message to the entire world, what was ahead should have come as no surprise. Andraé said as much that year in an unusually open interview with Norma Simpson with the African American newspaper the *Los Angeles Sentinel*:

> I feel, today, many people come to Christ and feel like all their natural-supernatural-artistic ability is supposed to be restricted. But the scripture says, "He whom the Son sets free is free indeed." We are free to expand, but it's only in the ministry that people make these stipulations or these boundaries on a Christian. Now, if I were a Christian artist, surely I shouldn't be bound to maybe painting churches or crucifixes.[48]

NOTES

1. "Best-Selling Gospel LPs," *Billboard*, January 6, 1979, 62; "Best-Selling Gospel LPs," *Billboard*, February 3, 1979, 46; "Best-Selling Gospel LPs," *Billboard*, March 3, 1979, 65; "Best-Selling Gospel LPs," *Billboard*, April 7, 1979, 65; "Gospel Scene," *Billboard*, February 3, 1979, 46; "Lexicon Blooms via Restructuring," *Billboard*, January 6, 1979, 62.
2. Karl Dallas, "Caught in the Act: Andraé Crouch," *Melody Maker*, February 17, 1979, 46; Glen Myerscough, interview with the authors, June 18, 2021; Jaymes Felix, interview with the authors, August 21, 2021; Marge Barnett, "Gospel Time," *Record World*, February 3, 1979, 101–102.
3. https://www.youtube.com/watch?v=Xlaz-VTZEuo.
4. "Andraé Crouch Brought 'Live in London' to the U.S.A. and Blew 'Em Away!" *Billboard*, April 7, 1979, 29.
5. David Jackson, "James Cleveland Sings the Horns Off the Devil," *Village Voice*, April 16, 1979, https:www.villagevoice.com/2019/08/30/black-music-james -cleveland-sings-the-horns-off-the-devil.

I'LL BE THINKING OF YOU

6. Jacqueline Trescott, "White House Salute to Black Music: Concert, Supper and 1,000 Guests," *Washington Post*, June 7, 1979; Joanne Ostrow, "White House Hosts Black Music Night," *Cash Box*, June 23, 1979, 7, 54; "Presidential Honor," *Billboard*, July 7, 1979, 36.

7. Jean Williams, "Crouch Deal Spurs WB's Gospel Debut," *Billboard*, June 9, 1979, 3, 106.

8. Bill Maxwell, interview with the authors, February 24, 2023; "Black Oriented Singles," *Record World*, March 15, 1980, 48; "Black Oriented Singles," *Record World*, April 12, 1980, 46.

9. Gerry Wood, "A Joyful Noise Rises to New Heights," *Billboard*, July 28, 1979, R-3; Pearl Williams-Jones, "Black Gospel Blends Social Change & Ethnic Roots," *Billboard*, July 28, 1979, R-12, R-16.

10. "Best-Selling Gospel LPs," *Billboard*, April 7, 1979, 65; "Best-Selling Gospel LPs," *Billboard*, May 5, 1979, 45; "Best-Selling Gospel LPs," *Billboard*, June 2, 1979, 55; "Best-Selling Gospel LPs," *Billboard*, July 7, 1979, 36; "Best-Selling Gospel LPs," *Billboard*, August 4, 1979, 39; "Best-Selling Gospel LPs," *Billboard*, September 1, 1979, 32; "Best-Selling Gospel LPs," *Billboard*, October 6, 1979, 75; "Best-Selling Gospel LPs," *Billboard*, November 3, 1979, 8.

11. "Christian Artists Meet Planned for August," *Record World*, February 17, 1979, 81; "Live Appearance," *Billboard*, August 4, 1979, 39; Jean Williams, "Soul Sauce," *Billboard*, July 14, 1979, 81; "Light-Lexicon Disks and Music: Release Spanish Versions," *Billboard*, September 1, 1979, 34; Margie Barnett, "Gospel Time," *Record World*, September 1, 1979, 52; Mike Hyland, "Gospel Scene," *Billboard*, November 3, 1979, 80.

12. Jaymes Felix, interview with the authors, August 21, 2021.

13. Glen Myerscough, interview with the authors, June 18, 2021.

14. Andraé Crouch, *I'll Be Thinking of You* (Light Records LS 5763).

15. The McCrarys, *Sunshine Day* (Light Records LS-5606, 1972); Linda McCrary, interview with the authors, August 19, 2021.

16. Kristle Murden, interview with the authors, November 8, 2020.

17. Linda McCrary, interview with the authors, August 19, 2021.

18. Howard Smith, interview with the authors, August 31, 2021.

19. Tammie Gibson, interview with the authors, December 28, 2022; Bill Maxwell, interview with the authors, February 24, 2023.

20. Howard McCrary, interview with the authors, February 18, 2022; Howard Smith, interview with the authors, August 31, 2021.

21. Bill Maxwell, interview with the authors, February 24, 2023.

22. Bill Maxwell, interview with the authors, February 24, 2023.

23. Bill Maxwell, interview with the authors, February 24, 2023.

24. Paul Grein, "Cross 'Wind' Hit, Number Two, Mastered Digitally a Year Ago," *Billboard*, May 17, 1980, 16, 52–53; Bill Maxwell, interview with the authors, February 24, 2023.

25. Robyn Wells, "Patrick Henderson Multi-Faceted Producer-Songwriter Plans to Cut NewPax Solo LP," *Billboard*, August 1, 1981, 49; David Ritz, *Messengers: Portraits of African American Ministers, Evangelists, Gospel Singers and Other Messengers of the Word* (New York: Doubleday, 2005), 198–200; Bill Maxwell, interview with the authors, February 24, 2023.

26. The authors are grateful to Rachel Wilhelm and Phillip Ferrell for this insight (March 1, 2023); Howard McCrary, interview with the authors, February 18, 2022; Bill Maxwell, interview with the authors, February 24, 2023.

27. Bill Maxwell, interview with the authors, February 24, 2023.

28. Howard Smith, interview with the authors, August 31, 2021; Howard McCrary, interview with the authors, February 18, 2022.

29. Howard McCrary, interview with the authors, February 18, 2022.

30. The authors are grateful to Debbie Mercado for this insight (March 1, 2023).

31. Bill Maxwell, interview with the authors, February 24, 2023.

32. Howard McCrary, interview with the authors, February 18, 2022.

33. "Crouch Premieres 10th Album," *Los Angeles Sentinel*, September 20, 1979, 9.

34. "Gospel Album Picks: *I'll Be Thinking of You*, Andraé Crouch, Light LS 5763 (Word)," *Record World*, November 10, 1979, 55; "Soul/Gospel Albums," *Billboard*, December 22, 1979, TIA-40; "Soul/Gospel Artists," *Billboard*, December 22, 1979, TIA-40.

35. Jean Williams, "Music Folk Brush Off Image Fete," *Billboard*, December 20, 1980, 56–57; Tammie Gibson, interview with the authors, December 28, 2022; Howard McCrary, interview with the authors, February 18, 2022.

36. Abraham Laboriel, interview with the authors, August 19, 2021; Bill Maxwell, interview with the authors, June 9, 2023.

37. Alfie Silas Durio, interview with the authors, June 18, 2021.

38. Russ Taff, personal correspondence with the authors, July 28, 2021.

39. "Perfect Blend," *Billboard*, March 19, 1980, 104; "King Tribute," *Hollywood Reporter*, December 27, 1979, 3; Eliot Tiegel, "Talent in Action: The Orchestra, Dionne Warwick, Maureen McGovern, Andraé Crouch," *Billboard*, January 26, 1980, 49; "Gospel Grammy Nominees Announced," *Record World*, February 9, 1980, 51; "Gospel Scene," *Cash Box*, February 2, 1980, 33; Kristle Murden, *It Took a Miracle and Then Some* (New Providence, NJ: Bowker Books, 2019), 101; Don Cusic, "A Powerful Medium for Spreading the Word and the Music," *Billboard*, September 27, 1980, G-10; "Gospel Scene," *Billboard*, April 19, 1980, 74; "Crouch on 'Today'," *Cash Box*, February 2, 1980, 33.

40. "Light & Lexicon Sales Rise 51%," *Billboard*, February 2, 1980, 30; "Coast-Based Publishers," *Record World*, March 8, 1980, 20; "Gospel Is Good News at Light/ Lexicon," *Record World*, March 29, 1980, 18.

41. https://www.onesnlaiday.com/2018/11/24/may-24-1980-buck-henry-andrew -gold-andrae-crouch-and-the-voices-of-unity-s5-e20/ (The episode is available via iTunes and the Peacock streaming platform).

42. Edward Morris, "From Choir Stalls to Cruise Ships," *Billboard*, September 27, 1980, G28, G30, G31; "Best-Selling Gospel LPs," *Billboard*, April 5, 1980, 70; "Best-Selling Gospel LPs," *Billboard*, May 3, 1980, 24; "Best-Selling Gospel LPs," *Billboard*, July 5, 1980, 44; "Best-Selling Gospel LPs," *Billboard*, August 2, 1980, 33.
43. Ed Ochs, "A Traditional Music Challenged by Change: The Reverend James Cleveland," *Billboard*, September 27, 1980, G6, G22; Ed Ochs, "A Traditional Music Challenged by Change: Andraé Crouch, *Billboard*, September 27, 1980, G6, G22.
44. Personal collection of Perry Morgan, loaned to the authors.
45. "A Traditional Music Challenged by Change: Andraé Crouch, *Billboard*, September 27, 1980, G6, G22; "All-Star Concert in L.A. Benefits Voter Education," *Record World*, November 8, 1980, 6; Robyn Wells, "Jones Gospel Cable Show Breaks Barriers," *Billboard*, November 29, 1980, 8; "Television Review: Barbara Mandrell & the Mandrell Sisters," *Hollywood Reporter*, December 3, 1980, 8.
46. "Best-Selling Gospel LPs," *Billboard*, January 5, 1980, 20; "Best-Selling Gospel LPs," *Billboard*, August 2, 1980, 33; "Spiritual Albums," *Billboard*, December 20, 1980, TIA-38; "Spiritual Artists," *Billboard*, December 20, 1980, TIA-38; "Soul LPs," *Billboard*, December 20, 1980, TIA-34; "Crouch Television Schedule Crowded," *Billboard*, January 10, 1981, 82; Sharon Allen, "Gospel Scene," *Billboard*, January 10, 1981, 82.
47. Kristle Murden, interview with the authors, November 8, 2020.
48. Norma Simpson, "Andrae Crouch: Modern Psalmist," *Los Angeles Sentinel*, October 4, 1979, B3A.

14

Don't Give Up

"It's Gonna Rain"

When Bill Maxwell and Andraé returned to the studio in mid-1980, the musicians and singers who had been touring steadily with Crouch were as tight and creative as any group, religious or mainstream, in the country. Recording in Paramount Recording Studio, Sound Lab Studios, and United Recording, they quickly produced two songs, "Please Come Back" and "It's Gonna Rain." "It's Gonna Rain" was released as the A-side of the 45 and, while it never charted, the song was later nominated for a Grammy. (Also nominated in the "Best Gospel Performance–Contemporary/Inspirational" category was Reba Rambo and Dony McGuire's *The Lord's Prayer* project, which included a song sung by Andraé, "Lead Us Not into Temptation.") Several well-known musicians were involved in the "It's Gonna Rain" sessions, including bassist James Jamerson Jr., son of legendary Motown bassist James Jamerson. Maxwell said that Jamerson was a consummate professional in the studio. At the end of the day, Jamerson asked Maxwell and Crouch if he could make a copy of the song and take it home with him to work on it some more. "James came back the next day and redid his bass track in one take and did not charge us again," Maxwell said. "He was a wonderful person who just wanted to do his best." "It's Gonna Rain," in particular, is one of Maxwell's favorites, an old gospel song that Andraé had been performing since his COGIC days, though with a different arrangement. The song featured only three singers (Phyllis St. James, Howard Smith, and Maxi Anderson) and a small band that included Jamerson, Don Grusin, David Williams, Wil Keene, Alex Acuna, and

Maxwell, with horn parts by Glen Myerscough and Allen Gregory. "I really liked the way it sounded," Maxwell said.[1]

Like many of Crouch's songs, "It's Gonna Rain's" deep up-tempo funk groove in E♭ minor would be extremely difficult to reproduce in churches. Its accompaniment and orchestration call for Clavinet, Rhodes piano, and electric bass, instruments closely associated with the funk music of the era. Andraé was among the first to take gospel to pop music; in time, the evangelical church would bring this style of West Coast Tower of Power horn pop music into the sanctuary.

The B-side, the gentle "Please Come Back," echoes the old hymn "Softly and Tenderly Jesus Is Calling." In the key of D minor (for the time, these jazz chord progressions were ultra-progressive—D-minor 7th, G-13th, C-11th, F, E-minor 7th to A-dominant 7th), the sequence unfolds over Andraé's almost pleading vocals that sometimes end with an inarticulate moan. For a change of pace, Crouch chooses to blend the heartfelt lyrics and sentiment to a soul funk power ballad groove.

The February 25 telecast of the 23rd Grammy Awards featured several gospel and CCM artists, including the vocalists from *The Lord's Prayer* album, Crouch, Cynthia Clawson, B. J. Thomas, Reba Rambo and Dony McGuire, the Archers, and Tramaine and Walter Hawkins. *The Lord's Prayer* received the Grammy in an awards ceremony now best remembered for Christopher Cross's upset wins in multiple categories.[2]

A New Venture

As for Andraé, his restless pursuit of musical expressions continually led him toward new directions. He recorded and performed the theme to an ABC Television production on the life of baseball legend Satchel Paige, *Don't Look Back*, which aired May 21. Composed by Jack Elliott and Norman Gimbel, the influential *Hollywood Reporter* called Andraé's vocals on "Don't Look Back" one of the production's "assets." Crouch also met with Motown legend Smokey Robinson. Robinson had written two faith-based songs and approached Andraé about the possibility of recording one of them, "A Molehill to a Mountain." At the time, Robinson said that Crouch might possibly record the song, even though it was suggested that the song might reach a wider audience if Robinson himself released it. "I've thought about that," Robinson said. "In fact, I recorded a track on it at one time. But I think Andraé can do a better job than I can." Crouch never released "A Molehill to a Mountain."[3]

Privately, however, Crouch expressed trepidation about the prospect of reaching a wider, non-gospel audience by recording for one of the largest secular labels in the world. Abraham Laboriel, who had become one of his closest friends, said that he sensed "genuine fear" in Andraé during the recording sessions. "Andraé confessed to me, 'This is my first album for Warner Bros.,'" Laboriel recalled, "'and I am really scared because I don't think I have what it takes to do what they're expecting of me.'" Laboriel said he replied, "Andraé, everything that you have done thus far was done by the Lord and not by you. So you have no right to have fear because the talent, the ability to play, the ability to write is not you—it's something that the Lord wanted to do through you." Laboriel said he reminded Andraé had he had originally been given the gift of music in order to play for his father Benjamin's church. "And I said, 'Andraé, there's no reason why the Lord will deny you that gift now that you're in a recording company that actually expects you to be gifted.'" Laboriel said that Crouch then returned to the studio to resume work on *Don't Give Up* with Maxwell.[4]

New Venues

Andraé's seemingly never-ending tours now took him to a host of new venues, both in the United States and abroad, including a stint headlining the two-day Family Joy Festival in Chicago's Great America Theme Park, May 16–17. Crouch returned home only long enough to receive the National Association of Recording Merchandisers' NARM Award for *I'll Be Thinking of You* for the best-selling Gospel-Spiritual Album of the previous year, before going on the road again. In August, he joined Stevie Wonder, Ashford & Simpson, and other artists performing at the Black Music Association Family Fair before 50,000 people in the Rose Bowl. The event raised $100,000 for the BMA and featured an unprecedented partnership among Black radio stations in Los Angeles. Clearly, the days of singing in small churches for love offerings, quite obviously, were long since behind him (Image 14.1).[5]

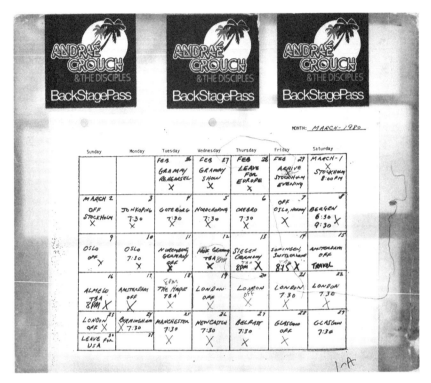

Image 14.1 March 1980 calendar, with Grammy rehearsals and performance and then beginning a long European tour. Courtesy of Stephen "Bugs" Giglio.

More of the Best

The mid-1981 release of the *More of the Best* collection from Light Records came as *I'll Be Thinking of You* was slowly descending the *Billboard* sales chart. *More of the Best* peaked at #11 in October and November and finished as the thirty-fifth best-selling "Spiritual Album" of 1981. In addition to "Please Come Back" and "It's Gonna Rain," *More of the Best* featured "Praises," "Sweet Love of Jesus," and "They Shall Be Mine" (from *Take Me Back*), "Soon and Very Soon" and "Quiet Times" (*This Is Another Day*), "I Just Want to Know You" (*Live in London*), and "I'll Be Thinking of You" and "Jesus Is Lord" (*I'll Be Thinking of You*). Light's dilemma with *More of the Best* was to include as few songs as possible from either of the previously released live albums or *The*

Best of Andraé Crouch. The other issue potentially impacting sales was that the much-publicized first Warner Bros. album, *Don't Give Up*, was released in late September with an "extensive advertising, merchandising and promotional campaign" on behalf of the LP. Warner Bros. promised an "advertising blitz aimed at trade and consumer print, in-store materials in the promotion" which would include "store streamers, 1×1 displays and full servicing for in-store play," as well as a "special emphasis on reaching Black contemporary radio on a national basis." Warner Bros./WEA also entered in a "special agreement" that would enable Light Records to "exclusively" distribute *Don't Give Up* in Christian bookstores. The article quoted Tom Draper from Warner Bros. as saying that the label was "confident" of its ability to work with the Crouch organization to "bring his music to a wholly new and potentially enormous audience." Almost simultaneously, Light announced a separate arrangement with Elektra/Asylum Records for a long-term distribution agreement, effective on February 1, 1982.[6]

A Warner Bros. Release

Maxwell said that there "wasn't really any tension" behind the decision—Andraé's move to Warner Bros. was prompted solely by a desire to have bigger recording and promotion budgets—with the hope of reaching a wider audience. "He ended up still doing gospel music," Maxwell said, "but the Warner Bros. album had a little more pop-oriented musical style." Maxwell said that the meetings with Warner Bros.' head of A&R Lenny Waronker were extremely positive. "There had been some discussions about having other producers do his album," Maxwell said, "including David Foster. But Lenny said, 'Give me another album like *I'll Be Thinking of You* and we'll be thrilled'—which took a lot of pressure off." But Crouch did not want to do another *I'll Be Thinking of You.* Maxwell said that Andraé was already listening to music with more of a "street funk" groove, like Michael Jackson. "But it wasn't Andraé's audience," Maxwell said, "and you didn't want to lose Andraé's audience—you wanted to keep it and build onto it." So while *I'll Be Thinking of You* had "I Got the Best," it also had the gospel-oriented "Jesus Is Lord." "But we didn't get that with *Don't Give Up*," Maxwell said.[7]

By servicing both the album and the first single, "Start All Over Again," to gospel, R&B, and pop radio stations, Warner Bros. execs hoped the LP would generate airplay on soul stations, but not alienate his longtime gospel music fans. Kent Crawford of Warner Bros. said that the message on the album was "consistent" with Andraé's earlier gospel releases. "But this music and production are more mainstream," Crawford added. According to Light Records, 40 percent of Andraé's audience had been white. With that in mind, Crawford said that "Waiting for the Son" might "have some appeal" during the upcoming holidays. Warner Bros. vice president Tom Draper said that the label's goal was to not, at the same time, "destroy Crouch's gospel base by promoting him to a secular audience." "We didn't sign him on the basis of being a gospel artist." Nor did Warner Bros. plan on releasing one of the two controversial songs on the album, "Hollywood Scene," at least not initially. "We didn't want to be the ones to appear to be making the break," Draper said.[8]

Warner Bros. was true to its word: beginning in October, *Don't Give Up* received star treatment, including glossy full-page color advertisements for the album in national music-related magazines. One ad bannered the headline "Don't Give Up. Discover the power of positive playing" and concluded, "Andraé Crouch's new music is for everyone with a taste for tunes they can sing, strut and shout along with. It's called spirit." Conspicuous in its absence in the advertisement was any reference to faith or religion. The LP received a coveted "Featured review" in the "New Album Releases" page in the "Soul" section:

> Is it gospel? Certainly not in the traditional sense—even by contemporary gospel standards. What we have here is an album filled with positive message tunes that one might expect George Benson or Stevie Wonder to record. There is, of course, Crouch's distinctive gospel flavoring. There are tunes like "Hollywood Scene" where the only connection with the gospel field is the artist singing it. Crouch, who wrote or cowrote all but one tune, uses a powerful horn section and background singers who complement his vocals with tight, smooth harmonies. This LP is as much pop as it is gospel. Best Cuts: At least seven of the nine are excellent.

Elsewhere, the first single release from the album, "Start All Over Again," with a writing credit by Marvin Winans, also received a generous promotional push:

> Although Crouch's popularity has been predominantly in the gospel field, this Warner debut should spread his appeal to secular audiences. Crouch's strong voice is supported by female harmonies and while the midtempo track has a sermon-like quality, it is nonetheless a commercial r&b tune.[9]

The album also received a coveted "Hits Out of the Box" designation in *Cash Box*'s review of the album, noting the "special spirit and energy" of the "Christian-oriented . . . but in a subtle-way material." The reviewer also raved about the "brilliantly arranged R&B/Pop/Gospel fusion that should attract listeners all around the dial" and that *Don't Give Up* could be "the Gospel breakthrough that the secular market has been waiting for." The review tabbed "Waiting for the Son" and the "raucous and foreboding R&B rave up 'Hollywood Scene'" as the most likely singles. However, in the "Feature Picks" of the "Single Reviews" section, the first single choice, "Start All Over Again," received a decidedly less optimistic review.[10]

One significant difference with virtually all previous gospel LPs, including Andraé's, was the appearance of a review in the influential *Variety* entertainment newspaper, which noted that Crouch, while continuing to record gospel for Light Records, was targeting a different audience with his first "major" label release. "Crouch expresses a deeply felt spiritual commitment in a variety of soul and pop/jazz contexts here," the uncredited review states, "and may succeed in getting significant airplay for the Christian message with songs like 'Hollywood Scene' and 'Handwriting on the Wall.'"[11]

Don't Give Up's packaging, however, was fairly generic, especially when compared to Light's visually arresting album jackets. Andraé is photographed in a wide-lapeled white suit with pink shirt on the cover, faintly smiling at the camera. On the back is a photo of Crouch taken on a cliffside in Santa Monica overlooking the ocean.

The album sleeve, printed white on black, lists the dozens of musicians who contributed to the project with Crouch and Bill Maxwell and contains the lyrics to the songs. Many of the same musicians from the previous LPs returned for the *Don't Give Up* sessions: Hadley Hockensmith and Dean Parks (guitars), Abraham Laboriel (bass), and Joe Sample (keyboards). Several well-known newcomers, including Steve Porcaro (synthesizer), David Paich (keyboards), Louis Johnson (bass), Greg Phillinganes (keyboards), and Phil Keaggy (guitar), also made significant contributions. Vocals were provided by a large group of singers, many of whom had already toured and recorded extensively with Andraé: Maxine Anderson, James Felix, Tommy Funderburk, Tammie Gibson, Alfred McCrary, Linda McCrary, Howard McCrary, Phyllis St. James (vocal coordinator), Alphanette (Alfie) Silas, Howard Smith, and former COGIC Edna Wright, along with members of the Winans family (Carvin, Marvin, Michael, Ronald, and CeCe) on several tracks.

"You" Songs

Despite the fears of some in the gospel community, words, and concepts integral to Crouch's Christian faith appear on virtually every song throughout the album. The lyrics "Waiting for the Son" were strongly religious and nearly all of the songs had some Christian terminology: "Don't Give Up" ("Father," "Lord"), "I Can't Keep It to Myself" ("God"), "Hollywood Scene" ("God"), "Handwriting on the Wall" ("Lord"), and "Start Over Again" ("Lord"). Lyrically, "Save the People" would have fit on any previous Andraé album. Unlike earlier Crouch LPs, however, there is no direct reference or mention of "Jesus" or "Jesus Christ," the direct focus of most of his previous compositions. This "lyrical ambiguity," as one writer termed it, reflected on the practice by some gospel and contemporary Christian music artists to write "you" lyrics— songs where a capital "Y" in "you" meant that the singer was singing to God or Jesus. Without the capital "Y," of course, it could have been a pop radio love song. Claudrena Harold traces Crouch's use of "you" songs back to "Quiet Times" and "Perfect Peace," but said that the practice occurs most often on *Don't Give Up*.[12]

The *Don't Give Up* Sessions

In the nearly two years of sometimes intense studio sessions leading up to the release of *Don't Give Up*, none of the musicians was likely aware of the tempest that was to come. Instead, most eagerly jumped at the opportunity to again record with Andraé, including Laboriel, who had quickly become a much in-demand studio bassist. "Whenever Bill Maxwell called, I had to say 'yes,'" Laboriel said, "because it is an appointment with the Lord. And the first thing that would happen is that we would pray in general, then pray for specific needs that people had." In his forty years as session musician, Laboriel said he has not encountered another producer who was simultaneously able to both play an instrument *and* serve as producer like Maxwell. "It is an uncanny ability Bill has," he said, "because somehow while playing he could keep track of what all of us were doing and make suggestions that were appropriate at the end of the first take. And then sometimes, we were so in tune that he would keep the first take." Laboriel said that because of Maxwell's extensive preparation for each song, the number of takes, at least in the rhythm section's sessions, were minimal. "Bill always made sure that we as a rhythm section would express our first impressions," Laboriel said. "He tried very hard to keep those first impressions in order to keep the performances fresh and exciting. In Hollywood, they have this terrible saying, 'Let's keep playing it until we get past it'—or, until there is no music left in the song. Bill never believed in that approach" (Image 14.2).[13]

Howard McCrary said informal auditions for singers for *Don't Give Up* were conducted over several months as Crouch searched for the exact voices he heard for each song. "Andraé surrounded himself with amazing talent," Howard said, "but he didn't take any prisoners. You came and auditioned and sang 'Precious Lord, Take My Hand.'" But if Andraé didn't "hear" the connection, he could be abrupt in his dismissal. "He'd say, 'All right. We'll see you later. Don't let the door hit you on the way out.' It's not because of his ego, but because the songs were so important to him. And the vessels that had to bring the message had to be the best there was." Tammie Gibson said that, like Stevie Wonder, Crouch was very demanding when it came to his background vocalists. "All of us had to sing soprano, C over high C," she said. "All of us had to sing contralto. All of us could sing tenor. You had to be able to sing all ranges and very quickly understand what the process of a blend was to make it work while recording." Gibson said that Andraé particularly enjoyed working with Linda and Howard McCrary because, as siblings, they possessed an innate understanding of vocal training and ability in the studio. "Andraé was a stickler for your blend," she said. "He would bring out the very best in you. He always took the time to say, 'Let's identify what we should do and how we should go about doing it.'"[14]

Phyllis St. James said that her strongest memory of *Don't Give Up* is that during the "intermittent sessions at his home studio" she came to understand that virtually every song on the album had an intensely personal connection. "Andraé could look at people and his antenna just wired into them," she said. "Every song on the album is connected with somebody. It wasn't just 'Hollywood Scene' or 'I'll Be Good to You, Baby'—he's talking about somebody. It's not just a concept he came up with. It relates to a real flesh-and-blood person."[15]

There was one other significant difference between *Don't Give Up* and everything that had gone before. Maxwell said that none of the songs on the LP had been "crafted in front of audiences," unlike most earlier releases. "Previously, they'd been tried out—and none of these had been tried out," he said. Until

```
                    TODAY IS:  Wednesday, October 8, 1980

      DEPARTURE                    ARRIVAL                GROUND TRANSPORTATION

                   NON-TRAVEL DAY



      SURFACE MILES_____-0-_____          TIME CHANGE_____None_____


      FACILITY                 OPENING ARTIST(S)              PROMOTER
                                                        DAN FIALA
   SPOKANE COLISEUM              HUEY LEWIS &            TOM HULETT
   1101 Howard Street            THE NEWS               (206) 455-9160
   Spokane, Washington



           CAPACITY_____9,000_____        SHOWTIME_____8:00_____
           SEATING_____G.A._____          D.B._____9:15_____


                                   HOTEL

   BAND & BAND CREW:           RAMADA INN
                               Spokane Internation Airport
                               Spokane, Washington 99219
                               (509) 838-5211
                               Bee Jay Hatch
```

Image 14.2 Daily travel log for October 8, 1980, with Huey Lewis and the News as the opening act. Courtesy of Perry Morgan.

now, most of Crouch's songs had been workshopped in real time, with Andraé carefully gauging each audience's response to the in-progress compositions. Maxwell said that half-finished songs might be completed in the studio—but not on the stage.[16]

But while *Don't Give Up* is secularized with pop sounds, Andraé's approach is still worshipful, even if that spirituality isn't always readily apparent. Those who knew him best suggested to the authors that by this point in his career, he had felt creatively restricted by Light Records' protocols, both cultural and financial. Even at this early stage, it appears that Crouch's relentless need to innovate was increasingly dissatisfied with the sameness of what was already becoming the norm in what was beginning to be called praise & worship services—a genre he had helped establish. As theologian D. H. Tripp suggests:

> The practice of worship, not least when it has passed the stage of thrilled discovery, and moved into the realm of dryness and boredom, is a process in which the participants grow through the repeated alignment of their being with the vectors of faith.[17]

It is clear from his interviews in support of the album that Crouch felt he *had* to move to Warner Bros. as an act of faith—he needed, he said, to rediscover "rediscovery." As a worshipper and artist, he was compelled to move from his increasing sense of spiritual dryness to a renewal and he wanted to act on the "vectors" of his faith: Christian scripture, the COGIC tradition, practical evangelism, and his personal journey as a believer. Andraé found that freedom through *Don't Give Up*.

However, in doing so, he ceded away much of his distinctive input in the music itself. *Don't Give Up* is the product of what the authors call the "Crouch Creative Team." The engineering, mixing, all-star rhythm section, synthesizer programming, and rhythm chart arrangements add an even higher level of sophisticated orchestration to the music, just as it generates different combinations of funk, pop, jazz, R&B, Motown, and grassroots gospel in the vocals. The influence of these genres, along with the work of Herbie Hancock, the Crusaders, Marvin Gaye, Stevie Wonder, Earth, Wind & Fire—and yes, Steely Dan—are strongly felt through the album's tracks. But more than any LP before it, Maxwell (and others) assert that these songs were co-composed with the instrumentalists, vocalists, and array of top-flight arrangers. And, as Maxwell noted earlier, unlike previous releases, these songs were not honed and crafted in front of audiences. The overall result, the authors believe, is less Andraé himself than what listeners have heard in more than decade. At the same time, this deep level and depth of collaboration with "outside" artists and arrangements was twenty years ahead of its time in the gospel music industry.[18]

Don't Give Up

Side I

"Waiting for the Son"

With "Waiting for the Son," Andraé plays with the words "son" and "sun," "sunshine" and "Son shining," in yet another song that celebrates what Crouch believes is the imminent return of Jesus. The song's impressively modal jazz-flavored opening progressions (D-minor 11th, E-augmented 7th with a sharp 9th, B♭ chord superimposed over an A♭ in the bass, A♭ major 7th with a bass pattern outlining the chord) finally resolve in the highly sophisticated F-Lydian jazz scale, a sound-world that fans of progressive jazz artists Weather Report or Return to Forever would immediately recognize. This adventuresome harmonic progression represents something outside what even Crouch has presented before—and announces to all listeners that this isn't your grandmother's gospel music! And yet, this is more than showy virtuosity for its own sake; it is unmistakable that his intent is to reach people who do not listen to gospel music. Perhaps more than any previous album, *Don't Give Up* explores new and different keys and tonalities.

By this stage in Andraé's career, Maxwell said he tried to record Crouch's complicated and continually evolving background vocal parts first "because then that let you know what you could do with the rest of the arrangement to fill in." For the first time, the session was contracted through the union, with St. James coordinating the vocalists. "We spent a fortune on background vocals," Maxwell said. "It was something like $50,000 just on background vocals because you're getting to pay for each 'stack' and Andraé would keep you there all day. It was like a party for him, having all those vocalists try this, try that." Fortunately, with Warner Bros., the studio budget was much higher than previous albums. Many of the vocalists, including Linda McCrary had worked with Crouch through multiple tours and recordings and knew what he was looking for. During the recording sessions for "Waiting for the Son," she said that she remembered Crouch using colors to help the singers understand the sounds he was hearing in his head. "I remember that 'Waiting for the Son' was definitely a 'yellow' sound," she said. "He was very adamant about this great expression of the sun and if you listen to it, you can feel it. He would pull stuff out of his heart and that's how he would get it there with us, to give us the example." McCrary said that with each song, Andraé was keenly aware of whom he wanted to reach. "He dug deeper than the surface of just a beautiful voice," she said. "He wanted the purity of your soul inside the music he was creating to reach people. That was his whole thing—he wanted to reach people for Christ."

McCrary said that Andraé's passion for his faith permeated every aspect of the sessions, whether they were at the much larger Paramount Recording Studio on busy Santa Monica Boulevard or the smaller, more intimate Mama Jo's. "The vibes in the studio were so amazing," she said. "The Holy Spirit would come in all of the time when we would do stuff. At the end of the day, we would sit back and listen and just praise God. I just thank God I was even chosen to be in connection with a man like this."[19]

Like his sister Linda, Howard McCrary said he remains in awe of Andraé's ability to craft music and a mood to match the lyrics on a song like "Waiting for the Son." "That was the thing about Andraé," he said, "you never could put him in a box. He always thought outside the box: a little calypso here, a little jazz there. This song has a tropical feel to it, almost Brazilian. And, of course, the best one to convey that was [bassist]Abraham Laboriel. Abraham not only plays the music, he *is* the music."

Marvin Winans said that he's long felt that "Waiting for the Son" "doesn't get its due" in Andraé's catalogue. "Watch the melody," Winans said, "[the] background coming in . . . those little things . . . Abraham Laboriel driving that bass. And then the idea of doubling his lead, singing in one pass and then doing the exact same thing the second time—the Winans borrowed all of that."[20]

"Don't Give Up"

The title track "Don't Give Up" features a duet between Andraé and Edna Wright, one of the quartet of talented vocalists from his first group, the COGICs. After leaving the COGICs, Wright's career included masterful backup vocals for such diverse artists as Andy Williams, the Righteous Bros., Ray Charles, Cher, Michael Jackson, the Beach Boys, and many others. With the Honey Cone in 1971, she enjoyed a number one hit with "Want Ads." Even while touring in support of "Want Ads," Wright returned regularly to her father's church, King's Holiness Chapel, where she told *Jet* that she worked with the young people in the congregation.[21]

Howard McCrary said that "Don't Give Up" was written specifically to inspire the Blacks of South Africa, still in the throes of fighting for their freedom under apartheid. "He chose a shuffle for this one," Howard recalled: "'Don't give up, stand and fight for what you know is right.' That line came out of the blue in a vamp we were doing. We were singing in English, but it didn't sound like it." To convey these sentiments, "Don't Give Up" (in the key of A♭ major), Tom Keene's radio-friendly arrangement uses horns and flutes to accentuate the slappin' bass guitar and punchy drums in the mix. In response, Andrae's impassioned vocals range from conversational to what is essentially an urgent falsetto as the background vocalists vamp out repeating "everything's gonna be all right." "Don't Give Up" features Crouch's first "ghost" reprise of the chorus, sung with just drums, bass, synthesizer, and vocals.[22] Ultimately, it is crafted to move a listener from passive hope for the future to actively participate in God's kingdom. Writer Sharleen Kato suggests that the song is a call to Christians to share the gospel message with what Crouch believes is a "broken and hurting world."[23]

"I Can't Keep It to Myself"

"I Can't Keep It to Myself," performed with an E♭ key signature (though the closing vamp switches to G-minor), opens and closes with strong female group vocals. Lead vocalist Howard Smith said he remembered when "I Can't Keep It to Myself" first emerged one evening at Andraé's house on Wells Drive. "I remember a few of us singing around the piano as he wrote this," Smith said. "We're kind of noodling around on stuff. We were thinking, 'Philly sound, Stylistics, Delfonics, that whole Thom Bell kind of vibe.' The whole time we're talking, we're all singing, all throwing stuff out and he pulls it together and he comes out with an idea of a song. And that's how we ended up with the falsetto approach to that song." Smith said that Crouch listened intently to the popular music of the era, especially Steely Dan. "In all of those songs, all of those sounds, you can hear—I can hear—his influences," he said. The mix and mastering of the instruments and vocals especially in the vamp on this and other songs is expressly designed to mimic classic Steely Dan—the chunky chords on the Rhodes, the staccato plucking of the guitars and bass, and the deep groove of the drums all prepare the way for the trademark horn blasts that complement the vocals. "If you go back in your mind now, you'll hear it." As for Marvin Winans, when asked about the "totality" of *Don't Give Up*, he flatly declared, "That was his Steely Dan days."[24]

"Hollywood Scene"

"Hollywood Scene," in E♭, is a collaboration with frequent Michael Jackson guitarist David Williams and reflects Crouch's admiration of Earth, Wind &

Fire. With its vibrant synthesizer lines, the strong rhythm section propels the vocals as Andraé sings some of the most controversial and challenging lyrics of his career. Vinesong ministry's John Watson said he was at Crouch's house when Andraé returned one evening from the recording studio. "Andraé told me, 'I've got to have one more song for the album and they're all waiting for me in the morning,'" Watson recalled. The two talked for a time before the discussion turned to the sad array of male prostitutes standing on the streets each day near the studio. It was then that the phrase "Young and clean on the Hollywood scene" emerged. "I said, 'Quickly, sit at your piano,'" Watson said. "I said, 'Be relevant. What is it that you see on Hollywood Boulevard?'" Crouch sat at his piano and "straight away" wrote the song. "Then he fell asleep," Watson said, "because God had given him another song."[25]

Soprano Maxine Anderson, who had been recruited by St. James, had done some vocal arranging prior to working with Crouch and said her experience in the studio with him "expanded" her knowledge of the craft. But even more revelatory was Andraé's ability to incorporate what he saw into song that could come together in a single day, such as "Hollywood Scene." *Don't Give Up*, she said, was "so far ahead before its time and people didn't accept it or receive it well." "They were upset with him and thought that he was not really dealing with Christian things," Anderson said, "but he'd always been sensitive to those issues."

Anderson said that when she and the other singers heard some of the lyrics, especially "Hollywood Scene" and "I'll Be Good to You, Baby," they expected pushback from some segments of his audience. "We all knew that," she said, "because we knew that Andraé was *before* his time. Especially, on that particular album, people weren't ready for it and didn't understand what he was saying. He was groundbreaking. He knew he was going to get criticism, but that's why he was put here."

"Andraé got a lot of flak for that song," Maxwell said. "He felt like this was his chance to make an album for the people, not the church—and that's not who his audience was." [26]

Side II

"Handwriting on the Wall"

Set to a Clavinet-heavy funk-jazz arrangement by Motown veteran Jerry Peters, and in the key of C minor, "Handwriting on the Wall" boasts a melodious, danceable five-note sonic hook, reminiscent of the fat Parliament/

Funkadelic chorus sound. Midway through the song, the singers invite both family members and the community to shout to others, "There's a handwriting on the wall." In doing so, Crouch returns to his perennial theme that the Lord will soon return and redeem humanity. For the recording sessions for "Handwriting on the Wall," Linda McCrary recalled that Andraé relentlessly searched for a certain sound with the vocalists. "He just sent three of us in and said, 'Sing this and do it eight times,'" she said. "Then he'd pick another three singers and he'd say, 'You know what, I need to put octaves on that,' [especially on] 'Handwriting on the Wall,' which was a really fiery piece. Or he'd say, 'Linda, sing this and double and triple and quadruple it—and then I want everybody to follow that.'" It also marked, Maxwell said, the recording debut of CeCe Winans, who also tripled her unison and octave parts.[27]

"I Love Walking with You"

The soft, slow lullaby for *Don't Give Up* is "I Love Walking with You." In F major, the arrangement suggests a tropical island feel in its warm, gentle interplay among Phil Keaggy (electric guitar) and Abraham Laboriel (acoustic guitar) and Dorothy Ashby's *glissandos* on harp. The singers who would be credited as "background vocalists" on most albums (Phyllis St. James, Tammie Gibson, Alfie Silas, and, unusually, Andraé himself) actually take the lead here, singing lyrics that speak to a personal relationship with Jesus Christ, celebrating the simple joys of walking, talking, and singing together. "I Love Walking with You" is one of the very few songs in Crouch's entire catalogue that does not feature keyboards.

"Save the People"

One of the most striking aspects of the up-tempo "Save the People" (in the key E♭/B♭) is the unabashedly synthesized-driven disco beat, but one coupled with a manic New Wave intensity. Few songs have had the benefit of Steve Porcaro's early mastery of synthesizer programming, Greg Phillinganes's piano (already noted for his work with Michael Jackson), Maxwell's rock-steady beat, and a bass line as propulsive as this one by Laboriel. The vocals are a duet between Crouch and Wright, whose distinctive voices are bracketed by a strong male trio of Howard Smith, James Felix, and Tommy Funderburke. Andraé returns to scripture for the lyrics, using the story of the disciple Peter's misadventure of trying to walk on water to illustrate the need for believers to keep their eyes fixed on Jesus.

"I'll Be Good to You, Baby (A Message to the Silent Victims)"

Crouch follows "Save the People" with an abrupt about-face in tempo and attack. Without the lyrics, "I'll Be Good to You, Baby," which hovers on the key of B♭ minor, intentionally sounds like a slow dance pop song for romantic couples. But the gentle and light jazzy sound belies the message of the lyrics, focusing on an issue that was tacitly considered taboo in Christian music circles—abortion. Beginning with the cries of a baby, the haunting instrumental accompaniment support lyrics that paint a picture of both a God who cries *for* unborn children and the unborn children who cry *to* God.

Looking back on *Don't Give Up* from the lens of forty years, Linda McCrary said that she was still frustrated that so many people, particularly in the church, "missed" the point of "I'll Be Good to You, Baby"—that it was not in favor of abortion. "He had a personal friend who had aborted a baby," she recalled. "A lot of people came against him on that song. He was writing what was in his heart." The authors believe that in the final sixty seconds of the outro, Crouch sings and speaks an imaginary musical dialogue where God assures these children that "I'll be good to you, baby."[28]

"Start All Over Again"

The album closes with "Start All Over Again," returning, once again, to the theme of the need for a personal relationship with Jesus Christ. Marvin Winans's lyrics speak the first-person voice of a believer who has strayed in their relationship, posing the question: "Should I stay on my faith journey or turn away?" Winans suggests that the act of remembering that lost closeness, including the intimacy of morning and evening prayers, will prompt a welcome return. Winans said that "Start All Over Again" was a song he and his brothers had written and performed before singing it for Andraé at one of the album's recording sessions, where Crouch immediately loved it. "We had a different vibe that went with it," Winans said, "and Andraé just made it more Andraé." The background vocals, as was often the case, were worked out in the studio. "Back then, we were doing two, three, four takes," he said, "and even as we sang the background, there was no such thing as singing one and then flying throughout. The backgrounds actually got better as the song progressed."[29]

Maxwell said that the song was recorded "live" in Paramount Studio and featured instrumentation by David Williams, Sample, Laboriel, and Parks. He then overdubbed Andraé's vocals. "Then we overdubbed the synthesizers with

Greg Phillinganes," Maxwell said, "then harp and percussion. Then we recorded the background vocals and finally replaced Andraé's lead with a better performance."[30]

Musically, hovering in the keys of G major/E minor, "Start All Over Again" highlights Winans's distinctive harmonic language and progressions. Ultimately, these chord progressions, which follow and support the lyrics' five questions, create something that sounds much more like a Winans song than a Crouch song. Even so, "Start All Over Again" again declares Andrae's passion for reconciliation amid the chaos and turmoil reflected in *Don't Give Up*'s lyrics. And, because of that, the song closes the LP with an expression of hope, rather than despair.

Reception

In the Black religious community, the reception to *Don't Give Up*'s songs about abortion and street hustlers ranged from outraged to incredulous. As for Andraé—at least publicly—he said that level of response was predictable. "Every album I've done has been controversial," he told one writer. Despite the prospect of future all-gospel albums for Light, he said he had regularly been condemned from the conservative pulpits of African American churches. Even as Crouch tried to make a distinction between his gospel albums and his Warner Bros. LPs, he admitted that he knew in advance that the decision to record some of these songs would cost him fans and sales. "Light has a certain exposure and it would be like trying to sell snow skis in Honolulu," he said. "I feel this album has the potential to reach a different kind of person than the Light Records audience." Andraé told Cary Darling that some of *Don't Give Up*'s songs had been several years in the making. "It's not anything new to me," he said. "It's just time for me to say it." The choice of the more religiously oriented "Start All Over Again" as the first single was an effort to avoid "creating a gap between his gospel and pop areas," Warner Bros.' Tom Draper said. However, the second projected single, "Hollywood Scene," with its depiction of desperate young street people, was almost guaranteed to cause an uproar, despite the redemptive nature of the chorus. The song's lyrics were "prompted," Crouch said, by what he saw on the streets of Hollywood each morning during the recording process at Paramount Studios. "So many people have put them down and said God has written them off," Andraé said. Another difficulty arose in that *Don't*

Give Up was released nearly two years after Crouch's previous album, in part, he said, because of his nonstop touring schedule. "I'm glad for it because different ideas came and I've changed," he said. "If I was still doing it, I would probably put another song and take another off." As for the presence of pop music stars like members of Toto and Louis Johnson on some of the tracks, Andraé said that it came about not because he was looking for "star power," but because one musician would enjoy the process so much that he would invite another. "Louis Johnson said he accepted Christ through my last album," Crouch said, "so when we called him, he wanted to do it." Andraé's critics had condemned his earlier releases as well, to the point that one "Christian" magazine accused him of "going disco" on "Perfect Peace." "People are so surprised to hear the name of 'Jesus' on this album," he said. "They thought Warner Bros. wasn't going to let me say 'Jesus.' Warners said, 'Hey, we like the way you make records. Just bring us the finished copy.' They didn't come down and listen. They just told me to be Andraé Crouch."[31]

Liturgy

And yet—almost magically—pressed into the entire opus is what the authors believe appears to be a liturgical format:

> *Introit*: "Waiting for the Son"
> *Sermon*: "Don't Give Up"
> *Testimony*: "I Can't Keep It to Myself"
> *Prophetic Warnings*: "Hollywood Scene," "Handwriting on the Wall"
> *Prayer Song*: "I Love Walking with You"
> *Laments*: "Save the People," "I'll Be Good to You, Baby"
> *Call to Discipleship*: "Start All Over Again"

A Misstep?

But despite the first of several appearances as both a cohost and a performer on TV's popular *Mike Douglas Entertainment Hour*, Crouch's *Don't Give Up* only debuted at #35 on the "Best-Selling Spiritual LPs" chart in December 1981. It debuted at #59 on the "Best-Selling Soul LPs" chart on November 7, rose to #52 a week later, then fell rapidly until it was off the chart by December. When the single "Start Over Again" never charted, Warner Bros. then released

"Hollywood Scene." It too never charted and barely received a mention in *Billboard*'s "Top Single Picks" in the "Pop" category on December 5.[32]

As 1981 drew to a close, whatever success—or lack of it—Crouch was experiencing in the secular sales charts did not impact his national visibility. Andraé was one of several artists, including the Commodores and the Pointer Sisters, featured on singer Mac Davis's NBC special *Christmas Is a Song*. Filmed at Pasadena's "opulently beautiful" First United Methodist Church, the *Hollywood Reporter* reviewer enthused that Andraé "really knows how to rally a crowd into a spirited mood."[33]

But a less jolly appraisal of the rush by the various secular labels to embrace and distribute gospel music emerged at *Billboard*'s second "Gospel Music Conference" in December. One religious exec said that his label had experienced "minimal" sales gains from the arrangement. Other religious label heads noted a similar lack of results. Likewise, they said, secular labels had "no idea" how to "make the most" of the gospel copyrights they had inherited with their deals with gospel labels. In an effort to boost sales, Light's Ralph Carmichael said that Andraé Crouch would "re-record some of his albums in Spanish" and those LPs would be marketed in Spanish-speaking markets. But the primary issue noted by multiple panelists at the conference was that "theological purists remain unwilling to compromise with the demands of the secular marketplace," which resulted in splits between "the spiritual and secular elements" and "among avowedly Christian artists and entrepreneurs." On an artists' panel, James Cleveland took the opportunity to, again, say that Andraé's appearance earlier that year on *Saturday Night Live* "wouldn't have been right for me." Cleveland, who had appeared earlier in 1981 with Elton John and Olivia Newton-John, claimed that he was not "criticizing" Crouch for doing so, however. Crouch, who was on the same panel, took a different approach:

> We have a great responsibility to speak the Word. We are in a great position. We may have to speak Chinese or have a harder drumbeat, but we have to get the word out. People ask me if I'll lose any of my old fans with my new album. I tell them that I'm not losing as many as the church is losing now.

In what may have been a direct dig at Andraé and the songs on *Don't Give Up*, "someone" on one of the panels, Edward Morris writes, "suggested" that "writers should not hedge their bets and look for crossover by substituting 'he' or 'you' for 'God' so that a devotional song might be acceptable as a love song."[34]

The pointed, sometimes hostile, comments would become worse in the days ahead. In major feature in *Ebony* magazine, a writer noted Andraé's Mercedes-Benz, his "lavish" home in "exclusive" Woodland Hills, his condominium, and a "devoted, racially mixed entourage constantly jockeying for his attention." While the writer admits that Crouch is "remarkably unaffected by all this show biz hoopla," he asks Andraé about the "resistance" he's faced from his "beloved church members" who say that with *Don't Give Up* he's gone "too far" with his music and lyrics:

> Sometimes the church wants you to stay the same. But the Bible says for us to "go into the world and preach the gospel." So what do all those good church people think that means? To keep pouring water into the ocean? The ocean already has plenty of water. We need to pour some of that precious water into some dry spots.

Like many writers before him, writer Walter Burrell could not resist asking Crouch about Cleveland ("Cleveland has his place," Crouch responded. "There's room in the body of Christ for all of us. There's always a need.") and Cleveland about Crouch ("Our paths seldom cross mainly because Andraé's audiences are 50 to 70 percent white while mine are 95 percent Black," Cleveland said. "In the long run, I think his exposure is helpful for all of us gospel artists.")

As for the criticism from the Black church, Andraé wryly responded, "sometimes Christians are the ones to stab their wounded."[35]

A Different Reception Among Musicians

But for those who knew him best, *Don't Give Up* was a logical expression for an artist who had always fought to expand gospel's horizons, not calcify them. "With this album, Andraé was trying to reach more people in the secular world," Linda McCrary said, "not that he was trying to be secular, but he was trying to crossover to that." The success in multiple markets of *I'll Be Thinking of You*, she said, had emboldened him to continue attempting to further his music's reach. "He never really, really, really stayed inside the box, even with the COGICs," McCrary said. "A lot of people in the COGIC world didn't like what he was doing, but he was following the Word of God. If God is speaking to you and you're listening [then] you are writing what your heart is telling you." Even the title of the album, *Don't Give Up*, she said, was as much written to himself as to his audience. "He was struggling with the church," she said. "He was going through a lot. He was saying, 'Don't give up. Stand and fight for what you know is right.'" Laboriel is another musician who still holds the album in high regard. "It's an album about affirming what we have always known about the Lord," Laboriel said, "that nothing can separate you from the love of God."[36]

Looking back on the project, Winans, who was closely involved in the album, said that the word "bravery" still comes to mind. "And a willingness to push the envelope," he added. "With gospel music, there are rails. There are confines. There's a radius that you have to stay in. And I think it was very brave to try and deal with the *Roe v. Wade* decision." But in the end, *Don't Give Up*'s sales in both the secular and religious marketplaces were "lackluster" at best and none of the singles charted or made any headway on Black radio.[37]

Don't Give Up on Tour

It quickly became obvious that few of the songs from the album "worked" in the subsequent tours supporting *Don't Give Up.* Maxwell said they tried opening with "Waiting for the Son," including at a date in Radio City Music Hall. When the song ended, the audience "barely" applauded. "It was like, 'What is he trying to do?'" Maxwell said. "Andraé knew he had to get them back, so we'd go with 'Jesus Is the Answer' and the things that would get the audience back." A few songs, including "It's Gonna Rain" and the title track, did engage audiences. "Only because Andraé would really sell it," Maxwell said. "He'd say, 'don't give up no matter what you're going through—you've got to rely on the Lord' and have them singing. But the rest of the songs dropped off [the playlist] pretty quickly." And some songs, including "Handwriting on the Wall," "Save the People," and "I Can't Keep It to Myself," were never performed live. "Those songs didn't work, really, with the audiences," Maxwell said. "They were not crafted for that."[38]

As for Crouch himself, several years later he still maintained that the album was his "favorite," even though being a "pioneer" means you "get all the kicks." "Sometimes I feel like a journeyman in an apprentice position," he said. "What I feel and really see put me too far ahead."[39]

Ultimately, Maxwell said, *Don't Give Up* "bombed." "It just didn't do well," he said. "I believed in the project. But I didn't realize how great 'I'll Be Good to You, Baby' was until Andraé's funeral [in 2015]." Maxwell said that producer/songwriter Tommy Sims cornered him in the back of the church during the services:

> Tommy said, "Let me play you something" and he started playing and singing to me, "I'll Be Good to You, Baby." He just sang his heart and I listened to it harmonically. He said, "People don't get this." He was really right. Tommy said, "I understood what you guys were trying to do."[40]

With the knowledge of everything that's happened in gospel music since 1982, *Don't Give Up* directly confronts listeners with Andraé's almost single-minded quest to explore new cultural issues with his lyrics, as well as new musical sounds and horizons.

The authors believe that despite the negative reception afforded *Don't Give Up*, Crouch was at the vanguard of a new genre, fusing different, sometimes widely varied, genres. Black musical stylings in pop music, Black gospel music in secular liturgies such as jazz, as well as Black praise & worship in liturgies in the marketplace, all paved the way for still *more* fusion where hip-hop, neo-soul gospel and other hybrids would soon become normative. These musical stylings provided fresh new locations for African Americans in particular to both praise *and* worship God.

The authors believe that Crouch essentially saw *Don't Give Up* as his praise offering on behalf of the people of God. More than with any other release, Andraé is sharing the stories of other people in his compositions. In this, and other ways, Crouch's praise is creative. Worship is for God alone because—as Andraé sings—God doesn't give up on God's people.

NOTES

1. "We Wish to Congratulate Our Artists on Their Recent Grammy Nominations," *Billboard*, January 31, 1981, 17; https://www.rollingstone.com/music/music-lists/50-greatest-bassists-of-all-time-1003022; Bill Maxwell, personal correspondence with the authors, January 20, 2023; Bill Maxwell, interview with the authors, April 4, 2023.
2. "Gospel on the Grammys," *Billboard*, February 21, 1981, 44; Paul Grein, "Cross Collects 5 Grammys in Major Upset," *Billboard*, March 7, 1981, 3, 8; "Gospel Grammy Winners," *Record World*, March 21, 1981, 47.

SOON & VERY SOON

3. Gail Williams, "Don't Look Back," *Hollywood Reporter*, June 1, 1981, 9; Paul Grein, "Robinson's Career: A Study in Stability," *Billboard*, June 20, 1981, 40.

4. Abraham Laboriel, interview with the authors, October 28, 2021.

5. "Crouch in Fest," *Billboard*, May 23, 1981, 71; "Crouch Wins NARAM Award," *Record World*, June 20, 1981, 47; "Concerts & Clubs," *Hollywood Reporter*, August 6, 1981, 11; Jean Williams, "In Pasadena Rose Bowl: 50,000 Attend 1st BMA Family Fair," *Billboard*, August 29, 1981, 36, 64.

6. Jean Williams, "Polygram and Simmons Deal Snagged," *Billboard*, August 8, 1981, 53–54; "Warner Bros. Bows Major Promotion for Crouch Album," *Cash Box*, October 3, 1981, 16; "Light Records Pacts with E/A," *Record World*, October 3, 1981, 6.

7. Bill Maxwell, interview with the authors, May 18, 2019; Bill Maxwell, interview with the authors, February 24, 2023.

8. "WB Tries to Break Crouch via Regular Commercial Avenues," *Variety*, October 21, 1981, 89; Rose Clayton, "Stars Book Themselves: Underground Network Helps Promote Live Talent," *Billboard*, October 3, 1981, 18; Robert K. Oermann, "Barriers Fall as Black Gospel Eyes Pop Venues," *Billboard*, October 3, 1991, G-33.

9. "Don't Give Up," *Billboard*, October 10, 1981, 108; "Top Album Picks," *Billboard*, October 10, 1981, 88; "Top Single Picks," *Billboard*, October 10, 1981, 98.

10. "Album Reviews: Hits Out of the Box," *Cash Box*, October 10, 1981, 13; "Singles Reviews, Feature Picks," *Cash Box*, October 17, 1981, 9.

11. "Record Reviews: Albums," *Variety*, October 21, 1981, 89; "Don't Give Up," *Cash Box*, October 24, 1981, 96.

12. Howard Smith, interview with the authors, August 31, 2021; *Don't Give Up*, Andraé Crouch (Warner Bros. Records BSK 3513); Claudrena R. Harold, *When Sunday Comes: Gospel Music in the Soul and Hip-Hop Eras* (Urbana: University of Illinois Press, 2020), 56.

13. Abraham Laboriel, interview with the authors, August 19, 2021.

14. Howard McCrary, interview with the authors, February 18, 2022; Tammie Gibson, interview with the authors, December 28, 2020.

15. Phyllis St. James, interview with the authors, January 23, 2021.

16. Bill Maxwell, interview with the authors, April 4, 2023

17. D. H. Tripp, "Liturgy and Pastoral Service," in *The Study of Liturgy*, ed. Cheslyn Jones, Geoffrey Wainwright, Edward Yarnold SJ, and Paul Bradshaw, rev. ed. (London: Oxford University Press, 1992), 582.

18. Bill Maxwell, interview with the authors, April 4, 2023.

19. Bill Maxwell, interview with the authors, April 4, 2023; Linda McCrary, interview with the authors, August 19, 2021.

20. Howard McCrary, interview with the authors, February 18, 2022; Marvin Winans, interview with the authors, December 8, 2020.

21. Cordell S. Thompson, "Edna Wright Got to Spend Her Life Singing: Honey Cone Trio Finds It Pays to Advertise," *Jet*, September 2, 1971, 56–60; David

Henckley, "Edna Wright Got to Spend Her Life Singing, Put That in the 'Want Ads,'" *The Culture Corner,* September 13, 2020.

22. Howard McCrary, interview with the authors, February 18, 2022; "Don't Give Up" by Andraé Crouch, Lexicon Music, Inc., courtesy of Capitol CMG.

23. Sharleen Kato, interview with the authors, March 2023.

24. Howard Smith, interview with the authors, August 31, 2021; Marvin Winans, interview with the authors, December 8, 2020.

25. John Watson, interview with the authors, October 6, 2021.

26. Maxi Anderson, interview with the authors, October 30, 2020; Bill Maxwell, interview with the authors, April 4, 2023.

27. Linda McCrary, interview with the authors, August 19, 2021; Bill Maxwell, interview with the authors, April 4, 2023.

28. Linda McCrary, interview with the authors, August 19, 2021.

29. Marvin Winans, interview with the authors, November 6, 2020.

30. Bill Maxwell, personal correspondence with the authors, April 4, 2023.

31. Cary Darling, "Warner Bros. Issues New Controversial Crouch LP," *Billboard,* November 7, 1981, 62–63.

32. "Douglas Salutes Gospel Music," *Record World,* December 5, 1981, 52; "Best-Selling Spiritual LPs," *Billboard,* December 5, 1981, 44; "Best-Selling Soul LPs," *Billboard,* November 7, 1981, 62; "Best-Selling Soul LPs," *Billboard,* November 14, 1981, 96; "Best-Selling Soul LPs," *Billboard,* December 12, 1981, 67; "Top Single Picks," *Billboard,* December 5, 1981, 72.

33. Gail Williams, "TV Review: Christmas Is a Song," *Hollywood Reporter,* December 11, 1981, 8.

34. Edward Morris, "Gospel Meet Studies 'Adjustment' Issue," *Billboard,* December 12, 1981, 3; Edward Morris, "Rifts Emerging as Gospel Pursues Mass Acceptance," *Billboard,* December 26, 1981, 8, 73; Cary Darling, "Gospel Performers Take Stand on Ministry-Show Biz Clash," *Billboard,* January 23, 1982, 59.

35. Walter Rico Burrell, "The Gospel according to Andraé Crouch," *Ebony,* September 30, 1982, 57–58, 60.

36. Linda McCrary, interview with the authors, August 19, 2021; Abraham Laboriel, interview with the authors, October 28, 2021.

37. Marvin Winans, interview with the authors, December 8, 2020; Harold, *When Sunday Comes,* 61.

38. Bill Maxwell, interview with the authors, April 4, 2023.

39. "Andraé Crouch," *CCM: Contemporary Christian Music,* June 1988, 71.

40. Bill Maxwell, interview with the authors, May 18, 2019.

15

Finally

If the record-buying public wasn't enamored with *Don't Give Up*, Andraé's peers still loved him. The album received the "Best Soul Gospel Performance Contemporary" Grammy at the 24th annual awards show in 1982. Crouch remained the most visible gospel artist in the mainstream press as well. In an article on the improved financial aspects of gospel music over the previous year, the *Hollywood Reporter* noted Andraé's clout in the industry, saying an "artist like Andraé Crouch can easily make $2 million in personal appearances." For Crouch, that also meant a guest appearance on the popular CBS comedy series *The Jeffersons* on February 7. Andraé, who played himself, sang "Can't Nobody Do Me like Jesus" while backed by four singers. When the audiophile-oriented *High Fidelity* magazine suggested that religious music could help the recording industry escape an ongoing recession, Crouch was cited as the "Stevie Wonder of the field." *HiFi Stereo Review* magazine furthered the analogy in its review of *Don't Give Up:* "Like some of Stevie Wonder's finer creations, Crouch's upbeat songs carry messages on the themes of love and concern for humanity."[1]

South Africa

Unfortunately, about the same time, in an interview with the powerful African American newspaper *New York Amsterdam News*, Andraé had blithely talked about his two recent solo tours of South Africa—despite the country's universally condemned policy of apartheid, which enforced segregation of the races and exploited the majority African population. When a reporter asked Crouch if he was aware of the boycott by American corporations and entertainers and South Africa's treatment of Blacks, Andraé admitted that he was, but said that the boycott didn't apply because he was not an "entertainer." "Yes, I performed, but I'm a minister," he said. "I was delivering a message." He then called the boycotts "stupid" and said that one South African Black urged him to tell African Americans *not* to honor the boycott, saying, "you are the only ones to keep us together and singing in the midst of everything happening." The *Amsterdam News* ended with an ominous note to the newspaper's readers: "The opportunity for those who want to talk back to Andraé will come August 19 when he will be appearing at Radio City Music Hall."[2]

Response to Crouch's comments was swift and devastating, as typified by an editorial in the *Amsterdam News* by historian William Seraile two weeks later. Seraile called Andraé "a poor student of history." "The racist regime is using entertainers such as Crouch to make the progressive people in the world think that changes are coming with the next sunrise," Seraile writes in the editorial.[3]

Crafting *Finally*

Bill Maxwell and Andraé had begun work on Crouch's next Light Records project in early 1982, long before the fallout from *Don't Give Up* or the pushback from his statements on South Africa. As had been the case on previous albums (save for *Don't Give Up*), some of the songs that would eventually appear on that LP spontaneously emerged during Andraé's frequent tours. Other songs were crafted at his increasingly crowded Woodland Hills home, with its ever-shifting array of friends and musicians, and what *Ebony* magazine had called "a devoted racially mixed entourage constantly jockeying for his attention." Longtime friend Linda McCrary said that the song "He's Waiting" came out of one such evening at Crouch's home at the piano with her brother Alfred and singing the old quartet song "How Long Has It Been" with Andraé. "I turned to Alfred and said, 'Why don't we write something new from that?'" Linda recalled. "That's how 'He's Waiting' came about. Andraé absolutely loved it and said, 'Oh, I just want to write the bridge.' It's very compassionate, just trying to bring people back into an awareness that God is waiting for you" (Image 15.1).[4]

Kathy Hazzard, who had appeared on several previous albums, was not available for the recording of *Finally* but was present at several of the spontaneous songwriting sessions in Andraé's home for the album. Among her strongest memories are of Howard Smith singing an early version of "We Are Not Ashamed." "Howard was there when we spent the nights on the floor

Image 15.1 Bill Maxwell grabs a quick bite while on tour, circa 1981–1982. Courtesy of Stephen "Bugs" Giglio.

under the piano and at 3 o'clock in the morning, with Andraé frying chicken with his favorite hot sauce while we were working out this song," Hazzard said. "And sung by Howard with that silky voice of his? I mean, you couldn't get better than that."[5]

340   SOON & VERY SOON

The intermittent sessions at different recording studios meant, once again, that a wide variety of musicians and singers eventually participated in the project. Among those who returned was bassist Abraham Laboriel, who said that the recording sessions for the *Finally* album were among the most religiously intense of his long career. At one point, he recalled, drummer Buddy Miles found his way into the studio with Bill Maxwell and Crouch and "just fell on his knees in the control booth and started to worship." Laboriel said that he believed all the musicians knew that what they were hearing in the studio was "a gift from God." "We would start learning the songs and capturing the arrangements," he said, "and then because of the trust that we all had for the Holy Spirit, once we had played [the songs] one time, we would take the arrangements to a different place with the freedom that we all had been granted." The sessions for the song "Let's Worship Him (Vamos a Alabar)," which Laboriel co-wrote with his wife Lyn, were particularly satisfying, he said, because of the "special gift" that Maxwell had in the studio. "Bill had a natural way of doing a rough mix that really sounded like a final record," Laboriel said, "so that we all could hear and enjoy the interaction among all of us. That made those recordings more special."[6]

New Studios, New Countries

Linda McCrary said that while the basic tracks had been recorded at Weddington Studios in North Hollywood, Maxwell and Crouch chose to record many of Andraé's vocals and mix and master the songs while in Europe, including Musikland Recording Studios in Munich, which had been recommended to them by Donna Summer. Maxwell and Crouch experimented in other ways as well, including on "That's Why I Needed You." The song featured an all-star lineup of vocalists, Linda McCrary, Howard Smith, Edna Wright, and Danniebelle Hall, all of whom had gone on to become notable recording artists on their own. Unlike other vocal tracks, McCrary said "That's Why I Needed You" was recorded live in the studio. "This was the first song we recorded," she said, "and I don't know why, but it was the first ad-lib vocal I ever did for Andraé—and it was one of the scariest moments of my life. I wasn't raised Pentecostal or COGIC—I was trembling with fear."[7]

Cost considerations prompted the move to Munich to record Andrae's vocals. Maxwell and Crouch found a sympathetic ear in engineer Benedict

Tobias, who had worked with David Bowie, Depeche Mode, and other English bands. Unfortunately, Andrae's now-obsessive retakes of his vocals meant that the sessions stretched on for three weeks. When the recording sessions finally wrapped up, Maxwell said that Light's financial issues meant that Musikland's bills were left unpaid. "I told Light, 'You don't get Andrae's masters unless you pay the bills,'" he recalled. Eventually, Light found the money and Maxwell wrangled the two-inch tapes through customs. When he returned, Maxwell said that Light's relationship with Word Records had ended—which meant that Crouch and Maxwell had a completed album—but no distribution.[8]

McCrary said she also has particularly fond memories of the recording sessions for the Latin-flavored "Let's Worship Him (Vamos a Alabar)." "This song was just a party," she said, "a complete worship party. We had so much fun recording this and we did get to do it live a few times." One of McCrary's frustrations with working with Crouch was his prolific songwriting—just as the group would grow attached to certain songs live, he would introduce a whole new set list. "By then he's done another album and you're on to the next one and those songs get forgotten," she said, "but I was just in love with that song and doing it live."[9]

Negative Reviews and Views

During this period, Andraé's new music began to receive some of the first mediocre, even negative reviews of his career. The *Washington Post*'s Richard Harrington, a longtime advocate of gospel music, writes that while Crouch had been a "trendsetter" in the past, *Finally* "subsumes the passionate heart of gospel under the weight of pop production." In an attempt to sound more like contemporary music, Harrington suggests that Crouch fell "into stylistic ruts" on the new album. One song, "Sweet Communion," "has a corny/majestic melody, *a la* Neil Diamond." Despite the "skilled production," he closes, "*Finally* leaves much to be desired." *Variety*'s review of Crouch's concert September 1 in the Music Hall in New York is even more scathing: "Gospel-goes-disco and ends up a wallflower best describes Andraé Crouch's 60-minute turn of pop/secular music." While reviewer "Mur" praises his supporting vocalists, Andraé "lacked charisma, intensity and direction on stage." The review ends with an equally dismissive note: "Crouch was clearly no match for Shirley Caesar's previous set, which had drained the crowd."[10]

Trouble in the Religious Music Industry

Crouch, of course, wasn't the only gospel artist who was suffering in a "sinking economy." Even *Billboard*'s usually upbeat annual gospel music section admitted that labels and artists were "hopeful" about soon emerging from a "period of retrenchment." Or, as Benson's Michael A. Blines noted, "I think we've seen once and for all the end of the myth that the Christian music market is insulated during bad economic times." While Benson, Word, Priority, and the other labels cut staff, artists, marketing and advertising, and—in some cases—even affiliated record labels, Crouch's label Light Records was quietly having even worse problems. As early as May, severe cash flow problems had forced Ralph Carmichael to lay off nearly two dozen employees and scale back dramatically. More layoffs followed and in his biography *He's Everything to Me*, Carmichael details the frantic days that followed as the once-prosperous company sank closer to bankruptcy. Support for all Light/Lexicon product, including Andraé's upcoming LP, was suspended. More staff cuts followed through the remainder of 1982.[11]

One area where gospel *was* finding success was in increased television exposure. Andraé in particular was cited by booking agent Bill Leopold for his recent appearances on programs on both the PTL and Trinity Broadcasting networks, as well as specials for Glen Campbell and Ray Charles. "What's interesting," Leopold said, "is that he's doing the same material on all shows."[12]

Even so, the controversial appearance on *Saturday Night Live* and *Don't Give Up*'s mostly critical reception continued to dog Crouch. In an interview prior to a September appearance at the Irvine Meadows Amphitheater, Andraé "vigorously" defended his music and choices to the *Los Angeles Times*'s Dennis Hunt. "Yes, a lot of them do think my music is trash," Crouch said of gospel music "traditionalists" who criticized his songs:

> Many of these people call me a rebel. But that's mild compared to what some of them have called me. But they can call me rebel, radical, anything they want. That doesn't bother me. I'm going to do what I think is right.

Through the interview, Andraé's tone transitions from resignation to annoyance to even resentment. He tells Meadows that "a lot" of traditional church music "bores" him and that his "enemies" in the church "cast people aside" who don't agree with their beliefs. At one point, Crouch adamantly dismisses critics who claim that he's only interested in a "hit record" with his recent releases:

> I like my records played on gospel stations but I also want to be in the Top 40. Why not? Why make music just for a few people? I want to be heard all over the world. Not that many people listen to gospel on the radio or buy gospel records, but many people listen to pop radio and buy pop records. I want to be part of that pop market, too.

Finally, the interview turns to Crouch's "pop-star aspirations" and "elegant Woodland Hills home," the Marina del Rey condo, and the Mercedes with personalized plates. "Should I drive a jalopy and live in a shack just to get them off my back?" he responds. "What matters is that I'm a man of God and I want to spread His word as best I can." Then, as a closing shot: "I pray for these people. They need all of the help they can get."[13]

Even interviews in the Black press, which had been supportive in the past, took a more direct turn, forcing Andraé on the defensive once again. In a September interview in the *Los Angeles Sentinel* that again mentioned his "plush, yet comfortable living room" in Woodland Hills, Crouch was asked about the "controversies" related to *Don't Give Up.* He responded by noting that prior to his relationship with Warner Bros. Records, his releases "could only be found in Christian bookstores." "It's not important how people learn and benefit from the Lord's wisdom," he said. "What is important is that they understand it and do benefit from it." He insisted, once again, the Christian message in his latest releases was "not diluted" in any way and might be better "understood" by younger listeners. "It's important to be of the world and not apart from it," Crouch said. "The Lord's Word is not lost in the modernization of the gospel sound."[14]

The Arrest and Fallout

Life, of course, can turn on a dime. Perhaps it was the sight of Black men, in the aforementioned silver-gray Mercedes, driving at night in pricey Marina del Rey. Or perhaps it was just random happenstance that caused the policeman to pull over Andraé and his unnamed friends. On the floorboard, a white powder had spilled from a can. The policeman, who called for assistance, searched Crouch's tracksuit, and pulled a length of a drinking straw "dusted with a residue" of what appeared to be cocaine—about .05 of a gram, or one twenty-eighth of an ounce. Andraé was arrested, spent a few hours in jail, then was released after posting $2,500 bail. Police quietly dropped the charges a few days later for lack of evidence, but by then news of the arrest had swept through the gospel community, was broadcast on major radio and television outlets, and even warranted a small paragraph in the *New York Times*. "I was innocent, as far as the accusation being me," Andraé told radio station KBE. For all his accomplishments, the specter of his arrest would continue to follow Crouch the rest of his life, even to the point of appearing in many of the obituaries that followed his death in 2015, more than twenty years later.[15]

Several of Crouch's friends had long expressed concern about Andraé's long-standing habit of inviting people he'd just met to stay with him, either in the Marina del Rey condo or his "sprawling San Fernando Valley home." Longtime friend Howard Rachinski said that because Crouch loved people, he would open his homes to anyone, anytime. "If people came to his concerts and they're addicts or they're coming off the streets and didn't have a place," Rachinski said, "he would just say, 'Hey, come on. Hang at our place for a couple of days.' And this included people who hadn't kicked the cocaine habit." Crouch's longest, most detailed interview on the topic—though he responded to questions on the subject for many years to come—was with *CCM* (*Contemporary Christian Music*) magazine later that year. There had been some friends from his past staying in the Woodland Hills home and, upon a return from New York, Andraé said he had found the vial and straw in question. Crouch told writer Davin Seay that he had only pocketed the items to confront the offenders later that evening. When news of the arrest spread over the radio, Crouch said, "I felt like I wanted to die." The arrest and subsequent furor, he said, "felt like the end of a long road" in his life:

> I'd felt so rejected by the church for so long—so rejected by people who didn't understand what I was trying to do with my music—that I'd separated myself from all of it. I'd tried so hard on my last album, *Finally*, to tell my brothers and sisters how I really felt, and I was beginning after a long time to start to feel loved again. Then the devil did his number and I thought, "I'm through." I felt there was no way I'd ever be able to get close to any community of Christians again.[16]

While the police quickly dropped the charges when prosecutors said that they "did not have a case they could take to court to prosecute him," some elements in the religious community never forgave him. Maxwell was among those who rushed to Andraé's side and found him in his bedroom sobbing.

"That was probably one of the biggest hurts in his life," Rachinski said. "It was like the whole church just turned their back on him." Forty years after the fact, Sherman Andrus said that memories of the incident still pain him. "Gospel is a tougher field than any other," he said. "People almost want to bring you down, to destroy your reputation. I don't think they understand what it means—but they only remember some of the bad stuff. They don't remember the great stuff you've done."[17]

Regardless of Andraé's innocence or guilt, through the harrowing experience and subsequent public shaming that followed, Crouch began writing a series of songs that were among the most intimate, most vulnerable of his long career.

A Final Serendipity

Ultimately, 1982 had been a year to forget—lackluster sales, Light/Lexicon's near-bankruptcy, the South Africa controversy, and, most crushingly, the arrest. But 1982 also ended on an unexpected grace note. The hippest late-night show on television was *SCTV*, a cutting-edge comedy based on an imaginary low-budget television station in Canada. *SCTV* was the launching pad for a host of talented actors, many of whom would soon become major stars on their own: Eugene Levy, Martin Short, Catherine O'Hara, Rick Moranis, John Candy, and others. In the final sketch for December 1982, Candy again portrayed the egocentric "Johnny LaRue." Down on his luck and suicidal at Christmas, LaRue encounters Crouch as an angel who operates a soup kitchen. As writer Arsenio Orteza recounts it, Andraé saves LaRue through "sympathetic acts of kindness" and—of course—a riveting performance of "Soon and Very Soon." Orteza ends his tribute this way: "Surreal though the skit was, Crouch was going where no Christian had gone before—and bringing Jesus with him in the process. It was, essentially, the story of his life."[18]

1983
Sandra Saves the Day

Entering 1983, things hadn't gotten better for Light/Lexicon. Carmichael was now facing serious tax issues and even foreclosure of his family's beloved ranch. The label released a few already-recorded albums but needed more product—and quickly. In his biography, Carmichael writes that during his darkest moments, "the truly gifted soloist and composer" Sandra Crouch suddenly called. Sandra was aware of the label's problems, in part because Light was delinquent on its royalty payments, including those to her brother. Sandra offered to write and produce an album at her own expense, recorded live with the choir from her father's Christ Memorial COGIC Church. *We Sing Praises*, and its accompanying choral book, provided the label with an unexpected infusion of cash and credibility. "Dear Sandra," Carmichael writes in his biography, "I'll aways be grateful." The influx of revenue enabled Light to release Andraé's *Finally* in the Christian bookstore marketplace, though the LP received virtually no promotional support. When private financing for Light/Lexicon Music "failed to materialize," Carmichael returned to his friend Jarrell McCracken and asked Word Inc. to resume sales and promotion of his records and songbooks in Christian bookstores, then began to search for buyers for the label—and its debt.[19]

The lyrics for what would be called *Finally* had always been crafted to be overtly Christian, Maxwell said, and Andraé brought back both Edna Wright and Sondra "Blinky" Williams from the COGICs for solos and background vocals. Light was so happy with what it heard on the recordings that the label rush-released a track written by Sandra Crouch, "We Need to Hear from You," as a single to put it forward for Grammy consideration.[20]

Recording *Finally*

As in previous years, the composition of the band and singers changed from tour to tour, and the song selection—which often varied nightly—was often influenced by the available singers. Among those who joined Andraé regularly in 1982–1983 was Alfie Silas (Durio). Silas's four-octave soprano gave Crouch the opportunity to revisit "My Tribute (to God Be the Glory")," which he had recorded previously both on *Keep On Singin'* (with Bili Thedford) and *Live in London* (with Perry Morgan), as a duet on *Finally*. Maxwell said that they were not happy with the production on the *Keep On Singin'* album and, with Silas available, "wanted to give it one more crack." "Many times when I would finish singing that song, I could not move afterwards," Silas said. "The anointing of the Lord was so powerful [and] the atmosphere was just charged with the presence of the Lord in such a way I had never experienced before." Silas said she loved "My Tribute" as a closing song because it was a "moment when everyone would stop and we could sing together." "Wherever we were," she said, "whatever the weather or location, people knew that song. So that was the moment where there was this community of singing together, worshipping God." It was also the first song to be recorded for *Finally*.[21]

Finally continued the trend that had begun with *Don't Give Up* as Andraé ceded most of the arrangements and production to others. Instead, the tracks on the album represent, at least in the opinion of the authors, "themes and variations" on Crouch's original contributions, with the arrangers and some of the musicians having much more pronounced input and influence on the stylistic and artistic musical decisions in the studio. For Andraé and his arrangers, form now follows function. Most of the songs on *Finally* begin with a chorus, then a repeat of the chorus, followed by some form of the verse accompanied by subtle harmonic variations of the chorus. Most of the songs are also in $\frac{4}{4}$ common time, with a few song introductions featuring irregular metrical modulations.

Finally

Side I

"We Need to Hear From You"

The form of "We Need to Hear from You" is composed like a palindrome: chorus, chorus, verse, chorus, chorus, then vamp, and reprise. It is performed in the key of D♭ major with a $\frac{12}{8}$ time signature, interposed with a distinctly Black church triplet feel. As on most of the songs on the LP, the tonal centers are in proximity with what the authors have called black key pitch centricity. For Silas, the studio recording of "We Need to Hear from You" typified Crouch's "attitude songs." "Andraé would say, 'Put your hand on your hips for this particular song,'" Silas said. "He wanted a particular attitude conveyed in our voices." If the approach wasn't working, she said that he would have the sopranos sing the alto parts and the altos sing the soprano parts "to get more grit." "He would also let us put our own little pieces in there," Silas said. "He'd give us something and we'd be allowed to put our personalities in it and interpret it. By the time you left the studio, you were tired but happy."[22]

"Finally"

In the key of F major, the title track begins with a symphonic overture with a piccolo trumpet and orchestral strings arranged by the talented Allyn Ferguson. After a few bars, "Finally" fuses this symphonic sound with straight-ahead, medium-tempo funk shuffle. The form is, again, highly unusual for any kind of popular music, much less gospel, as each section has eight bars with an introduction—chorus, chorus, verse, chorus, verse, chorus, and outro to fadeout. The song is a good example of Crouch's new interest in developing music using a "theme and variation" format as opposed to gospel's standard verse, verse, chorus form.

"Everybody's Got to Know"

Also with a sweeping orchestral opening, this time lasting forty seconds, featuring strings, bells, harp, and French horns, "Everybody's Got to Know" (in the key of B♭ major) highlights one of Andraé's most unusual song forms: introduction, chorus, chorus, verse, verse, chorus, verse, verse, linkage, chorus, and vamp. The complex structure creates a tension and release for listeners to hear Crouch's lyrics emphasize the message of the "Great Commission" of Matthew 28 ("Go therefore and make disciples of all nations"). Andraé's brilliant chorus of singers declare "everybody's got the right to know who Jesus is," reinforcing his long-held belief that his music should be for everyone, not just churchgoers.

"We Are Not Ashamed"

"We Are Not Ashamed" begins, yet again, with Ferguson's lush orchestral arrangement of piano and strings, an approach that later artists, such as Lionel Richie, will embrace on similar power ballads. It features the velvety smooth voice of Howard Smith, before turning to the powerful testifying vocals of Wright. In G♭ major, this is one of the few songs with Andraé himself on the piano, accompanied by a small combo of top musicians—Larry Muhoberac (keys), Dean Parks (guitars), Abraham Laboriel (bass), and, of course, Maxwell (drums). Crouch's compositional genius is on full display here on a song that—unbeknownst to Crouch (and probably anyone present at the time)—would provide the archetypal praise & worship format for future songwriters, especially in the format: four-bar introduction in $\frac{4}{4}$ time, chorus, chorus, bridge (a shouted, emphatic "God's Word!"), and closing with free-style gospel variations and improvisations on the words "we are not ashamed."

"Sweet Communion"

The last song on Side I of the LP, "Sweet Communion" is the centerpiece of *Finally*, a reverently soulful, slowly building accompaniment for a Christian

FINALLY

349

communion service based on I Corinthians 11:24, though laced throughout with some of Crouch's most mystical musical allusions. The song is dominated with jazz fusion influences, and a vocoder/synthesized voice singing, "This you do in remembrance of me/So you won't forget/I love you," suddenly appears midway through. The format is radically different from the other songs in Crouch's catalogue and uncommonly intricate, even by Andraé's standards: twelve-bar introduction, verse, verse, bridge 1, bridge 2, chorus, post-chorus with synthesizer, verse, verse, bridge 1, bridge 2, chorus, post-chorus with percussion section, and closing *codetta* with non-syllabic words.[23]

Bill Maxwell said that "Sweet Communion" was one of the last songs written and recorded for the album and remains a personal favorite. "I just felt the presence of the Lord when I was cutting it," he said. "I felt inspired just doing the track." As both producer and drummer, Maxwell said the drum tracks were typically the last ones recorded. When studio time was a factor, he often played it "safe" to avoid multiple retakes. "Mostly I just tried to hold the songs down as a drummer," he said. "So, I play a little bit like a traffic cop— 'No, don't go too fast! Watch this turn!' But on "Sweet Communion," unlike previous albums, time was not an issue and Maxwell said he was able to play with more freedom and creativity.[24]

Side II

"All the Way"

The side-opening "All the Way" represents a return to the urgency of some of Crouch's earlier LPs in its funky Spinners-styled attack and use of all-male unison vocals (including old friend Perry Morgan). In the keys of A minor and C major, the lyrics reference Roman 8:31 ("If God is for us, who is against us?"). Buoyed again by the swooping strings of a classic disco number, this time arranged by Bruce Miller, "All the Way" is still another track that is compositionally complex in form: sixteen-bar dance/disco intro, chorus, verse, bridge 1, verse, chorus, bridge 2, verse, chorus, bridge 3, bridge 4, closing *codetta*, and vamp fadeout.

"He's Waiting"

The verses of "He's Waiting" pose personal spiritual questions for listeners concerning their relationship with God. Composed in the key of G♭ major and presented in the key of F major, the song is co-written by Andraé with friends

Alfred and Linda McCrary and features Linda's distinctive voice in a duet. Its musical form is in a more familiar style—orchestral intro, verse, chorus, verse, chorus, bridge, vamp, outro. "He's Waiting," with its overtones of the old hymn "Softly and Tenderly Jesus Is Calling" (which he has referenced before), extends another open invitation to listeners to deeper Christian discipleship.

"Let's Worship Him (Vamos a Alabar)"

The dance-oriented "Let's Worship Him (Vamos a Alabar)," co-written by Abraham and Lyn Laboriel and Crouch, begins—unusually—with bass patterns by Laboriel and is heavily spiced with Latin percussion, including timbales, congas, bongos, and cowbells. In the key of D major, each chorus in "Let's Worship Him" has slight variations in both the lyrics and vocals in yet another intriguingly creative arrangement: intro, chorus, chorus, verse, channel, chorus, verse, channel, and chorus variations. "Let's Worship Him" also features most of the members of Maxwell's group Koinonia: Harlan Rogers (synthesizer), Hadley Hockensmith (guitar), Alex Acuna (percussion), Laboriel (bass), and Maxwell.

"That's Why I Needed You"

In the key of A♭ major, the ballad "That's Why I Needed You" includes, especially on the reprise, vocals by some of the singers who had sung with Andraé for decades—Edna Wright, Danniebelle Hall, Howard Smith, and Linda McCrary. Once again, the arrangement turns the familiar gospel verse/verse/chorus/repeat until vamp format on its head: intro, verse, chorus, verse, chorus, turnaround, ritard to a false ending, then a chorus reprise with six variations, and fade.

For Crouch, the emotional lyrics to "That's Why I Needed You," which responds directly to the criticism and controversy that had bedeviled him since the release of *Don't Give Up*, may have been the most important track on the album. "It came out of a pondering between me and God," he told the *Louisville Defender*. "My voice cracked a little while I was singing it in the studio—it was a deep-felt thing." Andraé insisted, again, that all of his lyrics, including those on *Don't Give Up*, were deeply biblically based:

> I know that if I write from my heart, it will eventually reach people. My greatest goal is to communicate with as many of them as I can. Sometimes I'm talking to church-going people, other times to those who aren't, who need to be reminded that there is a God.[25]

"My Tribute (to God Be the Glory)"

The album ends with Alfie Silas's soaring rendition of "My Tribute," which first appeared on Andraé and the Disciples' *Keep On Singin'* album in 1971. This version would become Crouch's preferred closing number at concerts for the next few years. Silas said that the lush orchestral track by the London Philharmonic that accompanied "My Tribute" was one of the very few times Andraé used a backing track in concert. The orchestra was recorded at C.T.S. studios in London, though the other musicians in the band always performed the anthem live. "Andraé just loved that arrangement," she said, "and he wanted to hear that sound."[26]

Of the songs themselves, Crouch told the *Louisville Defender* that the songs he chose to perform and record always had to answer one question:

> Does it reach you? I sense the feedback from an audience if the song is working. I know what is real, that's what I got from being raised in church. I believe, however, that the lyric of a song and the music, the actual feel, are two different things.[27]

The Lost Album

Finally was released with little fanfare in the summer of 1983. It only debuted at #30 on the *Billboard* "Best-Selling Spiritual LPs" charts in August. It would rise as high as #14 in October but never crack the Top 10, hampered in no small part by the unrelentingly bad publicity from the arrest and Light/Lexicon's financial woes and lack of support. *Finally* did not appear among the "Top Spiritual Albums" year-end charts. It also marked the beginning of the end of long tours for Andrae. Maxwell said from this point on, Crouch would primarily schedule individual dates or very short two- or three-date engagements.[28]

Response

The dates that did follow the release of *Finally* included, at least for a time, many of the singers from the recording sessions, including McCrary and Silas. Edna Wright's other commitments, however, kept her from performing with Crouch on a regular basis. McCrary said one of the challenges was performing "We Are Not Ashamed" live in place of Wright—who she said had "just killed" the song in the studio version. "We were like, 'Why do I have to sing this behind her?'" McCrary said. "Edna had the perfect voice and perfect attitude to proclaim that we are not ashamed of the gospel. That's why everyone was intimidated if you had to do it live."[29]

Kathy Hazzard said she has a host of fond memories of the concerts in support of *Finally*, including a well-attended performance at Melody Land Theater in Anaheim on a night that was heavily marketed to the Hispanic community. "Abe [Laboriel's] "Let's Worship Him" had such a great Latin feel," she said, "and it was so popular among Hispanics that when we'd get into the beats, Andraé would start it over and play it all over again—and we'd walk off the stage on that song."[30]

McCrary said that no song on *Finally* impacted her more when performed in concert than "Sweet Communion," especially on the few occasions when the song was performed during an actual communion service. "This song gave me another level of understanding about what communion really is," she said. "And to sing it during a service creates this very real ambiance of the Holy Spirit. Once, I had to sing it live after Andraé passed and I had to leave the stage. I had to go backstage and cry, it was so heavenly." According to McCrary, "Sweet Communion," along with the spiritual "Let Us Break Bread Together" and "Always Remember Jesus," is one of the very few songs in any genre that celebrates the communion service. "And when we would do it live," she said, "a reverence came over the whole band. I ain't even talking about the people—just the band and singers alone. That was one of the greatest things I experienced with Andraé was [that] you're experiencing what the people are experiencing. You're getting blessed as the people are getting blessed."[31]

But Hazzard said her most lasting impression of the *Finally* concerts were the highly charged closing performances of "My Tribute (to God Be the Glory)," featuring Silas. "It was almost like experiencing a full concert, a full movie, or even a roller coaster in just those few minutes," Hazzard said. "That, to me, embodies what Andraé was trying to do. It was almost like 'The Hallelujah Chorus' every night."[32]

A Special Concert

Even as *Finally* sank in the charts and with Light unable to meet its financial obligations, including royalties, Crouch doggedly returned yet again to the road just to pay his bills, invariably facing the same questions about the arrest at virtually every performance. He had also resumed writing songs for his second, as yet unnamed, Warner Bros. album, along with continuing to piece together an informal home recording studio. In August, Andraé returned to Israel for the One Nation Under God International Gospel Festival, staged at an open-air auditorium just outside the walls of Jerusalem's Old City by the Sultan's Pool. Andraé was joined by "frenemy" James Cleveland, Shirley Caesar, and Barry White, and the event was organized by White and Rod McGrew, general manager of a California radio station. Additional dates were planned for Mann Auditorium in Tel Aviv and the Roman Theater in Caesarea. Crouch said that he would perform with his full band, one that included, according to Phyllis St. James, Sandra Crouch, Kristle Murden, Linda McCrary, and Howard Smith. "No small trio will do," Andraé said. "The people love hot music." Crouch said that he had visited Israel early in 1983 in preparation for the concert. "What most people do not know is that my mother's folks are Jewish," he said, "my father's great-great grandfather was Jewish. So you see, I have an untold love for the Jewish people." During his whirlwind earlier visit, Crouch said he also visited several Israeli radio stations. "And the disk jockeys were stimulated and impressed by my song, 'Jesus Is the Answer.'" *Ebony* magazine's extensive coverage of the events reported that the night had "the Israeli audience jumping and cheering and dancing in the chilly night air." One photograph featured a broadly smiling Andraé surrounded by fans in Jerusalem.[33]

As before, Andraé's struggles with the church and some gospel music fans didn't impact his visibility in the wider world of mainstream music. He was among several top guest artists—including Joe Cocker and Glen Campbell—tapped to perform for a taped special honoring Ray Charles's fortieth year in show business. The two-hour special, produced in association with the Dick Clark Company, was taped in the Coconut Room of the Ambassador Hotel in Los Angeles. In December, Crouch was even featured on the TV series *Solid Gold*'s Christmas special, resplendent in a black tux singing "Joy to the World" and, later, joining Peter, Paul, and Mary for "Go Tell It on the Mountain."[34]

Finally's Impact

In retrospect, *Finally*'s impact, like its reception at the time, was mixed. The Baltimore *Afro-American* reviewers loved it and were "so impressed that some wanted to give it more than that allotted amount [*sic*] of stars available. Naturally, this one is an absolute must." Another chronicler of the era called it a "worship-oriented project" and noted the "bouncy" title track, the remake of "My Tribute," and "We Need to Hear from You"—and not much else. Still another writer said that it was a "disappointment" and lacked the "superb musicianship" of earlier albums, though "We Need to Hear from You" and "We Are Not Ashamed" were cited as two of Andraé's "more popular compositions." One encyclopedia-styled book on gospel music, however, doesn't bother to mention the album at all.[35]

From the vantage point of forty years, the authors believe that the lightly regarded *Finally* is a release of new musical song forms not previously explored in gospel. Within the too-often predictable confines of contemporary gospel in the 1980s, *Finally* contains more musical variation than any of Crouch's previous LPs and it is the most colorful variety of keys/tonal centers yet heard on a gospel release. "Sweet Communion" not only marks the first-time use of a vocoder on a gospel song, it is also the first time drums were used as a principal instrument with such freedom in the coda/outro. In these and other ways, Crouch and Maxwell set a standard for theme and variation development for the artists who followed them. At the same time, *Finally* marked a conscious effort to include more "church songs" for the singing church and featured more vocals by Andraé himself. In later years, when it is referenced at all, it has been celebrated for including a song focused solely on the sacrament of communion/the Lord's Supper/celebration of the Eucharist. Crouch, an ambassador for reconciliation, composed a song that united Protestant and Catholic listeners in what could have been a theologically divisive interpretation and discourse. And the LP also marked the first time a major gospel album featured a song sung in Spanish.

Created amid the intense personal drama of the previous year, *Finally*'s musicality and tightly focused, biblically based lyrics, and challenging song forms contrast vividly with *Don't Give Up*'s obvious mirroring of the popular music of the day. The frequent use of symphonic orchestral sounds on *Finally* is reminiscent of the approach by the producers on *Keep On Singin'*, released more than a decade earlier. In this and the overtly evangelical tone of the lyrics, *Finally* may well be, the authors suggest, Crouch's attempt to deeply reconnect with the original church audience that had sustained him since the beginning of his musical ministry.

Regardless of the reception, looking back, Maxwell said that he's proud of *Finally*. "These records are passion projects," he said. "We put our whole heart in it, whether it worked or not."[36]

As for Crouch, after a time apart to recover from the dark days of 1982 and 1983, he once again threw himself into the rigors of performing and writing. When a sympathetic writer later asked Andraé and Sandra about the controversies of the previous two years, he made a quick analogy between his troubles and the more relaxed "dress codes" he was now seeing in Black churches. "You can't dress bad enough for God not to love you," he said. "You can't dress good enough to make God love you."[37]

NOTES

1. www./grammy.com/awards/24th-annual-grammy-awards; Ruth Robinson, "Financial Rewards for Gospel Growing," *Hollywood Reporter*, February 25, 1982, 16; "Andraé Crouch Joins Jeffersons," *Los Angeles Sentinel*, February 4, 1982, B5; Davin Seay, "Christian Music: The Record Industry's Saving Grace?" *High Fidelity*, February 1982, 72; "Record of Special Merit: Andraé Crouch: *Don't Give Up*," *HiFi Stereo Review*, April 1982, 70.

2. Marie Moore, "Andraé Crouch Thinks S. Africa Boycott 'Stupid,'" *New Amsterdam News*, August 21, 1982, 4.

3. William Seraile, "What Message Did Rev. Andraé Crouch Deliver in S. Africa?" *New York Amsterdam News*, September 4, 1982, 45.

4. Walter Rico Burrell. "The Gospel according to Andraé Crouch," *Ebony*, September 1982, 57; Linda McCrary, interview with the authors, November 9, 2021.

5. Kathy Hazzard, interview with the authors, November 30, 2021.

6. Abraham Laboriel, interview with the authors, August 19, 2021.

7. Linda McCrary, interview with the authors, November 9, 2021.

8. Bill Maxwell, interview with the authors, May 20, 2023.

9. Linda McCrary, interview with the authors, November 9, 2021.

10. Richard Harrington, "A Soft Crouch, an Uncertain Mills," *Washington Post*, August 20, 1982, 37; Mur, "Andraé Crouch (12), Shirley Caesar," "The Winans," *Variety*, September 1, 1982, 76.

11. Bob Darden, "Christian Labels Emerge Hopeful from Period of Retrenchment," *Billboard*, October 2, 1982, G-4, G-12, G-16; Ralph Carmichael, *He's Everything to Me* (Waco, TX: Word Books, 1986), 165–171.

12. "Religious TV Helps Viewers Keep an Eye on the Star," *Billboard*, October 2, 1982, G-20; Sharon Allen, "Nashville This Week: Television Specials in the Works," *R&R (Radio & Records)*, August 26, 1983, 66.

13. Dennis Hunt, "Pop-Gospel: Rebel with a Cause," *Los Angeles Times*, September 24, 1982, G1, 13.

14. Phyllis Bailey, "Crouch Updates the Message," *Los Angeles Sentinel*, September 30, 1982, B7.
15. "Police Arrest Gospel Singer on Drug Possession Charge," *New York Times*, November 15, 1982, A17; UPI Archives, https://www.upi.com/Archives/1982/11/12/Award-winning-gospel-singer-and-composer-Andrae-Crouch-was-arrested/4569405925200/; David Seay, "The CCM Interview: Andraé Crouch," *CCM*, November 12, 1982; "Singer Andraé Crouch Denies Drug Charge," Baltimore *Afro-American*, November 27, 1982, 1.
16. David Seay, "The CCM Interview: Andraé Crouch," *CCM*, November 12, 1982; Bill Maxwell, interview with the authors, February 24, 2023; Howard Rachinski, interview with the authors, October 20, 2023.
17. Howard Rachinski, interview with the authors, October 20, 2023; James H. Cleaver, "Andraé Crouch Cleared," *Los Angeles Sentinel*, November 18, 1982, 1, 6; Sherman Andrus, interview with the authors, September 5, 2020.
18. Arsenio Orteza, "Joyful Noise Maker: Andraé Crouch Sang with an Indefatigable—and Soulful—Optimism," *World*, February 7, 2015, 30.
19. Carmichael, *He's Everything to Me*, 170–179; "Light/Lexicon Returns to Word," *Billboard*, January 22, 1983, 50.
20. Bill Maxwell, interview with the authors, May 20, 2023; "25th Annual Grammy Awards Final Nominations," *Billboard*, January 22, 1983, 67.
21. Alfie Silas Durio, interview with the authors, June 18, 2021; Bill Maxwell, interview with the authors, May 20, 2023.
22. Alfie Silas Durio, interview with the authors, June 18, 2021.
23. "Sweet Communion" by Andraé Crouch, Lexicon Music, Inc., courtesy of Capitol CMG.
24. Bill Maxwell, interview with the authors, May 20, 2023.
25. "Andraé Crouch Takes Gospel Music to a Higher Level," *Louisville Defender*, October 21, 1982, A9.
26. Alfie Silas Durio, interview with the authors, June 18, 2021.
27. Tim Walter, "The Pros Tell How to Write a Hit Song," *Louisville Defender*, January 7, 1982, A8.
28. "Best-Selling Spiritual LPs," *Billboard*, August 8, 1983, 39; "Best-Selling Spiritual LPs," *Billboard*, October 29, 1983, 61; "Top Spiritual Albums," *Billboard*, December 24, 1983, 78; Bill Maxwell, interview with the authors, May 20, 2023.
29. Linda McCrary, interview with the authors, November 9, 2021.
30. Kathy Hazzard, interview with the authors, November 30, 2021.
31. Linda McCrary, interview with the authors, November 9, 2021.
32. Kathy Hazzard, interview with the authors, November 30, 2021.
33. Phyllis St. James, interview with the authors, January 23, 2021; Itour Gelbitz, "Kolleck Finds 'Promised Land' for Screen," *Hollywood Reporter*, August 16, 1983, 12; Titania Polk, "Borders Blur as Black Gospel Takes On Global Issues," *Billboard*, August 27, 1983, G-10, G-16; Charles L. Sanders, "Gospel Goes to the Holy Land," *Ebony*, December 1983, 37–38, 42.

FINALLY

34. Leo Sacks, "Radio: Featured Programming," *Billboard*, August 27, 1983, 19; https://rhino.com/artists/rhino-factoids-a-solid-gold-christmas.
35. Pamela Littlejohn, 'Record Review Ratings," Baltimore *Afro-American*, November 27, 1982, A27; Mark Allan Powell, *Encyclopedia of Contemporary Christian Music* (Peabody, MA: Hendrickson Publishers, 2002), 212; Claudrena N. Harold, *When Sunday Comes: Gospel Music in the Soul and Hip-Hop Eras* (Urbana: University of Illinois Press, 2020), 61; Bil Carpenter, *Uncloudy Days: The Gospel Music Encyclopedia* (San Francisco: Backbeat Books, 2005), 107–108.
36. Bill Maxwell, interview with the authors, May 20, 2023.
37. Von Jones, "Gospel Greats Have a Message," *Los Angeles Sentinel*, March 14, 1985, A1.

16

No Time to Lose

The Road Back

Perceptions shift. Time changes things. While there would always be those in the church who never forgave, never forgot, Crouch family fortunes began to change in 1984. Sandra's album *We Sing Praises* was awarded the "Best Soul Gospel Performance, Female" Grammy in late February. On March 17, the LP hit #1 after spending twenty-five weeks on the charts. As for Andraé, after the firestorm of criticism from some religious music circles for daring to address topics like prostitution and abortion in his songs, gospel artists like the Winans, Commissioned, the Clark Sisters, and a few others received praise for releasing similar songs. It rarely pays to be the first, it seems.[1]

The success of *We Sing Praises*, strong advance sales for Andraé's upcoming release (distributed, once again, by Word's large sales force), the Crouch-produced Winans LP *Long Time Comin'* and Tramaine Hawkins's *Determined*, meant that parent label Light found itself amid an unexpected resurrection in mid-1984. Ralph Carmichael reported that Light would pay off its $2 million indebtedness by mid-year. "If there was a turning point, I think it was [Sandra] Crouch winning the Grammy and the Dove Awards this spring," Carmichael said. "I think that had a lot to do with us perceiving ourselves winners again."[2]

The *No Time to Lose* Sessions

The recording sessions for *No Time to Lose* had begun earlier, in late 1983. Andraé's management renegotiated their financial arrangement with Light, with the studio budget now administered by Crouch Productions. Maxwell said, as before, that Crouch's constant experimentation in the studio with the background vocals quickly depleted the budget, limiting Maxwell's options. "As producer, spending studio time for three days on the background vocals on one song was torturous," he said. "For Andraé, he's having a party and he's the host—everybody is there and they're singing. 'Let's do this, let's try that.' He's not thinking about the money." Eventually, Maxwell was forced to move to a much cheaper home studio, Redwing, in nearby Tarzana to complete the album.[3]

Despite the circumstances, Howard Smith said that the relaxed *No Time to Lose* sessions were particularly fun for the singers. "Andraé was very appreciative of us being there," Smith said, "and those were great, great songs with great singers. Just business as usual." Like Kristle Murden, who had already released a solo album by this point, Smith had begun working on his own solo LP and had accrued much more experience in the studio. "We had all become solo artists and we could all arrange," Smith said, "and Andraé was open to our ideas. He'd say, 'OK, what do you hear?' He'd say, 'OK, let's do that' and then we'd all do it." The result, Smith said, was that the singers were essentially co-producers of the vocal tracks:

> When you have a bunch of lead singers who can adapt and who are willing to, for the sake of the project and the sake of the blend, sacrifice their best stuff to blend and to match tones—man, that's fun. Andraé mentored us, groomed us and brought us in. He had a knack for surrounding himself with the best singers and the best musicians—they were drawn to him and he to us.[4]

Alfie Silas's recollections of the *No Time to Lose* sessions were also uniformly positive:

> It was fun, it was silly, it was godly because I think these things were all of what the combination of the people who were in that room were. It was a small group of people. We had been through things, we knew the Lord, we loved Him with all of our hearts, and we were happy to be together, happy to be singing together and being a part of something so unique and so special with Andraé—and enjoying every minute of it.[5]

On the instrumental side, Crouch and Maxwell again recruited several "regulars"—Abraham Laboriel, Joe Sample, Larry Muhoberac, and others—for the sessions, as well as several new names, including Scott V. Smith, bassist Andrew Gouche, synthesizer/keyboardists Rhett Lawrence and Michael Ruff, woodwind player John Phillips, and guitarist James Harrah. Harrah said it was

[Scott V.] Smith who introduced him to Maxwell. "I knew it was going to be a blast," Harrah said, "to get to play with really professional, super-credible world-class musicians, I was really pumped. Bill Maxwell gave me so much room. The sessions were relaxed and there was a great flow." One of his favorite memories was working on songs with Sample ("I was a huge Jazz Crusaders fan in those days"), as well as Gouche, Muhoberac, and Maxwell. "It was just the four of us, two or three basic tracks, eight hour-ish days," Harrah said. The musicians worked from Smith's detailed rhythm charts on their songs. "There were a lot of details written in the music, but [they were] still open to interpretation, and Bill would guide as we went and talked details as we played through," Harrah said. "I was the really young guy and he was very generous with me."[6]

Laboriel's recollections of the songs he recorded during the sessions including a "special" time when he and Crouch prayed as the song "Jesus Come Lay Your Head on Me" was coming together. Laboriel's other strongest memory was of the enormous amount of time Maxwell spent preparing each session, which minimized the number of takes for each song. This preparation was particularly evident in "Right Now," where he recalled being present for the recording of the earliest tracks. "It was like hearing the actual song being born," Laboriel said in retrospect:

> We just had a skeleton of the melody and what it became was absolutely mind-blowing because it started in such a simple way. And then, as the layers of singing appeared, one of the great things about Andraé's signature as a musician is his impeccable sense of rhythm. I learned, as a musician, how legato and staccato both could be incredibly exciting, and not just the contrast of articulation. We learned to play with intensity and, at the same time, with a delicacy—without losing the excitement.[7]

For the vocalists, Howard Smith said that Crouch once again tried repeatedly to "give away" his lead vocals during the sessions. Maxwell continued to argue with him, including on the song "Always Remember," which Maxwell insisted Andraé sing. "There were some songs that Andraé wouldn't fight on," Smith said, "but Bill had to watch him to keep him from giving everything away to whoever was his new muse, such as 'Always Remember.' There was some stuff on that song that went in the 'can' on alternate takes that was powerful, powerful stuff."[8]

The sessions, which wrapped up in early 1984, took place during a period when the recorded music industry was gradually switching to more and more

362   SOON & VERY SOON

of the time-consuming computer sequencing of instrumental tracks, instead of recording live with musicians in the studio. *For No Time to Lose*, Scott V. Smith contributed the rhythm arrangements and sequencing to several songs. Despite the budget constraints and Crouch's need to continually tinker, Maxwell was able to get the tracks recorded and mixed. "Andraé was a budget-buster," Howard Smith said. "Bill Maxwell is a master. We'd get it right and whatever that track was, that was pretty much it. There wasn't a whole bunch of gluing stuff together because of Bill's ear. We would fix whatever needed to be fixed, stack it, and move on."⁹

Light Records gave *No Time to Lose* the most handsome packaging of any of Andraé's solo albums. In addition to the credits and a long list of "thanks" on the back side of the jacket, it features a beautiful, colorful photograph of a smiling Crouch on red reclining chair with matching ottoman, surrounded by some of the artists on the LP: Sandra Crouch, Alfie Silas, Tata Vega, Howard Smith, Kristle Edwards (Murden), Rick Nelson, Martin "Tuffy" Cummings, and Rodney Wayne. Phyllis St. James again served as "Vocal Contractor."

A Return

No Time to Lose signaled Crouch's return to singing the name of Jesus in virtually every song. The songs directly cite or rephrase passages and stories from the Gospel of Luke in particular, along with the Gospel of Matthew and the Old Testament books of Job, Proverbs, and the Psalms. He also returns, once again, to his favorite topics: the invincibility of God's truth, the Lordship of Christ, the nurturing of an intimate relationship with Jesus Christ, and the end times and eschatology. Andraé's continual restating of the evangelical church's belief in the return of Jesus Christ—the "Second Coming"—is reflected in the choice of the album's title. As he has done since "It Won't Be Long" from *Soulfully* more than a decade earlier, Crouch uses his musical platform to urge listeners to live their lives as if that return is imminent.

But where the lyrics and music employed in the previous three albums, *I'll Be Thinking of You*, *Don't Give Up*, and *Finally*, represented Andraé's long-stated desire to take that message to believer and nonbeliever alike, often using the song-forms of the early 1980s to do so, *No Time to Lose* marked a return to a more clearly Black gospel music–oriented sound. On this album, Crouch blends his arranging and composing skills through classic ecumenical church hymns, returning to old-school gospel songs and, intriguingly, Black spirituals. Maxwell said that more than with the previous albums, Andraé found inspiration in his church past:

> He dug from his roots in the Church of God in Christ and songs he'd sung as a young boy. He was always aware of them. He'd used those things that he remembered, [then] totally modernized them with different harmonies and slightly changing the chords. This was all in him. He knew all of the old songs. He could remember every song.[10]

No Time to Lose features affectionate musical and lyrical references to several spirituals, including "All Night, All Day, Angels Watching over Me," "I Want to Be Ready," and "Jesus Come Lay Your Head in the Window." Several older hymns are cited, including "The Battle Hymn of the Republic" and "The Solid Rock," as well as older gospel songs, such as "If We Ever Needed the Lord Before (We Sure Do Need Him Now)" and "Somebody Prayed for Me." Crouch even revisited the themes of his 1972 song "You Ain't Livin'" in "Livin' This Kind of Life."

In the mid-1980s, sales of songbooks based on popular albums remained a viable share of the marketplace. Light's Lexicon Music publishing division had pioneered the concept, and for the previous twenty years, songbooks and octavos could be found in the piano benches for family singalongs and in the hands of the directors of thousands of youth choirs across the country. Maxwell and Crouch's friends Carrie Gonzalo and Lennie Niehaus provided many of the transcriptions, which were geared more toward families gathered around a piano than professional performance. The multitalented Scott V. Smith is credited with the transcriptions for the *No Time to Lose* songbook, and the simplified arrangements featured much more accessible keys, suitable for mixed chorus with simplified piano accompaniments and vocal arrangements. The differences between Smith's transcriptions and the actual recorded versions sometimes reveal valuable clues as to Andraé's thought process in composing the biblical and theological messages found in the lyrics. The songbooks made the music more accessible to a much larger audience.

Despite the traditional source material of many of the songs, the vocal arrangements and orchestration of the vocals in particular sit on the precipice of some of the most strikingly edgy, even futuristic, gospel singing yet recorded in the genre. Throughout *No Time to Lose*, Crouch's impressive group of talented singers masterfully brings to life the sometimes otherworldly harmonies he is hearing in his head. These vocal sounds will set the tenor and the tone for gospel singing, vocal colorings, articulation, and creativity for the next forty years.

No Time to Lose

Side I

"Got Me Some Angels"

"Got Me Some Angels" is one of the most upbeat, propulsive (with quarter notes that range from 112 to 120 beats per minute) songs in Crouch's catalogue and immediately became a live concert staple. The score is in the now-familiar key of D♭ major and the song begins on the G♭ major 9th, though the melody actually begins on the major 7th. This signals a new direction for arranging spirituals, infusing them with rich, innovative gospelized harmonization and a decidedly disco feel. The overall form—introduction, chorus, pre-chorus, chorus, verse, post-chorus, chorus, chorus, bridge, disco vamp, and outro—continues Crouch's practice of employing unusual (and challenging) song formats from the *Finally* sessions.

Maxwell said that he replaced some of Smith's programmed instruments with Andrew Gouche's funky bass and James Harrah's guitars, as well as "real" drums. "Everybody's still trying to capture the backgrounds on songs like this one, even to this day," Linda McCrary said. "The way Andraé layers backgrounds and puts them together, you didn't know what was coming." The instrumentation, particularly the timbales and cowbell in the outro, vividly reflect Andraé's Latin-fusion sensibilities and—again—echo his lifelong desire to blend and bridge multiethnic cultures.

The song was later performed live on *The Tonight Show with Johnny Carson* on June 12, 1986, with a band that included Maxwell, Lou Pardini (keys), Geary Faggett (keys), Gouche (bass), and vocalists Tata Vega, Jean Johnson, Rose Stone, Voncielle Faggett, and Sandra Crouch (vocals and percussion).[11]

"Jesus, Come Lay Your Head on Me"

The old spiritual "Jesus Lay Your Head in the Window" provides a historical context for Crouch's more personal approach in the power ballad "Jesus, Come Lay Your Head on Me." The key lines in Andraé's version reference Jesus' final hours before his trial and crucifixion. Crouch brings Kristle Edwards (now Murden) to serve as storyteller and *griot*, reinterpreting the story in Luke 7:36–50 with a gentle, compassionate invitation. The concept that, in his humanity, Jesus could need someone in his most desperate hour is startlingly original in gospel music and is made possible by Edwards's eloquent improvisation of the lyrics. The song, in D♭ major again, features yet another one of Crouch's complex, yet ultimately satisfying, arrangements: intro, chorus 1, chorus 2, verse, bridge, chorus 3, bridged vamp, and outro. "Jesus, Come Lay Your Head on Me" ends with a twist as it fades into a highly rhythmic light funk bossa nova, spiced by Joe Sample's Fender Rhodes interpolations and more innovative percussion. "I didn't get the beginning concept of that song at first until Kristle put her vocal on it," Linda McCrary said. "She brought that thing to life. There is an old saying, 'God blesses us all of the time, but we can also bless Him.'"[12]

"Right Now"

For Maxwell, the inclusion of the bouncy "Right Now" gave the group another popular gospel shuffle for their live performances, along with "Got Me Some Angels" and "Livin' This Kind of Life." "That song was gospel-driven," Howard McCrary said. "It set a new standard for contemporary gospel singers—that's all. And Andraé was actually playing the piano that fast in real time." The recording, in the key of G♭ major, is a case study for vocal improvisation and theme and variation development—all packaged in Andraé's fascination with vocal jazz fusion and experimentation within the context of contemporary gospel music.[13]

"His Truth Still Marches On"

"His Truth Still Marches On" is a clever fusion of Julia Ward Howe's classic patriotic hymn "The Battle Hymn of the Republic" arranged with Black gospel music stylings. At first it sounds improvised, but the song form steadily develops from within the text and musical accompaniment. Andraé and his colleagues slowly build the arrangement from the introduction, strengthened by Howard Smith's resonant voice amplifying and riffing on Crouch's melody. (Forty years later, Linda McCrary vividly recalled the moment in the studio: "Howard Smith did the first verse and I'm thinking, 'Do I really want to come behind Howard Smith?' You've really got to be ready.") McCrary's masterful vocal coloring on the second verse both contrasts with and reinforces Smith's, creating a strikingly original blend. The background vocal tracks have five-to-eight-part layering harmonic textures, with thirds and fifths intervals doubling in the octave. At the same time, the "inner" voices sing intervals of seconds and suspended fourths, resolving to the third. Even with the prime unison singing, this is yet another example of Crouch's genius for a large choral arrangement. This vocal "stacking" in the studio, as expensive as it may have been with the studio "clock" running, is simply unprecedented in gospel music. The entrance of the pipe organ at the 3:30-minute mark unexpectedly introduces the classical European organ sound to mainstream gospel music. It is, the authors believe, another illustration of Andraé's sometimes single-minded intentionality to bring disparate Christian cultures together. God's truth, Crouch asserts, draws *everyone.* "His Truth Still Marches On" closes with octave unisons— congregational singing—to the familiar line "his truth still marches on."[14]

The participants in the recording session said they knew that even as the tapes rolled that something special was happening in the studio. "We were very blessed and the anointing began to fall," McCrary said. "You just go in and sing the story and make it into something believable for people to take into the core of their very being. I think Howard and I did it in one or two takes." Howard McCrary said he "marveled" at Andraé's ability to make a song "resonate" with those who heard it:

> Not every writer has that ability. It's not a patented thing or a scientific thing as much as it is just resonation, just resonating with the heart. What do people want to hear? Songs that get into their minds and their hearts. That's something that's very rare. That's why Andraé, I think, was so loved and appreciated.

During the process of recording the song, Linda recalled that Crouch allowed the singers to embellish the melody and even change some of the notes to make them a better fit with the orchestration. "I allowed, Howard allowed, Kristle allowed, we all allowed the Holy Spirit to take that melody and bring it to life," Linda said, "because what Andraé's giving you is coming from the Holy Spirit. So you want to do it right. I was privileged to learn how to arrange backgrounds because of Andraé. There was no stress—the backgrounds were just fun because we got to create wisdom."[15]

Side II

"Oh, It Is Jesus"

The lyrics of "Oh, It Is Jesus" retell the story of Luke 8:43–48, where a woman suffering with a painful "issue" of the blood creeps through a crowd of jostling people to touch the hem of Jesus' garment—and is instantly healed. This is the only $^6_8$ compound meter song on the LP and, from the opening notes, Crouch's piano and the energized background vocalists launch into a more traditional Black gospel performance. "Oh, It Is Jesus" sits in the middle of the nine-song album, and the name of *Jesus* is at the center of it all, while the lyrics declare "and His blood has made me whole." The recorded version of the song is in D♭ major, which allows Andraé to play the piano. The result is a song that Maxwell said he remains particularly fond of, years later. "I like that things are pared away and it's really Andraé playing," he said. "It's really the gist of what Andraé is—that's Andraé and it's nobody else." Like "His Truth Still Marches On," the singers said that the recording session was packed with emotion. "When we sang it in the studio, the Holy Spirit came down on us," Howard McCrary said. "The *Shekinah Glory* was right there in the studio that day when we sang. We couldn't stop crying, we couldn't stop singing, we just kept singing over and over again, 'Jesus, something about that name.'"[16]

Tata Vega's ferocious vocal prowess and ability to convey a narrative through song is one of the highlights of "Oh, It Is Jesus," which allows listeners to imagine that *she* is the woman in the story who is desperately reaching to "touch the hem of His garment." Maxwell said that Vega sang every song, whether in the studio or in concert, with total abandon, which often meant she would be hoarse by the third take. As a result, Maxwell said that he usually assumed that one of the first takes of a given song would be the one used on the final recording. "Tata was a 'one-hitter quitter,'" Linda McCrary marveled. "She would get in there and get it done in one take."[17]

"No Time to Lose (I Wanna Be Ready)"

The title track is one of the more offbeat inclusions on *No Time to Lose*, with enough musical and lyrical references to confound a seasoned musicologist. There is the subtle shout-out to Larry Norman's seminal Jesus Music anthem, "I Wish We'd All Been Ready," as well as the old spiritual "I Wanna Be Ready." Yet the music is decidedly of the era—disco-styled orchestrations and groove with an electronic techno-influenced arrangement. "No Time to Lose" is in the key of B minor and the song is driven, unusually, by the guitars and synthesizers, with musical echoes of Gary Wright, Steve Winwood, even ToTo. The result is the groove of Steely Dan, but with a touch of Parliament. The vocals, however, are reminiscent of Earth, Wind & Fire, filtered through Andraé's distinctive gospel harmonies. There is even a hint of a reggae beat!

The message of this musical gumbo, however, is resoundingly clear: Christians need to be ready for the impending return of Jesus Christ. Guitarist James Harrah's strongest memory of these sessions was the unusual guitar sound. "Bill wanted to simulate [on the guitar] a clock ticking," Harrah said, "marking the seconds going by, I suppose. When we heard the playback, it was 'Wow!'— that really communicated the clock ticking."[18]

"Livin' This Kind of Life"

In the key of A♭ major, "Livin' This Kind of Life" is a splendid Detroit gospel funk shuffle and signals Andraé's strong connections to the Winans, who were already making a significant impact in gospel music. The song is presented as Crouch's testimony. It is possible, the authors suggest, that the song was written as Andraé's response to the bad press and allegations of the previous years. The lyrics, delivered almost conversationally, including the line "no more walking in sinking sand," reference the beloved hymn "The Solid Rock," and the vamp allows the text to develop—"It's a good life, such a sweet life, you know/I like livin' this kind of life."

Musically, the song is filled with instrumental breaks, prime unison vocals, and staccato horn hits. Even the chord progressions on the vamp are influenced by the new contemporary gospel approach spearheaded by the Winans. Like the singers, "Livin' This Kind of Life" allows the instrumentalists a great degree of improvisational latitude, and they respond with Harrah's pointillistic rhythmic guitar bites and Gouche's agile, engagingly funky bass line.

By *No Time to Lose*, recording studio technology was in the midst of a digital transformation, introducing MIDI technology, drum loops, and other innovations to the producer, arranger, and musicians. The result of this collaboration with Scott V. Smith and Maxwell is a song quite beyond the capabilities of all but the most accomplished Black church at the time. The album would join a select handful of others that would herald the direction of contemporary gospel music.

"This is one of the songs where he took the background vocals and made everybody a lead [singer]," Linda McCrary said, "then put it together as a background vocal. Now, of course, Kirk Franklin and a lot of other people do it, but Andraé was doing it forty years ago. Sometimes he'd send me in and say, 'Linda, sing this and double and triple and quadruple it—and then I want everybody to follow that.'"[19]

"Somebody Somewhere Is Prayin' (Just for You)"

"Somebody Somewhere Is Prayin' (Just for You)" also marks something new in the Crouch canon. This is his first published song to focus on a practical theology of prayer, and its format mirrors a multistep process designed to teach effective praying, improvisation, testifying, and preaching. This "theology" of prayer resonates with the words of St. Theophan, "Prayer is the test of everything." In retrospect, the song sounds like a testimony, with a touch of desperation—Andraé *has* to believe that in this difficult time that there are friends, family members, and a host of others praying for him. Even the brief musical modulations sprinkled through the song—to G♭ major from E♭— signal (the authors suggest) the idea that the prayers and supplications are for Andraé himself. At the very heart of the composition are Larry Muhoberac's lovely keyboard patterns. Maxwell called Muhoberac a musical "genius" who, among other gifts, could chart and arrange songs as fast as Crouch could play them. "His ears were astonishing," Maxwell said. "Andraé brought the best out in Larry and I think Larry inspired Andraé."[20]

"Always Remember"

The hymn-like "Always Remember," with its four-part open voice chorale reminiscent of the boy choirs of English cathedrals, Maxwell said, immediately connected with many Black musicians and singers. Unusual among Andraé's compositions, the song fades *in* as if it is a processional or entrance to the sanctuary. With its open chord hymn styling, the song sounds as if it was written specifically for an ecumenical audience. "Always Remember" is unusually basic and yet, in many ways, ahead of its time, providing another template for the praise & worship movement that will eventually come to provide the primary music format for many churches, Black, Latinx, and white.

As one of the last songs recorded, it also serves as a postlude to prayer and possibly a farewell. The album title *No Time to Lose* refers once more to the angels mentioned in the opening track. On "Always Remember," listeners hear voices that sound like celestial angelic "ohhs" underneath the verses. The words, "terror by night" and "angels charge over you," are drawn from several disparate sources, including Psalms 91:5, Isaiah 28:19, Job 4:18, and Job 27:20. From those references, it may be inferred again that Andraé wrote "Always Remember" in response to his constant battles with public opinion, the marketplace, and the media, reminding himself to always keep his eyes set upon Jesus even as the song instructs his listeners to "always keep Him on your mind."

"'Always Remember' was so awesome because it kept your heart in a humble place," Linda McCrary said. "Only what we do for Christ lasts anyway. Andraé always remembered where it all came from, wherever it all started, no matter what his ups and downs were. He always came back to that." "Andraé tapped into heaven when he wrote that song that day," Howard McCrary said. "There's something just angelic about the whole scale of that song."[21]

A Cry for Help?

Despite the presence of upbeat, bouncy songs like "Right Now" and "Livin' This Kind of Life," it is also possible to hear *No Time to Lose* as a heart-cry, a lament. Crouch's lyrics often reflected what was going on in his life, great highs sometimes followed by crashing lows. The narrative of "Jesus, Come Lay Your Head on Me" may refer directly to Christ's moments of despair in the Garden of Gethsemane but—on an intensely personal level—could also refer directly to Andraé's own trials. He has given his life to ministry. In his time of greatest need, who ministers to the minister? Who pastors the pastor? "I think to me in some ways, this album was Andraé crying for help," Maxwell said, "for who he really is and what he really stands for. After everything that had happened, he felt his good name wasn't a good name anymore. He was hurt and it destroyed his confidence." With that in mind, then, the closing pastoral benediction "Always Remember" is addressed to Andraé himself. Ten years later, Andraé would find *himself* unexpectedly serving as pastor of Christ Memorial Church of God in Christ.[22]

Touring Again

Crouch supported *No Time to Lose* with a series of short tours, each with fewer dates than in previous years. Several of the new songs quickly found their way on the regular setlists. Linda McCrary remembered how much fun "Living This Kind of Life" was to perform as Andraé quickly got into character:

> It was almost like you were bragging—"Hey, I'm living this kind of life and you can, too, if you trust God." Andraé would put his thumbs in the lapels of his coat

and strut across the stage, just being so proud that he was privileged, we were privileged, to know the Lord. Even though he went through things and had a lot of stuff happening to him, he was very proud to represent Christ—and I loved that man for that. The other song that was so much fun to perform was "Right Now." People would just go bonkers.

Vocalist Jackie Gouche, who sang on the *No Time to Lose* tours, also said that "Right Now" was her "favorite" song to perform. "Every time we sang this song there was a power and a presence on the song itself," she said. "People relate to a message that sticks, that when you say it makes a powerful point, a simple point. It stays with people. With 'Right Now,' 'we need him right now.' Even if you don't know all the lyrics, simple messages that stay with people have a lasting effect."[23]

The addition of the dynamic Tata Vega to the recording sessions and touring band added a new visual element to the concerts. Vega was particularly "demonstrative" on stage, according to Alfie Silas. "I remember during 'Oh, It Is Jesus,' she would hit her arm like she had been shooting up—and talk how the Lord now has made her whole. She would do all kinds of visual things that would help you understand what she was singing about." Some of James Harrah's strongest memories on the *No Time to Lose* tours also include Vega's show-stopping performances of "Oh, It Is Jesus," crawling across the stage floor with a towel over her head, trying to touch Andraé's pants leg, vividly recreating the story of the woman with the blood issue from Luke 8:43–48. Maxwell said that that the rest of the band was in shock. "James Harrah told me, 'I haven't seen someone crawling around the stage since I was with Madonna.'" "Tata's performance on that is awesome," Harrah recalled, "but she was such a character."[24]

Harrah, however, was increasingly in demand for recording session dates and soon had to return to Los Angeles. His replacement was his longtime friend, guitarist Wayne Brasel. "As James moved up the studio ladder, he kept throwing me his old gigs," Brasel said. "I was happy to take them." His first performance with Andraé was at an open-air concert in Jamaica before 10,000 people. Brasel said he immediately had a crash course in *No Time to Lose* but was forced to learn and perform some of the older songs while on stage. Brasel was also featured in tours of Scandinavia in 1984 and 1985, which included a jazz festival in Sweden and a concert in Larvik, Norway, broadcast on Norwegian television. Brasel said some of his best memories of that tour are spending time with his friend and keyboardist Lou Pardini, who would later join the band Chicago. "The musicians and the singers in that band were so good," Brasel said, "I was just happy to be with them. I was a little concerned because I didn't grow up in the Black church and whether I would be 'authentic' enough for Bill Maxwell." Fortunately, Brasel said he quickly discovered that Crouch "wanted something fresh. "They didn't really expect me to play the old way that James had played on the record," he said.[25]

The Larvik concert, which was uploaded to YouTube by longtime Crouch family friend Johnny Tarberg, is dated "Winter 1985." Five songs were featured on the video, though Brasel said they played more: "Got Me Some Angels," "Right Now," "We Are Not Ashamed," "Livin' This Kind of Life," and "Let's Worship Him." Both the audio and visuals are of a high quality, offering an excellent introduction to Andraé's incredibly tight touring ensemble at the time: Sandra Crouch (vocals and percussion), Maxwell (drums), Andrew Gouche (bass), Geary Lathier Faggett (piano), Lou Pardini (keyboards), and Tata Vega, Rose Banks, Maxine Anderson, Vonciele Faggett, and Jean Johnson on vocals.

Vonciele Faggett said that the tours following *No Time to Lose* were particularly creative times for all involved. "It was always a party because Andraé was a prophetic writer," she said. "He would end up writing after every performance. It was going to be new and different than the previous time, so the excitement was always there. I looked forward to that." Faggett said the instrumentalists and singers would watch Crouch closely after the opening, usually preselected numbers. "We'd ask, 'What is he going to do? How do you top last night's performance?'" she said. "And sure enough, he'd get some inspiration and we'd start having fun and making stuff up as we go along." Andraé, Faggett said, fostered that sense of creativity. "If something creative would come to me or to Tata or to Jean, he'd say, 'Do it! Go for it!' Every night was different, every night was fresh. And I loved, loved, loved that about him."[26]

Brasel continued to tour with Crouch for several more years, once as the group even followed the legendary Miles Davis on a revolving stage in Chicago. "Of all of the people to follow—and yet Andraé's music was so unique it really didn't matter," Brasel said. "And there was never any question whether Andraé would just electrify the band and the audience. He just turned on, like a light." As had been the case throughout Crouch's career, Brasel said the group never knew the set list from night to night, save for some of the songs from *No Time to Lose*. "You didn't know when suddenly he'd sit down at the piano and start playing a bunch of songs that you'd never heard before," he said. "But that was

A Strong Comeback

The combination of Light's increased support, the quality of the songs, and Andraé's live performances buoyed *No Time to Lose*. It debuted at #20 on the "Best-Selling Spiritual LPs" chart, hit #2 by October, and reached the #1 position by December. The album's success was in stark contrast to his previous release, *Finally*, which had debuted at #30 in 1983, never charted higher than #14, and was off the charts completely by April 1984.[28]

The reviews were equally positive. *Billboard* gave it a featured review, saying that *No Time to Lose* "demonstrates that Crouch is on the cutting edge of mainstream pop/gospel." Vocals by Crouch, Kristle Edwards, Tata Vega, Howard Smith, and Linda McCrary "give this album broad appeal." The Baltimore *Afro-American* stated that the LP "was sure to be a success."[29]

But instead of taking a victory lap, Crouch used the success of the album to lament what he considered an increasing separation between Black and white audiences, something he blamed on the Christian music industry's use of separate sales charts and promotional practices and the "scarcity" of Black gospel music on the primarily white CCM radio stations. Ecumenism and inclusivity, of course, had been two of Andraé's primary concerns from the earliest days of his ministry. "The world should know that we are all brothers and sisters and that we all have a song," Crouch said. "Some of these innovative artists, if they could play the way they want, could really reach the kids on the street—which means the devil wouldn't get at them." The inclusion of more Latin-oriented music on *No Time to Lose*, he added, was intentional, in part to make the public more aware of the "untapped pool of Hispanic gospel talent." "It's ludicrous for us to ignore these other styles of music," Crouch told *Billboard*.[30]

At year's end, Sandra's *We Sing Praises* was the best-selling "Spiritual" album, followed by the Winans' *Long Time Comin'* (#11) and Tramaine Hawkins's *Determined* (#13). While the chart only listed the top twenty-five-selling LPs, the success of *No Time to Lose* in the second half of 1984 doubtless meant it would have been one of the next few entries on the list.[31]

The End of the Partnerships

However, the year also marked the end of two of the most significant collaborations in the history gospel music. It would be Andraé's last album of original material for Light Records. The difficulties of the previous years, Crouch said, had been too much to overcome. "Light was a label that was very non-appreciative to their artists," he told *Rejoice!* magazine a few years later. "They didn't try to accommodate them." Andraé noted virtually all the remaining Black artists left the label shortly thereafter. "Ralph Carmichael never came to one of my concerts in all the years I was there. They were strictly business—a nine-to-five operation. They didn't support their artists beyond what was required by contract."[32]

It would also be Crouch's last album with producer/drummer Bill Maxwell. Since *Live in London*, Andraé's need to constantly tweak material, especially the vocals, had consumed more and more studio time. Some of the background vocalists, who asked that their comments be considered background only, told the authors that the time required to "experiment" and do seemingly endless "retakes" in the studio made working with Crouch increasingly difficult, from both a financial and a career standpoint. Maxwell said that the albums following *Live in London* had exclusively become "studio projects," producing songs that were increasingly difficult to replicate live. "With *No Time to Lose*, my involvement was over," Maxwell said. "Andraé just got worse and worse about doing his vocals and redoing his vocals. The song would be ready to master and he'd want to redo a vocal. There wasn't money for all the time you're putting in. Money wasn't really the issue, though, it was just wearing me out emotionally."[33]

Meanwhile, in addition to becoming a much in-demand producer, especially on television, Maxwell's band Koinonia signed with Sparrow Records and soon headlined jazz tours, especially in Western Europe and Scandinavia, where they were particularly popular. The group reluctantly disbanded in 1990 when the much in-demand musicians could no longer afford to miss so many lucrative studio dates, though Maxwell and Laboriel continued with a group called Open Hands.[34]

The tipping point, though, was the hit television series *Amen*. Maxwell had been contracted by producer Ed Weinberger as "music director" for Carson Productions and assembled a stellar recording team for the session to record Andraé's composition "Shine on Me," including vocalist Vanessa Bell Armstrong, Andrew Gouche (bass), David Williams (guitar), Pardini (piano), Crouch on organ, Maxwell on drums, and a small choir contracted by Rose Stone. The theme song was a success and launched Armstrong's career. Maxwell and Crouch worked on the music for *Amen* for the entire season. "It wasn't a falling out," Maxwell said:

> But by the second season, because Andraé wasn't disciplined to do something like that regularly, they didn't keep him on—but they kept me on. He got hurt, but we got over it. It was never really bad between us. I switched and began to do more television. I would still go out and do tours with him every now and then until the early '90s.

In the years that followed, Crouch worked with a variety of producers, arrangers, and music directors, with varying degrees of success. "Andraé couldn't exist without Bill back in those days," longtime friend and singer Perry Morgan said. "Bill took charge. Andraé did the songs and everything, but Bill knew the tempo it was supposed to be. He knew everything musically."[35]

"I tried to protect him," Maxwell said:

> I tried to protect his music, the integrity of his music, the integrity of what he was given. I tried to get it on tape as good as I could. I tried to bring the songs to life as good as I could. Tried to help him on stage as good as I could. But there was only so much you could do with the talent.

Decades after *No Time to Lose*, Maxwell said he was working with singers Ryan Tedder and Jessie J when Tedder asked how he managed to master the sound boards in the recording studio. "I said, 'Andraé Crouch,'" Maxwell recalled. "And I didn't touch the surface of what his talent was at this. He gave me a skill I didn't know I had."[36]

NOTES

1. Paul Grien, "Thrilling Eight Grammys for Michael Jackson," *Billboard*, March 10, 1984, 1, 72; "Best-Selling Spiritual LPs," *Billboard*, March 17, 1984, 37; Claudrena Harold, "Almighty Fire: The Rise of Urban Contemporary Gospel Music and the Search for Culture Authority in the 1980s," *Association for the Student of African American Life and History* 1, no. 1 (2012): 34.
2. Bob Darden, "Carmichael Marks 20 Years of Light," *Billboard*, September 15, 1984, 54; Bob Darden, "Major Labels: Poised on the Brink of Breakthrough with Pop Music's Fastest-Growing Genre," *Billboard*, September 29, 1984, G-5, G-20.

3. Bill Maxwell, interview with the authors, June 10, 2023.
4. Howard Smith, interview with the authors August 31, 2021.
5. Alfie Silas Durio, interview with the authors, January 18, 2021.
6. James Harrah, interview with the authors, August 19, 2021.
7. Abraham Laboriel, interview with the authors, August 19, 2021.
8. Howard Smith, interview with the authors, August 31, 2021.
9. Bill Maxwell, interview with the authors, June 10, 2023; Howard Smith, interview with the authors, August 31, 2021.
10. Andraé Crouch, *No Time to Lose* (Light Records LS 5863, 1984); Bill Maxwell, interview with the authors, June 10, 2023.
11. Bill Maxwell, interview with the authors, June 10, 2023; Linda McCrary, interview with the authors, November 9, 2021; https://m.imdb.com/name/nm0189 428/fullcredits.
12. Linda McCrary, interview with the authors, November 9, 2021.
13. Bill Maxwell, interview with the authors, June 10, 2023; Howard McCrary, interview with the authors, February 18, 2022.
14. Linda McCrary, interview with the authors, November 9, 2021.
15. Linda McCrary, interview with the authors, November 9, 2021; Howard McCrary, interview with the authors, February 18, 2022.
16. Bill Maxwell, interview with the authors, June 10, 2023; Howard McCrary, interview with the authors, February 18, 2022.
17. Bill Maxwell, interview with the authors, June 10, 2023; Linda McCrary, interview with the authors, November 9, 2022.
18. James Harrah, interview with the authors, August 19, 2021.
19. Linda McCrary, interview with the authors, August 19, 2021.
20. Igumen Cariton of Valamo, *The Art of Prayer: An Orthodox Anthology* (London: Faber & Faber, 1966), 51; Bill Maxwell, interview with the authors, June 10, 2023.
21. Bill Maxwell, interview with the authors, June 10, 2023; Linda McCrary, interview with the authors, November 9, 2022; Howard McCrary, interview with the authors, February 18, 2022.
22. Bill Maxwell, interview with the authors, June 10, 2023.
23. Linda McCrary, interview with the authors, November 9, 2022; Jackie Gouche, interview with the authors, November 13, 2020.
24. Alfie Silas Durio, interview with the authors, June 18, 2021; James Harrah, interview with the authors, August 19, 2021; Bill Maxwell, interview with the authors, June 10, 2023.
25. Wayne Brasel, interview with the authors, August 28, 2021.
26. http://www.youtube.com/watch?v=OlG11j5jjAw; Wayne Brasel, interview with the authors, August 28, 2021; Vonciele Faggett, interview with the authors, October 21, 2021.
27. Wayne Brasel, interview with the authors, August 28, 2021.

28. "Best-Selling Spiritual LPs," *Billboard*, August 4, 1984, 52; "Best-Selling Spiritual LPs," *Billboard*, October 27, 1984, 46; "Best-Selling Spiritual LPs," *Billboard*, November 24, 1984, 56.

29. *Billboard* August 25, 1984, 73; Eddie King, "Gospel Greats," Baltimore *Afro-American*, September 22, 1984, 11.

30. Moira McCormick, "The 1984 Crossover Crusade: Marching at the Front of the Talent Parade," *Billboard*, September 29, 1984, G-3, G-18, G-24.

31. "Top Selling Spiritual Albums," *Billboard*, December 12, 1984, TA-32; "Best-Selling Spiritual LPs," *Billboard*, December 28, 1985, T-31.

32. Edwin Smith, "Catching Up with Andraé Crouch," *Rejoice!*, August/September 1992, 7.

33. Bill Maxwell, interview with the authors, May 18, 2019.

34. Bill Maxwell, interview with the authors, January 20, 2023.

35. Bill Maxwell, interview with the authors, January 20, 2023; Perry Morgan, interview with the authors, May 18, 2019.

36. Bill Maxwell, interview with the authors, May 18, 2019; Bill Maxwell, interview with the authors, June 10, 2023.

17

The Final Years

The end of the Crouch–Maxwell work relationship marked the conclusion of the most successful, most enduring partnership in the history of gospel music. An appropriate comparison in popular music, the authors believe, would be the end of the relationship between producer George Martin and the Beatles. In both cases, both producer and musician or musicians would go on to additional acclaim—but it would never be the same.

Bill Maxwell remained an accomplished, much-in-demand producer (and drummer), and the central, much-beloved touchstone to the host of musicians and singers who worked and toured with Andraé Crouch. Many of the musicians and singers interviewed for the book said that Maxwell's firm but loving hand reined in at least some of Andraé's perfectionist—some used the word *compulsive*—qualities in the studio and gave direction to his unquestioned compositional genius.

But for Crouch, the dissolution of the musical partnership, coupled with the continued repercussions from the arrest in the often unforgiving world of religious music, and even the rapidly changing musical landscape in gospel music that Andraé himself had helped create, meant that Crouch would not record another gospel album for more than a decade following the release of *No Time to Lose*. Instead, he would turn—often quite successfully—to a variety of other projects.

Projects Outside the Gospel Bubble

Quincy Jones soon invited Crouch to participate in Steven Spielberg's prestige film project *The Color Purple*. Spielberg requested several gospel songs for a sequence involving a rural Black church and needed them within twenty-four hours. Andraé called his closest musical collaborators and together they composed fifteen songs in one night. The highlight, "Maybe God Is Trying to Tell You Something," featured both Tata Vega and the Christ Memorial Church of God in Christ Choir. "Some of [the older church members] couldn't sing particularly well," Crouch told *Billboard*, "but it sounded *right*. Those old church mothers don't care how pretty something sounds—they just *sing*." Included in the choir was eighty-nine-year-old "Mother" Dora Brackins in her wheelchair. According to Kathy Hazzard, Crouch instructed Brackins, "Do like they do in all-night prayer—no music." "And that's what they did," Hazzard said. "Spielberg had never heard anything like that. It's a moan. They call it the 'War Cry.'" The album received an Academy Award nomination for "Best Original Score" but did not win.[1]

Through Quincy Jones, Crouch and the core group of talented singers under his direction also recorded songs with Michael Jackson during the King of Pop's run of iconic albums in the 1980s and 1990s, including "Man in the Mirror" (from *Bad*, 1987), "Keep the Faith" and "Will You Be There" (from *Dangerous*, 1991), and "Earth Song" (from *HIStory: Past, Present and Future*, Book I, 1995). Andraé's collaborations with the legendarily eccentric Jackson led to some memorable music—and stories. One biographer called Jackson's vocal performance with Andraé, Sandra, and a small choir of handpicked vocalists on "Man in the Mirror" "one of the highlights of Michael's recording career." Hazzard also recalled that during the "Man in the Mirror" sessions, Crouch, as was his custom, began each session with a group prayer. While the prayer was in progress, she saw Jackson—who ordinarily stayed in the studio's recording booth—on the floor filming the prayer circle with a small camera. When Andraé asked Jackson about his faith, Hazzard said Michael replied, "I'm still searching."[2]

"Like a Prayer"

In 1989, Crouch and his vocalists recorded the background vocals for the song "Like a Prayer" by controversial pop artist Madonna. While the song itself raised a few eyebrows in the Black church, the accompanying music video, which featured "a scantily clad Madonna singing in front of burning crosses, suffering wounds on her hand like Jesus and kissing a saintly statue that turns into a man" was widely denounced by a host of religious organizations, including

THE FINAL YEARS   381

the Vatican. Crouch, offered a part with the gospel choir in the video, declined to appear. Regardless, the backlash against the song was swift and savage and the events further alienated Andraé from the more conservative elements in his audience. "It's a song that explores the word 'prayer,'" Andraé told *The Guardian* newspaper. "Madonna wanted something very churchy, so I tried to blow up what she did and make it as powerful as I could." In a later interview, Crouch said that he recorded the song because he "saw it as an opportunity to share the Lord" with Madonna and her producers.[3]

James Cleveland and Other Losses

After a brief illness, the Reverend James Cleveland, Andraé's longtime friendly rival, died on February 9, 1991, allegedly from complications of the AIDS virus. Gospel royalty packed the Shrine Auditorium in Los Angeles as a visibly shaken Crouch spoke at the funeral. He called Cleveland "his idol" and recalled how it was at Cleveland's home that he wrote his first song, "The Blood (Will Never Lose Its Power)," before singing "Through It All" to the rapt audience.[4]

In the early 1990s, Crouch and sister Sandra suffered a series of even more devastating personal losses. Their mother Catherine died on April 6, 1992. Fourteen years later, Andraé said that his mother's death by cancer was the "lowest day of my life." Bishop Benjamin Crouch Sr. died of prostate cancer just over a year later, on December 16, 1993. The Bishop's death meant that eldest son Ben, who had health issues of his own, reluctantly assumed the pastorate at Christ Memorial, which caused a split in the congregation.[5]

In the midst of the turmoil and loss, Crouch released his first gospel album in a decade in 1994, *Mercy*, for Quincy Jones's Warner Bros.–distributed Qwest label. Andraé explained the long absence as being due, in part, to his original desire both to establish his own record label (to be called Stomp Records), and to produce other artists before deciding to record and release with Qwest. *Mercy* was produced with Scott V. Smith and featured some of the instrumentalists and especially the singers from his Light Records years, including Kristle Murden, Linda McCrary, Maxi Anderson, Alfie Silas, Vonciele Faggett, Tammie Gibson, Tata Vega, and Hazzard and debuted at #29 on the April 16, 1994, *Billboard* gospel charts. But the album never really gained traction in the marketplace and by year's end, it finished as the thirty-fifth ranked gospel album on the list. Crouch told Lisa Collins that with *Mercy*, he felt as though he was "starting from the beginning in so many ways" and admitted that many young gospel fans were probably not aware of his music and asked, "'Who was this guy we've heard about?'" (Image 17.1)[6]

Andraé Crouch

P.O. Box 1248 San Fernando, CA 91340   www.NewCMC.org

Image 17.1 Undated Andraé Crouch promotional photograph, circa 2000. From the authors' collection.

Crouch's next high-profile engagement was working with producer Hans Zimmer on the award-winning film soundtrack to *The Lion King*. Kristle Murden (as Kristle Edwards) was featured as one of the lead vocalists on "Can You Feel the Love Tonight," and Alfie Silas (later Durio) contracted the vocalists for the gospel choir. Silas said that Zimmer, who had worked with her on the *Thelma and Louise* film soundtrack, told her, "I want you to help bring that 'Andraé sound' to *The Lion King*." "I told him, 'Well, why don't we get Andraé?'" Silas responded. Zimmer said, "Oh, do you think he'd do it?"[7]

But two years after accepting the call to pastor what was now called New Christ Memorial COGIC, Benjamin Crouch Jr. passed of prostate cancer as well, on February 7, 1995. Andraé then assumed the pastorate, following a ceremony and concert September 22, 1995, that included Michael Jackson, Quincy Jones, Stevie Wonder, Marvin Winans, and others. The official installation and consecration services took place at the church the following day. Crouch, who had been ordained in 1980, told the *Los Angeles Sentinel* that he was "excited" about the prospect. "I really want God to use me," Andraé said, "and he does through my music and my ministry. My goal is to reach the world with my ministry and music." Andraé soon left his home in the West Valley, moved into his parents' small house near Christ Memorial, and even declined the pastor's salary as he attempted to juggle the ministry of the church with performing and recording during the week. "It was just a big, big, big job for him," Tammie Gibson said. "To be traveling, recording, and integrating that into preaching and preparing for these services, a lot of that can take a big toll on your body." Singer Voncielle Faggett said that Andraé's ministry "inspired" her to later become the worship leader at the church. "He would lose himself in the worship," she said, "and it could go on and on. He just basically talked when he preached. Having Andraé in the pulpit was like sitting down and having a conversation with him." At other times, recalled theologian Jamal-Dominique Hopkins (who had attended the church as a young man), Crouch would stay at the piano and "sing" the sermons, sometimes improvising as he went along. "Those are the times I miss most of all," LaVern Moore said, "when he would sit at the piano and talk and praise and play. And it would be straight from the throne."[8]

Crouch again teamed with Smith to produce *Pray*, which Qwest/Warners Alliance released late in 1997. Once again, Andraé surrounded himself with many of the singers from his previous releases and left the production duties with Smith. But like *Mercy*, none of the songs on *Pray* caught the attention of gospel music consumers and the album finished as #32 on the year-end "Top Gospel Albums" sales chart in *Billboard* and did not chart at all in 1998. For

Silas, *Pray* marked significant changes in Andraé's life, both musically and ministerially. "He had become more entrenched in the ministry at his father's church," she said. "And you could hear the music change a bit. He had been on the road at that point for forty years." The most haunting moment on the album is the final track, the ballad "Until Jesus Comes," where Crouch calls out the names of loved ones he will see again in heaven: "My mother! My father! My brother!"[9]

Ordaining Sandra

In August 1998, Andraé challenged Church of God in Christ tradition and ordained Sandra, who in the previous year had already become active in the ministry as "assistant pastor." "I believe that when you have a sense within yourself that God is calling you to work in a particular part of the ministry," Sandra said, "that no matter what gender you are, you should be able to answer that call." The three-hour "very joyous occasion" was not attended by either the COGIC leadership or New Christ Memorial's supervisory bishop, Bishop J. Bernard Hackworth, who called the event "unofficial." "I'm not taking a man's place. I'm just taking my place," Sandra said.[10]

Health Issues

By now, however, it was clear to those closest to him that Crouch's health issues were accelerating. In addition to surgery to remove cancerous growths from his colon in the late 1990s, decades of nonstop touring, bad sleeping and eating habits, and marathon composing and recording sessions were catching up with him. He delegated more and more of his singing and performing duties on stage and left most of the production duties, save for the background vocals, with Smith. Even with stellar vocal performances from Yolanda Adams, Chaka Khan, Tata Vega, Patti Austin, Daniel Johnson, and many of his beloved "crew" of singers, *The Gift of Christmas* (Warners-Alliance, 1999) charted only briefly in December and failed to even appear on the either of the year-end "Top Gospel Albums" charts in 1999 and 2000.[11]

In the early 2000s, Crouch suffered through another round of treatments for cancer and while still in the very early stages of recovery was invited to receive an award from the International Worship Institute. Longtime friend Howard Rachinski said that Andraé insisted on attending, and Rachinski was forced to nearly carry him from his hotel room to the ceremony. But when he was asked to sing, Rachinski said "he comes alive, he pours out his heart." Howard and Sandra then physically supported him back to his room.[12]

Despite the lack of sales and an ever-decreasing touring schedule, the name *Andraé Crouch* retained its magic. There were songs and performances on other movie soundtracks ranging from *The Passion of Christ* to the animated *Yertl the Turtle*, more TV performances, a tribute album composed primarily of CCM artists, induction in the Gospel Music Association Hall of Fame, and even a star on the Hollywood Boulevard Walk of Fame in 2004, but no more gospel albums until 2006, when Verity, one of the most powerful labels in gospel music, took a chance and released Crouch's *Mighty Wind*. Since Andraé's stamina had waned dramatically following another stomach surgery, Linda McCrary said she enlisted Markita Knight and Kristle Murden to work with new producer Luther "Mano" Hanes to complete the project before offering it to various gospel labels. "I just wanted to do what I felt the Lord was telling me to do without anyone giving me [direction] as to what the industry wanted," Andraé said. "I wanted something cutting edge. Verity spoke my language." Despite considerable star power from guests that included Marvin Winans, Karen Clark-Sheard, Fred Hammond, and others, *Mighty Wind* failed to capture the public's imagination and it too barely grazed the lowest levels of the sales and airplay charts.[13]

"Let the Church Say Amen"

Crouch's health was now of a concern beyond his circle of closest friends. He doggedly continued to write, but it soon became obvious that even short tours were beyond him. In 2010 and 2011, Andraé enlisted Linda McCrary and others to record one more studio album, again produced by Hanes, *The Journey*. Only Hanes's recently founded Riverphlo label was interested. Again, his friends and longtime fans rallied around him, and the album included performances by Kim Burrell, Take 6, Tata Vega, Rance Allen, Sheila E., and Chaka Khan. McCrary worked long hours over several months with Crouch to finish the songs. Crouch's compulsive need to tinker with "completed" recordings and frequently "impromptu" recording sessions meant that Hanes and business partner Kevin Raleigh were forced to reschedule the release on multiple occasions. However, *The Journey*—and Andraé—contained one final surprise. The song "Let the Church Say Amen" became Andraé's last widely requested and performed song. At Crouch's request, Marvin Winans, by then a pastor himself, had flown to the Fantasy Studio in San Francisco where Andraé had composed a single line to a song, "Let the church say amen," written in the dark days following his brother Benjamin's death. "That's all he had," Winans said, "my brother's gone." The Crouch family had been praying for Benjamin, and when it happened, Andraé said, "God has spoken. So just let the church say amen." Winans said that he then contributed verses to the existing recording created by Crouch and Hanes. McCrary said that the musicians in the studio knew the song was special, even if Andraé himself didn't. "I mean, everybody around the world is still saying, 'Let the Church Say Amen,'" she recalled. But McCrary said that when Crouch tried to record his vocals, she was forced to write the lyrics out in large block letters so he could see them. She was also deeply involved with Hanes in the numerous overdubs after the basic tracks had been completed. Though the song "Let the Church Say Amen" spent four weeks at the top of charts in April 2012, Riverphlo's limited distribution was not strong enough to boost *The Journey*'s overall sales.[14]

Crouch, who had been suffering from diabetes for years, now suffered from extreme foot pain. According to McCrary, the pain eventually made it impossible for him to play the piano. "The only reason he stopped performing was because he couldn't get up and go to that piano," she said. "That's when I think he kind of started giving up." "When he got to the point where he could not play and it was so painful for his feet to press the pedals, I knew that he would not be with us very much longer," LaVern Moore said. "His heart was just removed when he could not worship [that] way."[15]

Crouch rarely took the stage and when he did, Bill Maxwell said that Andraé would often launch into long, sometimes incoherent monologues. On their final brief tour together, Maxwell said the band was reluctantly forced to play over him after Andraé had rambled for forty minutes. Afterward, Crouch sadly told him, "I don't remember how to do what I did." Crouch was determined, however, to release one last live album and with the heroic assistance of McCrary and others, was able to record the tracks for what would become *Live in Los Angeles*, released by Riverphlo in 2013 with an accompanying concert DVD. Poor distribution and limited publicity meant that Andraé's final album barely caused a blip in the marketplace and even used copies remain difficult to find. "I'm just grateful that I was there in that last season of arranging and writing and assisting him and standing by him," McCrary said. "I'm so blessed, you wouldn't even believe." Producer Raleigh said that Crouch's health meant that the recording of the accompanying concert film was accomplished on a soundstage in Burbank before a small "controlled" audience. It was understood by the cast and crew, Raleigh said, that this might have been one of Andraé's last performances. "I think that was the reason that everybody wanted to make this as perfect as possible," Raleigh said. "Nothing was left on the table with this. Andraé's health issues weren't going away and he knew that as well." "He could hardly sing and move," Rachinski recalled of the concert, "but it was powerful."[16]

Last Days

Crouch began spending more and more time in doctors' offices and even the hospital than at home. During one extended hospital stay, Sandra said her brother begged for a small piano and led a worship service in the hall. "People were coming in wheelchairs just to hear Andraé play," she said. Original Disciple Bili Thedford was among the host of people who visited Andraé regularly, both when he was bedridden at home and in the hospital. In addition to the diabetes and painful foot ulcers, Thedford said an infection from an earlier gastric bypass surgery had seriously further weakened him. "He was getting sicker and sicker in 2013, 2014," Thedford recalled. "He didn't take care of himself and he didn't take care of his diabetes." In late 2014, an all-star concert tour honoring Andraé, featuring Marvin, Bebe and CeCe Winans, Marvin Sapp, Rance Allen, Israel Houghton, and others, was scheduled and postponed several times because of Andraé's reoccurring and increasingly serious health issues. Another original Disciple, Perry Morgan, also visited him repeatedly but said that by December he knew that Crouch's time was limited. One evening in the hospital, two weeks before his death, Morgan arrived to see Andraé bedridden but still witnessing about Jesus to the young technician working the nearby monitors. Moments later, Morgan said, a doctor entered, humming a familiar song: "I said, 'Andraé, the doctor's singing your song.' The doctor said, 'What? You wrote that?' Andraé smiled and agreed." In the final days, Maxwell said he brought recordings of Crouch's favorite artists to play when he visited the hospital. Abraham Laboriel also visited with his guitar and played and sang for him. Andraé was particularly fond of gospel artist Doovie Powell's version of "Always Remember," Maxwell recalled. Despite his weakened condition, Crouch was so moved by the recordings that he called Powell and asked him to sing on his next album. Crouch suffered a heart attack on January 3 and was admitted to Northridge Hospital Medical Center in Los Angeles. When Andraé was slipping into a coma, Sandra and Bill were at his bedside. When Maxwell again played "Always Remember," tears ran down Andraé's face, Maxwell said. On January 8, 2015, he was gone. "Today my twin brother, wombmate and best friend went home to be with the Lord," Sandra Crouch said in a prepared statement. "I tried to keep him here but God loved him best." Andraé's passing was extensively covered by every major news media outlet and both President Barack Obama and Michelle Obama and former president Bill Clinton issued statements celebrating Crouch's life and lamenting his passing. Andraé Edward Crouch was just seventy-two.[17]

Celebration of Life

As is the tradition in gospel music circles, Crouch's Celebration of Life service was a massive two-day affair, with more than 4,000 people packing West Angeles Church of God in Christ to hear songs and sermons by Stevie Wonder, Kirk Franklin, the Reverend Jesse Jackson, Shirley Caesar, and many others, as well as virtually all of the artists and singers who had known, performed, or recorded with Andraé. Bishop Kenneth Ulmer officiated, and the service was broadcast on the BET network. The artists rehearsed for two days before the service. Among those in the choir was Tammie Gibson, who followed in Sandra Crouch's footsteps to become one of just a handful of women pastors in the Church of God in Christ. As the artists were filing in to the spacious West Angeles Church of God in Christ sanctuary for the service, Gibson said she was finally overcome with emotion and fled the building. "I just could not process it at that time," she said. "That was my private time to grieve over a friend that I lost. If you really, really knew him, you felt the blow of his demise in a very, very personal way" (Images 17.2–17.4).[18]

Image 17.2 Program cover, Andraé Crouch Celebration of Life, January 8, 2015. Courtesy of Perry Morgan.

Crouch's passing immediately brought a renewed interest in his music. "Let the Church Say Amen," featuring Marvin Winans, debuted on the "Gospel Digital Chart" at #5 with more than a thousand downloads. "Soon and Very Soon," "Take Me Back," "Through It All," and "My Tribute" also returned to the charts.[19]

Kirk Franklin's response to the funeral, in many ways, represents what Crouch's contemporaries thought of him—and his passionate, life-spanning

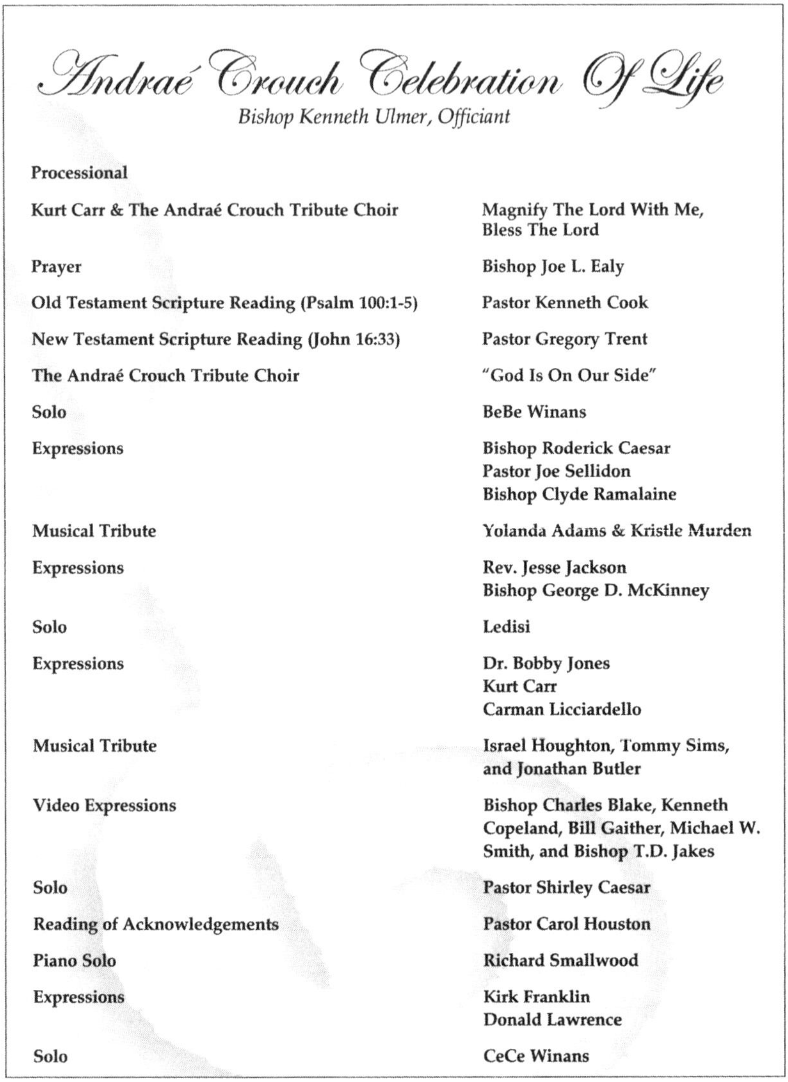

Andraé Crouch Celebration Of Life
Bishop Kenneth Ulmer, Officiant

Processional	
Kurt Carr & The Andraé Crouch Tribute Choir	Magnify The Lord With Me, Bless The Lord
Prayer	Bishop Joe L. Ealy
Old Testament Scripture Reading (Psalm 100:1-5)	Pastor Kenneth Cook
New Testament Scripture Reading (John 16:33)	Pastor Gregory Trent
The Andraé Crouch Tribute Choir	"God Is On Our Side"
Solo	BeBe Winans
Expressions	Bishop Roderick Caesar Pastor Joe Sellidon Bishop Clyde Ramalaine
Musical Tribute	Yolanda Adams & Kristle Murden
Expressions	Rev. Jesse Jackson Bishop George D. McKinney
Solo	Ledisi
Expressions	Dr. Bobby Jones Kurt Carr Carman Licciardello
Musical Tribute	Israel Houghton, Tommy Sims, and Jonathan Butler
Video Expressions	Bishop Charles Blake, Kenneth Copeland, Bill Gaither, Michael W. Smith, and Bishop T.D. Jakes
Solo	Pastor Shirley Caesar
Reading of Acknowledgements	Pastor Carol Houston
Piano Solo	Richard Smallwood
Expressions	Kirk Franklin Donald Lawrence
Solo	CeCe Winans

Image 17.3 Program page, Andraé Crouch Celebration of Life, January 8, 2015. Courtesy of Perry Morgan.

relationship with his faith. Reflecting on the service a few days later, Franklin writes:

> To my embarrassment, some of the songs sung that day I grew up believing were just hymns found in the dusty hymnbooks in the backs of church pews. I was

New Christ Memorial Church Remarks	**Pastor La Vern Moore**
Solo	**Tata Vega**
Expressions	**Bishop Barbara Amos**
Musical Tribute	**Donnie McClurkin & The Disciples Tribute Ensemble**
Remarks	**Pastor Sandra Crouch**
Congregational Song— The Blood	**Donald Lawrence & the Andraé Crouch Tribute Choir**
Eulogy	**Pastor Marvin Winans**
Recessional	**"Let The Church Say Amen"**

INTERMENT PRIVATE
Final Arrangements provided by Angelus Funeral Home

PALLBEARERS
RAYMOND MILES
TORY DEHAAN
KIYOSHI KINOSHITA
FRANK GONZALEZ
NOAH BROWN
SAMUEL CAMPBELL

On behalf of the family of Andrae' Crouch, there are no words to express how thankful we are for you support during this difficult time. Your prayers have truly been felt and your presence helped to make the weight a little lighter. Whatever sacrifice you made to help us celebrate the life of our dear Andrae' Crouch we say THANK YOU, we love you and may God bless you!!

Special thanks to...

Demetrus Alexander	Kurt Carr
Howard Rachinski	Kenneth Copeland Ministries
Mano Hanes	Ray & Barbara Miles
Bill Maxwell	Fred & Suzi Wehba
Linda McCrary	David Byerley
Every singer and musician	Bill & Judy Dodson
Brian Mayes - Nashville Publicity	Nathan DiGesare
Pat Shields - Black Dot & Team	Carman
Edna Sims - Public Relations & Team	Bishop Charles Blake & the West Angeles Church staff
Lisa Collins - LA Focus	Bishop Kenneth Ulmer & the Faithful Central Bible Church staff
Valerie Williamson	Donnie McClurkin
Gwen McClendon - New Act Travel	Richard Gumbs
Robyn Hill – Personal Assistant to Sandra Crouch	Morris Chapman
Tee Garlington	Suzanne Cadena
Cynthia Evans-Joseph	Ejugwo Omakwu

Image 17.4 Program page, Andraé Crouch Celebration of Life, January 8, 2015. Courtesy of Perry Morgan.

brought into another musical dimension when I was told, "Those are Andraé's songs." Donnie McClurkin even told me to be quiet after I kept asking in shock, "That's his song, too?"

I had no idea his pen was so thick with God.[20]

NOTES

1. Bob Darden, "Gospel Lectern," *Billboard*, March 3, 1986, 60; Kathy Hazzard, interview with the authors, January 17, 2022.
2. Michael Jackson, *Bad* (Epic EK 40600, 1987); Michael Jackson, *Dangerous* (Epic EK 45400, 1991); Michael Jackson, *HIStory: Past, Present and Future, Book I* (Epic EK 59000); Steve Knopper, *MJ: The Genius of Michael Jackson* (New York: Scribner, 2016), 166, 346; Kathy Hazzard, interview with the authors, August 19, 2021.
3. "Madonna's 'Like a Prayer' Clip Causes a Controversy," *Rolling Stone*, April 20, 1989, 22; Lucy O'Brien, " 'We Argued a Lot': Inside the Making of Madonna's Stormy Divorce Album," *The Guardian*, March 30, 2019, https://www.theguardian.com/culture/2019/mar/30/we-argued-a-lot-inside-the-making-of-madonna-stormy-divorce-album/; Edwin Smith, "Catching Up with Andraé Crouch," *Rejoice!*, August/September 1992.
4. Lisa Collins, "James Cleveland Dead at 59," *Billboard*, February 23, 1991, 4, 65; Alisha Lola Jones, *Flaming? The Peculiar Theopolitics of Fire and Desire in Black Male Gospel Performance* (Oxford: Oxford University Press, 2020), 14–15; https://www.youtube.com/watch?v=qakR8G-Y3E.
5. "Benjamin Crouch: Church Founder," *Los Angeles Times*, December 23, 1993; "Catherine D. Crouch, Singers' Mother," *Los Angeles Times*, April 11, 1992; Jerri Menges, "I Love Walking with Him," *Decision*, August 8, 2006, https://i-love-walking-with-him/; Jamal-Dominique Hopkins, interview with the authors, October 15, 2022.
6. Lisa Collins, "In the Spirit," *Billboard*, April 30, 1994, 49; "Top Gospel Albums," *Billboard*, April 16, 1994, 45; "The Year in Music: Top Gospel Albums," *Billboard*, December 24, 1994, YE-70; Andraé Crouch, *Mercy* (Qwest D 103005).
7. Alfie Silas Durio, interview with the authors, June 18, 2021.
8. "Andraé Crouch Installed at Christ Memorial," *Los Angeles Sentinel*, September 21, 1995, C-6; Mark Allan Powell, "Andraé Crouch," in *Encyclopedia of Contemporary Christian Music* (Peabody, MA: Hendrickson Publishers, 2002), 213; Tammie Gibson, interview with the authors, December 28, 2022; Vonciele Faggett, interview with the authors, October 21, 2021; Jamal-Dominique Hopkins, interview with the authors, October 15, 2022; LaVern Moore, interview with the authors, March 21, 2022.
9. Andraé Crouch, *Pray* (Qwest/Warners Alliance 9 4524-2); "Top-Selling Gospel Albums," *Billboard*, December 27, 1997, YE-84, YE-86; "Top-Selling Gospel Albums," *Billboard*, December 26, 1998, YE-98: Alfie Silas Durio, interview with the authors, June 18, 2021.
10. Adelle M. Banks, "Prominent Gospel Singer Breaks Tradition, Ordains Sister," *Religious News Service*, October 1, 1998, https://www.religionnews.com/1998/10/01/news-story-prominent-gospel-singer-breaks-tradition-ordains-sister.

THE FINAL YEARS   393

11. Powell, "Andraé Crouch," 213; Andraé Crouch, *The Gift of Christmas* (Warners Alliance 9 47091-2, 1999); "Top Gospel Albums," *Billboard*, December 25, 1999, YE-104; "Top Gospel Albums," *Billboard*, December 30, 2000, YE-100.

12. Howard Rachinski, interview with the authors, October 20, 2022.

13. Deborah Evans Price, "Crouch's 'Mighty' Career," *Billboard*, May 27, 2006, 46; Andraé Crouch, *Mighty Wind* (Verity VR 73645); "Top Gospel Albums," *Billboard*, December 23, 2006, YE-78; Marvin Winans, interview with the authors, November 6, 2020; Linda McCrary, interview with the authors, February 24, 2022.

14. Kevin Raleigh, interview with the authors, January 26, 2022; Andraé Crouch, *The Journey* (Riverphlo RIVER 002); Marvin Winans, interview with the authors, November 6, 2020; Linda McCrary, interview with the authors, February 24, 2022; "Top Gospel Songs," *Billboard*, December 17, 2011, 89; Howard Rachinski, interview with the authors, October 20, 2022; LaVern Moore, interview with the authors, March 21, 2022; Wade Jessen, "Crouch's Death Impacts Charts," *Billboard*, January 24, 2015, 127.

15. Linda McCrary, interview with the authors, February 24, 2022; LaVern Moore, interview with the authors, March 21, 2022.

16. Bill Maxwell, interview with the authors, May 18, 2019; Andraé Crouch, *Live in Los Angeles* (Riverphlo RIVER 020, 2013); Linda McCrary, interview with the authors, February 24, 2022; "Top Gospel Songs," *Billboard*, December 21, 2013, 136; Kevin Raleigh, interview with the authors, January 26, 2022.

17. Andy Argyrakis, "Andraé Crouch: Saluting Gospel Music's Godfather," *CCM*, April 1, 2015, https://www.ccmmagazine.com/features/Andraé-crouch-saluting-gospel-musics-godfather/; Sandra Crouch, interview with the authors, February 25, 2021; Bili Thedford, interview with the authors, March 18, 2021; Bill Maxwell, interview with the authors, May 18, 2019; Effie Rolfe, "The World Says Farewell to Andraé Crouch—Father of Modern Gospel Music," *Chicago Defender*, January 28, 2015, 11.

18. Argyrakis, "Andraé Crouch"; Rolfe, "The World Says Farewell to Andraé Crouch," 11; Tammie Gibson, interview with the authors, December 28, 2022.

19. Wade Jessen, "Crouch's Death Impacts Charts," *Billboard*, January 24, 2015, 127.

20. https://www.patheos.com/blogs/kirkfranklin/2015/01/Andraé-crouch-the-man-who-raised-the-goal/.

18

Conclusion

The struggles of Andraé Crouch's final years, we believe, do nothing to diminish his legacy—that is, the *transformative* nature of his music and ministry. The outpouring of love and tributes following his passing, and the accounts by some of gospel music's biggest stars of how Crouch changed music, are compelling, of course. And not just in gospel music. Rock and Roll Hall of Fame legend Al Kooper told us that he was one of Andraé's biggest fans and how he had stayed up most of the night prior to our scheduled Zoom interview listening to Crouch's albums while "bouncing around" and "rocking like crazy at 4 in the morning." "When I heard him," Kooper said, "the thing that really got me was his originality. He was just perfect. There was nobody like him. He influenced a lot of people, me being one."[1]

But ultimately, of course, testimonies and tributes are still, essentially, personal and anecdotal. However, there is one area where a composer's impact *can* be reduced to numbers. Craig Dunnagan, who spent decades on the publishing side of sacred music with the Capitol Christian Music Group and Integrity Music before starting his own management publishing company, shared with us charts of the CCLI (Christian Copyright Licensing International)'s listings of the most performed Christian songs—and in 2023 Crouch retained multiple spots in the top 2,000 songs, despite the fact, Dunnagan said, that many Black churches are not affiliated with the CCLI. Howard Rachinski, who founded CCLI and remains connected with the organization, said that Andraé's "evergreens" continue to be performed. "Clearly now," Rachinski said, "there are people who know who Andraé is."[2]

How else can an artist's impact be measured? As an innovator, and pathfinder, the scope and scale of Crouch's influence abroad is unique in gospel music. Bill Maxwell said that during his tours with Andraé, particularly in

396   SOON & VERY SOON

Europe, the packed auditoriums rocked with people singing Crouch's songs—
old and new—in their own languages. Monique Ingalls, who has written extensively of gospel music abroad, said that Andraé's music is widely known
and sung by the gospel community choirs in the United Kingdom. Linda
McCrary, who has toured Africa on five occasions with various artists, said her
tour of the continent with Crouch was the most memorable of all because of
the uniformly enthusiastic response—in country after country. And for much
of his career, Andraé was one of the very few gospel artists consistently touring
abroad.[3]

As for Crouch's influence in sacred music in the United States with the
Disciples, he integrated the ranks of the predominately white Jesus Music/
contemporary Christian music world. He added an extended harmonic language, influences from World Music forms, syncopation, and polyrhythms to
gospel, enriched it, and made it possible to reach a much wider audience. As
one scholar described it: "What Thomas Dorsey was to the gospel world in the
1930s and 1940s, Crouch was to the world of contemporary Christian music
in the 1970s and 1980s." Andraé's music took his message out of the church
into what evangelical Christians call "the world" and, in doing so, as gospel
executive Teresa Hairston notes, he "brought whites and Blacks together in a
time when white and Black didn't mix." Not that it was easy. Famed session
bassist and frequent collaborator Abraham Laboriel said that Crouch's successful entry into both worlds proved a "challenge" for Christian communities
that could "no longer think of him as just a Black gospel entertainer." Instead,
wherever he went, Crouch brought unity and diversity. "Andraé always came
not as a Black gospel entertainer, he came as a messenger of God," Laboriel
said. Reflecting on Crouch's legacy, pastor and longtime friend Val Gonzalo
emphasized to us that it was Andraé's unique ability to break down both musical *and* racial barriers that ultimately set him apart:

> In Christianity, there was a Mason-Dixon Line where a white audience never
> mixed with a Black audience. I believe he was called to this. If he had never heard
> or answered the call to really stretch out and take the risk . . . gospel music would
> still be stuck in the Black church. But he ventured out and crossed that line and
> said, "I'm going to risk it only because everybody needs to know Jesus. I don't
> care the color of your skin—white, red, brown, yellow, Black. I'm going to do
> this because I hear the call." He was the pioneer who said, "I will be the one.' And
> there would have been a lot of artists who would not have stepped across that line
> unless it was for Andraé Crouch. He was the forerunner.

CONCLUSION

And when compared to the many talented gospel and CCM artists of that era, Claudrena N. Harold writes simply, "Andraé Crouch was in a class by himself."[4]

The restless nature of Crouch's faith-inspired muse was such that revolutionizing CCM and challenging deeply held perceptions about race in the church were only the first steps in the odyssey of his musical ministry. Over the course of a handful of early albums—*Take the Message Everywhere* (1968), *Keep On Singin'* (1971), *Soulfully* (1972), *Just Andraé* (1972), and *"Live" at Carnegie Hall* (1973)—he created and opened doors to the sonic possibilities of what would soon be called *contemporary gospel music* as well. Today, most scholars and writers call him the "founder" of the genre. Gospel music executive Vicki Mack Lataillade put it even more bluntly: "He ushered in a genre of music." Certainly Edwin Hawkins's "Oh Happy Day" (1968–1969) and the early albums of the Mighty Clouds of Joy and Jessy Dixon were part of the process, but when it came to transforming traditional gospel, Andraé was the most consistent, most relentless innovator in the field, experimenting, adapting, incorporating, and—if necessary—creating an astonishing array of musical styles, instrumentations, formats, and colors for his songs. At Crouch's massive two-day funeral celebration in 2015, most of the tributes from the who's who of gospel music—Richard Smallwood, Donald Lawrence, Israel Houghton, Donnie McClurkin, BeBe and CeCe Winans, Yolanda Adams, Kirk Franklin, Edwin and Lynette Hawkins, Marvin Winans, Dr. Bobby Jones, and many others—whether spoken or performed, all referenced in some way Andraé's position as the father of contemporary gospel.[5]

"In the process of becoming a successful performer," adds Jean Kidula, "he has affirmed tradition while celebrating innovation."

Along the way, Andraé is widely credited with writing and popularizing yet *another* genre, what is now called "praise & worship" music. According to Deborah Smith Pollard, early CCM artists like Danny Lee and the Children of Truth joined Crouch and "opened the door" for "today's praise and worship explosion." "Crouch created a body of work that would become foundational for praise and worship music," Harold adds, "a genre that transformed the Black gospel sound and continues to do so." CCM historian Paul Baker credits Andraé with creating many of the original "classics" of what he calls "victorious praise music—vertical music"—"The Blood (Will Never Lose Its Power)," "Jesus Is the Answer," "Bless the Lord," and "My Tribute (to God Be the Glory)," though he could have easily also included "Hallelujah" and

"Praise God"—songs that continue to be sung in churches both Black and white today.[6]

For those who knew him best, this aspect of his creative output was a direct representation of the man and his core beliefs. "Andraé was a worshipper," pastor and friend LaVern Moore told us. "Whenever I speak of him, I say that he was the greatest worshipper this side of King David. There is just such an anointing and such a revelation of what God can do when you give Him a life. And Andraé certainly gave Him a life."[7]

From a musical standpoint, four threads in particular link Crouch's innovations in all three genres:

A. The sheer caliber of the musicianship performed by Crouch, the Disciples, and the ever-shifting array of musicians and singers in his studio recordings and performances;

B. The otherworldly creativity, the outlandishly catchy melodies, coupled with the bedrock-solid Biblical truths embedded in every song;

C. His uncanny ability to compose lyrics that theologically unified, rather than divided, listeners from dozens of different denominations and belief systems; and

D. The family-oriented networking that he and Maxwell established, creating vast webs of "related" musicians and singers who, even today, continue to keep in close contact with each other, encourage each other, pray for each other. As we would complete one interview, the interviewee would invariably say, "You know who you need to talk to next? Let me get you her number."

For the performance and recording musicality, Crouch and Maxwell insisted on the best players—and the best players flocked to play and record with him. Virtually every musician who worked with Andraé would enjoy subsequent (and sometimes concurrent) success on their own or in other groups, beginning with his very first group the COGICs (Billy Preston, Edna Wright, Sondra "Blinky" Williams, Sandra Crouch, and Gloria Jones) to the performers and artists on his final tours and recordings. All fell under Andraé's spell.

For compositional genius, as we have tried to show throughout with our observations and analysis of his music, that while we can dissect individual songs and suggest *what* he did in those three or four minutes, we are at a loss to be able to discern *how* he did it. Our shorthand for Crouch's creativity

CONCLUSION

throughout this book has been both "Duke Ellingtonish" and "Mozartian"—that Andraé was a prodigy, a savant. In the Church of God in Christ and other denominations, the word is "gift," as in "God gave Andraé this *gift*." And that's the word many chose to use when describing him:

> Andraé will never be out of time. You could not put him in any category. He was a gifted, God-given man. The hand of God touched that man.—singer Tammie Gibson

> I appreciate Andraé's gift of spiritually speaking and cutting through so much with his message, words, and melodies. When I hear one of his songs in church, it triggers memories. They cut right to the heart.—guitarist James Harrah

> He had a way of seeing and hearing Jesus above the noise of the masses and getting lost in intimacy with Him while the heaven-dipped notes flowed with abandonment. This gift was forged in heaven.—artist and composer Reba Rambo McGuire

> "As for the melody, like all of his melodies, they were sent from the Lord," Linda McCrary told us. "He was an open vessel to be able to hear it and then relay it to us. It is like an apostolic gifting." —singer Linda McCrary[8]

Maxwell was Andraé's friend, confidant, arranger, producer, and drummer, and he has seen and heard more than his share of genius in his professional life in music. Additionally, Maxwell's ability to recall specific, detailed memories of the hundreds of recording sessions he produced borders on the miraculous itself. When remarkable songs would suddenly appear, as if plucked from the ether, only Crouch did not seem surprised. "Whatever happened, happened," Maxwell told us. "He was gifted. He didn't think. Perry Morgan used to say, 'Where *did* these songs come from?' Andraé'd just show up and come out and he'd sing. He was extraordinarily gifted."[9]

That said, throughout this book, we have attempted to identify, wherever possible, Crouch's specific innovations, instances where he is the first known gospel artist to do *this*. Or *that*. If Andraé believed that a certain set of lyrics needed a specific musical accompaniment, regardless of the genre, rhythm, chord progression, instrumentation, or tempo, then that's what came out on his piano. For bassist/composer Jaymes Edward Felix, spending time performing and recording with Andraé was an incredibly freeing experience musically. "The major thing for me meeting and playing with Andraé and seeing how he wrote was that there weren't any boundaries," Felix said. "He opened a whole 'nother thing for being a Black musician or a gospel artist."[10]

Throughout his career, Crouch simply refused to be held to the artificial compositional or stylistic boundaries that, for many years, defined traditional gospel music. And, in the process, was able to create compelling, memorable, sometimes hauntingly beautiful music.

Crouch was also at the forefront of a revolution in the use of lyrics in gospel music. Andraé's lyrics reflected the issues that had shaped him from an early age while listening to his father, Bishop Benjamin Crouch Sr., both in the pulpit and in his love of street-level preaching and ministry, sermons which included a wide and welcoming ecumenism, international evangelism, the imminent arrival of the Second Coming of Jesus, and a deep, abiding love for all people, including—and maybe *particularly*—society's outcasts. All this, both Andraé and his father emphatically believed, was rooted solely and unequivocally in Christian scripture and sound doctrine.

During virtually every interview we conducted, particularly with the singers who accompanied Crouch for years, we were told repeatedly of Andraé's love for the Bible and how he spent every minute (when he wasn't composing) reading and making notes in his well-worn Bible. Pastor Tammie Gibson vividly recalled for us a representative incident early in Andraé's career during an impromptu songwriting session with Voncielle Faggett, Alfie Silas, Perry Morgan, Bili Thedford, and Gibson all clustered around Crouch's home piano. Andraé was reading and commenting on the famous passage in the Book of Acts where Saul was struck blind on the Road to Damascus during an encounter with Jesus—and how the incident transformed Saul into the beloved Paul the Apostle. "He was very spontaneous in his discourse," Gibson told us. "And what he felt biblically ultimately led to his interpretation of a God-given song." Gibson said that after reading about the incident, Andraé turned to her and said, "Tammie, this is what I get out of that," and began spontaneously composing a song based on the story. "His thoughts from the Word of God were constantly activated as he began to talk about what he'd just read," Gibson said, "and then he would write it right there on the spot."[11]

According to Laboriel, Crouch was both intellectually gifted and a keen student of the Bible, carrying a well-loved copy with him everywhere. "He always came across as a very humble servant who loved to make music," Laboriel told us, "but he really, really knew and understood the 'why' of the Bible." Singer Valerie Doby said, as a lifelong scholar of the Bible and as a "master" composer, Crouch's inspiration came directly from the God of his Bible. "I finally really know that all of that came from God," she said. "He didn't write

CONCLUSION 401

anything mediocre. No filler. With his songs, you knew it was from another place. And people will be singing his music until the end of time."

"God placed a horn in his spirit," Gibson told us at the end our interview, the awe obvious in her voice, "and he blew that horn so beautifully."[12]

Again, as we have analyzed the songs in Crouch's canon, we have repeatedly been struck by the sophistication of the compositions, his uncanny ability to know what "works" musically to best support and enhance the theological statement, not to draw attention to the complexity or the elegance or the cleverness of the musical accompaniment, but instead to emphasize above all the words and the message. Singer and pastor Donn Thomas said one of the distinctives of Andraé's songs was how much Crouch valued an unambiguous "clarity" of expression in creating and combining music and words to present a certain biblically based message—and nothing more. "He kept the music in a place where it didn't get in the way of the message," Thomas said. "And then, at the end of the song, he might take you somewhere and he might put you in a groove, but it was always married to the message."[13]

Promoter and manager Wes Yoder was present at the beginnings of the Jesus Music movement and closely followed Andraé's career throughout his life. Yoder said the key to Crouch's widespread acceptance was that his songs were always "Christological or Christocentric" in every way. "Andraé didn't go down rabbit trails of theology but kept the central core of a belief system in Christ intact," Yoder said:

> It was Christocentric without having this other way of measuring yourself—you just were invited. This would be true every time I saw Andraé—you were being invited to a party and it was God's party. It was a good party and we were the friends who were invited to the party. We were the prodigals who were invited by the Father to come. And that's why it hit so broadly around the world.[14]

This project has been a journey of discovery for both of us. Each new interview answered a few questions and raised several more. So strong were their feelings for Andraé, many of our interviewees prayed for the book—and for us—at the end of our time together.

As we end this book, we come away with a few observations—"conclusions" seems too definitive a word. The authors between them know many, many people—we've both been fortunate (or *blessed*, to use Andraé's parlance) to have wide circles of friends and associates. But in both of our cases, we've come to believe that there are few people in our spheres who have loved God more passionately than Andraé. In our interviews, that defining aspect of Crouch's life came up again and again:

> I know that Andraé truly loved God. And I know that he was blessed by God to write those words because they would just come to him. I believe that he was special.—singer Gloria Jones

> He loved God. He loved people. And he loved, loved, loved music. There was no strategy to it. For these years that I've been in the gospel music business, I tell people all the time, "If you've got to aim at something, if you've got to work towards making something work, then it's contrived. When it just does what it does, then it's downloaded." Andraé took what was downloaded to him and that was the thing that taught me, if you just do what you do, they will come.—music executive Demetrus Alexander

> With his music, with his life, what I saw was somebody so in love with God. It wasn't like, "This is an event, this is a gig [that] I've got to do, I've got to do this recording." It was something that was drawing him, a yearning for the Lord. He was always in that place where he was creating, talking to God, singing to God, hearing God.—Donn Thomas[15]

The other aspect of Crouch's life that we came to quickly understand is that when someone is so totally in love with God, then they feel *compelled* to share that message. They have no choice. At least, that is how Andraé responded. He'd found the Good News and couldn't wait to share it, whether in restaurants or on stage or on network television. He couldn't help himself. Like his father Benjamin, he was at his happiest, at his most fulfilled when he was sharing the gospel of Jesus Christ. Composer Jeffrey LaValley was adamant on this point—it was that evangelism and evangelism alone that drove Crouch above all else. "His lyrics reach the simplest man's heart," LaValley told us. "He reached your heart through what he was trying to say. That was his goal. Andraé said, 'Tell them,' which I honestly believe was inclusive of everybody. Get the word to everybody that they're loved."[16]

As a result, many of our interviewees said that more than anyone else they had ever known, Andraé was supremely confident in his calling. "I believe he knew exactly what he came here on earth to do," singer Alfie Silas Durio said. "The yearning and the relationship with God, everything came out of that relationship with Andraé. He wasn't perfect by any means. He knew it. But it was still this perfect relationship between Andraé and his calling. Nothing could rival that."[17]

CONCLUSION 403

We have read every interview with Andraé Crouch we could find, using the wonderful resources of multiple libraries and search engines, dozens of databases, and the deep connections of his small army of friends, family, and fellow musicians. For readers and viewers who don't share his particular strand of Christianity, the jargon in those interviews is sometimes a bit dense or even off-putting. But virtually every time, Andraé's transparency and sincerity managed to somehow shine through. One of our favorites is a filmed interview with producer Mark Joseph. Crouch is clearly at ease—the two are old friends—and the conversation soon turns, as it almost always does with Andraé, to his favorite topic:

> For me, that's what it's all about. We're here to win souls. When He uses me to win the last one, I'm out of here. Until then, all you're going to hear from us is how can we win that person to Jesus Christ. I don't even want to think I know a person that went to hell. I don't even want to think that our paths cross and they ended up in hell.
>
> I've been happiest when I'm doing stuff for the Lord. I have no interest in most things. I'm probably one of the dullest people you'd ever meet. But I have this passion for Jesus and for people to fall in love with Jesus at least as much as I do.[18]

Perhaps that line—"I don't even want to think that our paths cross and they ended up in hell"—helps explain Andrae's career-long fascination with the End Times, the evangelical concept of the Second Coming of Christ to gather all believers in heaven, manifests itself in so many songs on the subject: "It Won't Be Long," "Soon and Very Soon," "Tell Them," "No Time to Lose," and others. That conviction, in many ways, was at the heart of many of his albums. He was happy to talk about it when someone asked.

At times, however, we would get the sense that Crouch only tolerated the interviewers' questions about his music, his new album, his latest tour, or whatever so he could get back to his favorite topic—Jesus.

Andraé Crouch was a change agent. That he manifests that change through one of the smaller subsets of popular music—gospel—makes what he accomplished even more remarkable. "At the height of his success," Harold adds, "he redefined the sonic, spiritual and even social possibilities of American religious music." "Andraé was known for being an innovator," Teresa Hairston told us. "He's one of the most creative musical geniuses of our time." And Weekes sums it up this way: "In these ways, Crouch's career embodies the music,

404   SOON & VERY SOON

social, and cultural 'integration' of modern gospel music reflective of the social realities of the 1960s and 1970s."[19]

We believe all this is true.

Looking back, we fully recognize the quixotic nature of our quest—to de-
fine and categorize the undefinable. If humanity understood what genius is
and how it came about, perhaps there would be more geniuses. We believe that
the genius of Andraé Crouch, while not something we're any closer to understanding, is certainly something worth celebrating.

A final story, from our interview with gospel scholar Deborah Smith
Pollard:

> When we had a television show, Andraé was doing a concert at a downtown
> theater in Detroit and we had the opportunity to interview him. But before we
> interviewed him, we talked to people coming into the theater and asked, "Why
> are you here?" And a woman in her late twenties, early thirties said, "I joined the
> church but the music they were playing was so tired. I said, 'If this is all you have,
> I can't stay here. And then I heard Andraé Crouch and that's what made me
> stay with the church.' I was trying not to laugh out loud because I was thinking,
> "Yeah, I understand." I absolutely understood what she was saying. And I think
> there were a lot of people who felt that way about his music as well."[20]

Ultimately, Andraé Crouch's understanding of practical theology, scripture, the role of worship, evangelism, and the Christian concept of God's
kingdom on earth was entrenched in every song he ever wrote. He believed
that music was a gateway to the world. He believed, from a practical standpoint, that theology was not supposed to be disconnected from the heart.
Theologians are trained to articulate theology with words, academic rigor, and
intellectual prowess. Crouch used music as a way of defining humanity and
the heart of God. He used music as a way of defining theology in the marketplace for the common person. From his very earliest songs, Andraé was deeply
concerned about the soul of humanity and the heart of God—and music was
his change agent.

For Crouch, Bible study was accompanied by music. He heard music every
time he opened his Bible. He married scripture, melodies, theology, and even
his purpose and justification for advancing God's kingdom in his songs. And
he faithfully recorded those songs as long as he was physically able. Sandra
Crouch once told us that Andraé had 1,500 songs on cassettes in various

CONCLUSION   405

rooms in their house and church—songs no one has ever heard.[21] We believe that he wrote some of those songs of hope and encouragement to himself, for himself, in his darkest hours. He was compelled to write them. And, for as long as he could, share them.

Every song that Andraé wrote was either inspired by scripture or speaks to scripture verbatim. Virtually alone of his peers in gospel music, he had a way of bringing lament, exhilaration, exhortation, deep reflection, and even a gentle humor into gospel music. His contemporary gospel music stylings were much more than the familiar call-and-response, verse-and-chorus format. His music responded to God's call. This is why so many people, regardless of race, religion, or even nationality could relate to his songs. For instance, the spontaneously composed "You Don't Have to Jump No Pews" is both whimsical and profound. Through it, Andraé declares that being "born again" is not something that is based on "emotional feeling." Instead, it is both doctrinally *and* theologically forthright. His theology is supremely practical. Andraé desperately wanted people to be born again, to accept the message and call of Jesus Christ.

During his career, Andraé had the opportunity to look into the eyes of people on nearly every continent. Each time, without exception, he saw that person as an image-bearer of the Wise Creator. Through the Gospel of Jesus Christ, Andraé created music that valued all of God's Kingdom without dismissing the diversity of that Kingdom. For Andraé, the gospel preached reconciliation, not division, not pride, not prejudice—and he reflected that belief in his life, in his preaching, and in his music. Racism in the 1960s and 1970s divided America, and during that period Andraé worked tirelessly to unite the church through his music. Everyone, he believed, bled red. Everyone could relate to "The Blood (Will Never Lose Its Power)." And that's why songs like that one have remained staples in the world's churches, regardless of denomination or creed.

And that's why, we believe, nothing could have made Andraé Edward Crouch happier than to hear the words of that unnamed concertgoer in downtown Detroit:

> "And then I heard Andraé Crouch and that's what made me stay with the church."

NOTES

1. Al Kooper, interview with the authors, November 9, 2021.
2. Craig Dunnagan, interview with the authors, October 6, 2022; Howard Rachinski, interview with the authors, October 2022.
3. Bill Maxwell, interview with the authors, May 18, 2019; Monique Ingalls, interview with the authors, January 12, 2021; Linda McCrary, interview with the authors, February 24, 2022.
4. Claudrena N. Harold, *When Sunday Comes: Gospel Music in the Soul and Hip-Hop Eras* (Urbana: University of Illinois Press, 2020), 64; Teresa Hairston, interview with the authors, September 11, 2020; Abraham Laboriel, interview with the authors, August 19, 2021; Val Gonzalo, interview with the authors, October 10, 2020.
5. Vicki Mack Lataillade, interview with the authors, October 8, 2020; Jean Kidula, "A Black Angeleno: The Gospel of Andraé Crouch," in *California Soul: Music of African Americans in the West*, ed. Jacqueline Cogdell DjeDje and Eddie S. Meadows (Berkeley: University of California Press, 1998), 313.
6. Deborah Smith Pollard, *When Church Becomes Your Party* (Detroit: Wayne State University Press, 2008), 25; Harold, *When Sunday Comes*, 64; Paul Baker, *Contemporary Christian Music: Where It Came From, What It Is, Where It's Going* (Westchester, IL: Crossway Books, [1979], 1985), 168.
7. LaVern Moore, interview with the authors, March 21, 2022.
8. Tammie Gibson, interview with the authors, March 23, 2023; James Harrah, interview with the authors, August 19, 2021; https://www.rambmcguire/news/tag/Homecoming+Magazine; Linda McCrary, interview with the authors, November 9, 2021.
9. Bill Maxwell, interview with the authors, May 20, 2023.
10. Jaymes Edward Felix, interview with the authors, August 21, 2021.
11. Tammie Gibson, interview with the authors, December 28, 2022.
12. Abraham Laboriel, interview with the authors, August 19, 2021; Valerie Doby, interview with the authors, April 4, 2023; Tammie Gibson, interview with the authors, March 23, 2023.
13. Donn Thomas, interview with the authors, August 21, 2021.
14. Wes Yoder, interview with the authors, September 22, 2021.
15. Gloria Jones, interview with the authors, December 23, 2020; Demetrus Alexander, interview with the authors, October 10, 2020; Donn Thomas, interview with the authors, August 21, 2021.
16. Jeffrey LaValley, interview the authors, August 29, 2020.
17. Alfie Silas Durio, interview with the authors, June 18, 2021.
18. Mark Joseph, http://www.mjyoung.net/weblog/242-disciple-andrae-crouch.
19. Harold, *When Sunday Comes*, 64; Teresa Hairston, interview with the authors, September 11, 2020; Melinda E. Weekes, "This House, This Music: Exploring the Interdependent Interpretive Relationship Between the Contemporary Black Church and Contemporary Gospel Music, *Black Music Research Journal* 25, no. 1/2 (Spring–Fall 2005), 51.
20. Deborah Smith Pollard, interview with the authors, September 26, 2020.
21. Sandra Crouch, interview with the authors, February 25, 2021.

Index

For the benefit of digital users, indexed terms that span two pages (e.g., 52–53) may, on occasion, appear on only one of those pages.

Abbey Sound Ltd., 156–57
Abbington, James, 241
Acuna, Alex, 299, 311–12, 350
Adams, Yolanda, 1–2
Addicts Choir
    creating album, 62–64
    Disciples as precursor to, 51–54
    early performances of, 54–55
    rare four-song 45 of, 55–59
    Teen Challenge Addicts Choir (album), 64–70
    and Teen Challenge Center, 59–52
"Addict's Plea, The" (*Teen Challenge Addicts Choir*), 65–66
Adler, Lou, 101
African Americans, 8, 86–87, 94–95, 119, 133, 139, 164, 191, 219, 252–53, 333, 337–38
African American Theology, 270
African Methodist Episcopal (AME), 40
Aja (album), 246
Akers, Doris, 9–10, 29, 64, 69
Alexander, Demetrus, 223
A-listers, recording, 288–91
Allen, Tex, 199–200
"All I Can Say (I Really Love You)" (*Take Me Back*), 204–5
AllMusic.com, 117
"All That I Have" (*This Is Another Day*), 253
"All the Way" (*Finally*), 349
"Along Came Jesus" (*Keep on Singin'*, LP), 113
"Always Remember" (*No Time to Lose*), 369–70
Amazing Grace, 39
AME. *See* African Methodist Episcopal
Amsterdam News, 337–38
Anderson, Maxi (Maxine), 381–82

contribution of, 317
    at Larvik concert, 372
    part of "It's Gonna Rain," 311–12
    recording sessions with, 291
    vocals for "Hollywood Scene," 325
Anderson, Robert, 8–9
"Andraé Preaching" (*"Live" at Carnegie Hall*), 184–85
Andrews, Inez, 40, 54
Andrews, Ola, 19
Andrus, Sherman, 53, 61, 75, 79, 107, 227–28
    departure of, 90–91
Annual NAACP Image Awards, 298–99
Ants'hilvania, 78–79
apartheid, boycotting, 279
Arguinzoni, Sonny/Julie, 60–61, 71–72
Armageddon Experience, 126
arpeggios, 57
arrest, 343–45
Ashby, Dorothy, 295–96, 297, 326
audience, finding, 94
    distribution agreement, 94–95
    equal commitment, 97
    Midnight Musicals, 95–96
    white audiences, 96
Australia, touring in, 190–92, 221, 254–55

Bacharach, Burt, 166–67
Bachmann, Scott, 117, 143–45, 154, 172
Bailey, Philip, 288–89
Baker, Paul, 132
Baltimore *Afro-American*, 353–54
Banks, Rose (Stone), 364, 372, 374–75
Barbara Mandrell & the Mandrell Sisters, 161
Beard, Naomi, 202
bebop jazz, 232
Benson Records, 130–31

408 INDEX

Berry, Chuck, 285–86
Best of Andraé, The (album), 227
  changes to packaging for, 227–28
  charts, 238–39
  in concert, 235–36
  and end of 1976, 240–41
  new home of Crouch, 233–35
  new horn section on, 230–33
  new media, 239–40
  song selection on, 228–30
  songwriting, 237–38
Bethel Gospel Tabernacle, 104–5
Billboard, 70, 79, 102, 117, 120–21, 125–26, 131, 135–36, 373, 381–82
Billy Graham Crusades, 66–67
Black gospel, 36, 69, 77–78
  Crouch version of, 38
  in "Nobody like the Lord," 57
  song closest to, 67
  traditional, 36, 67, 77–78, 80–81, 86, 96, 129, 366–67
Black Key Pitch Centricity, 36
Black Theology & Black Power (Cone), 138–39
Black Theology of Liberation (Cone), 138–39
"Bless His Holy Name" (*Just Andraé*), 171
Blind Boys of Mississippi, 96
Blines, Michael A., 342
"Blood (Will Never Lose Its Power), The" (*Take the Message Everywhere*), 83–84
blood songs, 83–84
Blue Streak, 108
Blumberg, David, 253
Boone, Pat, 126
Bowles, Lillian, 69
Boyer Brothers, 13
Boyer, Horace C., 10–11, 255–56
Boyer, James B., 11
Bradford, Alex, 104
Branham, John L, 9
Brasel, Wayne, 371–73
Brewster, William Herbert, 173
"Bringin' Back the Sunshine" (*I'll Be Thinking of You*), 293–94
Broadcasting magazine, 187–88
"Broken Vessel, The" (*Take the Message Everywhere*), 81

Brown, James, 285–86
Burrell, Walter, 331
bus, life on, 213–14. *See also* touring
Butler, Jerry, 31–32

CAC. *See* Christian Artists Corporation
Caesar, Shirley, 54, 352–53
Campbell, Glen, 353
Campbell, Lucie, 57, 173
Campus Crusade for Christ (CCC), 125–26
CAM Sound Studio, 145–46
"Can't Nobody Do Me like Jesus" (*"Live" at Carnegie Hall*), 185
Caravans, 40
Carlton, Larry, 201
Carmichael, James Anthony, 137–38
Carmichael, Ralph, 216, 221–22, 229, 238, 257, 265, 278–79, 283, 330, 342, 359
  end of partnership with, 374
  finding audience, 121
  and influence of *Keep On Singin'*, 117
  interview with, 110–12
  issues in 1983, 345–46
  and Light Records, 77–78, 135–36, 302
  as new friend, 54–55
  preparing and composing *Just Andraé*, 155–58
  recording *"Live" at Carnegie Hall*, 178–79
  recording studio A-listers, 288–91
  and *Soulfully* (album), 136–38
  and *Take the Message Everywhere* session, 78–80, 84–87
  and trouble in religious music industry, 342–43
Carpenter, Bil, 134–35
Carr, Bea, 104–5, 145–46, 221, 245, 284
Carson, Johnny, 134–35
Carter, Jimmy, 258, 285–86
Cash Box magazine, 101–2, 256–57, 266–67, 285–86
Cash, Johnny, 126–27, 131
CCC. *See* Campus Crusade for Christ
CCM. *See* contemporary Christian music
Celebration of Life, 388–91
Challenge Temple, 60
Challinor, Frederic Arthur, 167–68

INDEX

Chandler, Russell, 276–77
Charles, Ray, 92–93
charts, 238–39
Cheetham, Betty, 127–28
Chieftains, 276–77
childhood, Crouch and, 14–19
Children of the Day, 126
"Choice, The" (*This Is Another Day*), 254
chords, creating, 159–63. See also *Just Andraé* (album)
Chosen Gospel Singers, 9–10
Christ Hymn, 295
Christian Artists Corporation (CAC), 216
Christian Booksellers Association, 257
Christian Copyright Licensing International (CCLI), 92
Christianity Today, 154–55, 177
"Christian People" (single), 103, 104
Christian Youth Travel Association, 221
Christ Memorial Church, COGIC, 19–20, 258
Christ Memorial Radio Choir, 251
Christology, 38
Church of God in Christ (COGIC), 3
    aspects of, 11–14
    Christ Memorial Church, 19–20
    early musical missionaries and influences, 11–14
    emergence of, 10–11
Clarin, Paula, 117–18
Clark, Mattie Moss, 12–13, 95–96
Clark, Twinkie, 95–96
Cleveland, James, 1, 9–10, 25–26, 31–32, 54, 277–79, 352–53
    Crouch *versus*, 284–85, 303–4
    death of, 381–84
Coates, Dorothy Love, 31–32
Cobb, Ed, 45–46
Cobham, Billy, 253
Cocker, Joe, 353
codetta, 80, 348–49
COGIC. *See* Church of God in Christ
COGICs (gospel group)
    early days with, 29–31
    end of, 45–47
    female vocalists for, 27–29
    first producer, 31–32
    greatest influence, 34–35
    great "lost" album, 35–44

It's a Blessing (album), 32–34
    overview of, 25–29
    and Vee-Jay Records, 44–45
Cole, Bill, 108–12, 157, 192
Cole, Nat King, 26
colors, achieving, 159–63. See also *Just Andraé* (album)
"Come and Go with Me to My Father's House" (*Songs of His Coming*), 62
"Come On Back My Child" (*Just Andraé*), 168
Come Together: A Musical Experience, 78–79
Como, Perry, 82
concerts
    Andraé Crouch and Disciples in, 87–88
    Best of Andraé concert, 235–36
    Explo '72 Saturday Concert, 126–27
    for "*Live*" at Carnegie Hall, 177
    for *Live in London*, 267–68
    performing at One Nation Under God International Gospel Festival, 352–53
Cone, James, 39, 138–39, 165
Consolidated Talking Machine Co. of Chicago, 11–12
Contemporary Christian Music (CCM), 193, 261, 344
Contemporary Keyboard magazine, 260–61
Coolidge, Rita, 126
Coomes, Tommy, 126–27
Cotton Bowl, 126
Cottrell, Bob, 131
Cowper, William, 41
Coy, Beverly, 145–46
Craik, Jan, 191
Craik, Kevin, 191
Crawford, Ken, 315–16
Crockett, Anna B., 37
Crosby, Fanny, 115, 208–9
Cross and the Switchblade, The (Wilkerson), 55
Crouch, Andraé, 179–80
    and Addicts Choir, 51–72
    arrest of, 343–45
    asking for "gift" of songwriting, 20–21
    assuming pastorate, 383
    Best of Andraé (album), 227–41
    and "call" to Evangelism, 20

INDEX

Crouch, Andraé (*cont.*)
Carnegie Hall album recorded by, 177–93
childhood of, 14–19
chords and colors, 159–63
versus Cleveland, 284–85, 303–4
and COGICs, 25–47
collaboration with Madonna, 380–81
in concert, 87–88
creating Addicts Choir album, 62–64
criticism leveled against, 164–65
cry for help by, 370
deteriorating health of, 385–87
Don't Give Up (album), 311–33
early days with COGICs, 29–31
early days with Disciples, 76
and end of 1976, 240–41
and end of 1977, 258–59
and end of partnership with Light Records, 374–75
Finally (album), 337–55
final years of Crouch-Maxwell work relationship, 379–91
as friend, 216–17
gift of, 398–99
greatest influence, 34–35
and great "lost" COGICs album, 35–37
growing dissatisfaction of, 145–46
health issues, 384–85
I'll Be Thinking of You (album), 283–306
innovations of, 398
Keep On Singin' LP, 101–21
last days of, 387–91
legacy of, 395–405
Liberty Records and, 101–2
Live in London (album), 265–80
magic of name of, 385
meeting Ralph Carmichael, 77–78
musical innovations of, 1–5
negative reviews and views of, 341
new home of, 233–35
new media, 239–40
No Time to Lose (album), 359–75
onstage with, 288
other losses of, 381–84
overseas with John Haggai, 88–90
Pittsburgh Courier interview, 257
pivotal events in life of, 285–88

pursuing new ventures and venues, 312–13
recording *Just Andraé* (album), 153–74
recording with Bill Cole, 108–12
response to dual approach of, 286–87
signaling return of, 362–64
Soledad State Prison performance, 259–60
songwriting by, 237–38
Soulfully (album), 125–48
and South Africa controversy, 337–38
Southern California upbringing of, 7–21
Take Me Back (album), 197–223
Take the Message Everywhere (album), 75–97
This Is Another Day (album), 245–61
and trouble in religious music industry, 342–43
and year-end flurry, 279–80
Crouch, Benjamin, Sr., 219, 241
Crouch, Catherine, 155
Crouch, Catherine Hodnett, 14–15
Crouch, Samuel, 11–12
Crouch, Samuel Martin, Jr., 15–16
Crouch, Sandra, 2, 3, 4, 7–8, 362, 398, 404–5
Best of Andraé (album), 227–28, 232
brother singing "The Blood (Will Never Lose Its Power)," 20–21
and call" to evangelism of Andraé, 20
celebrating brother, 388
childhood of, 14–19
and Christ Memorial Church of God in Christ, 19–20
and Church of God in Christ, 10–11, 14
creating Addicts Choir album, 62–64
driving Ford Falcon, 27
early days with COGICs, 29–31
Finally (album), 352–53, 355
and first Disciples, 51–54
on four-song 45, 55–59
greatest influence of, 34–35
health issues of brother, 384–85, 387–88
I'll Be Thinking of You (album), 284, 287–88, 291
It's a Blessing session, 32–34
joining Disciples, 106–8

Just Andraé (album), 155, 156–57,
  161–62, 169, 172–73
Keep On Singin' (album), 101–23
lead vocals on "Won't It Be Sad," 40
Live in London (album), 268, 273, 276
Live" at Carnegie Hall (album), 179–
  81, 184, 191
meeting Frankie, 25
No Time to Lose (album), 364, 372
ordaining, 384
personal losses of, 381–84
projects outside gospel bubble, 379–80
questioning Willaims, 28
and Richard Simpson, 31–32
saving day in 1983, 345–46
Soulfully (album), 125–51
Take Me Back (album), 198, 202–4,
  218, 221
Take the Message Everywhere (album),
  75–100
and Teen Challenge Center, 59–60, 61
This Is Another Day (album), 245, 249,
  250–51, 258
winning Grammy, 359, 373
Crouch Creative Team, 321
Crouch Productions, 359–60
Cruz, Nicky, 60
Curry, Terrence, 12–13, 272

Dallas, Karl, 266
Danny Lee and the Children of Truth, 126
David, Hal, 167
Davis, Jerry, 177
Davis, Jessie Ed, 254
Davis, Jimmie, 191
Davis, Miles, 372–73
Davis, Tramaine, 91–93, 101–2, 103,
  110–12, 284
  departure of, 105–6
Department of Evangelism, 14
Diangelo, Danny, 90–91
Dick Clark's American Bandstand, 104
Disciples, 2
  arrival of Tramaine Davis, 91–93
  Carnegie Hall album recorded by,
    177–93
  in concert, 87–88
  creating *Just Andraé*, 155–58
  criticism in 1975, 215–16

demanding touring schedule of, 256–58
departure of Sherman Andrus, 90–91
early days with, 76
and end of 1976, 240–41
and end of 1977, 258–59
finding audience, 94–97
first live album of, 179–81
first photographs in national magazine,
  101–2
increased exposure of, 187–88
Liberty Records and, 101–2
life on bus, 213–14
Live in London (album), 265–80
live session of "Satisfied," 127–29
major tours and appearances of, 197–98
on national television, 134–35
new hurdles of, 119–20
new media, 239–40
overseas tour of, 190–92
overseas with John Haggai, 88–90
performing Explo '72 Saturday concert,
  126–27
resuming touring schedule, 188
Sandra Crouch joining, 106–8
singles of, 101–5
Soledad State Prison performance, 259–60
and Sonlight quartet, 129–31
Sonlight quartet joining, 153–55
touring prior to *Take Me Back*, 212–13
Tramaine Davis departure, 105–6
Dixon, Jessy, 181, 256, 258
DjeDje, Jacqueline, 8–9
DJM Records, 256
Dolvin, Gloria, 145–46
Don DeGrate Delegation, 145–46
"Don't Give Up" (*Don't Give Up*), 323–24
Don't Give Up (album)
  liturgical format, 329
  packaging of, 317
  as potential misstep, 329–31
  producing "It's Gonna Rain," 311–12
  pursuing new ventures and venues, 312–13
  reception of, 328–29, 331–32
  sessions leading up to release of, 318–21
  side I, 322–23
  side II, 325–28
  tour version of, 332–33
  Warner Bros. release of, 315–17
  "You" songs on, 318

412   INDEX

"Don't Let It Be Said Too Late" (*It's a Blessing*), 37
"Don't Stop Using Me" (*It's a Blessing*), 43, 44
Doran, Elve, 11–12
Dorsey, Thomas, 1, 8–9
Dorsey, Willa, 126
Dosey, Thomas, 173
Douroux, Margaret Pleasant, 272–73
Dove Awards, 187–88
Dranes, Arizona, 11–12, 173, 255–56
Draper, O'Landa, 223
"Dreamin'" (*I'll Be Thinking of You*), 296–97
Durio, Alfie Silas, 291, 300, 346–47, 351, 383, 400, 402
Dylan, Bob, 249, 301

Early Hits of 1965, 46
Earth, Wind & Fire, 230, 232, 246–47, 292, 294, 321
Ebony magazine, 15–16, 331, 338, 352–53
Eckler, Greg, 254
Eckstine, Billy, 75, 82, 285–86
Electric Symphony, The, 109
Elektra, 297–98, 302, 305, 314–15
Emmanuel Church of God in Christ, 15–17
Escalante, Michael, 231, 245, 284
eschatological frames, 38
Eshleman, Paul, 126–27
Evangelism, "call" to, 20
"Everybody's Got to Know" (*Finally*), 348
"Everything Changed" (*Soulfully*), 139
"Everywhere" (*Take the Message Everywhere*), 80–81
Exodus Records, 44–45
Explo '72
   aftermath of, 131–34
   influence of, 131–34
   performing live version of "Satisfied," 127–29
   Saturday concert at, 126–27
   Sonlight quartet performing at, 129–31

Fagen, Donald, 292, 293
Faggett, Geary, 298–99, 372
Faggett, Vonciele, 234, 298–99, 372
"Faith Unlocks the Door" (*Teen Challenge Addicts Choir*), 62, 68

family, emphasizing importance of, 18–19
Fedco Audio Labs, 177
Felder, Wilton, 202, 206, 248, 253, 254
Felix, Jaymes, 399–400
   Don't Give Up (album), 317, 326
   Live in London (album), 267–68, 271–72, 273, 274–75
   with new horn section, 230–33
   onstage with Andraé, 288
   in pivotal events, 287–88
   on road again, 283–84
This Is Another Day (album), 245, 249, 250–54, 255, 257
Fernandez, Ruben, 61, 75, 79, 107
Fidler, Richard L., 37
Finally (album), 337
   arrest and fallout while crafting, 343–45
   crafting, 338–40
   entering 1983, 345–47
   impact of, 353–55
   negative reviews and views before release of, 341
   recording, 346–47
   recording in other countries, 340–41
   release of, 351
   response to, 351–52
   side I, 347–49
   side II, 349–51
   and special concert, 352–53
   and trouble in religious music industry, 342–43
"Finally" (*Finally*), 347–48
final years
   deteriorating health of Crouch, 385–87
   health issues, 384–85
   last days of Crouch, 387–91
   losses, 381–84
   Madonna collaboration, 380–81
   ordaining Sandra, 384
   overview, 379
   projects outside gospel bubble, 379–80
Fitzgerald, Ella, 221–22
Flash Cadillac & the Continental Kids, 212–13
Floria, Cam, 216
Fonda, Jane, 221–22
Ford, Roger, 126–27
Forerunners, 126
Four Seasons, 31–32

INDEX

Fourth Annual International Gospel Song Festival, 188
Franklin, Aretha, 18–19, 286–87
Franklin, Kirk, 1–2, 147, 389–90
Frazier, Thurston G, 9
Frye, Theodore R., 69
Full Gospel Businessmen's Fellowship International, 154–55
Funderburke, Tommy, 326

Gaither, Bill, 146–47, 265
Garrett, Snuff, 101
Gassman, Clark, 109, 110, 112, 113, 114, 116, 137–38, 198, 209, 249, 252–53
Gaye, Marvin, 221–22
Gay Sisters, 13
genre fusing, 57
George, Cassietta, 9–10
Gershwin, George, 250
Gersztyn, Bob, 94
Giglio, Stephen "Bugs," 119, 218–21
Gipson, Revé, 33
glissandos, 42, 296–97, 326
"God Loves the Country People" (*Just Andraé*), 170
Godspell, 160–61
"God Will Never Leave You, No, No, No, No," 76
Gonzalo, Carrie, 93f, 103f, 115–16, 217f, 234, 363
  early days with COGICs, 29
  meeting, 54–55
  on promoting "The Blood (Will Never Lose Its Power)," 64
  recording *"The Broken Vessel,"* 81
  Take the Message Everywhere session, 78, 85–86
Gonzalo, Val, 87–88, 233–34, 396
Gospel Harmonettes, 31–32
gospel music, 1–4
  Black gospel music, 67, 83, 96, 172–73, 197, 210, 333, 362–63, 365–66, 373
  creating new sound in, 58
  in Crouch childhood, 14–19
  emergence of, 8–10
  immersion in, 34–35
  COGIC influence, 11–14
  projects outside bubble of, 379–80

Richard Simpson, 31–32
Southern California style of, 53–54
"There Is a Fountain" uniqueness in, 40–41
traditional, 67, 71, 86–87, 94, 303, 399–400
transforming, 36, 41
Gospel Music Association, 187–88
Gospel Music International, 256
Gospel Music Workshop, 235–36
Gospel Pearls, 9–10
"Got Me Some Angels" (*No Time to Lose*), 364
Gouche, Andrew, 360–61, 372
Gouche, Jackie, 371
Graham, Billy, 64–65, 125–27
Graydon, Jay, 249
Great Commission Company, 126
Greater Pittsburgh Charismatic Conference, 257
Great Migrations, 7
Green, Keith, 237–38, 256
Green, Melody, 147
Greene, Jeannie, 129–31
Greenlee, Jeanie, 25–26
Gregory, Allen, 230–32, 256
Gregory, Dick, 31–32, 267, 284
Griffin, Bessie, 9–10
Grusin, Don, 311–12

Hackworth, J. Bernard, 384
Haggai, John, 88–90
Haines, John, 132, 133
Hall, Danniebelle, 117–18, 126–27, 155
Hall, David, 59–60, 63, 221, 350
Hallelujah, I Am Free" (*Teen Challenge Addicts Choir*), 67
"Hallelujah" (*"Live" at Carnegie Hall*), 184–85
"Hallelujah" (*Live in London*), 273
Hancock, Herbie, 249
"Handwriting on the Wall" (*Don't Give Up*), 325–26
Handy, W. C., 26
Harlem Renaissance, 7
Harmony Recorders, 32–34
Harold, Caludrena N., 117, 397
Harrah, James, 360–61

INDEX

Harrington, Richard, 341

Harris, Emmylou, 249

Hawkins Family, 238

Hawkins, Edwin, 13, 62, 91, 134–35, 145–46, 232, 238, 287–88, 397

Hawkins, Tramaine, 13, 221–22, 227–28, 283, 302, 359, 373

Hawkins, Walter, 13, 37, 91, 105, 145–46, 221–22, 238, 240–41, 258, 260, 278–79, 283, 287–88, 298, 302, 312, 331

Hayes, Isaac, 75

Hazzard, Kathy, 104–5, 238, 252–53
  on Andraé's house, 233–34
  Disciples performing "Country People," 161
  on Explo '72 aftermath and influence, 132–33
  and growing dissatisfaction of Andraé, 145–46
  on message of "What Does Jesus Mean to You," 160–61
  "Perfect Peace"/ "My Peace I Leave With You," 246–48
  Quiet Times," 249–50
  response to *Just Andraé*, 172
  talking about horn sections, 232
  talking about *Take Me Back*, 198–99, 202, 204, 205, 208–10, 219

"This Is Another Day," 248

Hearn, Billy Ray, 64–65, 187, 237–38

Heavenly Tones, 91

"He Included Me" (*It's a Blessing*), 42, 44

"He Included Me" (*Teen Challenge Addicts Choir*), 68–69

"He Lives" (*It's a Blessing*), 43, 44

"He Looked beyond My Fault" ("*Live*" at *Carnegie Hall*), 183–84

Henderson, Patrick, 288–89

"He Never Sleeps" (*Take the Message Everywhere*), 80

"He Proved His Love to Me" (*Soulfully*), 140

He's Everything to Me (Carmichael), 342

"He's Waiting" (*Finally*), 349–50

He Touched Me (album), 109–10

HiFi Stereo Review magazine, 337

Higgins, Billy, 51–52

Hines, James Earle, 9

Hines, Stuart K., 64

"His Truth Still Marches On" (*No Time to Lose*), 365–66

Hockensmith, Hadley, 189f, 268, 284, 292, 295–96, 299, 317, 350
  chords and colors, 159–63
  creating *Take Me Back*, 198, 200
  and growing dissatisfaction, 145–46
  impact and influence of *Just Andraé*, 163–64
  and life on bus, 213–14
  "*Live*" at *Carnegie Hall* recording, 178–79
  "*Live*" at *Carnegie Hall* songs, 183
  at Mama Jo's, 201
  and national television, 134–35
  preparing and composing *Just Andraé*, 155–58
  songs of *Just Andraé*, 165–71, 172–73
  and Sonlight, 252–53
  touring, 212–13
  touring overseas, 191

Holiness beat, 8–9

Hollywood Reporter, 301, 312–13, 330, 337

"Hollywood Scene" (*Don't Give Up*), 324–25

Holy Ghost Songs: Church of God in Christ Standard Hymnal, 37

Honeytree, Nancy, 94

Hooker, John Lee, 31–32

Hopkins, Jamal-Dominique, 34–35, 383

horns, domination of, 230–33

Humbard, Rex, 154–55

Hungate, David, 199–200, 202

Hunt, Dennis, 342

Hymnary.org, 146–47

Hymns Speak for the Organ, 46

"I Cannot Tell It All" (*Teen Challenge Addicts Choir*), 69

"I Can't Keep It to Myself" (*Don't Give Up*), 324

Ichthus Music Festival, 132–33

"I Come That You Might Have Life" (*Soulfully*), 141

"I Didn't Think It Could Be" ("*Live*" at *Carnegie Hall*), 184–85

"I Don't Know Why Jesus Loved Me" (*Keep on Singin'*), 112

INDEX 415

"I Don't Know Why" (*"Live" at Carnegie Hall*), 181–82
"I'd Rather have Jesus" (*Teen Challenge Addicts Choir*), 66–67
"If Heaven Was Never Promised to Me" (*Just Andraé*), 168–69
"I Find No Fault in Him," 57
"If I Was a Tree (The Highest Praise)" (*Live in London*), 272–73
"I Just Want to Know You" (*Live in London*), 273–74
"I'll Be Good to You, Baby" (*Don't Give Up*), 327
I'll Be Thinking of You (album), 283
    and 1980, 301
    broader audience for, 297–98
    Crouch *versus* Cleveland, 303–4
    eventful end to 1980, 305–6
    Koinonia originating from, 299
    more never-ending tours following, 304
    onstage with Andraé, 288
    performing on *Saturday Night Live*, 302
    pivotal events in life of Crouch, 285–88
    recording approaches in studio, 291–92
    recording studio A-listers, 288–91
    road warriors, 298–99
    side I, 292–93
    side II, 293–97
    success for Light Records, 302
    touring schedule, 283–84
    touring sessions following release of, 300–1
"I'll Be Thinking of You" (*I'll Be Thinking of You*), 292
"I'll Keep on Loving You Lord" (*Live in London*), 274
"I'll Never Forget" (*Take the Message Everywhere,* LP), 83
"I'll Still Love You" (*Take Me Back*), 203
"I Looked for God," 58
"I Love Walking with You" (*Don't Give Up*), 326
"I'm Coming Home Dear Lord" (*Keep on Singin'*), 113
"I'm Gonna Keep On Singin" (*Keep on Singin'*), 112
Imperials, 78, 90–91, 109–10, 172, 216, 300

improvisation, spirit of, 106–7, 153–60
"I Must Go Away" (*Keep on Singin'*), 76, 113, 116
"In Remembrance" (*Just Andraé*), 166
InterVarsity Fellowship, 125–26
"Invitation" (*"Live" at Carnegie Hall*), 185
"I Serve a Risen Savior" (*It's a Blessing*), 43
"I Shall Never Let Go His Hand" (*Teen Challenge Addicts Choir*), 68
"I Surrender All" (*Live in London*), 271
"It Ain't No New Thing" (*Take Me Back*), 207–8
It's a Blessing (album), 32–34
    and end of COGICs, 45–47
    and great "lost" COGICs album, 35–37
    side I, 37–40
    side II, 40–44
    and Vee-Jay Records, 44–45
"It's a Blessing" (*It's a Blessing*), 43–44
"It's Gonna Rain" (*Don't Give Up*), 311–12
"It's Not Just a Story" (*Just Andraé*), 167–68
"It Will Never Lose Its Power" (*It's a Blessing*), 39, 44
"It Won't Be Long" (*"Live" at Carnegie Hall*), 185
"It Won't be Long" (*Soulfully*), 142
I've Got Confidence, 109–10
"I've Got Confidence" (*Keep on Singin'*), 111t, 114–15
"I've Got It" (*Take the Message Everywhere*), 81–82
"I've Got Jesus" (*Teen Challenge Addicts Choir*), 67
"I've Got the Best" (*I'll Be Thinking of You*), 292
Ives, Burl, 64–65

Jackson 5, 253
Jackson, Jimmye, 117–18
Jackson, Mahalia, 1, 84–85, 134–35
Jackson, Michael, 193, 255–56, 315, 323, 324–25, 326, 380, 383
Jamerson, James, Jr., 311–12
James, Phyllis St., 126–27, 191, 202, 221, 319, 352–53
J. C. Power Outlet, 30
Jenkins, Margaret Aikens, 9–10

Jerome, Benjamin, 14–15
Jessy Dixon Singers, 181
"Jesus, Come Lay Your Had on Me" (*No Time to Lose*), 364–65
"Jesus (Every Hour He'll Give You Power") (*Keep on Singin'*), 113
Jesus Christ Superstar, 160–61
"Jesus Is Lord" (*I'll Be Thinking of You*), 294–95
"Jesus Is the Answer" (*"Live" at Carnegie Hall*), 184–85
Jesus Movement, 125–26
Jesus Sound Explosion (album), 131
Jim Crow, 7
Johnson, Jean, 298–99, 372
Jones, Gloria, 25, 27, 28, 398, 402
  "The Blood (Will Never Lost Its Power)," 83–84
  and end of COGICs, 46
  and first Disciples, 53
  and great "lost" COGICs album, 38
  "Precious Lord, Take My Hand," 85
and rare four-song 45, 58
Jones, Quincy, 379–80, 381–82
Jones, Wilbert, Jr., 17
Journey, The (album), recording, 385–87
Journey through the Secret Life of Plants (album), 298
"Joy Bells," 58–59
Just Andraé (album)
  album as liturgy, 171
  chords and colors of, 159–63
  composing, 155–58
  impact of, 163–64
  influence of, 163–64
  and issue of race, 164–65
  legacy of, 172–74
  overview of, 153
  preparing, 155–58
  reception of, 172
  side I, 165–69
  side II, 169–71
"Just Like He Said He Would" (*Take Me Back*), 204
"Just Like He Said Would" (*Live in London*), 274

Kaiser, Kurt, 64–65, 77, 216
Karl, Frankie, 25–26, 27

Keaggy, Phil, 326
Keene, Wil, 311–12
Keep On Singin' (album), 138–39, 144, 145
  back-cover interview, 110–12
  "Christian People" (single), 103
  Danniebelle Hall and, 117–18
  finding audience, 120–21
  impact and influence of, 117
  Liberty Records and, 101–2
  new hurdles, 119–20
  recording with Bill Cole, 108–12
  Sandra Crouch joining Disciples, 106–8
  side I, 112–13
  side II, 114–16
  stylistic differences, 110
  "Too Close" (single), 104–5
  Tramaine Davis departure from Disciples, 105–6
Kessler, Irv, 101, 104
Khan, Chaka, 141–42
Kibble, Mark, 206, 249, 255–56
King, Evelyn, 285–86
Kingdom of Tonga, touring in, 192
Knight, Gladys, 253
Knight, Marie, 13
Koinonia, 299
Kristofferson, Kris, 126
Kuhlman, Kathryn, 154–55

Laboriel, Abraham, 257–58, 299, 348, 360–61
Larvik, Norway, concert in, 371–72
Lataillade, Vicki Mack, 272
Late, Great Planet Earth, The (Lindsey), 114
LaValley, Jeffrey, 95, 206, 250–51
Lawrence, Donald, 1–2
Lawrence, Rhett, 360–61
"Leave the Devil Alone" (*Soulfully*), 142
Lennon, John, 168–69
"Let the Church Say Amen" (song), 385–87
"Let's Worship Him" (*Finally*), 350
Lexicon, 135–36, 265
Lexicon Music, 363
Lexicon Publishing, 77–78
Liberty Records, 101–2
L.I.F.E. Bible College, 17–18
Life magazine, 133

INDEX

Light Records, 4, 77–78, 135–36, 153, 179, 200–1, 202–3, 258, 266, 277, 283, 289–90
  end of partnership with, 374–75
  More of the Best (collection), 314–15
  sessions leading up to release of *Don't Give Up*, 318–21
  success for, 302
Lightner, Gwendolyn Cooper, 8–9
"Like a Prayer" (Madonna), 380–81
Lion King, The (soundtrack), 383
liturgy
  Just Andraé album as, 171
  Soulfully album as, 142–43
"Live" at Carnegie Hall (album), 219
  album components, 179–81
  concert memories, 177
  distribution of, 187
  impact and influence of, 192–93
  increased exposure of, 187–88
  overseas tour, 190–92
  promotion of, 187
  recording album, 178–79
  responses to, 186–87
  resuming touring schedule, 188
  songs, 181–86
Live in London (album)
  evangelical statement of, 269–70
  as game-changing release, 266–67
  musicians of, 268
  original concerts, 267–68
  reception of, 276–79
  set list for, 268–69
  side I, 270–72
  side II, 272–73
  side III, 273–75
  side IV, 275–76
  touring context for, 265
  and year-end flurry, 279–80
Live in Los Angeles (album), 386–87
"Livin' This Kind of Life" (*No Time to Lose*), 368
London, England, 241, 260–61, 351
  Black people in, 268–69
  concerts in, 267–68
  I'll Be Thinking of You tour in, 283–84
  pivotal event in, 287–88
  recording string parts in, 291–92
  recounting memory in, 300

"Lookin' for You" (*I'll Be Thinking of You*), 283–93
Look magazine, 127–28
"Lord, You've Been Good to Me" (*Just Andraé*), 169
Los Angeles Gospel Music Mart, 8–9
Los Angeles Sentinel, 59, 297, 306, 343
Los Angeles Times, 276–77, 342
Louisville Defender, 350, 351
Love Center Choir, 221–22, 238, 240–41, 278–79, 283
Love Is the Thing (album), 109–10
Love Song, 94, 126–27
"Lullaby of the Deceived" (*Just Andraé*), 170–71

Madonna, 380–81
Make Up Your Mind (album), 230
Mall, Andrew, 132
Malone, Tom, 199–200
Mama Jo's
  recording *This Is Another Day* album, 227–28, 246, 251, 252–53, 254
  Take Me Back sessions, 198, 199–203
Manchester, England, 267, 268–69, 273–74, 351
Mann, Johnny, 277
Manna Music, Inc., 64, 77–78
Mansion Builder (album), 257
Maranatha, 177
Marini, Lou, 199–200
marketplace, 214–15
Martin, Sallie, 31–32
Martin, Stillman, 38
Maslow, Steve, 156–57
Mason, Charles Harrison, 10
Matthews, Randy, 126, 129–31
Mavis and the Staple Singers, 101–2
Maxwell, Bill, 4, 166, 167–68, 198, 400
  and all-star studio lineup, 199–200
  in Australia, 221
  back on road, 188
  Best of Andraé (album), 227–38
  chords and colors, 159–63
  creating *Just Andraé*, 155–58
  creating *This Is Another Day* (album), 245, 246–55
  and Crouch songwriting, 237–38

418 INDEX

Maxwell, Bill (*cont.*)
  Don't Give Up (album), 311–33
  end of partnership with, 374–75
  Finally (album), 337–55
  final years of Crouch-Maxwell work
    relationship, 379–91
  growing dissatisfaction of Andraé,
    145–46
  I'll Be Thinking of You (album), 283–306
  impact and influence of *Just Andraé*,
    163–64
  Keep On Singin' (album), 114– –15
  and last days of Andraé, 387–88
  Live in London (album), 265–81
  Mama Jo's and, 200–3
  and national television, 134–35
  and new horn section, 230–33
  No Time to Lose (album), 359–75
  overseas tour, 188
  preparing *Take Me Back*, 198–200
  recording *Finally*, 346–47
  recording *"Live" at Carnegie Hall*,
    178–79, 185
  on road again, 256–58
  on responses to *Take Me Back*, 210–12
  in Sonlight, 129–31, 153–55
  Soulfully (album), 136–47
  Take Me Back songs, 203–10
Mayfield, Curtis, 246–47
McCall, Marti, 300
McClurkin, Donnie, 1–2, 223
McCracken, Jarrell, 64–65, 187, 257
McCrary, Howard, 288–92, 296, 298–99,
  319, 352
McCrary, Linda, 399
  crafting *Finally*, 338
  dinner/songwriting gatherings, 289–90
  Finally songs, 349–50
  heading to Los Angeles, 9–10
  health issues of Andraé, 385–86
  losses, 381–82
  No Time to Lose songs, 364–65, 367,
    368, 370, 373
  recording at different studios, 340
  remembering Sandra and Andraé, 19
  special concert, 352–53
  touring, 370
  Warner Bros. release of *Don't Give Up*,
    317

  working on *Don't Give Up*, 322–23,
    325–26, 327, 331–32
McCreary, Gentry, 277
McGee F. E., 12–13
McGovern, Maureen, 301
McGuire, Barry, 126
McReynolds, Jonathan, 1–2
Medema, Ken, 216
Melody Maker magazine, 266
Mercy (album), 381–82
metered music, 57
Midnight Musicals, 95
Mieir, Audrey, 29, 54, 64–65, 69, 78–80,
  87–88, 94, 229
Mighty Clouds of Joy, 301
Mike Douglas Entertainment Hour,
  329–30
Monday Musicals, 54–55
Moore, LaVern, 53, 62–63, 96, 398
More of the Best (collection), release of,
  314–15
Morgan, Perry, 51–53, 61–62, 75, 79,
  84–85, 119, 126–27, 155, 179–80,
  202, 221, 245, 284, 298–99
  on creativity of Crouch, 234–35
  on finding audiences, 96
  Sandra Crouch joining Disciples, 106–8
Most Exciting Organ Ever, The, 46
Muhoberac, Larry, 159, 201–2, 246–48,
  252–53, 254, 348, 360–61
Murden, Kristle, 289–90, 301, 352–53, 360
Murray, Bill, 105
musicians, *Live in London* (album), 268
Musikland Recording Studios, 340
musique concrète, 293–94
Myers, Laura Lee, 68–69
Myerscough, Glen, 231–32, 248, 251–53,
  267, 268, 271, 272–73, 275, 284,
  288, 295
"My Peace I Leave With You" (*This Is
  Another Day*), 246–48
"My Soul Loves Jesus," *It's a Blessing*, 39,
  44
My Story! My Song! Blessed! (Andrus), 53
"My Tribute" (*Finally*), 351
"My Tribute" (*Live in London*), 276
"My Tribute" (to God Be the Glory)"
  (*Keep on Singin'*), 115–16
Myrrh Records, 287–88

INDEX

National Association of Recording Merchandisers, 313
national television, 125–26, 134–35, 197–98, 305
Newby, Stephen, 3, 172–73
New Church Hymnal, The, 265, 287–88
New Hebrides, touring in, 192
Newton-John, Olivia, 212–13
New York Times, 133, 343–44
Niehaus, Lennie, 363
1980, performances during, 301
1982, events of
   arrest and fallout, 343–45
   final serendipity, 345
   negative reviews and views, 340–41
   South Africa controversy, 337–38
   trouble in religious music industry, 342–44
"No, Not One" (*Take the Message Everywhere*), 82
"Nobody like the Lord," 56–57
Norman, Larry, 94, 126–27, 131
Norwood, Dorothy, 40
"Nothing Is Greater," (*It's A Blessing*), 40
No Time to Lose (album)
   as cry for help, 370
   and end of partnership with Light Records, 374–75
   overview, 359
   recording sessions for, 359–62
   short tours supporting, 370–73
   side I, 364–66
   side II, 366–70
   signaling return of Crouch, 362–64
   as strong comeback for Crouch, 373
"No Time to Lose" (*No Time to Lose*), 367–68
NRK, network, 284

Obama, Michelle, 1
Ochs, Ed, 303
"Oh, I Need Him" (*Soulfully*), 140
"Oh, It Is Jesus" (*No Time to Lose*), 366–67
"Oh Savior" (*Take Me Back*), 208–9
"Oh Taste and 275, See" (*Live in London*)
OKeh Records, 11–12
Olson, Nat, 65
100 Greatest Albums in Christian Music, The, 144–45

O'Neal Twins, 13
One Nation Under God International Gospel Festival, 352–53
"One Touch of Venus," 45–46
Otis, Johnny, 51–52
Owens-Collins, Jamie, 77
Owens, Jimmie, 216

Paramount Recording Studio, 311–12
Pardini, Lou, 371–72
Parker, Lillian, 177
Parker, William Henry, 167–68
Parks, Dean, 202, 249, 253, 295–96, 299, 348
Patterson, Deborah Mason, 37
Patterson, Gilbert Earl, 15–16
Pentecostal Christ Sanctified Holiness Church, 53
"Perfect Peace" (*Live in London*), 270–71
"Perfect Place" (*This Is Another Day*), 246–48
Peters, Jerry, 325–26
Philips, John, 299
Phillinganes, Greg, 326
Phillips, John, 360–61
Pickett, Wilson, 101–2
Pinding, Lyndon O., 256–57
Pittsburgh Courier, 257
planning, 81, 248
"Please Come Back." *See* "It's Gonna Rain" (*Don't Give Up*)
Poitier, Sydney, 221–22
Pollard, Deborah Smith, 272, 397–98, 404
"Polynesian Praise Song" (*This Is Another Day*), 254–55
Powell, Mark Allen, 117, 172
"Power in the Blood" (*Live in London*), 273
"Power of Jesus, The" (*Teen Challenge Addicts Choir*), 66
"Praise God, Praise God" (*Live in London*), 275
"Praises" (*Take Me Back*), 203–4
Pray (album), 383–84
"Precious Lord, Take My Hand" (*Take the Message Everywhere*, LP), 84–87
Preston, Billy, 20–21, 25–26, 36, 56, 68, 172–73, 206, 207, 215–16, 221, 288–89, 295–96, 398

420 INDEX

Preston, William Everett, 26–27
prison, performance at, 259–60
Psalm 150, 230–32, 254, 268
"Psalms 40" (*Teen Challenge Addicts Choir*), 69
PUSH for Excellence, 287–88

QuestLove and the Roots, 294–95
"Quiet Times" (*This Is Another Day*), 249–50, 260–61

race, issue of, 164–65
Rachinski, Donna, 216–17
Rachinski, Howard, 92
Raincross Square Auditorium, 235–36
Ralph Carmichael Presents Clark Gassman, The Electric Symphony, 109
Rambo, Buck, 118
Rambo, Dottie, 181
Rambo, Reba, 129–31
rare recordings (*Teen Challenge Addicts Choir*)
    overview, 55–56
    second rare recording, 62
    side I, 56–57
    side II, 58–59
Ramscy, Guthrie, 248
Raspberry, Raymond, 9–10
reception, 328–29, 331–32. See also *Don't Give Up* (album)
Record World magazine, 102, 257, 258, 266, 277–79, 297–98
religious music industry, trouble in, 342–43
"Revive Us Again" (*Live in London*), 273
"Right Now" (*No Time to Lose*), 365
ritard, 57, 67, 350
road warriors, 298–99
Robinson, Smokey, 117, 285–86, 312–13
Rock Garden, 177
Rogers, Harlan, 129–30, 145–46, 156–58, 178, 191, 212–13, 268, 292, 295–96, 299, 350
Ross, Diana, 92–93
Ruff, Michael, 360–61

Salvo, Patrick, 239
Sample, Joe, 327–28, 360–61, 364–65
    hiring, 199–200

piano part of, 249, 252–53, 317
Sande, Robert L., 62
"Satisfied" (*Soulfully*), 127–29, 140
Saturday Night Live, 302, 330, 342
"Save the People" (*Don't Give Up*), 326
"Say Yes" (*Soon & Very Soon*), 41–42
Scott, Samuel T., 62
2nd Chapter of Acts, 94, 256, 257
Sensational Nightingales, 96
separate-ness, COGIC, 10–11
set list, *Live in London* (album), 268–69
Seymour, William, 8
Sgt. Pepper's Lonely Hearts Club Band, 114
Sharp, Rick, 245
Shea, George Beverly, 66–67
Shindig, 46
shout serenade, 42
side I. *See various albums*
side II. *See various albums*
Silas, Alfie, 298–99, 346–47, 360
Simmons-Akers Singers, 9–10
Simpson, Norma, 306
Simpson, Richard, 31–32, 46
    and *It's a Blessing* session, 32–34
Sinatra, Frank, 53, 82
"Since I Found Him" (*It's a Blessing*), 39–40
singability, concept, 255–56
Singing Rambos, 118
16 Yr. Old Soul, (album) 26
Sjöholm, Lennart, 291–92
Sly and the Family Stone, 101–2
Smallwood, Eugene, 9
Smiley, Tavis, 180–81, 251
Smith, Connie, 126, 129–31
Smith, Fred, 31
Smith, Howard, 288–89, 317, 373
    "It's Gonna Rain," 311–12
    No Time to Lose sessions, 360, 361–62
    recording lead vocals, 296, 324, 326, 348, 350
    religious experience of, 290
    singing early version of "We Are Not Ashamed," 338–39
    in special concert, 352–53
    in touring group, 298–99
    vocals on "His Truth Still Marches On," 365–66
    vocals on "That's Why I Needed You," 340
Smith, Scott V., 360–61, 381–82

INDEX

Smith, Utah, 13, 350
Soledad State Prison, performing at,
    259–60
solo album, recording. See *Just Andraé*
    (album)
"Somebody Somewhere Is Prayin' (Just for
    You)" (*No Time to Lose*), 369
"Someday I'll 66, See His Face" (*Teen
    Challenge Addicts Choir,* LP)
songwriting, 20–21, 237–38
Sonlight, quartet
    joining Disciples, 153–55
    performing at Explo '72, 129–31
"Soon and Very Soon" (*This Is Another
    Day*), 250–51
soteriology, 38
soul, concepts of, 142–43
Soulfully (album), 105–6, 147–48
    Explo '72 aftermath and influence,
        131–34
    Explo '72 Saturday concert, 126–27
    formation of Light Records, 135–36
    growing dissatisfaction, 145–46
    impact of songs on LP, 146–47
    Jesus Movement, 125–26
    as liturgy, 142–43
    live version of "Satisfied," 127–29
    national television, 134–35
    other message of, 138–39
    recording album, 136–38
    responses to, 143–45
    side I, 139–41
    and Sonlight quartet, 129–31
soul power, adopting concept
    of, 126–39
Sound Lab Studios, 311–12
South Africa, controversy regarding,
    337–38
Southern California, Crouch in
    asking for "gift" of songwriting, 20–21
    call" to Evangelism, 20
    Christ Memorial Church, 19–20
    Church of God in Christ (COGIC),
        10–11
    Crouch childhood, 14–19
    early COGIC musical missionaries and
        influences, 11–14
    gospel music, 8–10
    overview, 7–8

Southwest Michigan State Choir COGIC,
    13
Sparrow Records, 256
Speer Family, 126
Spencer, Tim, 64, 77
Spielberg, Steven, 379–80
Spinners, 212–13
Springs, Frankie C., 25–26, 32
Staples, Mavis, 25, 285–86
"Start All Over Again" (*Don't Give Up*),
    315–16, 327–28
Steely Dan, 46, 139, 246, 283–93, 321,
    324, 367–68
Stowe, David W., 131, 186–87
Sunshine Day (album), 288–89
surge singing, 40–41
Sutherland, Sam, 177
Swaggart, Jimmy, 69
Swan Silvertones, 31–32
"Sweet Love of Jesus" (*Take Me Back*), 207
Sweet Spirit, 104–5, 127, 154, 197,
    198–99
"Sweet Communion" (*Finally*), 348–49
Swisher, Phyllis, 117–18, 156–57

Tackett, Fred, 246
Taff, Russ, 300–1
"Take a Little Time" (*Keep on Singin'*), 114
"Take a Little Time" (*Live in London*), 272
Take Me Back (album), 197
    all-star lineup sessions, 199–200
    Christian Artists Corporation (CAC),
        216
    criticism in 1975, 215–16
    Crouch as friend, 216–17
    as enduring classic, 222–23
    and life on bus, 213–14
    major tours and appearances preceding,
        197–98
    Mama Jo's and, 200–3
    in marketplace, 214–15
    preparing album, 198–99
    responses to, 210–12, 217–18
    side I, 203–5
    side II, 205–10
    and Stephen "Bugs" Giglio, 218–21
    touring prior to, 212–13
    year in review, 221–22
"Take Me Back" (*Take Me Back*), 205–7

422 INDEX

Take the Message Everywhere (album), 78–79, 138–39, 145
  Andraé Crouch and Disciples in concert, 87–88
  arrival of Tramaine Davis, 91–93
  departure of Sherman Andrus, 90–91
  early days with Disciples, 76
  finding audience, 94–97
  meeting Ralph Carmichael, 77–78
  overseas with John Haggai, 88–90
  overview, 75
  recording session, 78–80
  side I, 80–82
  side II, 83–87
Taylor, Danny, 177
Taylor, James, 249
T-Bone Burnett, 130
Teen Challenge Addicts Choir, album
  aftermath, 70
  as modern liturgy, 70–72
  overview, 64–65
  side I, 65–67
  side II, 68–69
Teen Challenge Center, 59–52
  fund-raiser, 92
  Teen Challenge Addicts Choir album, 64–70
"Tell Them" (*Live in London*), 272–73
"Tell Them" (*Take Me Back*), 209–10
Terrill, Marshall, 132, 133
Tharpe, Rosetta, 13, 173, 286–87
"That's What it's All About" (*Just Andraé*), 166–67
"That's Why I Needed You" (*Finally*), 350
Thedford, Billy, 346–47, 387–88, 400
  arrival/departure of Tramaine Davis, 91, 105
  in Australia, 221
  best of *Andraé* album, 227–28
  at concert for *"Live" at Carnegie Hall,* 177
  creating Addicts Choir album, 63
  creating *This Is Another Day* album, 245
  departure of Sherman Andrus, 90–91
  early performances, 54–55
  Explo '72 aftermath and influence, 131–34
  and impact of *Soulfully* LP, 147
  on influence of Explo '72, 132

and life on bus, 213–14
"Live" at Carnegie Hall album, 179–86
live version of "Satisfied," 127–29
at Mama Jo's, 200–3
memory of *"Live" at Carnegie Hall* concert, 177
nomination of, 301
as one of first Disciples, 51–54
and overseas touring, 89, 191, 192
photographs of, 101––2
pivotal events, 287–88
preparing and composing *Just Andraé,* 155–58, 164, 169–70, 172–73
recording with Bill Cole, 108–12
Sandra joining Disciples, 106–8
Soon and Very Soon songs, 276
Soulfully album, 127–29, 147
Take Me Back album, 203–10
Take the Message Everywhere, 75, 79, 84–85, 88
and Teen Challenge Center, 61
vocals on *Keep On Singin'*, 112–17
"There Is a Fountain" (*It's a Blessing*), 40–41, 44
"There's No Hatred" (*I'll Be Thinking of You*), 295–96
"They Shall Be Mine" (*Take Me Back*), 208
This Is Another Day (album)
  continuing demanding touring schedule, 256–58
  creating album, 245
  and end to stellar year, 258–59
  impact and influence of, 260–61
  recording at Mama Jo's, 246
  response and impact of, 255–56
  side I, 246–55
  Soledad State Prison performance, 259–60
"This Is Another Day" (*Live in London*), 275
"This Is Another Day" (*This Is Another Day*), 248
Thomas, B. J., 302
Thompson, John J., 186–87
Through It All: Andraé Crouch (Crouch), 14–15, 20, 89
"Through It All" (*Soulfully*), 140–41
Thurman, Howard, 269
Tiegel, Eliot, 301

INDEX

Time to be Born, A (Vachon), 127–28
Time magazine, 125, 259
"To Be Used of God" (*Teen Challenge Addicts Choir*), 69
Today Show, 301
Tonight Show with Jimmy Fallon, The, 294–95
Tonight Show with Johnny Carson, The, 54–55, 134–35, 136–37, 154
"Too Close" (single), 104–5
"Touch Me" (*I'll Be Thinking of You*), 292–93
touring
    Don't Give Up on tour, 332–31
    life on bus, 213–14
    never-ending tours, 304
    supporting *No Time to Lose*, 370–73
    for *Take Me Back* album, 197–98, 212–13
Trefetehn, Tom, 246
Trent, Mattie, 257
Tribbett, Tye, 1–2
Tripp, D. H., 321
"Try Me One More Time" (*Soulfully*), 141–42
Turley, Richards, 126
Turner, Steve, 193
23rd Grammy Awards, 312

Ulmer, Kenneth, 388
Uncloudy Day: The Gospel Music Encyclopedia, 172
United Recording, 311–12
United Western Studios, 273–74

Vachon, Brian, 127–28
Van Woodward Associates, 90–91
Variety, 276–77, 317, 341
Vee-Jay Records, 31–34, 44–45
Vega, Tata, 371, 372
Vereen, Ben, 276–77
Village Voice, 284–85
Visser, Joop, 13
Voices of Eden, 9

"Wade in the Water" (*Take the Message Everywhere*, LP), 84
"Waiting for the Son" (*Don't Give Up*), 322–23

Walker, Albertina, 40
Walker, David T., 201, 253
Walker, Hezekiah, 1
Walker, Wyatt Tee, 57
Ward, Clara, 9–10, 134–35
Ward Singers, 9–10
Ware, Frederick, 250
Warner Bros., 329–30, 343, 381–82
    act of faith moving to, 321
    being in contact with, 286
    budget with, 322–23
    distinction between gospel albums and LPs with, 328–29
    first album with, 313, 314–15
    move to, 315–18
    recording contract *Take Me Back*, 212
    release by, 315–17
Waronker, Lenny, 315
Waronker, Si, 101
Warwick, Dionne, 301
Washington, Ernestine B., 12–13
Washington, Grover, 276–77
Washington Post, 341
Waters, Ethel, 64–65
Way Inn. *See* Soledad State Prison, performing at
WDIA (Memphis), 94–95
"We Are Not Ashamed" (*Finally*), 348
Weddington Studios, 340
Weekes, Melinda E., 146–47
"We Expect You" (*This Is Another Day*), 251–53
Weinberger, Ed, 374–75
"Well Done" (*Live in London*), 275
"We Need to Hear From You" (*Finally*), 347
WERD (Atlanta), 94–95
Whalum, Kirk, 223
"What Does Jesus Mean to Me?" (*Just Andraé*), 169–70
"What Makes a Man Turn His Back on God?" (*Take the Message Everywhere*, LP), 84
"What Ya Gonna Do?" (*Keep on Singin'*, LP), 114
White, Barry, 352–53
White House, visiting, 285–86
Wilde, James, 259

424 INDEX

Wiley, Fletch, 198, 227, 254, 256
adding solos, 178
in Australia, 221
and *Best of Andraé*, 227–28
at Explo '72, 126–27
in horn section, 230
at Mama Jo's, 200–3
in new horn section, 230, 232
at new house of Andraé, 234
performing with Sonlight, 129–31, 153–54
preparing and composing *Just Andraé*, 155–58, 164, 172–73
recording *"Live" at Carnegie Hall*, 178
song arrangement by, 154–55, 246–47, 254
Take Me Back sessions, 199–200
Take Me Back songs, 203–10
Wilkerson, David, 55, 60
Williams, David, 311–12, 324–25, 327–28, 374–75
Williams, Jean, 277
Williams, Marion, 13
Williams, Riley F., 11–12
Williams, Robbie Lee, 26
Williams, Sondra "Blinky," 25, 28–29, 31, 46, 61, 126–27, 179, 346
Williams-Jones, Pearl, 287
Wilmington Assemblies of God, 29
Winans, Marvin, 316, 323, 385–86, 389, 397
Winfield, Paul, 301
Wise, Raymond, 180, 204, 222
"Without a Song" (*Take the Message Everywhere*), 82

WLAC (Nashville), 94–95
Wonder, Stevie, 253, 285–86, 288–89, 319
Wonder Teens, 25–26
Won't It Be Sad" (*It's a Blessing*), 40
Woodstock, 126, 128
Word Records, 64–65
Wrecking Crew, 138
Wright, Edna, 25–26, 28, 47, 317, 340, 367–68, 398
and Addicts Choir, 58
commitments of, 351–52
duet in "Don't Give Up," 323–24
and end of COGICs, 45–46
great "lost" COGICs album, 37
It's a Blessing session, 33
Sandra saving day in 1983, 346
vocals in "Save the People," 326
vocals of, 348, 350

Yoder, Wes, 128, 133–34, 401
"You Ain't Livin'" (*Just Andraé*), 165–66
"You Can Depend on Me" (*Take Me Back*), 205
"You Don't Have to Jump No Pews" (*Live in London*), 271–72
"You Don't Know What You're Missing" (*"Live" at Carnegie Hall*), 182–83
"You Don't Know What You're Missing" (*Soulfully*), 141
"You Gave to Me" (*Live in London*), 274–75
"You Gave to Me" (*This Is Another Day*), 253
Youth with a Mission, 125–26